ANGEL
of ALTA
LANGA

Also by **Suzanne Hoffman**

LABOR OF LOVE:
WINE FAMILY WOMEN OF PIEMONTE

ANGEL of ALTA LANGA

A Novel of Love & War

S UZANNE H OFFMAN

UNDER DISCOVERED
PUBLISHING, LLC
Edwards, Colorado

Published in the United States of America

Under Discovered Publishing LLC
Edwards, Colorado
www.publishcolorado.com
www.suzannehoffman.net

First Edition: November 2021

Library of Congress Control Number: 2021917355

ISBN: 987-0-9972359-2-0
eBook-ISBN: 987-0-9972359-3-7

Cover and Interior Design: Ellen Pickels, Communication Arts, Midlothian, Virginia
Back Cover Art: Clare O'Neill, Minneapolis, Minnesota
Editor: Elatia Harris, Cambridge, Massachusetts
Cover photograph of young woman: Jane Weihman Block
Cover landscape images: Adobe Stock (stock.adobe.com)

Dedicated to

Beatrice Roggero Rizzolio, Rina and Demetrio Veglio,
Maria and Carlo Rivera, Giulia Pellizzari di Grésy,
Giuseppina Rabino, Maria Badellino Oddero, and those
whose names shall never be known who stood against the wave
of evil that swept their land during the Nazi occupation.

"Senza memoria si cancella la storia di un territorio e non c'è possibilità di capire il passato, di vivere il presente e di progettare il futuro." [To live in the present and prepare for the future, the memory of the past must not be erased.]

— Giacomo Oddero, patriarch of Poderi e Cantine Oddero,
Santa Maria La Morra (Barolo)

"Be on guard. Stand firm in the faith. Be courageous. Be strong. And do everything with love."

—1 Corinthians 16:13–14

TABLE *of* CONTENTS

DEAR READER,

Welcome to the world of the fictional Fiore, Giordano, and Bottero families of Piemonte. Soon you will travel in these pages to the expansive northwest Italian region the House of Savoy ruled for centuries. But the Piemonte of 1918 through 1946 that you will enter is quite different from the one today known for its food, wine, and stunning natural beauty. It is the Piemonte of those who lived under Mussolini's repressive fascist regime during the interwar years. It is the Piemonte of the people who survived a brutal foreign occupation aided and abetted by their own countrymen. It is the Piemonte inhabited by those upon whose shoulders today's successful wine families stand.

Before you begin, a few words about the material I have included to enrich your reading experience and fully immerse you in this bewitching land's culture and history.

You will find a glossary in the back matter of the book. My mission was to write an engaging story with compelling characters, but most importantly, to use my *Angel* to spread an understanding of Piemonte in the first half of the twentieth century and pay homage to those who sacrificed so much and suffered greatly during that dark era. My characters in *Angel of Alta Langa* speak three different languages—Italian, German, and Arbëresh—and one dialect—Piemontese. And, of course, Latin was the language of the Catholic Church before the conclusion of the Second Vatican Council in 1965. Arbëresh—or Albanese as it was known in Italian before the 1990s—and Piemontese are dying out. Although unification of Italy was in 1861 (completed in 1871), it was not until the twentieth century that Italian was spoken as the country's standard language. Italian dates to the third century, but the dialects of the various Italian territories were spoken until the early twentieth century. In 1922,

Mussolini outlawed dialects, and Italian was taught in schools, furthering the standardization of Italian as the country's language. Today, there remain over twenty different dialects in Italy, but like so many of Italy's rich traditions, they are dying out among the younger generation. I chose to weave into my prose and dialogue some of the words, phrases, and sayings my characters would have spoken. They are noted first in italics and can be found in the glossary in the back matter of the book.

Piemonte is Italy's second largest region. The diverse landscape of rugged mountains, fertile plains, and vineyard- and forest-carpeted rolling hills give the region its character. Since *Angel of Alta Langa* is set across this expansive land and other locations in Italy, Switzerland, France, and Germany, I have included three schematic (not to scale) maps for you to follow the footsteps of my characters across the twenty-five-year period between the ends of the two cataclysmic world wars.

The population of *Angel of Alta Langa* is quite large, and Italian names usually end in *a, o,* or *i,* making it a bit confusing to follow at first. Although you will quickly come to know them, I have provided you with a cast of characters in the front matter.

To maintain authenticity, I chose to break one of the conventions of *The Chicago Manual of Style* regarding the titles of my characters. For example, Cesare Costa's title of "dottor" is not capitalized in Italian when used in a sentence. However, as my language advisor, Anna Olivero, pointed out, God's title—Signore—is always capitalized. Ironically, so are tyrants such as Il Duce.

Buona lettura! Happy reading!
Suzanne

HISTORICAL TIMELINE

1848–1861
- Unification of Italy.

1861
- March 17: The First Italian Parliament meets in Turin and proclaims King Vittorio Emanuele II of Sardinia (House of Savoy) the first king of unified Italy.
- March 23: Piemontese statesman, Camillo Benso, Conte di Cavour is named the first prime minister of Italy.

1914–1918
- The Great War (World War I)

1917
- The Balfour Declaration announcing Great Britain's support for a Jewish homeland in Palestine.

1918–1919
- The Great Influenza pandemic rages around the world, killing between fifty and a hundred million people.

1918
- November 11: Armistice ends the Great War at 11:00 a.m.

1920
- February 24: National Socialist German Workers' Party (Nazi) is formed in Munich.

1921
- November 9: National Fascist Party is formed (Partito Nazionale Fascista) in Rome.

1922
- October 27: March on Rome begins.
- October 28: Mussolini called to form a government in Rome.
- November 25: Parliament grants Mussolini full powers.

1925
- Fascism is fully established in Italy.

1929
- Wall Street stock market crashed, beginning the Great Depression.

1932
- Franklin D. Roosevelt is elected 32nd president of the United States.

1933
- January 30: President von Hindenburg names Hitler chancellor of Germany.
- February 28: Emergency powers are granted to Hitler after the Reichstag fire.
- March 22: Dachau concentration camp for "enemies of the regime" is opened near Munich.

- March 23: Hitler gains dictatorial powers after the German Parliament passes the Law to Remedy the Distress of the People and the Reich ("Enabling Act") giving the Reich government the power to pass laws without consent of the Reichstag.
- July 14: The Law Against the Founding of New Parties declares the National Socialist German Workers Party (Nazi Party) the only legal political party in Germany.

1934

- August 2: German President von Hindenburg dies. Hitler unites the chancellorship and presidency under the title "Führer." He is now the absolute dictator of Germany with no constitutional or legal restraints on his power.
- Mussolini declares, "There has never been anti-Semitism in Italy."

1935

- September 15: The Reich Citizenship Law and The Law for the Protection of German Blood and German Honor (known collectively as the Nuremberg Race Laws) are enacted.

1936

- January 20: King George V of Great Britain dies.
- August 1–16: The Berlin Olympics

- Franklin D. Roosevelt is elected to a second term as president of the United States.
- December 10: King Edward VIII of Great Britain abdicates; he is succeeded by his brother Bertie, King George VI.

1938

- March 12–13: Nazi troops enter Austria, and Hitler announces the Anschluss with Austria.
- July 6–15: The Evian Conference of delegates from thirty-two countries fails to reach consensus on providing relief to Jewish German refugees.
- July 14: The ten-point Manifesto on Race is published (Manifesto della razza) in Il Giornale d'Italia.
- August 22: Special census of Jews in Italy begins.
- September through December: The first of the racial laws (le Leggi Razziali) are enacted in Italy.
- September 30: British Prime Minister Neville Chamberlain declares "Peace for our time" after the Munich Agreement is reached between Germany, France, Great Britain, and Italy whereby Germany is allowed to annex the Sudetenland in western Czechoslovakia.
- November 9–10: Night of the Broken Glass, known as "Kristallnacht."

1939

- March 15: Germany invades Czechoslovakia.
- May 22: Nazi Germany and Italy sign the "Pact of Steel."
- September 1: Germany invades Poland.
- September 3: Great Britain and France declare war on Germany.

1940

- April 9–June 22: Germany's Blitzkrieg moves across Western Europe.
- May 10: Winston Churchill becomes prime minister of Great Britain.
- May–June: First prisoners categorized as "professional criminals" arrive at Auschwitz.
- June 10: Italy declares war against France and Great Britain.
- September 27: Berlin Pact (also know as The Tripartite Pact) is signed by Germany, Italy, and Japan.
- Franklin D. Roosevelt is elected for a third term as president of the United States.

1941

- June 22: Germany attacks the Soviet Union. Operation Barbarossa begins.
- September 3: The SS tests Zyklon-B for the first time on Soviet prisoners and other weak or infirmed prisoners at Auschwitz 1.

- December 7: Japan attacks Pearl Harbor, drawing America into the Second World War.

1942

- January 20: Wannsee Conference and the beginning of the implementation of Hitler's "Final Solution"
- February 15: Industrialized mass murder begins at Auschwitz-Birkenau with the arrival of the first transport of Jews who, upon arrival, are immediately gassed by the SS using Zyklon-B.

1943

- July 10: Allies land in Sicily, ending the persecution of Jews in liberated zones of Italy.
- July 25: Mussolini is deposed and arrested. The Fascist regime falls. King Vittorio Emanuele III appoints Marshall Pietro Badoglio as prime minister.
- September 3: Armistice of Cassibile (Sicily) is signed between the Allies and the Kingdom of Italy.
- September 8: Armistice of Cassibile is announced.
- September 10: The Nazi occupation of Northern Italy officially begins.
- September 11: German troops enter Turin.
- September 12: German troops rescue Mussolini from his prison in Campo Imperatore in Abruzzo ▶.

- September 23: The German puppet state of the Italian Social Republic is proclaimed with Mussolini as head.
- September 16: Round up and deportation of Italian Jews with the help of the Fascists begins in Merano.
- October 13: Italy declares war on Germany.
- October 16: Roundup of Jews in the Rome Ghetto begins.
- October 18: 1,035 Jews from the Rome Ghetto are deported to Auschwitz.

1944

- June 4: The American Fifth Army liberates Rome.
- June 6: D-day Allied invasion of Normandy
- Franklin D. Roosevelt is elected to a fourth term as president of the United States.

1945

- April 12: President Roosevelt dies in Warm Springs, Georgia.
- April 25: Italy is liberated.
- April 27: Mussolini is captured by Garibaldi partisans in Dongo near the Swiss border.
- April 28: Mussolini is executed in Giulino di Mezzegra.
- April 30: Hitler commits suicide in his bunker in Berlin.
- May 7: Germany unconditionally surrenders to the Allies.

- May 8: V-E Day—End of the war in Europe.
- August 14: Japan accepts the terms of unconditional surrender to the Allies.
- August 15: Japan's Emperor Hirohito announces the unconditional surrender of Japan.
- September 2: Japan's formal surrender is signed aboard the USS Missouri in Tokyo Bay.
- World War II ends.

CAST *of* FICTIONAL CHARACTERS

Monviso (il Re di pietra): Monte Viso, The Stone King

The Fiore Family of Ca' dei Fiù in Asili
Nicolas (Nico) Fiore, head of the Fiore household
Luigia Capra Fiore, wife of Nico
Luciana (Luce) Capra, sister of Luigia; nurse in Alba at Ospedale
   San Lazzaro
Mirella Canta Fiore, mother of Nico
Dina Capra, mother of Luigia and Luciana
Sara Fiore, eldest daughter of Luigia and Nico
Maria Fiore, second oldest daughter of Luigia and Nico
Letizia Fiore, third oldest daughter of Luigia and Nico
Giovanna Fiore, youngest daughter of Luigia and Nico

The Bottero Family of Altavilla, Cascina Asili, and Bossolaschetto
Cornelia (Madama Lia) Ferri Bottero, widow of Alessandro Bottero
Alessandro Bottero, husband of Cornelia
Giulia Bottero, daughter of Alessandro and Cornelia
Giuseppina Molino Rocco, longtime housekeeper and companion to
   Cornelia
Gianni Rocco, chauffeur to Cornelia Bottero and husband of Giuseppina

Giordano Family of Turin
Gabriele Giordano, patriarch of the Giordano Family
Daniela Dalmasso Giordano, matriarch of the Giordano Family
Doretta Giordano, eldest child of Daniela and Gabriele
Michele Giordano, middle child and only son of Daniela and Gabriele
Elena Giordano, youngest child of Daniela and Gabriele
Eduardo Dalmasso, great uncle of Daniela and Silvana
Ida Pellegrino, housekeeper in the Giordano household

Becker Family of Germany
Silvana Dalmasso Becker, wife of Fritz, younger sister of Daniela
Fritz Becker, husband of Silvana
Friedrich Becker, son of Silvana and Fritz
Gisele Becker, daughter of Silvana and Fritz
Lorelei Vogel, aunt of Fritz in Rosenheim, Germany

Olivero Family of Alba

Stefano Olivero, attorney and consigliere to Cornelia Bottero
Marina Olivero, wife of Stefano
Franca Olivero, mother of Stefano
Luca Olivero, son of Marina and Stefano

Bosco Family of Contessa Entellina, Sicily

Antonino Bosco, head of Bosco family household
Anna Bosco, wife of Antonino
Francesco Bosco, youngest child of Antonino and Anna
Renzo Bosco, cousin of Francesco (in New Orleans, Louisiana, USA)

Volpe Family of Turin

Dino Volpe, head of Volpe family household
Flora Volpe, wife of Dino; Daniela Giordano's dressmaker
Baldo Volpe, son of Dino and Flora
Sofia Volpe, daughter of Dino and Flora

The Bader Family from Strasbourg

Ernst Bader, head of Bader family household
Talia Bader, wife of Ernst
Rachel Bader, daughter of Talia and Ernst

The Priests and Nuns

Don Pietro, priest of the Latin church in Contessa Entellina
Papas Nicolas, priest of the Arbëresh (Greek Byzantine) church in Contessa Entellina
Don Rocca, priest in Alba
Don Paolo, priest in Barbaresco from 1905–1934
Don Emilio, priest in Barbaresco from 1934–1946
Don Bartolo, priest in Serravalle Langhe
Suor Angelica, sister of don Pietro, teacher and nurse in Alba at Ospedale San Lazzaro

Other Fictional Characters

Frieda Stern, boarding school friend of Cornelia Bottero
Renata Goren, boarding school friend of Silvana Becker
Dott. Cesare Costa, young doctor in Barbaresco
Dott. Adriano Pera, retiring doctor in Barbaresco
Cinzia Strega, Alba Fascist policewoman whose family is from Barbaresco
Gunther Schliessen, Waffen-SS officer from Berlin stationed in Turin
Volker von Ebnerberg, aristocratic Wehrmacht officer stationed in Langhe
Pipo Merluzzo, caretaker at Cornelia Bottero's Bossolaschetto farm
Ornella Merluzzo, wife of Pipo, cook at Cornelia Bottero's Bossolaschetto farm
Paolina and Fabrizio Pratto, owners of Hotel Paradiso in Bossolasco
Zeus, Sara Fiore's black Hanoverian horse
Romeo, Fiore family farm horse
Milo, Nebbia, Fufi, Fiore family dogs

Real Life Character

Suor Giuseppina de Muro, nun in Le Nuove Prison in Turin

MAPS

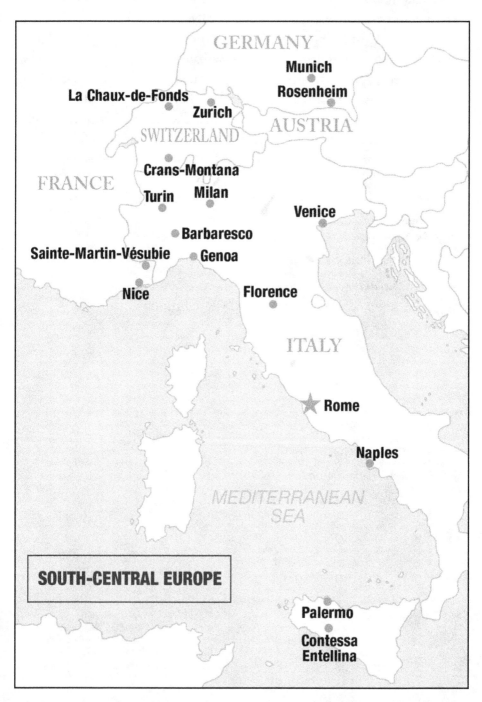

SOUTH-CENTRAL EUROPE

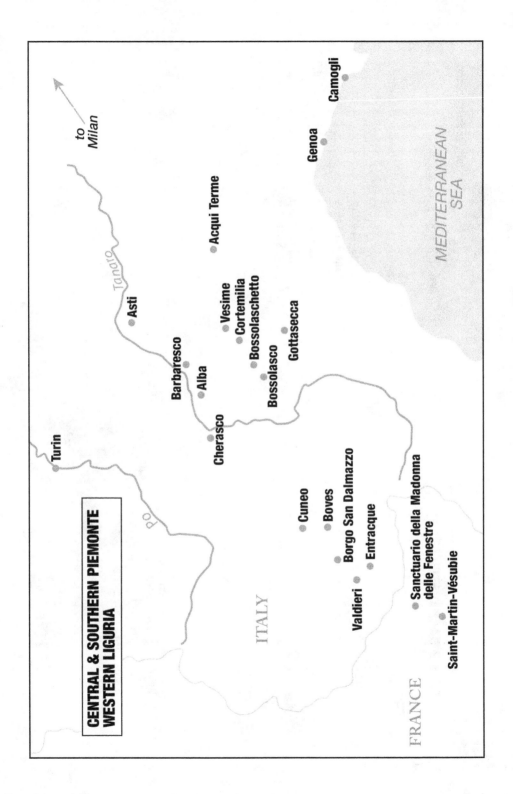

CENTRAL & SOUTHERN PIEMONTE
WESTERN LIGURIA

to Milan

Tanaro

Po

Turin

Asti

Barbaresco

Alba

Cherasco

Vesime
Cortemilia
Bossolaschetto
Bossolasco
Gottasecca

Acqui Terme

Genoa

Camogli

MEDITERRANEAN SEA

Cuneo

Boves

Borgo San Dalmazzo

Valdieri

Entracque

Sanctuario della Madonna delle Fenestre

Saint-Martin-Vésubie

ITALY

FRANCE

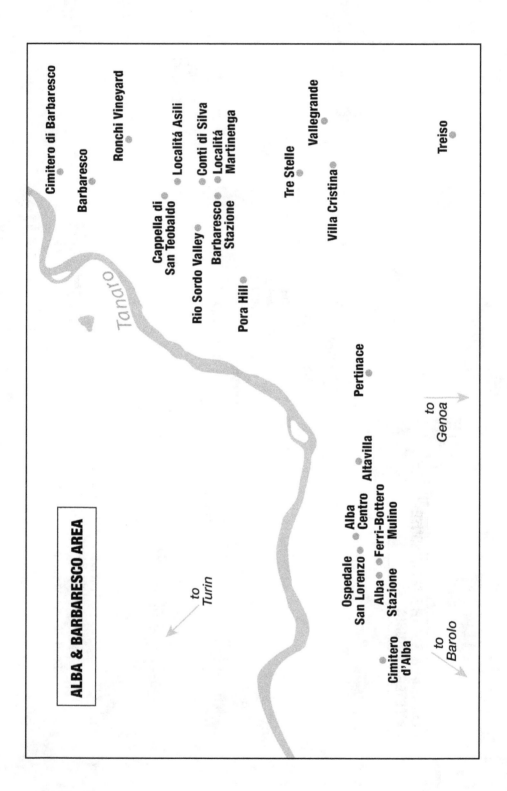

ALBA & BARBARESCO AREA

Cimitero di Barbaresco

Barbaresco

Ronchi Vineyard

Cappella di San Teobaldo

Località Asili

Conti di Silva

Località Martinenga

Rio Sordo Valley

Barbaresco Stazione

Tanaro

Pora Hill

Tre Stelle

Vallegrande

Villa Cristina

Pertinace

to Turin

Altavilla

Alba Centro

Ospedale San Lorenzo

Ferri-Bottero Mulino

Alba Stazione

to Genoa

Treiso

Cimitero d'Alba

to Barolo

PROLOGUE

Ceaseless ringing in her ears and jackboots reverberating on the stone floor of the hall woke her from a fitful sleep. How many were there this time? With each thud, the sounds grew louder and nearer. They were coming for her.

She rolled over on the putrid mattress, willing her body to ready itself for them. Bedbugs had feasted on her since her first night in Le Nuove Prison. Mice fought one another for morsels of her paltry rations. It was as though the vermin in her cell were allied with her torturers.

Blood from the wounds they had inflicted and her monthly blood that had come early stained her trousers. She touched her cracked lips, the scabbing gash on her head. The manacles they slapped on her when she was taken for interrogation cut into her swollen left wrist that now constantly throbbed—no doubt a fracture from the fall when they pushed her from the truck that night.

Her face, struck more times than she could remember, was swollen. Was she even recognizable? Even one of her most distinctive features, her soft, wavy hair, was now a dark, greasy snarl caked with blood from the gash on her head. That was the idea, she knew—to strip her of her dignity until she felt meaningless to herself and easily gave all she knew. Despite inflicting pain beyond telling, they were unable to break her.

They marched past her door, spreading terror throughout the cells, keeping the advantage of surprise. For whom would they come? Anyone, everyone. And when? Anytime.

The days since her capture probably numbered ten. Each time she returned to her cell, she scratched a notch in the thick grime covering the walls, but with consciousness ebbing and flowing, she was uncertain of the passage of time. Frigid air whistled through the wind-tunnel corridor. The naked bulb overhead and the glaring blades of light from the hall illuminated her world at night. It was always dark when she was taken for the sessions where, through torturous means, they attempted to extract information. Three times, she had been dragged into a truck and driven to a distant house of horrors where German, not Italian, was spoken. It was there they inflicted the worst of her pain. Otherwise, she never left the infamous Le Nuove prison.

When she no longer could restrain her screams, which she tried desperately to suppress lest giving the demons more pleasure, *suor* Giuseppina de Muro would play *Ave Maria* on a ramshackle piano. The dissonant strains calmed her. Long ago, the nun had come to Le Nuove as a nursing sister. Now she was the only source of comfort in the wretched place. Would the saintly woman ever know the far reach of her music? She sang to herself the comforting words of the blessed song she had learned from a loved one, praying for release from her agony, but if not, for protection of those whose lives were at risk if her resolve failed. And for her family, wherever they were.

Had all but the one partisan with her been slaughtered at the *cascina* that night? So it appeared from the silence as she was dragged, drifting in and out of consciousness, through the frigid darkness. The blasts of orange light shooting from the barrels of machine guns were all the warning the partisans had received. Then stillness. And flames. She heard a woman's shrill voice call her name before she sank into unconsciousness from a blow to the side of her head. Who had betrayed them? Whoever it had been, she knew she had been spared that night for one reason: only she knew the names. Only she knew the location of the one they sought—the one she knew had survived, hidden in the forest.

All of a sudden, it was quiet. The jackbooted tormentors had stopped at her cell.

It was indeed her turn. Keys rattled, the lock turned, and tired, dry hinges squeaked as the iron door was opened. Through her swollen eyes, a vaguely familiar face she could not discern in the dim light came into focus.

"*Alzati! Adesso!*" one of the Blackshirts shouted. "Stand up, I said!" Before she could will her body to respond, someone dragged her to her feet, but her legs disobeyed. Down she went on the hard, filthy floor. Again, the Fascist screamed, "Up!" This time when she staggered, a male prison guard, who often leered at her and whose foul breath blended with the stench of the cell, slapped her bruised face and pinned her against the wall with his body. Suor Giuseppina often interceded when the lecherous guard was on duty. Not this time. She did not appear. "Wake up!" he shouted, his face pressed up against hers and his over-sized hands roaming her body, close to her breasts. "Enough!" ordered the man whose words gripped her throat like talons. The guard relented, and though bile rose in her throat, she willed her legs to obey.

No shackles this time. Did they believe they had broken her will to escape? To survive? She took her first tentative steps toward the open door when the owner of the still-obscured face spoke in that same menacing tone. "We meet again," he hissed, contempt dripping with each word. "Did you really believe you would not be caught?" She knew the voice, and it filled her with dread. She tried to see his face in the hall light, but the Blackshirt jerked her left arm, pain and weakness sending her to the ground once again.

As they approached the outer door of the prison, fresh cold air brought into focus a world she believed she would never see again. The amber light the rising sun cast on the distant mountains signaled that it was early morning. She squinted in the unaccustomed sunshine. Overhead was a pale-blue, winter morning sky—its purity a blessing. In the distance, the familiar snow-covered Monviso called to her. The forested valleys of *il Re di pietra*, as the mountain was called, had given the partisans shelter in their fight against the Germans and the Fascist Blackshirts.

Now, the king of mountains was powerless to protect her, but the majesty of the early morning was speaking, and the gratitude in her heart was a comfort.

They stuffed her into a truck where the Blackshirt held her, clenching her fractured wrist. She cried out. He tightened his grip. Thankfully, her legs, though weak, remained intact, ready to spirit her away if opportunity arose. Did anyone know where she was? The partisans were known to save their comrades, to save those who saved them, but Le Nuove was a fortress.

Although it had been impossible for her to see their route on previous journeys, this time she sensed a different destination. The man whose face she still had not seen spoke her name again as though to cleanse his mouth of a foul taste. "I should have put a bullet in your head in the forest for all the help you've been. But it was pleasant to finally demonstrate the power I have over you—power I have always had. But when I catch that bitch who shot me…" he growled. So that's why he had not appeared at Le Nuove for days after he had captured her. He would be dead had his assailant not been injured herself, struggling no doubt to hold the gun.

When they dragged her off the truck, she looked about at her unfamiliar surroundings, recognizing the unmistakable stench of death. The guards marched her to a bullet-riddled wall where, in slush mixed with human excrement, a high-backed, wooden chair sat facing the redbrick wall. A guard pushed her onto it and grabbed her arms, tying them tightly behind her back. She was now beyond pain. The awareness of her circumstances washed over her. She had heard of partisans who faced this favored form of execution once nothing more could be wrung from them. The place, they said, was known as il Martinetto.

The rope was tight enough to hold her steady. She tilted her face toward the blue sky and thought of those whom she dearly loved and whose lives she had protected. Yes, no doubt the partisans at the cascina were gone, but others who fought with them to free Piemonte from the Germans and their Fascist collaborators were safe. The work would go on and Piemonte would be free. Soon. This time, she heard, the Allies were coming.

Someone approached through the slush. She turned her head. Ah, the man. Finally, in the daylight, she saw his true demonic face she knew all too well. Those dark eyes, windows into Hell. He grabbed her matted hair and jerked her head to face the wall. *I will meet the moment without malice*, she resolved. And she felt the cold steel of his pistol at the base of her skull. He spat out her name.

PART ONE:

1918 – 1937

CHAPTER I

Alba
November 1918

Cornelia Ferri Bottero's eyes were dry and hot, her tears spent even before sweet Giulia breathed her last. It had all happened so fast. Just when they thought the influenza was behind them, the second wave came with the harsh winter of 1918. The war was finally over, but the battle against the contagion still raged.

She sat, her hands folded in her lap, and took in every last detail of Giulia's four-year-old face. Even in death, she had the same endearing expression that had defined her personality from birth. The child's red curls were now tangled and dark from her final fever. Cornelia tidied a lock. Cold already. She shuddered.

Was it days or hours since they came to San Lazzaro hospital in Alba? She no longer knew. It had been dark. Sometime before midnight, Giulia's temperature skyrocketed. Cornelia rushed to wake Gianni. He and his family had been with hers for years, and he dearly loved the little girl who followed him around the house as he did his chores. "Pity her father is gone," he murmured when he saw her.

Gianni carried the swaddled, unconscious child as though she were a porcelain doll and placed her on Cornelia's lap in the carriage. The short ride down the hill from *località* Altavilla and through Alba in the wind-driven snow had been an eternity for her. Who had not prayed that the horror that had killed so many in Langhe would not invade their homes? Yet here it was. "Mamma is here, *carissima*," she said over and over, trying to force back the night. Could Giulia hear her?

The hospital doors swung open, and Cornelia cried out with relief when her beloved childhood friend Luciana Capra appeared at the far end of the long, narrow hallway. It was no surprise since nurses rarely left the hospital as the number of influenza cases mounted. From the moment Gianni laid Giulia on the gurney and heard the squeaking of its wheels as it was rolled along the black and white marble-tiled floor, all sense of time ended for Cornelia.

"Lia, come with me," Luciana said as she rose from prayer beside the dead child's bed. Not wanting to startle her, she brushed Cornelia's shoulder. "Sadly, the bed is needed. They must take her away now."

Luciana Capra, though only twenty-nine years old, was a woman of great wisdom and strength. Over the past year, Cornelia had busied herself with organizing shipments of portable altars to the front for the Catholic Women's Union, yet she often wondered how she would have survived her first years as a young widow without her childhood friend's support.

Cornelia nodded and spoke the first words Luciana had heard from her for hours. Not taking her eyes off Giulia, she murmured, "I am now alone, Luce, all alone." Words fled from Luciana. She could only listen and order her eyes to remain dry as she observed her anguished friend. "First, Alessandro—now, my precious angel."

During the Great War, Cornelia's husband had served as an aid to the Italian Second Army commander, General Luigi Capello. Alessandro had died the prior year in the disastrous Battle of Caporetto that created thousands of widows throughout Italy. It was Alessandro's second war as a high-ranking officer. Life had blossomed for them when he returned home from Libya in 1913 and resigned his commission. But that had been cut short when an assassin's bullet in Serbia plunged Europe into a cataclysmic war. No husband. No child.

She bent to kiss little Giulia farewell.

Cornelia dug deep for the energy to rise from the chair she had occupied for hours. She forced up the edges of her mouth and kissed Luciana's cheek. It was time once again to meet her trusted consigliere, Stefano Olivero, and prepare to bury another loved one. Somehow, life would go on.

CHAPTER 2

Alba
December 1918

hree weeks after watching the pallbearers slide Giulia's tiny coffin
into the vault beside Alessandro's—with room for her own on Giulia's
other side—Cornelia woke to a bright, sunny day. Even through her
deep grief, she recognized its beauty. Snow from the series of storms that had
battered Langhe for weeks blanketed Alba below her home in Altavilla. The
Roman city of towers appeared purified, but the pestilence that had stolen
Giulia from her and kept so many fearful mourners sheltered in their homes
still prowled.

On any normal day during Advent, Cornelia would have taken time from
her work to stroll with Giulia along via Maestra to make their final Christmas
preparations. Only a week ago, Giulia was full of life. Now, she was gone.
Such was the nature of this brutal, unseen killer.

Cornelia stood at the bedroom window under the spell of majestic Monviso,
far away across the plains. Giulia's had been one of many solemn services in
Alba's churches that day. The surge of death, particularly among Langhe's
youth, continued with no relief in sight. Despite the flow of stricken citizens
filling the hospital, Luciana had walked the short distance to San Lorenzo's
Cathedral in Piazza Duomo to comfort Cornelia. Her devoted friend sat beside
her with one gloved hand in hers and the other fingering the crystal beads of
her rosary as she mouthed the prayers. It was a scene they had repeated far too
often in recent years. Cornelia longed to share happier times with Luciana again.

Their friendship was made and sealed in girlhood in the cool hills of Alta
Langa near the Capra farm where Cornelia's family had a summerhouse.

Whenever Luciana broke free of her household chores and minding her baby sister, Luigia, she dashed to Cornelia's grand house on the ridge at Bossolaschetto to spend hours talking and wandering through the thick forests and hazelnut groves that carpeted the hills. The barren forest floor amazed Lia. *How clean.* Luciana explained that nothing went to waste in Alta Langa. Farmers scooped up fallen leaves they used as forage for the cows. Broken branches and twigs became firewood.

Often, in a forest clearing, they would be struck as one by the way the light fell, the trees reached for the sky, or the mushrooms clustered. Each knew the other sensed a secret order—the hand of God—and they were not afraid to speak of it. Once, a she-boar approached a clearing with her piglets, and Lia, the city girl, wanted to bolt. "No, they are part of Creation too," Luciana said, her voice serene. "The wolf shall dwell with the lamb, and the leopard shall lie down with the young goat; and a little child shall lead them." She took Lia's hand and calmly led her away. "Lia, do you believe we will live in a time of peace?" Luciana then asked. The girls looked at each other as if they knew something no one else knew.

Now, as she prepared to begin her first day of work after her loss, she wondered whether that life illumined by simple pleasures would ever return. She would have to try hard to believe in it. Even her appetite had disappeared with Giulia. A strong *caffelatte* was all her longtime housekeeper, Giuseppina Molino, could persuade her mistress to take in the morning.

"Signora Cornelia," Giuseppina pleaded at each mealtime, "you must eat, or you will get sick." Most Italian women believed no problem was too great not to be cut down to size with food. Cornelia did not concur with that, particularly now. Only work would distract her from her grief, at least during the day.

"Please ask Gianni to ready the carriage, Giuseppina. I'm going to Alba."

Displeasure with her mistress's decision drew the housekeeper's eyebrows together. She stood with her hands planted on her generous hips, one foot tapping. "It's too cold today. Please rest a few more days and return to work after Epiphany. It's too soon now," she added, growing heated. "Besides, what will people say?"

"They'll say that I've not changed," Cornelia snapped. "Those whose opinions matter to me know now more than ever that I need my work. Now please, give Gianni my message." It was unusual for her to snap at the loyal woman who had served as her nanny and then as Giulia's, but she had no patience for admonishments this morning.

Since Giulia's death, Giuseppina had assumed the role of a lady's maid, helping Cornelia dress and spending more time with her. Alma, her cook, now ruled the kitchen. Cornelia was independent and at first brushed her away, but she found that Giuseppina, who had cared for Giulia night and day, needed comfort too. Truth was, though she loathed admitting such dependence, Cornelia needed Giuseppina now. The care, the loving touch.

As Gianni maneuvered the carriage along the steep, slick road from Alta-villa, golden-yellow morning sunlight spread across the eastern, snow-covered slopes of the Alpes-Maritimes to the southwest. Winter was brutal for her now, making the days all too short and the lonely nights endless. Only another week of ever-shortening days was left before the sun reversed its course to track north again.

Before they left the villa, Cornelia had instructed Gianni to drop her at Piazza Duomo. She wanted to light a candle in the cathedral before she walked to her lawyer's office on Piazza Savona. Thankfully, he simply nodded without any reproach when she told him not to wait. Had that horrid night when they frantically raced to the hospital deepened Gianni's understanding of his mistress whom he had watched grow into such a capable woman? He might be learning to read her need for time to herself.

Cornelia hoped a walk in the bracing air would lighten her mood. The shops were still closed, so she had the street to herself. Better not to meet anyone yet. Although money and food for Christmas celebrations were scarce, via Maestra was festooned in Christmas decorations. A young boy scampered around delivering *panettone* to cafes and shops. Was it a mistake to stir the happy memories that she, Alessandro, and Giulia had created during their brief time together? It would make too sad a mood for the meeting, perhaps. But by the time she reached Piazza Savona, she felt prepared to meet with Stefano Olivero to face the future.

"*Buongiorno*, signora Bottero," he called from behind her as she climbed the stairs to the office. She started and, glancing over her shoulder, saw that *dottor* Olivero must have walked behind her from the Duomo, leaving her to her thoughts. There was no need for him to ask her how she felt. Even in the dim light of the stairwell, she knew her swollen eyes and gaunt face made her grief all too obvious. "Welcome back, signora Bottero. We have much to discuss." Her long-time lawyer knew that work would ease her mind.

From the landing, Cornelia wiped her eyes and forced a brittle smile. "Yes, dottor Olivero, I am ready."

Greeting her at the office door was her lawyer's eldest son, Luca. Still a young boy, he would follow in his father's footsteps. Whenever he managed to escape school—and his mother—he shadowed his father. "I have no better teacher than my papà," he'd proclaim. Today would no doubt be filled with valuable lessons as his father prepared Cornelia to return to the land of the living. Lessons, too, in what not to say. How to quietly observe. When he grew up, Luca would aim to speak as seldom, and as to the point, as his father did.

Olivero men had served as legal counsel to Cornelia's family since the unification of Italy more than five decades earlier. At first, Stefano Olivero was skeptical about working for a woman. A lawyer who possessed a sharp financial mind, he guided Cornelia through the turbulent years of the war. The economic calamities of the pointless conflict the European monarchs triggered had left Cornelia intact, for he had structured her wealth to survive them.

Wealth for *one* as it turned out. What would she do with it?

In 1914, a month after Giulia's joyous January birth, pneumonia took Alessandro's mother, Federica. Cornelia cherished her relationship with mamma Fede, who differed greatly from the typical *suocera*. Then came the devastating shock on an early summer Sunday morning in Alta Langa in 1915. A fatal carriage accident along the muddy ridge road to church in Bossolasco orphaned Cornelia. Before her mourning period had ended, Alessandro was called up and deployed to Austria. The year did not end without another loved one taken from her. Alessandro's father, Giulio, who had never recovered from the loss of his beloved wife, died from what his doctor called "a broken heart."

Through it all, Stefano Olivero steadied Cornelia. As an only child, she inherited the entire Ferri fortune. Although hoping for a boy, Domenico Ferri was besotted with the only child his wife, Ludovica, was able to produce. Even before she reached the age of ten, her father recognized her quick wit. He affectionately referred to her in Piemontese as *la mej*, the best. Despite his wife's protestations that it was unseemly for a young woman, Domenico gave her a classical education with a tutor and involved Cornelia in the running of the family's store in Alba. Alessandro knew he had married a strong, intelligent woman, and he found that a gift—something to rely on in bad times. When he left for Austria, he executed documents that gave her full power over the couple's finances in his absence. It was a good thing to have a wife who was no fool.

Alessandro was given leave to attend his father's funeral. Upon his departure, he advised Cornelia to leave the money both recently had inherited in the bank until he returned. "Lia, the war won't last long," he reassured her, "and you've had a difficult time these past years. Signor Olivero can manage the store, so rest and enjoy Giulia." But Cornelia had her own ideas about protecting their fortune.

The war plunged the rural community into deeper poverty as able-bodied men went off to war. Without strong men to work the fields and vineyards, crop yields plummeted, leaving many to starve. Lia was fortunate to be among the landowners who received Austrian prisoners of war to work their land. She was generous in sharing her crops and was kind to the prisoners, hoping, as many women did, that somehow their counterparts in Austria would hear of it and do the same for Italian men who might be working on their farms. As the war dragged on, Lia saw others suffer as inflation devalued savings thought safe in the banks. Having managed to hold her own through clever investments, she would hardly alarm Alessandro by not following his advice.

Alessandro's late *nonno* Angelo, a wealthy landowner and passionate farmer at heart, had cultivated wheat at Cascina Asili in Barbaresco and on his farm south of Turin. He sold his grain to the gristmill in Alba, taking partial payment in flour and the rest in cash that was slow to come at times. Knowing food production would always be a safe investment, Cornelia purchased the Alba mill. Not only did she increase her profits from her wheat crop, she ensured a steady supply of flour for the generations-old bakery she inherited from her mother's family. Food was the key to survival. Between the mill, the bakery, and her farm in Barbaresco, she, and all those who relied on her, would have food.

"Signor Olivero," she said now, continuing to study the ledgers spread before her on the desk, "I want to buy another mill."

Astonished that she was considering such a thing at this time, dottor Olivero simply asked, "But where? There are no more possibilities in Langhe."

"Look further afield or build a new one. Nizza Monferrato?"

She amazed him. "Then I shall begin a search," he said. He now had a clear understanding of her strategy. The lessons of the war had been too stern for anyone with foresight to feel released from worry. In truth, things did not look rosy now, particularly with that rabble-rouser Mussolini gaining notoriety.

Cornelia knew the grief that gripped her heart was unshakable, but at least now she had a new plan. Childless, she was nevertheless born to make things grow. Time would tell the reason for this lonely need to flourish. What would it bring?

CHAPTER 3

Asili (Barbaresco)
January 1919

Luigia Fiore's labor pains began earlier and were sharper than she expected. It would not be long before her first successful pregnancy was brought to term. She was hoping for a few more days to ready the house before life changed forever, but God had other plans as she had once learned.

It was Sunday and the workers were away, so her husband Nico chose to pass the time and ease his anxiety by pruning the vines close to the cascina. They welcomed the azure blue skies after weeks of bitterly cold weather and blowing snow, making the tedious, hand-numbing job much easier. Nico reveled in Barbaresco's mid-winter days, when the snow-covered Alps dominated the horizon far across the plains to the west, and in the time that he spent alone with his thoughts in the vineyards. He was close enough that he would hear the call from the cascina but far enough barely to hear Luigia's wails as the baby's arrival grew closer. He prayed that, this time, joy would be on the other side of Luigia's intense pain, but the sounds of his wife's anguish clawed at his heart. It reminded him all too well of her first pregnancy, which ended too soon.

Theirs had been a love match. From the moment Nico spied Luigia in the Alba *mercato* with her father, he knew the only work his *baciale* would have to do was to seek a proper introduction and complete the dowry agreement. He worried that, like most girls, she sought a husband from the city instead of a farmer from Barbaresco. His fears vanished the moment they sat across from one another in her parents' home in Bossolaschetto. It was as if they had sat down together to their own married life, a feeling of being fated to one another. By late spring 1917, they were married. The war raged and he worried that he would be called up, but after his two older brothers died in Caporetto, it seemed his family's loss would prevent his conscription. Sorrow mixed with joy—it was the common emotion these days.

Now, nearly two years later, he admired Luigia's courage throughout her second pregnancy. The pain of losing their first child only weeks before the expected birth had lingered. A boy it was. He recalled how Luigia fought back the tears as don Paolo blessed the lifeless child, unable to christen him before he died. "There will be more boys, Luigia," he said as much to assure himself as his wife. "Just rest."

Working along the row of barren vines, finishing the pruning he began in December, he cut the spent canes and dropped them to the ground. Nico's heart soared at the thought of sharing this work he loved so much with his son. He gave no consideration to the possibility that a girl might soon arrive. Teaching a son to prune was an important moment in a vintner's life and one for which Nico ached. The skill linked generations of vine-tending families all throughout Langhe. He whispered to himself, "My son will carry our farm into its fifth generation." True, though sons were important, Nico often said he would be happy with a daughter or two for Luigia's sake but only after the legacy of the Fiore farm was secured with a son.

Langhetti believed sons were indispensable, and girls were akin to a curse. A brood of only girls would be as though Satan himself visited them to cast an evil spell. Daughters married then left home with dowries of land carved from their parents' farms to live on and work for their husbands' families. What was a dowry but a gift to your daughter's in-laws? Sons helped keep the land intact for future generations, and their marriages brought more help to the family. They surely were not cursed, Nico believed, since life had been good to him despite the widespread poverty in Langhe, despite Luigia's miscarriage.

They were by no means rich, but they owned land, something rare for Langhe farming families. Over seventy years earlier, tired of working on land he would never own, Nico's *bisnonno* Aldo Fiore, the youngest of six boys, left the relative security of Calosso d'Asti in Monferrato to make a new start. No surprise—his father thought him crazy to leave a land that even the Savoy royal family loved for the blighted Barbaresco hills. The Piemontese were known as *bogia nen*, people who do not move, but Aldo was not to be dissuaded. All farmers who tended others' land dreamed of owning their own farms. It was a dream rarely fulfilled. Aldo had been determined to be one of the few who succeeded.

Along with his two young sons, Aldo threw himself into the task of clearing forests of the Rio Sordo valley in the enclave known as Asili near Martinenga.

With proceeds from each sale of wood from the cleared forests, he bought vines. Little by little, the Fiore family's farm took shape.

Nico scanned the panorama of vineyards and narrow fields of wheat below and the truffle-rich forests of Pora hill in the distance. His heart swelled with pride for what the Fiore men had achieved in only four generations despite all the odds against them. Soon, the next Fiore heir would come into the world.

"Nico!" came an urgent call from the cascina, "*Vieni qui! Subito!*" Such a blessing his sister-in-law was a nurse. He knew, if Luciana had left her sister's bedside even for a moment, the baby had arrived. Nico dropped his knife, shed his gloves, and ran to the cascina through the quagmire of clay mud and snow.

"First take off your boots!" Luciana ordered as she summoned him upstairs to the bedroom.

Her happy demeanor made it clear to Nico that all was well with mother and child—a relief, but what of the gender, he wondered. "Luce?" he asked as he struggled to pull off his boots, but she had already disappeared up the stairs.

Luigia sat up in their bed, smiling, glowing, bathed in sunshine beaming through the window. Still dressed in his work coat, Nico eagerly reached for the child, but Luciana stepped between him and the bed. "Hands first and coat off, Nico," she commanded, pointing to the basin of water on the dresser.

It seemed an eternity as he washed his hands, but finally he could receive his heir. Luigia handed him their newborn. "We have a beautiful daughter. A little angel."

Crestfallen, Nico held the child close and with his eyes caressed her face, one of immense sweetness and beauty. Within seconds, the child bewitched him utterly. He raised his eyes to Luigia, his face bright with extraordinary and unfeigned happiness.

"Not to worry, Luigia, our sons will have an older sister to guide them," he assured her. "What shall we name her?"

"Sara, after your papà's maternal *nonna*. And, most important, it is the name God Himself gave to Abraham's wife. Such a courageous Biblical figure, so I'm sure that will please Luciana."

"Sara," Nico whispered as he put aside thoughts of a boy and kissed the forehead of the angel who had entered their lives.

On a stool in the bedroom corner, Luciana bowed her head in prayer.

CHAPTER 4

Barbaresco
Evening next day

The ascending full moon lit the colorless, snow-covered landscape beyond the bedroom window. Yesterday, Nico's day had begun with feeding the animals before dawn, no differently from all the others. By noon, Luigia had delivered a healthy daughter, and he had hardly strayed far from her all day. He worked in the barn the next day, only footsteps from his wife and child. The vineyards could wait. Now he craved male company. How doggedly bitter his mother had been, scolding Luigia to her face for giving birth to a daughter. He would postpone sleep to celebrate his first child's arrival at the tavern in Barbaresco. But what would his friends say about a girl child?

Nico stole another look at Luigia and Sara, both far off in their dreams while Luciana sat in the corner, eyes closed, lips moving in silent prayer, with her hands resting on her well-loved Bible. Although she had to leave early for the hospital in the morning, nothing would keep her from her sister's side these first nights.

The two sisters were practically inseparable. When Luigia miscarried early the previous winter, Cornelia Bottero sent Gianni with the *landò* to take Luciana to Barbaresco. Gianni raced in the over-sized carriage from San Lazzaro hospital through the winding, hilly road to Asili. In no time, she was by Luigia's side. Luciana assured her that God had other plans. Luigia wished her sister would come to live in Barbaresco. Her nursing skills were desperately needed in the countryside, but she never would leave Alba and the hospital, at least not now.

Luciana was a spinster, a *tota*, who devoted all her time to nursing and serving the less fortunate of Alba. Nico once asked Luigia why her sister had not taken her vows. There was no answer, only a knowing smile that crossed her face. Perhaps it was for moments like this when she ministered to her family without the constraints of convent life.

Luciana opened her eyes and smiled at him. "Good night, Nico. God will give you all you need. Be patient."

The peace and satisfaction evident on all the faces in the room, including the tiniest of all, warmed him. He wished it would melt his mother's heart. He waved at Luciana on his way out the door.

At the base of the stairs, Mirella Canta waited for him, arms folded. She had neither spoken to nor embraced her first grandchild before she left the bedroom minutes after Sara arrived. Tomorrow, Luciana would return to Alba, leaving her sister in the care of her mother-in-law until Luigia's mother arrived from Bossolaschetto. Normally, the paternal nonna cared for the new baby, but Mirella had made it clear that Sara's nonna Beatrice should take the responsibility. She had too much to do around the farm with Luigia now confined to bed. A storm was brewing. Nico sorely missed his father, who always had a way to dull the sharp edges of Mirella's tongue.

"Nico!" she barked, "I won't let Luigia forget she owes a son to the memory of your dear departed father, Ernesto." She crossed herself as always at the mention of her late husband's name.

Nico studied the short, hunched woman whose face bore the etchings of deep pain: sons lost in a senseless battle and her husband in a farming accident. Since then, her farm animals received greater kindness than she gave the people in her life. Nico often heard his mother and aunts voice disdain for women who were childless—or worse, produced only girls. When a woman failed in her duty to produce males, she was shunned. Luigia should know what to expect of the older generation. Her own mother had been the mother of daughters, not sons.

"She must rest now, Mamma. Let us accept God's gifts in God's time." Mirella's scorn-twisted lips opened, but Nico walked away, too weary to argue with her. Since his father's death, Luigia had taken over the running of the household, and, although she was a strong-willed woman, she often deferred to Mirella to keep the peace. Now she would have to endure thirty-nine more days of confinement until don Paolo came to bless her and remove the sin of childbirth. Until then, he would ignore his mother's hounding and do all in his power to deflect Mirella's wrath. Nico pleaded with Luciana to stay longer, at least until Beatrice arrived, but with influenza still raging and Luigia safe from childbirth, her duty was to the sick of Alba.

Outside, the damp air held close to the ground the scent of burning wood from fires lit to consume the spent vines. The smell stirred Nico's memory of vintages past with his papà and nonno. Thin, wispy clouds slinking over the Alps to the northwest dimmed the light of the full moon. Snow on the way. Did this mean the warmth of the past two days was not the harbinger of spring after all? Much work remained in the vineyards before the vines were ready for the magic of bud burst in March.

The war had left him with few workers. The Austrian prisoners of war had been good vineyard workers, but after the Armistice, not enough Langhetti returned to fill their place. Managing both Cascina dei Fiù and Cornelia Bottero's farm, which he had taken on when her husband left for war, was sometimes too much of a burden. But Nico believed it was a matter of honor to repay the kindness and generosity of her late husband's family through the generations since the Bottero family had come from Nizza Monferrato to Barbaresco.

Nico chose to walk the mile to the village, hoping to cleanse his mind of his mother's grievance before he faced his friends. Would they echo her sentiments? Everyone knew: he must have a son. How else would he hold onto Cascina dei Fiù and make it produce?

The fading moonlight on the skeletal remains of last year's vintage cast ghostly shadows on the muddy road. Snorting *cinghiali* running through the vineyards were the only sound in the still night. Despite Luigia's successful delivery, foreboding plagued him. What sort of world would his daughter face? A chill ran up his spine. From the treaty table, the Allies had thrown Italy some scraps, sowing the seeds of discontent. He had heard in the mercato that hundreds of thousands of soldiers, half of whom were peasants, likely died in battle and from the influenza that paid no heed to the Armistice. Who would work the fields and vineyards now?

Stefano Olivero brought news to Nico on his regular trips to signora Bottero's farm. The sage lawyer spoke with urgency to Nico of political discord spreading throughout Italy. This wasn't the usual farm management talk. There were forces at work, he said, that threatened the House of Savoy or, at a minimum, would transform the king into a puppet. In 1914, a former socialist journalist in Milan, Benito Mussolini, formed a group that called themselves Fascists. In the months since the Armistice, Mussolini's influence had been growing. And then there was the economy. What was a farmer to do? Remain aware, Stefano had counseled him. Hold on to your land. It will keep its value through inflation. And, more than anything, choose your associates wisely.

The money Nico made from his crops was barely enough to buy what they didn't produce and pay the few workers he employed. What sort of world was ahead for them, for his daughter and the sons to follow?

He stopped at the church of San Giovanni Battista near the bar on via Torino to say a prayer of thanks for the good health of his wife and new child, throwing in an extra prayer that a brother would soon follow her. The fragrance of incense was a comfort, and he hoped it would sanctify his prayer. As he stood in front of the church, looking up at the silhouette of the medieval tower of Barbaresco, Nico let it sink in: he was a father now.

From the entrance to the tavern, he spied his childhood friend Primo Barbero sitting with three other men in the far corner, cards in hand, cigarette stub dangling from his lips, a near-empty pitcher next to him. No telling how many pitchers of Dolcetto Primo had drunk, and no telling the *lire* he had lost this evening alone.

Primo's family had been sharecroppers before fortune smiled. His father married a woman with a dowry of land on the far side of Barbaresco, giving the family a rare step up the economic ladder. The Barberos' luck nearly ran out when six daughters arrived before his mother's last pregnancy. They named their first son and last child Primo. Now Primo would inherit the farm in Ovello, provided he didn't lose it at the card table as so many in Barbaresco had. Nico often gave thanks to his departed nonna Dina, whose temper flared at the sight of playing cards. Vehemently against gambling of any sort, she had tossed into the fire many a deck she snatched from Nico and his brothers.

"Nico, come sit!" Primo boomed as he pulled a chair for him and ordered another pitcher of wine.

"Wait, it's a celebration. Let me order," Nico said to the proprietress. "Nebbiolo and five glasses," he called to the barkeep.

Primo's bloodshot eyes widened. He grinned and slapped Nico on the back with his large, weatherworn hand. "A boy! You have a son, Nico. Why else would you drink Nebbiolo on a weeknight?"

Nico's smile flickered before he puffed his chest and announced, "No, Primo. A girl. Sara. And she will be the big sister to guide my many sons in the years to come."

The scornful looks of Primo and his three card-playing partners answered Nico's question. Yes, of course they shared his mamma's disapproval.

The wine arrived with days-old *biova* bread and a generous board of *salumi* and *tuma*. Nico poured for everyone at the table, even the thin, sullen man with narrow, scornful eyes across from him who bore no resemblance to a *Langhetto*. Who was he?

"Not to worry, Primo, boys will come. Look how long it took your mamma," Nico joked wondering whether he was trying to convince himself or the others.

"So let's drink to Nico's last daughter and all the sons who will follow," Primo said as raised his glass. "*Salute!*"

"Girls!" the stranger growled. "What use are girls other than to make sons for Italy?"

Nico sipped the wine to seal the toast then set his glass on the table. He glared at the man who quashed his celebration with his pronouncement. Primo cut in, "Oh, Nico, meet my cousin Ettore Barbero from Milan." The man, whose dark and pointed gaze bore into Nico, reached across the table to shake his hand. Nico hesitated an instant but offered his, not wanting to insult Primo.

"Yes, of course, girls have their uses," Ettore repeated with a tinge of contempt buried under his feigned attempt to apologize, "except Italy needs sons and lots of them. We must rely on ourselves in the future—not so-called allies and certainly not the monarchy."

Primo, whose ample body occupied more space than his wobbly chair could accommodate safely, fidgeted as he drained his glass and searched the room for a way to divert the conversation. Nothing came to him.

"The *Risorgimento*," Ettore continued, "is unfinished business. We are not yet unified. The work of a manly life is to father sons, restore Italy's pride and strength. We must crush the Bolsheviks!"

Well, well, this was someone Stefano Olivero would counsel him against supporting. "We're unified under the House of Savoy," Nico responded. "Whoever loves Italy has had enough of fighting and misery."

Before his cousin responded, Primo waved his hand in the air, "Nico, Ettore, enough of politics," he ordered. "I still have to win my money back, so deal another hand, Ettore."

Nico stood. First his mother and now this belligerent stranger who spoke of a new movement that would create more misery. He had wanted a little male company. This was not it. "Good night, Primo. Good night, all. Enjoy the wine. It's on me."

After paying at the bar, Nico glanced at the men in the corner now absorbed in their card game, except for the stranger who glared at him. For the second time that evening, a chill ran up his spine.

CHAPTER 5

Genoa
October 1932

F rancesco Bosco savored the crisp morning air from his perch near the ship's bow. The seasickness that plagued him all through his night on deck had finally subsided. They had sailed from Naples a day before as an approaching storm churned the seas. The skies were clear now, land was in sight, and his new life was beginning.

He studied the scar across the palm of his left hand. The ragged mark would never disappear, nor would the memories. Six years earlier, Francesco began the journey he was now close to completing although, at the time, he had no idea what was to come. Though strong for his age, tending horses when he was ten years old had left Francesco vulnerable to injuries such as the one that nearly severed his hand. Wincing, he recalled the day the stallion lurched from him, the rope slicing through his young flesh. He loved animals, but he knew then that a life caring for them was not his future. Soon after, Francesco discovered the vines, a life-changing moment the painful injury made possible.

This was Francesco's first time at sea. His only travels in Sicily were to work the vineyards on Etna with his papà. He knew so little about the world beyond the Belice Valley and his village of Contessa Entellina. Soon he would debark at Genoa, a huge port welcoming ships from all over the world. From there he planned to travel by wagon over the salt road to his new home in the vineyards of Langhe. Barbaresco awaited him.

Barbaresco. What a strong name for a little village. Don Pietro, the maverick priest of the Latin church in Contessa Entellina, told him the village was named for barbarians who once lived in the nearby forests. The old, tattered photo of the village's medieval tower transfixed him. Don Pietro gave him the photo to show his mamma where he was going. The good priest wove many tales about the hundreds of castles and vineyard-covered hills he would find there. Soon he would make that magical place filled with promise his new home.

Francesco was too old for tears, but a lump formed in his throat each time he thought of leaving his family, particularly his mamma, but he had no choice. At sixteen, he knew that, if he didn't leave Sicily now, he never would. Piemonte was far away from his home in the rugged mountains of the Belice Valley, but America was much further, across an ocean he was told. Some were leaving Contessa Entellina for America, but there was no money for him to make it that far. All on his own, he had the ambition to escape the imprisonment of poverty, but as for the plan, he owed it to don Pietro and his own parish priest, papas Nicolas, the author of his journey's itinerary.

In the absence of schools, papas Nicolas, the priest of the Arbëreshë church, gave basic instruction to children who showed a willingness to learn. Francesco was one of the most eager and inquisitive boys that papas Nicolas had ever tutored. Albanians, like many of the families in Contessa Entellina, had come to Sicily hundreds of years earlier, fleeing the Ottoman Turks. They had kept their own Arbëreshë language and folk ways, but they were as Sicilian as anyone else. Even at a tender age, village children were put to work, and few had the time to attend papas Nicolas's lessons, challenging his ability to provide them with the keys to a better future.

Work never interfered with Francesco's desire to learn. From the time he was six years old, whenever he finished his chores, usually well before his siblings, he would slip away to Piazza Matrice. In the back of the church, he would find papas Nicolas in his office, light from a high singular window illuminating the dark room and the portraits of generations of Arbëreshë popes that adorned the walls. It was here that the priest ignited Francesco's imagination of the world outside the Belice Valley where hardship, not wealth, abounded. Francesco was shocked when he discovered that his Arbëreshë language wasn't spoken everywhere, not even in all of Sicily.

Francesco hid his studies from his sisters, who he knew would tattle to his mamma, Anna. He worried she would uphold his father's prohibition on studies. Antonino Bosco shared the skepticism of many of the men in the valley who believed skills and hard work, not book learning, were the only way forward. But in a small Sicilian village, it was impossible for children to hide secrets from their mammas. There were too many watchful eyes from windows above the narrow streets and alleys—eyes that witnessed what the women's whispers shared in a flash. Francesco marveled at the speed at which news and gossip spread like wildfire throughout the village.

The truth emerged at dinner one evening when his mamma asked Francesco what he had learned from papas Nicolas that day. Without thinking, Francesco was quick to answer. "More words in Italian, Mamma," eliciting a burst of giggles from his older siblings. His face reddened as he stared at the meager plate of dry bucatini and one thin slice of salami she had placed before him—holding his breath, waiting for his mamma's response. Anna glared at the impertinent girls, who immediately quieted in response to her all-too-familiar stern look.

"I am very proud of you, Francesco. It cannot be easy to do your chores so well and so quickly and still find time to study. You are the first in our family to learn Italian."

Relieved, Francesco gazed into his mother's loving eyes—framed by wrinkles that aged her far beyond the number of her years on earth—and responded in Italian, "*Grazie*, Mamma." He loved her dearly.

Anna Bosco showered her youngest and remaining son with affection she rarely had time to show the others through the years of closely spaced pregnancies. Her two late-term miscarriages that preceded him had given her a rest from caring for infants. This boy, her only redheaded child, Anna had prayed would be different. Francesco would succeed. He would have many sons. Perhaps one day, God willing, he would own the land generations of Boscos had farmed for others.

As though reading her thoughts, Francesco said, "Mamma, I promise to care for you always. Things will be different for me, I know. Papas Nicolas said so."

"*Na do madh'in'zot*, Francesco." *If God wills*, she answered in their native tongue.

Literacy was the greatest gift of all that papas Nicolas gave to his young students. He knew that the Italian he taught them would be of little use in their native village where Arbëreshë was the common language. He was preparing them, in fact, to emigrate. Most would join the steady stream of villagers in their exodus to America, never to return. Francesco sought to learn and studied hard. Where was his future, the priest wondered? Elsewhere, he knew. And from the boy's passion, he knew the vines would be part of it.

Shortly after his tenth birthday, Francesco's lessons ended when he was sent to work for the Inglese family at the Abbazia Santa Maria del Bosco far above the village. The wealthy Inglese family from Palermo, the largest landowner in the valley, was kind to him, and he liked his work alongside their *stalliere* caring for the horses and the *vaccaro* tending the cows.

Their kindhearted cook, Lilli, grew fond of him and made sure Francesco had a warm place to sleep in the cowshed. Each evening she treated him to sweets she had squirreled away for him. It was Lilli who tenderly cleaned and bandaged the torn flesh of his hand the day the stallion bolted from him. To Lilli, Francesco was the son who never lived past his teens, struck down in the Great War.

Francesco was sent home to heal. He didn't want to return to the animals, but he sorely missed Lilli. Soon after, instead of returning him to the Inglese family, his father took Francesco to work with him in the vineyards near Sambucca, west beyond Monte Genuardo. Though his hand was still weak, he had nimble fingers that would be useful in the delicate work of tying vines, cutting grape bunches, and pruning in winter. Antonino Bosco wasn't a particularly kind father, but watching his youngest child working beside him touched his heart, reminding him of himself as a boy discovering the vines.

Father and son were away from home for weeks at a time. As was the custom at the time for sharecroppers and laborers, they were paid their paltry wages annually in September, often not in money, but in what they produced which, in turn, they sold. It was subsistence living, but they were grateful for what little they had.

Francesco didn't mind the long absences from home or the grueling work under the hot Sicilian sun. But he did miss his mamma and the lessons with papas Nicolas he had squeezed in while his hand healed. It was a far better life than most boys his age knew. His three brothers had been sent to the sulfur mines when they were young. One died there, while the others later answered the Mafia's siren call of promised riches. They found only death. His three brothers, two of whom he never even knew, were gone before Francesco was five.

Although his father opposed his book learning, Antonino reveled in teaching Francesco skills he believed would serve his son well in life. Little did they know that the amalgam of papas Nicolas's lessons and his vineyard training one day would free Francesco from the Belice Valley.

Shortly after Francesco's fifteenth birthday, the seeds of his escape were sown. Each month, papas Nicolas and don Pietro sat in the shade of the olive trees in the Arbëreshë priest's garden, sharing their parishioners' gifts of wine. They spoke about the families they had lost to America, mostly to a hot, humid city in the south where many had already made fortunes.

When papas Nicolas told don Pietro the story of a young parishioner who wanted to go to the vineyards of the north, the rotund priest's face lit up.

"What is it, don Pietro?"

"The north is home to much wealth." The smile waned as he continued. "Here we have the Mafia and the wealthy landowners standing in the way of a better life for the peasants. But in the north, I've heard, a man can buy land and be his own boss."

"How do you know?"

The sagacious, older priest's mouth turned up again. "My sister, Angelica, is a nun in Alba, a small city not far from Turin in Piemonte. She's written me of how men who came to the area and worked hard were able to buy land. In fact, she's friends with one such family."

Papas Nicolas was overjoyed to hear this. As an outsider, owning land was out of Francesco's reach, but maybe a better job awaited him. He would never go far in the vineyards of Sicily no matter how hard he worked.

The two clergymen quickly hatched a scheme, employing the help of suor Angelica and her dear friend and fellow nurse, Luciana Capra. A year of exchanging letters—with long, painful silences between each one—passed. Finally, in early summer 1932, the letter they had been waiting for arrived. Luciana's brother-in-law, Nico Fiore, had four young daughters, no sons, and a farm in Barbaresco. Times were tough. Money was scarce. Though all he could promise him was food and lodgings in exchange for work, Francesco was welcome.

Francesco's thoughts shifted to the scene before him as the Genoa port appeared through the early morning autumn mist. Someone called out the name of a small fishing village, Camogli, and pointed to colorful houses that clung to the steep hillside above it. He understood most of their excited Italian as they spoke of returning home to the village. The calm sea mirrored the reflection of small boats as they slowly moved from the village's marina out to the fishing grounds in the Golfo Paradiso.

The *moli* were beehives of activity. Crowded along the docks were ships of all types from across Europe and North America. As the sun rose higher, a dark orange-yellow light washed over the silhouette of the mountain of grain sacks being off-loaded from a cargo ship. Flocks of voracious seagulls swarmed behind incoming fishing boats. Baggage-laden passengers struggled along the vast boardwalk of the *molo* to an awaiting steamer. Were they headed to America? Genoa was the only flat land visible along the coast. Colorful, elegant buildings like none he had ever seen before, not even in Palermo, lined the waterfront like soldiers guarding the port. Palatial villas dotted the rolling landscape above the city. Lush green slopes of steep mountains dusted with early autumn snow from the overnight storm plunged into the sea. Green was a color rarely seen briefly in springtime in the drought-plagued, craggy mountains of his home except for the gnarly, twisted trees in the forests of Monte Genuardo and Monte delle Rose above Contessa Entellina. The explosion of color and grand buildings before him presented a world so unlike the one he had left behind. The splendor of it all moved him, much to his surprise. *Perhaps one day I'll make enough money to send for Mamma.*

His mamma's sobs had echoed on the narrow stone road through the canyon of houses as he ambled down the hill away from her. For fear he would lose his courage, he never looked back. He simply said a prayer that he would see her again.

When Anna Bosco's youngest and last remaining son left home, wanting something more than Sicily had to offer him, the pain was nearly as deep as if Francesco had died. There would be no grave for her to visit on All Saints Day—only an old photo they had taken on a singular trip to Palermo. Would he prosper and aid the family? Or would he simply vanish from their lives?

When he had broken the news to his father, Antonino had studied his son's youthful face, yet to bear the creases of a life of poverty, embraced him as he never had before, and said, "God go with you, my son." That was well over a month ago. With the grapes ripening and the growing season coming to an end, Antonino had left shortly after for the *vendemmia* and would not return for several more weeks.

The bright flash of light on the water from the rising sun as it broke above the mountains to the east snapped Francesco from his melancholy reverie. The reek of fish entrails from an onshore factory welcomed him to the port city. Francesco took his first steps on dry land and scanned the horizon to the south one last time. His mamma's tearful words as he left his childhood home returned: *"Chrishti të bekon, kaha vete e kaha vjen." May God bless and protect you wherever you go and on your return.* They were words he would never forget. Would he return? Sicily was now his past. Barbaresco and its mysterious tower awaited him.

CHAPTER 6

Asili
October 1932

S ara raised her eyes from the meticulous work of cutting Nebbiolo grape bunches to drink in the poignant autumn beauty all around her. Her perch atop the Asili vineyard offered her a grand view of the Rio Sordo valley and the beehive of harvest activity on its slopes. The green leaves of the Nebbiolo and Barbera vines were already fading, showing tinges of gold. In some spots, the Dolcetto leaves were changing to crimson before they dropped—the last sign of life on those vines until bud burst in springtime. Across the valley to the east lay the hunting lodge of the San Benedetto family, Villa Cristina, at the summit of vineyard-carpeted Monte Silva. It was the highest point in Barbaresco with a grand view for miles around. Beauty everywhere.

Sara was grateful she could return to Barbaresco for the harvest, her favorite time of the year. In February, after her thirteenth birthday, she had begun school with the Dominican nuns in Alba where she was studying to become a nurse. Life in the city with her *zia* Luce differed greatly from her country routine in the vineyards and *cantina* with her papà and nonna. A convent education was a rare opportunity for a farm girl like her, but she missed her family, most of all her baby sister, Giovanna, and her nonna Mirella.

A breeze ruffled the vine leaves. Sara glanced at the western sky and frowned at the appearance of wispy cirrus clouds over Monviso.

"Nonna, look at those clouds over il Re," she exclaimed to Mirella, advancing from down the row to work beside her.

"Rain, Sara," Mirella somberly replied. "Not much time to finish these rows before bad weather arrives tonight."

"So soon? How do you know?"

"My old bones, *cara*," Mirella groaned. "I know when I begin to hurt more than usual that it won't be long until a storm arrives." Since experiencing her first vendemmia when she was five, Mirella Canta had helped bring home the grapes for six decades. Even when she was heavily pregnant with Sara's papà, she did not stop tending the vines until two days before he was born. That was how it was done in Langhe. The vineyards and the crops did not wait.

"Nonna, are you all right? You seem sad today."

"No, child. I'm not sad, only tired. This is my last vendemmia."

Sara was horrified to hear her beloved nonna say such a thing. Nonna Mirella lived for pruning and harvesting. Although all the Langhe women helped in the vineyards, no woman in Barbaresco had spent as much time tending the vines as Mirella. When Sara was five, her nonna taught her how to prune the spent canes in winter, tie off the unruly vines and peel away the sucker shoots as the canopy exploded in early June, and cut the bunches in autumn.

The vines and the farm animals were Mirella's true children. The vineyards were her territory. Sara's mamma, Luigia, on the other hand, was a *casalinga*. As such, the house was her domain. Luigia had taught Sara all the domestic necessities a farm girl needed to know like skinning and cooking rabbits, making *tajarin* and *agnolotti del plin* for special occasions and *minestre da bate el gran* after the grain had been threshed in Neive. Mirella taught Sara the world of nature in the vineyards and the barn. Her papà Nico delighted in teaching her the secrets of wine making. What a world for such an inquisitive, nature-loving girl to live in! The close study of nature on the farm would help her to become an excellent nurse, she knew. She would owe that success in part to Mirella. But it had not always been such a harmonious existence for Sara and her nonna.

Sara knew that Mirella had not welcomed her into the world. Once, she overhead her mamma say to zia Luce that before she lost her husband and eldest son, Mirella was a strong but kind woman, that in her bitterness she had held a grudge against her for not being a boy. Yet with time, her heart softened, and she showered affection on Sara who, from a tender age, sensed the true nature of her nonna.

"I'm growing old, Sara. Like the vines, I'm in the autumn of my life. I've given everything I have. Now I shall go to sleep this winter."

The old woman's words baffled Sara, but she sensed that her nonna's forebodings were not something she could help with or even understand.

"Nonna, are you still angry that I wasn't a boy?" Sara asked as she plucked a few berries off the vine and popped them into her mouth.

Mirella's back stiffened.

"I know Mamma went many times to the church to pray with don Paolo for a son. She really tried, Nonna. But God took them to Heaven. She couldn't help that."

Mirella lost herself in the intense, cornflower blue eyes of her eldest grandchild, who peered deep into her soul, in places invisible to Mirella. In the changing world she would never inhabit, perhaps a girl as strong and clever as Sara had the ability to succeed with the farm the way Madama Lia Bottero had done here in Barbaresco, and tota Virginia Ferrero in Barolo.

"Sara, why do you ask me such a question?"

"I heard Mamma and Papà talking after Giovanna was born. Mamma was crying. She said she couldn't have more babies. Mamma said that she had failed you and Papà. Why would she say that?" Sara asked, her tone a touch accusatory.

"Sara dearest, I will not lie to you. You asked, so I'll tell you a story. First, know this and never forget it: I love you dearly."

Mirella held her *coltello serramanico* in one hand and turned over an empty wooden crate to rest her painful back. There still were two rows of grapes to be harvested before the rain came. But right now, that seemed to her less urgent than her favorite granddaughter's curiosity. Mirella's eyes rolled skyward as if seeking guidance and then at the thickening clouds on the horizon. Finally, her eyes settled on Sara's sweet teenage face wreathed by unruly blonde curls. It was time Sara knew the truth about the day she was born.

She motioned to Sara to sit on the ground before her.

"I remember so clearly the day you came into this world, Sara. It was a cold January day with a sky so blue it seemed unreal. We had a ferocious storm the day before, a tempest. Your mamma woke with pains. It was a little soon, but you were coming. I knew the bright sunshine after such a vicious storm meant a grandson would come before the sun set. I was so happy."

Mirella's voice cracked and she closed her eyes, willing a tear to stay put. More than ever, she needed to shed the guilt she had carried for so long. Soon enough, her Creator would judge her.

"Your zia Luce had already arrived from Alba before the storm, so she cared for your mamma all day. She prayed the rosary in between your mamma's pains. All morning, I cooked to soothe my nerves. I had even saved some eggs to make tajarin for such a special occasion. Then, without warning, in the early afternoon, your mamma screamed like I have never heard a woman scream. You were there when Letizia and Giovanna were born, so you know the pain your mamma experienced. But this was something much more."

Luigia's animal-like screams still haunted her. Such a sweet, quiet woman in a flash wracked with unbearable pain. The sound haunted her still.

"I ran from the kitchen up the stairs to her room. Luce's rosary was on the floor. Your mamma was lying on blood-soaked sheets. Just like when your sweet brother was born before you," she paused, looking away, her voice somber. "But he was born dead."

Sara knew that. Zia Luce said the angels took him before he opened his eyes to see his mamma, but that he would see all of them in Heaven.

Mirella could no longer restrain her tears. Sara's touch was soothing, and she had felt it many times when the child sat on her lap and hugged her.

"Please don't cry, Nonna," Sara softly pleaded as she pulled a pale blue handkerchief from the pocket of her tattered apron and dabbed her nonna's eyes.

Mirella saw that Sara was no longer a child, if ever she had been. Her granddaughter was born an old soul with a gift of empathy to which Mirella had been blind. This was almost a young woman before her, one who possessed compassion and understanding greater than most adults Mirella had known. She would tell Sara—now.

"Grazie, *mia cara*." Mirella took a deep breath and looked again past Sara to the horizon where the clouds had darkened, now ominous. The wind had picked up. The scent of rain. Nico would come soon.

"Your papà was in the vineyard not far from the house. I told Luce I would call him. 'No,' she calmly said. 'This time will be different.'"

"Your zia had such a serene, knowing look. She sat on the bed next to your mamma and wiped the sweat mixed with her tears from her face." Her pale, nearly ghostly face—Mirella shook her head as though to banish the image. She remembered Luciana's calm demeanor as she softly prayed for her writhing sister who grew weaker. Or was Luigia at peace, reassured by her sister's presence and prayers? Water, not blood, now flowed. The baby was coming.

"Luce saw you were not in the right way to come out. She was so careful as she positioned you. Then, with one final scream from your mamma, you came to us, crying as if to say *sono arrivata!*"

"But Mamma was fine then, wasn't she?"

"Yes, of course. Your zia Luce saved her…and you. She helped your mamma through your horrible birth." Mirella stopped when her face flushed with shame. She had described Sara's birth as horrible. But Sara's expression didn't change.

"The bleeding stopped and although your mamma was very weak, she was smiling. Luce pulled back the *caul* from your face—a veil, just like the one I had—washed and swaddled you, then handed you to your mamma, saying, 'Here's your angelic daughter, Luigia.'"

Another pause. There was no turning back now.

"Sara, the things that I said then were as though Satan had come into my body and would not leave." The tears returned. "I didn't mean to say I hated you and your mamma. You must believe me," she begged both her grand-daughter and her God. The words came to her in fits. But if she broke down, she might not finish.

Sara embraced her nonna.

"Nonna, please don't cry. I know you didn't mean it."

"Oh, but I did Sara. I really did. At least I meant it then."

"Do you now?"

"No, my dearest. No. You must believe me."

"Then why did you say that, Nonna?"

Mirella had to release the rest of the bitterness that life with Sara as she grew had helped to wash away.

"Sara, when I lost your nonno Ernesto, I was so frightened. Only recently I had lost two sons in the Great War and now..." For a moment, she was still. "Your papà was now the patriarch, so your mamma was head of the house. I was nobody. I blamed her in a way for your nonno's death. Your papà was with her when Ernesto died in the forest. Your brother was coming, so he stayed behind in the cantina to be near her. My dear Ernesto never should have gone alone to cut wood in the forest. I blamed her."

Mirella was now spent, weak from such deep emotion and tears.

"For years, I refused to forgive your mamma. I knew she was not to blame, but I hurt her. I couldn't stop it. But always she was good to me. You know your mamma—strong and willful—but there was a kindness, a sort of under-standing that seemed to shield her from my anger."

"What happened to change things, Nonna?"

"You, Sara. You. As each daughter was born, I saw that God was punish-ing me for my sin of hatefulness, for not seeing that you were a gift He had given us. You changed me."

Sara kissed Mirella on her cheek and once again dabbed her grandmother's tears. "I love you, Nonna. Do you think you can be happy now?"

By unburdening her soul, she felt truly happy for the first time in over thirteen years. Mirella used her cane to stand. As she reached with her coltello serramanico to free the vine of another heavy grape bunch, she winced. Her hands, for so many years nimble, were failing her.

"Nonna, go back to the house. Papà is coming, and together we'll finish these rows."

"No, Sara, I won't..." It was pointless to argue with her granddaughter, so much like her she was. The harvest was over for her. She had taught Sara everything she knew about the vines, about life. Sara had much still to learn, but others would teach her. Life itself would teach her. With that thought, Mirella handed Sara her knife, kissed her cheek, and turned for home. She would need the coltello serramanico no more.

Sara watched her grandmother lumber through the vineyard rows, leaning on her cane a bit more than usual. What a day it had been. Once again, she drank in the scenery around her. How she loved the Barbaresco tower, on the bluff above the Tanaro River and splendid against the backdrop of the Alps, already white with early autumn snow but fast disappearing in the clouds. Although no longer used as a refuge from marauding bands, the tower, with its impossibly high entrance, was still a safe haven in Barbaresco, a place Sara often went alone to enjoy the panorama from its base. She missed it and all the splendor of the Rio Sordo valley when she was in Alba. But the city was her home for now, and one day she would return to Barbaresco.

Madama Lia had said the world around them was changing fast. How long before the changes swept beyond Turin and Alba into the villages of Langhe?

Sara often wondered how her good fortune was possible, enabling her to live in the city and study. It cost money, but zia Luce said not to worry and looked away to discourage further talk. She must have a benefactor—but who? She worried that Mamma and Papà needed her back on the farm, but they kept telling her that the village needed a nurse, that she was doing something for the greater good. Who other than Mamma and Papà thought she was capable of acting for some greater good beyond the farm? Would she be called to such a cause? As well to be ready then. Meanwhile, the identity of her benefactor remained a mystery.

Just then, Nico's trusted truffle hound, Milo, came baying up the hill, announcing the arrival of his master. With autumn rains beginning, soon Nico and Milo would be hunting for white truffles in the Pora woods across the valley. Sara caught a glimpse below of Mirella entering the *cappella* di San Teobaldo.

Nico arrived. Together they clipped the remaining Nebbiolo bunches as a light rain began. The rain and the thought of Luigia's harvest feast awaiting them at home hastened their work. Another vendemmia was finished, always such a joyous moment and one made even more special by sharing it with her papà. Soon Sara would return to Alba, and Nico would begin the alchemy of transforming the harvest bounty into wine. She would miss the countryside in autumn and the beauty of the rolling landscape preparing for its winter slumber. But the city, filled with new experiences and adventures, was awaiting her.

CHAPTER 7

Turin
Autumn 1932

The wall clock competed with the metronome on the piano as Baldo Volpe's stern teacher, professor Eduardo Dalmasso, stood watch behind him. Grieg's "Notturno" would be Baldo's finale—how fitting. Nighttime. The end of a day and the end of these blasted lessons. Now he would concentrate on what mattered most to him: advancing through the Fascist youth group, the Avanguardia. At sixteen, he was the size of a grown man and far too old for the music room. It was time to concentrate on preparing to serve Il Duce in the battle to redeem Italy's honor.

"Pay attention, Baldo. Finish well!" Professor Dalmasso tapped his baton on the opulent baby grand piano.

But how could he? This mattered not at all to him. Only for Flora, his mamma, had he tolerated the lessons from the insufferable old man all these years. Sadly for her, his father had put an end to this folly by refusing to allow his mamma to finance it any longer. "Baldo must prepare himself for battle, not for concerts!" he bellowed during dinner one recent evening. "These ridiculous lessons must end now! It will make him weak. And with a Jew teacher at that!" Flora had cringed at those words, but Baldo was relieved to be done with the lessons.

Finally, the three and a half minutes it took him to reach the end of the melancholy piece had passed. And the curtain fell on his lessons.

"Estimable, Baldo. You have done quite well," professor Dalmasso said. "Your technique is excellent, but you must put more passion into your music. I do hope your father will change his mind and you will return to develop your gift."

"It's a gift I don't want," Baldo scoffed. Even if Mamma convinced his father to allow him to return to the piano, he vowed he never would touch a keyboard again.

With a heavy heart, professor Dalmasso dismissed him. *Such anger in one so young and so talented. Shouldn't the love of music die harder than that?*

Baldo left his open music book on the piano and hurried out the door with a mere nod. *Good riddance!* was his last thought as he left.

Professor Dalmasso lived near the Great Synagogue of Turin. Since King Carlo Alberto emancipated the Jews in 1848, they were free to live wherever they wished. In 1880, some of the newly rich Jews moved away from the ghetto and built the synagogue close to Turin's center. Baldo hated walking through the area, but it was the fastest route to the tram on Corso Vittorio Emanuele II. Wherever he walked, there they were. Increasingly they dominated his thoughts night and day.

They were even allowed in government, something Baldo's father repeatedly condemned. Dino Volpe had served under a Jewish officer at Caporetto and blamed him for their defeat. "We lost the war because of the Jew generals," his father often grumbled, "and yet they were rewarded with medals. Even that Jew officer of mine, Giordano, who led us to capture, was awarded the Gold Medal for so-called heroism during the battles of Monte Grappa."

Those with long memories assured Baldo that Dino Volpe had not always been such a tyrant. Not even to break free of the poverty of her mountain village in Alto Adige would Flora have married such a man. He had left for war in the summer of 1915 a trustworthy and reasonable man, they said. But the battle of Caporetto, brutal captivity in an Austrian prison, and the long grueling winter trek home changed all that. He returned the man that Baldo knew.

All Baldo wanted now was out.

The stinky old men near the synagogue bothered him most of all. Why did some Jews dress so strangely? Had they never shaved or cut their sideburns? And what was it with the tall fur hats the men often wore? Baldo would never understand these people his Südtirol-born German language teacher said were not Italians, although they claimed to be.

Baldo proudly wore his Fascist youth group uniform that day, an excellent change from his schoolboy clothes. He always felt strong and bold, as his name implied, when he was dressed as a member of the Avanguardia. Many couldn't afford one, but his mamma sewed his uniform. As he rounded the corner, a group of giggling schoolgirls his age exited the Hebrew school next to the synagogue. He knew they were snickering at him; he sensed it. They were snobs, and he hated them for that. As he walked past, he mumbled, "Dirty Jew." One girl overheard him. She ran in front of him and turned, blocking his path.

She stood with her hands on her hips, glaring at him.

"What did you say?" she demanded.

"You heard me." Then he spat on the ground in front of her. "*Sporca ebrea!*" Dirty Jew! "One day we will chase you out of Turin! Out of Italy!" Something had changed in the short time since cutting himself off from professor Dalmasso's droning about Beethoven, Mozart, and Rachmaninoff. Ah, not having to face the old Jewish *professore* allowed him to say exactly what he thought about these people, exactly what his German teacher and youth group leader had said many times to him. The freedom to express how he truly felt stirred his manhood. But the girl showed no fear and didn't run from him. She stood her ground and bore into him with her blue eyes, so unusual for a Jew, he thought.

"We will meet again one day, but the hunter shall become the hunted," she said.

He laughed. What a ridiculous thing for a girl, much less a Jewess, to say to him, a unit leader in the Avanguardia! But it was unsettling all the same, especially because she seemed so familiar. He spat again and walked past her.

Baldo took a few steps and glanced back. The girl stood glowering at him, her eyes narrowed and arms crossed. He took a few more steps, turned, and strode back to within a few feet of her. Her friends, no longer giggling, had stopped and stared at them.

"I'm not afraid of—" Before she could finish, one of the other girls grabbed her and pulled her away.

"You had better be afraid. One day we'll come for you and your Bolshevik Jew friends. I warn you!"

Baldo boarded the tram at Porta Nuova for the ride to his squad meeting. The girl's blue eyes, so familiar, hounded him. He was certain he had seen her before, but where? He pushed her face out of his mind when the tram passed Le Nuove prison. The hellish building intrigued him. He fantasized about the punishments given to enemies of the state. *One day I will be the one interrogating the Bolsheviks there! How I will pay them back for seeking to undo all the great work of our Fascist leaders.* What would have become of Italy if

Il Duce and his Blackshirts had not marched on Rome in 1922? A glorious decade of Fascist control. But even so, Bolsheviks, many of them Jews, were the enemies of the state and remained a threat to the regime.

LATER THAT EVENING, WHEN BALDO WALKED HOME THROUGH HIS OWN DRAB quarter, he wondered in what condition he would find his mamma that evening. She was a kindhearted woman caught in a hellish marriage to a brute. The only joy she had was to hear Baldo sing in the choir at *Chiesa* di Santa Giulia and to know that his musical gift was being nurtured to praise God. He did not like to take that away from her, but the time had come for him to be a man. After her long days teaching unruly primary schoolers, Flora spent her evenings sewing fancy clothes based on the latest Parisienne fashions, mostly for wealthy Jewish women, to earn extra money for Baldo's lessons. No more. Poor Flora, she stood her ground to ensure that Baldo would continue singing at church. It had cost her, though. The bruise on her cheek still showed despite the heavy makeup she applied each morning. And how long would singing in church last? He was no choirboy now. He was a young man on fire to restore Italy's former glories, to restore the glory of Rome. And the fire would be purifying.

As he climbed the five flights of stairs to the tiny apartment, he heard his father shouting. Drunk again. No job, but somehow money to drink. One day soon, he swore, he would put an end to his father's violence against his mamma, as he had for himself. Dino Volpe would never lay a hand on him again. It was such a puzzle. Baldo despised his father but approved of and shared his politics. If Dino could ever make himself useful again, his deep dedication to Mussolini would mean something.

Appetizing aromas welcomed Baldo. "*Buonasera*, Mamma," he said cheerfully as he entered the kitchen. He ignored his father, who grumbled and left the room. Baldo went to Flora, gently wiped her cheeks wet with tears, and kissed her forehead. She was much shorter than Baldo and seemed increasingly fragile. "It will be all right, Mamma. I promise."

Flora quickly gathered her composure, wiped her hands on her apron, and handed him an envelope. "You have a letter, Baldo. It looks official." Baldo ran his finger over the tricolors of the Italian flag and the *fasces*, the symbol of the National Fascist Party. This was definitely something official.

Baldo ripped open the envelope and pored over the contents of the short letter. "Mamma, I'm going to Berlin!" he exclaimed as he swept her up in his arms.

"Baldo, put me down! What's wrong with you?" Flora knew any trip was unaffordable, even with her seamstress money. "It is not possible, Baldo."

"Mamma, it is. I'm being sent there by the Party. I've been chosen to study German in Berlin and work at our embassy. I leave after Epiphany. Imagine that!"

Although Baldo saw no use for his musical gift, his talent for languages had earned him honors in school. As one of the Avanguardia *scelti*—the chosen ones—he had the opportunity to impress many local Fascist party leaders. And now this. Not only would he be able to study his favorite foreign language, but he also would do so in a country where great changes were happening. His group leader had assured him that Hitler would be Germany's next chancellor. With time, Baldo believed Mussolini would ally himself with Hitler and he, Baldo Volpe, would be in an enviable position.

Flora's smile crumpled. "How long will you be away?" She returned to her pot on the stove, not able to look at him. Her heart hurt. This was the end of her hopes that music, not the way of the Blackshirts, would be his future. He was smart enough to be an engineer or a professor and lift the family into the middle classes, but all he wanted was to consort with vicious rabble. Day and night, Flora worried about the increasing violence of the Fascist youth groups and her son's involvement with them. And his growing hatred of Jews was unfathomable. Yes, his father went on night and day about them, but she taught many sweet Jewish children and made lovely clothes for kind Jewish women. They were Italians like everyone else. They even spoke Piemontese!

Baldo read the letter once more. "They don't say how long." His mind spun. He didn't care about the duration. But in an instant, his elation evaporated. Mamma. Who would protect Mamma from his father? His older sister, Sofia, had moved away from Turin for a job in Milan. She had had enough of her father's paws, and Baldo had been too young to protect her. Now Flora would be alone with Dino.

Baldo would have to show Dino how things stood, or he would never be able make a break. Come to that, didn't he have reliable friends to keep Dino in line? He folded the letter and cached it under a pitcher in the kitchen dresser. He made fast strides to embrace his mamma at the stove. The frightened look in her swollen eyes ignited his smoldering hate. Today outside the synagogue, he proved what a man he was. Now he would defend his mamma.

"Papà!" he shouted, walking down the hall.

With one hand on the gas knob, Flora stared into the pot before her as though in a trance. Slowly, she increased the flame. Bubbles broke the surface of the minestrone that was to be dinner. Soon droplets of hot liquid flew from the pot, some landing on her cheeks. She felt no pain. Baldo was once such a sweet boy. So kind. Perhaps he was like the soup—once calm, now boiling. What had ignited that flame of hate burning within him? And now he would be in the midst of those hate-filled Nazi youth groups in Berlin that she had heard some of her Jewish clients discuss among themselves. Her mind whirled. Flora closed the gas and watched the surface of the soup calm. "Oh, if extinguishing Baldo's flame was as easy," she murmured.

Flora removed her apron, replaced it with her coat, and willed herself to the door without so much as picking up her handbag. As she descended the stairs, the noise of men shouting in their apartment grew louder and echoed through the stairwell. That hideous bark came from her son, the choirboy. She continued out into the cool early evening air. Flora Volpe was a woman with no place to go, no one to turn to.

CHAPTER 8

Barbaresco
Late Autumn 1932

Francesco was on the last leg of his weeks-long journey to his new home. Six days earlier, at the port of Genoa, he had discovered how far from Barbaresco he was. How to get there was a difficulty he had not considered. On board the ship, a fellow Sicilian boy told him of a labor market held near the port in the early morning. Once ashore, Francesco sped to it and read a handwritten sign that was an answer to a prayer: Conducente Gep Raimondo. *Your labor for a ride.* He gladly offered to help the aging Piemontese make deliveries of heavy crates of *baccalà* and salted anchovies and barrels of olive oil. The exchange was fair and provided him with transportation as far as Alba. It was rough going in the old wagon along the narrow dirt roads that wound through the Ligurian Apennines to the hills of Alta Langa, but it helped him conserve what little money remained in his pocket.

They slept under the stars, and Gep shared with him some of the savories they were transporting. Mostly, their sustenance consisted of his wife's gamey wild boar salami, luscious tuma from goat's milk, and bread Gep called biova that had long since gone stale. They washed it down with a tasty red wine unfamiliar to him that Gep's brother had made. Dolcetto, he called it.

Francesco woke to splendid new vistas each day. Even though it was late autumn, there was still much greenery—so unlike the home he had left. While the Belice Valley was mountainous, and he had even traveled to Mount Etna on Sicily's northeast coast, nothing he had ever seen compared with the soaring, snow-covered peaks across the plain as they entered the wild, rolling hills of Alta Langa.

Gep pointed to the tallest of the mountains he called "Alps" and exclaimed, "il Re!" With its pyramid-shaped peak soaring above the surrounding crags, Monviso was undeniably the king. It was majestic and seemed always to be directly to his left, no matter how far north they traveled.

Although Gep talked nonstop, Francesco welcomed the company after so many weeks of lonely travel. At first, he struggled to understand the harsh-sounding words of the Piemontese dialect. Gep finally settled into serving up a verbal soup of Piemontese and Italian so that slowly Francesco's comprehension improved.

At close to midnight on the fourth day, Gep dropped him at Alba train station. Exhaustion gripped him. The station waiting room was locked, but Francesco found a sheltered corner outside where he managed a few hours of sleep before the first train to Barbaresco in the early morning.

WHEN THE TRAIN EXITED A TUNNEL INTO THE VALLEY, THE BRIGHT SUNLIGHT snapped Francesco awake. As his eyes adjusted, it was as though a curtain lifted to reveal brilliant images unlike any Francesco had seen in Sicily. Under the cobalt-blue sky, dense forests of oak and poplar trees lined the tracks and climbed up the hill to his right. Past the forests, the scene abruptly changed to rolling hills carpeted with golden and red vine leaves glistening in the morning sun. Here and there, he spotted fruit tree orchards and neatly planted, stubby round trees Gep had identified as hazelnuts, from which many Piemontese sweets were made. The vines had already surrendered their bounty, but even now, they appeared lush. Planted in orderly, narrow rows, they looked nothing like the unruly vines he tended in Sicily.

Were they nearing Barbaresco? Up the hill to his left, he saw several farmhouses nestled in the vineyards. Where was la *Torre*? Since he arrived in Langhe, he had seen many hills topped with either a castle or fortress, but he had yet to see the Barbaresco tower of the postcard image papas Nicolas had shown him.

Francesco had no idea that one had to request the stop at the tiny Barbaresco station. Fortunately, another passenger pulled the cord and alerted the engineer. Soon the train rolled into a station that looked like a small, fine house. Where was the village? He had only seen vineyards and forests. And people.

The station was buzzing with activity. Wagonloads of *damigiane* filled with wine were arrayed next to the tracks, awaiting the westbound train that would transport them to Alba and south to Ligurian customers. A few rotund, gray-haired women with empty baskets impatiently waited for the same westbound train to take them to Alba. It was Saturday, and he had seen streams of people arriving in the city by foot, donkey, car, *cartun*, and two-wheeled carts that Gep had referred to as *birocc*. Groups of people carrying brimming baskets, some leading donkeys laden with wares slung across their backs, walked beside the tracks in the opposite direction. No doubt, they were headed to the mercato to sell what they produced.

The only information Francesco had was two names: Nico Fiore and *Ca' dei Fiù*. He didn't even know how to contact don Pietro's sister, suor Angelica, who had made this all possible for him. Luciana Capra, he was told, was another link in the chain that connected him to the Fiore family. He would seek her help if he were unable to locate the Fiore farm. No one he heard spoke Italian, but days of Gep's nonstop gabbing left him with a few useful phrases.

"Bondì, monsù, an dua ca alè la cassin-a dei fiù?" he stammered in Piemontese to a burly man off-loading a large *damigiana*. The stranger twisted his bushy mustache and narrowed his dark eyes as he scrutinized Francesco. Was it that he was so tall, particularly for his age, or that he was an outsider who spoke barely comprehensible Piemontese that prompted the man to study him so? After a pause, he removed the scrawny unlit cigarette dangling from his lips, pointed up the hill to a road below the vineyards before returning to his work. *"Mersi,"* Francesco responded, hoping he had chosen the right Piemontese word to thank him.

The road was muddy from the recent rain. As he climbed from the shade in the valley into the sunshine, Francesco finally shed the chill from the night. And there was Monviso once again. Il Re was now a familiar landmark. Thick, dark-gray mud like none he had ever seen clung to his boots. Soon, passing wagons and a shiny black automobile unlike any in Contessa Entellina splashed muddy water from the deep puddles. The black jacket and pants his mamma had made for his trip were now dingy gray and the worse for wear. A scruffy beard and wiry moustache—his first ever—had grown over his sunburned face. No surprise the man scrutinized him so.

The road that passed through the località Martinenga above the station gradually climbed as it meandered through the vineyards and orchards. He wondered whether he had understood correctly. Where was the village? It wasn't long before he came to a tiny chapel at an intersection. Unsure which path to take, Francesco decided to rest and take in the sprawling landscape of his new home. Don Pietro told him that, although Piemonte had the blessings of fertile plains and good terroir for grapes, Langhe was a poverty-ridden farming community. To Francesco, the land spoke of prosperity. Squinting in the bright, morning sun, he looked across the valley to the next hill and, finally, he saw it. La Torre! Now he knew he was nearly in Barbaresco.

The tower and the snow-covered mountains in the distance bewitched him and claimed all of his attention. Excited and hurrying now to reach the village, he collided with a petite, blonde-haired girl as she emerged from the chapel. Down she went with a splash. Unfamiliar words poured through her gritted teeth. He looked at her sitting in a puddle on the road, her dress now covered with mud that had also spattered her face and hair. "Excuse me," he stammered in Italian as he bent to offer his hand. She swatted it away and scrambled to her feet.

The girl appeared a few years younger than he was and yet on the cusp of womanhood. Her face was crimson, the edges of her mouth curled downward, but her captivating blue eyes framed by long, dark-blonde eyelashes expressed a different, kinder emotion. Francesco had seen a few Sicilians with blue eyes, but hers were like the *fiordalisi* he loved to collect in spring for his mother. His heart jumped. Is this what cousin Renzo meant when he once described to Francesco what love felt like? *Colpo di fulmine?*

She looked unnerved but not intimidated as she snapped at him in Piemontese. "Who are you?"

Her belligerent tone was a bit brazen for someone so young and so small, particularly when addressing a tall stranger like him. Why was he breathless? Despite her disheveled appearance and her unfriendly, abrupt demeanor, she appeared like an angel to him.

Wiping her muddy hands on her dress, she again demanded, "Who are you?"

His mind whirled. Words escaped him. Even his native Arbëreshë tongue eluded him. *My name—she must be asking my name.* "Francesco. *Mi chiamo* Francesco Bosco." She threw back her head and giggled. In a flash, his face under layers of dirt and hair burned. Was it his accent?

"You're *the Sicilian*! I'm Sara. Sara Fiore," she responded. "We were wondering whether you would ever appear, and now the harvest is over."

What great fortune! This angel was a Fiore, the family that had offered him a job. He hoped her ire would fade.

"*Anduma*, Francesco. Let's go!"

Francesco rushed to keep up with Sara as she led him up a short road that ended in a cul-de-sac. There, across a broad *cortile*, sat two very different farms, one with a grand two-story cascina painted creamy yellow, and the other with two rustic stone buildings. Such a contrast. Four horses, two of which were fine and well-groomed, nuzzled hay and regarded them from the paddock between the farms. Paying no attention to Francesco, Sara walked ahead of him to one of the stone buildings. As she pushed open the heavy wooden door, familiar smells conjured images of a place he had left behind. He was far from home, and these vineyards, so neat and well-kept, were unlike Contessa Entellina's, yet the heady aroma of fermenting grapes was the same. Ah, the cantina.

"Papà, the Sicilian is here," Sara shouted into the darkness.

A little girl no more than four or five bounded out of the humbler of the two houses, giggling and running to Sara, who swept her up in her arms and spun her around. "Giovanna, look, the Sicilian has come." She kissed the child, set her down, and disappeared into the house. Should he follow?

Francesco assumed the bundle of energy before him was Sara's sister. She possessed the same heart-shaped face and blonde curls, but her eyes were a lighter shade of blue. Standing with arms crossed and brow furrowed, Giovanna repeated Sara's question. "Who are you?" Ah, a familiar phrase. "Francesco, mi chiamo Francesco Bosco," which sent her into a fit of giggles once more.

"Giovanna! Where's Sara?" A stocky man with a broad smile on his weatherworn face emerged from the cellar.

Without answering, Giovanna scurried back to the cascina. "You must be Francesco. Welcome. You've met two of my daughters. The eldest and youngest. I'm Nico Fiore," His new employer's shining brown eyes were warm and welcoming as he extended his calloused, red-stained hand. Francesco, once again befuddled by the language, simply grinned and shook Nico's hand. The two men had only communicated through don Pietro and suor Angelica, but Nico's warm expression welcomed him.

Two women emerged from the house—one of a maternal age with smiling hazel eyes, brown hair in a braid pinned atop her head, and a lustrous complexion and the other, deep creases in her weathered face, ambling behind her, leaning heavily on her cane—their labor in the kitchen having cloaked them in rich culinary aromas and spotted their aprons. Francesco's belly grumbled. He had eaten the last of his stale bread and cheese after reaching Alba and nothing since. The younger woman, Sara's mother perhaps, seemed shy, but like Nico, her face exuded kindness. He shivered as his longing for home and his mamma rushed over him for the first time in days. The older, gray-haired woman stood apart from the others, rubbing her hands together and eyeing him with the same wary look that Sara and the man at the station had given him. Two other girls, somewhere between Giovanna and Sara in age, came no closer than the entrance to the cascina. Where had the angel gone?

"Francesco, this is my wife, Luigia, and my mamma, signora Fiore." Nico made the introductions in Piemontese, but noting the lost look on Francesco's face, switched quickly to Italian, *"Mi dispiace,* Francesco. Our dialect must be difficult for you. Although children must learn Italian in school now, it's still unusual to find people in Langhe who speak it. Piemontese is still our language." The Italian Nico spoke sounded so different from what papas Nicolas had taught him that Francesco wondered whether he would be able to communicate with his new employer. But he was a fast learner, he must never forget. All the moves he needed would come—and fast.

"Thank you, signor Fiore. I've already learned a few words during my journey to Alba," he replied with a shyness that was foreign to him.

Luigia, who was also gifted with the Italian language, beckoned to him. "Come, you must be exhausted after the long journey. Sara will show you to your room. I'll boil some water for you to wash." *Hot water!* He would get cleaner than he had been since he left home.

"We finished the harvest last week before the rains came. Your arrival under sunny skies is a sign, is it not?" Nico chuckled and slapped Francesco on the back. "So now we celebrate tomorrow after church. Luigia and Mamma have been cooking for days."

"Nico!" A woman, close in age to Luigia—elegantly dressed all in black and not much taller than Sara—called out as she emerged from the pale yellow cascina. A wiry, bald man leading two fine horses, their coats gleaming and odd-looking saddles on their backs, followed her. "Where is Sara?" she asked. "She promised to ride with me to Villa Cristina to visit the contessa."

The woman stopped before Francesco. Her eyes narrowed as she studied him. Nico made the introductions. "Madama Bottero, may I present Francesco Bosco of Contessa Entellina, Sicily?"

Francesco had forgotten to remove his hat for the Fiore ladies, so he grabbed it off before responding, *"Piacere,* signora Bottero." He nodded. Should he bow? Did he say her name wrong? He had never met a real lady before and felt tongue-tied. She had a pleasant smile, though, and seemed amused at the sight of him.

"Piacere," she responded.

"Francesco, Madama lives in Alba, but her farm is here, next to ours. I manage her vineyards and make her wine."

Francesco's cheeks flamed and he fidgeted with his cap. Would he have to say more to her? She relieved him of his anxiety when she abruptly turned to Nico and once again asked for Sara.

"I don't know, Madama Lia, she disappeared into the house."

Madama Lia turned to the man leading the horses. "Gianni, this is Francesco. He's Nico's new farmhand," she said. "Nico, please go see what is keeping Sara. Francesco, hold Sara's horse while Gianni helps me up," she directed. Gianni gave her a leg up and she settled on the horse with both legs on one side. Francesco marveled to see a woman on a horse and riding in such a manner.

Sara came striding out of the house, dressed like Madama Lia except her clothes were deep blue. The fit of her jacket revealed that she was closer to womanhood than Francesco had realized. Her previously unruly hair was now neatly tucked under a dark blue silk hat, and a thin veil attached to it obscured her face. And her eyes. That breathlessness returned! He tried to hide it.

"Sara, hurry, we'll be late."

"Francesco, help me up," Sara ordered as she bent her left leg to be lifted. When he touched her booted leg, electricity coursed through his body. He thought he would faint, so he quickly lifted her slender, light body into the saddle. As she gathered the reins, she informed Francesco that her sisters Maria and Letizia would show him to his room. Her voice was kinder. Did she smile at him behind her veil? Perhaps he had completed his punishment for knocking her into the mud.

Francesco watched as the two women cantered off on the vineyard road. Nico, observing Francesco's gaping mouth and the besotted expression on his face, shook his head. "Let's go, my boy. You have quite an education awaiting you."

CHAPTER 9

Asili
Sunday, late October 1932

A sliver of sunlight penetrated the wide crack in the shutters and shone on Francesco's face, stirring him from a leaden slumber. Even the opera of feisty roosters calling out to each other across the valley had failed to wake him hours earlier.

He had not paid much attention to the room the day before, but as the light grew brighter, details of his surroundings emerged. Tucked under the roof of the building that housed the cantina and barn, the room was small, but its comforts were grand, particularly compared to the sleeping quarters of vineyard workers in Sicily. The simple chair in the corner would make donning his boots easier. There was even a chest of drawers and a small armoire, although he didn't have much to put in either. He didn't need many clothes anyway. Best of all was his narrow bed with a mattress and soft bedding fit for a king. His head felt as though it floated on the pillow stuffed with downy feathers—a perfect spot to rest after a long day's work. This was his new home.

Francesco's arrival in Barbaresco the previous day had been filled with expected challenges—most notably his struggles with the Piemontese dialect that he was confident he would overcome—and unexpected delights including his chance encounter with an angel. Sara had not behaved like one as she sat in the mud, shouting unintelligibly at him, but she warmed a little to him as the day progressed. The breathless, near-giddy feeling he experienced when he first met her returned each time he looked into her luminous eyes. Sara was so petite; he was so tall. Sara was mature, soon to be fourteen years old. He was almost sixteen but unversed in so many things she seemed to know. The biggest difference, however, was one that shook his confidence. Sara was unlike any farm girl he knew, different even from her sisters. Had he met Sara elsewhere, he would have thought her the daughter of a lady like Madama Lia, not of a farm family, even one that owned land. He overheard Letizia discuss with her mamma Sara's return to Alba soon, but he wasn't sure what that meant or when exactly "soon" was. He hoped her absence would not be for long. Sara had won his heart, and he was certain he would eventually win hers. Time was on his side now that he was living at Ca' dei Fiù. In the short time since their lives collided, she had become his polestar. How could he lose her from his sky?

Giovanna, who worshiped her big sister, quickly took to him. The four-year-old followed him everywhere, giggling every time he spoke. Surely, that gave him a boost with Sara. At dinner, she demanded to sit next to him instead of Sara. When he sat for his first Langhe meal, Francesco was washed, clean-shaven, and dressed in his work clothes—his only clean clothes. One time at dinner when he was speaking with Nico, he spied Sara out of the corner of his eye, wrinkling her nose and studying him from across the table. When he returned her gaze, she quickly turned away. Maria and Letizia, who were closer to Sara's age, were not as effusive as their baby sister was, but they were kind as they helped him settle in. They made him—a stranger, an employee, and not least of all, a Sicilian—feel welcome. Don Pietro had warned him that the Piemontese, though kind, were reserved with outsiders, and being accepted, if it ever happened, took a long time. But, other than Sara, everyone had been warm to him since his arrival in Barbaresco. Don Pietro also had mentioned that Luigia had lost three sons at birth. Was it too improbable that he might be a son to them one day? *Stop dreaming.*

Francesco sat up, rubbed his crusty eyes, and looked around the room—his own room—again. Eight times, distant church bells rang. It was late! This would be the last morning he would rise after the sun until the springtime. He shivered and wrapped himself with the blanket Letizia had given him. The last embers in the small iron *stufetta* in the corner were all the heat he had. Stoking them with the rod next to it failed to reignite the flames. He needed more wood. Perhaps the sunshine would help warm the east-facing room.

Francesco threw open the shutters. Under the radiant blue sky, farm animals milled about in the barnyard below, and beyond the fence stretched a sprawling amphitheater of vines. Was he dreaming? No, he wasn't. The small room with more comforts than he had ever known was his home now. Tomorrow he would begin earning it.

He opened the door. The sweet fragrance of hay permeated the space under the long roof. From the opening steps from his room, an exterior staircase led to the barnyard. Someone had left a pitcher of cold water and a few pieces of wood outside his door. Sara, perhaps?

Francesco added the wood to the stoked embers. The stufetta came to life. He buried his hands in his blanket, pulled it tighter, and walked to the window again. No human sounds, only the animals below. Surely, everyone was awake. It seemed a good time to explore.

The room warmed up quickly, so Francesco shed the blanket and tidied the bed. His mamma would be pleased although he rarely did so when he was home. After a quick refresh with the water left for him, Francesco dressed and headed outside.

Before he reached the bottom of the stairs, noisy chickens and sniping geese fled to the opposite end of the yard near cages filled with rabbits. One cage was open and empty. A large, bloodied knife on a worn tree stump was a familiar sight to him. He remembered the first time he had seen his nonna kill a rabbit, swiftly slicing its neck. He shivered. Animals were for food, she always said, but witnessing the executions sickened him. Pecking around the vines, a fat rooster stopped to take in the stranger in his domain. Francesco wondered why it had not crowed that morning. Surely, he would have heard it.

He peered into the barn. A milk cow and the two horses he had seen Sara and Madama Lia ride raised their heads. Such a luxury on a farm like this to have saddle horses whose only labor was to transport fine ladies. Horses were prized in the countryside but usually for their strength, not their beauty. Four other horses, already shaggy with their growing winter coats, huddled next to one another in the far corner of the yard. No doubt, they spent their days performing tasks more arduous. At dinner, when Francesco asked about the saddle horses, Nico told him they were from Germany and belonged to Madama Lia. He also told of an eccentric *contadino* on the other side of the eastern ridge in Vallegrande who loved fast horses. Luigi Grasso was known not only for his wine but also for his bay horse and his passion for racing him. Nico said that, although he shunned gambling, it was popular in the countryside. Many a farm had been lost, he said, at the card table or before the dust settled after races on long dirt roads. "Stay away from the card tables, Francesco," Nico had warned.

Up the hill beyond the paddock sat Madama Lia's grander cascina with the name elegantly written in white paint: Cascina Asili. He decided to return to the Fiore house. For him, the paddock fence was the border beyond which he would not venture—at least for now.

As he climbed back to the hayloft, giggling girls approached the farm. He peered around the corner and saw the four Fiore sisters in their Sunday finest walking toward the house, the older Fiores close behind them. He marveled at the old woman who, despite her age and need for a cane, walked briskly with the others. Mirella had yet to grace him with a kind word or gesture. Of all the family, she was the coolest to him.

"Francesco! *Bondì!*" shouted Giovanna as she let go of Sara's hand and ran to him. At least he knew that Piemontese word, so he returned her good morning greeting. Before he left the family the night before, Sara told him that Giovanna had always lamented she had no big brother, so she had decided he would do. "Don't let her pester you, Francesco," Sara had warned. Giovanna tugged at his heart. He cursed his inability to speak with her better. She spoke no Italian, and he struggled with Piemontese. Maybe she would be his teacher, although he preferred to let Sara help him. No doubt, she had much to teach him. What would his mamma say? "Oh Franco, such thoughts, and on Sunday! You should be ashamed of yourself." He blushed. Did anyone notice?

"Buongiorno, Francesco," Nico said. "We decided not to wake you for Mass this morning."

"Will you come with us to Mass next week?" Luigia asked. "You are Catholic, aren't you?"

Francesco was uncertain how to answer. "Oh yes, signora Fiore, I do go to Mass, but I am Arbëresh, so I go to the Greek church."

Luigia tilted her head. "What do you mean, Francesco? Are you Greek Orthodox? There is only one Catholic church. And don Pietro is your priest, correct?"

Once again, Francesco's face flushed, which was happening far too often since he arrived. He had always known the other church in Contessa Entellina as the Latin church. They had the same pope, they were both Catholic, but they prayed in a different language of which he knew not one word. Papas Nicolas was a priest, but he had a wife. Don Pietro was also a priest, but he was forbidden to marry. It was all so confusing. Did he have to defend himself among these kind people for being a little different the way he had with boys from the Latin church in Contessa Entellina?

"Signora, I really don't know how to explain, but I'm Catholic. Papas Nicolas said our ancestors came from Albania over four hundred years ago and that the pope allowed them to keep their traditions and still be part of his church. Don Pietro is a priest, but at the Latin church." He hoped that would satisfy her because that was all he knew. It was something he had accepted as fact all his life and never questioned.

"I see," Luigia said, looking like she still did not truly understand but perhaps realizing her questions caused discomfort. She must have seen that he crossed himself after grace, although in a different manner, so she knew he was a Christian. He glanced heavenward, showing his relief that she had not probed further.

"Now, girls, come. We have lots to finish for *pranzo*."

Francesco watched the four girls disappear into the house, Sara never turning to acknowledge him. With his attention fixed on Luigia, Francesco had not seen her scrutinizing him while he spoke with her mamma. If he had, he might have seen the dewiness in her blue eyes and the slight blush that appeared on her cheeks.

"Come, Francesco," Luigia called from the cascina entrance.

He followed Luigia into the kitchen where she laid out on the table a steaming cup of strong coffee with hot milk, a slice of crusty bread, and a hunk of hard cheese. He had barely finished when Nico tugged on Francesco's arm. "Come, the train from Alba will be arriving soon, and I must fetch my *cognata*, Luciana. Luigia's sister is coming to lunch to give thanks for our bountiful harvest—and, of course, to meet you."

"*Arrivo*, signore."

"Francesco, please—Nico. Call me Nico. We're not so formal here on our farm."

For the trip to the station in the valley, Nico took the 1923 Fiat 501, of which he was proud. What a relief that Nico took the automobile and not the cartun. Francesco had had enough of sitting on the hard wagon bench with Gep for four days. He welcomed the luxury of his first time ever in an automobile of this type.

The train was late, which Nico said was unusual since Mussolini had come to office. "One of the few good things about him," Nico said, but then thought better of it. "Certainly he's done a great deal for the country, but we're still struggling here in the countryside. I'm certain it's simply a matter of time before things improve." Had he said too much? It was dangerous these days to speak openly against the Fascists. They barely knew Francesco. Nico would have to hold his tongue and warn Sara—in the habit of speaking her mind—to do the same. Too many alert eyes and ears these days.

52

Francesco remained by the car while Nico waited trackside. The peaceful surrounding contrasted with the bustle the previous day when everyone rushed to and from the Alba mercato. Luciana stepped from the two-carriage train attired in an understated black dress longer than most women were wearing. As they walked closer, Francesco noted her serene presence. Nico had told him that she was a nurse and a pious single woman, a tota. In contrast to her sister and her oldest niece, Luciana was tall, appearing more so because of her slim figure. Francesco immediately noticed that, like Luigia, her brown eyes twinkled even when the rest of her face was passive.

"Signorina Luciana Capra, may I present Francesco Bosco. He's the young Sicilian who'll be working for me now."

Francesco grabbed his cap off his head, held it close to his chest, and gave a nearly imperceptible bow. *"Am fa piasì cunosla*, Madama," he said, once again stumbling through a dialect phrase that Gep had taught him.

"Piasì, Francesco." Luciana replied. "But please, I understand you speak Italian, as do I. Our dialect is difficult, and I am impressed you learned some words so quickly."

Relieved, Francesco quickly added in Italian, "Thank you for helping to make this all possible for me, signorina Capra."

The language barrier was thrown up again as Francesco sat cramped in the backseat of Nico's tiny car for the short ride to Asili. He only understood names, especially the one repeated most often—Sara. He was eager to be back at table with the family but still had not been invited to lunch.

During the excited greetings, hugs, and kisses between the sisters and their aunt at Ca' dei Fiù, Francesco kept his distance. He stepped away as the women, chatting between themselves and not noticing him, returned to the cascina. Was he to join them at the celebratory harvest lunch?

"Francesco," Sara called from the entrance. "Don't be late for lunch or nonna Mirella will be cross"—adding after a short pause—"and so will I. Be here at noon." No warmth came from her, only an order, but it was one that he would willingly obey.

Francesco decided to walk into the vineyard near the house where the delectable aromas wafted through the open kitchen door that led to the barnyard. He was hungry. The vineyards were quiet, a southerly breeze warming the air and rustling the golden vine leaves. The beauty overwhelmed him.

"Buongiorno, Francesco."

Startled, Francesco turned to see Madama Lia.

"Isn't it lovely here?" she said without breaking her gaze of something in the distance.

"Bondì, Madama Lia." Nico had told him a great deal about her, including that she was a childhood friend of tota Luciana. For one so powerful, she was petite like Sara. He towered over her but felt small in her presence.

"You may speak Italian to me. Soon enough you will be challenged with communicating in dialect with the *contadini* in my fields and vineyards."

With nerves freezing his thoughts, he spoke not in Italian, but in Arbëreshë. Blessedly, the church bells of San Giovanni Battista in the village pealed. It was noon, and Giovanna called from the kitchen door.

"Francesco, *ven sì*!" she ordered, hands on her hips. "*Ura ed disne*!" He stifled a chuckle. One so young, yet already strong and demanding—no different than her big sister.

"Lunchtime. We must go, Francesco."

He followed Madama Lia obediently to the front of the Fiore cascina, grateful to have been spared conversing with her.

Giovanna raced to him before he set foot in the house. She grabbed his hand and again ordered him to sit next to her at the middle of the long, exquisitely set table. There was an odd, musky scent in the air. It wasn't unpleasant—on the contrary, it was appetizing. It smelled a bit like the wet forests of Alta Langa he had driven through with Gep. Mushrooms?

The table, with long benches on either side and a chair at each end, was the most elegant he had ever seen. An embroidered white tablecloth now covered all the cracks and scratches years of love had etched into the wood. Bright red and golden vine leaves scattered down the middle of the table added color. Francesco counted ten settings of elegant blue-and-white dishes. The forks and knives were the same as before, but next to each plate were white napkins and stemmed glasses that sparkled like the crystal chandeliers in the Arbëreshë church in Contessa Entellina. Francesco had never attended a grand harvest celebration. He glanced at his big, clumsy hands then tugged at his collar. How would he hold the delicate glass without crushing it?

Madama Lia took her place to the right of Nico, who always sat at the head of the table. Luciana and the three younger sisters all sat as Mirella and Luigia busily worked at the *putagè*.

"*Setesse*, Francesco!" nonna Mirella barked, but he waited for Nico to sit first. Sara brought platters of an unfamiliar dish to the table. When was Sara going to sit? And where? There were three empty places at the table, one of which he knew was Luigia's at the head opposite Nico, one next to her, and the other next to him. Oh, dear Lord, I know I didn't go to Mass today, but please let Sara sit next to me. He prayed the dour nonna would not fill the empty seat to his left.

The torture continued as Sara shuttled more food to the table. Finally, all were seated, with Sara slipping onto the bench next to him.

Heads bowed while Nico gave thanks for the harvest, the food, the family and, to his surprise, for Francesco's safe arrival. Francesco added to himself thanksgiving for his great fortune, far beyond his dreams, and for the blue-eyed girl whose nearness stirred him.

Sara motioned to him to take one of the long, thin breadsticks spread in bunches on the table. "Grissini," she said as he hesitated. She took his plate and served him thin pieces of poached meat over which a velvety sauce was spooned. "*Vitello tonnato,*" she said. "It is where the sea meets the farm: tuna sauce and meat."

Veal! Beef was a rarity on his mamma's table, and never in his life had he eaten tender cuts.

The red wine Nico served wasn't in a flask like the inky Dolcetto had been the night before, but in a bottle. Exceptional. "My Barbaresco, Francesco," Nico proclaimed, "from 1922. An extraordinary vintage. It's still young and will only improve with age."

Francesco's hand shook as he took the glass. As his nose settled over the delicate crystal rim, it was as though the window to the barnyard had been thrown open. Was that tobacco he smelled too? The red color was much lighter than the intensely dark Nero d'Avolo from Mount Etna that he drank last Christmas.

Nico raised his glass, signaling a toast. Even Giovanna raised hers with a splash of wine at the bottom. "May we celebrate many more vintages together, and may they be filled with joy, health, and abundance! Salute!"

"Salute," all responded as they clinked glasses.

"Francesco! You must clink your glass with everyone. It's bad luck if you don't," Giovanna chided as she lightly touched her glass to his. "No, look in my eyes when you toast."

Francesco turned to Sara, and they lightly clinked glasses. Following Giovanna's instruction, his gaze dipped into Sara's eyes, feeling again his heart skip a beat.

His first taste of the noble Nebbiolo grape was a pleasant introduction to a wine named for a humble village. Francesco peered over the edge of his glass, sensing all eyes were on him. In an instant, his mouth was dry, as though he had eaten grape seeds. Flavors of black cherries and even chocolate followed, something he had tasted when Gep shared his creamy *gianduja* with him. Giovanna giggled.

"I saw your face," she proclaimed. "Tannins!" Sara interrupted Giovanna's attempt to educate Francesco about the wine that dominated their lives. "It's not always easy to drink Nebbiolo at first, but like dialect, you will soon come to know it. And love it."

"I do already, Sara. I love it all." *I love you, too,* he nearly added but caught the words before they escaped his mouth.

"Francesco," Nico called out, calming the chatter in the room. "Although you didn't work this harvest, you'll celebrate it with us to know what awaits you after the long months of hard work. It's rare that a stranger comes to live in Barbaresco, especially a young one who left his family and traveled so far. You have much work ahead of you."

Over the next three hours, Francesco feasted, occasionally feeling a pang of guilt that his mamma and sisters were not here to enjoy such an array of food, and in such abundance. Several *antipasti*, including *agrodolce* peppers with anchovies, *insalata piemontese*, and a creamy flan with melted Fontina cheese followed the *vitello*. Sara dished out thin, golden noodles she called tajarin topped with creamy fresh butter. *Butter on pasta? What a decadent luxury!* Sara told him the pasta was an extra special treat because it was made with many eggs, a treasured farm product that fetched a good sum at the mercato. The pungent, woodsy aroma that had greeted him when he entered, grew stronger. Nico reached from behind and ran a pale, odd-looking mushroom across a blade set into a small wooden board, shaving paper thin slices of the mushroom over the pasta on Francesco's plate.

"*Tartufo bianco*, the diamond Milo hunts in the forest of Pora hill," he said before continuing to shave the truffle onto everyone else's plate.

More bottles of Barbaresco appeared. The 1917 vintage from Madama Lia's cellar was more elegant and smelled not earthy but of roses, and even a bit like his mamma's cookies at Christmas.

The real feast came as the *secondi*—not one, but three meat dishes and a stew! The first was *coniglio* cooked with vegetables. That explained the empty cage and bloody knife in the barnyard. Next came a thick slice of beef that Luigia had cooked for hours in Nebbiolo, served atop creamy polenta. "*Brasato al Barbaresco*," she called it. In autumn, after the harvest, Nico hunted hares, wild boar, and pheasants that Mirella loved transforming into dishes generations of Piemontese women had cooked. With her chin held high and her face beaming as Francesco had not yet seen, Mirella presented platters of roasted pheasant and autumn vegetables from the garden. He had reached his limit before the first *secondo* was served, but for more than one reason, it was impossible to say no to the food Sara continued to serve him.

Finally, il *dolce*! Mirella placed before Francesco a bowl of pears from Madama Lia's orchard cooked in Nebbiolo, and a plate of light, crispy meringues made with the egg whites left from making tajarin. Nothing in a Piemontese kitchen was wasted, not even a pig's head, Luigia said. Eggs were particularly prized. With each of her dishes that Francesco devoured, Mirella's chilly disposition thawed ever so slightly. Now a ghost of a smile flitted across her face.

More wine. This time, however, it was the color of straw, slightly bubbly, and delicately sweet, not at all like Zibibbo, the muscat from Pantelleria he had once tried. The Moscato's aroma was like springtime, like the orange blossoms in Contessa Entellina. Perhaps when he was lonely, the wine would transport him home to the Rocca di Entella, where he loved to scale the rocks in springtime. But for now, this was home. He said a silent prayer of thanksgiving, asking God that his life here would always be filled with such warmth and generosity. Don Pietro was mistaken about the Piemontese. This wasn't at all the reception he anticipated.

As the three oldest sisters rose to clear the dishes, Francesco noticed that Giovanna had slipped away. She was fast asleep in the chair by the fireplace, Nico's loyal truffle hound, Milo, at her feet. Nico bade Francesco to sit next to him for a *digestivo* and offered a small glass of something thick and dark red.

"Drink up. Chinato is good for the digestion."

The aroma of spices from the mercato in Sambucca had always reminded him of the syrup his mamma made to stop their winter coughs, just like the Chinato. But Nico's orders were to be obeyed. Francesco drained the glass in one gulp and smiled. Medicine had never tasted so good.

As Nico wove yarns about the local history of Chinato, Francesco's mind wandered. Where was Sara, he wondered? She was nowhere to be seen. Although throughout lunch she made certain he was well fed, they had not spoken much during their feast. Over twenty-four hours had passed since he first laid eyes on Sara, but he knew so little about her and about the entire family. He longed to know everything.

Madama Lia rose from her place and smoothed her dark blue dress. "It is time to go, Luce. Girls, fetch your sister, please. The sun is setting, and it looks like rain. I do not like Gianni driving the new car back to Alba in the dark."

Go? Was Sara leaving? He had heard Sara speaking with Letizia about the nuns, but he wasn't sure what that meant. Surely, she wasn't studying to be a nun! The girls scurried up the stairs, calling for Sara.

The sisters returned shortly with Sara trailing them. Why had she changed from her lovely lavender Sunday dress into a white shirt and black skirt? She carried a valise, Letizia a satchel of books.

"Back to school now, Sara," Luigia sighed as she took her eldest child in her arms. "The harvest passed too quickly this year, *carina*."

"I know, Mamma. Suor Angelica said that, when I return, I'll have much to do to catch up before exams."

Suor Angelica? Wait! Was she don Pietro's sister? Before he asked, Gianni appeared at the door and took Sara's valise from her.

"The car is outside, Madama Lia."

"Nico, cara Luigia, cara Mirella. Thank you for another lovely *pranzo domenicale*. I treasure celebrating the harvest with you."

"Everything's ready, Madama," Gianni said with a touch of impatience in his voice. "The fog's rising from the valley. Rain is coming."

Mirella pointed to two large baskets brimming with fruits and vegetables for Madama Lia's cook, Alma, in Altavilla. "There's a little something sweet in there for you and Giuseppina, Gianni. I know how much she loves Moscato and my hazelnut cake."

At the door, Madama Lia stopped and turned to Luigia, "I am so blessed to have Nico tend my vines and look after my farm. When Alessandro left for the front, he assured me that, should anything happen, the Fiore family would manage the farm. Little did he know how you would fill the void in my life he and Giulia left. Thank you for sharing Sara with me."

Luigia nodded, and the two women who so dearly loved Sara embraced. Madama Lia was a kind, generous woman, but rarely did she share such deep emotions. Most women in Luigia's position would harbor jealousy toward a wealthy widow who showered on her daughter so much she was unable to give her. But Luigia was different than most. And Sara was special. She knew from the moment Luciana handed her daughter to her that she would have to share her with many.

Francesco had barely understood her words, but he knew they were discussing Sara. His heart sank to learn she was leaving, not knowing when she would return.

Gianni helped Madama Lia and Luciana into her shiny black Balilla.

"It has been nice meeting you, Francesco," Sara said curtly. "I'm certain you'll work hard for my papà. He needs your help."

"Sara!" Giovanna came running from the house, panicked and on the verge of tears. "Sara, you didn't say good-bye. Why must you go? Can't you stay longer?"

"Carina, mi dispiace." Sara pulled the child to her and gave her a strong embrace. "You were sleeping so soundly, and I must get back to school. I'll see you in Alba soon. Mamma said she would take you with her to Mass at the Duomo on All Saints' Day." Giovanna pulled away, her lower lip quivering, eyes downcast.

The tearful leave-taking reminded Francesco of his own weeks earlier. Seeing Sara depart now, all joy of the day evaporated.

"Arvëdsi. Arrivederci," Sara called. His throat thickened and blocked his words. Before he could respond, she was gone. How he wished that he could ask where exactly she was going in Alba and when she would return.

Despite the drizzle, Francesco didn't budge. He watched the car disappear. From the doorway, Luigia studied him. He was a handsome, kind young man, eager to please, but he was still a stranger to them. They only knew what little suor Angelica had told them. Sara was far too young to think about anything except her studies although Luigia had to admit that he was probably the handsomest boy Sara had met. No, life as a farmer's wife was not what Luigia wished for her eldest daughter, nor did Madama Lia. But she knew Sara was taking Francesco's heart with her back to Alba. Would he be yet another with whom she would have to share Sara? Certainly not. All that hard work only to return to the farm was not what she wanted for Sara.

As if reading his wife's mind, Nico pulled Luigia close to him and kissed her brow. "She will be gone for two months—plenty of time for Francesco to meet other girls. Sara has no interest in him." But Nico was not convinced. In the brief time Francesco had been with them, Nico had grown fond of the boy. Who knew what the future would bring? He hoped for Francesco to make a good match with a Langhetta, but not necessarily with Sara. Maria would make a better farm wife for him. "All is in God's hands, Luigia. Nature will take its course."

CHAPTER 10

Turin
November 1, 1932

Although days had passed since Doretta Giordano's encounter with the uniformed boy outside the synagogue, his face and words haunted her. When their eyes met, she sensed he recognized her. But how could that be? Since then, Doretta had not ventured far alone. She even asked her siblings' nanny to walk with her to school, never revealing the reason she suddenly needed company. It wasn't that he frightened her, exactly, but why tempt fate?

Doretta's bedroom was now her sanctuary. The soothing cream-colored walls and robin's egg-blue curtains and linens cocooned her. Upon her bat mitzvah, at her father's insistence, her mother changed all the furniture to the modern Art Deco style. The big hardwood bed and armoire with full-length mirrored doors were her favorites. Her mother even filled the armoire with new dresses her seamstress had made for her. Although the dresses were still too childish for her taste, it was a sign that her mother recognized she was growing up. Now she promised that, for Doretta's sixteenth birthday, she would take her shopping in Paris for an entirely new wardrobe.

Her baby sister, Elena, still slept in the nursery with her *bambinaia*, so for now Doretta had her room to herself, a quiet space to be alone and to ponder the world she was growing into. Doretta found comfort looking at photographs of family and arranging her porcelain dolls, who had always been her trusted companions. And her books, of course. The big atlas her papà had brought from London recently was her favorite. Each day after school, Doretta settled into her window seat perched high above Corso Re Umberto, where trams rattled along under the chestnut trees. With the atlas spread out before her,

Doretta let her mind transport her on journeys to places far from Turin. Far from Germany. She was hoping the adventures would erase the image of that boy's face, but it seemed a hopeless task.

Doretta knew she would always remember that day, the end of the week-long Sukkot holiday. Although her family wasn't religious and only attended temple on high holy days—if then—they belonged to the Great Synagogue and sometimes joined in community activities there. Her mother had insisted that Doretta should make her bat mitzvah. Now, a year later, although her friends were mostly Catholics, she felt drawn more than ever to the socials where she met Jewish teens. Like her parents, she considered herself Piemontese above all, but her bat mitzvah did feel like a coming of age. For the first time, she understood what it was to be Jewish. Was this what her mother had had in mind? Doretta hadn't discussed it with her yet. The awful boy had not only insulted her but had cursed this new way of being she was only now beginning to understand.

The Christmas season loomed. Would this year's celebrations her family shared with their Catholic friends feel different? Would they sense a difference in her? She was, same as always, Doretta Giordano, the banker's daughter— good student, fun-loving companion, with a prosperous and gracious family welcoming everyone—but an invisible barrier had arisen. Did those Jews who preferred all these years to live separately from Christians, like those in the Rome ghetto, have a point? Until recently, she never would have considered the question.

Most intriguing to her were the Zionists. Once, she heard her papà and nonno Davide discussing them. She hadn't caught much of the conversation other than to note her papà's disapproval. A friend gave her a copy of the weekly Florentine newspaper, *Israel*. In it, she read that Zionists believed now more than ever was the time for Jews to return to their homeland. Hitler, they warned, was dangerous to every Jew in Europe. When she showed the paper to her papà, he scolded her and said she was not to read such drivel. There would be no discussion. The paper ended up as ashes in his study's fireplace. Although her papà disapproved of them, she found it exciting to imagine a place where Jews would be safe forever—not in spite of their being Jews, but because they were—a place where people like that boy could not harm them.

The boy had been dressed in black shirt and shorts, the uniform of the Avanguardia. Doretta mostly remembered his sneer and narrowed, angry eyes. Once, when she had been early for her piano lessons with *zio* Eduardo, an older boy had stormed out of the studio muttering under his breath. All she understood at the time was "old Jew." Of course. As he spat the slurs at her in front of the synagogue, she had recognized the voice but not his face. But then, at the studio, he had been looking down, and she hadn't seen those eyes.

Now Doretta was determined to speak to her zio Eduardo about the boy. Her nonna's twin brother and her favorite zio, he needed to know about the hate that consumed the boy. The thought of zio Eduardo alone with him worried her.

That night the opportunity arose when her zio came to their house for erev Shabbat dinner. She waited for him at the entrance of their apartment building, ready to catch him before he rang the bell.

Right on time, as usual, zio Eduardo appeared with a bouquet of fragrant pink roses, her mamma's favorite. Doretta hugged her zio before leading him up to their apartment and into a nook near the entrance.

"Slowly, Doretta, why the rush? Do you have a surprise for me?"

Eduardo Dalmasso had a special place in his heart for his great-niece and they often had memorable conversations about music and art. But something was different tonight. Her need for secrecy was unusual.

Without any further pleasantries, Doretta asked Eduardo about the about the boy with such black eyes. A shadow passed over his face.

"It's best not to speak about another music student, Doretta, even one who no longer comes for lessons."

Doretta did not yield. "Zio Eduardo, my friends and I saw him on the street a few days ago. He was angry. He was vile."

"How so, child?" Eduardo asked.

"We came out of the synagogue where we had been helping prepare the Sukkah for that evening. As he walked by us, I heard him say…" Doretta shivered, swallowed hard then blurted the disgusting words. There, she said it. Such words she had never spoken. Tears welled in her eyes, but she willed them back, until that is, zio Eduardo put his arms around her.

Eduardo Dalmasso knew much about this kind of pain, his late wife having fled Kiev for Italy after her parents were murdered in the pogroms of 1881. Fifty years later, he feared it was happening again, but this time in modern Europe, not the Russian Empire of old. With each letter from Silvana Becker, his niece in Berlin, came news of how the Nazis tightened their grip on power. Recently, he heard more and more about incidents of thuggery against Jews on Turin's streets. Despicable caricatures began appearing in Italian publications.

Though Mussolini said he did not share his fellow fascist's views on biological superiority of the Aryan race, few trusted him. Eduardo did not discount Doretta's concern. In fact, he admired that someone so young had become aware of the political storm just beyond the horizon while so many, like her father, ignored it.

"I'm sorry, but I can't tell you his name. It would be impolite of me. Although he has innate talent to create heavenly music, he's chosen a different and, I fear, sinister path." Zio Eduardo sounded defeated, adding, "Perhaps I failed in nurturing his gift."

"Why did he quit, zio?"

"It doesn't matter, child. What matters is that you avoid him and all those like him. Now, it's ill-mannered of me to wait much longer to greet your parents."

At dinner days later, Mamma mentioned a letter that she had received from her sister Silvana in Berlin. Silvana lived in Berlin with her Christian German husband and two children. Surely, there was no need for them to be alarmed.

"No!" Daniela exclaimed, dropping the letter from her baby sister on the table as though it had burned her. In a way, it had. "Silvana and Fritz are leaving for America before Christmas. She has no time to come to Turin beforehand." Her voice trembled. "Those horrible, hateful Nazi fascists!"

"Your sister's imagination has gotten the best of her again. There is nothing to fear," her husband said, waving his hand as if to dismiss her while he poured himself a glass of Moscato d'Asti. As a loyal member of the National Fascist Party, Gabriele Giordano banned criticism of the Fascists, including the Nazis, in his home. Doretta often wondered how her papà found common ground with those men and boys in black shirts.

"Anyway, we are quite safe here in this house under Mussolini's protection." All their neighbors knew that Gabriele was an official in the party and had even met Il Duce. But his assurances did not allay Daniela's concerns, nor Doretta's.

Ignoring her husband's comments, Daniela pulled the letter from her dress pocket and read aloud her sister's words.

We have a close Jewish friend who is a journalist. He was beaten by Röhm's Brownshirts for writing negative things about Hitler, including his hatred of the Jews. He continued to write about the dangers of a dictatorship like in Italy. Now he has disappeared. His wife has not heard of him for weeks.

Others have disappeared too.

After she spoke the last words, Daniela bit her lip and rubbed her throat. She usually disapproved of unpleasant talk at the table. It impaired one's digestion, she believed. This letter warranted the exception. Gabriele appeared not to be listening although the furrow in his brow deepened and his eyes narrowed. He said nothing as he dissected with his fork the slice of *torta di nocciole* on the delicate Meissen dessert plate. Doretta sat far back in her chair. She was all ears. Her brother, Michele, had left the table to finish painting his pewter soldiers, and little Elena had been put to bed before the family sat to dinner. Doretta's parents were so intent on their discussion that neither noticed she was there, partially hidden by the large candelabra between them.

Daniela took a deep breath, not about to stop reading her sister's letter aloud. "*Ascolta*, Gabriele!

Renata Goren's family closed their German textile factory and consolidated all work in Turkey.

"You remember Silvana's boarding school friend, Renata, don't you Gabriele? Her mother and Fritz's zia Lorelei grew up together in Hamburg.

Renata even confided in me that her father and uncles placed most of their fortune with Union Bank of Switzerland in Zürich. I'm sure it will be safe there. Her father was worried there might be currency restrictions now that the Nazis have gained so much power in the Reichstag. The Gorens are leaving for Palestine soon even though the British are making it more difficult for Jews to enter. The Americans have tightened immigration since the war, so Fritz believes we should—

"*Basta*, Daniela! I've heard enough of your sister's paranoia," Gabriele shouted as he threw his fork and napkin onto the table, sending his full glass of Moscato tumbling to the floor. Fire flashed in his eyes, and his crimson face contorted, blood vessels bulging at his temples. Doretta thought for a moment it was time to slip out of the room, hopefully still unnoticed, but decided to remain, never having seen her papà in such a rage. He was nearly unrecognizable. She caught a glimpse of their longtime housekeeper, Ida Pellegrino, peering into the dining room before disappearing. No doubt, the shouting shocked her as well. Doretta decided to stay for her mamma.

Silence. Both parents stared into a space neither occupied. Only each swing of the old grandfather clock's pendulum kept total silence at bay. Doretta heard the pounding of her heart. After what seemed like an eternity, Gabriele stood as though to leave. But no, he walked to Daniela, kissed her cheek, then tucked behind her ear an errant black curl that had escaped her tight chignon.

Gabriele's tone softened. "Cara, I've told you many times that Mussolini is not an anti-Semite. Yes, he has some around him as advisors—I even know a few here in Turin—but they are powerless in this matter. Il Duce would never harm us."

Unable to look at Gabriele, Daniela continued to stare at some point that appeared far beyond the room as though she hadn't heard him.

"We Giordanos are one of the wealthiest and most respected families in Piemonte's banking and silk trades. We have been faithful Piemontese, faithful Italians, and faithful soldiers who fought bravely for Italy, as did I in the Great War. And don't forget, my nonno supported Camilo Cavour and the Risorgimento. *Italianità* has been a part of the Giordano family for over four hundred years. We are safe. Nothing will change that, Daniela."

Once again, Gabriele bent to kiss Daniela's cheek. To Doretta, he appeared mechanical, unfeeling. He paid no attention to his wife's distress—so unlike Papà.

"Now, I will be in my study if you care to join me, cara."

Daniela had no intention of doing so. The dining room spun. Her thudding heart sent tremors through her body. Never had her once kind, gentle husband raised his voice in such a manner. Now, ten years after the Fascists marched on Rome and grabbed power, Gabriele practiced a new religion, the most sacred tenet of which was blind devotion to Mussolini and to the party. "Mussolini is never wrong," he often said. She had read that some of his fellow party members in Turin had begun to speak well of Hitler, expressing hope that Mussolini would soon realize the need to answer the Jewish question in Italy.

Finally, Doretta spoke. "Mamma."

Daniela startled and gripped her chest, her long pearl necklace. Her young daughter had just seen the worst thing that had ever happened between her parents. "Doretta, what are you doing here? Why aren't you in bed?"

Ignoring her mother's question, Doretta asked one of her own. "Mamma, why is Papà a Fascist? Nonno Davide doesn't like that he is."

"You have discussed that with him?" Doretta, at thirteen, continued to surprise her.

"Yes, I went one day to see him at the bank on the way home from school. He always has *biscotti* and hot chocolate for me when I visit. You know that, Mamma. Anyway, I asked him to tell me why he wasn't a Fascist. I wanted to know why those young men in black uniforms were so mean, why they are always so angry.

"I told him how, recently on a side street near Porto Nuovo, I saw several Blackshirts beating a man as they screamed 'socialist swine!' He was on the ground and bleeding, but they kept hitting him with a big stick and kicking him. There was no one else around, so I hid behind a parked car. I was worried they would come for me because I saw them do it."

"Why haven't you told me before?"

"I didn't want to worry you. I know how frightened you are of these people."

"You do? I assure you I don't like them to frighten my children. So why tell nonno?"

"I wanted to know more about these people, the socialists, and why the Fascists hate them so much. He started to tell me, but Papà came into the room and nonno stopped talking. After Papà left, nonno told me not to tell him or you that we discussed such things."

Most of the candles had burned down. How did they miss seeing her there? Maybe they didn't. Maybe they counted her as an adult since her bat mitzvah, and they were letting her in on the big things now without being ready to admit it.

"*Vieni qui*, cara," Daniela said in Italian rather than the Piemontese usually spoken in their home.

Doretta walked to her mother, distressed to see her red-rimmed eyes in the fading candlelight.

"We are living in very difficult times, carissima. Your job is to study hard so you can go to university. I know the Fascists do not like women to be educated and have important work, but you are smart and strong. Remember: one day things will be normal again."

"Not if they hurt the Jews, Mamma, like they're doing in Germany."

The pounding in Daniela's head that Gabriele's reaction to her sister's letter had triggered became sharper, and her vision blurred. "Time to sleep now, Doretta."

"But Mamma, I want to—" Doretta stopped, knowing this wasn't the time to tell her mamma about that horrid boy.

"No, Doretta. *Basta così*. I'm sure nonno Davide has much to explain to you."

Doretta's eyes widened. "Do you mean you don't mind me speaking with him about these things?"

"It is time you learn. Your nonno Davide is a very wise man. I would rather you learn from him for now." Daniela hoped that, although he was unable to open his son's eyes to Mussolini's duplicity, at least Davide Giordano would prevent the Fascist ideology from poisoning her daughter. "Best not to mention anything about it to Papà, though."

Doretta hugged Daniela and kissed her cheek, now dry.

"Now, again, it is time to sleep."

Hand-in-hand, mother and daughter left the room, stepping over the shards of crystal, a jagged reminder of Gabriele's fit of rage. Daniela walked past Gabriele's study, having said all she would say to him tonight. "*Buonanotte*" was not a sentiment she wished to express to him.

"Tell your father good night, Doretta," Daniela said barely over a whisper. She did not want Doretta to harbor ill will against her papà. One day, Daniela was certain, Gabriele's eyes would be opened. She prayed it would not be too late.

As Doretta walked down the hall to her room, her sanctuary, once again the boy's face, his voice, returned. Knowing his name would give him an identity she would not forget. But how to convince zio Eduardo to tell her? She meant what she had said. He will one day be the hunted one. Though her papà was blind to it now, the battle had begun. She swore to herself she would be ready to fight, to protect her family, when the time finally arrived.

CHAPTER 11

From her small room in her zia Luce's apartment, Sara watched the bustling activity on via Maestra below. Christmas was coming, and everyone seemed filled with the festive spirit despite continuing dire economic conditions. Sara had finished her exams with top marks two days earlier, giving her a chance to stroll among the shoppers, enjoying the unusually mild and sunny Advent weather. It had been a long and difficult year adjusting to life in the city and the strict discipline of the nuns. The transition from farm life in Asili to the long hours of instruction and study had not come easy for her. For now, she put thoughts of school aside and focused on her return to the vineyards and rejoining her family—and Francesco—for the festive celebrations.

It had been six weeks since she had been home and no word about Francesco. Had he settled in? Was he thinking about her? When she had seen Giovanna at Mass in Alba on All Saints' Day, she only divulged that Francesco was working hard with Papà in the cantina. Her normally chatty little sister hadn't been the fountain of information she usually relied upon. Sara even tried to extract information from suor Angelica, but the nun wasn't forthcoming.

She regretted being haughty to Francesco at their parting that Sunday in Asili. It wasn't like her to act that way, even with strangers. Although he had knocked her into the mud, that was an accident, and he had immediately apologized. Was it that she had not seen any boys near her age so tall—or handsome? Yes, he was handsome all right, so why was she so rude? She vowed to make it up to him when she returned to Asili.

68

Zia Luce broke into her daydream. "Sara, Gianni is here."

"Coming, zia." She tingled with excitement at the thought of going home. Handing her valise abruptly to Gianni, she threw on her coat, and started out the door.

"Sara! No good-bye?" Luciana said.

"Mi dispiace, zia Luce!" That jolted her. Where was her mind that she would run out on the woman who had cared for and encouraged her the entire school term, and who shared her own nursing knowledge with her, even allowing her to shadow her at the hospital? She had better calm herself before she reached Asili. Her eagerness to return home and begin again with Francesco was difficult to contain.

"I will see you soon in Barbaresco, Sara. Next term will be more difficult for you when you start your nursing classes, so enjoy your holidays."

Sara embraced her aunt and followed Gianni—dapper in a new chauffeur uniform she hadn't noticed at first—down the stairs to the waiting Balilla.

"We must hurry, signorina Sara," Gianni said. "Madama Lia is waiting for us." Gianni smiled at Sara in the rearview mirror. He relished his role as chauffeur. Madama Lia had sent him to the Fiat plant in Turin to learn how to care for a car, and he found tinkering with the car's unreliable engine and waxing its shiny exterior far more enjoyable than brushing horses and cleaning stalls. This was Fiat's latest model, and he could tell that Sara felt like royalty riding in the plush four-seater.

A driver from the *mulino* had already taken Giuseppina with Madama Lia's Christmas presents and special holiday foods up to the farm earlier in the day, so there was plenty of room in the car. Although two weeks of Advent remained before Christmas, Madama Lia liked the quiet, reflective peace of Cascina Asili over the busy city during the holidays. That had been her way ever since the death of her daughter Giulia. Sara would be good company for her in the car.

In Altavilla, Madama Lia was already waiting in the villa's cortile when Gianni drove through the gate. She was not Piemontese in her punctuality; timeliness was next to godliness with her. Gianni jumped out to open the car door for her.

"Gianni, you're late!" Madama Lia snapped.

"Mi dispiace, Madama Lia." Gianni knew explaining his delay would not be helpful since it was Sara who was late, having forgotten the book she was assigned to read over the holidays.

"Buongiorno, Sara. How were your exams?"

"Buongiorno, Madama Lia. My exams? Tiring, but I scored high marks on all of them. Zia Luce warned me next year will be more difficult."

"Yes, I believe so. Suor Angelica said you will be studying many science courses and have reading to do over the holidays. I recall when your zia Luce finished her science classes. We had a big celebration in Bossolaschetto that summer."

"But I'm looking forward to it. We'll learn about microbes and how so many died from one in the Great Influenza—" Sara caught herself. She knew Madama did not like to discuss those dark times. "Mi dispiace, Madama Lia. What an awful thing for me to say." Sara cringed, knowing she must have unsettled Madama Lia.

Though Sara knew her heart ached for Giulia, Lia's gaze into the distance did not change. To Sara's relief, her expression didn't change and indicated no sign of distress at the memory of her sweet Giulia. For a while, no one spoke.

"Sara, it is a fact that many people died. Like me, many parents lost their children. But much has been learned since then. I've learned…I'm certain that should such a thing happen again, you will be one of the brave nurses who tend the sick like your zia Luce did."

Lia was silent again. She took in the landscape as they crested the hill and the Alps came into view. Like an old, trusted friend, Monviso always lifted her spirits. Sara, though not her own daughter, was a blessing. Would Giulia have been like her? The similarity in their looks was uncanny.

A heavy but not uncomfortable silence descended. No one broke it for the rest of the trip along the winding, hilly roads. The drive through Pertinace and Tre Stelle took longer than the train, but the views of the mountains and vineyards on such a clear day were so much nicer than the long tunnel between Alba and Barbaresco. Sara resolved not to dwell on her thoughtless comment, which Madama Lia had appeared to take in stride. Her spirits soared as the Rio Sordo valley, Villa Cristina, and the Barbaresco tower came into view along the ridge through Tre Stelle.

As Sara expected, Giovanna was the first to greet them. From her perch in the hayloft, she had kept watch in the last hour for the shiny black car to appear across the valley. As soon as Gianni passed Villa delle Rose in Tre Stelle, beginning his descent into the valley, she scurried down the stairs and ran to the chapel to await them at the turn to Asili. Gianni stopped to pick up the excited six-year-old. Even the ride the few hundred feet to the farms was a thrill for Giovanna.

"Sara!" she screamed as she jumped onto her sister's lap, paying no attention to Madama Lia who winced from the high-pitched sound of Giovanna's peals of joy.

"You're home! We've missed you so." Giovanna wrapped her arms around Sara's neck and clung to her for the duration of the short ride.

"Giovanna, have you forgotten your manners?" Sara asked sternly.

Giovanna's face reddened. "*Ca ma scüsa*, Madamin Lia. *Bon-a seirà*. Um, buonasera." Giovanna quickly switched from Piemontese to Italian. Teacher had told them in school they must now speak the language of their country. Il Duce decreed it.

Lia smiled and thanked the child, always in awe of the sisters' bond. She wished she had not been an only child, but God at least sent her Luciana, who was there for her when it most mattered.

"You must tell me everything you've been doing, Giovanna. It seems like forever since All Saints' Day."

"So much to tell you. Francesco—" Before Giovanna could continue, they had arrived. Sara's heart sank. *What about Francesco?*

Maria and Letizia came running out of the house as they pulled into the cortile. Now that her three sisters stood together, Sara observed in her short absence that they had all grown a bit. Maria was eighteen months younger than Sara, and the first signs of womanhood had begun to take shape on her body. Letizia looked up to Maria, but the three-year gap with her sister that should have been filled by a brother was becoming a challenge for Letizia to bridge as Maria's eye turned to boys.

The remaining two Fiore women emerged from the house, both in flour-covered aprons. Sara had forgotten that today was the weekly bread baking in the communal *forno a legna* in Barbaresco. Once, when she asked her papà why he hadn't built a wood oven at Asili, he laughed and said it would deny nonna Mirella and her mamma the opportunity to catch up on Barbaresco news.

Nonna Mirella, walking slower than usual, trailed Luigia. Unlike before, she was using the cane she formerly reserved for long walks to the village or vineyards. Something wasn't right. Her face was nearly ashen.

Before Sara was able to greet her or her mother, Nico threw open the cantina doors and emerged from the shadows. His oldest child was home at last. And what a change in her. She was more a woman each time he saw her.

Nico would not admit to anyone, least of all Sara, that the year had been difficult for him. During Sara's short summer break at home, he was grateful for the long days that allowed them *passeggiate* through the lush vineyards after dinner. Their walks were special to him. Nico relished telling her the family history about their four generations of ties to the land. He often repeated the stories, but Sara never seemed tired of hearing them. It was true that all his dreams for a son were dashed when dottor Pera told them that Giovanna must be the last child, but Sara was the light of his life. How blessed he was with these wonderful women around him! And now, he had a young man on the farm to learn what he would have taught a son had God sent him one. *Perhaps, He did after all*, Nico sometimes thought. Time would tell.

"Madama Lia, thank you so much for bringing my angel home to us."

"Papà!" Sara ran to Nico and threw her arms around him with the same exuberance as her little sister.

"Sara, no. I'm dirty from racking today."

"Oh, Papà, but you smell heavenly, like wine!" She took his brawny, wine-strained hands in hers and kissed them. The hands of a farmer were God's gift to the land, zia Luce always said. Sara glanced over Nico's shoulder toward the cantina door, hoping to see Francesco behind him.

"Francesco is in the vineyards. He's pruning."

"What do you mean?" She felt a deep blush wash over her cheeks. How had her papà guessed?

Sara's defensive tone did not fool Nico. Anyway, with Francesco in the vineyards, he would not have to compete with him for Sara's attention.

"Why now, Papà? You always prune in late January."

"Francesco wanted to practice, so I sent him out to the Dolcetto vines. We'll save the Nebbiolo for him to do with me in January when his skills have improved."

Disheartened, Sara returned to the women. She had forgotten to thank Madama Lia, who was now in deep discussion with her mamma. Did she hear Mamma mention Francesco?

Sara walked to them and they stopped talking. "Madama Lia, *grazie mille per tutto*! I'm so grateful to you for your support and generosity."

"My pleasure, Sara. Now I must go. The Giordano family is coming to Asili on Sunday for their annual wine-buying visit, so I must see what Giuseppina has planned. *Buona serata a tutti*."

The rest of the day passed all too slowly for Sara. Where was Francesco? He had not come to the house for lunch and now, as night fell, she still hadn't seen him. Catching up on all the local news about babies, sad departures, and planned weddings after next year's harvest kept her thoughts of Francesco at bay.

Finally, minutes before dinner, she heard his heavy footsteps across the hayloft floor above her room. He was back! As she raced to dinner, she scolded herself for being so eager to see him. Seven places set on the table? Who wasn't eating tonight?

"Letizia, why only seven places?"

"He's with that fascist family again. He—" Before Letizia said another word, Luigia cut her off.

"Francesco is going to the village tonight," her mamma said. "He's having dinner with some friends he made."

"Who, Mamma?"

"Please add some wood to the putagè, Sara."

As she waited for the wood stove to come alive, the kitchen door opened. "Bon-a seirà," Francesco said as he walked in from the barnyard. Although far from being that of a Langhetto, his Piemontese accent had improved.

When Francesco stepped into the light, Sara's heart skipped a beat. Now, dressed in finer clothes than she had seen in October, and his beard and moustache shaved, he was even more handsome.

"Buonasera, Francesco. How are you?" Was it the heat from the roaring fire in the putagè that seemed to scald her cheeks? In an instant, her self-confidence evaporated—so unlike her. What was it about this boy whom she barely knew?

With Francesco's sudden appearance, Sara forgot to close the door to the putagè. Flames licked out, nearly igniting her dress. Francesco leaned toward her, brushing her arm as he closed the iron door. The heat she felt in her face intensified despite the cold air rushing in through the open door.

"All is good, Sara. Same for you, I hope." Those were the only words he spoke to her as he turned his attention to her mamma.

"Signora Fiore," he still found it difficult to refer to her as Luigia, despite her approval of the familiar *tu*. "I repaired the latch on the cage door. That should keep the fox from helping himself to the rabbits."

"Grazie, Francesco. You look very nice. Enjoy your dinner in the village."

Before Sara uttered another word, he was gone, having only glanced at her as he disappeared into the darkness.

Luigia had scrutinized the two teenagers. She hoped the Strega girl from Alba now visiting her family would keep his mind off Sara. Cinzia was closer to Francesco's age and far more developed than Sara would ever be. Sara had her studies ahead of her. Francesco would only be a distraction. Luigia had hoped Francesco's attentions would turn to someone else—they were far too young—and fortunately, they had, at least for Francesco. Or so it seemed. Nico, however, hoped otherwise since he had quickly grown attached to the boy.

"*Tutti a tavola*," Luigia called. And the night, at least for Sara, was over. Clearly, Luigia wasn't going to talk to her about Francesco. He was such a different person from when she left. And what did Letizia mean? The only possible family he could be visiting were the Stregas. But that was impossible. They had no one his age here since the younger Stregas now lived in Alba. And they were a family set apart, particularly in their allegiance to Mussolini. Surely, Francesco hadn't become a Fascist too! Tomorrow she would press Giovanna on the matter. The six-year-old was a gifted spy.

The next few days passed with Sara catching only fleeting moments with Francesco at meals, though he never sat next to her. When she asked Giovanna about Francesco's new friends, Giovanna feigned ignorance. But Sara knew otherwise from her sister's fidgety behavior every time she mentioned him. Giovanna never was able to keep a secret, especially one like this. Eventually the dam would break, and Giovanna would spill all.

The answers came on Sunday, and Giovanna did not have to tell Sara anything. Francesco left early for church, something odd since Giovanna did say Francesco was often late. Clouds had thickened overnight and the wind from the south had increased. Nonna Mirella foretold of snow. Sara's stomach quivered, and an uneasiness washed over her, but she discounted it, instead blaming it on the gloomy day after so many weeks of sunshine.

San Giovanni Battista church at the base of the medieval tower of Barbaresco was festively decorated for the season. Advent was Sara's favorite time of year. She loved the anticipation of Christmas and was glad to be back home with family and the simple, tiny church of her childhood. The Duomo in Alba, with its tall, banded columns and blue vaulted ceiling, was glorious but too grand for Sara's taste. The church of her ancestors was her spiritual home.

No sooner had she walked into the church, than she solved the mystery. A girl! Francesco had met another girl. This one looked about his age. Though she looked familiar, Sara couldn't say for sure she knew her although she did know the Strega family and that they were not to be trusted. Rumor had it that the patriarch, Secondo Strega, cheated, aiding in his ability to win prized vineyards at the card table. What was the girl's name?

Francesco and the girl were seated with Secondo's wife Graziella in the back of the church to the left. His eyes were fixed straight ahead. He appeared ill at ease although the girl seemed delighted to be seen with him. Giovanna grabbed Sara's hand and pulled her up the opposite side of the church, the family following behind as though they were in on the secret as well. Had the little brat told them she had quizzed her about Francesco last time she saw her in Alba? She wanted to run, but within moments, she was squeezed into the pew between Giovanna and nonna Mirella. No escape.

Mass seemed endless. Although forced to learn Latin in school, she still was unable to follow the Catholic liturgy. Besides, her thoughts were on Francesco. This was all wrong. Surely, he didn't care for the girl who dug her claws into him. Did the girl shoot Sara a nasty look as they went to communion? Her face didn't seem to have the spirit of the Mass written on it. Chills crawled up Sara's spine. Was that the uneasiness that had nagged her earlier? Francesco walked up the aisle behind the girl, his gaze never wavering, as though he were looking to see where he would kneel at the communion rail. Giovanna squirmed. The little spy had better tell her all after Mass.

Finally, after nearly two hours, don Emilio dismissed them. The congregation spilled into the piazza as the first snowflakes swirled in the air. From nowhere, the girl appeared in front of Sara, a smirk on her face. Why was this nasty slut treating her like a child? Francesco wasn't to be found.

As if to rescue her, Luigia called to her. "Come, Sara, we have much to finish preparing for pranzo."

Sara looked back and the girl was gone. But there she was, walking with Francesco along via Torino. The girl glanced back then snaked her arm through Francesco's. No, there is something dark, even sinister, about her. What did Francesco see in her?

Giovanna was once again by her side. Putting her tiny hand into Sara's, her face scrunched, Giovanna said, "I don't like her."

"Why, Gio?"

"She doesn't seem very nice. Just look in her eyes if you see her again. You have pretty eyes. How could Francesco like hers? Mean eyes, I tell you. Mean."

Sara stifled a giggle at her sister's simple sage explanation, well beyond her years. Nonna Mirella always said the eyes were the windows to the soul. Perhaps there was something in the familiar saying that led Giovanna to dislike this girl.

"Giovanna Caterina Fiore, you know it's not nice to judge someone. Mamma would not approve. Besides, when did you ever see her so close that you could look in her eyes? You better tell me what you know."

"It was on a Sunday a few weeks after you left. I saw Francesco talking to her after church. I ran up to say *ciarea*. She didn't seem very nice, Sara. She gave me a mean look with her beady eyes. I don't think Francesco wanted me there, so I ran to catch up with Letizia and Maria."

Sara knew Giovanna had a vivid imagination, but she had the same feeling when her eyes met the girl's. Like Sara, Giovanna sensed things others did not. It was one of the many reasons the two sisters were so close.

"Do you know her name?"

"Cinzia. Her name is Cinzia Strega. And like her last name, I think she's a witch. Just look at her pointy chin. She cast a spell on Francesco. How could he ever like her? He loves you, Sara."

"Did he ever say that? Why would you say such a thing? He barely knows me."

"No, but I could tell. The way he looks at you when you aren't looking. He thinks I don't see, but I do." Giovanna wasn't imagining his dreamy eyes when he looked at Sara. "That's the way Papà looks at Mamma sometimes. We know how much Papà loves her."

A child's fantasy, no doubt. Wishful thinking on her part? Again, that feeling that stirred Sara's stomach returned.

"Come, Gio. I want to get home before the snow covers the ground."

The sisters held hands as they walked silently home to Asili. Giovanna fiercely protected her big sister from being hurt. At least she tried to. She had come to love Francesco like the big brother she never had. Giovanna convinced herself that they were meant to be together. There had to be some way to get him away from that girl, to break that witch's spell. Sara, lost in her own thoughts, was plotting as well. There was no time to lose.

CHAPTER 12

Barbaresco
Mid-December 1932

Madama Lia waited until all the village congregants had entered San Giovanni Battista before stepping out of her car. She enjoyed driving alone. The privacy was matchless, considering she was also getting where she needed to go. During the short drive to Barbaresco, she had contemplated the challenging day ahead. She slipped into church and sat at the end of the last row of pews as Mass began. Her plan was to leave immediately after don Emilio's homily. Dressed for Mass as she was for business, everyone would recognize her, the *piccola vedova* under the heavy black veil, but there would be no time for the usual conversation with parishioners. She seated herself before noticing Francesco Bosco two rows in front of her. Why was he sitting with that troublesome Strega family?

Lia's thoughts strayed from Francesco and the Latin rite to the discussions she would have later that day with Gabriele Giordano. The Giordanos' December visits to Asili during Hanukkah and Advent were always festive. No business, other than wine, was discussed. But this year would be different. After a recent trip to Turin, Lia's long-time attorney and trusted advisor, Stefano Olivero, related a disturbing conversation he had had with her banker, Davide Giordano. Though circumspect, the patriarch of the Giordano family seemed concerned about his son's increased involvement with the Fascist Party. Gabriele now handled all Madama Lia's financial affairs. Any distractions during these trying economic times, especially in the dangerous world of the Fascists, were cause for alarm.

The Giordano and Ferri families' century-old relationship transcended business. As loyal bankers to the Savoy family, Davide's great-grandfather,

Salomone, was the head of one of the first Jewish families allowed to settle outside the Turin ghetto. The early nineteenth century was an age of enlightenment when wealthy Jews such as Salomone were welcomed into the salons of Turin, most notably that of Giulia Colbert Falletti and her husband Carlo Tancredi, the Marchesa and Marchese di Barolo. It was there Salomone met Vincenzo Ferri. Lia envied her great-grandfather his opportunity to be among those brilliant reformers.

The two men followed the lead of the Tancredis and became supporters of the Risorgimento. Shortly after unification, Vincenzo moved his fortune to the Giordano bank, which managed the assets of some of Piemonte's leading industrialists. Out of the two families' close business ties and shared political views grew a friendship that continued to this day. For that reason, news of Gabriele Giordano's nearly fanatical devotion to Mussolini alarmed Stefano Olivero. Madama Lia shared his concern.

After slipping away from Mass, Lia motored to Asili as it flurried. She hoped the deteriorating weather would not hamper the Giordanos' drive from their country home in Cherasco. The bridge over the Tanaro River was perilous in icy conditions.

Gianni was waiting for her as she pulled into the cortile of the cascina.

"Will you be needing the car again today, Madama?" Gianni knew the answer, but lately Madama Lia had not been herself, often taking long drives alone to destinations unknown. On warmer days, she went riding through the vineyards, but increasingly the car was her preferred mode of transportation when she sought solitude and distance. Giuseppina told him that conversations with her mistress were short and that she was often distracted. These moods of hers were reminiscent of the dark time.

"No, Gianni. With the snow, it's best to put the car away."

Lia sat in her sunroom overlooking the valley and tried to make sense of it all. The falling snow, now covering the vineyard floor, matched her emotions— cold and colorless. Gabriele might say it was none of her business, but the two families had lived through so much together she should not discount the seriousness of Gabriele embracing fascism with such fervor.

Lia and Gabriele were childhood friends and often confided in one another. Although she had known of Gabriele's fascist sympathies even before the March on Rome, Lia discounted it as his belief that siding with the Fascists would be helpful for the family's large businesses. "Easier to keep an eye on them," he once said of his involvement with the Fascist Party in Turin. However, according to Stefano, it went further. Like many of her friends and business associates, Lia tolerated the Fascists but never trusted them. Mussolini had fast become a dictator, and there were ominous signs that he had imperial aspirations.

He wasn't the only fascist in Europe creating concern in her circles. From what she had heard on the radio, Hitler's frenzied supporters were increasingly dangerous and taking to the streets. Would Hindenburg name Hitler as chancellor? That was the question on many of her Jewish friends' minds. What did Gabriele think of another fascist government in Europe, this one ruled by a man filled with hate for Jews? Did he not see that Hitler's rise to power could only mean a return to darker days? It was as though fascism was a new religion sweeping Europe. Lia believed Gabriele was fast becoming a zealot.

Giuseppina slipped into the room. "Madama Lia, signor e signora Giordano have arrived."

Lia followed her, saying not a word.

The scene in the cortile lightened Lia's spirits. Giggling girls danced about in the snow. The Fiore sisters reveled in the Turinesi children's visits to Asili. Giovanna enjoyed little Elena's company and the few hours when she wasn't the youngest. Michele was twelve years old and soon to make his bar mitzvah. He found being with so many girls tiresome, so he remained with the adults, much to Maria's chagrin. In contrast to the gaiety all around her, Daniela was unusually subdued. Lia had not seen her since the summer. This was not the happy woman she last saw in Cherasco on *Ferragosto*. Were Gabriele's politics the cause? She had known for years Daniela was strongly opposed to the Fascists but that as a dutiful wife said nothing. Was she worried about her sister Silvana, now living in Berlin? Obviously, there was more cause for concern in the Giordano family than Gabriele's political activities.

"Welcome, Gabriele, Daniela. Pity the snow finally came today of all days. Was the drive difficult?"

"Not really. The roads are still clear. This will pass."

Lia hoped the other storm clouds would pass as well. "How are things in Cherasco, Gabriele?"

"Quiet, as always this time of year. I prefer the long summer days in Cherasco."

Out of the corner of her eye, Lia caught the darkness in Daniela's face. Were things quiet in the Giordano family?

"When Daniela's zio Eduardo decided to keep the Dalmasso family home in the former ghetto, I was against it. Better to forget those times. But now, we are truly Piemontese with nothing to fear."

Lia was not so sure but said nothing.

"Besides," he went on, "it provides a nice escape from the city and makes collecting my Barolo and Barbaresco bottles so much easier. Yesterday we paid a visit to Cesare Borgogno in Barolo. And now, you."

"Well, let's get out of the weather, shall we?"

A hint of a smile appeared at the corners of Daniela's mouth, but she remained quiet, detached. Her solemn demeanor was in stark contrast to Gabriele's cheerful mood. The young girls were collecting snow to build their first snowman of the winter. Doretta and Sara, arm-in-arm and deep in conversation, slipped into the Fiore cascina. Lia was glad that Sara corresponded often with Doretta, who as a well-educated city girl was a good influence. Sara seemed melancholy; her winsome expression when they arrived from Alba had vanished overnight, but with Doretta's arrival, her spirits appeared lighter. Gianni helped Michele carry Christmas gifts from his family into the cascina, then the two disappeared into the garage. Cars fascinated Michele, and no one enjoyed talking about them more than Gianni. Lia led Gabriele and Daniela into the house.

Gianni had prepared the sunroom table for a tasting. Even though Gabriele always bought the most recently released wines, it had become a ritual to first taste with Lia. They made small talk about the winery and the results of the recent harvest, which helped pass the time before lunch. Gabriele did most of the talking while Daniela remained silent.

Giuseppina called the Giordano children to lunch. They shed their wet coats and boots and joined the adults in the dining room. The snow had lessened to light flurries although the temperature had dropped precipitously. Winter had finally arrived in Langhe.

Giuseppina had laid an elegant table with generations of Ferri and Bottero family crystal, china, and silver. Although not of the same faith, the Giordanos enjoyed celebrating the month-long Advent and Christmas festivities with their Catholic friends, particularly in the countryside with Madama Lia. The pranzo domenicale Giuseppina had spent days preparing disappeared within three hours. Wine flowed and adult tongues loosened. But abundant food and the pleasure to be found in it did not lift the strangeness at the table.

After devouring Giuseppina's crunchy meringues with chestnut puree and Chantilly creme and slices of delectable panettone, her holiday labor of love,

Michele and Elena asked to be excused. Only Doretta remained with the adults. She thought it odd that the adults didn't discuss politics since there was so much in the news these days. Madama Lia freely shared her opinions, but today the discussion was more about the unusually warm weather and the vineyards than anything interesting. With dismay, she studied her mamma as she folded her napkin, avoiding eye contact with her papà across the table. Why was Mamma not speaking to Papà? Had more unkind words passed between them? In fact, she had let Michele sit in the front seat of the car, a rare treat for him. The frigid atmosphere between her parents had become unbearable for Doretta. She wished she had someone with whom she could discuss this. Madama Lia? No, it would be a betrayal of Papà's trust to speak with such an important client. If it went on much longer, she would speak with nonno Davide as her mother had advised her to do.

Finally, Daniela spoke. "Madama Lia, as always, this was an exquisite lunch. Thank you so much. I know you and Gabriele would like to visit the cantina, and I have not had an opportunity to greet Luigia Fiore and her suocera. Will you excuse me?"

Doretta sprang from her chair. "I'll go with you, mamma," she said a little too excitedly. "Madama Lia, thank you so much. And thank you for the lovely locket. What a special Hanukkah gift! May I be excused as well?"

"You are most welcome, Doretta. It suits you. You may be excused."

"Don't be long, Daniela," Gabriele barked in a tone Madama Lia had never heard from him, at least not directed to his wife. "The roads will be dangerous, and it will be dark soon."

Daniela ignored his command, took Doretta's hand, and left the dining room.

Madama Lia was finally alone with Gabriele. Before she poured more Chinato into their glasses, she allowed the silence to hang in the air while she decided how to broach the subject. The small talk that had gotten her through the day was over.

"Gabriele. What is it? We were friends long before we stepped into our fathers' shoes in business and have always confided in one another. Tell me." His behavior toward Daniela gave her the opportunity for an indirect approach to the issue that concerned her most.

"Lia, nothing is wrong, why do you ask?"

"I've never seen Daniela so glum." As concerned as she was about Daniela's behavior, she was grateful to have a way to initiate an uncomfortable conversation with him.

"Oh, don't worry, Lia. It's her sister Silvana, you know, the one who lives in Germany. She's filling Daniela's head with all sorts of drivel."

"About what?" Lia knew, but wanted to hear it from him, to hear his tone.

"Hitler, of course. It's all nonsense that he will harm the Jews if he gets into power. Besides, she's married to a Christian. Her children were baptized no less. There is no way they would be in any danger." There was the opening Lia needed.

"But Gabriele, aren't you concerned about the German fascists and their avowed anti-Semitism? Jewish fascists must be worried there are Hitler sympathizers in Mussolini's inner circle too."

"Of course not, Lia!" The deepening red of his flush was evidence that she had hit a nerve. "Mussolini is no anti-Semite. And in any case, Hitler is all bravado. Hindenburg and Papen will keep him reined in."

"That's not what I hear from my friend Frieda Stern. You met her here once. You remember—the Swiss watchmaking family in La Chaux-de-Fonds?" No response. He fiddled with his glass. Was he listening? "Their relatives in Strasbourg are so concerned about the increased anti-Semitic attacks that they may join the rest of the family in Switzerland."

Still no response. She took a deep breath. It frustrated Lia that Gabriele, a husband and father of three, had less concern about anti-Semitism than she. "How can you be so sure, Gabriele, about the Fascist Party not harboring anti-Semites? Aren't you concerned about the violence of the Blackshirts and *OVRA*'s increased surveillance both at home and abroad? The secret police are brutal toward anyone suspected of being an anti-Fascist. Imprisonment first. Proof maybe never. Or worse."

"As they should be! Mussolini has done so much for Italy. He stopped the Bolshevik strikes in 1922, didn't he? And he prevented them from poisoning our youth with their dangerous revolutionary propaganda. Can you imagine if they had succeeded in toppling our monarchy the way those blood-thirsty communists did in Russia?" His voice grew harder as it grew louder. "No, the Fascists are our only hope for Italy to regain her pride and strength."

"Gabriele, I'll ask you again—aren't you concerned about the increased violence? I heard from a friend in Turin how Blackshirts and even some of those despicable Avanguardia teens are randomly beating people in the streets. Surely you've heard."

"Again, Lia. Lies. Nonsense. Such talk is dangerous. I'm surprised at you." A veiled threat, perhaps? Lia wasn't retreating.

"Gabriele, could it be you've become too close to the party's inner circle in Turin? I know you believe it serves your business interests to be close to those in power, but are you dismissing the dangers as a way to…to fit in with them?"

Silence once again. Gabriele's face was blood red, the muscles of his jaw working. He made no attempt to hide his rising anger. Whatever cordiality existed earlier had evaporated. He drained his Chinato and stared at the empty glass as if contemplating whether to dash it to the floor. She hoped he wouldn't toss it. Now Lia grasped what must have transpired to have Daniela in such a state. Undeterred, Lia continued. She was, after all, not only a friend. She was a major client of his family's bank.

"You know Mussolini is a master politician. He has no ideological beliefs other than power at all costs. And now, if he allies himself with Hitler, things will only get worse, particularly for Jews. He will make use of the Jews of Italy in any way that helps him. Don't you see?"

Gabriele turned his icy glare on Lia. Had Daniela seen it too?

"Lia, as you said, we've been friends for many years. Our families have been friends for generations. But I must warn you. That sort of talk is very dangerous. I will forget I ever heard it. Now, it is late, and we must go."

Lia was not ready to surrender—she rarely did—but decided she had gone as far as possible today. It was late, as he said, so best to assuage his ire and leave this discussion for another day. In time, he would remember it in a different light, and perhaps his vision would clear.

As though he had not spoken harsh words to her, Gabriele rose. "Lia, you haven't shown me your new *botti* from Slavonia. While Gianni is loading my wine into the car, I'd like to tour the cellar."

When they returned to the cascina, Daniela and the children were donning their coats, ready to return to Cherasco. Daniela appeared refreshed as though she had unburdened her soul. Had she shared her angst with Luigia? Daniela had known her for many years but not as a confidante. They were from two different worlds. But women in desperation find safe harbor in other compassionate women such as Luigia.

"Again, thank you, Lia, for such a lovely lunch. Please tell Giuseppina she outdid herself this year. She must share with my cook her secrets for such an airy panettone."

"I'll tell her, Daniela. I do hope when I am in Turin in late January, we'll have time for a chat. I missed that today."

"Thank you, Lia. I can't wait to share the wine with my friends," Gabriele said as he kissed both of Lia's cheeks. "Come children."

Sara joined her to bid the Giordanos farewell. What was it she and Doretta had been discussing so intently? It was snowing again. She would not be able to ride with Sara if it continued all night. Something was upsetting the girl, and Sara always opened up to her on their long rides. Lia pulled her fur coat tight as she watched Daniela climb into the backseat with her daughters. Was it a curse to see clearly the shape of things to come? Lia was rarely wrong in her reading of events on the horizon, but now she prayed she was.

Watching her angel walk home across the cortile, in the dim light Lia saw Francesco at the cantina door, his eyes fixed on Sara. Although she questioned his choice of the Strega girl, she was determined that nothing should impede Sara's studies, especially a relationship with a farm boy. But now, watching him, she wondered whether Francesco did have eyes for Sara. And did Sara's melancholy mood have anything to do with him?

But Lia did not like that the handsome boy who lived and worked among them seemed taken with the Strega girl. That was another family the Fascists had bewitched. Lia had no fear of her old friend Gabriele Giordano; he only wanted to end a conversation that had cut too close. But she would not want the Stregas to know of her political thinking or that of the Fiore family.

Lia went up to her sala where Gianni had laid a crackling fire and left a glass of Moscato and a small plate of *baci di dama* for her. It was just what she needed as she composed herself to look forward to the new year that she hoped would prove all of her misgivings wrong. Surely, 1933 would bring some relief from the hardships that she knew many across Europe were suffering. Would they finally see an end to the mad career of that aspiring despot in Berlin? Then, Italians would soon tire of the thugs in Rome, and Sara's generation would be spared what their parents endured when the world went to war. It was unbearable to imagine the fate that, otherwise, awaited them.

CHAPTER 13

Turin
January 31, 1933

The three months since that autumn day when Baldo truly became a man, and protector of his mamma, had passed in a blur. He spent weekends with his Avanguardia squad trekking in the mountains of Val di Susa, even after the winter snows finally arrived in mid-December. It was good training, helping them to become strong for the day they would assume the role of protectors of the Fascist Party. Maybe once he fulfilled his dream of being a member of Organization for Vigilance and Repression of Antifascism, he would even be sent to Rome. To join the feared secret police at the seat of power was his deepest wish.

Now, amid the early morning bustle of Porta Nuova Station, he boarded the express train that would take him from Turin to Milan. He was so excited that he didn't know how he would be able to sit still for such a long trip, ultimately to Germany. Well, he would pace the corridor, he would think. He looked forward to the grand views of the fertile Po River Valley, which he would not see again until Christmas. With great certainty, he knew his time in Germany would forge his future. Fortunately, he was able to dissuade his mamma from coming to the station with him. She would have embarrassed him by breaking down, and he was highly emotional too. An Avanguardista doesn't get teary or wave too many times to his mamma on the platform.

Surely now that Hitler and the Nazi Party were in full control of Germany, the alliance between the two fascist nations would grow. His superior German language skills and proven loyalty to the party destined him to rise in the ranks. How he hoped war would come so Italy would finally redeem herself!

The British and the French would not easily accept the new order, one governed by fascist principles, even if it was the best thing for them. Bloodshed, not diplomacy, would be the only way for Europe. In Germany, he was certain to find many who agreed with him.

He settled comfortably into a window seat in a second-class compartment—a luxury for him. Hopefully he would have the same luck for the longer, overnight portion from Milan to Berlin. He had never traveled outside Italy, and he didn't know what to expect.

At least he would not have to worry about his mamma while he was away. No more beatings. The neighbors had heard the shouts. They saw him throw his father's meager belongings down the stairs, then push him out onto the street, drunk and bleeding. He didn't care what they thought. But what would happen if Dino discovered he had left the country? Would he return? He had already once tried to worm his way back in, bullying his mamma at the mercato for money. Fortunately, Baldo was with her that day. It was the last time he had seen his father.

For years, since Dino had lost his job after the Jewish-owned bank foreclosed on his employer, Flora had been the family's sole breadwinner. She was a primary school teacher and a gifted seamstress with a client list of some of Turin's finest women. Baldo wished she didn't have to make clothes for Jewish women, but he was more than happy for her to take money from them. Now, with his father gone, she would have money to spend on herself—and on him. Times were difficult, and food prices were soaring. Flora was lucky to have work. He was lucky to have her.

She had already begun to smile as she had when he was a little boy, and they had enjoyed many good moments in the apartment. He would miss that, away in Germany. But she would work hard and live prudently.

His group leader had offered to watch over Flora in his absence. As an Avanguardista, a shining young star of the local Fascist Party, he should expect no less. If Dino attempted to re-enter Flora's life, the fit and devoted teenagers would give him what he deserved on Baldo's behalf.

Flora was sad Baldo was leaving for so long, and going so far from her. She spent the Christmas holidays doing what she loved best: sewing and knitting, day and night. Although he mostly would wear his Avanguardia uniform, his mamma had sewn him a new suit and other clothes she believed would be useful when the warm weather returned. Berlin would be much colder than Turin, so she knitted him two wool scarves and two thick wool sweaters. For

Christmas, with the money she had earned sewing a New Year's party dress for one of her Jewish clients, she bought him a pair of Florentine black leather gloves lined with cashmere.

He wished she wouldn't make such a fuss about what he would do when his clothes—particularly his uniform—no longer fit. Although he was seventeen years old, he was still growing. Since October, he had grown another two inches. And the mountaineering with his squad had hardened him. They were taught three key principles to guarantee success as soldiers: suffer without crying out, do more than asked, and serve without expecting rewards. He had learned them all well. No longer the skinny boy who, before he became an Avanguardista, had often been bullied, he was much taller and stronger than most other boys his age. And most handsome, Flora told him, with his sandy blonde hair and dark brown, nearly black eyes. Too bad they weren't blue. He then would fit in perfectly with his Aryan brethren in Berlin.

Blue eyes. That girl outside the synagogue—but it was impossible for a Jew to have blue eyes! Some weak Aryan woman poisoned his bloodline with a Jewish husband no doubt. No Aryan man would do such a thing. The thought of those eyes stirred a memory of a lucky discovery he made before Christmas.

A week after their encounter, Baldo had returned to the synagogue, hoping it was her routine to be there at that time. He waited an hour. She never appeared. He persevered, and finally one day, his luck changed. Peering around the corner, he spotted her among a group of girls who emerged from behind the synagogue. He recognized her voice. Unlike the previous time, she left the group and walked toward Corso Vittorio Emanuele II. Given the time of day and the early winter darkness, he presumed she was going home. He followed her, determined to discover more about her. Baldo suspected she was an anti-Fascist, perhaps even a Communist, so if she didn't live near the synagogue like so many Jews, she was probably going to a working-class district such as his.

That day he wore civilian clothes, dark colors to match the weather. No need to make himself more recognizable, although she, in her rust-colored coat and matching hat, made herself an easy mark to follow. A light rain fell, so he opened his umbrella. It allowed him some protection from discovery as he hid under it and followed her up the narrow via Sant'Anselmo. Corso Vittorio Emanuele II was only a block away from the synagogue. Was she headed for the tram as he had been that day? She stopped to window shop. He darted into a recessed entryway not far behind her before she glanced in his direction. Did she suspect she was being followed? If she was boarding

Tram 7 on Corso Vittorio Emanuele II, he would run the risk of either being discovered while waiting at the stop or he would lose her. What luck! The tram rolled to a stop as she crossed the street. She entered through the front of the car without hesitation. No, he was certain she didn't suspect someone was following her. Sweating and jittery, Baldo fumbled with his umbrella and darted through the rear door. The girl was already seated near the driver, reading something, probably some Bolshevik propaganda. Although there were many empty seats, Baldo stood in the back where he would not be noticed and kept an eye on her. The crowd of passengers that boarded at Porta Nuova train station nearly thwarted his plan. Workers returning from the Fiat plant in Lingotto filled every space—standing and seated.

Finally, he was rewarded for his height. Over the heads of passengers who crowded the aisle, he caught a glimpse of her reddish coat as she rose to get off. He leapt for the door, not bothering that in the process he knocked an elderly man off his feet. Baldo ignored the epithets the other passengers hurled at him. This was too important to care about some old man. He had to find out who she was, where she lived.

No one else got off. Would she notice him? It was pouring now, so she dashed under the arcade. He waited for a moment at the stop to see her next move. Blending into the throng of people rushing home through the arcade, he watched as she walked in the opposite direction. He kept his distance and followed her as she rounded the corner. There she was, walking along the chestnut tree-lined street, alone. He tilted his umbrella to shield his face. No chance to lose her now. He nearly collided with her when, without warning, she stopped in front of a door with shiny brass fittings and knocker, framed in marble. She was searching her handbag—no doubt for her keys—so he kept walking, slowly, not looking at her. When he heard the door click shut, he chanced a glance back toward the building entrance. She was gone.

Hidden under his umbrella, fixated on his mark, he had failed to note any landmarks. Wherever he was, he knew by the opulent Piemontese Baroque facades that it was where rich people lived. The four-story building she had entered was grand—not at all what he suspected of a Communist. But Jews were rich now. Too rich. He noted the brass numbers affixed to the marble door frame: 15A. Now, all he needed was the name of the street, and that was easy enough. Corso Re Umberto. His squad leader would be proud of his tracking skills. It was a skill he knew he would use many times in the years to come as a member of the secret police.

A month later, as Christmas approached, orders for fancy holiday dresses kept his mamma busier than ever. School was out for the holidays, so she sewed day and night. Word had spread among the wealthy women of Turin—mostly Jews—about Flora Volpe's creative flair. She copied the most recent styles from Paris and Milan, improving the designs through the magic she worked with her Singer sewing machine.

One morning Baldo woke to find his mamma folding several dresses into one of her handmade sateen bags before placing them into a large box.

"Baldo, you're awake. Finally. After you've had something to eat, I need you to take these dresses to a client. She is expecting them this morning. I truly don't have a minute to spare away from my sewing today."

"Certainly, mamma." She went to her clients' homes for fittings and then delivered the dresses herself when they were finished. He hoped they paid her well for her long hours bent over her machine or delicately sewing sequins and rhinestones by hand onto the dresses she created.

"Now listen, Baldo, signora Giordano is a very important client, one of my first. You must be polite."

"Is she a Jew too, Mamma? Why do you work for those people?" he said with no effort to hide his disdain. She knew his thoughts about them.

"I won't have any of that talk, Baldo," she snapped. I need your help. Signora Giordano has been very generous to me. And to you." Flora regretted those last words as soon as she spoke them.

"To me?" He was aghast. "What did she ever do for me?"

Flora ignored his question. She saw no reason to divulge the relationship between his music teacher and Daniela Giordano, or that it was Daniela who gave her extra money for the lessons. Even with her dressmaking work, after Dino lost his job in 1929, she barely had enough money to pay their rent and food bills. His drunken habits consumed what she hoped to spend on Baldo's lessons. Flora didn't want to accept signora Giordano's generosity, but both women recognized the talent buried deep inside the angry boy. That was in the past. Professor Dalmasso should never have mentioned him to his niece, but his compliments on her stylish gowns opened the door for him to conclude that his hostile student was her dressmaker's son. Signora Giordano would not accept her refusal. Such a kind woman.

"Baldo, here are the directions. The address is 15A Corso Re Umberto. Best to take Tram 7. You only have three stops after Madama Cristina. It's the first stop after Porta Nuova. You'll see Caffè Platti and it's right after that in the direction of Piazza Savoia. Ring the bell. Someone will let you in. Go to the top floor…*Baldo!* Are you paying attention?"

The address was the last thing he heard. He knew exactly how to get there from the tram stop. What luck!

"Once again, she is a *very* important client of mine. The Giordanos have been in Turin for many centuries. They own one of the most important banks in Piemonte. It's an honor for a woman of her stature to wear my couture. You must not make any mistakes. Please." Flora heard herself pleading with him. Perhaps it wasn't a good idea to send him.

He sensed her concern. The last thing he wanted was for her to change her mind. Now he would gain entry to the mystery address. "Don't worry, Mamma. Tell me her name again."

"Giordano. Signora Daniela Giordano." He let the name sink in. Giordano didn't sound Jewish, but those clever Jews had long ago tried to be like Italians. He knew better, though. They were *not* of Italian blood.

"Perhaps you've heard of her husband, Gabriele Giordano. I recently read he is an important member of the Fascist Party. I've been to their home many times, but I have never met him. I thought you might be interested to know this."

His mind raced. What if this was the girl's family?

"Baldo, she will give you one hundred and eighty lire. It's a large sum of money and I am counting on it to pay some bills. Tuck it away carefully inside your coat and come straight home. No stops along the way."

"Yes, Mamma."

An hour later, Baldo was standing in the back of Tram 7, holding the bulky box. Lost in his thoughts, he nearly missed the stop. Within minutes he slipped past the doorman, busy helping an old lady, and climbed the stairs to the Giordano apartment. His pulse raced, not from the exertion—after all, he was fit—but from anticipation. If this was her apartment and she answered the door, what then? He hadn't thought of what would happen if this woman was the girl's mother. What if she recognized him? His mamma would lose one of her best clients. Well, so what? She barely has time to do the work she has now. Besides, there were many other rich women in Turin. Aryan women. After learning her client's husband was a powerful Fascist, it was more important than ever to discover whether the mystery girl was a daughter of this house.

The brass nameplate on the door at the top of the stairs read "Giordano" and some strange object was diagonally affixed to the frame on the right side of the door. He rang the bell. No answer. As he was about to ring a second time, a man dressed in a tuxedo opened the door. "Signor Giordano?" His voice cracked.

"Good sakes, no, boy. Who are you? How did you get past the doorman downstairs?" the man demanded as he appraised him with narrowed eyes and a curled upper lip.

Ignoring the man's questions, Baldo uncharacteristically stammered, "Buongiorno, I am here…uh, I'm here to deliver dresses to signora Giordano from signora Volpe." He paused, then puffed out his chest. "She is *my* mother, a great dressmaker."

"Oh yes, Madamin is expecting you. Your name?"

"Baldo. Baldo Volpe." A butler no less. And so pompous. He had underestimated the Giordano family's wealth.

"Wait here," he ordered.

The man disappeared into a room across the hall. From the little Baldo observed, it was a brightly colored room with far-too-realistic paintings of nude women on the wall. Pornographic! No surprise they would have such obscene art. Shocked to be in the home of a rich Jew, and a Fascist at that, Baldo took in his surroundings. The many large paintings hung in the long hall to his left were nothing like the great masters of Italy. These canvases were portraits of people, but their shapes were strange and angular. Who was Picasso? Never heard of him. Didn't Italy have Renaissance masters? To the left of the room across the hall, there was a carpeted staircase with a carved light wood balustrade. One apartment with two floors? Such vulgar opulence. Peering back into the room across the hall, he spotted an ornate baby grand piano similar to the one professor Dalmasso had in his studio. He long ago banished thoughts of that vile old man who always reeked of pipe tobacco. Although he was glad to be done with lessons, he had to admit that he missed playing. But he had no piano of his own, and it wasn't a manly enough activity for an Avanguardista anyway.

The tuxedoed man reappeared. "Come this way."

Before he made any introductions, a woman in an elegant dark-blue dress that hugged her figure and that he recognized as one of his mamma's creations greeted him. "Baldo, I've heard so much about you from your mother. You are much taller than she described. And handsome. I've known her for several years, so I've heard many stories about you."

"Um…" All of a sudden, his mouth went dry, and words stuck in his throat. The woman was not at all what he had expected. She had a kind face, and she was pretty, almost a beauty. No hooked nose like he had seen in cartoons in the issue of *Der Stürmer* his squad leader shared with him.

"I was so sad to hear you stopped piano lessons with my uncle. I spoke with him about you. He believes you have a gift."

Uncle! Spoke about me? Baldo's head spun. Not wanting to spend more time than necessary with her, he stammered, "Signora Giordano, I have your dresses."

"Yes, of course. I know you must be busy helping your mother with deliveries. Such a busy time of year. Lay them down here please."

Why couldn't she take the dresses and give him the money? He placed the box on the semi-circular pale green divan and laid the bag next to it. What manner of furniture is this? He untied the bag and freed the three dresses.

She took her time—painfully for Baldo—inspecting each gown. "They are exquisite. Once again your mother has outdone herself." She laid them back on the divan. "Everyone will be so envious."

Feeling as though the room was closing in on him, pressing on his chest and making it hard to breathe, Baldo cleared his throat. "Here's the invoice, signora. It's one hundred eighty lire."

"Oh, but I am sorry, Baldo. Of course. I have the money here. Let's see." After counting out the bills, Daniela handed the money to him. Anxious to leave, he stashed the money in his inside coat pocket.

In a voice devoid of emotion, he said, "My mother says to thank you and that she appreciates your business." It made his stomach turn to have to say that to her. Even if she was nice, and pretty, she was a Jew for whom his mamma worked too hard.

"Renaldo will see you to the door. Please give my best to your mother and wish her a Merry Christmas."

Baldo reddened, forced his tight lips to curl into a smile, and followed the butler. But he stopped in his tracks. The girl! It's her! In a silver frame on a table next to the divan. He couldn't miss it. The blue eyes. And the man! Professor Dalmasso. It all made sense now. She wasn't merely another pupil of the old Jew; she was his niece. So this was *her* family, *her* house. This was much more than he ever expected to discover.

Voices came from upstairs. A young boy called out, "Doretta, you promised to go with me to the museum today."

"Michele, I promised to take you in the afternoon. What time is it now? I have errands to run this morning."

That voice! She had spoken only a few hostile words to him that day, but he recognized her voice, her face in the photo. Doretta. Now he knew her name, where she lived, *and* that she was the daughter of a powerful Fascist. Could he not control his daughter? What would he say if he knew how she had threatened him, an Avanguardista, in public? He couldn't believe his luck to have discovered this scandalous information.

Footsteps fast approached from the second floor. Time to dash before she discovered him there. It would be the end of his mamma's work since all the Jewesses would talk no doubt. Someday, he was certain, the knowledge would be extremely useful. Who knows, in time he might even return to this place to arrest her. The Jews would be properly controlled once Hitler convinced Mussolini of the danger they posed.

Before Renaldo the butler opened wide the door, Baldo bolted out of the apartment, skipping stairs as he rushed to the ground floor. A wave of satisfaction washed over him as he stepped out into the late morning and drew the cold, fresh air deep into his lungs. Completing his first covert mission had so invigorated Baldo that he burst out laughing.

BALDO HAD GOTTEN LOST IN HIS MEMORIES OF THAT GIRL. THE MOTION OF the train was soothing, and he felt quite satisfied with himself. The near encounter with Doretta Giordano and the discovery that she was the daughter of a powerful member of the Fascist party gave him food for thought all through the holidays. Even now, on the train to Milan, he could not shake the memory of those blue eyes and the fancy rooms where no one labored even to open doors for themselves.

Doretta Giordano was old enough for evening parties. He imagined the fabric his mamma sewed touching her body. As his train slowed in the outskirts of Milan, he vowed to keep an eye on her when he returned. And when he had attained membership in OVRA, he would make sure the secret police interrogated her thoroughly. Who knew—perhaps he would be the one to open her up and make her talk.

A strange feeling washed over him. He shuddered and rushed to the toilet. Oh that girl! She was already trying to cast her Jewish spell. He had read about such things in German magazines. He had to shake her memory. There was no way he would defile himself with her.

CHAPTER 14

Turin
May 26, 1933

S ara knew that reading foreign papers was perilous, but she had no other
source of truthful reporting. Besides, she found it great homework for
her English class although today she didn't even need to understand the
words. The image in the New York Herald Tribune, the American newspaper
printed in Paris, was all the proof Sara needed. It was happening as Doretta
had predicted.

The flames leaping from burning books reminded her of Girolamo Savon-
arola's Florentine Bonfire of the Vanities centuries ago she learned about in
school. This latest act of German censorship eclipsed even their suppression of
press freedom. What sickened Sara wasn't the ring of uniformed Brownshirts
and Nazi officials around the pile of incinerating books—that was expected
of them—but the joyous faces of civilians, cheering, raising their right arms
in the Nazi salute. It showed the Nazi propaganda she had read about was
working. Although she had seen the salute in Italy, there was something far
more sinister, even demonic, about regular people saluting the destruction
of literary works deemed "Un-German." German civilians were now willing
participants in the madness that began on January 30 nearly four months
earlier when Hitler became chancellor. When would it touch her world? Sara
would write Doretta and ask about her zia Silvana in Berlin. Hopefully Silvana
and her family had left for America.

After Doretta's trip to Barbaresco in mid-December, the two girls corresponded regularly. That day, as they sat alone in Sara's bedroom, they discovered
the many things they had in common, the important things. The differences

that others might have noticed about their lives seemed not to matter. Madama Lia herself had told Sara that Doretta would make a good friend. At times Sara did wish that she had something more exciting to write about to her friend than the goings on at the convent school and her hospital chores, especially when she received Doretta's letters filled with news about parties and concerts in the city.

Despite this, Sara would not have missed Doretta's weekly letters for anything, filled as they were with fun details about boys and descriptions of her mother's custom-made party gowns that she hoped her mother would let her wear when good times returned. As most women in Turin, Doretta and her mother ignored Mussolini's directives that they dress as members of the *Massaie Rurali*, the largest group of women in Italy. Dressing as peasant women–ladies of the field–was unthinkable, especially in a country as fashionable as Italy. Sara quizzed Doretta once about why her mother didn't travel to the fashion houses in Paris or Milan, choosing instead an unknown woman to create her wardrobe. She was, after all, a woman of means and someone well known in Turin high society. Doretta answered that her mother always sought ways to help those in need in Turin. The economic promises of the Fascists had yet to be fulfilled. Unemployment and inflation crushed the middle and working classes. Once Daniela heard about Flora Volpe and discovered her talent, she wanted to help her build her business, especially after her husband left her with a boy to raise on her own. Though Sara only saw her a few times each year, she sensed Daniela Giordano was a kind and loving person. In these past six months, Sara discovered Doretta had inherited many of those same qualities.

Each week when a new letter arrived, Sara shared the contents with her zia Luce over dinner. They vicariously enjoyed a charmed city life through Doretta. In early March, weeks after the Reichstag fire helped Hitler gain more power, the tone of Doretta's letters darkened. They became a frightening window on a world going mad. She related increasingly worrying news from her zia Silvana in Berlin. In the last month, her letters were joyless, echoing a desperate tone from far away.

The doorbell rang, and Sara quickly folded the paper, covered it with her schoolbooks, and answered the door. Those caught reading banned publications would experience the wrath of *polizia* politica. Censorship was strict, and the eyes of the PolPol, as they were known, were everywhere.

"Sara Fiore?" the courier asked.

She held out her hand, noticeably trembling. Sara had never received a telegram nor known anyone who had. Surely, the news could not be good.

Who would send me such an urgent correspondence? She ripped open the telegram: Doretta.

Please come to Turin today for the weekend.

That was all her dear friend had written. How strange she would send a telegram and ask her to come on short notice. Was there more to her invitation?

Sara had looked forward to a quiet weekend preparing for exams, but how could she resist a weekend with Doretta in Turin during such beautiful spring weather? It had been a long time since they had seen one another. Why not have some fun before her grueling exams began?

Sara grabbed a few clothes suitable for the city from her armoire and stuffed them into her small cloth valise. Something was missing—of course, hazelnuts. A tin of *nocciole tostate* from her nonna Beatrice's farm in Bossolaschetto was the perfect gift for her hosts. When she stopped at the hospital to say good-bye to her zia Luce, Sara reassured her all was well although she had begun to wonder herself if there was more to it. Was it that Doretta was merely tense about her zia Silvana's situation in Berlin after the book burning? She promised Luciana that she would make up for the lost time studying, kissed her good-bye, and was off.

From there, Sara stopped at Madama Lia's mulino next to the train station. The flour mill had the only telephone she could access. Doretta should know she was coming. Madama Lia had gone to Nizza Monferrato for the day, so Sara was spared hearing her disapproving tone when she told her she was going for a weekend in Turin with exams looming.

When the train pulled into Porta Nuova station in the late afternoon, Doretta surprised Sara by waiting trackside. Through the crowd of passengers crammed on the platform, Sara noticed that, in the six months since she was last in Asili, Doretta had developed the figure of a young woman. Her thick chestnut mane, usually in a single long braid, was now short and wavy in the latest style. Dressed fashionably in a form-fitting, bright-yellow dress, Doretta now appeared more like a grown woman—not a girl in her early teens. Sara worried her own growing days were past. She accepted she would always be petite but lamented that her girlish figure would never change. Did that explain Francesco's preference for the buxom Cinzia Strega? Sara quickly banished thoughts of those two. Although Doretta smiled as she waved, Sara read signs of despair in her expression. Why did she scan the area as though looking for someone else? Doretta gave her a long and sisterly embrace, reminiscent of Giovanna clinging to her when she was frightened. Though she flashed a big smile, Doretta's cheeks were moist when Sara kissed them. Had she been crying?

"Doretta, how did you know I'd be on this train? I only told Ida to tell you I was coming."

"I didn't. I guessed. If you hadn't been on this train, I would have waited for the next one. You're an angel to come on short notice." Doretta turned away, avoiding Sara's bewildered expression. When she turned back, her eyes were indeed red, tears welling, her smile gone.

"Cara, *dimmi*, what's wrong?"

Doretta blinked hard, and a weak smile reappeared. "We'll talk at home. I hope you don't mind walking. It's not far, and it's such a lovely day."

"Of course. I've been either in class or in the hospital all week. Spring will be gone before I've had a chance to enjoy it." Maybe all Doretta wanted was her company after all. But why the tears and sad face?

Under the cerulean sky, the two young girls walked arm in arm along Corso Vittorio Emanuele II with Doretta peppering Sara with questions about Asili. Sara was happy she avoided inquiries about Francesco. Many months had passed since he arrived, and the two had settled into a cordial relationship that was neither friendship nor enmity. Only Cinzia Strega's frequent appearance on the train with her from Alba to Barbaresco stirred her emotions.

As they walked in the arcade of the avenue lined with budding plane trees, Doretta constantly glanced about as though looking for someone. Their stroll reminded Sara of the only time she had been to Turin on a springtime day. Then, she was a little girl, clinging to her mamma's hand, a bit overwhelmed by all the people, cars, and trams. And the soaring trees had seemed to her like a forest in the middle of the city. Now, with her dearest friend clutching her arm, telegraphing that something did in fact trouble her, Sara wondered whether they were facing a world that would make them both grow up far too fast. At least they had each other.

Once inside the street entrance to the apartment building, Doretta relaxed. She had been edgy the entire walk from the station, her lighthearted conversation betrayed by her body language. With Doretta's arm through hers as they walked, Sara felt her taut muscles, like a cat ready to spring. Something—or someone—was frightening Doretta.

This was Sara's first visit to the Giordano apartment. How grand! It reminded her of something she had seen once in a silent movie. As she walked across the threshold, the parquet floor of the stairwell gave way to a dizzying chevron pattern of black and white marble. The furniture was unlike theirs in the countryside. Such strange, light-colored wood with lots of swirls and lines. And so highly polished. It was like entering another era.

"Doretta! How beautiful."

"You like it? Art Deco. It's all the rage now, so of course Papà wanted our home to be in fashion."

"Of course I like it. It's just that, it's so…so different."

"Come, let's find Mamma. She's probably upstairs in her sitting room."

A two-level apartment? Never had Sara imagined an apartment as large as a cascina. Not even Madama Lia's villa atop Altavilla overlooking Alba was this grand, and she was one of the wealthiest citizens of Alba.

Upstairs, Sara noted the family's bedrooms, a room for the nanny connected to Elena's, and two separate sitting rooms for each parent. There were even two bathrooms—with indoor plumbing, no less! Whatever was upsetting Doretta, a lack of comfort was *not* the cause. Halfway down the long hall, they found Daniela in her sitting room, bathed in sunlight from the large open windows, writing at her desk.

"*Scusami*, Mamma. Sara is here."

Daniela turned to them, and her face came into view. Doretta had grown into a beauty, but her mother had aged beyond her years in the six months since Sara last saw her. She had not lost her beauty, but under her eyes, her skin looked like dark half-moons, and more than a few strands of gray invaded her thick, dark brown hair that had lost its luster. And she was thinner than Sara remembered. Was she ill? Was that the reason for Doretta's summons? Oh, how she longed to speak alone with Doretta. After her skittish behavior walking home from the station, Doretta now appeared relaxed, puzzling Sara even more.

"Sara, buonasera. *Benvenuta*! What a delight to see you here in the city for a change." Despite the changes in her visage, Daniela Giordano was still in control of her flair for style and elegance. Her fitted, embroidered, white cotton blouse—that showed a bit more cleavage than Sara had seen women dare in Alba—over a mid-calf pencil skirt of red linen emphasized her hour-glass figure. Doretta now bore a striking resemblance to her mother—all but her blue eyes and chestnut hair.

"Buonasera, signora Giordano. Happy to be here. Thank you. Here, I brought you something from Bossolaschetto I thought you'd enjoy."

"Oh, Sara, how thoughtful. You remembered how much I enjoy your nonna Beatrice's toasted hazelnuts. How is your nonna?

"She's fine, much better now that spring is finally here."

"I do hope we can drive to Alta Langa this summer to see her. Thank you, Sara. Doretta has been missing you so much. I'm so happy you came. Please, sit."

They made small talk until Daniela suggested the girls rest before Shabbat dinner. It would be a new experience for Sara. In recent years, Doretta had told her, Daniela convinced her husband to observe erev Shabbat in their home. She strongly believed it was important for the children to have some Jewish traditions. Too many families she knew were slipping away from the culture that had held their people together in the Diaspora. Doretta said she didn't mind as long as it pleased her mother.

Precisely at eight o'clock, the girls and Doretta's siblings, Michele and Elena, went to dinner. Sara had tried once again to discover the reason for Doretta's request that she come to Turin and for her tears in the train station, but Elena insisted on her sister's company before dinner. She entered without knocking, climbed up on Doretta's outsized bed, and thumbed through her Paris fashion magazines. No matter what Doretta tried, it was impossible to shoo her away without a fit of tears erupting. Sara empathized as she had frequently experienced the same with Giovanna. Doretta assured her they would talk later.

As he did each Friday, Daniela's zio Eduardo arrived minutes before dinner. Well into his seventies, the former concert pianist still cut a fine figure—quite dapper. He appeared capable of continuing his illustrious career, but Doretta had said his arthritis prevented the long hours of practice he would need for a demanding concert schedule. He still played, however, and enjoyed teaching young students and composing. Hopefully he would play tonight. Never had she met a famous musician. Everyone was so kind to her.

The dining room was elegant simplicity. No heavy, dark wood or overstuffed chairs like those in Madama Lia's villa. Four large windows framed in pale blue silk curtains overlooked the avenue. The last rays of sun cast a red-orange glow on the paneled cream-colored walls, giving the room a warm feeling. Although there were only seven of them that evening, the table appeared long enough to seat fourteen people.

Before they were seated, Daniela lit the Shabbat candle and said a blessing in a language unfamiliar to Sara. Doretta whispered it was Hebrew. Sara sat to Daniela's right and her zio Eduardo to her left across from Sara. He shared fascinating stories about traveling the world and meeting famous musicians and composers when he was active in his concert career. She so dreamed of traveling far away one day, hoping the tempest brewing in Germany would not prevent that. The long table emphasized the distance between Doretta's parents that Sara detected as soon as they were seated. They were so spread out at the long table that Sara barely had an opportunity to speak with Doretta. She would have to wait even longer.

The lavish dinner resembled a *festa*, not a weekly dinner. Most of the dishes were familiar *cucina piemontese* fare although there were some new foods like *Rebecchine di Gerusalemme, polpettone di tonno cotto*, and the shiny braided bread that was soft and golden inside. The challah, as Doretta called it, was nothing like the tasteless, soft-crumb biova her nonna Mirella used to bake once a week in Barbaresco. Nonna—Sara's thoughts drifted away. It still pained her to think of her departed nonna, now gone more than four months. How had she known she would not live to see another harvest? She once told Sara that she, too, had the gift of knowing the future. Like her, she said, Sara had been born with a veil that gave her the power. Sara knew that Luce called her *en caul birth* rare, but she wasn't sure what that meant. Although she often sensed things more than others did, she had dismissed her nonna's talk as superstitious.

After dinner, Michele excused himself to retreat to the battleground in his room; his pewter soldiers awaited their general. The rest of the family, including little Elena, joined zio Eduardo in the library. Elena settled onto Doretta's lap as their uncle worked magic at the piano. Sara recognized *Für Elise*, a piece that Madama often played on the phonograph when she was at Cascina Asili. The music was so romantic; she thought it might have been a song Madama Lia enjoyed with her late husband.

After three lively pieces by Chopin, Liszt, and Mozart, Eduardo called Doretta to the piano. Finally, Sara would get to hear Doretta play.

"Doretta, come join me. We haven't played a duet for some time."

Doretta blushed but slid Elena off her lap and jumped up to join him. Sara knew Doretta's favorite times at the piano were those with her great-uncle by her side. "What shall we play, zio?

"You are my favorite duet partner for Chopin's Polonaise in A-Major. Shall we?"

The music mesmerized Sara as her dear friend displayed a talent beyond what she expected. There still was much about Doretta she didn't know.

"*Bravi*! Now for a Rachmaninoff, please," Daniela asked. "You know I love his Piano Concerto Number 2, zio."

"Oh, cara, but I have no orchestra with me. You know it is not a solo piece and it is just not the same. Why not one of his Etudes-Tableaux? Perhaps Opus 39, Number 2?"

"Too sad, zio. Not even a bit of the first movement of the concerto? Just to watch your hands. One of my fondest memories of you in concert was when you played it with the Berlin Philharmonic. Such a memory!"

"Yes, a sweet memory. We shall need such memories." His melancholy tone betrayed the smile that creased his face.

As his hands struck the keyboard, it was as though church bells rang. Sara felt the music reverberate within her. Soon the bells quieted, and rolling, lyrical music flowed from the instrument. Sara found herself lost in the sonorous melody, slightly swaying in rhythm with the music.

All at once, Eduardo stopped playing. "Okay, that's enough without the orchestra. Time for more brandy."

"Thank you so very much, zio."

"I do love that piece. Rachmaninoff was a genius. You know, I had the privilege of meeting him and performing many of his great works in Moscow... before the Revolution."

Gabriele spoke for the first time since the music began. Sara had noticed how quiet and brooding he was, sitting with cigar and brandy in hand. "If not for Il Duce and the Fascists, the same would have happened here in Italy after the war. The Bolsheviks were poisoning our youth."

Daniela's back stiffened. The muscles in her face quivered, drawing away her smile.

"Gabriele, surely you are informed about the recent events in Germany," said Eduardo. "In less than five months, Hitler has begun what many fear will be a reign of terror. First the boycotts of Jewish businesses, the non-Aryan laws, and the book burnings over two weeks ago."

Sara noticed Daniela's and Doretta's faces darken. Doretta squirmed and cast sideways glances at her mother. Neither seemed comfortable with the discussion.

"And I hear his Brownshirts are brutalizing non-compliant journalists," Eduardo added.

"There is nothing to it, Eduardo. Simply a bunch of thugs out to cause mischief."

The newspaper photo Sara saw that morning contradicted Gabriele's comment. Yes, the Sturmabteilung—known as the Brownshirts and no different from Mussolini's Squadristi and Avanguardisti—were there, but so were adult civilians—many of them—all cheering. Sara wanted to know more about the book burnings, but she didn't ask for fear they might think her ignorant. Doretta's father, her host, was a Fascist who seemingly failed to see the danger posed by people who shared his political ideology.

"Perhaps." Eduardo rested his empty glass on the table next to him and contemplated his smoldering pipe before he spoke. "Gabriele, those thugs were once simply lost boys brainwashed by Hitler's SS—no different than the Avanguardisti whom the Fascists are grooming to become Blackshirts and even members of the OVRA secret police. Cruel they are."

Doretta fidgeted and eased a now-sleeping Elena off her lap once more and onto the divan before she reached for her glass of Moscato. Good, Elena was sleeping. The conversation would give any child nightmares. Sara feared such talk would disrupt her sleep as well.

"Eduardo, wasn't my dressmaker's son a pupil of yours? I recall you said he showed so much talent." Sara noticed the look of surprise on Doretta's face when her eyes met her uncle's before he turned away from her. "Signora Volpe was quite sad he quit, and she worried about him getting mixed up with these thugs."

"No doubt all that hate churning within him is aimed at Jews. I felt it. Have you any idea what happened to him?"

"Baldo? No, I don't. I met him only once, right before last Christmas. He came here to deliver dresses for his mother. He was polite and seemed nice…" Doretta's glass crashing to floor interrupted her.

"Mi dispiace *tanto*, Mamma. It slipped out of my hand." Doretta slid out from under Elena's head and picked up the thin crystal shards from the floor. Her hands shook.

Daniela turned her attention back to Eduardo. "He is an Avanguardista. I know the Fascists require all the boys to join their youth groups, but I was surprised to hear from his mother how zealously he had taken to it."

"Yes, I recall his last lesson in October, days before Sukkot. He was dressed in that awful uniform. He stormed out." Eduardo returned his ivory pipe to his lips and puffed while he relit the tobacco. Sara noticed Doretta bit her lip and her hands continued to shake as she scooped up the last shards of broken glass.

Gabriele opened his mouth to speak, but Daniela interjected. "His mother told me he was awarded a prized scholarship to study German in Berlin for a year. He returns before Christmas, she said."

Eduardo glanced over at Doretta, now clearly distressed. Before Daniela prolonged the uncomfortable conversation, Eduardo rose, signaling the evening had come to an end as far as he was concerned.

"Cara, it is late and I must go. Please thank Bruna for the delicious brasato. The Barbaresco from Cascina Asili was a perfect pairing."

With a conciliatory tone in his voice, Eduardo said to Doretta, "You played splendidly tonight, carissima. Choose another duet for next week. Perhaps something from Bach or Mozart—something cheery?" He kissed her cheeks, gazed into her eyes, and left.

The evening ended abruptly. Sara sensed an unspoken understanding had passed between Doretta and her great-uncle. Did they share something dark?

Doretta carried Elena upstairs and laid her in her bed. Nanny would come later to change her into her nightclothes and tuck her in. As they walked to Doretta's room, Sara thought, *Now she'll have to tell me.*

Alone at last—"Okay, Doretta. Time to tell me why I'm here. It's been nearly twelve hours since I received your telegram. What's upsetting you so?"

Doretta ignored the question. Instead, she pulled out a small envelope from the drawer of her nightstand. Her tone darkened as she motioned Sara to join her by the unlit fireplace. "Sit here, Sara. Read this."

Sara studied the envelope as Doretta settled on the floor next to her. There was no return address, but the postmark was Berlin. Probably from her zia with more disturbing news about the Nazis. The flimsy typewritten page inside was folded several times. It reminded her of the notes she and her classmates passed around in class when suor Angelica wasn't looking.

"But, Doretta, it's in German. You know I don't speak it much less read it." Sara chided herself for her impatient tone. Something distressed Doretta, and she needed comfort.

Doretta took the letter from Sara and translated, her voice tense.

My dearest Doretta.

She stopped and swallowed hard.

I heard you speaking German once at the cafè near your house, so I know you will understand my words.

Did Doretta shiver?

As you can see, I know who you are and where you live. There is nothing about you that I do not know. There are many people watching you, no matter where you go. We will always be watching. You and your Jew family in Italy will soon be the hunted ones.

Panic flashed in Doretta's eyes. She murmured to no one in particular, "The hunter becomes the hunted."

"Doretta, is this why you asked me here?" Doretta's teary, frightened eyes answered Sara's question. "But who would write *that*...and in German no less? Who do you know in Berlin besides your zia?"

"It's him. I know it's him."

"Doretta. I'm confused. Who?"

"Baldo Volpe," she answered, empty of emotion, staring at the dark fireplace as though in a trance.

"You mean the son of your mother's seamstress?" Doretta nodded. "How do you know?"

"I suspected it was from him, but until tonight I really didn't know for sure. When Mamma said signora Volpe's son had gone to Germany to study..."

"But I still don't understand. Why would he write such a letter to you? How do you even know him?"

"Remember when we were together in Asili and I told you about what happened to me in front of the synagogue? I never thought he... And now tonight to learn he was here...in my home. With my mother's dresses."

"He was vile, you said." Sara's mind raced as she tried to put all the pieces together. Perhaps it was simply a coincidence. Sara didn't know what frightened her more: a total stranger stalking her friend or someone she had encountered and later discovered her mother knew. Both were frightening possibilities. How could she best advise Doretta?

"Somehow he discovered where I lived. I don't know how, but he did. Sara, he did." Doretta stopped, caught her breath, and continued. "And I don't know whether he knew my address when he came here." Sara slid from the chair and sat beside Doretta, taking her hands. They were so cold. And still trembling. She put her arms around her shoulders and tried to calm her. "Oh, but what am I to do?" she cried in despair. "I can't prove the letter was from him. It's typewritten. If I accuse signora Volpe's son without proof... Well, I just can't."

"Doretta, didn't your mother say he was away until Christmas? If it was him, at least until then you're safe."

A phone rang in the hall. Gabriele called to his wife.

"Doretta, you're safe tonight," Sara whispered. "No one can harm you now."

The girls sat silently. Sara prayed for guidance on the best advice to give her dear friend. Doretta's breathing slowed, and her muscles relaxed. Just then, Daniela shrieked.

"Now do you believe the danger, Gabriele? Do you now?"

Hurried footsteps approached. The door flew open. Doretta's mother rushed in, raw panic in her voice. "He's dead. Oh, Doretta, he's dead."

"Who, Mamma? Not zio Eduardo. Who?"

"It's Fritz. Silvana called to say they found his body floating in the Wannsee. His neck was broken. Oh, Doretta…" Daniela reached for the bed to steady herself. Doretta sprang up before she swooned. She sat her on the bed and put her arms around her, comforting her as Sara had done for her.

"But I don't understand. Who would do such a thing, Mamma?"

"Fritz was one of the journalists who had been criticizing the Nazi party. According to Silvana, he was warned. Since March, other Berlin journalists have been sent to Sachsenhausen, one of the four concentration camps they've set up around Germany. They send dissidents and others the Nazis consider undesirable there. They threatened to send him to a camp. But he kept writing, mostly about the unfair treatment of Jews after the non-Aryan decree in April."

Gabriele stood at the door, listening. Finally, he entered.

"Daniela, what can I say? I am so sorry."

Daniela glared at him, her face crimson. "Say nothing, Gabriele!" Through gritted teeth, she lashed at him, "You wouldn't believe these people were dangerous. You wouldn't believe Silvana. You even ridiculed her as being hysterical. Well, now she *is* hysterical! She's hysterical because her husband has been murdered!"

"Daniela, we have no idea that this was anything other than a robbery. Maybe he resisted and—"

"Gabriele! Enough!" Daniela turned away from her husband and saw Sara as she sat quietly in the shadows, not wanting to remind them of her presence. Suddenly aware of the scene unfolding before their guest's eyes, Daniela continued, calmer. "This was no accident. It was no random crime. He was targeted. Silvana received a call this morning telling her that her husband was finished denouncing the Party. 'He has been silenced,' they said."

"Nothing more?" Gabriele ventured to ask.

"No. Later a policeman came to the house to say he had been found. He was the only policeman, she said, who had been kind to her when he went missing. Tomorrow I will take the train to Berlin."

"No, Mamma! You can't. They are doing terrible things to Jews there." Doretta's panicked expression told Sara that the thought of her mother alone in Berlin horrified Doretta.

"I must. My sister is alone now. Fritz's family will not shield her, not even her children because under the new law they are non-Aryan. Jews. *Mischlinge* they call them. She told me they blame *her* for his murder. And it was because of *his mother* they did not leave for America! Why didn't the old witch die earlier?" Hearing the hateful words from Doretta's mother shocked Sara. Surely, she didn't mean it.

"I'll go with you, Mamma. I can protect you." Michele, who had been listening unseen in the hall behind his father, walked to the bed, sat beside his mother, and took her hand. "I've been practicing maneuvers with my army. I know how to fight." Daniela smiled at her only son—a fearless boy he had become. She took the pewter soldier out of his hand, studied it, and kissed his cheek. "I know you can, Michele, but you are needed here. Your army needs its general."

"I will go with you, Daniela. Together—we'll face this together." Sara glanced at Doretta's father who earlier that evening appeared so haughty, so self-assured these fascists in Germany were harmless. Now he seemed crestfallen.

"If you must." Daniela said with resignation. She kissed her children, nodded at Sara, and walked past Gabriele toward her room, Michele following close behind. Gabriele walked in the opposite direction to his own bedroom, apart from his wife.

A heavy silence descended on the room.

"Mamma!" Down the hall, Elena had awakened. Sara knew the child would experience nights far more disturbing than this. It was only a matter of time. The Jews of Turin would be the hunted ones. Sara recalled the final words of the letter from the hateful boy—the boy who stood for the rising tide. She shivered even though the room, its windows closed, was warm. Had she sensed the future as nonna Mirella had predicted? Or did they all feel as she did even if they seemed afraid to talk about it openly? When she returned to Alba, she would seek out Madama Lia who was worldly and wise.

Still seated on the bed, utterly drained, Doretta regarded Sara knowingly as if to say, *so you see how it is*. And then it came to Sara: this was only the beginning.

106

CHAPTER 15

Alba
August 1936

"Dona eis réquiem. Amen." And with those final words of the Catholic graveside prayer under the blazing August sun, don Rocca commended Stefano Olivero's soul to God. Lia heard none of it. Stefano should be in Val Maira now with the living, escaping the summer heat of Langhe. But her friend and counselor of decades was gone.

Lia watched the pallbearers slide Stefano's casket next to his father's in the Olivero family crypt. Luca, now the young patriarch of the Olivero family, stood between the two women he most loved—his grief-stricken mother and nonna—holding them close. Stefano Olivero had been fifty-six years old and still vital when his heart stopped beating without any warning. No one expected that his walk to work that day along the via Maestra would be his last. He never made it to Piazza Savona.

Stefano's patient, sage guidance through the devastating years following Alessandro's and Giulia's deaths freed Lia from the bad decisions that might have come with grief, making it possible for her to build a business empire—quite a feat for a woman, particularly in the difficult economic times that followed the Great War. She had the courage and will to persevere and prosper, but Stefano had steadied her and paved the way to success.

And now he was gone. Stefano had groomed his son Luca for the legal profession from a young age. Four years earlier, he had finished law school in Padua and returned to Alba to join his father's practice. The time came early and unexpected for the young lawyer to step into his father's role as a trusted member of the Olivero family, a confidante in service to Lia. Could

107

he handle it? On his face was a look of passionate sorrow, and he was still very young.

Lia remembered clearly the day she returned to Stefano's office after Giulia's death. She saw in Stefano and Luca her present and future. Luca, nine years old at the time, yet already so astute, listened quietly, watching as his father attended to matters that he confided in him later were the most difficult of his career: counseling an anguished mother still suffering the raw pain of loss from her husband's death.

Lia's thoughts returned to the grieving family. Marina Olivero and her mother-in-law, Franca, stood clasping hands as mourners passed them, each offering condolences, some lingering longer than Lia believed proper. Behind their thin black veils, their faces remained stoic. Lia knew all too well the desire to keep the world at a distance, to hide the pain and share only in private with those they loved.

"Marina, Franca, I've been praying for you." Lia took Marina's gloved hands in hers. Steady they were—no surprise to Lia. "You know how deeply I valued Stefano, both as my adviser and my loyal friend. He shone a bright light for me in the darkness of my own despair." She paused, allowing the tightness in her throat to abate. "And the sacrifices you made as well, Marina. I believe my father and I took far too much of his time from you and the children."

Marina, her eyes warm and knowing, lightly squeezed Lia's hands. "Thank you for those words, Madama Lia. Stefano loved his work. He loved your family as did his father and grandfathers. You need not worry. He was a loving husband and father. He made the most of every moment with us."

Lia returned her smile, relieved to hear that Marina Olivero held no ill will toward her for the countless holidays and celebrations her needs often disturbed. She kissed the two women then took her leave.

"Madama Lia, one moment. Scusami, Mamma." Luca stepped away from his mother. "May I walk with you a moment?"

"Certainly, Luca." So much like his father in looks and manner. Now she would have to comfort him. In truth, they would need to comfort each other. "What is it?"

"I know I have only four years of experience and there is so much I have left to learn, but I promise I will not disappoint you." Although Luca spoke in his usual confident manner, his rushed words signaled to Lia that he was nervous.

"Of course, Luca. I know you are quite capable. As soon as you feel your mother can spare you, I will be ready to meet with you."

"I'm ready now, Madama Lia. Today even." The nervous undertones disappeared. Now he was eager. Lia stopped and turned to Luca. The dark circles under his eyes emphasized his need for sleep, not work, but the sorrow on his face had passed. How like a lawyer to exert that control.

"Absolutely not, Luca. You are the patriarch of your family. You must attend to the needs of your mother and nonna. At least today." Lia could see that, in Luca, Stefano Olivero was still with her. "Tomorrow is Saturday. Spend the Ferragosto holiday with your family as was planned." She swallowed, battling the tightness in her throat once more at the thought of what should have been. "Then we can start the Monday after. Now, back to your mother." Lia turned and continued toward her family's crypt. She needed a moment with them, but even so, he followed her. Footsteps crunched on the gravel path.

Lia had only walked a few steps before he plaintively called out to her. "But Madama Lia"—he drew closer and lowered his voice—"the Jews. What about the Jews?"

She stopped and turned to him. "What do you mean, Luca?" Lia was taken aback by his timing, but his question did not surprise her. Stefano had agreed not to involve Luca, not yet at least, but it was like him to prepare for any eventuality. *"I am not indispensable,"* he recently said to her. Did he have a premonition? The doctor said his heart stopped beating, and most likely, there was no warning. Obviously, Luca knew a good deal.

"Madama Lia, I know about the Jews. They need our help."

Lia looked about and lowered her voice, cautious of ever-present spies. "Luca, come to the office tomorrow morning. I am going up to Asili tomorrow afternoon and won't be back in Alba for two weeks, or at least until the end of the holiday. Now, tend to your mother." She would need to educate Luca in short order, but he was well on his way to discovering the full extent of her clandestine activities. "And say nothing of this to her."

At her family's crypt, Lia sought shade on a nearby bench under a plane tree. It was here she often found peace. She shed her black straw hat and veil and pulled off her gloves. The torrid heat made everything harder to endure. *Oh, Alessandro. First Papà, then you, now Stefano.* She would meet the dark future on the horizon, but she longed for her husband and Stefano, her connection to her father—for the counsel of all three men.

In the three years since his appointment as chancellor, Hitler had become a despotic dictator, the Führer. She and her confidants feared Hitler intended to purify all Europe of Jews, not only Germany. It was obvious to her that the persecution of German Jews was only beginning. How far beyond Germany's borders would he dare go before someone stopped him?

News reports from the Olympic Games spoke nothing about the violent repression, only the great victories of the Aryan athletes of the super race. The event proved little more than an extravagant propaganda ploy to curry favor with the international community. As the eyes of the world turned to Berlin, anti-Semitic signs disappeared, and the pressure on Jews eased. Lia believed it was fleeting. When the flame in the Olympic cauldron was extinguished, Hitler and Goebbels would again stoke the fire of hate, and Jews would once again be in their crosshairs.

Frieda. Lia had yet to inform her of Stefano's unexpected passing. There had been no time. She would have to send Luca to Switzerland to finish his father's task once he was fully briefed.

Frieda Stern had swept Lia into the Jewish relief efforts days after the Nazis remilitarized the Rhineland the previous year. Now, more than the usual amount of time had passed since she had spoken with her Swiss friend. Twice Lia had called, and twice she was told that Frieda was out of the country. These days, rarely did a week pass that they were not in contact. The two women had become close at boarding school in Lausanne and had kept in touch since then. In retrospect, Lia believed it was fated that they should have met.

Before Frieda entered her life, the Giordanos were the only Jews Lia knew. Each summer, the family escaped the heat in Turin for the cooler climes of Alta Langa as guests of Lia's parents. During their annual sojourns in Bossolaschetto, Lia discovered the only thing that set them apart was that they did not join them for Mass on Sunday. Gabriele, who was her age, explained that their views about Jesus were not the same as hers. She was only a child and did not comprehend at the time what that meant. Their ancestors had settled in Piemonte four hundred years earlier, so the Giordanos were Piemontese first and foremost. That's what mattered above all, wasn't it? The Swiss boarding school she attended was strict though meant only to prepare girls for society with etiquette, history, and language education. However, there was a dark side some German students hid from the teachers but exposed to Frieda on a regular basis. They hurled scornful, hateful words at her that bound the girls together. Lia had defended her friend even though Frieda was more than capable of fending for herself, and Lia found that she became more alert than most to any sort of injustice.

Both Frieda and Daniela Giordano, whose sister Silvana had not yet left Berlin, had told her that conditions were worsening for Jews in Germany. The brutal riot in Berlin's posh Kurfürstendamm district in July of last year was the first time anti-Semitic violence had touched Frieda. That night, two hundred young thugs dressed in civilian clothes, but suspected of being Nazi Storm Troopers, indiscriminately beat men and women they believed were Jewish. Even foreigners suffered their wrath. A longtime client of Freida's family was savagely beaten as he locked up his watch shop. The blows to his head had left him comatose, and doctors gave his wife little hope that he would ever wake.

With a growing number of countries limiting Jewish immigration—even America—many German Jews sought refuge in Italy. Initially, Lia believed, as did many, that with time the Americans and British would end Hitler's continued violations of the Versailles Treaty. Wasn't the Rhineland occupation earlier that year a warning to all? The Allies had done nothing other than raise objections. The Nazis only grew stronger. They were emboldened while the danger to German Jews and those who were swept into the Reich from other countries increased. If Hitler failed to cleanse the country of Jews by disenfranchising them, some feared he might use violent tactics to achieve his sick vision of a *judenrein* Germany. Despite the stifling heat, she shivered.

Gianni cleared his throat. "*Mi scusi*, Madama Lia. It's lunchtime. And it's too hot out here. Wouldn't you like me to drive you home?"

Lunch was far from Lia's mind. Giuseppina had been hounding her to eat since Luca's phone call on Monday with the shocking news of Stefano. For decades, her loyal housekeeper had attempted to cure all her ills—emotional or physical—with food.

"No Gianni. I'm not hungry. You return to the mulino. I will walk."

"But Madama, the heat. Let me drive you—"

"No, Gianni!" Softening her tone, she said, "Thank you, but I prefer to walk. Now go along."

Gianni, of course, was right. It was noon, and her damp black linen suit clung like sackcloth to her small frame. She opened her parasol and handed her hat, veil, and gloves to Gianni who continued his pleas for her not to walk. Lia would have none of it. Time alone to contemplate how best to integrate Luca into her covert pursuits was what she craved. The future beckoned. The fifteen-minute walk in the fresh air would clear her head. Frieda Stern's most recent call had alarmed her. Luca would have to learn quickly.

ANOTHER SLEEPLESS NIGHT FOLLOWED THE FUNERAL. RELENTLESS HEAT AND her concerns for Luca kept Lia turning in bed. After another battle with

Giuseppina, she was off to the mulino on her own. She loved driving her Alfa Romeo cabriolet in the summer, not caring whether people said it was improper for a woman to drive a bright red convertible with her hair blowing in the wind. This afternoon she would drive it along the winding roads to Barbaresco. Had she developed a passion for cars to be closer to Alessandro's memory? Ah, he would have enjoyed this car.

Luca was waiting outside the gate of the mulino office when she arrived. He must have walked over from his own office in Piazza Savona to see if she was in yet. Much of Albese life occurred in the piazza, but when Lia had driven past today, it had been eerily empty. Townspeople had already fled the heat to the sea or mountains for the Ferragosto holiday that would stretch for the next two weeks.

"Bondì, Madama Lia."

"Buongiorno, Luca. How is your mother this morning?"

"She took breakfast in her room, so I haven't seen her today. She and nonna will leave for Val Maira this morning."

"The mountain air will no doubt do her good. Aren't you going too?"

"I haven't decided yet."

"Luca, you really..." She didn't continue, knowing he shared his father's stubbornness and dedication to work. Best to get to work.

The cortile, normally alive with activity as delivery trucks and horse-drawn wagons came and went, was empty today. The mill was silent. Each morning as Madama Lia approached her office, she would be greeted by a line of ordinary people waiting to sit in one of the chairs facing her carved mahogany desk and seek her counsel. Daily, she fielded requests for money, food, lodging, and the like. Many came for her wisdom to settle disputes. No problem was too small or too large for her to counsel. If money was needed, with a cluster of keys only she possessed, she would unlock a drawer in her desk, remove the cashbox, and take what was needed. The routine was repeated numerous times a day. Only a handshake and meeting of the parties' eyes executed the contract to repay her when possible. In fifteen years, no one had ever failed to honor their debt to her. Stefano preferred she not lend money in this fashion, but she adopted the practice when she bought the mulino to honor her father and grandfather, who had done the same in their time at the family store she had long since sold. Because of the late-summer holiday, the mulino was closed, and no one waited for her.

Lia motioned to Luca to sit down. This would be their first meeting with an empty chair beside him. She gave him a brave smile, took her notebook and pen, and came from around the desk to sit where Stefano would have been. Stefano's absence weighed heavy on them.

"I'll get to the point, Luca. As you know, I am involved in funding relief efforts for German, Czech, and Polish Jews. You are now the only other person in Alba with this knowledge. For their sake, I've not even shared this with Gianni and Giuseppina. I intend to keep it that way for as long as possible."

She paused to emphasize the gravity of her statement. As an attorney, he was duty bound to guard client confidentiality, but never had he been confronted with information that might have dire consequences. "Do you understand, Luca?"

"Yes, Madama."

"Currently, relief operations are conducted in the open in Italy. The Fascists are aware of it. They're more than happy to allow rich Jews *and* their foreign currency into the country. However..." Was all the secrecy necessary? Or was she being an alarmist? Stefano had agreed that the future was fraught with danger since both dictators were unpredictable megalomaniacs vying for power. The anti-Semitic advisors in Mussolini's inner circle might ultimately convince him the best way to ally himself with Hitler was to share his vision of a Europe cleansed of Jews.

"Undoubtedly, our relief efforts would become illegal, and immigration of foreign Jews would be banned. I have every intention to go underground with my work if that should happen. The fewer people who know of this, the better our chance to continue unnoticed." The Fascists may rule Italy, but Lia Bottero would not allow them to interfere with her work, no matter the danger.

"Madama Lia, may I ask how you became involved in this? I know your banker in Turin is Jewish. Do they have relatives in Germany?"

"Yes, they do. The younger sister of signora Giordano lives in Berlin. But she is not the reason I became involved, although she is now someone whom we are trying to help leave Germany. It was Freida Stern, my Jewish boarding school friend from Switzerland who called. She needed my help to settle family members from Strasbourg in Italy. Switzerland has strict quotas, but Italy has an open door, for now. It was impossible to say no to her, particularly when so many lives are in danger."

"Strasbourg? Has Hitler threatened to invade Alsace-Lorraine as he did the Rhineland?"

"Not publicly, but there's no reason to doubt he intends to reclaim what Germany lost in the Great War."

Luca would need more background, especially since he would soon meet Frieda in La Chaux-de-Fonds. "Let me explain the connection," she went on. "Madame Stern's family left Alsace in 1871, following the Franco-Prussian War. After the German annexation, her great-grandfather and fifty thousand other French citizens—Catholics, Protestants, and Jews—opted to leave the region rather than renounce their French citizenship. Those who refused were expelled. Her bisnonno, a wealthy watchmaker, was among the lucky few allowed to settle in Switzerland. With other Alsatian and East European Jews, he contributed to creating one of the greatest watchmaking regions in the world."

Seeing Luca where once his father sat, and so much like Stefano, her mind wandered a moment. Tall and handsome, yet still unattached. She hoped he would soon find someone like his mother who understood his passion for the law.

As though to banish the distraction, she blinked hard and continued the Stern family saga. "After the Great War, distant relatives of Madame Stern's bisnonno who had settled in France across the border from Basel returned home to Strasbourg. Life was good for a time. With the sudden German aggression to their north, they worried Alsace would be next. Only this time, there would be no options for them. German Jews were already disenfranchised in their own country, so they feared they would be serfs of the Reich without any rights of citizenship. They wanted out, but no one, except Italy, would accept them. That's when Madame Stern called me."

"What were you able to do?"

"Your father arranged for the two families, sixteen people in all, to move to Milan. They're not rich, but they were able to pay their way. What they needed was logistical help. Jobs. Lodgings. As you know, your father is"—her pause was imperceptible, but her throat tightened once more—"*was* brilliant when it came to logistics. Since they were highly skilled in optics and watchmaking, finding jobs for them was easy. But that was only the beginning."

"What's now the urgent problem with Madame Stern?"

"Last year, a longtime client of her family's watchmaking business was beaten during a rampage of suspected young Nazi Storm Troopers in Berlin. He died two weeks ago. Seventy-five years old." Lia studied the look of horror on Luca's face. This, she believed, was only the beginning of what he would witness. "His widow has no family left in Berlin. She wants to leave Germany. The challenge for us is to help her leave with her estate intact."

"How are we to help?"

We—it pleased Lia that he already thought of himself as part of their team. She knew that the team in Alba would have to grow eventually, at a minimum adding Gianni and Giuseppina who were tightly woven into her life. Had he heard her not just as a lawyer but also as a man who shared her convictions? The emotion in his voice and his expression as he leaned forward on the edge of the chair, his eyes fixed on her, told her what she needed to know. Stefano would be proud.

"There are rumors the Nazis are planning to heavily tax German Jews' assets. And they are making it difficult for emigrating Jews to take their fortunes with them. Your father was working with Madame Stern to help the widow. I have stayed out of the particulars. You must go to Switzerland after the holiday. Madame Stern is at her family's villa in Crans-sur-Sierre in Valais now. The Grand Saint Bernard pass is clear this time of year, so you should have no problem driving. I would drive you, but I have much to attend to here."

Luca handed Lia a folder marked "Watchmaker," no doubt his father's code for the mysterious Swiss woman. "Is this the entire file?"

"There is another folder." She went to unlock the large drawer in her desk that also held the cashbox. "These are the rest of the documents. You have Madame Stern's number in there. She will be expecting your call next week but not before."

Luca's furrowed brow betrayed his emotions under his calm demeanor. This was obviously not the sort of work he had expected as his first task as head of the firm.

"Now, when you have finished reading the information in here, lock it in the safe behind the *stufa*. Then go to the mountains to be with your mother and nonna. This may be the last long break you'll have for some time. And your family needs you."

He started to speak, but Lia stopped him. "That will be all, Luca. Thank you."

Luca tucked the folders under his arm and, with his hat in hand, said his good-byes. Madama Lia was right. Two weeks in the alpine terrain would clear his head of grief and ready him for the tasks ahead.

Lia was pleased with the meeting. At least now, for the duration of the Ferragosto holiday weeks, she, too, would have time to grieve for Stefano. She was grateful that he had sufficiently prepared Luca to take over, even though he couldn't have known that it would be this soon.

LIA LOVED THE VIEW OF THE ALPS FROM THE LARGE WINDOW BEHIND HER desk. Only the train station roof impaired the vista. As she reached to close the window, a lone couple on the train platform a short distance away caught her attention—a tall, red-haired young man and a woman partially hidden by a column. They were facing each other. She moved closer to him, a tall, slender girl in a black coat. He stepped back. She reached to touch his face. He brushed her hand away.

"But I love you, Francesco! Haven't I shown you that?" she shouted. Francesco? Of course. The red hair. On any other morning, she would not have been able to hear them, but with the streets empty, the sound traveled from the station unimpeded.

Lia watched as the woman stepped closer to the man that she believed was Francesco Bosco. Not many other men in Langhe had such red hair, much less one named Francesco. Cinzia Strega! As Francesco turned away, she lunged at him, clasped her arms around his neck, and kissed him. Unlike before, he didn't resist. He held her forearms as though to pull them away but slid his hands down her arms, grazed her full breasts pressed against him, and held her waist with one hand on the small of her back. He pulled her closer as his other hand moved slowly over her hips until he caressed her buttocks. Lia shut her eyes. But curiosity got the better of her. In a flash, more forceful than before, he grabbed her wrists and pushed her away.

"No, Cinzia! I won't. I can't do that to…" He pushed her away. Before he moved, she lunged at him again, her shouting angry not lustful. She clawed at his face and he shielded himself from further damage. Had she drawn blood?

"To *her*? You mean to her, that *stronza arrogante*, don't you? That bitch! You used me while you waited for her to finally notice you as someone other than her father's Sicilian farm boy!" Her shrill voice rose. "I thought you loved *me*."

"I never said that! Cinzia, how many times have I told you we're not suited for each other?"

"I'm a woman, Francesco. I can give you so much more than that child you're pining for."

Though his face was obscured, Lia observed resignation in Francesco's posture. He removed his neckerchief and, with his left hand, held it to his cheek. Was he bleeding? He walked away to the far end of the platform.

"You'll be sorry, Francesco. I can—and I will—make your life hell," she shouted. "And that bitch's too."

Francesco stopped, spun around, and strode back to her. The train from Barbaresco was pulling into the station, preventing Lia from hearing the words he spoke although, even from a distance, she could see the rage in his crimson face. Cinzia fled the station. With his head hung, still dabbing his cheek with his kerchief, Francesco boarded the train for its eastward return to Barbaresco.

Cinzia Strega was a dangerous woman, deeply involved in Fascist activities in Langhe. The company she kept was not the sort one should cross. Francesco should not have become involved with her, and now he might have to pay the price for that poor judgment. But Sara? She was an innocent. And Lia would do whatever was needed to help keep her safe, always.

The wind had picked up, and clouds appeared in the sky. She closed the window. It was time to head to Asili, her oasis. The vineyards were now lush and the vines heavy with grapes. Inspecting them from the saddle would be a comfort. Black clouds on the northwest horizon hurried her along. Not an omen she wanted to see after such a day.

CHAPTER 16

Barbaresco
Ferragosto—August 1936

From Alba, Lia raced up the winding, hilly road to Barbaresco. The storm she had seen from her office brewing on the horizon blew in faster than she anticipated. Being caught in an August thunderstorm, particularly with the top down on her sports car, was unthinkable.

As soon as she pulled into the driveway at Cascina Asili, the heavens exploded. The wind rushed through the vines, and sheets of rain fell. Darkness descended on the landscape, changing mid-afternoon into night. Bolts of lightning struck nearby in the vineyards. The crash of thunder reverberated in the valley seconds after each flash of light.

Gianni waited at the open door to the newly built garage, worry deepening the wrinkles on his face. No doubt, he would scold her for taking such a risk. As he stood, holding the car door open for her, his lips moved but she could not hear him. The rain pounded on the tin roof, and thunder rumbled nearby. She cupped her hand behind her left ear. When she turned toward the cortile, a curtain of wind-whipped rain hid the vineyards. Or was it…?

"Hail!" Gianni shouted.

Large hailstones danced on the pavement outside and pounded the roof. The tender vines, heavy with maturing clusters of grapes, would be helpless against this onslaught.

Together they watched nature ravage the Nebbiolo vineyard next to the farm. Within minutes, the cortile turned white as shards of ice covered the ground.

"Oh no, Gianni, look at the size of them!" Lia shouted. "Like eggs."

Hail this size was merciless and would strip plants to their rootstocks, in most cases leaving the vineyard unproductive for several vintages. This was the fruit that two months later would have come home to the cantina, and now they stood watching it destroyed. Months of hard labor gone in a flash.

Gianni had witnessed each harvest in Asili since Lia's marriage to Alessandro over twenty years earlier. He only worked the vineyards during the harvest, but he loved the vines as though they were members of the family, the children he and Giuseppina never had. During harvest, Nico often chided him about how slowly he cut clusters from the vines, saying "Mi dispiace" to each one. There would not be a vendemmia in Asili this year. Tears welled in his eyes, and Lia saw that his lower lip quivered. They both stood shocked at the destruction before them.

In less than fifteen minutes, the hail stopped. The wind subsided and a gentle rain fell, signaling that the storm was nearly past. Over six inches of jagged hail covered the ground, transforming the verdant landscape to white. In winter, they relished the magical, snow-carpeted vineyards. The snow hydrated the vines, helping to assure their health when buds broke in March. But scenes like this in August meant economic disaster for vineyards and orchards.

Lia spotted Nico standing at the open cantina door, his eyes wide with horror. He knew how hail could decimate one vineyard while leaving an adjoining one unscathed. When he saw the size and depth of these hailstones, he feared the worst. Already rivulets channeled water into the vineyard as rain melted the ice. Lightning still flashed. Their survey of the damage would have to wait until morning after a restless night.

Nico, shoulders slumped and rubbing his neck nervously, walked through the slush and rain to join Lia and Gianni. The 1936 vintage for these vines ended abruptly. A farmer worked when his crops needed him, which meant nearly every day after the lush canopy of vines exploded in late May. For Nico, cleaning up the vineyards after a hailstorm was the most painful task of farm life. A funeral of sorts. He would mourn the loss of the grapes that had showed great promise.

"It's not safe to go into the vineyards now. I'll check the buildings. No telling the damage. The roof surely has damage from both the wind and hail."

"Tomorrow I'll ride out to see the vines for myself. Perhaps it was highly localized, Nico." Lia did not believe such a violent storm damaged only a few rows in the vineyard, nor, she was certain, did Nico, but it felt good to hold out hope. "At least, Nico, it isn't as bad as *Festa di Maggio* in 1922. Remember?"

"I certainly do. Two feet of hail we found here when we returned from the May fest in Alba." He paused. Another painful memory of a truncated vintage although several of his rows of Nebbiolo in Ronchi were spared, enough for some bottles from the exceptional vintage. The grain harvest had been poor, and they sacrificed a great deal to make it through the year. "Seeing most of the fruit destroyed weeks before the vendemmia begins is harder. Same result: no crop. All those hours tending the vines and sleepless nights worrying about hail, mildew, and pests for nothing."

"There is always next year, Nico," Lia said, trying to keep her voice light. A failed crop spelled ruin. At least, unlike in 1922, the wheat and grain harvest in July had been a success. Although grape production was lucrative for the contadini and *mezzadri*, Langhetti still measured wealth not by their vineyard production, but by the numbers of sacks of grain a family produced each year. Nico had produced over twenty-five thousand pounds this year, so the Fiore family would be able to survive.

Lia studied the vineyard and the dark clouds moving away toward the southeast, continuing to spread heartbreak. How many others stood as they were, staring at their lost harvest? Nico made a steeple with his fingers, placed his wine-stained fingers to his lips, and closed his eyes. Perhaps when he finished his prayer, it would all have been a dream. Yet when he opened his eyes, the denuded plants were still there.

"Francesco was going to the sea this weekend, but I heard him upstairs in his room. He must have returned on the afternoon train. Good thing he changed his plans."

Lia hadn't known about his planned trip to Liguria. Was that the spark that ignited the argument between Cinzia and Francesco? He had had no valise with him, which she found odd for someone going on a weekend trip, unless he had decided to change his plans before he arrived at the station. Was it meant to be a weekend away from prying eyes?

She glanced over at Gianni, standing modestly some distance away. She knew he needed to occupy himself, not stand and brood over the vineyards. *What's done is done.* There would be other vintages.

"Gianni, there's a wheel of Castelmagno in the boot. Please make sure to give it to Giuseppina." He nodded and opened the trunk. "By the way, Giovanni Oddero was sending my Barolo order straight to Asili. Has it arrived?"

"I haven't seen it, Madama, but I'll check with Giuseppina." Gianni removed her valise and the precious, heavy wheel of cheese from the trunk, and plodded through the slush to the house.

Nico shook his head and turned to her. "Madama Lia, are you here in Asili for the entire holiday?"

"For now. That's my plan, but business always seems to intrude on my holidays. Is Sara here?"

"She was earlier, but she went to Villa Cristina. Sara's been there nearly every day this week to tend to the Contessa's bronchitis. Should I have her call on you when she returns?"

"In the morning. Have her come for breakfast. It's been some time since I have seen her. She's always so busy with dottor Pera when I am here." She hoped talking about Sara and the warm reception she had received in Barbaresco when she returned as a nurse would take his mind off the vines. "Luce tells me she's doing a splendid job. She said locals call her *il piccolo angelo*. She certainly is an angel."

Nico liked the nickname villagers had given Sara. It suited her. Since she returned home last Christmas, she had worked alongside the aging dottor Pera in his office or made house calls mostly on horseback and in all sorts of weather when his own health prevented him from attending to patients. Hopefully, she had reached Villa Cristina before the heavens opened. Nico worried about her working too much. Perhaps Madama Lia would help them find a younger doctor to succeed dottor Pera. A doctor closer to Sara's age would solve many problems. He had long ago given up hope on Sara and Francesco. Many times, he spied longing looks Francesco gave her that she failed to notice. Or the times she returned to Alba and he sulked for days. Their close proximity over the last eight months since her return home had failed to ignite a spark.

"Between your support and Luce's tutoring, Sara has become a dedicated nurse. How will we ever repay you, Madama?"

Lia snapped at him. "Nico, you promised we would never speak of that. We agreed that Sara must never know about my involvement." Lia thought she heard a door close and looked about to see whether anyone had overheard them.

"Yes, of course, Madama. Mi dispiace. It's just…just that Luigia and I are so grateful to you. We've always known she was too bright to be simply a farm girl. Now she's able to give so much to our village. All thanks to you." Lia's face softened and she touched his shoulder, a gesture she rarely made.

"She loves being back here with her family. Yes, I miss her in Alba, but seeing her happy and successful gives me great joy, Nico. Hopefully she will… will return soon to Alba." Lia left it at that.

The rain stopped, and the sun broke out of the clouds to the west. Such was the nature of these summer storms. Sadly, only a few minutes of hail had wreaked havoc in the vineyards.

Francesco emerged from behind the Fiore cascina. He stopped at the edge of the vineyard, stooped, and picked up a severed grape cluster from the mud. For a few minutes, he studied the mangled fruit then let it fall to the ground. Francesco joined Lia and Nico at the entrance of the garage. His face mirrored their distress.

"Bondì, Madama Lia."

"Buonasera, Francesco." Was that blood on his hands? And the scratch across his left cheek. Cinzia had drawn blood! How close to his eye she came. The long scratch had opened, and again it bled. And now she saw another smaller, but deep scratch under his right eye unlike the other smaller contusions that appeared to be more recent, from the hail perhaps.

"Is that blood on your hands?" Nico asked as he took Francesco's right hand and studied the mixture of mud, blood, and…feathers.

"I didn't see the storm coming until it was too late." His voice cracked. "I tried to shoo the chickens to safety, but they ran in the opposite direction of the barn and the henhouse. I'm so sorry. Most are dead." He hung his head as tears pooled in his eyes. "The hail was huge, like stones."

Nico sighed. "All right. That was good of you. What's that, did the hail do that to your face?"

"The pieces were sharp," Francesco said, averting his eyes. "The poor chickens."

"Well, you should see to those cuts. Sara isn't here now, but she should be home for dinner soon. Go ask Luigia for now."

"I hate to tell her about the chickens." He nodded at Lia and turned toward the house.

"And I must finish in the cantina, Madama Lia. Ca ma scüsa."

As Lia watched Francesco remove his muddy boots at the entrance to the Fiore cascina, she wondered whether Sara's feelings for him had changed. No longer the gangly, shy boy that he had been three years earlier—illiterate in their dialect and clumsy in his manners—he had grown into a handsome, self-assured young man. Though at nearly nineteen he towered over Sara, she was growing into a winsome young woman. The age difference between them appeared to have shrunk as she matured.

Cinzia was right. He was pining for Sara. Whether she would ever return his feelings, Lia was uncertain. She believed the two were well suited and that their personalities complemented one another. But when she set out to fund Sara's education, she intended for her a settled city life away from the farm and its vulnerabilities—a life for Sara, near her in Alba, she had to admit. It was enough that she involved herself in Sara's education. Or was it? Yes, she had given Sara an opportunity at a vocation, but what then…? What about a husband, a companion with whom she would share her life and raise children? To live the life *she* lost. No—Sara was not Giulia. Hadn't she vowed not to interfere with her life beyond her education?

When Lia opened the car and reached for her purse and gloves, her knees weakened. She steadied herself and sat. The week of sorrow, new beginnings, and intrigue had left her drained before she even left Alba. And now—catastrophe. Her heart ached for Alessandro though he'd left for battle two decades earlier, never to hold and comfort her again.

And for Giulia, who now would be a grown woman. This week, for the first time since those awful years, doubt gripped her. Could she do this all alone? Should a woman have so much responsibility without the support of a husband? Even with Stefano by her side, she rarely admitted when she needed counsel. But now she did. She buried her face in her hands, leaned forward against the steering wheel, and wept as she had not allowed herself to do since the evening after she said good-bye to Giulia.

Two hours later, with the last rays of sun shining on the devastated vineyard, Sara arrived on horseback. She spied Madama Lia's car through the partially closed garage door at Cascina Asili. Not wanting Madama to see her in pants, she trotted her horse, Zeus, into the barn, jumped off, and slid the door closed. When she began working with dottor Pera, she had exchanged her formal, and expensive, riding habit for trousers for her rides across the countryside making house calls. It still shocked many Langhetti that a young girl would ride astride and that she dressed like a man, but Sara didn't care. It was quicker and easier to reach the remote farms by horseback. Besides, dressing like a rich girl would not endear her to poor farmers. She would let her work speak for itself. Wasn't tota Virginia in Serralunga, a revered woman in Barolo, known as the "woman in pants?" No one dared criticize her. Times were changing. Mussolini's incessant propaganda that Italian women were meant to be wives at home, making sons for battle, had not succeeded. The Great War had changed everything. Sara, however, did care what Madama Lia thought.

Whenever she rode with Madama Lia, she maintained the image of a perfect equestrian lady. If she had to ride out on a house call when Madama Lia was in Asili, Sara snuck out through the vineyards behind their cascina. Sooner or later, she would be discovered, but she saw no reason to disappoint the woman who had been so kind to her when she lived in Alba, showering her with gifts each Christmas and birthday.

As she walked into the dimly lit barn, Zeus's ears pricked. She barely recognized the man in the far corner next to the stalls.

"Francesco, what are you doing here now?"

"Oh, ciao, Sara. Just plucking the chickens. The hail. So many dead."

Sara cross-tied Zeus and approached him. He stepped back further from the light.

"Almost finished. There. All done." He grabbed several carcasses by the neck and hurried past her, avoiding eye contact. "Scusami, Sara. I must take these to your mamma right away. Glad you're home okay."

"Francesco, I thought you were... Are you coming to dinner?" Before she could ask him why he hadn't made the trip to Liguria to see his old friend Gep, he was gone. How odd. He had talked a great deal about how much he looked forward to seeing the old cartun driver for the first time since their journey together. Well, she thought, Papà must be pleased to have him here to help after the storm.

Sara finished unsaddling and grooming Zeus, her Hanoverian gelding Madama Lia had presented to her the Christmas after she finished her studies. She spoke to him about Francesco as she often did, leaning close to his neck. Zeus was a trusted friend with whom she spent hours alone each day, and he did seem to listen. She only hoped no one ever overheard her. They would think her *pazza*.

Although it was nearly dark, she could see the chaotic barnyard scene from the rear door of the building. Feathers mixed with mud everywhere. Hail had stripped vegetation from the peach trees her nonno Ernesto had planted between the rows of vines thirty years ago. Nonna Mirella said the money from the peaches helped feed them after phylloxera killed their vines. *Pesche della vigna*, she said, were the most delicious of all. Fortunately, her sisters had picked most of the fruit last week. The shredded plants in her mamma's vegetable garden were unrecognizable. Mamma would have to buy vegetables to put up for winter. Without the egg money, she would serve the family spartan dishes until spring.

After she washed, Sara unbraided her hair and brushed it out, letting the soft waves drape over her shoulders. Normally, she wore a simple blouse over her khaki pants in the evening, but tonight she changed into a baby blue dress much more to her mamma's liking. But her real motivation was the hope that Francesco would join them for dinner.

When Sara entered the dining room, she noticed that Maria had only set out six places, leaving Francesco's usual place empty. Luigia kissed her, said nothing, and returned to her pots. The shock of her losses in the barnyard had set in, and Sara sensed she struggled to hold back tears. Sara knew her mamma rarely fired up the putagè on hot August evenings, but cooking always soothed her. They would all suffer the heat for her sake. Sara would brew a special *tisane* for her after dinner that would help her through the night. Things would be difficult as they all adjusted to the losses. But this wasn't the first time, Sara knew, that they had faced such challenges. Nor would it be the last.

"Sara, Milo's hurt," Giovanna said as she took her hand and led her to Nico's beloved truffle dog curled up on Luigia's discarded blankets in the corner of the *tinello*. Blood stained the hairs of his brown and white coat. He seemed subdued but awake.

"What happened, Gio?"

"He was outside with Francesco when the storm hit. I called and called, but he wouldn't come in."

Sara wasn't surprised. Although he was Nico's constant companion, Milo had bonded with Francesco not long after he arrived. "Don't you think Milo was trying to herd the chickens, Sara? I do." Giovanna, tears welling in her eyes, nodded at Sara.

"No doubt, Gio. He's a smart dog, and I'm not surprised he wanted to help Francesco." Francesco—where was he? They should all be together. She had been relieved to see him in the barn and had looked forward to his company at dinner.

Giovanna cuddled up on Sara's lap, and together they sat on the floor next to the dog, stroking his head and speaking to him. Giovanna loved all the animals on the farm, even those in the barnyard that eventually ended up on their table. Milo was her favorite. Sara examined his wounds. A glob of ointment covered a deep gash above one eye.

"I cleaned him up with alcohol, Sara, just like you taught me to do. He was such a good boy. Never cried. And look—I took the healing medicine you gave me and put some on his big cut." Sara beamed. Giovanna always looked over Sara's shoulder when she tended to scrapes and cuts.

After Nico said grace, no one spoke as they waited to hear what he would say about the grapes.

"Where were you when the storm hit, Sara?" he asked.

"Villa Cristina, saying good-bye to the housekeeper. A huge bolt of lightning struck a tree next to the Grasso's cascina below in Vallegrande. Another struck near the villa. Zeus was all I thought of at first, but the farm hand had already led him to the barn. Zeus is so brave. He didn't even try to run."

Luiga blanched. "Sara, is it really necessary to ride all the time, especially when the weather is so uncertain? Why not use the Topolino?"

"Yes, Mamma, I know. I did see the dark clouds toward Turin as I rode from Treiso, but the Contessa has been so sick. I couldn't pass the villa without stopping. She's much better today, so she insisted I have some Moscato and torta di nocciole with her."

"What did you see on the way back?" Nico asked.

"Oh, Papà, so sad. There were mudslides everywhere. Had I not been on Zeus, I don't think I could have made it home, at least not through Tre Stelle."

"Was there damage in the vineyards of Martinenga? What about the Contessa's vineyards on Monte Silva? Could you see?"

"The Dolcetto vines below the villa were damaged but not nearly as bad as here in Asili. I don't believe there was as much hail there. Mostly wind and lightning. As I rode down from Tre Stelle, I saw that the west side of Martinenga closest to Asili was white. Not a leaf on the vines, but the east side looked untouched. Papà, it was strange. I'm sure they must have had some damage, but not like what I saw between Martinenga and home."

"Tomorrow we'll know more." From what he had seen, Nico believed his parcels of Nebbiolo vines in Asili had been stripped bare, but he held out hope that his few rows of Barbera on the other side of Barbaresco in Ronchi were spared. In the last few years, the demand for Barbera had grown, and the wine had become lucrative. Without the Barbera, he would likely have no wine from the vintage.

There was a knock on the door, and Francesco asked to join them. Giovanna jumped up and set his place, now permanently assigned next to her. She placed the flask of Barbera next to his plate while Luigia set a platter of vitello tonnato on the table. The cold veal dish had become one of his favorites. Without looking at the family, Francesco went straight to Milo to check on the injured dog.

"Bravo, *cane*, Milo, bravo. So brave, so good." He placed his face next to the whimpering dog and continued to whisper to him until Milo rolled on his back for a belly rub.

It wasn't until Francesco took his seat at the far end of the table that Sara saw his injured face and bandaged right hand. Her parents' eyes were on her.

"Francesco! What happened?" She jumped up and rushed to him. With his wine glass in his left hand, he kept his eyes on his plate, trying to avoid looking at her.

To his surprise, she first asked about his hand. "What happened?"

"The hail was jagged and cut like knives."

Still not looking at his face, she took his right hand and unwrapped the gauze bandage. She had tended to him before, but for some reason, this evening her nearness and gentle touch sent heat pulsing through his body. He knew, if she looked at him now, she would not only see the scratches but also his flushed face. The heat was unbearable.

"Did Mamma dress these cuts?"

"Your mamma—and Giovanna, of course—did an excellent job tending to me. Maybe one day Giovanna will be a nurse like you." He turned toward Giovanna, who beamed. He meant it but also wanted to deflect attention from his face.

"Very good, Gio. Very good." She re-wrapped his hand and placed it on the table, holding it a bit longer before she pulled her hand away. Francesco knew he was the center of attention and wished that he had gone to the tavern instead. Against his better judgment, he had decided to join the family. He hoped to see Sara. He *needed* to see Sara. After the scene with Cinzia at the station earlier that day, he longed to be near her, if only in the same room. And now, here she was, touching his hand, standing close to him.

"Francesco? May I see those cuts on your face?"

He gulped his wine to settle his nerves and buy some time. Unlike the others, she would know that not all the wounds were of the same origin.

"It's nothing, Sara. As I said, Milo and I were out in the storm trying to corral the chickens under cover. I guess we both got pelted badly."

Not giving in to his protestations, Sara leaned closer to him. Her clean scent and her small breasts so close to him sent his pulse racing. She placed two fingers of her right hand firmly on the far side of his chin, but then she drew back.

A tingling sensation shot from her fingers up her arm. Sara touched him again and turned his face toward her, holding him firmly in place. He didn't resist, obediently turning in his chair to face her. With her hand cupped under his chin, she raised his head slightly until their eyes met. She saw only his eyes, not his wounds. Why had she not fallen for his eyes, the color of the sea, and that dark red hair when they first met in front of the cappella so long ago? And his smile, so warm, so genuine. Many times, Sara had dressed wounds on his hands after minor accidents in the cantina or vineyards, but this was the first time she had touched his face, her own so close to his, her eyes penetrating his.

Everyone was quiet. No one touched their food. Her heartbeat quickened, and her eardrums pulsated with each beat. She hoped no one, particularly Francesco, noticed her blooming flush. The night air through the open door to the barnyard had cooled the room, but to her, the heat had become unbearable. Francesco jerked away.

"Please, you're badly cut. Giovanna, get my bag from my room."

"No, Sara, really I'm fine." He waved her off and turned back toward the table away from her. "Your mamma—"

"Gio," Sara barked, "do as I said. Now!"

When Giovanna returned with her medical bag, Sara directed Francesco to Nico's chair in the tinello and pulled up a stool next to him while the family resumed their dinner. He looked down on her, studying her small frame. They were not only alone in the room but in the universe. Or so he wished. No one else mattered, only Sara. She was petite, not much taller than Giovanna, but she had an alluring figure all the same. He longed to trace her heart-shaped face with his fingers, touching her as she now touched him. To caress her and kiss her full lips. Was she aware of his intent contemplation of her body? She had missed the top button of her dress, exposing the edges of her ivory lace camisole. Francesco tried not to look, but it was impossible not to imagine what lay underneath. If only time stood still, even for a moment. He desperately wanted to hold her breasts close to his body as he had Cinzia that morning.

Cinzia! He broke into a cold sweat. Why had he been so stupid? Nico was right. The girl was vicious, as dangerous as the scorpions that crawled in the rocky soil of Contessa Entellina. If there ever was any hope for him, if there ever had been any at all, Sara must never know. He believed that, if Sara discovered he had been with Cinzia as he so longed one day to be with her, this tender moment with her would be his last. He tried to look away, but she held his chin tight.

Sara touched his cheek, trying to focus not on his eyes but on his nasty cuts. "This one is still bleeding, Francesco."

Taking an alcohol-soaked wad of cotton, Sara dabbed at the long cut. He winced and tried to pull away.

"Don't be silly, Francesco. Sit still. I know it stings, but this is such a nasty cut." Sara held his chin in place as she attended to the wound. All of a sudden, she stopped and studied his face as though seeing it for the first time that evening. The cut under his right eye and the long one across his left cheek looked different, and even older, than the others that pocked his face. Something wasn't right. These two wounds were scratches, not the sort that jagged ice pellets caused but as though from nails—a woman's fingernails! She let go and sprang up.

"Sara, really I'm all right."

She was spent. Whatever tender feelings had pulsed through her as she closely examined his wounds had vanished. The day had been exhausting. And now this. She tossed everything back in her bag.

"Here, Francesco, make sure you put this ointment on your scratches before you go to bed. It will help prevent an infection." She smacked the small jar of ointment on the small table next to him. Moments ago, she would have handed it to him, perhaps touching his hand again. No more.

Her voice turned frosty, no different from when she spoke her first words to him. What had changed? Scratches. Had she seen what the others had not? He wanted to excuse himself—go back to his room—but to hurt Luigia's feelings was unthinkable. It would be hard to swallow, but he had no choice but to rejoin the family and finish his dinner.

Sara went to her mamma, then to her papà, kissed each, and wished them buonanotte before storming up the stairs. Heavy footsteps overhead. The door slammed.

Nico broke the silence. "Francesco, tomorrow at first light, I want to drive to Ronchi to check the Barbera vines. Then we'll start in Asili."

Francesco nodded mechanically, lost in thoughts about allowing himself to be swept up in a relationship with a woman who hated Sara, who threatened her. Sara, the angel he loved from the moment he set eyes on her, had now become the target of a vengeful scorned woman. But surely, she would not harm Sara because of him. He would never forgive himself if she did. Sara wanted nothing more to do with him. Perhaps it would be best if he left—to return to Sicily or join his cousin in America.

Francesco finished his meal without speaking and even forgot to thank Luigia. Later, Maria and Lucrezia went to bed, but Giovanna settled down in the corner with Milo. She stroked the dog's ears and regarded Francesco. What did she suspect? Luigia busied herself preparing vegetables to roast with the chickens the following day. Where was Nico? He had slipped away. Francesco stood to do the same.

Luigia continued cutting onions for a moment but then turned to him, concern in her eyes. She set her knife down and embraced Francesco as his mamma had four years ago when he said good-bye, perhaps forever. He missed her so.

She said nothing as she held him like a child of her own. When Luigia released him, she searched his eyes and brushed away a lock of hair from his face. Though of a different color from Sara's, Francesco saw the same compassion and warmth in her eyes. It was as though he was back in Contessa Entellina in the care of the only woman, before Sara, that he loved.

"*Caro* Francesco, you must know how loved you are in this family. All of us love you. God saw fit to take the sons of my body to Heaven far too soon. But then He blessed us with you. For you to have come so far, to have overcome so many obstacles, it was no doubt God's will for you to be here with us." She took his uninjured hand in hers and squeezed it. "Be strong. She is not easy. You know that. But I believe it is also why you love her so. Be patient. If it is God's will, one day you will be together, but for now, let her go, Francesco."

Caro. No one had called him that since he left Contessa Entellina. These were all words of wisdom his mother would have said to him. Did Luigia believe he had any future with Sara? He had heard Luigia once say to Nico that, though she loved having Sara near to her in Asili, she believed because of Sara's education, she would flourish in the city, even Turin where Gabriele Giordano could help her get a job in the hospital. How he wished to prove his worth as a husband for Sara and a great father to Nico and Luigia's grandchildren, but why would Sara throw away her education to be a farmer's wife?

"All in good time, Francesco."

Someone knew how he felt. It was impossible to share with Luigia his concern about Cinzia Strega, but at least he knew he had an ally who also loved Sara.

"Now, run along, Francesco. Nico will want you up early."

Francesco rushed out to hide the tears he fought back.

"Mamma?"

Luigia glanced toward Milo. She had not noticed that her child had been sitting there, no doubt taking in everything. "Yes, Gio?"

"I never told you before, but I prayed every night since zia Luce taught me to say my prayers that God would give me a brother. Do you think Francesco was the answer to my prayers?"

"Yes, Gio. I think he was."

"So, do you believe if I pray hard enough that God will make Sara love Francesco?"

"Prayers are always helpful, cara, but only Sara can make Sara love Francesco. Perhaps you can ask God to open Sara's heart to him."

Giovanna pondered her mamma's wisdom for a moment.

"Where is Papà?"

"He went outside. Would you take him this? Sara made a good-night tisane for me and there is a cup for him as well."

When Giovanna opened the front door, she saw Nico at the edge of the vineyard, sitting on the bench Gianni had made for Madama Lia to watch the sunset. She went to him and sat, putting her arm around his waist, resting her head against him. Shredded grape clusters lay among the twisted vines at their feet.

"Here, Papà. Mamma said for you to drink this. To sleep better."

"Grazie, Gio. *Molto gentile da parte tua.*" He sipped the warm aromatic drink. "So kind of you. So kind, Gio."

"Papà?"

"Yes, Gio?"

"I love you. I'm sorry you lost all your grapes today. But God will give you more. He gave you Francesco, so He loves you, I'm sure."

In the moonlight of the now clear skies, Nico saw the love that filled her eyes. So much like Sara, my first to live. Gio, my youngest. Perhaps God did love him after all. It had not felt that way earlier when it seemed as though Hell's fury was upon them, but he knew in his heart he was loved. By God and by his family. In the end, wasn't that all that mattered?

CHAPTER 17

Turin
April 1937

oretta woke earlier than usual for a Saturday morning. She had a busy day ahead—one she prayed would be the beginning of the end of her zia Silvana's nightmare in Nazi Germany. A murdered husband, in-laws who shunned her, and two small children to care for were nearly unbearable challenges. But for Silvana—and the children because her blood mingled with Fritz's in their veins—there was the added curse of being Jewish in Germany, a hostile country where danger grew daily. With each new edict that further disenfranchised Jewish Germans, their situation became more alarming. The lives of Silvana and tens of thousands of others hung in the balance.

Daniela and Doretta had pleaded with Silvana to leave for America in 1932. Fritz could follow, they suggested. Or why not stay with them in Turin? Even Fritz urged her to leave. But Silvana was stubborn and had insisted that her place was with him. Besides, Silvana reasoned, it would take years for Hitler to carry out the anti-Semitic threats against Jews he had made in *Mein Kampf.* And surely, the German populace would not stand for fellow citizens to be targeted so brutally. Reality hit them in early 1933 when Paul von Hindenburg appointed Hitler chancellor. After the Reichstag fire, it took weeks—not years—for Hitler and his cronies to show the world their wickedness. Why, then, were the Allies not acting to stop him?

If only they hadn't stayed for the sake of Fritz's terminally ill mother. Once he was gone, his family turned their backs on Silvana. Four years had passed since his murder, yet they still blamed her for his death. They spurned their own grandchildren. After Fritz's murder, the authorities confiscated her passport on a trumped-up charge that she was an accomplice. No doubt, his family claimed, without her urging, he would have stopped his illegal criticism of the party. Now—unable to leave the country, her meager assets heavily taxed, and forbidden as a Jew to work for German employers—the little money she had was gone. Luca Olivero was their last hope. And Doretta was the link.

With the spring sunlight flooding her bedroom, Doretta had had enough of drab winter wear. She chose a mandarin-orange linen dress decorated with white embroidered flowers. Her mamma had given it to her for her birthday in February. She loved bright colors, and the dress fit perfectly, showing off her figure. She had not asked her mother whether signora Volpe had made it. She did not like to think of her because of her son, that awful Baldo Volpe. Her mamma had mentioned once that signora Volpe lived alone now that her husband had died, and her son was in Germany. Zia Silvana had related horrible stories about the Brownshirts there. Yes, she was sure that Baldo Volpe would fit right in. She hoped he would never return.

Elena entered Doretta's bedroom without knocking. She had begged her mother for a lock on the door, but she had refused. Elena climbed up on Doretta's unmade bed, sat cross-legged, and then launched into her usual interrogation when she saw her sister dressing up to go out.

"Who's the boy, Doretta?" she asked with more than a hint of mockery in her voice.

"There's no boy, Elena. I have to meet someone from Alba for coffee this morning."

Elena rolled her eyes and plopped onto the stacked down pillows, making herself comfortable in her sister's grand bed. Doretta was always the belle of the ball and had lots of boys calling on her. Not one escaped Elena's attention.

Daniela, still in her robe and slippers, came through the open door, a large envelope in her right hand.

"Good morning, girls. My, Doretta, but that dress is lovely on you. I knew it would be." Daniela worried that the neckline was a little low when she ordered it from Flora Volpe. Doretta was, after all, only eighteen, and though she was well endowed, some things were better not displayed in such a manner.

"Thank you, Mamma. It's dazzling out today. I need color." She admired her womanly figure in the mirror while fixing the matching French beret she wore low on one side. Doretta loved Greta Garbo's style and followed the Swedish film star's fashion trends closely. Yes, the dress was from Paris, she allowed herself to believe.

"Anyway, I'll keep this on for tonight." Doretta smoothed the skirt over her thighs. Even though it was the last day of Passover, she was grateful she did not have to attend services at the synagogue this morning as many of her friends did. Her parents had never insisted on that.

"Is zio Eduardo coming? He promised to play some Scott Joplin songs for four hands with me. It's been too long since we've sat together at the piano."

"Yes, Doretta, he's coming. But you shouldn't push him. He hasn't been feeling well lately, and I know his hands are bothering him."

"Growing old is so awful, Mamma. Poor nonno Davide. Look how he suffered before the end last year."

Daniela shook her head. "That's the price we pay for a long life, cara. And why we should enjoy each day—each moment." She looked past Doretta out the window. *Will my children have a long life?* she wondered. *And what world will they live in?* The chestnut trees had yet to sprout any leaves. Winter seemed to grip Turin longer than usual this year. But today would be mild and fair. Doretta was right, it was time to seek color in their lives. "Elena, would you please excuse us?"

"What do you mean, Mamma?"

"To leave, Elena, that's what," Doretta snapped.

"Mamma, is that—"

"Yes, Elena. Please go now."

With that, Elena stalked out the door. As soon as she was safely past her mamma, she turned and stuck out her tongue. Before Doretta could cross the room to push her out and close the door, Elena was gone. At last, they were alone.

"Really, Mamma, she's becoming impossible. She still needs a governess. You should have replaced Fraulein Hofbauer."

"Enough of that, Doretta." Daniela did not want to explain the lack of any new staff members in the house. Not now. Who can one trust these days, particularly since the brutal anti-Jewish press campaign that began the previous autumn? People actually believed those despicable claims. "You really need to be more patient with her. Anyway, we have more important things to discuss. Please sit."

Daniela handed an envelope to Doretta to give to Luca for his mission to Germany. If all went well, Silvana and her children would soon be with them in Turin.

Doretta still didn't understand why her mamma wanted all the secrecy. Why hadn't Luca come to the apartment as he had on previous occasions with Madama Lia? And anyway, carrying so much money in her purse made her nervous. But she had no choice. Zia Silvana was desperate. This was the least she could do.

AS SHE STEPPED OUT ONTO THE STREET, HER STOMACH REMINDED HER THAT she hadn't eaten breakfast. Too late to go back. Perhaps she would pop into the Caffè Platti around the corner for a cappuccino. As she paused to check her watch outside the café, a large man rushed out, bumped her, and nearly sent her tumbling. Although she regained her balance, she dropped her purse, which held the envelope. She snatched it up and gripped it tightly across her body. He didn't even excuse himself. The fat man must have pushed past others in the crowded café since a man was cursing him. Well, better to skip the coffee and continue to the station. Anyway, she was anxious to be rid of the envelope and the responsibility of guarding it. Luca should take possession of it as soon as possible. She tapped her purse, made sure the strap was secure across her body, and continued through the arcades along Corso Vittorio Emanuele II to the station.

Perfect timing. The train was pulling in as she arrived at the platform. Luca smiled and waved as he disembarked and merged into the crowd of passengers pouring out. Although he was ten years older, Doretta felt a bit giddy whenever she was around him. So handsome he was with his thick hair and warm brown eyes, and he was taller than most men she knew. And *very* unmarried. And it was spring. Like the bears in the Alps, she was coming out of hibernation.

He pushed through the throng and kissed her politely on both cheeks. "Doretta! You look…well, I'm tired of seeing pretty women dressed in dark colors. You do know that you're violating the dress code for subservient Fascist women, don't you? You're certainly not dressed like a peasant!" They both had a good laugh. He had spoken in a low enough voice, but she put her index finger to her lips and gently shushed him.

"Luca, be careful. There are eyes and ears everywhere. In any case, have you ever known me to be subservient?" Again, they laughed, then linked arms, and walked out of the station, her free hand clutching her purse against her. "Since it's so pretty, why don't we walk to Caffè San Carlo? Most likely, they have tables outside today. And I have to pick up a cake for dinner tonight. Mamma insists on unleavened baked goods during Passover. Everyone's dying for cake tomorrow."

As they walked through the arcade on via Roma, Doretta paid close attention to her surroundings amidst the crush of people, but Luca seemed nervous.

Twice he stopped to peep into a window, looked around as though he was shopping, and then continued walking with her.

"Are you really flying to Germany, Luca, to bring them here?"

"That's the plan," he said, barely audible. "There really is no other way. Neither Madama Lia nor Madame Stern trusts anyone else. Carrying false identity papers, particularly in a foreign country, is dangerous for everyone. The children will need false documents as well since it would be dangerous for them to travel under a different name."

"When will you go?"

Abruptly, but gently, he pulled her to a shop window and pointed out some items.

"Luca, what—"

"Just look at these lovely hats, Doretta! Let's go in." He opened the door and ushered her in, looking back in the direction they had come before slipping into the millinery shop.

Doretta hesitated at the door. "Luca, I don't need a hat. Why did we come in here?" He slipped his arm around her narrow waist and guided her into the shop.

"Buongiorno, signora." He greeted the shopkeeper before whispering to Doretta, "Please, play along with me." A loving tone replaced the edginess in his voice as he continued playing the part of a doting boyfriend—or perhaps husband. "Summer is coming soon, cara, and I know you would love a new straw hat. It's all the rage in Hollywood, I hear."

"Hmm, I don't know. You said you liked me in a wider brimmed hat, with a ribbon around the crown." She had no idea what he was up to, but she had to admit her pulse quickened when he called her "cara" and whispered in her ear. She quivered when his warm breath touched her cheek.

He kept watching the street. "Well, it's obvious you're not in the mood for shopping. And we're late. Grazie, signora. *Buona giornata.*"

With that, they were back on the street and resuming their stroll to Piazza San Carlo.

"Luca, what was that all about?"

"Later, Doretta. You'll have to learn not to ask questions like that and assume there is a good reason."

"But, Luca, you were the one who wasn't careful at the station with your talk about Fascist women."

"I know. It was your orange dress. I forgot myself. Anyway, times are changing here too. Enough talking for now." He *had* forgotten himself and the reason they were meeting today. His thoughts were on Doretta—her perfume and her lovely orange dress that skimmed her body, accentuating the rounded curve of her hips—not on the business at hand. And this was serious business. People's lives were at stake. Also, she was very young, and this was not the time for romantic entanglements.

For the next few minutes, they walked silently to the café, Luca continuing the act of the doting lover. He took her hand and led her to the table on the side farthest from the arcade. "Much quieter for us there, cara, don't you think? I have something important I want to ask you."

Well, if he was going to keep up the act, so was she. "It's perfect, caro."

As she started to sit in the chair facing the arcade, he quickly pulled the other chair across for her. "Cara, no. Sit here. It's so much nicer to have the view of the piazza." Luca wanted his eyes on the arcade, watching for any further signs of a stalker.

As patrons filled the café, Luca ordered the specialty of the house: hot, thick, dark chocolate and a beaker of water. Doretta chose her favorite: bicerin with lightly whipped crème on top.

"Luca, enough with the mystery. I mean, you're quite the romantic and all, but…" She stopped as the heat rose in her cheeks. Perhaps the dress she chose wasn't such a good idea to wear for this meeting. The problem, she realized, was that she enjoyed and wanted the attention Luca was giving her.

He leaned forward and slipped his hands into hers. Though his face seemed relaxed and he smiled at her, his voice was so low that she could barely hear him.

"Doretta, when we crossed into the piazza, I had a strange feeling that we were being followed. That's why I stopped a few times. I pulled you into the shop because I thought I saw someone following us. But he just walked past. I have nothing incriminating on me today. Maybe I'm a little paranoid. It was probably just my imagination."

Doretta opened her purse, but then snapped it shut as the waiter arrived with their drinks. Once he left, she pulled the envelope out and slid it to Luca. He quickly slipped it into his briefcase.

They talked for a while longer with Doretta giving him details about Silvana and the children. He had wanted to pose as her husband, but Madama Lia prohibited that idea. It was enough that he was carrying false documents and a large amount of cash needed for bribes when they crossed the border from Austria into Italy. Traveling on his own passport was easy, so there was no need to increase the danger. They would travel together but apart.

"Luca, I can't thank you enough for this risk you're taking. My family cannot. Well, Mamma, that is. Papà still doesn't know."

"Madama Lia mentioned his political opinions were…um…let's just say, they were different than ours. That's all she said."

"He's a Fascist, Luca. A Jewish Fascist. And he has been for many years. I still can't believe he's hanging onto a thread of hope that the train barreling toward us will stop. Mussolini is and always was an anti-Semite. Zia Silvana is running away to Italy. Soon we may be running for our lives as well."

They sat quietly for a moment.

"One question, Luca. Why?"

"I don't understand."

"Why are you doing this? You could be a successful lawyer, running a powerful Piemontese woman's businesses and not risking your life."

"It's hard to explain, Doretta." He finished his water and studied the etched glass for a moment before continuing. "I've known Madama Lia all my life. I was there the first day she returned to work after her daughter, Giulia, died. Although I didn't understand the business she and my father were discussing, I saw her courage and compassion. And since my father died, she's been my mentor. I guess, if she's risking everything, I might as well follow her."

Doretta shuddered to think of anything happening to him, or to Madama Lia, all on account of them.

"I really don't know what to say to that, Luca. We'll never be able to thank you enough for taking this risk. Let's hope this madness will end soon. If not, I shall join you in the fight."

"Doretta—" But there was no use telling her more about the dangers that might soon be at their doorstep. Perhaps she knew. Let her enjoy these last years, or months, of innocence. It would disappear soon. Then she would have to grow up fast. "We should follow Madama Lia's orders and not draw attention to ourselves. It's a dangerous road we're travelling. Quite dangerous."

It was getting late. Time to get home.

While Luca was returning his journal to his briefcase, Doretta wove her way through the tables, back to the arcade. She didn't want to forget the cake. A young man dashed in front her at the café entrance. She stopped. It had been years, but was that…? No, he was in Berlin, Mamma said. She dismissed the specter of Baldo Volpe. Probably, like Luca, it was her imagination running wild after their charade. She turned back toward Luca, feeling light-headed.

"What is it, Doretta?" he asked. "You look like you've seen a ghost."

"Oh, it's nothing. I thought I forgot my purse. And look, here it is." *Calm your nerves.* There was no need to tell Luca. Not now, at least. If that demon had returned to Turin, she would call Sara for advice. Sara always knew best.

"Not to worry, Doretta—when you see me next, you will also see your zia e *cugini.*" With those words, he smiled, kissed her cheeks again, and left for Porta Nuova station.

Godspeed, Luca, she said to herself as she watched him turn onto via Roma. *Godspeed, caro.*

ON THE DESK BEFORE HIM LAY A *CASELLARIO POLITICO CENTRALE* FOLDER WITH a name in black block letters stenciled on the cover: DORETTA GIORDANO. The recently created file had joined thousands of others kept on anti-Fascists and other enemies of the party. Only a single sheet of paper and an old photo of her were inside—for now. Baldo was sure that the contents would soon grow. He would see to that. There was much about her and her anti-Fascist sympathies that would interest OVRA, the secret police whose methods were unknown by most but feared by all.

"Beware, Doretta," he whispered as he ran his palm over the folder, the thrill he now associated with thoughts of bringing her to heel warming him. The first time he experienced it, four years earlier, he had been shocked and ashamed of himself. But soon he came to realize it as a sign of his masculinity—a sign of his power over this woman. He leaned back in his chair, easing the pressure in his groin as he stared off into space. *Soon we will come for you, Doretta.*

When Baldo first left his home, he had assured his mamma that he would be home by Christmas. He was, but three Christmases then passed before he saw her again last December. He had sorely missed her, but his life was dedicated to the Party, to Italy. Sentimentality caused weakness. Weakness caused mistakes.

After he finished his German language and history studies, Baldo had remained in Berlin as an intern attached to the senior political officer at the Italian Embassy. In the four glorious years he spent in Germany, the Nazi whirlwind had begun to sweep the inferior races from Germany and retake lands the Allies wrongfully seized at Versailles. America, England, and France had defeated Germany and duped Italy at the treaty table, yet now they were feckless in the face of Hitler's brave actions in the Rhineland. What luck to have a front row seat to the great opera that was the rise of the Third Reich.

Baldo's time in Berlin had helped to launch him in his career as a member of OVRA. Now his goal was to reach the pinnacle of power, such was the importance of OVRA in protecting Mussolini and the state. As a feared officer of the secret police, he would defend the country against those trying to undermine the government, primarily the socialist anti-Fascists. Baldo admired the cleverness of the name—OVRA sounded like *piovra*, the mythical giant octopus. Like an octopus, OVRA's tentacles reached in all directions, even beyond the country's borders. Wherever enemies of the party were found, they would be severely punished. Soon he, Baldo Volpe, would wrap Doretta Giordano in his own OVRA tentacle.

In Berlin, Baldo had run with a circle of friends who were Brownshirts, soon to be commissioned officers in the SS. They spent hours in beer halls, debating how their generation would rule Europe…and countries far beyond. Fascist youth at its finest. And he, as fit and as tall as they were, had felt right at home. What a time that was!

It had taken time, but Mussolini finally recognized that, to return Italy to glory and to resurrect the Roman Empire, he needed to ally himself with Hitler. In October, the two great men created the Berlin-Rome Axis. When Heinrich Himmler and Arturo Bocchini, the father of OVRA, entered into a cooperation agreement, Baldo was ecstatic. There was much for him to learn. With his OVRA superior, he spent hours in the presence of Himmler, one of the greatest men in Hitler's circle. Together, the Gestapo and OVRA would bring conquered European countries to heel and cleanse the continent of Jews and undesirables. And he, Baldo Volpe, would do his part.

Already, Baldo had made use of his power and connections. Back in 1933, he grew concerned over a letter from his mother. He could tell she was afraid. So he asked his childhood friend, Umberto, now a fellow Squadristi, to visit her, ostensibly to wish her *Buon Natale*. Umberto soon confirmed Baldo's suspicions. Dino had returned to her life.

He had not gone to the apartment but had assaulted her in broad daylight. The incident occurred in the crowded Porta Palazzo market on the last Saturday before Christmas. He grabbed her purse and pushed her to the ground. Umberto reported this to Baldo and told him that his mother still lived in fear at the thought of coming across her husband from whom divorce was impossible. In early spring that year, when water from melting alpine snows had transformed the Po River into a torrent, police recovered Dino Volpe's body downstream from Ponte Vittorio Emanuele I, caught up in the thicket at the river's edge. The police investigation was closed as quickly as it was opened.

When Baldo received news of the report from Umberto, he smiled. Dino Volpe would no longer harm his mother. Yes, they had eliminated his father, but when had he ever said a kind word to him? It surprised him to learn that Flora, despite the anguish Dino had caused her through the years, had cried over his death. He was, she said, her husband, without whom she would not have such a loving, kind son.

Baldo paced the large, smoke-filled room he shared with other OVRA officers, stopping now and then to look out the window toward the Po, the river that helped put an end to one distraction and a huge threat to the only person he loved. He had not meant to upset her, but he knew that she was better off now. All that mattered was that she was finally safe. There were other important issues requiring his full attention.

Though younger than his peers and only a junior officer, his time in Berlin brought him more respect and responsibility. Three months earlier, he had been assigned to surveillance. Sensing his advantage, he used Doretta Giordano—a Jewish woman with suspicious associates, cloaking herself in the safety of her high-ranking Fascist father's house—to inaugurate a surveillance operation for himself. How appropriate that he began his OVRA career investigating her.

He returned his attention to the folder. The sheet inside only gave basic information about Doretta Giordano that he already knew from his own clever surveillance work before he left for Germany. At the top of the page, he read, *"Father is Gabriele Giordano, a prominent Jewish member of the PNF in Turin."* That was the juiciest bit of information he had recorded: a Jew member of the Fascist Party with an anti-Fascist daughter. Although Mussolini was finally ridding himself of Jews in his government, people like Gabriele Giordano still had power. That would soon change.

Recently Baldo discovered that, in 1934, Doretta had attended meetings of an outlawed anti-Fascist group. At least that was the assumption when she was seen carrying a copy of the socialist anti-Fascist newspaper *Giustizia e Libertà*. The paper, printed in Paris, was banned in Turin. Surely, she was too young for them to accept her into their organization and, no doubt, they would not trust a daughter of such a prominent Fascist Party leader. No, most likely she was only a sympathizer of the organization filled with intellectuals and bourgeois Jews from Turin, not an active member. However, the reported sighting of a daughter of Gabriele Giordano with anti-Fascist propaganda was sufficient evidence for his superior when he approved Baldo's request to assign an informant to her file.

With a little bit of money to grease palms, finding someone to spy on her was easy. But trusting the nameless, numbered informant, someone who claimed to know her, was another thing. What if he was himself an anti-Fascist seeking to derail OVRA's investigations into others like him? In any case, Baldo relished the moments he followed her himself as he had a few days earlier. What a productive day that had been, and now he would track down the man she had met.

He returned to his desk, lit a cigarette, and sat back, relishing the memory of stalking Doretta Giordano as he blew smoke rings, nooses around her neck, into the air. He had to admit he enjoyed following her, watching her swaying hips and shapely calves as she strutted through the arcade. Even from a distance, Baldo could see that she was no longer a child. Gone was the long schoolgirl braid. Now her wavy chestnut hair was short, almost mannish. The cocky way she wore her beret and strutted in her bright orange dress were unbecoming for a woman. How obscene to expose so much of her flesh. If she were his woman, he would forbid such behavior. If only…but she was a Jew, for God's sake. His friends in Berlin had told him that Jewish women were known to seduce Aryan men and cast spells on them. Maybe that was what happened that day in front of the synagogue even though she was still a schoolgirl. He would deal with her when the time came. An interrogation session would free him from her evil clutches. Never would she escape him.

And he would deal with the mystery man from Alba. He looked far too old to be her boyfriend. Of course. The man was cheating on his wife with this Jew harlot. It didn't surprise him one bit. Another unsuspecting non-Jew, although not an Aryan, caught in a Jewish woman's sorcery. But what if their amorous behavior was all a ruse? Or were they lovers in on the same anti-Fascist mission? Whatever their relationship, Baldo believed he had witnessed an exchange of illicit information. He would continue to follow her. There had to be more to what he had seen.

He crushed his cigarette in the ashtray and loaded paper into his typewriter. As he started composing his report, he smiled, enjoying once again that warm feeling in his groin he had whenever he contemplated his power over her. One more document in her file, one more piece of the puzzle that was Doretta Giordano. He looked forward to adding others and watching the file grow as he tightened his OVRA tentacle around her and those conspiring with her. It would no doubt be useful one day. Soon, he believed.

CHAPTER 18

Turin to Rosenheim, Germany
April 1937

L uca glanced at his watch. Already the Ala Littoria flight from Venice to Munich was fifteen minutes late. Although flying through clear skies, the inbound flight had landed late. Now they sat, the air in the cabin hot and stuffy. In the past, Luca had often flown the Rome-to-Berlin express, the pride of the government-owned airline system. Those flights were always on time, taking off with un-Italian precision. Well, at least today his flights from Turin to Milan and onward to Venice had been uneventful, and he was now safely on board for the final leg. If only they could get going.

Early that morning in Turin, his heart sank when he pulled back the curtains in his hotel room. He saw nothing but the famed Po River valley fog that one could cut with a knife. Would he have to scrub his mission before he even left Piemonte? It seemed like a bad omen, but by the time he arrived at the airport for his flight, the sun had broken through. The plane took off on time, and he was on his way to meet Silvana Becker. By now, she and her two children should be safe in Rosenheim, southeast of Munich, with Fritz's *Tante* Lorelei, the only Becker relative who had not shunned her.

While they waited, Luca extracted a tattered envelope of fine stationary from his suit pocket. The oft-read letter inside was one he needed to read again as he set off on the most dangerous journey of his life. Would more follow if he lived through this one? The last paragraph of the letter he had committed to memory, but seeing his father's handwriting now comforted him.

I look forward to many more years with you by my side. Although I never wanted to push you in that direction, practicing law with my son was a dream of mine. But you chose it early, and for that, I am truly blessed. And so my dear son, although I pray this last war truly was one to end all others, I fear it was not. Your generation, I believe, will be called upon to fight the forces of evil that took root in the ashes of the Great War. As you go forward, I know you will use your intellect and all that you've learned from me, from Madama Lia, to do what is right. Never question yourself, but be quick to question others' motives if not aligned with those values we have instilled in you. I love you, caro Luca, and I am immensely proud of you.

Buona fortuna,
Papà.

He returned the letter to the place near his heart and stared out on the tarmac. *Papà, please watch over me.*

Minutes later, a heavyset man in a tailored suit swaggered into the cabin with a buxom blonde clinging to his arm and a young assistant following with their bags. Once they settled into their seats at the front, the stewardess closed the cabin door. A thirty-minute delay for a Fascist Party official didn't surprise Luca. The three propellers of the Savoia-Marchetti S.73 started spinning as the engines coughed and sputtered. He would keep his briefcase wedged between his feet. Why did he feel again as though a giant bull's-eye was painted on it? On him? All he carried were false identity papers for a Jewish German woman, now persona non grata in her own country, and her two small *Mischlinge* children. *What could go wrong?* he asked himself. Too much to contemplate.

He still could not shake the feeling that someone had been following him on Saturday with Doretta. OVRA was powerful and omnipresent. Even a neighbor's reported suspicion could result in a prison sentence—no proof needed. Luca knew this had become a means of retaliation against any enemy, including family members and adulterous spouses. These were dangerous times. But if someone had been following them, he hoped that he was the mark, not Doretta. Until now, Madama Lia had not involved her in any of their activities. Surely, as the daughter of a prominent party member, Doretta was safe.

It had been easy enough to collect the forged identification documents from Madama Lia without arousing suspicions. Her priest in Alba regularly visited the mulino on Monday afternoons for an *aperitivo* and a chat. Who could have imagined that he would be able to use his expert forgery skills, learned during the Great War, to help Jews like Silvana? Tuesday afternoon, Luca paid his own weekly visit to the mulino. Her calm demeanor about her involvement in the daring rescue impressed him.

With more Jewish families and political dissidents needing Madama Lia's courage and largesse, Luca knew many more like Silvana and her children would seek out her help. After Hitler remilitarized the Rhineland, the number of Jews emigrating exploded. Only Italy kept its doors wide open to them, but not always with a pure heart and concern for their safety. Lia often said money, specifically foreign currency, proved a greater motive for the Italian government than humanitarian relief. Together with her childhood friend Frieda Stern, Lia would spread their safety net far and continue to help resettle Jews in Italy as long as Italy remained safe for them.

Once airborne, Luca gladly accepted the glass of Riesling the stewardess offered. Long day. Frayed nerves. When they reached cruising altitude in the clear sky, he gazed down at the Austrian Alps, still covered in a thick blanket of snow. No matter how many times he had made this journey on Madama Lia's flour-mill business, the majestic peaks seen from this angle always moved him. Each spring, he hungered for the snows to disappear in Val Maira so he could resume trekking in the alpine meadows. Long summer days spent among cows grazing on tender grass and sweet flowers lightened his spirits, particularly in those days after his father's sudden death. But today, it was impossible not to imagine that the long chain of rugged, towering mountains stretching across southern Europe had become a great fence, impossible to scale if the border crossings slammed shut. But he would soon pass through with Silvana, Friedrich, and Gisele—born Becker, now Frei. He smiled at the irony of Silvana's new last name. If all went well, they soon would be free.

Escaping Germany now, through Austria to Italy, ensured they would not be among those Jews trapped within the Reich. Austrians were Nazi sympathizers but not yet under Berlin's control. How long it would remain a corridor to freedom between Germany and Italy depended on when and where Hitler struck next. Madama Lia and Madame Stern believed Hitler and Mussolini wanted nothing short of war. Luca agreed. The Allies were sleeping through the opening act of this tragic play. Luca feared it would be too late when they finally woke.

Men in military uniforms, wearing red armbands emblazoned with the loathsome black Nazi swastika, occupied half of the other sixteen seats. As for the Italian insignia, Luca found Mussolini's obsession with symbols of imperial Rome's power a bit comical. But he would never accept the swastika as something legitimate. Better to close his eyes and rest. He would see enough of the perverted cross soon.

Fritz's Tante Lorelei lived in Rosenheim, a village just north of the Austrian border that provided a safer option for a rendezvous with Luca. Far less German soil to cross. Always a kindhearted soul and a bit of a black sheep in the family herself for her choice of husband, Lorelei preserved ties with her beloved nephew's widow long after her sister and brother-in-law excommunicated Silvana from the Becker family.

They had crafted a simple plan. On March 23, five days before Easter, Silvana would arrive for a month—or so she would say—and tell her aunt a tale of Luca's planned visit to Rosenheim. Luca would be in Munich on business the week of April 4 and would deliver to Silvana a precious heirloom from a recently departed uncle. Daniela had wanted to send it, but she did not trust the post. Luca would be the perfect courier, although the precious gifts he would transport *from* Rosenheim were more important than the one he would deliver. Their escape would begin when Luca and his driver picked up Silvana and the children in the morning for a drive and lunch along the shores of the Chiemsee. When they left Tante Lorelei's house, whatever they had on their persons would be all their worldly possessions when they left Germany.

The lunch, of course, was a ruse. Madama Lia had been adamant that Luca was not to travel with Silvana and the children, but there was no other way. By train or plane, they could sit apart, allowing Luca to appear detached though nearby should something go awry. However, flying would involve additional checkpoints manned by more experienced guards—perhaps even under Gestapo surveillance—and more opportunities for searches. Going by car and, thus, limiting contacts with police was the safest way to travel.

Luca opened his eyes at the familiar sound of the changing pitch of the propellers as they began their descent. Shortly after one o'clock in the afternoon, the plane touched down at Munich Oberwiesenfeld Airport. As he pulled his small valise from the overhead netting, his briefcase tipped over. With his hands full, he was unable to quickly grab it. The stewardess retrieved and handed it to him.

"*Vielen Dank*," Luca said in German without thinking but quickly corrected himself. "Mi scusi. Grazie, signorina."

"*Bitteschön*," the shapely young Italian stewardess answered as she winked and handed Luca the briefcase.

As he made his way through customs and immigration, he silently thanked Madama Lia and his father for insisting that he study languages in university. Being Piemontese, he already spoke French, the language of the Savoy family who had ruled the region for centuries. But it was not enough in his father's opinion. German, he feared, would become the most important foreign language he spoke.

During the flight, he had overheard a chilling conversation between the two Nazis sitting behind him about the "Jewish question." They voiced their frustration over Mussolini's slow pace in coming around to Hitler's correct thinking when it came to ridding Europe, perhaps the world, of the Jewish race. *Judenfrei* was not enough for the Nazis. Luca believed their endgame was *judenrein*—draining Jewish blood from mankind. "Mussolini is a weak pompous ass," one hissed under his breath. Luca marveled at their arrogance, speaking that way on an Italian government-owned aircraft. Already it was obvious that the Nazis had no intention of being Mussolini's partner in battle. They intended to rule Europe and make a puppet, at best, of Il Duce. The thought of Nazi occupation chilled Luca's blood.

Outside the terminal, a chauffeur fitting the description Madame Stern had given Luca stood with a placard bearing his name.

"*Guten Tag*, Herr Olivero. *Ich heiße* Dieter."

As Dieter reached to take Luca's valise, he spotted the long scar he had been told about on the man's right hand. The day was proceeding as planned.

During the ninety-minute drive south, Luca avoided small talk. The less said, the better. Dieter also remained quiet. A good sign. A professional who understood the need for discretion.

Luca checked into a *Gasthof* in Frasdorf, a small village near Rosenheim. Having spent most of the day in stuffy airplanes, he longed for a stroll to explore the Bavarian village, but he erred on the side of caution and remained in his room. After a sleepless night, Luca had a small breakfast at the inn and waited outside for Dieter. At precisely 10:00 a.m., he arrived. Luca's long day with an uncertain ending began.

Lorelei Vogel, a war widow, lived in a modest house in the Am Salzstadl section of Rosenheim, a picturesque neighborhood not far from the town center. As they drove through the center of Rosenheim, Luca admired the tidy and quaint Bavarian town. He caught a glimpse of the huge marketplace of Max-Josef-Platz and the onion-domed spire of the Saint Nikolaus church. Brightly colored tulips lined the roadway. But when they passed the grim, rectangular police headquarters, all the charm vanished. Inside, he knew, the Gestapo were at work.

A plump lady of medium height, her silver-gray hair pulled back tightly from her face in a bun, answered the door. Her warm, welcoming smile and the smell of freshly baked bread wafting through the open door calmed Luca's nerves.

"Guten Tag, Frau Vogel. Ich heiße Luca Olivero." She smiled with her full rosy cheeks at his German. "*Ich bin hier für* Silvana."

"Yes, of course. I am Silvana's Tante Lorelei. Do come in, Herr Olivero."

"I am very pleased to meet you, Frau Vogel." He was well trained in the protocols of the German language, the most important one being how someone older than he should be addressed. "Please do call me Luca."

She guided him into her bright sitting room off the front hall. The fire glowing in the small fireplace took the chill from the air. Next to it, toys were scattered about. Father dead. Mother living in a virtual prison. And now they must flee even from the seeming safety of Bavaria.

Silvana soon joined them in the parlor. Luca had only met her once, in the summer of 1932, less than a year before she became a widow. In those days, she was a lovely woman whose deep dimples appeared when she smiled, which was often. Her large, laughing, brown eyes were now weary and sad. Although she was six years younger than Daniela, her face was taut and thin, as was her body on which a black day dress hung far too loosely. Flecks of dull gray in her dark brown hair, pulled into a Dutch braid, aged her. Luca wanted nothing more than to see her safely to her sister in Turin.

"Luca, what a pleasure to see you here in Germany. Such a coincidence." She greeted him with a kiss on each cheek before taking his hands in hers. Her voice turned somber. "I was so sorry to hear about your father's sudden passing last summer. How is your mother?" She searched his eyes, her soft voice gentle and sincere as though seeking reassurance that her nightmare would soon end. He lightly squeezed her hands and her face brightened a little.

"Thank you. She is doing quite well, Frau Becker, despite the shock. My nonna and my brother's children keep her busy."

"Are you married, Luca? I hear from Daniela that the party is tough on men your age who remain single. Is that true?"

"No, I'm not married yet. But sadly, it's true that Mussolini wants babies, lots of them, preferably sons to fill his army. I'm taxed each year until I marry and have children. But first, I would need to find a woman to love. Madama Lia keeps me far too busy." Enough talk about marriage. It stirred too many thoughts of Doretta. "Here's the package from Daniela." Luca handed her a tiny box wrapped in brown paper that Daniela had included in the envelope Doretta passed to him.

"How dear of zio Eduardo to think of me in his will." She hoped speaking of him as though he were dead would not curse her beloved uncle. How long before she would once again hear the beguiling music he made? Silvana stared at the box, longing to open it. "Excuse me for a moment, Luca, while I put this in my room and get the children." She smiled at her Tante Lorelei. "I'll open it with you later this evening." The deception cut deep into Silvana's heart. Would she ever forgive herself for dragging her into this intrigue? But what other option did she have to save her children?

Silvana left her aunt and Luca to chat as she rushed up the stairs, locking her bedroom door behind her. She ripped off the wrapping paper and opened the wooden box inside. *Oh, Daniela—my sage, loving sister.* The box contained the locket she had given Daniela on her wedding day, tucked in the same small, pink, satin bag. A photo of their beloved departed mamma when she was Silvana's age replaced the one of Gabriele. Silvana read the note accompanying it.

Wear this close to your heart, out of sight. Always remember that I am with you and Mamma is watching over you.

Silvana squeezed her eyes shut and willed herself not to release the tears she had held back for years—tears of joy. There would be time for that when she was reunited with Daniela. She took the safety pin Daniela had included, reached into the top of her dress, and pinned the bag securely to the inside of her brassiere, next to her heart. With one last look at the meager possessions her kind aunt would have to dispose of, she picked up her purse, turned, and left the room.

She called for the children. They would not at first understand, but they were about to embark on the voyage they would always remember.

After quick introductions with Friedrich—who considered himself the man of the house and greeted Luca with a firm handshake—and Gisele, shy and wary of the stranger, Luca checked his watch. It was time to leave.

When Silvana hugged her aunt and said good-bye, she tried not to let her emotions betray that she was leaving for good. But when Lorelei kissed her and whispered in her ear, "Godspeed, *meine liebes Schatzli* until we meet again," the dam holding back her tears nearly broke. She knew! But how had she discovered her deception? Lorelei held her close, continuing to whisper as the children watched, appearing puzzled at such a display of emotion for a simple good-bye for a few hours.

"Shh. *Keine Worte.* Did you think I would fail to spot the desperation of a woman I know and love to save her children?" She stepped back, rested her hands lightly on Silvana's flushed cheeks, searched her eyes, and flashed her a mischievous grin. "Besides, if you were truly having lunch at the Chiemsee, this nice young man would have asked me along."

A brief laugh broke through Silvana's lips. The muscles of her face relaxed under her aunt's soft hands; they telegraphed, she believed, love and concern. "Now, go with God, but never lower your guard, Silvana. Never trust a soul but Luca until you are safely under your sister's roof."

"Tante Lorelei, how will I—"

"Hush, child. Now go."

As he watched the scene, alarm bells rang in Luca's head. He noticed how Friedrich's eyes darkened as he studied the two women clinging to each other. At some point, Luca was sure, Silvana would be pummeled with questions from the eight-year-old. Gisele, clutching her brother's hand, glanced up at Luca, then slipped her other hand into his. He squeezed her tiny hand and smiled, trying to reassure her with his eyes that all was well. Hopefully, she could not sense his growing concern about the delay. They should be on their way.

Luca hurried the children along and settled them into the spacious backseat of Dieter's car. They had witnessed enough of the intense emotions the two women displayed. Finally, Silvana turned. Luca read panic on her face. Lorelei grabbed her hand and held it until the last possible moment as her niece walked to the car, her eyes glazed, all color gone from her face.

What had her aunt said to her? Luca worried this might be a revelation that someone outside their tight, secure circle knew of her plan to defy the brutal authorities and make a dash across the border—and under an assumed name. Was it foolhardy to risk the lives of Silvana and her children, or should she have waited in the relative safety of Berlin until the Allies finally put a stop to Hitler's mad plans? Luca wondered whether he was complicit in a disaster for the Beckers. Surely, this woman, who was a steadfast friend and a kind aunt for so many years, would not betray Silvana or the children of her blood. But this was Nazi Germany. He had heard of neighbors turning on neighbors, families renouncing relatives. Anything was possible.

Luca wanted to ask her more about what Tante Lorelei had said, but Silvana sat in the backseat with the children while he got in the front next to Dieter. Discreet conversation was impossible. He would have to wait until the next leg of their journey to quiz her.

Gisele wasted no time crawling onto her mother's lap then flicked her thumb over her lips and slid it into her mouth. Silvana extracted a small, stuffed dog from her large purse and nudged it into the girl's hands. She popped her thumb out and seized the toy, clutching it close to her chest. Friedrich studied his mother as though looking for a clue as to what might unfold now. When the boy's searching eyes met his, Luca turned back to face ahead. He had no answers he could give now. The weight of the responsibility he had undertaken settled heavily on him.

Once the doors were closed, a familiar fragrance filled the air. Roses! Doretta's perfume. Silvana was wearing it! He didn't need a reminder of her at this time, at least not of the memory he had made with her in Turin. Though he wanted to savor the fragrance and thoughts of Doretta a while longer, he quickly turned his attention back to the three people who depended on him. Too much was at stake for distractions.

Silence settled over them except for Gisele's soft whimpering and Silvana's cooing as she stroked the child's dark blonde hair. Their flight to freedom was underway.

CHAPTER 19

Germany
Later that day

After leaving Lorelei Volker standing at her front door, waving as they drove away, their silence continued as Dieter drove them along the shores of the Chiemsee to the picturesque town of Marquartstein. There, a car for Luca to drive would be waiting for them for the next leg of their journey. To get his mind off his concerns about what had transpired between Silvana and Lorelei, Luca reviewed in his mind the next step in the plan.

They would say good-bye to Dieter, and Luca would drive the remainder of the journey to Bolzano. If stopped and questioned, he was Silvana's brother-in-law visiting from Alba. The border crossing into Austria at Reit im Winkl was chosen because it was not heavily manned and was a popular spot on the Bavarian Alpenstrasse along the foothills of the Bavarian Alps. Madame Stern's contact reported that only regular border guards manned the crossing, not the feared SS soldiers. The German guards often left their posts unmanned at lunchtime, especially on warm, sunny days as was forecasted for their crossing. Although Luca was confident that don Riccardo's forgeries would hold up under scrutiny, he preferred not to test his theory. Dieter had already provided him with maps and further information he needed to cross Austria, eventually arriving in Bolzano where Gianni would be waiting. Easy. But there were many obstacles they might encounter: unbribable border guards, unexpected mountain snows, and car trouble not the least of them.

As expected, a small black Ford Köln had been left for them in Marquartstein. Once alone in the car, Luca spent a few minutes explaining where they were going and briefing the children on what to expect. He worried, knowing they could be unpredictable even in predictable situations. Gisele, he had noticed earlier, studied Friedrich carefully. If he appeared calm and unconcerned, she would follow his lead. And the trust she had put in Luca at her great-aunt's house reassured him.

Silvana sat next to him in the front with Gisele wrapped in her arms, sound asleep on her lap. Friedrich, alone in the backseat, set up for battle ten small pewter soldiers and horses Silvana had managed to slip into her purse. One stuffed dog and the pewter miniatures were all that the children had left of their past. They had even left their identities behind.

The drive from Marquartstein through the forested hills to the border village of Reit im Winkl was only ten miles, but each minute seemed an eternity as they made their way through the Bavarian countryside. Once out of Marquartstein, Silvana told him everything her aunt had said, her voice calm after having nearly two hours to compose herself. Various reasons for Lorelei's behavior ran through Luca's mind, the most chilling possibility was that she was an informant for the Gestapo. But though he only spent a few minutes with her, Luca dismissed that possibility. Anyone could see she loved Silvana and the children. In any event, they would know soon enough when they reached the border.

They were alone on the road but for a black Mercedes Benz he had spied some distance behind them, which now followed them closely. It appeared that there were only two occupants in the car, two men, both in the front seat. Every muscle in his body went rigid. He broke out in a cold sweat. Would they be stopped before they were able to get to the border? Barely twenty-four hours had passed since he arrived in Germany. He said a short prayer that, before another hour passed, they would arrive safely in Austria.

Luca knew, all too well, what would likely happen to Silvana and the children if they were caught. As a foreigner driving out of Germany with a family who had been under virtual house arrest and now carried forged passports, his own fate would be sealed as well. *Oh, Luca, why did you agree to this?* To keep his mind off the grim possibilities the car behind them presented, Luca told Silvana of the plans once they were safely in Austria. He kept his voice calm and tried to hide his growing concern with each mile they drove, only occasionally glancing in the rearview mirror.

They arrived at the Masererpass, three miles from the border on the far side of Reit am Winkl. The mysterious black Mercedes continued to follow them. At the top of the pass, Luca spied a perfect spot to pull off the road.

He might as well get it over with now if they were to be arrested. Although he considered the option of making a dash for it if they were stopped at the border, Austria offered no sanctuary from the Nazis for such an infraction.

The black car passed without slowing. Neither occupant seemed to take note of them. Relief—for now.

"Why are we stopping, Luca?" Silvana asked. "Shouldn't we continue?" She turned to Friedrich, still engaged in battle in the backseat, then cuddled her baby girl even tighter.

"Mutti, you're hurting me," protested Gisele.

"*Entschuldigung*, Schatzli." Silvana eased her embrace and kissed her daughter's hair. Gisele nuzzled her mother's chest and drifted off once more.

"I want to check my instructions to make sure we're on the right road." Luca pulled out the sheet of paper he had folded and stored in his suit jacket pocket, although the words were a blur to him. He knew where he was going. The question was whether anyone else did. "Yes, all good. We should be there shortly. It's just around the bend."

He eased the car back onto the road, behind another black Köln. As he drove into the clearing, the final leg of their journey in Germany, Luca's pulse quickened, and his breaths came too fast and shallow. He began to feel dizzy. He loosened his death-grip on the steering wheel and slowed his breathing. He could almost feel Madama's hand on his shoulder. She had told him that both the SS and regular border police were specialists in detecting nervous behavior. That was the last thing they needed.

Luca eased off the gas a bit and put some distance between themselves and the other Köln, though not enough to draw attention.

"Friedrich, remember what we discussed?" he said in a bright voice. "I am your zio Luca. We're going to visit the family in Italy. Most importantly, Friedrich, what is your full name?"

The little general sat as though at attention in the backseat and proclaimed, "*Mein Name ist* Friedrich Frei. It's really so easy, zio Luca," he said, giggling. "Zio Luca, that's funny."

"Excellent, General Frei." Luca breathed easier. "I believe it would be best for you to stay with your troops in the backseat when we arrive at the border. Yes?"

"But, zio Luca," Friedrich asked, "when are we having lunch?"

"Soon, Friedrich, soon. It's a little further up the road after we cross into Austria." Luca had not considered that, though the lunch plan on the lake was a ruse, the children would still need to eat.

"Gisele, dear," Luca waited a moment while she fully awakened. Having her sleep would be better, but he worried what might happen if she woke, startled, and cried. "What's your name?"

"Ich heiße Gisele." She smiled at him, her eyes still heavy with sleep, and searched her mother's face for approval.

"*Ja*, Schatzli. That is correct, but zio Luca would like you to say your full name. Do you remember?"

"Oh yes. Mein Name ist Frei, Gisele Frei." Again, she glanced at her mother for confirmation. Silvana stroked her hair.

"Excellent, Gisele. Now, the next thing to remember is to be quiet like a mouse as I drive through the crossing." Luca made eye contact with Silvana and nodded, trying to reassure her. And himself. They would be fine. He said it a few times to himself. An interrogator could easily extract information from the children, but he prayed it would not come to that.

They spoke not a word as they drove through the picturesque village of Reit im Winkl, still a winter wonderland with the sun reflecting off the melting snow on the ground. Here was another calm and peaceful place Luca would have loved to visit in a better time. Would that ever happen, or would Europe's borders become a demarcation between life and death? Luca suspected that he would never see this place again—would never want to.

And there it was. As he rounded the sharp left-hand bend, not far past the village, the border crossing loomed a few hundred feet ahead. The black Mercedes-Benz! It was there, off to the right side, next to the guardhouse. The two men he had seen in the black car that had followed them stood with two border guards next to the Ford Köln that had passed them on the Masererpass. Both men wore trench coats and were dressed in black from head to toe, a color Luca would never again associate with anything other than evil. At least the soldiers with them were regular border guards as he had seen in Munich, not SS. One of the men in black was studying documents, likely passports. They had to be Gestapo. Dread gnawed at his insides. He glanced at Silvana. The tense expression she had worn since they left Lorelei's home had disappeared. Now she looked every bit a relaxed, happy mother on an outing with her family. Impressive. She had been forced to learn quickly how not to give herself away.

Luca drove straight to the barrier and cranked the window down.

"*Pässe bitte!*" the guard barked.

Luca handed over the three forged passports and his own valid one. As the guard flipped back and forth through the pages, he stopped and looked at the faces in the car before turning back to the passports. Luca fought his nerves as he waited to be told to pull aside.

"Where are you going?"

"Italy." Luca nearly added Turin to his answer. His lawyerly instincts paid off. Answer only the question asked, and never volunteer information. The guard gave him a stern look and continued to flip through Luca's passport.

"You go often to Switzerland, I see. Why?"

Luca stiffened. What of his passengers' false documents? What if they were quizzed about the stamps? Luca had not thought to have Silvana look at the stamps of places she had supposedly gone. "I'm a lawyer for an important client who has business in Zürich." Perspiration broke out on Luca's brow. He wanted to blot it, but what if he drew attention to a sign of his nervousness?

Several times, the guard glanced over the car in the direction of the stopped car. He cleared his throat. "And where are you coming from? You flew into Munich yesterday, ja?"

"Rosenheim. I flew in so that I could drive my sister-in-law's car for her. Traveling such a distance alone would be dangerous for a woman and two children." Too much information. His heart fluttered. Calm yourself, Luca. The more time they spent under scrutiny, the greater the chance they would be pulled over for interrogation.

"No husband?"

Silvana, who had not spoken a word since they left the Masererpass, answered before he thought of a reply. "We're traveling to meet my husband, officer. He's in Milan on business." Luca glanced at Gisele's puzzled look when her mother answered, but she remained quiet.

Seemingly satisfied with her answer, the guard continued, "Car papers, please."

Luca's stomach sank as he extracted additional false documents from the glove box and handed them to the guard. Fortunately, Madame Stern's contact made certain that the car was registered in Silvana's name. To Luca's horror, the guard, with his passport and all the false documents in hand, walked around the car, stopped in front, and glanced back and forth between the car papers and the license plate. When he walked to the guardhouse, Luca fought the panic that struck him. He could not bear to watch as the guard stood in the doorway, speaking with someone inside, occasionally turning back toward him. Luca strained to hear their conversation, but they were on Silvana's side of the car, making it impossible to hear them. He sat frozen, looking forward at the closed barrier in front of him, fighting the urge to look back to see whether the men in black were still standing by the other black Köln.

Friedrich leaned forward over the front seat between Luca and Silvana. "Zio Luca, is everything—"

"Not now, Friedrich," Silvana snapped. She softened her tone. "Everything's fine. Now back to your soldiers."

Luca believed the boy had seen more than his share of soldiers checking papers and searching his mother's house, interrogating her. Luca's eyes met Silvana's before she looked back at Gisele, awake on her lap, concern showing on her small face.

Finally, the guard returned to the car. In the backseat, Friedrich barked orders to his soldiers. Did the guard's expression soften when he eyed the boy?

"How is the battle going, General…?" The guard flipped through the passports. "General Frei?"

"Very well, sir. We'll beat those bad Russians once and for all. No one can defeat our great Führer!" Luca stifled a chuckle. So young Friedrich had learned the art of deception after all.

With that, the guard handed Luca all the documents and gave a crisp Nazi salute. Luca swallowed hard and gripped the steering wheel. The young guard raised the barrier and ordered him to drive on.

With his mouth dry as cotton and his throat tight, Luca croaked a polite, "Thank you." Never would the words "Heil Hitler" cross his lips. They were through. Luca knew they faced danger in Austria and even in Italy, but the most perilous part of their journey was behind them.

Silvana, once again reprimanded by Gisele for hugging her too tightly, spoke. "Luca, I didn't want to mention it, but as you know, we have no luggage. What if he had searched the car?"

"We would not be on the Austrian side of the border, Silvana, that's what." He had not given that obvious point any consideration. Well, he had enough to worry about without that. They were through and that was all that mattered.

After they left Germany miles behind, Luca returned to the subject of Silvana's Tante Lorelei and quizzed her about her aunt's behavior since her arrival. Had she been nervous? Did she ask many questions? Did she have any unusual visitors? In Silvana's opinion, nothing appeared to be out of the ordinary. Her aunt was as warm and loving as always, Silvana said.

They drove on for another hour before stopping for lunch in a quiet, remote Gasthof. The rest of the day motoring across the bucolic countryside passed without incident until shortly after the village of Wolkersdorf on the southern side of the Hochtor tunnel. With Silvana and the children fast asleep, Luca had allowed himself for the first time that day to daydream about Doretta, about Turin. Tired and distracted, his attention drifted away. As he rounded a curve, two deer dashed across the road. Too late to stop, he swerved to miss them, hitting a deep pothole on the side of the road and then clipping a small tree.

"What was that!" Silvana asked, shaken awake by the incident.

"Some deer on the road. I swerved to miss them." Angry with himself, Luca got out to check the damage. A blown tire. Just then, a police car driving in the opposite direction up the Hochalpenstraße stopped. Once they had made it across the border, Luca was confident that, absent car trouble or a wreck, they would have an easy drive to Bolzano. And now this.

"*Was ist los?*" the older of the two Austrian policemen asked as they crossed the road toward him.

"Just a small accident, officer. Some deer—"

"Ja. Quite common along here with *outsiders* speeding down from the tunnel." Luca flinched. His emphasis on outsiders unsettled him. "Your papers, please. Where are you going?"

Having survived the border guard's scrutiny, would two deer now be their downfall? He handed the passports and car papers to the older officer while the other inspected the damage.

"Bolzano, officer. I'm going…" Luca hesitated. Again, he caught himself volunteering information.

"You won't be going anywhere on that tire," the junior officer said. "You'll have to go back to Wolkersdorf."

"No need for that. They can stay with us." Luca turned to see the kind face of a farmer who emerged from the shadows of the forest. "I'm happy to help the family, Officer Harl."

"Very good. Here." He handed Luca his papers. "Farmer Dunkel and his wife will take good care of you. *Auf Wiedersehen.*"

After a hearty supper and a night in warm beds under eiderdown covers, Luca set off for Lienz with Farmer Dunkel the next morning. A replacement tire would have to be sent from Salzburg, so for two more days and nights they enjoyed the alpine hospitality of Andreas and Clara Dunkel. Luca had to admit that traveling with the two children had been fortuitous. First the border guard, and then the middle-aged childless couple who took to Friedrich and Gisele. Having never been on a farm, the children found that unexpected days in the countryside meant two days of fun. They learned how to milk cows, fetch eggs from the henhouse, and even make butter. The time also seemed to help Silvana, although he knew that she still wondered about her Tante Lorelei.

On the third day after their escape from Germany, they were finally on their way again.

"THE FLOUR SHIPMENT HAS ARRIVED IN TRIESTE" WAS ALL GIANNI HAD TO say when he rang Lia the previous night. Trieste was their code for Bolzano. No need to give the precise details on the phone. Luca and the Becker family were safe in Italy. Gianni considered it best to drive in daylight, so they had stayed the night at a trusted friend's home in the vineyards near Trento before leaving at dawn for Turin. Shortly after midday, Daniela called to thank Lia for the gift.

"Bondì, Madama Lia. Thank you for three lovely crystal candlesticks. For something so fragile to be packed so beautifully and arrive unscathed is quite amazing." Lia detected genuine excitement in Daniela's voice. Silvana and her children were safe in Turin. Thank God.

"I'm happy to hear that, Daniela. Was the wrapping intact? Gianni meticulously packaged it."

"It was, although slightly torn. But no damage."

They made a bit of small talk before Lia hung up the phone. Slightly torn? She knew Daniela meant something had happened along the way. That explained the delay. Five days had passed since Luca had landed in Munich, two agonizing days longer than expected. What had happened? Now she waited in Asili, pacing the terrace. A walk in the vineyards would relax her. It always did on days like this. No, she would wait here. Not until she saw Luca and heard the details of the rescue would she rest easy.

She stood in her favorite spot on the terrace, watching for Gianni to drive up the lane. After the heavy rains two nights before, the skies had cleared, and the air had been washed clean. She so loved *primavera* in Asili and the rebirth of her vines. Happy sounds of Giovanna playing with her father's new truffle dog, Nebbia, drifted up from the cortile. Poor Milo. Old age came too soon for canine friends. At eleven, Giovanna reminded her more and more of Sara. She had begged her parents to let her go to school in Alba too, and Lia would love to have obliged her. Giovanna was not at all like the two middle sisters who seemed more interested in boys than books. And Sara had blossomed into an impressive young woman, a compassionate, dedicated nurse whose skills sadly might be needed for things other than delivering babies and bandaging farmers' wounds. No, times were too uncertain for Giovanna to leave Asili. One hoped her childhood would last a little longer.

In the distance, Lia's constant friend il Re stood majestically under blue skies in the afternoon light. Winter snows still clung to its steep, craggy slopes. Spring had taken hold in Langhe, but winter often reappeared without warning in the mountains. Was that the tear in the packaging Daniela had referred to? A delay of two days, all for bad weather—could it be that simple?

Luca's delay stirred painful memories of Alessandro's departure for Austria in 1915. As they stood on the platform at the Alba *stazione*, he had wrapped his arms around her and their little cherub Giulia that she held tight to her breasts. "Don't cry, carissima," he said, kissing the tears on her cheek as he stroked Giulia's head. "It won't be long before I'm back home. You'll have no time to miss me," he had assured her.

Luca's own assurances of his quick, safe return had given her no comfort. Had it been prudent to send Luca, so young and untested, on this dangerous mission? He could have turned her down, but maybe he had felt duty bound to his father's memory. She had really given him no choice. Yet even on the day of his father's burial, he had wanted to talk about the rescue work. She vowed that this would be his first and last assignment in Germany. Was it a vow she could keep? They would make good use of his legal and financial mind in the safety of Langhe. She heard the crunching of gravel on the lane into the cortile before her black Fiat came into view. Gianni had brooded when she sold the Balilla and bought a less showy car she thought more in keeping with the times. The car passed below the terrace with Gianni at the wheel and Luca slumped against the door, apparently asleep.

"Giuseppina! *Sono tornati!*" They were back. Giuseppina rushed from the kitchen, crossing herself and thanking God with each pass of her hand across her body.

"*Grazie a Dio.* Grazie a Dio," she repeated as she hurried behind Lia to the cortile below. Giuseppina was getting on in years, but she moved quickly to greet her husband. Although he had not crossed the border, transporting passengers with false identity cards within Fascist Italy was dangerous.

By the time they reached the cortile, Luca was walking about in the sunshine, stretching his long arms and wiping sleep from his eyes. His tie was askew and his handsome, hand-tailored suit, an Easter gift from his mother, was wrinkled from having been slept in for many nights.

His almost boyish, normally clean-shaven face was drawn from fatigue and covered with a days-old beard. But he gave her the smile of a triumphant warrior home from a faraway land. Giuseppina, normally as reserved as any Piemontese woman, ran to Gianni and clung to him as she wept tears of joy. Lia had to restrain her own desire to hug Luca and welcome him home almost as a mother would have. Seeing them, she felt the weight of the many lives that had been at risk to save three people, now political refugees.

"Luca, welcome back," she said as she gave him two perfunctory pecks on each cheek and squeezed his broad shoulders. She studied him, her brow narrowed. "You're exhausted, I know, but I'm anxious to hear details from you after you rest. I shall see you at six. Giuseppina, please show Luca to his room. He will stay in Asili tonight." With that, she joined Gianni, now free from Giuseppina's embrace, in the garage. Luca knew she would waste no time in getting the details about the delay from Gianni.

Luca felt as though he were sleepwalking to his room. But he breathed easier now that he was back at the farm, which had become a second home. He had absorbed Madama Lia's love for the Rio Sordo valley and sometimes stayed longer than he needed to for business.

As he lay in bed, thinking of Doretta and their chances for a life together, he remembered another Jewish woman who had stolen his heart when he was studying in Padua. The booming voice of her father when he discovered their love still echoed in his ears nearly ten years on. "Never!" he had shouted. "Never will my daughter marry a Gentile." Well, he should have known that loving the daughter of a rabbi held no future for a Catholic boy. But no one had come close to replacing Rachel in his heart. No one, until now. Yes, Doretta was Jewish, but in name only from what Madama Lia had said. After his experience in Germany hearing the Nazi's on the plane, he worried greatly for the Giordanos. He chased away the image of Doretta running for her life then drifted into a deep sleep.

At six, rested and washed up, Luca took the stairs three at a time to the sunroom for an apertivo. The evenings were still chilly, and the fireplace had been lit. Monviso was bathed in the rusty orange light of the springtime sunset. It felt good to be home again, safe in the vineyards.

To his surprise, Sara Fiore was there. No longer the lively girl who dragged him through the barnyard mud to see her baby rabbits, she had grown into a poised woman—petite like Madama Lia—without a hint of shyness or frailty.

Seeing her there next to Madama Lia, Luca was struck by the similarities between them, as if Sara was a younger (and frankly, better) version of the older woman. Yet he wondered why she had been invited to dinner. Surely, he and Madama Lia needed to have a confidential discussion.

"Buonasera, Luca," Madama Lia said as she poured him a glass of Arneis from Cecu Carbone. He learned long ago to drink whatever she gave him. She knew the farmers and their wines better, she always said. But of course she would. "You remember Sara Fiore, don't you?"

"Yes, of course. It's been a long time. Sara, you're a nurse now I hear."

"Yes, I am. I've been back in the village since I finished my studies in Alba last year."

"Dottor Fenocchio so wanted her to remain at the hospital in Alba, but she was determined to return to Barbaresco. At least I still get to see her here. Well, salute." They lightly touched glasses and followed her direction to sit.

"Luca, I'm sure you're wondering why I invited Sara to join us. Truth is, I've confided in her about our activities. I know the days are coming when our group will have to grow and organize. More refugees are coming, and will come, from Czechoslovakia and even Poland. Many of them are desperate—poor and ill, in need of medical attention."

"Luca, I was surprised too that Madama invited me," Sara said. "But Doretta Giordano is my closest friend, and her family has been kind to me. So I asked Madama Lia about the escape of her aunt and cousins. I think you're very brave, by the way."

Luca smiled at her and looked away. Brave indeed. And he had almost ruined everything because of a moment of distraction. Silvana's perfume, so much like Doretta's, had made the car smell like a garden of roses. A garden with Doretta in it. Fortunately, Silvana had not reapplied it during the journey. Still, the scent lingered in his memory.

"Thank you, Sara. I really didn't do much other than follow instructions. It was relatively uneventful. A few times I had to be creative, but it was easier than I expected."

Lia made it clear she was not in the mood for small talk. "I want to hear about your...creativity, Luca. But first, I want to you to tell us everything from the moment you arrived at Lorelei Vogel's house."

Before diving into the details of their journey, Luca took another sip of his Arneis and nibbled on a *grissino*. He had gone straight to his room when he arrived, and he was starving. Dinner, he knew, would be served at seven—still nearly an hour to go. Before he began recounting his journey, he put the glass down. Wine on an empty stomach would make him lightheaded.

"Most amazing story, Luca," Madama Lia commented after he finished speaking and paused to take a big gulp of wine. "But what happened to the car? And why were you delayed? Gianni said the front bumper was damaged."

Luca hated to deceive Madama Lia, but since Silvana had been asleep and had not seen anything, he gave in to the temptation to invent—a little—as he recounted the story. The deer, he told her, were standing in the road when he rounded a sharp bend.

"I'm sorry you worried, but with no phone at the farm, there was no way to call."

Luca's face burned. How would he explain that he ran off the road, caught up in a daydream about Doretta? He looked quickly at Sara, wondering whether she could tell the reason for his unease.

"Any further word from Silvana's zia?" Luca squirmed. He had left out the part about her exchange with Silvana when they left. "What is it, Luca? Is there anything else I should know?"

Yes, of course there was. He had not meant to omit it, but she did need to know. Luca filled in that missing piece of information and watched as Madama's face turned grim.

"How could she have known, Luca? Madame Stern sent express orders to Silvana through her intermediary about the dangers of anyone at all knowing. That is precisely what we did not want to happen."

Luca sighed deeply, once again picked up his wine glass, and drained it despite his gnawing hunger. "I know, Madama, but I don't know how to explain it. Neither does Silvana." Luca glanced at Sara sitting quietly in the chair next to him, her expression one of great compassion, her signature trait. "Silvana did everything she was told to do."

"What concerns me, Luca, is that Tante Lorelei is a member of Fritz's family, and we know how they feel about Silvana and even their own flesh and blood. How are you so sure she isn't an informant?"

"I'm not," he said, looking down, avoiding Madama Lia's eyes. "I didn't know what to do. I was quite afraid when it all poured out of Silvana. Both of us agreed we weren't sure who had more to fear. Her zia if the house had been watched and Silvana and the children had failed to return, or ourselves as we approached the border."

Luca tried to read Madama's expression. Was it anger? Concern? After a few moments of tense silence, her face lightened.

"Well, at least you're home safe. Well done, Luca."

Yes, he was pleased with his success, but he believed a guardian angel had watched over them. Nothing else explained their good fortune.

"Madame Stern will inquire for us. I believe you've had enough excitement for one lifetime. That is, until the next time, if you're needed."

Next time? Thankfully, he had pulled it off and the four of them were safely back in Piemonte, but he knew now that he would be of more use behind a desk than playing cat and mouse with the Nazis.

"*Allora, andiamo a tavola.*" With Madama's call to the table, Luca's tale was complete, and they were finally off to enjoy Giuseppina's delicious cucina. Madama Lia appeared satisfied for now. Luca knew that, while it had been a successful rescue, it had not been a perfect one. He was certain Madama Lia would quiz him further and that he would confess all in the end.

"Mi dispiace. I forgot, there is one more thing, Madama. Here's the cash you gave me." He handed her the same envelope Doretta had given him. "I had to pay for the tire, and I tried to give Farmer Dunkel some money for his troubles. He wouldn't hear of it. Unfortunately, I did have to bribe an Italian border guard. After so much worry about the Germans, in the end crossing into Italy was the problem. And to think, he claimed *my* passport was forged! It was a small price to pay."

Sara had sat quietly, seemingly enthralled with his account. He wondered what role she would play in the rescue organization Madama Lia was forming. Soon enough, he feared, he would know.

CHAPTER 20

Asili
November 1937

During summer, each rumble of thunder, each heavy rain pummeling the tin roofs of the *cantine*, triggered anxiety in Barbaresco. Summer tempests careened over the Langhe. Farmers were powerless to do anything except watch and pray when towering, deep-blue clouds massed on the horizon on hot, bright days. Nico felt guilty that his prayers for relief would mean someone else's torment; if the storm bypassed him, it would soon find another farm. Suffering was an all-too-common aftermath.

Only last year, the pearlescent clouds had darkened, unleashing egg-sized hail that beat his Nebbiolo crop to a pulp. The fruit from the current vintage was of good quality but not as plentiful as in previous years. The ice had destroyed the grapes and stripped many of the vines to the rootstocks. But much like the farmers who tended them, the Nebbiolo vines were resilient. They would regenerate and, in coming vintages, deliver bountiful harvests. The 1936 Ferragosto storm had spared Nico's Barbera vines and a few rows of Nebbiolo in the Ronchi vineyard on the other side of Barbaresco, giving him some fruit to vinify. The precious grapes of the Asili amphitheater, however, had been wiped out.

That horrible afternoon, as Nico and Madama Lia surveyed the destruction in the vineyards, she had been philosophical about the loss as she always was when Mother Nature unleashed her temper on the Langhe.

"Nico, I know how devoted you are to our vines, but it was a bountiful grain harvest in July. That is most important. The vineyards will recover, and we will again have great Nebbiolo vintages."

"And hail, Madama," Nico replied. "More hail."

"That's enough, Nico. How would we know to be thankful for the good if we hadn't suffered some loss first? I refuse to let Mother Nature defeat us. We have to work with her."

Now Nico smiled at the memory. Nothing ever seemed to undermine Madama Lia's optimism. How was it that someone to whom life had been so cruel at a young age only saw challenges, never defeat? She always gave him hope, no matter the loss. Well, as she said, that was the past. Even the shroud of dense fog that filled the Rio Sordo valley failed to dampen his spirits. Fog meant truffles in the Pora forest. Tomorrow he would take Nebbia on their first hunt of the season.

Today was the end of the harvest. Rain had come during the growing season at the optimal time and in the perfect amount. Once Francesco arrived with the last wagonload of grapes from Madama Lia's small vineyard across the valley, the only work left to be done was to make the wine. And that he truly loved.

Since his arrival, Francesco had taken to the vines as though he had been rooted in the Piemontese soil from birth. Two years earlier, Nico had turned over management of the vineyards to Francesco. Together they would decide when to prune and when to harvest, but Francesco was responsible for overseeing the day-to-day vineyard work. That gave Nico more time in the cantina and with his other crops and animals. They divided their labor with no qualms or arguments, resulting in a perfect partnership. If only Sara had treated him better when he arrived. What a partnership *that* would have been. Francesco as a son-in-law, the son he was denied, would be a blessing beyond all others. It was odd that, since parting ways with that Strega woman two years ago, Francesco had kept mostly to himself.

As he was scraping his boots off at the front door, he heard the car. Sara steered up the lane, the little Topolino skidding, splashing globs of dark gray mud everywhere. She brought the filthy car to a stop in the cortile and jumped out to greet him. "Bon-a seirà, Papà."

"Ciarea, Sara." He stepped back as she approached him for a hug. "No, Sara, look at my hands. All stained from racking today."

"Oh, Papà, when has that ever bothered me? After such a long day, I need a hug from you."

He wrapped his arms around her, lifting her from the ground with an exaggerated grunt. Sara was grateful that her papà took his houseful of daughters in stride. Unlike most Langhetti fathers, he showered his girls with affection.

She knew that he had to ignore the jokes made about him at the tavern. To Nico, daughters were not a curse although he worried about the dowries he would need to pay. He still needed a son to take over the farm, but he also needed the love and affection of each of his four daughters.

"I see the weather was too much for Zeus today."

"Not really, Papà. Zeus would have fared much better than the Topolino," she said as she grabbed her medical bag from the little Fiat. "I was worried coming home. So much mud washed over the road. But I had to see Leone Cigliuti on Bricco di Neive today. I knew, if I took Zeus, I'd be riding after sunset. I so miss the long summer days."

"You mean the long summer days when you work many more hours than you should?" Nico admired her headstrong convictions, even her inability to say no to someone in need, but sometimes it was too much.

"Sara, what took you so long?" Giovanna called from the open door, hands on hips in the habit of their mother and, sometimes, Sara.

Hungry and exhausted, Sara pulled her sister toward the heady aromas of Luigia's cooking in the kitchen. There had been no time for lunch. The salami and bread signora Cigliuti had given her, although delicious, only made her hungrier.

"Bon-a seirà, Mamma." Luigia stood at the putagè, its belly filled with a roaring fire. Two large pots on the flat top of the iron stove spewed delicious aromas into the room.

"What smells so good?" Sara held back her hair and leaned over one bubbling pot, inhaling the steam that rose from the hearty autumn dish. "Bollito! Oh, how did you know I needed something warm and filling tonight? *Che nebbia*!"

"*Pranzo della vendemmia*! But for dinner tonight. I didn't want to wait until Sunday to have it. We need to celebrate the harvest early, especially after last year. Some meat and broth will do us good."

"And *cugnà*!" Sara peeked into the bubbling pot of cooking grape must, hazelnuts from the Capra farm in Alta Langa, and apples from their orchards. The marmalade was one of her favorite harvest treats—enjoyed with the Roccaverano cheese her nonna Beatrice sent up to Barbaresco with the hazelnuts. She knew that it was one of Francesco's favorites too.

"Francesco brought me a pail of Nebbiolo must this morning," Luigia said, as if overhearing Sara's thoughts. "I could tell it was a hint for me to make a new batch. That Sicilian boy has become more Piemontese than many of our boys, don't you think?"

Sara ignored the question. Francesco's height and shy demeanor certainly appealed to the Piemontese girls, and many sought his attention at church or in the mercato. Yet he seemed oblivious to the hearts he made flutter in Langhe. "Where is Francesco, Papà? I didn't see the cartun outside."

"He's not back yet," the little guardian of the house proclaimed. "I've been waiting for him all afternoon!"

"Where was he today?"

"He took Romeo early this morning," Nico replied, "for the vineyard next to Villa delle Rose. Those were the last grapes to be harvested."

Giovanna wandered over to the window and pressed her forehead against the glass. "But, Papà," she said. "Romeo's right here. What's he doing loose?" She ran outside as the horse came to a stop at the barn. "Papà! Come quick. Romeo's alone!" Giovanna shrieked. "The cartun! It's gone…" She ran back to the house, shouting, "Papà…oh Papà, hurry!"

Nico ran outside and found the exhausted horse nosing the closed barn door. Pieces of broken wagon dangled from the harness. Nico grabbed the mud-soaked reins off the ground.

"Easy, Romeo, easy," Nico said, running his hands along the horse's hot, trembling neck. "You came home to warn us, didn't you? What happened now?"

Romeo's face was splattered with mud, his left flank nearly covered, but the right side seemed mostly clean. Such a stout draft horse, used to pulling heavy wagons at a slow pace, yet now breathed heavily, his bright red nostrils flaring. Blood oozed through the thick mud on his left hindquarters. Only a broken shaft would have caused such a gash. Nico knew the wagon had rolled. But where?

"Francesco…where are you, Francesco?" Nico whispered as he wrapped his arms around the horse's neck. Giovanna, standing in the doorway, saw her father's face and covered her mouth. "Giovanna. Call Sara. And tell Maria and Letizia to come quickly."

Before Giovanna could turn, Sara rushed past, draping her saddlebag filled with medical supplies over her shoulders. She had seen everything from the kitchen window. She knew well the conditions of the roads that day. "I'm here, Papà. I'll take Zeus and try to follow Romeo's trail."

She paused then, seeming to calm herself, and looked back over her shoulder at her sobbing sister. "Gio, back in the house. Be brave. Do as Papà says." She and her father exchanged a knowing glance, and together they went into the barn to saddle Zeus. The surefooted gelding was a far better option than the skittish Topolino that twice had stranded her in the past month. While Nico readied her tack, she threw her saddlebag over Zeus's back, and was about to pull him from the stall when she saw him flinch. She leaned her forehead against the big horse's shoulder and breathed against his bristly neck, fighting the rising panic. *No*, she prayed to the Virgin Mother.

As she gathered her reins, Nico came up behind her and squeezed her shoulder. "He could be anywhere along between here and Villa delle Rose. Or…" He looked away and dabbed at his brow with his kerchief. "He's most likely off the road, Sara, down the hill on the right-hand side." He imagined the wagon teetering on the edge, rolling down the embankment. Was Francesco thrown clear? Or was he lying trapped beneath the wagon?

"Ride slowly. It's almost dark. I'll be along behind you in the truck. I need Letizia to tend to Romeo's wounds. Where is that girl?"

"Bring some lanterns. And ask Mamma for some blankets and towels. And fill a damigiana with water. We don't know what we'll find." With that, she mounted Romeo and pulled the rein sharply. "And Papà? Send Maria to fetch dottor Costa. He was in the village today. We'll need him."

THE FADING LIGHT AND BLANKET OF FOG MADE IT NEARLY IMPOSSIBLE TO see beyond Zeus's nose. She loosened the reins and let him extend his neck to find the way as she tried to scan the side of the steep embankment into the vineyards. "Francesco!" she repeatedly called. With each step Zeus took, her throat tightened. Had she missed him? "Francesco!"

At times, the fog toyed with her and thinned a bit. But as she descended into the valley, it mercilessly enveloped them. Sara couldn't be sure where she was or how far they had come. This valley was her home, and she knew every inch of this road, but she was lost, unable to navigate in the sea of fog. She thought she might be near the turn up the hill to the Conti di Silva farm that lay at the bottom of the Martinenga amphitheater. If she could find it, she would ask the farmhands for help in the search, but she feared she had missed the turn. As she pulled Zeus to a stop to get her bearings, the fog thinned ever so slightly and, as though it were an apparition, a sign appeared: Martinenga. The turn to the farm! Soon she could see not only the sign but also a few paces in front of her. To the right, she spotted a place where the mud had been disturbed, and twisting, large skidding marks. Francesco!

Sara jumped down and sprinted to the spot with loyal Zeus trotting behind her. The heavy rains the previous night had washed soil from the vineyard across the road, creating a quagmire of ankle-deep mud. No surprise the draft horse had fallen.

"Francesco!" She called.

It was nearly dark. She felt the cold fog on her face and prayed it would not be Francesco's shroud. She removed her saddlebag and thrust her hand inside, feeling for her flashlight. Don't panic, she repeated to herself when she realized it wasn't there. She would have to manage in the dark until her papà arrived with lanterns.

Long ago, she had taught Zeus to stand like a statue when untied. It took a while to train him as he always followed her, nuzzling for treats. But it was for moments like this when she needed to leave him ground-tied, that she had persevered. Sara knew that, when her papà arrived, driving slowly, he would see the horse and know to stop. The embankment was not very steep across from the di Silva farm entrance, so she carefully picked her way through the dead, tall grass from the spot where she was certain Romeo had fallen. After a few steps, her hands no longer brushed against the grass, which had been flattened as though a giant had walked through. Having only taken a few tentative steps in the deep mud, her hands in front, feeling in the darkness, Sara stumbled against what she had feared most, the overturned cartun. "Francesco!" she called. No reply.

She dropped to her knees, sinking into the mud that sucked her in. The heavy saddlebag, slung around her neck and filled with medical supplies she would be too filthy to use, added to her burden. As she crawled around the perimeter of the wagon, she struggled to keep her balance as she groped for signs of life. He was nowhere to be found. She was on the far side of the wagon. Nothing. Was he thrown clear? With every step, her hands and knees drove recently harvested grapes into the mud. When she slid her left hand through the mud to find her way out from the cartun, Sara felt a hand, upturned in the mud. The fingers twitched as she gripped it.

"*Madòna*! Francesco!"

She ran her hand up the arm. A shoulder, a face. Warm! She threw the saddlebag down and moved closer to him.

"Oh, Francesco!" She placed her fingers on his throat, checking for a pulse. It was there, weak. "Can you hear me?"

A groan, a reply, barely a whisper, "Sara?"

"Francesco, caro mio." He was alive. He needed her. But the realization that she might lose him here in the dark without so much as gazing into his green eyes again made her freeze. Oh, Sara, you fool! She gasped, fighting a sob, but then heard a calm voice saying, *No. Not now.* She had work to do.

Sara deftly traced his face with her fingers then through his thick hair, touching his scalp, feeling for any wounds. Nothing. Alone in the dark, no one to help her, and fighting to keep panic at bay, Sara methodically went about checking the rest of his body, first brushing away the bunches of grapes covering him. She ran her hands across his broad, muscular chest and checked his other arm, his fingers twitching weakly in response to her touch, then over his torso to his legs. He winced as she pressed lightly on his left thigh. She reached across him, feeling the underside of his thigh. Her hands touched torn cloth. Wet torn cloth. A small piece of wood, a branch or even a piece of the cartun, had impaled his leg. She sat up again and continued her examination down his thighs, his knees… wood. Francesco's lower legs were pinned beneath the overturned cartun.

Sara gripped his hand and shook it. "Francesco, if you can hear me, squeeze my hand or wiggle your fingers." He curled his fingers ever so slightly, then extended them, twice. "Now signal to me you feel your legs." She waited. No response. "Francesco, you must help me." He closed his fingers around her hand—a good sign. It appeared that his back had not been broken.

Voices! Her papà wasn't alone. "Papà! I'm here Papà!" she shouted.

She reached to steady herself on the wagon and pulled herself up. Daggers of light, growing brighter by the second, sliced through the fog. "Papà. Francesco's here and badly injured."

"Sara, I don't see you. Keep calling…" Nico made his way through the sea of mud and grapes and rounded the corner of the wagon.

Three short, strapping men followed him, lanterns lighting their faces. When her father held up his lantern, Sara saw for the first time Francesco's dire predicament.

"My God! Sara. Is he alive? Only by chance, I saw the road up to Martinenga. Look, I've brought help from the di Silva farm."

After struggling in the mud, slipping and sliding as they fought to maintain their footing, the men managed to right the wagon. Francesco yelped as he tried to move.

Again, Sara knelt next to him. "Lie still. Don't move. The pain is a good sign, but we must get you out of this mud and back to the house." Francesco was beginning to shiver. Shock was setting in. She needed to get him home to Asili. Driving to the hospital in Alba with the treacherous road conditions was unthinkable.

"Sara," Francesco once again croaked her name. "I'm sorry, Sara. I was…"

She brushed his hair back off his forehead and met his eyes that searched hers. What was he trying to say? It wasn't important. "Francesco, be still. Save your strength."

One of the men, who had disappeared, came now with a long board he had brought from Martinenga, and laid it alongside Francesco.

When Sara lifted his left arm, he once again yelped. Broken. No blood. Good, not a compound fracture. She carefully straightened it and set it down along his side.

Now that she was certain he had not suffered a spinal injury, it was time to move him out of the filthy conditions and get him home to Asili.

"Papà, we must get him off this wet ground."

With one man at each end, they transferred Francesco to the board and Sara swaddled him in the blankets Luigia had sent. He lost consciousness. No time to lose. Once he was settled in the truck bed, Sara climbed up and knelt beside him. All through her frantic work, the cold had not gripped her. It did now. Her hands were tingling, numbness setting in, and, like Francesco, she shivered.

Nico mounted Zeus and they turned for home. The fog was thinner, so they traveled faster than before and were soon back in Asili. When they arrived in the cortile, Giovanna dashed out first, followed by Letizia and Luigia, wiping her hands on her apron.

"Sara, Maria rode to town on Madama's plow horse to fetch dottor Costa. He should be here any minute if he was in the village."

"Thank you, Mamma. It is too dangerous to drive to the hospital tonight. We have to stabilize him here." In the dim light of the cortile, Sara could see that the color had drained from Francisco's face. His shivering had subsided on the trip home as she stretched out next to him to share her body heat. She barked orders to the farm hands who had been like silent guardian angels since they arrived with her papà.

"Letizia, show them to my room. Gio, run ahead, switch on the lights, and pull down the covers of my bed. It will be easier to tend to him there, and he will be warmer."

Giovanna stood behind the truck with her eyes transfixed on Francesco.

"Gio! Go!" Sara growled. "And stoke the stufetta in my room. Now!"

As the men carefully slid the board out of the truck, a familiar car pulled into the cortile and stopped next to the truck.

"Cesare...dottor Costa." Sara was giddy with relief to see the new village doctor, who had come to Barbaresco after Easter to replace his uncle. Young, handsome, and educated in Turin, Sara always wondered why he had decided to come to a village like theirs. Her mind spun. They had spent a lot of time together and had grown close. Now, she could barely meet his eyes. "Thank you for coming, dottor Costa. The cartun overturned, and Francesco was pinned underneath." She continued to brief him while they followed the men and Francesco into the house. "He has feeling in his legs, but the puncture wound looks deep...."

"We'll take a look at him. I could barely see coming down from the village. We'll stabilize him here and get him to the hospital in the morning."

After they transferred him to her bed, Sara shooed away all the family except for her mother.

"Sara, look at you," Luigia said. "You can't tend to Francesco like that. Go wash up. Take something light to eat. I'll get him ready for the *dottore*."

While Sara changed and dottor Costa prepared his instruments and medical supplies on the small night table next to the narrow bed, Luigia laid a sheet over Francesco's naked body. Despite the fire burning in the stufetta, his violent shivers returned.

Giovanna, her voice quivering, called to Luigia from the hall. "Will he live, Mamma?"

Luigia knew it was better not to deceive her. She was old enough to deal with the pain of loss, the longing for a loved one taken from her too soon. This was Langhe. Life was hard, often cruel. And women had to be hard as well to survive.

"We'll know more later, Giovanna. Dottor Costa and Sara will care for him. Now go. It's late."

Sara met her tearful sister at the door. Seeing the child so shaken, small, and alone reminded her of the day she said good-bye to nonna Mirella when she wasn't much older than Giovanna. Sara pulled Giovanna close and embraced her.

"Gio, go now and pray as zia Luce taught you to do. Isn't Francesco here because God answered your prayers?" Giovanna looked into Sara's eyes, searching for reassurance. Before Sara turned to face the dreadful scene in her bed, she said her own short, silent prayer to the Virgin Mother. *Mother of Jesus, please help us care for Francesco. And help me to be strong.*

Luigia had long ago learned the basics of nursing—first from her sister Luciana and then from Sara—and she was a great help as they changed the sheets soaked with blood and dirty water. Each time they moved him, Francesco yelped. A patient in agony wasn't new to Sara, but she felt Francesco's cries in her own chest.

Dottor Costa moved between the women who prepared Francesco's leg so he could remove the branch. Infection from such a deep puncture wound presented the greatest threat to Francesco.

Despite the dose of morphine dottor Costa gave him earlier, Francesco cried out when the branch was pulled and Sara cleaned the deep wound. Then the dottore, speaking softly to Francesco, splinted his left arm and leg.

"That's all we can do for him here, Sara. Hopefully we can get him to the hospital first thing in the morning."

Later, Luigia stopped at the door and glanced at the scene. Francesco slept. Sara stood over him, gazing at him intently, her hand on his forearm. Behind her, Cesare Costa packed up his medical bag. Luigia stole out of the room.

"Sara, you were incredible tonight. I'm proud of your work and your cool head." Cesare placed his hands on her shoulders and squeezed her. She spun around, buried her face in his chest and released the tears she had bottled up inside.

Though sedated, Francesco struggled to open his eyes, if only a little. In the dim light, he saw Cesare Costa wrapping his arms tightly around Sara. His Sara. Or perhaps not. Sleep—and escape from the nightmare—finally overtook him.

CHAPTER 21

Alba
Days later in November 1937

"Sara." The soft voice sounded far away. Was it nonna Mirella again? She startled awake and slowly shook her arm, which had fallen asleep. Since she found Francesco—days ago now, although she didn't know how many—she had spent every night sitting beside him, first on the stool, listening to his labored breathing that first night in Asili, and then on the hard metal chair at the hospital. The first night had been the worst, of course. After he assured her that Francesco would sleep through the night, Cesare Costa had asked her to see him to the door. The house was quiet but for Nebbia sleeping by the warm stufa, yipping in his sleep. When Cesare leaned to kiss her good-night at the door, something she had enjoyed as recently as the previous evening, she placed her hand on his chest. This was all too confusing.

Cesare had been kind to her, she enjoyed being with him, and he was the first man she had kissed. She knew what he wanted from her; she only had to give the word. Now, Cesare nodded and said that she must be very tired. She looked away, unable to meet his eyes. He cupped her face in his warm hands and pressed his lips to her brow as he bade her good-night.

Back upstairs in her room with Francesco, Sara settled onto the stool next to his bed, on alert in the dim light for any signs of distress. Finally, exhaustion overcame her, and she slumped forward, resting her head close to Francesco's splinted arm as she drifted off to sleep.

FRANCESCO'S FERAL SCREAMS SHORTLY BEFORE DAWN WOKE THE ENTIRE household. Sara sprang from the stool and grabbed the lantern. Luigia rushed in and helped Sara restrain him, but he was delusional from morphine. The more he thrashed, the more intense his pain and his strength. At one point, he flung his left arm, landing a sharp blow to Sara's face with his wooden splint.

Sara screamed, "Papà! Come quick. I need you."

Nico burst through the door, his thick hair askew, and still fastening his pants.

"Help us. Here, Papà, you've got him." Sara rushed to the table to prepare the morphine. This was her fault. She should have given him the shot hours earlier.

Within seconds of the opioid entering his blood stream, his thrashing stopped, and Francesco went limp. The crisis was over, for now. Sara did not need to take his temperature to know that a fever had set in. His skin burned. Infection from the puncture wound and the danger of sepsis were their greatest fears. Even the smallest wound, if infected, could be life threatening.

"Sara, your cheek. You're bleeding."

"I'm fine, Papà. Really I am."

When all was quiet and her parents went back to bed, Sara sat listening as the roosters began their morning opera throughout the valley. Francesco was calm, dreamy, and smiled at her when she put the cool compresses to his forehead. At first light, they would finally take him to the hospital in Alba. Sara worried they had little time to spare, but Nico said it was too dangerous to drive before sunrise. Luigia brought her a caffelatte, and told her, sharply now, to let her tend to her wounded cheek. Although the cut was superficial, Luigia was certain she would have a black eye. Nursing, Luigia had seen with both her sister and daughter, was a hazardous profession.

At the hospital, dottor Costa gave Francesco *chinino* to drink to subdue the fever. Sadly, he had little else in his arsenal against infection, and it was nothing more than his nonno had used decades ago. Until the infection was under control, sepsis was their biggest fear. Cesare had used newly developed antibiotics as a battlefield surgeon in Ethiopia in 1935, but the miracle drugs were not available for civilian use, at least not in the poverty-ridden Langhe countryside. All they could do was clean the wound with a *spirito*, a witch's brew of ninety-percent alcohol, and *acqua borica*. And prayer that Luciana offered, both on her knees on the hard floor beside his bed and as she went about her duties on the ward. That, Cesare came to believe, was their only hope. He knew of no physicians who did not believe in prayer. He, too, whispered a prayer, not only for Francesco. For Sara too. Throughout the two days and nights since Francesco had been hospitalized, Sara only left his bedside to tend to her necessities and to fetch supplies and medicines. She would soon break under the emotional and physical strain. Anyone would.

"Sara, you must rest." Someone gently touched her shoulder. She gazed at the troubled, but loving face of the woman who had given her a home away from home during those difficult years of school in Alba—the woman she was certain had arranged for her education though how she afforded it still baffled her.

"Zia Luce, I'm all right. Truly I am." Sara never deceived her zia, not intentionally. Yet she knew zia Luce saw through her. During the night, she had chanced a glimpse of herself in the mirror over the sink in the nurses' changing room. An unfamiliar face stared back at her. Sallow skin, no longer creamy, with a touch of bronze from long days in the saddle. She traced the shadows like dark half-moons under her bloodshot eyes, the deep purple bruise that was turning yellow. Each time she blinked, the underside of her eyelids scratched across her eyes like sandpaper. Her hair was dark with grease and haphazardly pinned atop her head under her headdress. She knew zia Luce saw it all, as well as the hollowness she felt inside. If she lost Francesco, there would be nothing left.

"Sara, I know quite well how you feel." But Luciana wondered whether she really did. She had never had a great love like this, a young love. She couldn't fathom God's ways. Why did it take a near tragedy like this for her niece to open her heart? Luciana had always prayed for Sara's enlightenment, but this was not how she had envisioned it would happen. *Dear Lord, please let him live. Let them live as one.*

Luciana walked up beside her beloved niece and placed her hands on her slumped shoulders, surprised by how thin and delicate they were. "But you are a nurse, Sara, an excellent nurse. And that means you must care for yourself as prudently as you do your patients, particularly *this* patient." No response. She knew it was time to take charge for the sake of both Francesco and Sara.

Luciana straightened and folded her hands. "Sara, I am sorry to say this to you, but you must go now. Dottor Costa and I believe your health is suffering. We see it, and"—she paused to choose her words carefully—"we are concerned your judgment and skill *may* become impaired due to exhaustion." May become? Luciana already believed Sara was teetering on the edge of collapse.

"No! I won't leave him." Sara jerked away from Luciana's touch, forgetting for a moment who was scolding her. Nothing would pull her away from

Francesco until the crisis had passed—until their eyes met the way they had that awful night, the way she had prayed for ever since.

"You have no choice, Sara. It's enough that I have one seriously ill patient from Barbaresco. I don't need two." Unbeknownst to Sara, dottor Costa had entered the cubicle. He nodded at Luciana and handed her a file.

"You don't understand, dottor…" Sara was near tears and found herself barely able to speak.

"I do, Sara, I do. I understand far more than you realize."

Sara glanced up at him, wondering. He had been kind but distant these last days. Did he see what she had tried to hide?

Luciana saw that something had passed between them, but she preferred not to think about it. "Sara, there's an extra bed at the end of the ward. I've prepared it for you, and there is something light for you to eat on the nightstand. Go now. I'll stay with Francesco and call you immediately if anything changes."

A scowl deepened the lines on Sara's wan face. She rose from her chair, but lightheaded from lack of sleep and nourishment, she swayed. Dottor Costa caught her about the waist. "Let me help."

She balked, shaking loose from Cesare as though he had shocked her with his hand. "No, no thank you. I'm all right," she said as she regained her balance and smoothed her uniform. "Quite all right."

Francesco moaned as he moved against the traction wires connected to his left leg. Sara turned away from Luciana and dottor Costa and fumbled with the thermometer beside the bed. "It's time for me to check his vital signs. And he is due for more morphine and chinino. The quinine has been helping his fever," she said more to herself than those who sought to tear her away from her duties.

"I can handle that, Sara," Luciana said as she took the thermometer from Sara's shaking hand. "Now, you *must* go! The morphine will send him back into a deep sleep, far from his pain." Luciana clasped Sara's arm and led her away from Francesco's bed, closing the privacy curtain behind her. Rarely one to give in, Sara was unaccustomed to accepting defeat. She shuffled to the far end of the ward. The bed Luciana had prepared was far too comfortable for her. The food held no interest. Penance was all she sought, but sleep overcame her, releasing her for a while from the nightmare she was living.

"SARA! COME QUICK." WAS IT NONNA MIRELLA CALLING HER AGAIN TO COME in from the vineyards? She wanted to stay and view the sunset beyond the mountains. Rarely did she disobey her nonna, but the brilliant shades of orange and purple over the regal king of the mountains were entrancing. Hurried footsteps. "Sara!" Why was nonna Mirella shaking her? "Come now," Luciana ordered. She rolled on her back, blinked hard, and saw zia Luce's face, deep lines of concern etched in her otherwise smooth complexion.

"What's happened?" Fear gripped her throat and strangled her words. "Zia…"

But Luciana was rushing through the ward toward Francesco's bed. Disoriented, Sara leapt from the bed and struggled to follow Luciana. What she saw took her breath away.

"Sara, where were you?" Francesco asked, barely above a whisper. "I was waiting." Francesco! The spark of life had returned to his green eyes.

Joyous tears filled her own eyes as she rushed to his bedside. She touched his forehead that for the first time in days wasn't burning from fever. "Francesco, you're awake. Finally." Luciana stood on the other side of his bed, wiping her own eyes. "When, zia Luce? When did he awaken?"

"Just now, his fever broke. Dottor Costa believes the crisis has passed." Luciana crossed herself and kissed the fingers of her right hand. "He still has a struggle ahead, but he will live. He *will* live, Sara." Again, she swept her right hand over the four corners of the cross and whispered, "Amen."

Their prayers had been answered. Sara had to stop herself from dropping to the bed, next to Francesco, and burying her face in his chest.

"It's good to see both of you awake. These past eight hours were not easy for him."

Sara looked sharply at Cesare Costa, standing at the end of the bed. "Eight hours? Difficult?" She narrowed her eyes and stood with her hands her hips. "Suor Luciana," she said in her deepest voice, "you promised to wake me if his status changed."

Luciana lowered her eyes, acknowledging that she had broken a promise. If Francesco had succumbed while Sara slept nearby, she never would have forgiven her. Luciana would not have forgiven herself. "I did try, Sara. But we believed it best to let you sleep. There was nothing you could do."

"Sara," Francesco's words caught in his throat as he tried to reach for her, but the plaster on his arm restrained him. His dry, cracked lips turned upward in a weak smile. "I'm all right now. Cara, you can't always be in charge." Sara saw that Luciana, her dear sweet zia Luce, suppressed a grin. They all knew her so well. Too well.

"Sit by me, please, Sara."

"Not now, Francesco. Let her freshen up and have something to eat. She'll come to you soon."

Sara looked down at the uniform she had donned days ago. What a sight she must be! What did they all think of her? What did Cesare think? She looked for him, but he had gone.

Not able to stop herself, she bent and kissed Francesco's forehead. But he was already drifting off, the edges of his mouth still curled up.

Over the next week, Sara remained in Alba with Luciana but worked long hours at the hospital, always caring for Francesco thanks to the kindness of one of the other nurses who relieved her in the village. In those days, she had time to sit beside him and hold his hand. She asked him questions she had never bothered with before—especially about his life before coming to Piemonte. She wanted to know everything—most of all, why he came to them. Luciana and even little Giovanna always spoke of Divine Providence. Now, she, too, believed that the hand of God had been at play. Both she and Francesco had been blessed with someone of deep faith in their lives, someone who believed that they were meant for something other than the poverty-stricken farming life into which they had been born.

For all the hours of talk, however, neither had professed feelings for the other. She loved Francesco. But did he love her or was he merely grateful to her for saving him? And what of Cesare, who had told her more than once that he loved her? Never was she able to say it back to him, although in recent weeks her feelings for Cesare had deepened. The passage of time had not resolved her confusion. Were it not for Francesco's accident, she might have walked with Cesare into a conventional life in town, and honor would have prevented her from ever opening her heart to Francesco. Now she knew that could never be.

Francesco remained bedridden for two weeks after the accident, although he was slowly improving. Sara thought it a good time to leave on the morning train to Barbaresco and return later in the day. The mudslide that had blocked the tracks had been cleared, and she had so much to tell her mamma. Zia Luce would watch over Francesco while she spent the day in Asili. And she would thank the three wonderful men at Martinenga. How clever they had been to bring the board on which to transport Francesco. How awful she had been to them that night—Papà, too. Dear Papà. She missed him. Only once in the early days had he come to see her, unable to take more time away from the farm. Would Francesco have lived if he had not thought to bring help and the lanterns? Cesare said that, in the cold, wet conditions, he could have succumbed to shock.

Sara decided to walk home from the Barbaresco stazione. She had sequestered herself in the hospital for two weeks, and the cold air and sunshine invigorated her. During her absence from Asili, winter had arrived early. Two heavy snowfalls had blanketed the vineyards, dropping over a foot of snow that, when melted, would leave a reserve of water deep in the ground to help the vines through the hot summer months.

She stopped at the site where she had discovered Francesco. The snow that had purified the land had hidden all evidence of a struggle. A white mantle, not a shroud, covered the land. The last time she had seen the valley was that dawn when they loaded Francesco into the back of her papà's truck for the bumpy ride to Alba. Would he return to Asili? She wondered when ambulances, a common sight in the big cities, would finally arrive in Langhe. Few people had cars, and private trucks were even scarcer. Nico had done well, and they were lucky to have the truck. But the journey in the cold, damp air across the muddy roads had been hard on Francesco. After covering him with a down comforter and a woolen blanket on top, Sara had propped his injured leg on cushions and pillows.

The day passed quickly, much of it filled with eating, especially her mamma's autumn cucina, always like medicine for her soul. She was surprised to learn that Giovanna had chosen that day to visit a friend in the village. Sara missed her, and knew that she would want to hear how Francesco was faring. More puzzling were her papà's comments about the cartun harness.

Once he had cleaned the mud from the leather, he discovered that part of it had been cut, but only partially. The rest appeared torn. He suspected that as Romeo began the gradual climb from the valley floor, pulling the heavy wagonload of grapes, the harness had broken and the cartun rolled backward and off the road. The axel was broken, which Nico believed was why the wagon had rolled. Why hadn't Francesco jumped off? The thought crossed her mind that someone may have tampered with the harness. But that seemed ridiculous. It was all very puzzling. She would ask Francesco about it later, although he said that his memory was as foggy as the night had been.

It was nearly the end of visiting hours when Sara returned to the hospital. She changed into her uniform and rushed toward the ward, still tucking her hair under her cap. Then she heard a voice, a girl shouting behind the privacy curtain in Francesco's cubicle. Sara pushed past visitors lingering in the hallway and craning their necks. She flung the curtain open.

Gio, her face crimson and her eyes on fire, was staring down the Fascist policewoman.

"Get out! Leave him alone!" Little Giovanna stood between the loathsome woman who towered over her and her big brother. "Get out!" Cinzia Strega, the zealous Fascist youth, was now a policewoman. She had come far too close.

"Gio! Be quiet. What's happened?"

Sara rushed to check on Francesco who, oddly enough, appeared to be asleep. His morphine doses were still high enough to induce sleep, but she was surprised that Giovanna's screaming had not roused him. Instinctively, she checked his pulse. Normal. Where was zia Luce? Had she not heard the commotion? Sara stood between Francesco's guardian angel and the woman whose spiteful eyes had tortured her dreams since first seeing them outside the church in Barbaresco years ago. The woman had slyly advanced several inches toward her.

"What are you doing here, Cinzia?" Sara demanded, struggling to keep her voice calm and even. Although the woman had never harmed her, nor had they ever exchanged a word, Sara would not address her as signorina Strega nor acknowledge her title as a police officer.

Cinzia snapped the privacy curtains closed. "There. That's better. I heard about Francesco's misfortune, signorina Fiore." She seemed to spit out Sara's name, and her lips curled.

Sara eyed the Beretta pistol holstered below the ample left breast. The Fascist uniform itself was intimidating, but this was just Cinzia.

"Visiting hours are over. As you can see, Francesco is asleep."

"Yes, well. Another time," she hissed. "Another time."

"No, Cinzia. There won't be another time." Sara spat her words and pushed Giovanna behind her, holding her forearm.

Cinzia scrutinized the long, red-lacquered nails of her left hand. "Signorina Fiore...Sara, if I may." She approached, coming too close. Sara pushed Giovanna further behind her, though the girl was struggling to get in front. Cinzia seemed to be examining her face, her cut, and black eye. "Who would hurt such a pretty face?"

Fear froze Sara in place. Cinzia eyed Sara's flat chest made more so by her heavy cape. "Such a little girl. Not much of a woman, are you?" Cinzia reached out as if to touch her face but instead grazed her neck with her nails.

Just then, Luciana parted the privacy curtain. "Zia Luce!" Giovanna cried as she darted from behind Sara and ran to embrace her zia.

"What is going on here?" Luciana demanded. "Who are you? Come away from my niece! And Gio! What on earth are you doing here?"

Still looking at Sara, Cinzia straightened the collar of her cape and slowly pulled her hand away.

"Nothing, sister. I was just saying good-bye to your *little* niece. Francesco and I have been friends for years. What a shock to hear about the unfortunate accident that nearly took his…life. Well, sisters, carry on."

As soon as Cinzia left, Sara doubled over as if kicked in the stomach, fighting the urge to retch, her breath coming in gasps. She swayed, and Luciana grabbed her and pushed her onto the chair beside Francesco's bed.

"Giovanna, run to the nurse's station. Quick. Tell them to call dottor Costa. I don't believe he's left for Barbaresco yet."

Giovanna was off in a flash, her footsteps resounding as she ran through the ward. Luciana unbuttoned Sara's heavy wool cape. Her face had turned ghostly white and she had broken out in a sweat. Violent shivers racked her body. Luciana feared that her niece was reacting to something that Luciana had no idea how to treat. Where was dottor Costa? All Luciana could do was kneel and take Sara into her arms, rhythmically rubbing her back in an effort to calm her.

After a few minutes, Sara's shivering eased and her breathing slowed. Luciana sat back on her heels and held Sara's tormented face between her hands. "Sara. Please. You must tell me. Who was that awful woman?"

Wide-eyed and pale, Sara remained silent, her eyes fixed on something only she could see in the distance. The witch's spell was still upon her. Francesco stirred.

Giovanna returned, winded, her cheeks bright red. "She's gone. I didn't see her anywhere."

"But where is dottor Costa, Giovanna?"

"I didn't see him, zia Luce. The nurse said she would find him."

"Gio, pour a glass of water for Sara, please. And tell me, what happened? Do you know that woman?" Luciana turned her full attention on her young niece. "And later, Giovanna Constantina Fiore, you have some explaining to do about how you got here today."

Giovanna knew she was in trouble, but to her it was worth it to have caught that woman. There was no telling what she might have done to Francesco.

"Yes, I do know, zia." Giovanna's voice quivered from the vision of that woman next to Francesco, touching him. "Her name is Cinzia Strega." Knowing that she was the only one to have seen what happened, she continued, confident that the story would spare her punishment. "Zia Luce, when I came in, she was sitting on the chair next to Francesco, leaning over him, and stroking his hair. And she touched his face—you know, that place where he has a little scar?" The tremor in her voice returned, and she looked down. "I heard her say mean things to him—mean things about Sara."

"Such as…?"

Giovanna ran to Sara and wrapped her arms around her. "Sara, I won't let her hurt you. She said you would pay. For what, Sara?"

"Gio, is that you?" Francesco's voice was thick as he struggled to focus on the scene before him.

"Francesco! That mean woman was here."

Francesco's eyes opened wide. She *had* been there. He thought it a morphine-induced nightmare. But it was real. And that meant that Giovanna's screams were real.

"What's the trouble, suor Luciana?" Dottor Costa appeared, confused by the scene, and especially by Sara, who sat with her hair disheveled, her face wan. "Sara?"

"It's all right, dottor," Luciana assured him. "Francesco had an unwelcome visitor—someone who must not be allowed in again, even if she is claiming to see another patient."

"But what does that have to do with Sara?"

Luce moved away to allow dottor Costa to examine Sara. "Can you tell me what happened? Sara?"

She finally spoke though her voice sounded distant—not her own. "A woman," was all she would say as she continued staring past them as though on alert for the witch's return.

"Her pulse is rapid. She's still anxious." He moved on to check Francesco who had remained strangely quiet. "Do you know that woman, Francesco?"

"I—I must have fallen asleep after my last shot."

Unsatisfied with his answer, Cesare turned to Luciana. "I would like to know more about what happened, suor Luciana. Is that woman a danger to Francesco? We should check the visitor registry."

"Come, dottor Costa, let me explain what I know. I believe Giovanna can tell us more." Luciana led the doctor and Giovanna away after giving Francesco a pointed look. She closed the curtain, tugging it all the way to the wall.

Days ago, Sara had placed her chair on Francesco's right side, his good side. Often, he took her hand, which she willingly gave. But now she pulled back, unable to meet Francesco's eyes.

"Sara, please, what did Cinzia do to you? It had to have been her. What did she say?" Silence. "Sara, please. Look at me." He had never known Sara to be frightened. Though he could not remember much from that night, he did recall her eyes, her loving eyes, as she worked feverishly to care for him that night. Now she seemed terrified and also dazed.

Her quavering voice came softly as she stared at her knotted hands in her lap. "Threats. All threats. Though not in so many words."

Francesco understood. It had been years since Cinzia had lashed out at him, leaving a faint scar, a constant reminder of a recklessness that led to this need to protect Sara. Had she come to harm him? Had Cinzia planned also to strike at her?

Sara looked up and finally seemed to see him, tears welling in her eyes. She took a deep breath and finally said the words. "*Ti amo*. Ti amo, Francesco."

She fell upon him, buried her head against his chest where she felt protected, and wept. But her tears now were from fear, and that fear and worry eclipsed her joy that he had recovered. Francesco held her close, stroking her hair, as he had wanted often to do, until her weeping subsided and her body released its tension as she lay across his chest. The nearness warmed him.

"Sara, carissima mio, ti amo." He lifted her head and studied her face, her eyes that bewitched him from the moment he first saw her. "*Ti ho sempre amato, ti amerò per l'eternità!* Sara, cara, there has never been a time I didn't love you, nor will there ever be. I will love you for eternity." Francesco wanted to shout it, but he whispered repeatedly those same words she said to him. "Ti amo, ti amo." He kissed her head and stroked her golden hair as he prayed to the Madonna that he would always be there to protect his dearest Sara.

She rested her chin on his chest and smiled warmly. Her face was bright, and her glistening cheeks had recovered their bloom. He drew her closer and kissed her forehead, then each eye—each beguiling blue eye—her aquiline nose, and her cheeks, still damp with tears. He cupped her chin in his hand and traced her mouth with his thumb. She kissed it. As he had longed to do, his lips found hers, soft and silky. He kissed her softly, tentatively, though he longed to unleash the torrent of love he had held for so long. Would she now accept him? Would she, still, if she knew?

Sara snuggled her head under his chin, kissed his throat, and closed her eyes. Her breathing slowed, and Francesco sensed that she had fallen asleep. One day, one day soon, he would hold her like this in their own bed as husband and wife, as lovers forever.

The curtain rattled slightly, and Francesco's eyes met Cesare Costa's, the man who had saved his life. He had nearly taken Sara from him, but he wasn't to blame. Dottor Costa was a good man, and Sara would have been well cared for as his wife. But Francesco and Sara were destined for one another. He would give her a good life, and together they would hold the Fiore land for the next generation.

Cesare backed away. He had seen all needed to see. "Ti amo," Francesco whispered again, "ti amo," and closed his eyes.

CHAPTER 22

Turin
April 1938

Informant number 013 had not proven his worth. Doretta Giordano was too important a catch for Baldo Volpe to tolerate such incompetence. Or was the informant a double agent who had tipped her off that she was a target of OVRA surveillance? He had told his superior officer that trusting a Jew to rat on another Jew would not work. And it hadn't. Now with events cascading, he was not granted permission to hire another informant. He would have to do it on his own when time permitted—so much important work to do to protect the party and Il Duce from Jews, Bolsheviks, and bourgeois capitalists that had infiltrated the country's economy and government.

Watching for her from his familiar spot in the café across from the lecture hall at the university, he caught up on the new weekly magazine, *il Giornalissimo*. Oh, those cartoons—superb. And the articles were most enlightening. The extent of the threat to Italy from within was now an open book for those with eyes to read. The launch issue's article by the expert on the Jewish race, Giovanni Preziosi, set out everything Baldo had believed for years. Italy had a Jewish problem. The Fascist Party knew it. It was time for Italian citizens to wake up. But it would not happen instantly. Turin was still too much under the influence of Jewish Bolsheviks, and local Jews like Gabriele Giordano still enjoyed a high ranking in the Fascist Party. A purge was needed.

Preziosi had also produced a translation of *The Protocols of the Elders of Zion*. There it was—a great education about the treachery of the Jews. Of course, there was no anti-Semitism in Italy, as Il Duce proclaimed in 1934, but there was a Jewish problem, and he was finally doing something about it. Only through a strong alliance with Germany and adherence to the Nazi ideology would Mussolini be able to solve this problem that had been plaguing the peninsula since Roman times.

In February, Baldo had rejoiced when ordered to compile a list of Jews at the university—faculty and students, foreign and Italian. An order followed from the Ministry of the Interior to provide the names of all employees of the "Israelite religion" in various government offices in Piemonte. And just days ago, Mussolini had dismissed all Jews from government newspapers. Jewish journalists could no longer spread their lies. Was this just the beginning? So many great things happening! There were rumors of laws being drafted to defend the Italian race that would be as strict, if not stricter, than the brilliant Nuremberg race laws of two years earlier. Baldo admired Hitler's swift progress on this issue. Il Duce had been in power eleven years longer, but Hitler was far ahead of him in terms of freeing Europe from the Jewish curse.

There Doretta was as always—haughty with her immodest dress. At least she had let her hair grow and wasn't wearing it like a boy. Although he was concealed in a dark corner near the window inside the café, Baldo held the magazine high enough to shield his face should she walk by. There had been far too many close calls with her. And, of course, she was with her boyfriend, the man no doubt cheating on his wife with a Jewess. Baldo had been unable to discover anything useful about him in the files, but he would assign someone to follow him. He had not been seen with her at any suspected anti-Fascist meetings or carrying any forbidden literature.

Baldo had reached the conclusion that she had lured an Italian Aryan man into an affair. In fact, the man wasn't to blame if she was satisfying his needs. She had a body no man would be able to resist, especially in those dresses that clung to her curves. Baldo understood that the Jewess had bewitched him, but did the lover understand what had happened? Probably not. Baldo wondered why he visited her at home if he was having a clandestine affair with her. Did he have business with her father? More investigation was needed, but for now he would keep an eye on her while he completed his list-making tasks.

She was on his roster as was her zio, who still was listed as a member of the music faculty, old and decrepit though he was. Doretta Giordano and Eduardo Dalmasso. Along with the rest of their family, they would be the first he would see off to the camps like those in Germany he was sure Il Duce would build here.

Baldo sat for a moment, thinking of how long he had waited to get back at her. He dropped some coins on the table, waited for the couple to pass, then slinked away to his office to return to his lists.

Doretta had been locked away in classes since early morning, and now the library awaited her. Spring was flying past, and here she was, unable to enjoy the sunshine. Soon the Easter break would free her for a few days before she had to prepare for exams. As she walked out of the lecture hall, the bright sun momentarily blinded her. When her eyes adjusted, she was surprised to see Luca walking toward her, his face lined with worry. Usually, he called to let her know when he was in town.

"Luca, I didn't expect you!" Doretta kissed his cheeks and threaded her arm through his. "I'm in a bit of a hurry, so walk with me."

"I hadn't planned on being in Turin this week, but I have urgent business with your zia Silvana." A shadow passed over his face and there was a slight tremor in his voice.

She stopped short. The library would wait. She wanted to read Luca's face should he try to hide something from her. Why hadn't he learned that they were as one for the cause? There was nothing that would hurt her—nothing she couldn't handle. And he shouldn't keep secrets from her.

The shadow darkened across his face. "It's about her zia. Lorelei Vogel."

Nearly a year had passed since Luca had bidden farewell to the friendly old woman. Not a word since. Now, Luca looked everywhere but at Doretta. Her penetrating sky-blue eyes, now glistening with tears, read every nervous, rapid blink of his. He owed it to her to meet her gaze when telling her such tragic news. "She was murdered." His voice cracked as the painful image of Silvana saying good-bye to her Tante Lorelei flashed through his mind. He never should have doubted her loyalty to Silvana. Repeatedly in his prayers, he had asked Lorelei to forgive him. She had given her life for her beloved nephew's widow and children. And she had known when Silvana left that her own life might be in danger.

Doretta squeezed her eyes shut. "Madòna. Non è possibile!" She opened them again, now defiant. "I bastardi!" Without retaking his arm, she rushed to the tram stop. Luca caught up with her and grabbed her arm.

"Doretta, wait. Where are you going? Let's talk."

"Dai, Luca, dai! We can talk on the tram. I want to see Mamma before you come. This is news Mamma needs to hear from me. She has to be prepared when you tell zia Silvana. You can wait around the corner at Caffè Platti.

Signora Volpe planned to come for a fitting this afternoon, so Mamma is home. Dai, Luca, hurry!"

Luca followed her onto the tram an instant before the doors closed. Doretta didn't speak for the entire twenty-minute ride through central Turin. She was deep in thought, and they both knew that the tram was full of eyes and ears. Long ago, Luca's father had taught him the wisdom of silence, so he gazed ahead and said nothing to her. He could tell that she was contemplating how to rise to the occasion—how to protect her mother and aunt.

When they alighted from the tram at Corso Re Umberto, now a familiar stop for him, she said nothing as she turned toward home. Luca was dumbfounded. She had not given him the opportunity to provide more details. As though hearing his thoughts, she stopped. With fire still burning in her eyes but making an obvious effort to calm herself, she grabbed his forearm. Again, she searched his eyes for truth. "Luca, what happened to her?"

The arcade was crowded, and he was jostled against her. "Doretta, please, let's sit in the café. This isn't the place."

She rushed ahead, diving among the afternoon crowd for the corner table closest to the entrance. The waiter arrived.

"*Dell'acqua minerale, per favore*," Doretta ordered, not bothering to inquire what Luca might want. She turned to him. "Dimmi, Luca. Tell me."

The story of Frau Vogel's disappearance was a painful one for Luca to recount.

"Early last week, Madama Lia received a cryptic letter from Freida Stern." Having memorized the letter, Luca recited it to Doretta.

My dearest Lia, I regret to inform you the sender of the package you received last April is no longer in business. The owner has passed away. I know how overjoyed you were to receive the fragile items in such good condition, so I thought you would like to know that you will not be able to order from her again.

Doretta shivered as though someone had walked across her grave. Although she had never met Fritz Becker's aunt, zia Silvana's stories about her had brought her to life. The children had adored her. Nothing she was told led Doretta to believe she was an informant as Luca had worried she might have been. Now she was dead—a defenseless, elderly woman murdered.

Luca fidgeted in his small bistro chair. He was uncomfortable having to share this tragic news with Doretta in a public place, but she gave him no choice. "Madama Lia decided we were to go immediately to Switzerland to see Madame Stern and hear the details directly from her. She's vacationing at her villa in Crans-sur-Sierre in Valais until next week, after Easter and Passover." He shuddered, recalling Madame Stern's dispassionate manner as she shared the details of Lorelei Vogel's gruesome death. For Frieda Stern, violence was becoming all too familiar. He found her altered by it each time he traveled to Switzerland to meet with her.

"Why did it take so long for the information to get to Madame Stern? Nearly a year passed with no word, now this?"

"She didn't want to send anyone to Lorelei's home in case the Gestapo were watching. She was in the midst of orchestrating the dangerous passage of a family of Polish Jews through the same area. Any attention drawn to them because of Lorelei Vogel would have placed too many lives at risk."

"Did she not have a telephone?" Doretta scoffed, incredulous that no one thought to call her.

"No, she didn't. That and the other operation is what made this so complicated." Doretta's impatience wasn't making this easy on him. He had not seen her for months and wished to catch up, not discuss such hideous things. In another time and place, Luca would have explored a deeper relationship with Doretta. He was ready. But the work that brought them together, and the difficult times they faced, dashed his hopes for that. "In July, Madame Stern spoke with your mother's roommate at boarding school, Renata Goren, whose mother grew up with Lorelei in Hamburg. She told her that she was worried for Lorelei's welfare. The Gorens are wealthy textile merchants who left Berlin for Palestine in 1933."

"Yes, yes. I know all about that," she said, waving her hand. "They wanted Fritz and Silvana to leave too. What on earth does she have to do with this?"

"Doretta, *tranquilla*! Please wait. You're not making this any easier." Luca sat back and folded his arms. Then the waiter came again to take their order. The café was busy, and they were occupying a prized table in his section. Luca's head was splitting, and he was thirsty, but he dared not stop telling his tale to give his order.

"*Vai*, vai! *Dopo*!" Luca was surprised at the sound of his own voice as he waved the fuming waiter away. "Listen, when the plan was hatched to rescue Silvana and the children through Rosenheim, your mother gave Frau Goren's contact information in Tel Aviv to Madama Lia. She sent a letter to Lorelei in which she gave her new address in Tel Aviv and asked her to write soon. No reply. Nearly six months later, shortly after New Year, the letter was returned. Addressee unknown." The stress of Doretta's impatience had exhausted him. "I told you it was complicated. Everything is these days."

"I still don't understand, Luca, why did it take so long to discover the truth?"

"It's a very dangerous situation there, Doretta. Or didn't you know that?" Softer, after a deep breath, he continued. "No one wanted to be seen making too many inquiries about Lorelei. I hear informants are everywhere...like here."

Luca's comment sent blood rushing to Doretta's cheeks. She hoped he hadn't noticed. More than once, she had sensed someone following her to and from school, but she thought she was being paranoid. She had yet to share her concerns with him. "Get to the point, Luca. How did they finally discover the truth?"

"The *Rosenheimer Anzieger*—the only local newspaper. Frau Goren contacted a former business acquaintance, a close family friend in Munich they trusted." He preempted her question. "Sorry, I don't know his name. She asked him to inquire about a family friend they heard had been ill. In early March, Frau Goren received a newspaper clipping from Munich. There was no note in the envelope, only the clipping."

Luca extracted an envelope from his pocket and read from a typewritten page:

"June 24, 1937. The widow Frau Lorelei Gisele Vogel was found murdered in her home at Am Salzstadel 10a. A neighbor, concerned for Frau Vogel's welfare after not seeing her for several days, discovered her on June 22. Frau Vogel had been brutally beaten and her home ransacked. Police believe she had been dead for some time. They are now looking for two short dark-complected men with mustaches, approximately in their late thirties who are believed to be from a Roma camp in the vicinity of the Simmsee. They were reported to have been seen in the area that week. The police have surrounded the camp and are asking for the public's assistance in apprehending the murderers."

"Gypsies! They're blaming the gypsies for this? Luca, we know the Gestapo is above the law in Germany. They can do as they please. And it's always the Jews, the Communists, or the Roma."

They sat in silence for a few minutes. Then Doretta jumped up and checked her gold watch, a gift from her zio Eduardo for her bat mitzvah years ago— another lifetime.

"Stay here, Luca. Drink an espresso. Come to the apartment in half an hour."

Luca nodded. What a great general she would have made if Gabriele and Daniela Giordano's firstborn had been a boy. She may be an alluring university student, but Doretta had a fire burning that he had seen in few others. It was beginning to grow, and he was certain that, when the time came—soon, he feared—she would be a leader.

"Oh, and have some *gianduiotto* with your espresso. Simply the best in Turin!" And she was gone.

Luca had left his appetite in Alba when he boarded the train. This was personal for him, not like other rescues where the persecuted Jews on the run were simply faces in photographs given to him to pass on to don Riccardo for their false documents. Tante Lorelei was a breathing human being who had welcomed him into her cozy home on a chilly April morning. Now she was lying underground in Rosenheim. What sort of a world was this?

There were rumors, reliable he was afraid, of Mussolini's government enacting racial decrees that would relegate Jews like Doretta and her family to second-class citizenship, if that. In Germany, Jews were non-persons, even called subhuman. One thing was certain: if such Draconian measures were passed in Italy, mixed marriages between Aryan Italians and Jews would be forbidden. He squeezed his eyes shut to banish the image of Doretta on the run as Silvana had been. He was working hard and doing all within his power. Many people were. But he had to face the truth: it might not be enough.

The short walk from the café to the Giordano apartment gave Doretta little time to fully grasp the details of Frau Vogel's death. She had no doubt that this was the Gestapo's evil work. The stories refugees and foreign students had told her validated that assumption. She would first tell Mamma but leave it to Luca to provide the specific details. Hearing about it was enough for her. She knew she needed to be stronger, but for now, she would let Luca finish his mission.

Pausing in front of her own door, she jumped when it opened. "*Mi scusi*, signora Volpe. Buonasera. Leaving so soon?" Doretta struggled to separate this kindhearted woman from her contemptible son. Many a time, she fought the urge to tell her Mamma that her dressmaker's son was a fascist anti-Semite. But the words always caught in her throat. Mamma only knew that she was a widow and a hard-working woman. No, Doretta would guard that secret…for now. Besides, Mamma loved the clothes Flora Volpe created for her—as did Doretta, she had to admit. The pursuit of beauty in these times was a welcome distraction and didn't hurt anyone. "How was Mamma's fitting today?"

"All is good, signorina Giordano. But your mamma needs to eat more." Flora held up a sateen bag of hanging dresses. "I will have to take in most of the dresses I made for her last summer."

"We all try, signora Volpe, but Mamma is stubborn that way." She forced a smile, anxious to send her on her way and to find her mamma.

Flora scanned the entrance hall and lowered her voice. "Signorina Giordano, my apologies for not bringing your nightgown with me today, but I wasn't certain whether you would be home. I wanted to give it to you directly."

Doretta blushed at the secret she and Flora Volpe shared. No doubt, her mamma would disapprove of her purchase, but the lace was too exquisite to resist.

The hint of a smile broke across Flora's flushed face. She wished Doretta buona serata and disappeared down the staircase. Doretta knew it would be anything but a good evening. This news would drain energy and appetite from her mamma even more.

She bounded up the stairs two-by-two, no different from when she was a teen and Ida would scold her for her tomboyish behavior. "Mamma?" she called out in the long hall. Doretta was certain she would find her in her sitting room, hopefully alone. Her papà was in Rome – a good thing too. She couldn't help but love him, though at times she found it difficult to respect him. Increasingly he was distant, brooding about the Fascist Party's alliance with Hitler. The air circulating around her parents when they were together was frosty, difficult to breathe. This was a matter she needed to handle without his lecturing that the misfortunes of German Jews would never happen in Italy.

"Buonasera, Mamma." Flora Volpe was right. Her cheekbones felt hard against her face when Doretta kissed her. "Elena? Would you mind—?"

Elena displayed her usual eye roll and folded her arms. "I know. Would you mind *leaving*? Well, I *do* mind!" And she stomped out, slamming the door behind her.

"Mamma…" Doretta began to complain and then stopped herself. "Mamma, I must talk to you. Please sit." Doretta locked the door and joined her mamma next to the dark fireplace.

Daniela Giordano could always read her eldest child—every wrinkle around her mouth when she spoke or smiled, every emotion in her blue eyes. She stiffened when she noticed Doretta's hardened mouth, her down-turned eyebrows.

"Where is zia Silvana, Mamma?" She bit her lip, thinking how best to break the news. Luca would be here soon.

Daniela's empty stomach churned. "In her room, I believe. Why, Doretta?"

"Mamma." Again, she bit her lip. Don Riccardo warned her last time when she collected false documents that she would have to suppress any sign of emotions. "Mamma, there is bad news from Germany about her zia Lorelei. She's dead." There—it was out, if a bit too blunt. Softer, knowing the next word would shock her even more, she nearly whispered, "Murdered." Doretta was not going to tell her any details; Luca would handle that and probably with more tact. "Mamma…"

Daniela's face blanched. "How, Doretta. When?" Fear edged her voice although the long silence from Silvana's aunt could only have meant bad news. This was too close to home.

"Mamma, Luca will be here any minute. It's a complicated story, so I believe it's best that he explains everything to you and zia Silvana. I wanted to be alone with you…to tell you first." Coward. But Luca was gentle and knowing. Better to leave the rest to him.

Daniela clasped her hands in her lap, wringing them, fighting the tears brimming in her eyes, a battle Doretta had seen her mamma wage far too often these last years. "La *mia povera sorella. Troppo mal di cuore.*" Yes, her poor sister had seen more than her share of heartache, and though Mamma had aged beyond her years, she still appeared younger than her baby sister did. A year in the relative safety of the Giordano family's home had helped, but at times Silvana still seemed like a skittish mare; every loud sound and unfamiliar face, particularly those of men, frightened her.

Doretta answered the soft knock and twist of the knob of the locked door.

"Signorina Doretta, mi scusi," said the shy, formal Piermaria, who had been with them since before Doretta was born. "Signor Olivero is waiting in the library."

"Grazie, Piermaria. Where is signora Dalmasso?" Doretta asked. Silvana had retaken her maiden name, and the children were provided with new passports. Although Gisele was not an uncommon name in Italy, *Friedrich* Dalmasso would draw unwanted attention to him at some point. Easy enough to change his name to Federico. It was worth the money Papà had paid for their new identities. "Please find her and ask her to join us in the library. And, Piermaria, stay with the children, including Elena." The maid raised her eyebrows. "As best you can, Piermaria, keep Elena with Federico and Gisele. Tell her you need her to help with them." She turned to Daniela who was now standing in front of the dark, cold fireplace, dabbing at her eyes with the linen handkerchief Silvana had embroidered for her. "Anduma, Mamma."

"Please, Doretta. Let me have a moment alone to freshen my face. And please pull the door behind you."

Doretta went to her mamma and hugged her. Increasingly, she found herself the caregiver where her mamma's emotions were concerned. She kissed her and left her to her thoughts. As the door closed behind her, a deep, mournful sob erupted from the other side. Doretta worried it would be some time before she regained her composure. This was not only about Lorelei. This was not the first time Daniela had seen beyond the moment into the frightening future.

Silvana was waiting for Doretta at the top of the stairs, far from Daniela's sitting room. By all appearances, she had not heard her sister crying, but the cords of her neck were visible. Silvana twisted her wedding ring. Despite the refuge she had found, she still wore the face of a hunted woman.

"Zia Silvana, please join me in the library. Luca Olivero is here and would like to speak with you." What little color she had drained from her face. *What now?* her expression said. "Mamma will join us in a moment. She's freshening up after her long fitting with signora Volpe." Doretta nearly added assurances that all was well but trapped the words in her throat.

In the last thirty minutes, Luca had managed to lighten his expression and he greeted Silvana warmly as usual. Their trip through Germany and Austria had forged a strong bond between them. Luca was one of the few men Silvana trusted.

The two made small talk while they waited for Daniela. Doretta was anxious to be done with this. She caught Luca's eyes telegraphing her to be patient. What was keeping Mamma? Finally, Daniela joined them. How impressive she was to have regained her composure so quickly—to appear so serene.

Daniela greeted Luca then led Silvana to the divan. They sat close together, clutching each other's hands. Luca went immediately to the news of Lorelei's death, letting her absorb that shock first before proceeding to the details. Through it all, Silvana sat impassively, attentively listening as Luca explained how the information was obtained. Doretta was shocked that Silvana's eyes remained dry. Did she expect this news? Her mamma had sobbed despite never having met the woman. Lorelei's niece by marriage appeared all but unfazed.

"Is that all, Luca?" Silvana asked. He nodded and glanced at Doretta, his brow knitted, a pained expression on his face. "Will you excuse me? I shall return in a moment."

Doretta followed Silvana and listened at the bottom of the stairs for her to open the door to her room. She dashed back into the library and spoke barely above a whisper to Luca and her mamma.

"I don't understand. They were close. Lorelei risked her life so zia Silvana could be closer to the border." No response from Luca or Daniela. Only puzzled, sad silence.

Silvana returned shortly, holding what appeared to be a note folded into a small square. She stood by the mantel as she slipped her reading glasses from her skirt pocket and slowly unfolded the paper.

"May I?" she asked as she adjusted her glasses.

Meine kleine Schaztli, I hope when you read this that you are far away, safe in the company of your sister and those who love you and the children as I do. I knew when you wrote earlier this spring that my home would be a way station on your journey to safety. Know that I love you dearly and that it has grieved me to see you treated so unjustly by a family who should have embraced Friedrich, Gisele, and you when Fritz was so brutally murdered. Now so many others are being persecuted. This is not the Germany my beloved Wilhelm fought and died for. This is a Germany of monsters. I want no part of it. Don't worry about me. I will be all right. I am ready to face whatever happens. I am ready to join my dear Wilhelm in eternity.

Ich liebe dich für immer.
Tante Lorelei.

Doretta was dumbstruck. The eyes of her mamma and Luca were wide, no doubt sharing Doretta's thoughts. When did she receive the letter? Why didn't she mention this? So many questions. Silvana removed her glasses, slipped them back into her pocket, and refolded the note. From its tattered appearance, Doretta suspected Silvana had read the note many times before.

"I found it last June when I searched my bag for one of Friedrich's missing soldiers." She smiled. "I found it between the cloth lining and the leather. The fabric was cut only enough that the note and the soldier would slip in."

"Silvana, why—?"

She held up her hand to quiet her sister. "Daniela, I didn't see any reason to share this with you. The burden on your own heart is too great now, and you've done far too much for us to add to that. I prayed she was unharmed, but now I find relief in the knowledge she's at peace, although she didn't deserve to leave this world in such a brutal fashion." She pressed the folded note between her clasped hands and exhaled as though her breath purged her of a huge burden. "She knew we were not returning."

"Silvana, how so?" Daniela insisted.

"She whispered to me as we kissed good-bye. Why would she wish me 'Godspeed' simply for a day's outing? At first, I was terrified, not knowing whether she had turned on me." She finally slid the note into her pocket. "Luca, is there any idea of who might have informed on her? On me?"

"Yes. Madame Stern's people are fairly confident your landlady called the police when you didn't return as expected."

"Poverina Lorelei. My poor aunt. I never should have disclosed my destination to that loathsome landlady of mine although I was forced to report it to the police. She must have reported me when I failed to return. The police called the Gestapo as they always do in the new Germany." Her voice trailed off as she stared at the dark fireplace.

"Silvana, I am so sorry. What a dear woman," Luca said, remembering the brief moment he had spent with her, the sweet, buttery aroma of strudel baking in the oven, the children's toys strewn across the floor.

"Thank you, Luca. You've been very kind and brave. Now, if you would excuse me, I must speak with the children."

As she turned to leave, Doretta asked her to send Elena down. "Mamma will need to explain some things to her."

It was dark when Luca finally took his leave of Daniela. He had stayed to help her explain something unfathomable for one so young. Now Doretta walked Luca down to the street entrance, and together they stepped out onto the dimly lit sidewalk. Typical of April weather, it had been a warm day with a breeze that carried moisture that now pressed the dank odors of the city against the ground. A bright flash streaked across the sky, followed by thunder rolling toward them.

Luca checked his watch. "I must go, Doretta, before the rain comes. If I hurry, I can still catch the last train to Bra. Gianni said he would meet me there."

"Luca, why don't you stay the night? Papà is in Rome. It would be nice for Mamma to have a man in the house, particularly…you."

Doretta's eyes danced like fireflies, teasing him. He made a futile attempt to avoid looking into them. "Thank you, Doretta, but I have an early meeting with Madama Lia tomorrow. More work for Madame Stern. The work is increasing every day. As you know too well, the need is increasing too."

Doretta stepped closer to him, letting the door shut behind her. Her eyes, earlier raging with anger, now called to him. Or was he misreading her, seeing what *he* needed, not what she wanted? Closer still she came, studying his face, holding him captive with her gaze. He set down his attaché case, his face nearly grazing her breasts. Without thinking, he brushed an errant eyelash from her cheekbone with his thumb, and let his hand rest where the eyelash had been. He tentatively caressed her cheek, feeling her downy skin, warm under his touch, as a red bloom washed over her face.

He came to his senses and pulled his hand away, but she grabbed it, pressing it against her cheek as she smiled, telegraphing her desire for his touch. Tiny beads of perspiration appeared on her forehead and glistened in the light as her warmth through the thin dress flowed into his body. He let his hand slide past her jaw to her throat, where her rapid pulse beat beneath his fingers. His hand ventured farther still, touching the dewy skin above the scooped, lace-edge neckline of her dress. Still she said nothing although her breath quickened.

There was much he wished to say to her, but he let his body talk instead. Since their playful charade in Turin long ago, he had not touched her again except for polite, friendly kisses on her cheeks as he did with all other women friends, even Sara. But tonight, Doretta's perfume, a garden of roses, even the memory of which had tortured him on the long trip between Germany and Turin, electrified him. Tonight, that fragrance mixed with her musky, natural scent that rose as her skin grew warmer. It was reckless, he knew, but for this moment—reason be damned. He wrapped her in his arms, her firm breasts against him as her body heat seeped into him and her arms encircled his neck.

Did she feel his heart hammering in his chest, as though it would burst? He brushed his lips across her cheek, before finding her succulent lips she willingly parted for him, first softly, then insistent as she invited his tongue to dance with hers. Closer still, he held her, a warm wave of desire pulsing through his body. She wove her fingers through his hair and cradled his head while she caressed his scalp. His knees weakened as her touch melted the day's stress. She leaned into him, sliding her other hand over his spine to the small of his back. Her hand—squeezing, releasing, squeezing, releasing—each time firmer, pulling him close, each time lower until he felt their bodies meld. Did she feel it? Oh yes—this was too close, too much for him. His breath came in gasps. He was far too aroused for such a setting.

"Doretta...I..."

But she would have none of it. He was powerless to retreat. No, this wasn't right. On the street, in public. This moment had taunted him in his dreams and every time he was near her, but it was not to be like this, not when he had to release her while his desire burned. He must go. But he allowed the struggle between his heart and mind to continue for a few brief moments of sensual exploration. Finally, he uncoupled his lips from hers, ever so slowly relaxing his embrace though she showed no signs of surrendering to reason. Years had passed since he had known love, but never passion like this.

"Doretta, no. We really…"

She reluctantly released him, flashing a coquettish smile before she brushed his lips one last time and disappeared into the house. For a moment he stood, staring at the polished wooden door, the sudden barrier between them. There were far greater barriers awaiting them, he feared. As he bent to retrieve his attaché case, the door opened again. Only her silhouette against the soft light in the foyer was visible. She spoke, her voice thick with desire, stirring his own.

"Luca…Luca, ti amo." And once again, as though a spirit had haunted him, she vanished. She didn't wait for him to reply.

"*Anch'io ti amo,* cara. Anch'io, cara." Yes, he did love her too.

As he walked toward the tram stop on Corso Vittorio Emanuele II, he ached for more of her, for her lips, for her body against his, and to return to the garden of roses that he entered each time she was near.

But frightening thoughts nearly washed away the thrill of the moment. These were dark times; they knew it. Would the growing anti-Semitism in Italy destroy their chances to be together? She loved him. For now, that was all that mattered to him. Luca would hold on tight to these sweet, tender moments to sustain him in the dark days ahead. All of a sudden, the heavens opened up, and God's voice thundered. Was He warning them?

Hail, early for the season, pelted the skylight. Lightning transformed night into day in his tiny bedroom where before only the glowing tip of his cigarette pierced the darkness. His mamma had arrived late from her client. No doubt the Giordano woman again. But he had come home early, relieved to have the apartment for himself. He was in no mood for talk.

The message from his superior after lunch had shocked Baldo. Why was he ordered to cease his surveillance of Doretta Giordano? Was she not an important subject because of her apparent political sympathies? He had no proof, only conjecture, but it was enough that she did not respect him and had cursed him. The daughter of a Jew Fascist. An anti-Fascist herself. Was that not enough? He had memorized the shocking words.

His superior never would have ordered such a thing unless either pressured by a government official or bribed. The angry storm intensified. Lightning continually flashed, giving him no peace in the dark. He, too, was angry. Although he may have been ordered to cease *official* surveillance of the anti-Fascist—as he was certain she was—there had been no prohibition about him doing so on his own time. No, he would continue to follow her when possible. To watch her walk, like a prostitute, swinging her hips in form-fitting silk and linen dresses his mamma's own hands were forced to sew. In their own apartment. It was easy to spot her because of that. He noted each garment his mamma hung on a rack she labeled "Doretta Giordano." Although the garments hung for Doretta's mother were gone, he saw an item he had never seen his mamma sew before for Doretta. A silk negligee. Pale blue, long and flowing, with a sheer lace front. Had she made it for a liaison with that man? That would explain why his mamma had not taken it with her today. The bitch didn't want her mother to see it.

Baldo drew hard on the cigarette, feeling its calming heat between his lips. Not as hot as what he had enjoyed earlier. Again, he inhaled the bitter smoke, exhaling slowly as he relived the feel of the delicate material and the way it was shaped to hold her full breasts. His pulse had quickened as he closed his eyes, imagining her flesh under the fabric, and he ran his fingers along the outside then the inside of the nightgown. The lace that would lie against her breasts, the large nipples he had spotted once through a silk dress on a chilly morning. That pleasurable sensation he had come to know so well spread through his groin, and his pulse quickened as his masculine swelling pushed against the fabric of his trousers. *Oh, Doretta, you slut, you witch. What sort of spell have you cast on me?* He helped that feeling pass as he had before, but this time without fear of discovery. And he had something of hers that heightened the pleasure that flowed through his body. Not once, not twice. He had time to relish the pleasure without complications.

The gown was once again hanging on the rack where he had found it. He longed to retrieve it, to feel again the lace between his fingers, against his face, his body, but what if his mamma discovered him? No, best to leave it there. He crushed the cigarette in the ashtray, shed his clothes, and slipped back into bed. Reaching his hand under the covers, he had only one thought: Doretta. He closed his eyes, only to see her body, clothed in the sheer lace, before him. Your day will come.

END OF PART ONE

PART TWO:

1938 – 1941

CHAPTER 23

Barbaresco
August 5, 1938

Francesco sat alone in the vineyard on the courtyard's edge, watching the sun cast its orange-red light across Langhe as it sank beyond the mountains. It seemed as though the land and all who lived on it sighed in relief from the blistering August heat. The next time the sun set, Sara Fiore would be his wife.

Since Christmas, the season of their betrothal, nine months had passed more slowly than the six years after he first met the beguiling but furious girl. Now he wanted to forget all the pain and misunderstanding of those years. His life would be filled with joy.

How could it be otherwise? He heard talk of war, of cruel treatment of Jews in Germany, but together, he and Sara could face anything. Besides, if war did come as many predicted, his injuries would exclude him from service. He would fight the war, if it came, on the home front.

To escape the heat of the city, Doretta Giordano had spent the last month in Asili. During this time, she and Sara had renewed the friendship that began when they were girls. Doretta, now in university, knew more of the world than Sara did, but Sara was inquisitive, and they spent hours walking through the vineyards and orchards. More than once, Francesco was a little jealous of the time they spent together, usually talking about politics and things never openly discussed in Barbaresco. Nico often cautioned Sara to mind her tongue, but Francesco knew his soon-to-be wife. The passion she brought to her work nursing the sick of Langhe also fed the fire to help in what the two women called the "battle for justice and liberty." *Dear Lord, please keep us safe from this dark cloud on the horizon* was often his prayer.

Hard times were ahead, he knew. Luca Olivero often made trips to Asili after Doretta arrived. Francesco suspected that Luca shared more than politics with Doretta. When she was with Luca, Francesco saw the same dreamy look, at times infused with hunger, that Sara often gave him. The two were obviously in love. Did they try to hide it because Doretta was Jewish? Luca didn't strike him as that sort of man, but you never knew these days.

Sara had told him her worries about Doretta and her family. She had read some of the propaganda to him from a newspaper, so he knew there were people even in this country who believed that Jews were an inferior race.

Mussolini now parroted Germany's dictator who always, Sara claimed, hated Jews—calling for war, calling for the Jews to leave Germany. He knew that Sara hated fascism, as did he, but he could also see how it attracted certain people, especially one woman he would like to forget. All that, for now at least, he pushed aside. There would be no talk of such things, not on this joyous day and not during their time by the sea, loving her.

Giovanna called to him and soon found him sitting where she had often joined him and Sara, watching the summer sunsets after dinner. His future mother-in-law had banished him from the cascina, claiming they would tempt fate if they slept under the same roof the night before the wedding. Giovanna said she would make sure he obeyed her mamma's orders. He thought to spend the night at the Conti di Silva farm in the company of the three workers who had helped to save him that awful night of the accident. But Madama Lia insisted that he spend his last night alone in her cascina, claiming that the di Silva workers would ply him with celebratory drink, denying him the rest he needed. Madama assured Luigia that Giuseppina would keep an eye on him. Giovanna, for her part, appointed herself his jailer although she behaved more like a general ordering everyone around as they prepared for the wedding. She had come now to escort him across the cortile in case he thought to slip away to his room in the loft.

"Where have you been? I've looked everywhere!" Hands on hips, glowering, she appeared every bit the schoolteacher ordering a naughty student in from recess.

"Just sitting here, Gio, by myself. Watching the sunset. Your papà pushed me out of the house after dinner and ordered me not to feed the animals tonight. So here I am." He patted the tall grass next to him. "*Siediti, Generale...per favore.* Sit."

She dropped onto the lush grass between the rows of vines and leaned on her elbows. Against her mamma's wishes, Giovanna had taken to wearing pants around the farm, hand-me-downs from her big sister. Giovanna said she felt freer in pants and that they were more suitable for farm work.

She put her arm around him and rested her head on his shoulder. Her voice came soft and low, nearly in a whisper—a serious tone for Giovanna.

"Francesco?"

"*Dimmi, cara sorellina.*"

Giovanna flashed a broad smile. Since she had ordered him to sit next to her at his first meal with the family, she had sought the title of Francesco's little sister. She now believed that Sara came to her senses through her prodding, not the accident. Her face grew serious, and she slipped her arm off his shoulder. For a few minutes, they sat in silence as she feverishly pulled blades of weeds from the ground and made rings of them around her fingers—a telltale sign when they sat together like this that something troubled her.

"Francesco, you love Sara more than anything else in the world, don't you?"

Surely, the little matchmaker, of all people, could not doubt his feelings. "Of course, Gio, why such a question?"

"You'll never go away, will you?" Her weeding intensified. "Promise me you'll never leave." She paused. "I know you get letters from America. Tell me you're not taking Sara away from us." The welling tears transformed her eyes into blue pools that finally gave way. Her tears, so rare, always tugged at his heart. He wrapped his arm about her shoulder and drew her close. She snatched his kerchief from his shirt pocket to dry her tears, and resumed her weeding, avoiding eye contact with him.

"Gio, stop." He grabbed her hand. Tomorrow would be a joyous day for them all and no dark cloud should hang over his sorellina. "Look at me. I give you my solemn oath: I'm not going to America. I'll never take Sara away from here. *I* will never leave here."

Her wet eyes narrowed. Once she had settled on a conclusion, she could not be convinced otherwise.

"Those are just letters from my cousins in New Orleans. Sometimes I miss my family—my Sicilian family—Gio. That's natural, don't you think?" Giovanna's concern didn't surprise him after the many letters he exchanged with his cousins during the last harvest. Why tell her that he nearly left, but because *of* Sara, not *with* her? Now, with her as his wife, he would remain in Asili until his last breaths. Despite the August warmth, he shivered. "But you, Gio, you and all the Fiores, even Nebbia and Minoucat, are my family now."

He pinched her sun-freckled cheek, forcing her to smile and bat away his hand. Her spirit was endless, her determination strong for one so young and so small. Like Sara. So unlike her other sisters, who reminded him of his own. Only when they could cause trouble for him with his mamma, would they pay him any attention. If only they had loved him as Sara loved Giovanna... No, regardless, he would have left.

"Ascolta, mia sorellina, I don't have to promise because that would never happen. I don't see why we won't continue as we've been doing. Sara will make visits to the sick, Papà Nico and I will farm. Only when the angels above come for me, when I am old and unable to walk in the vineyards, will I leave." He leaned back to see her face and make sure she was smiling. "What about you? Surely you'll marry one day and leave Asili."

When she turned to him, defiance flashed in her eyes. "Never! I'll *never* leave Asili. I wanted to be a nurse like Sara and zia Luce. Mamma said I can't, but I'll never marry. If I did, I would have to leave Asili to go live with my husband's family and be a slave to my suocera. And I won't need babies because I'll stay and help raise yours, just like zia Luce helped Mamma after Sara was born."

"Well, Gio, you're still young, so you have time to decide all that. Someday, someone will come, and you'll fall in love..."

"I'll be thirteen in the spring. I'm old enough to know what I want! Sara was thirteen when she met you. *Amore a prima vista* it was, for her."

"Now you're talking nonsense. She certainly didn't love me at first sight. The lightning struck *me*, not Sara."

"Well, you're wrong." Giovanna's tone softened. "I know these things. She was just too snooty to admit it."

He laughed, leaned back on his elbows, and stretched to ease the soreness in his left leg, still sometimes painful even after months of healing. Giovanna knew her sister well. Sara had been haughty those years she lived in Alba.

But her work in Barbaresco tending to the poor had humbled her. After he returned to Asili, Luigia had told him that, during her stay in Alba, while he was in hospital, a rumor spread like wildfire through the villages and farms that the *angioletto* had returned to Alba for good. She was a lifeline for so many. Despite her youth, she understood them in ways that the new doctor could not. But she had come back and resumed her home visits, riding Zeus between the villages of Barbaresco, Treiso, and Neive even through the winter.

The last splashes of orange against the darkened sky had faded. Sara called to Giovanna from the cascina.

"Oh no! Sara! Stay here, you mustn't see her. After I go in, then you can leave." Orders from the youngest of the family were not to be ignored.

He hugged her good-night and pulled her braid to tease her as he often did. Now he grew serious. "Gio, Sara may sense things in the future and only God knows what's waiting for us, but for now, let's do as zia Luce always says. Let's take the joy as a gift from God. All will be well. I promise."

With that, she stood on her toes as he bent to kiss her cheeks. "Buonanotte, little angel." And she disappeared into the night.

To say the daily performance of Rio Sordo valley's roosters woke him the morning of their nuptials is to say he had slept. He had not. All night, in the sweltering darkness, he lay staring at the night sky through the open shutters, reliving the life he had led that brought him to Asili and, in a few hours, to Sara's bed.

In keeping with Langhe countryside tradition, no matter their betrothal date, couples had to wait to wed until after pruning in the cold, foggy early winter months. Although she respected the old customs, Sara never hesitated to ignore them when it suited her. She insisted on a summer wedding between the end of the wheat harvest and the beginning of the vendemmia. Their union, she argued, must be sun-kissed in the presence of the grapes that brought Francesco to her homeland, not in the bleak early winter that would remind her of when she nearly lost him forever. Arguing with her was futile. But the nine months had been hard on him. And soon, he knew, he would have to wait another nine months for her to bring him a son and Nico a grandson. He prayed that his mamma was watching him from above.

Anna Bosco's death in January from influenza dashed his hopes of traveling with Sara to Sicily to meet her. At least Mamma knew he was happy and that he had a good life in Langhe with people who loved him. The valley of his birth had only grown poorer, with no end in sight to the exodus of villagers to America. Most of the relatives he knew and loved had immigrated to America, most to New Orleans. Now he had no reason to return.

When the sun had risen over Monte Silva, Giuseppina tapped on his door and told him she had prepared a hot bath—such a luxury for him—and set out breakfast for him on the terrace. Madama Lia had gone for an early ride, so he would eat alone. That news relieved him. Despite her generosity to them both, she still unnerved him.

Francesco found Nico waiting in the cortile, already dressed for the occasion in his only suit. Neither man owned a tie or fancy shoes, so Francesco followed Nico in wearing his work boots, brushed clean. On this bright summer morning with the sun shining in their eyes, Francesco felt proud to be walking with his soon-to-be father-in-law. His *suocero*.

The warm summer days had left no time for the two men to talk. Crops and vines did not wait. But today, Nico said he wanted to show Francesco something up on the *bricco*. Often, as he had done the night before in the vineyards near the cascina, Francesco would sit with Sara on the bricco at the top of the Asili amphitheater. The grand panorama of Langhe, Roero, the Alps, and the faraway Apennines—the gateway to the sea to the south—seen at sunset always brought him peaceful sleep. He found renewal there.

He had even intended to propose to Sara on Christmas Eve there, but a heavy snowstorm had rendered the road up the steep hill impassable for the cartun. His leg had not yet mended, so he was imprisoned in the cascina as the snow blanketed the ground. The lane to the cappella was clear, however, so Sara had driven them the short distance in the Topolino. There, where their lives had collided and where today they would marry, she accepted his proposal.

Above the sea of lush vines, heavy grape bunches testing their strength, Nico once again told Francesco the history of Asili and which of his paternal ancestors had planted which vineyards and which orchards. Most important of all, he said, were those at the top, the bricco, where the best conditions existed for the grapes. Here, in Vigna Fiorina so named after Nico's *bisnonna*, the mamma of Giacomo who planted these first vines of Asili, the Fiore vision of transforming the wooded, hostile earth of Barbaresco into a prized wine region took root.

Then Nico turned to Francesco and said, "These vines are yours—yours and Sara's. And one day they will belong to your son. It's here I will teach your son, my grandson, the lessons of pruning that my nonno taught me. It's here we will tend the vines and harvest together in autumn."

Francesco had not given the idea of a dowry a thought. Nico had already given him a new life, and Sara's hand in marriage was priceless. But this, he knew, was not a bride price. It was Nico's assurance that he and Sara would add another link to the chain of Fiores that now stretched back nearly a century. Francesco studied Nico's sun-etched face, warm and loving, not at all like his own father, who had not even seen him off, choosing instead to leave for work in Sambucca. Francesco had not thought that to be unusual at the time.

"Thank you, Nico. I'm truly grateful to you and Luigia. I know what the Asili vineyard means to you, what it has meant to the Fiore family for generations, particularly these vines up here."

"I'm still a man of tradition, and these are our ways. I know I don't have to tell you how Sara is. But you should never underestimate the resourcefulness of a *donna di Langa*, my boy. And you are marrying one of the strongest, most determined ones I know."

Before Francesco spoke, Nico held up his hand.

"Anyway, you've worked hard. You earned it. And I'm bound by a promise I freely made to give you these vines. To Sara's nonna Mirella."

Francesco looked at Nico, puzzled. "What do you mean, Nico?"

"The Christmas of your arrival, not long before her death, she walked with me her last time to the *bricco* and chose this spot, these rows, for Sara's dowry. I'm honoring her wishes to pass Vigna Fiorina to you and Sara."

Francesco had arrived only three months before she died. And Sara had scorned him during those last months of her nonna's life. Once, Luigia had told him that Sara, like her nonna Mirella, was born with a veil. They sensed the future. That explained many of Sara's premonitions and her insistence on marrying in the summer before winter's chill gripped the landscape. Something about this coming winter worried her. But Mirella had seen something even Sara could not see.

Nico and Francesco walked down the hill to the cappella in silence, each lost in his own thoughts. Across the narrow valley stood the fabled Torre di Barbaresco. It had witnessed much joy and sorrow through the centuries. How many hailstorms had battered its walls? How many villagers had laid their loved ones to rest in its shadow? Today, a dusty, hot, August morning in 1938, the tower would bear witness to the union of Sara, a child of Asili, and Francesco, a son of Sicily who, against all odds, rooted his life in the vineyards of Langhe.

Don Emilio waited for them outside the cappella di San Teobaldo. For their small ceremony, they had chosen the tiny chapel, steps away from Sara's birthplace. Normally, couples married at San Giovanni Battista at the base of la Torre. But Sara begged don Emilio to allow them to wed in the cappella. Madama Lia's intercession facilitated the inflexible priest's consent. Sara, she said, had given much of herself to help the poorest and sickest of their community. Surely, he would grant dispensation. Madama Lia determined to do all in her power to ensure a perfect day for her.

Giovanna's happy singing and skipping with Elena Giordano heralded the arrival of the wedding party. She had shed her farm girl trappings. No longer dressed in pants and boots, at twelve years, Giovanna closely resembled Sara when he met her. In her blue dress—Sara's favorite color that Giovanna had, of course, adopted—and her hair unbraided, loose, long blonde curls framing her face, she looked the exact likeness of Sara the day he met her. The sweet memory evaporated as a nameless fear swept over him. Not at all a feeling that should eclipse the joy of this day, but something about seeing Sara again as she was six years ago chilled him. Icy fingers had grabbed him…and he saw them grab Giovanna too! What evil was lurking in their lives? The sight of the cheerful wedding party following Giovanna and Elena cast out the specter.

Far down the lane, the guests followed, the colors of their festive clothes a pleasant contrast to the usual black clothes seen in the countryside. Madama Lia's green linen suit matched the color of the lush, unruly vines. Francesco hoped her smile signaled that she accepted him as a suitable husband for her beloved Sara. The Giordano and Dalmasso families, summering in their ancestral home in Cherasco across the Tanaro River, trailed behind, talking animatedly. Luca Olivero walked closely alongside Doretta Giordano—tan from her month of walking and riding with Sara—and her brother Michele. Francesco had not seen him since the family's annual visit to Asili before Christmas, and in that time, he had grown taller than his sister. With war more a threat each day, he hoped that the battlefront did not await him after he graduated from the same military school his father had attended.

When Maria and Letizia appeared, Francesco knew that the bride would soon emerge from the cascina. Giovanna grabbed his hand, ordering Francesco and her papà inside the tiny chapel with don Emilio. Giovanna warned him not to look, but while she turned her attention to ordering people about, he turned away from the altar, hoping to catch a glance of Sara. Not twenty-four hours had passed since he had seen her last. Every part of him ached for her.

He grew impatient. The unbearable heat intensified his hunger to see his bride, to be with her that night by the sea. One last order came from Giovanna to face the altar. Then she appeared beside him. Sara. His bride, his angel, wore a cornflower blue cotton dress, a gift from Daniela Giordano.

No sooner had the priest begun the Mass than Francesco heard no more. Only Sara and he existed. The headstrong, small woman, his *taboret*, would soon be his wife. Sara handed her fragrant bouquet of lavender and white roses from Luigia's garden to Doretta. With his rough, calloused fingers, he dared to hold tight her delicate hands. What if this was all a dream and only by holding her would she not vanish? The light squeeze she gave as she discreetly brushed the ugly scar on his palm with her index finger calmed his nerves but awakened thoughts not suitable for the blessed setting.

"*Francesco, vis accípere Sara hic praeséntem in tuam legítimam uxórem juxta ritum sanctae matris Ecclésiae?*"

Before God and the people dearest to them, Francesco stood with Sara as don Emilio read the question he would answer, pledging his life, love, and fidelity to her. But he said nothing. Don Emilio rustled the pages in his prayer book as though he had lost his place. Doretta and Sara suppressed giggles. The bald-headed, rotund priest, not much taller than the bride, cleared his throat, and Sara, cara Sara, came to his rescue and whispered to him to repeat the question. Before the priest read again the vows and the most important question of his life, Francesco answered, "*Volo.*" Of course he would. He would always love, protect, and cherish her no matter what.

Then came Sara's turn. "Volo," she declared for everyone to hear, to know that she pledged herself to him.

"*Ego conjúngo vos in matrimónium. In nómine Patris, et Fílii, X et Spíritus Sancti. Amen.*" Don Emilio finished the blessing that no one understood, though the Latin liturgy was familiar to all. And they were married. *Signor e signora Francesco Bosco.*

After the nuptial Mass finally ended and the couple escaped the heat of the cramped chapel, Giovanna and Elena resumed their joyful singing and tossed pink rose petals in the air as they led don Emilio and the wedding party back to Ca' dei Fiù for the wedding lunch. All were grateful that the walk was short from the cappella in the stifling, late morning heat.

Luciana, who spent her August holidays in Asili, had joined Luigia and Giuseppina for days of preparations for this lunch. All for Sara, the one who had brought such joy to their lives that they gladly suffered the heat of their wood-fired stoves, preparing dishes—normally only eaten in cooler months—for Sara's *pranzo di nozze.*

They had set two long wooden tables in the shade of the long, vine-covered pergola that connected Cascina Asili with the garage. Pitchers of red and white roses were set along the middle of the white lace tablecloths Luigia's mamma made for her own wedding. These were difficult times, and food prices had soared under the Fascists. But in the countryside in summer, nature provided in abundance. Luigia's humble meal included Christmas and Easter favorites.

She and Giuseppina combined the hard work of their hens to prepare tajarin and agnolotti, storing them in the cold, lower reaches of both cellars, along with vitello tonnato, braised rabbit with peppers, and abundant fresh vegetables from Luigia's garden served with a sauce of Ligurian olive oil and salt. And no summer feast was complete without *merluzzo alla salsa verde*, anchovies, *risotto alle lumache*, and peach cake.

In late February, a letter had arrived for Luigia from Francesco's eldest sister, the kindest gesture she ever made to him. Before their mamma passed from influenza in late January, Anna Bosco asked her daughter to reply to Luigia's letter asking what she would have served had Francesco married in Sicily. *Rosolio*, a sweet homemade drink of rose petals, almonds, sugar, and spirits, she told Luigia, was Francesco's favorite sweet and one she would have served at his wedding if only he had stayed in Contessa Entellina.

After don Emilio blessed the meal, Gianni and Luca filled everyone's glass with a special gift from Madama Lia for the *brindisi*. Her dear friend Beppe Contratto had long ago given her a case of his 1919 *metodo classico*, the first vintage sparkling wine ever produced in Italy. The vintage, Sara's birth year, was foremost in her mind when she chose the wine.

Madama Lia's eyes glistened. Though her daughter was gone now for twenty years, she could not help but think of what might have been for Giulia's celebration. But as she raised her glass to them, Lia radiated joy. Sara beamed, filled with love for the woman who had blessed her beyond the imagination of any country girl. Never had Madama Lia sought to replace Giulia with Sara, nor to take Luigia's place as Sara's mother. But she was alone with no heirs, and she recognized in Sara a young woman like she hoped Giulia might have been—compassionate, responsible, and generous to her community. It gave her pleasure to share her blessings in her lifetime.

"Sara, Francesco," Lia's voice cracked, "I pray your days will always be joyous and filled with the love of this day. And in those times of trouble we all face in our lives, you must think back on this moment and remember your blessings, most importantly the love of family and friends. Salute!"

When it came time to serve the noble wines of Langhe, Nico produced four bottles of 1919 Barbaresco. It was unthinkable to keep wines for so long, particularly in these troubling economic times, but Nico believed four bottles for each daughter's wedding would make no difference in their lives except to bring them joy. Wine was part of their heritage. Their births and the vines of the vintage were inextricably entwined.

Francesco had no wine of his birth year to share, but Luca surprised him with four bottles of 1909 Barolo from Marchesi di Barolo, the winery of the late Giulia Colbert Falletti, the last Marquess of the great estate and the namesake of Madama Lia's only child. It wasn't Francesco's birth year, but not knowing what the future held, Luca thought it best to celebrate with it now. The other bottles, Luca hoped as he raised his glass to Doretta, would be drunk at his own wedding one day.

Madama Lia's generosity did not end at the table. She had given them a weekend wedding trip by the sea in Camogli. They thought it extravagant to spend anything more than a day in Turin to celebrate their marriage. Only wealthy couples honeymooned, particularly these days. But Madama Lia insisted they accept her gift. "My dear friend Freida Stern wishes for you stay at her family's villa on the Golfo Paradiso. She's in Valais now. So you will have the villa and the servants all to yourselves. Besides, memories of the fresh sea air, Francesco, will help you whenever you face adversity."

With several hours of train travel ahead of them, Luigia pushed the newly-weds out of the door at four o'clock. The younger girls had fashioned garlands of tuberose, lavender, and branches of juniper to festoon Madama Lia's landò for the short ride to Barbaresco stazione. Since Madama Lia's first horseless carriage arrived nearly twenty years earlier, the landò had rarely been out of the garage. For this short ride, Gianni was delighted once again to be holding the reins.

All the children jumped into the back of Nico's truck, and the adults climbed into their cars for the procession to the train station. Amid cheers and showers of rose petals, Sara and Francesco boarded the train for the short ride to Asti. From Asti, they still had several hours of travel ahead. As the train pulled away from the station, Francesco disregarded the black-clad crones who shared their car, drew Sara close, and embraced her. Before they would see the morning sun on the water, their bodies would join as one.

CHAPTER 24

Camogli (Liguria)
August 1938

After sleeping apart for the last time, Sara and Francesco had seen the sun rise over the vineyards of Langhe that morning. Hours later, now married, they watched the sun sink beyond the Alps from their Genoa-bound train. Tomorrow, together from their bed, they would see it set over the Golfo Paradiso.

Alone in the compartment, they cuddled, and Francesco stole many kisses from her. Then she slept peacefully for most of the trip between Asti and Genoa. The sea air in Genoa stazione when they changed trains refreshed her. The briny scent was like an old friend welcoming her back to a place of fond memories—a place she would leave changed, all for the better.

Now, on the last leg of their journey to Camogli, she sat across from Francesco, gazing into the darkness, straining to see the lights of the villages along the sea. Above them were the steep southern slopes of the Ligurian Apennines, which plunged to the Mediterranean.

As the train had pulled out of the station, a rotund, short man with a pencil-thin mustache had entered their compartment. He sat at the door, leaving empty the seat beside Francesco where Sara had sat. A chuckle rose from the man as he read his paper. Sara strained to see what he found so amusing. On seeing, she understood why Doretta had warned her that, away from Barbaresco, another frightening world existed.

Francesco had noticed her stiffen. Though the compartment was dimly lit, he could still see that her soft rose complexion flamed. Was her flushed face a sign that wedding night anxieties had settled upon her? Soon they would be at the villa, alone. But her narrowed eyes and her mouth that had compressed into a straight line transformed the amorous expression she had worn all day into one he knew well. She was fuming about something.

"Sara?" No response. Francesco decided to distract her. He wanted her to enjoy the journey as much as he was. They were nearly at Camogli where this part of the trip would be over.

"When Madama Lia mentioned Camogli, I had such *pelle d'oca*," he whispered to her, rubbing his arm. "Goose bumps, like the first time we kissed in the hospital. You made my skin tingle." Nothing. "Do you remember?" When she didn't react, he stared off into the ink-black sea then thought of the first time he saw the sun rise over Golfo Paradiso. "I remember the last time I saw the sea. It was from the ship's deck as we came into port. Sara…" Still no change in her brooding eyes—she was off somewhere dark. Rapidly, almost in one breath, he described the vision of that morning. "It was the first time I saw such dense, green forests. Belice Valley is mostly barren and rocky. A few forests…one day, you'll see." Enough of this. He reached and touched her knee. "Sara…Sara, are you all right?"

She blinked, her eyes brightening as she focused on him. "Sì, caro, mi dispiace. Dimmi."

Had she even heard him? "The forests clung to steep slopes that dropped straight into the sea. You'll see tomorrow, but of course, you've seen it before. Someone next to me on deck pointed to a tiny village with colorful houses like ornaments on a Christmas tree. 'Camogli,' they said. And soon I'll be in that village…with you."

Sara had returned to him. Her smile and raised cheekbones brightening her small face, longing in her eyes that no doubt read the same in his. He was hungry to touch her, to love her. The desire she expressed when she kissed him so passionately in the stable two nights ago told him she had no fear of the night ahead.

"You know," she said, "my life began today. There was no yesterday until today. Now you are my tomorrow."

He smiled but also turned his head away with embarrassment that the stranger might have heard her. Then he reached for her hand. Her full lips turned up in a playful smile. That familiar eagerness in her eyes returned. Yes, the engagement had been a torture, and now each minute that passed seemed an eternity. But then, they had eternity to be together.

"Sara," he began, but her attention had turned to the man by the door, her gaze hard and cold.

The train pulled to a stop at the small station. As he reached up for their valise, he turned and saw Sara sweep past the stranger, deliberately bumping his magazine with her hand, sending it to the floor. Francesco moved to retrieve it while she continued out of the compartment without an apology. He handed the magazine to the man, but before he could apologize for her, there it was—the headline. There was no mistaking what had infuriated his bride.

This is what Luca meant when he told him about the dangers he feared Doretta and her family would soon face. He remembered something Luca had said recently on one of his trips to Asili in July. "Francesco, I tell you these things because Sara, as you know so well, is a passionate woman who rushes in against any injustice. This could prove dangerous for her. And for you."

The large, bold letters stunned him: *Razzismo Italiano.*

Luca explained that scientists had published a manifesto of ten points that was being used to support racial edicts in Italy. Sara and Doretta Giordano had grown close over the summer, and the louder the anti-Semitic voices in Italy grew, the more protective Sara became even though Doretta herself showed no fear. What Sara had done was understandable but dangerous. Thankfully, the man ignored them and remained on the train.

On the platform, Francesco caught up with her. "Carissima, I know how upset these things make you, but you can't behave that way." Anger flashed in her eyes, and Francesco decided to leave the subject for another time. But he would not forget.

They walked hand in hand to the villa, located at the water's edge where the shore jutted out to a peninsula dominated by a small mountain. So strong were the scents of the sea in the humid evening that Francesco tasted the salt of the water over which the breeze had blown. The moon, still low in the sky to the east, cast its ethereal light on the towering, steep slopes. The air was filled with the pungent odor of fish—both freshly caught being offloaded from small, colorful wooden boats and that being cooked in a tiny restaurant near the beach. It made him hungry, but there would be no time for dinner tonight.

As they walked through the cortile of the villa, tucked away on its own at the head of the peninsula, Francesco let go of Sara's hand. Such luxuries were new to him. He would never be able to give Sara something like this. And, after her life in the city and the gifts Madama Lia showered on her, she might be expecting it. Yet, her humble roots were deep. For him, the luxury would be to lie with her, even on the beach. He wanted Sara and nothing more.

An elegantly dressed man greeted them at the villa entrance. "Buonasera, signorina Fiore. *Auguri!*" He slapped his mouth and corrected himself. The young girl he had met before when she had visited was no longer a maiden. "Mi dispiace, signor e signora Bosco, *ben arrivati.* Mi chiamo Mario. *Al vostro servizio.*" Madama Lia had brought Sara and her zia Luce here to visit Madame Stern and to celebrate the successful completion of her studies. Her friendly disposition endeared her to the villa staff. That and her small stature and piercing blue eyes made it hard to forget her.

Mario took them straight up a grand staircase to their room. The two glass doors leading to the terrace had been left open, sending a rush of sea air that embraced them as Mario opened the door to the room. Francesco had forgotten how invigorating it was, in contrast to Langhe's earthy aromas that defined the land. From this night onward, the scent of the sea would be a perfume he would associate with Sara.

Mario switched on the lights, illuminating the splendid furnishings. Francesco's jaw dropped. Madame Stern had given them a grand suite with a *letto matrimoniale* and a west-facing terrace over the water. Mario informed them that it would be a grand place to sit and view the sunset over the gulf. For now, all they wanted was for him to leave. Mario grinned and slipped away, switching off the lights as he left, leaving them in the soft moonlight.

Years of longing, months of waiting, were over. Francesco pulled her close, lifting her lithe body. Even in the pale light, her eyes shone. He set her down and began to undress her, but she pulled away.

"Sara…what are you…?"

"Caro. Wait. I'll be back."

She slipped away and Francesco heard the door to the bathroom close. Of course, it had been a long train ride. While he waited, he poured two glasses of water from the bottles left for them. After they were both refreshed, she turned her back to him and pulled her long hair to the front, draping it over her chest.

Daniela Giordano's dressmaker must not have considered the obstacle she created when she designed the long line of delicate buttons from the neck to the bottom of Sara's spine. Or perhaps she did. With each cloth-covered button he slipped from its loop, he fought the urge to rip apart the blue dress. As his thick, clumsy fingers moved down her spine, Sara's breathing quickened, as did his. His hands trembled with urgency, making the task all the more difficult. He bent to kiss her neck, two kisses for each button. The taste of her salty skin and the fusion of her warm scent with the briny air that had filled the room intoxicated him.

Nine, ten… "Sara," his voice quivered. This was torture. Was she suffering as much as he was? She was so small that he had to sit on the edge of the bed, holding her between his knees as his mouth followed his hands, kissing her salty skin as he painstakingly freed each button.

Eleven, twelve… Finally, he lost the battle with his passion and pulled the dress from her shoulders, freeing her arms. She pushed it off her hips, but held onto her slip, unwilling to reveal more. He swooped her up in his arms and fell back on the grand bed. Her damp, silk slip clung to her. Even through his clothes, he felt the heat rise from her featherweight body. It was as though her heart was in his chest, pulsing blood through his own body. He wanted to move but lay still, fearing she might roll away. Instead, she surprised him with a question.

"*Mio caro marito*, am I to be the only one free from hot clothes?" She asked in an unfamiliar voice, her eyes intense and luminous with desire. Since their engagement on Christmas Eve, they had kissed with abandon countless times, but she had always pushed him away, leaving him frustrated. Recently, in the stable she granted him brief explorations of her body through her clothes as they kissed, but always sent him home to the hayloft, alone. Their good-night kiss in the stable, the last before they married, was the first indication that a fire smoldered below.

Now, on her knees, she straddled him about the hips, her hands shaking as she worked to remove his damp shirt. He was powerless as she smothered his chest with kisses while she caressed his jaw and explored his lips with her fingers. She sat up and moved her fingers from his throat to his waist. The quivering peaks of her small breasts stood erect under the clinging slip. The straps had slid off her shoulders, making it easy for him finally to free her from the wet fabric. Once again, she stopped him. She took his left hand and traced the scar across the palm.

"I feel as though I should thank the wild horse that hurt you so." She kissed it and ran her fingers across it as she had in the cappella. "Would you have come to us and the vineyards, if not for this?" No, perhaps he wouldn't have, but the passage of time had convinced him that they were fated to be together.

He pulled his hand away and reached once again for the straps of her slip. "May I?" he whispered. She nodded before closing her eyes as he uncovered her. In the ethereal light of the half-moon, he wondered for a moment if she was a spirit. But no, she was real. Seeing her bared breasts and the first hint of shyness as she curled her arms over them only heightened his desire. He gently tugged at her arms, but she resisted.

"Sara, please." His desire reached a fever pitch, but he reminded himself that she had never shared her body with anyone. This was the first time a man touched her like this and caressed her nakedness with his eyes. He knew that they had crossed into a place unknown to her. He must tread lightly now and handle her delicately.

Not giving him a moment to enjoy the vision, she collapsed upon him. Tendrils of her tousled, wavy hair spilled forward, brushing his shoulders and neck as her lips sought his. What a surprise she was. Soon, she made quick work of his belt and the restraints holding back that which had been a long time ready to enter her. Then, in one abrupt move, she rolled off him and pulled the sheet across her bare chest.

This hunger mixed with shyness was driving him wild. Now he would take control. He sat up and removed his boots. He walked to the terrace doors and pulled the shutters closed, leaving the slats open so he would have enough light to see her, when she let him. His pants dropped to the floor, finally freeing him.

His silhouette showed her what she had not seen while nursing him. Luciana had bathed him and tended to his needs when he was in the hospital. And nothing Sara had read addressed this situation, exactly. She was so small, and a virgin. Mamma told her there would be pain—no pleasure the first time. Pleasure, she said, was secondary for a woman. Babies and satisfying her husband were her primary duties. Thus far, she had felt only pleasure of a kind she had never known, but now she feared that he would hurt her, and in a way she couldn't bear. Would she bleed? If she felt pain, she would. That much she knew about what would happen the first time he entered her.

He slid into bed beside her and slowly pulled the sheet away before nudging her slip and panties over her hips and onto the floor. She tensed and squeezed her eyes shut, grabbing the sheet and covering herself again.

"Sara, cara. Don't be shy." But she rolled away from him, her knees and the sheet drawn tightly to her chest. He leaned over her and nudged her onto her back. She didn't resist. He kissed her closed eyes and with his thumb wiped away a lone tear. "You've seen me before. You can't possibly be embarrassed with your husband."

She opened her eyes wide. "No, you're wrong. Mamma made certain you were covered at all times. She even made me turn my back one time when she was undressing you. And Luciana took over at the hospital."

SUZANNE HOFFMAN

He lay beside her and once again tugged at the sheet, but she clutched it in her hands. One quick pull was all he needed to tear it from her, but that was not how he wanted this moment to be for her. His voice was gentle but pleading as he tried in vain to coax her to let him unveil her. "Sara, what can I do with you covered like that? Let me…" He tugged again, this time a little stronger. "If you won't let me see you, please let me—not the sheet—cover you."

As quickly as she had rolled off him before, she threw back the sheet, pushed him onto his back, and rolled atop him. She clung to his shoulders and buried her face against his neck, her hair tumbling over his face. He brushed it away and caressed her tiny, muscular bottom, so tense now. The pain would be worse, he knew, with her this wound up. How could he calm her fears, though, when he didn't even know how much pain she would feel? He had never been with a virgin. He knew that pleasure awaited him, but at her expense. Now she bravely opened her legs and pressed firmly into his thighs. Such sweet pain. Now, how to pry her loose. "Ah, Zeus, what a life you have had," he moaned. A muffled giggle rose from her. At long last, she relaxed and nuzzled his neck as she worked her way to his jaw, his cheeks, his mouth. "Oh, Sara, I do love you so."

He waited, throbbing. It wasn't like Sara to be this frightened and wary. His patience was rewarded when she slid off him onto her back—this time uncovered but with her eyes still squeezed shut. He kissed her trembling eyelids and explored her lips with his tongue before they softened and parted. Patience might work. But he had a better idea. Numerous times, he had watched Sara break the young, skittish horses. The harder she pulled on the lead line, the more stubborn the horse became. When she stopped pulling, the horse always relaxed. Then she would reward him, put him in his stall, and try later.

"What a hot day it has been, don't you think?" She gazed at him as though surprised by the question. "Mario said we have a grand bathtub with lots of hot water, although cool water would feel better. What if I fill the tub for you?"

"Oh, but Francesco…I mean…are you sure?"

He smiled and slid off the bed. How it hurt him in every way imaginable, but no, he would be patient. While he drew her bath and sponged himself with cold water, he watched his frustrated arousal wither. He knew that, at the sight of her, even the smell of her, he would be ready again. Hopefully she would be too.

She stood at the door, wrapped tightly in the sheet, her blushing face so winsome.

222

"Here, Sara. All for you. And lavender-scented bubbles." Glowing, she walked to him, stood on her tiptoes, and gave him a kiss—not a passionate one as before but quite sweet, stirring him once more. She walked to the tub, and not waiting for him to leave the room, let the sheet fall to the floor. Before she slipped into the tepid water, she turned her head and gave him that mischievous grin he had seen. For a moment longer, he relished her beauty, pulled the door, and slid into bed to wait for her—however long it took.

Later, Francesco lay on his side, propped up on his elbow as he studied his sleeping bride. He had drifted off to sleep while she bathed and woke to find her alongside him, also sleeping, more at ease with her nakedness. The sheet she had clung to now only covered her waist and thighs. What lay between her parted legs remained hidden from him.

She moaned, stirring, her mouth edging up at the corners into a sweet smile. What was she dreaming about? Dawn was breaking, and the tide must be coming in, as he heard the clacking of stones on the beach in rhythm with the waves. The breeze was up, filling the room with the mysterious scents of the sea.

The first rays of sun peeked through the shutters, giving him enough light to see the silhouette of her small breasts and their tips she had hidden from him, firm against his chest when she had lain on him. Her sudden shyness had robbed him of the chance to explore her body with his hands, his eyes. With each deep breath, her chest rose, then fell, steadily, slowly. Lightly, he traced her collarbone to its junction with her breastbone. He paused. Lifting his finger ever so slightly, he hovered above her throat. Although hungry to kiss what his fingers touched, he did not dare lest he startle her.

His finger resumed its journey, through the shallow valley between her breasts—she shivered, he paused—onward to her navel. He fought the intense urge to cover her body with his. He would wait. She shivered again and straightened her legs, her feet pointing and relaxing, pointing and relaxing. Was she dreaming of him?

Less cautious now, he drew the sheet away and revealed what she had so closely guarded. He rested his palm on her belly and spread his fingers over her silky skin. As he moved lower, over her downy patch above the junction of her thighs, her hips arched, rose slightly to meet his touch, and fell again. She moaned but still seemed to be asleep. He watched as they rose again in the instinctive rhythm of love. His own hips involuntarily moved with hers. This time, not only would he be ready, but he would ensure that she was as well.

He inched closer until his pulsating arousal pressed against her thigh. She was so tiny, so petite. Earlier, he had not thought of how she might feel beneath him. Was he too heavy for her to breathe?

Goose bumps erupted across her skin. A soft groan from her beckoned him to continue exploring. He slipped his hand between her legs and cupped her thigh, nudging a tender place he had not yet touched. His fingers relayed the signals that her body was ready. Did he dare probe further? Light fingers brushed his hand. He froze. Was she stopping him? But they fluttered over his hand and moved past, searching. She wrapped her hand around his now throbbing fullness. As her fingers tightened around him, the eagerness and strength of her first touch nearly brought him to the point of no return.

"Francesco..." She whispered his name, but it was more a moan than speech. He reluctantly slid his hand out from between her thighs and she rolled to her side, toward him this time. Tentatively, he cupped her bottom to bring her closer to him. Her grip on him increased, driving him closer to the abyss. She drew him closer, tighter. When she rolled on her back, he gladly followed, resting on his forearms as he slowly lowered his weight onto her. When certain that he would not crush her, he allowed his body to settle onto hers. As he entered her, she took in a shallow, raspy breath. He slowly eased into her, deeper, but stopped when she turned her head. He froze for a moment, but then she wrapped her legs tight about him and pulled him closer, deeper, pressing her hands firmly on his hips. She let out a soft whimper.

"Sara?" She would not look at him. Tears oozed from under her squeezed eyelids. She bit her lower lip. "Should I stop?" he asked even though he knew he wouldn't be able to. He was deep inside her, and they seemed inseparable. But he could wait as long as possible. She freed her lower lip and searched for his mouth. He had her answer.

"Francesco" she said.

"What is it, Angel?"

"Don't ever leave me."

Together they moved in rhythm until damp heat from within her surged around him. With one more gentle push deep inside her, he was oblivious to all except the tidal wave of heat that consumed him.

"Never, Angel. Never shall I leave you." Still within her, he rolled onto his back, carrying her, wrapped tightly in his arms, along with him. Together, they surrendered to sleep as sunlight flooded the room.

The sound of children on the beach below woke her. Sticky heat had replaced the cool sea air. What time was it? They remained entwined—her top leg draped over his stomach, her face buried against his neck. It was now her favorite place, her refuge. She slid off him while he slept. The searing pain within her groin had subsided. The memory she had already banished, preferring only to remember how, inside her, he had experienced such pleasure.

She stretched her leg and rubbed a cramp in her calf. How long had they been lying together? By the fading light through the shutters, she knew the sun was low across the water. Had they slept through the day? Neither of them was covered. Sara sat cross-legged and looked over the body that had loved her. She kissed her finger and brushed it over the near-invisible scar on his right cheek. "*Perdonami amore mio. Perdona la mia gelosia,*" she whispered. For so long she had wanted to ask his forgiveness for having treated him poorly. What right did she have to be jealous after she had spurned him? That was the past. What mattered most was that he was here with her. And he loved her like no other.

Across his groin and on the sheet she saw dried blood. Her mamma had not been entirely right. Yes, it had been excruciating, but pleasure quickly followed. And she thrilled at the idea of pleasing him, her power over him. She gingerly touched herself. Still sore, but ready for him again.

The light weight on his body and feathers tickling his face woke him. Something warm and dewy pressed against his belly. And there were her eyes, filled once again with desire, her smile lusty, no longer mischievous. Wisps of her hair, not feathers, lay across his face, his shoulders. Her teasing lips finally chased away his grogginess.

"Oh, Sara, not so soon."

"Soon? The sun is already setting. Why not?" she asked as she squeezed her legs tighter around his. Her lusty laugh, something so deliciously new, stirred him.

"Seriously, love…" It was a losing battle. What had happened to his angel? Had he awakened a devil lurking within her? "You had your chance to soak last night. Now it's my turn, but I want company."

Her girlish giggle returned as she ran to the bathroom. After she closed the door, he heard the squeaking sound of faucets and running water. Moments later, she emerged, peeked around the corner, and crooked her finger to beckon him.

"Come, you can have your privacy, then I'll join you for some and fruit and cheese Mario left for us. I'm starving."

"My dear nurse, don't go. You first."

She slipped into the tub and waited for him to climb in behind her. He slid his arms around her and cupped her small breasts. Never had he known such bliss, such tender love. Lust, yes, but his all-consuming love for his wife took him to an unknown place.

"Francesco, what shall we name our son?" she asked in a matter-of-fact manner as she pushed bubbles over her chest. He pushed them away and pulled her closer, cradling her in his arms.

"So soon?"

"The time would be right though I would prefer we have time alone together first." Her fingers danced along his thigh. "You wouldn't want to be married and unable to…well…enjoy this, would you?"

"Nico. Our son should be named for his nonno, who will teach him all he taught me about the vines, the cantina. About life as a contadino in Langhe."

"But your father's name is Antonino. Surely you mean Nino."

He squirmed behind her, settled back again, and rested his feet on the edge of the tub. "Why are these tubs so short?"

"I fit perfectly. Answer my question."

"No, Sara. My papà is Nico and that's the name of our son. And if a girl?"

"Anna, after your mamma. We'll call our second daughter Luigia. Mamma won't mind. Always, you spoke with such love of her. I'm sad I'll never meet her."

He hugged her and kissed the top of her head. Her nearness between his legs stirred him again. "Either way, they are lovely names." He caressed her tiny breasts and nibbled her neck. "Back to bed now?"

"No, Francesco. I'm hungry, and I want to see the sunset." She stepped out of the tub, leaving him wanting, and wrapped herself in the plush robe left for her. He heard the cork of the Champagne bottle pop. The shutters creaked, and she called to him.

Mario was right: the sunset was magical from the terrace. The entire day had passed without their awareness of time except that the room was now stifling. She handed him a glass of Champagne and touched his glass with hers. Out on the terrace, not caring that the Champagne they sipped was now warm, he marveled at the beauty of the woman he loved against the breathtaking landscape. She put her glass down and turned toward the sea. He kissed her damp neck. So petite in size, but strong in character. Life with Sara would be a challenge. When they left Camogli, would he ever know such a moment of peace, of joy, again?

The clicking sound of jackboots on the strand broke the sea's spell on him. Blackshirts marching through the bucolic village. If they were here, in a secluded seaside village, how long before they marched on via Torino in Barbaresco? Sara's body against his stiffened. In the last vestige of daylight, her face reddened to the deep red of rage, no different than her reaction to the man on the train.

He turned her to him, away from the sight. They stood for a moment, wrapped in each other's arms. If he let her go, would she vanish? Was this all a dream and the Blackshirts their reality?

"Come, cara." He scooped up his lover and carried her back to bed, completely closing the shutters behind him. They were both starving, having only eaten the fruit and cheese while they soaked. But first, they would feed the insatiable hunger they had for one another. They would have to face the outside world again, but at least now, they would face it together. This time, there was no hesitation, no pain. Sara did not shiver. She shuddered under him. Her back arched as the heat from within her intensified and she tightened around him, as he had hoped she would. Her fulfillment unleashed a tingling, blissful surge of energy that flowed through his body, carrying him on a warm wave into euphoric blankness.

CHAPTER 25

Turin
September 1938

Carissima Doretta.

Those were the first words Doretta heard from Sara since waving good-bye to the newlyweds at Barbaresco stazione a month earlier. Doretta longed for news from her, now more than ever.

I'm sorry I have not written to you earlier. You have been on my mind since we returned from Camogli. It was short but, Doretta…well, when I see you next, we shall talk. The harvest is about to begin, so I barely see Francesco during the day. But our nights…

Doretta laughed, longing to hear the details from her strong-willed friend who, despite her knowledge of the human body, had blushed and giggled like a schoolgirl when Doretta told her about her passionate kiss with Luca.

Doretta longed for the countryside—not only to visit Sara and escape the turmoil in the Turin Jewish community but also to see Luca. The brief moments they stole during his visits to Asili in the summer were all she had seen of him in months. His infrequent letters were cordial and businesslike though he was warmer when they were together. He had yet to acknowledge her declaration of love, and she hesitated to raise it in Asili. It was all so confusing. For two years, helping German Jews flee to the relative safety of Italy had brought them together. Now, the anti-Semitism those Jews fled had erupted in Italy.

The events of the last six months ran counter to Mussolini's declaration in

1934 that there had never been anti-Semitism in Italy. Ironically, that claim had coincided with the beginning of an anti-Semitic press campaign by the Fascists, accusing Jews of being Communists who took Italian jobs and were responsible for the high food prices. Most Italians, including Doretta's circle of Catholic friends, discounted the campaign. But then *Il Giornale d'Italia* printed the ten-point manifesto on race on July 14.

Doretta was in Asili at the time, enjoying the summer with Sara and getting ready for her wedding. Luca brought her a copy of the manifesto and averted his glance as he handed it to her. The headline of the *La Stampa* article burned in her mind: *Il problema della razza nell'Italia Fascista*. First, in April, Mussolini had dismissed all Jewish journalists, and since then the press had mimicked German newspapers. Now, the "Decalogue of Racism" declared that Italians were of the Aryan race. Doretta read it as a decalogue of hate.

Although racial scientists and scholars were named as the signatories to the Manifesto, many suspected that Mussolini and his anti-Semitic stooge, Guido Landra, himself a self-styled "racial scientist," had penned it. Even her papà thought so, yet he clung to his unwavering loyalty to Mussolini. "He has a Jewish mistress, Doretta. How could he be anti-Semitic?"

On September 1, Mussolini lowered the hammer on Italy's Jews when le Leggi Razziali, the first racial laws, were announced. With King Vittorio Emanuele III's signature on these laws, he undid King Carlo Alberto's full emancipation of Piemonte's Jews in 1848. The king had sided with the anti-Semites. Many thought that would be the end of it, that this was all a way to curry favor with Hitler, but Doretta didn't believe it.

The grandfather clock in the hall chimed eight times. Time for breakfast. Her father had just returned from Paris, and she wanted to speak with him. She slipped Sara's letter into the textbook. She would read it later between classes.

Doretta looked at her parents on opposite ends of the long table, rarely speaking to one another anymore. She sat beside her papà while he read the latest news of the racial laws in *La Stampa*. Since Lorelei Vogel's death, her relationship with her papà had cooled. She missed their long talks and sharing her opinions with him. There was a time when she had hung on his every word. Now she found it increasingly difficult to hold her tongue. Mussolini had become a taboo subject. But this was different. He was going to strip Jews of their rights as Italians.

"Papà, do you see now? We finally have proof that Mussolini is an anti-Semite. I think he always was." She paused, waiting for his reaction.

He rattled his newspaper as he turned back to the front page but continued reading, avoiding her angry glare. "You have no idea what you're talking about, Doretta."

Doretta leaned in, lightly touched his arm, and pointed to the headlines. "Read, Papà! Do you see what they are saying? They claim we are of a different race and must be removed from Italian society."

"Teodora Giordano! I will not have that kind of disrespectful talk in my house," he shouted as he folded the paper and slammed it on the table. He paused, glaring at her before continuing, softer, but his voice still brimming with anger. "I was told that, as a result of being a loyal founding member of the Fascist Party and giving service in the Great War, we would not be subject to these laws." Calmer still. "Mussolini has said repeatedly he is for discrimination, not persecution. We are safe! Now enough of that talk."

Oh? So other Jews could be treated badly as long as he remained special himself? "But, Papà, don't you see, they counted us last month. That census was only for Jews. Now they know where each and every one of us lives. How long, Papà," she pleaded, "before we're required to change our identity cards to include Sara or Israel as our middle names like zia Silvana had to do in Germany?"

"That was nothing, Doretta. It was a part of the ongoing special census. Didn't you see on the questionnaire that I had to give my Fascist Party card number and details of my war record? These laws will exclude loyal Fascists like us."

Doretta's skin crawled at his inclusion of all family members as loyal Fascists. She certainly was not. "Papà. It was a *racial* survey. They aren't counting people based on religion. They are only counting Jews based on race. And Moslems have been excluded from the count. What does that say?" It felt as though she was seeing herself from afar. She could not stop herself at this point. "Papà, why don't you see the danger in that?"

He sat glaring at his plate, fiddling with his knife. His cheeks vibrated as he ground his teeth. Even the tips of his ears had gone red.

Yet Doretta knew that there was no going back. "Don't you see that Mussolini has turned Italy into an anti-Semitic state? What will it take to wake you up, Papà"—she paused then shouted—"blood in the streets?"

"Enough!" He slammed his fist on the table, upending his water glass. Thank God, Elena had already left for school. She glanced at her mamma, needing reassurance or some signal of comfort, but found none. Neither did she admonish Doretta for her disrespect.

"This is *my* house, do you understand?" Gabriele roared. "I will not have anyone, particularly a child of mine—a girl no less—speak to me in such a manner. Your anti-Fascist attitudes have no place under my roof. If you do not apologize for your disrespect and change your ways now, I will lock you in your room, do you understand?"

Still her mamma sad rigid, eyes narrowed as she glared at her husband at the far end of the table. Doretta's heart raced. Her breakfast, what little she had eaten of it, started creeping back up, burning her throat. All was now lost with her father. Thoughtfully, calmly, she folded her napkin, stood, and walked to her mamma. She kissed her dry, bony cheek and left the room.

DORETTA FOLLOWED HER CLASSMATES INTO THE LECTURE HALL, LISTENING to her friend Isabella's story of a holiday trip to Venice. For the first day of her second year of law studies, Doretta had chosen an understated, dark-blue dress and flat shoes. The professore of the international law class was known to be difficult and demanding. Best not to stand out. Everyone was afraid of him. But what better way to prepare to face judges, to face anyone?

Isabella sat next to her, whispering, as she continued jabbering about her trip to Venice. Doretta didn't want to be rude, nor did she want to miss her name in the roll call on the first day of class.

"Ginzburg, Primo."

"Present." A student seated two rows ahead of her raised his hand. The professor's next words caught everyone's attention, even Isabella's.

"Ginzburg. Jewish student. Take all of your things and go straight to the administration office."

"But, sir, professor…"

"Now!"

Doretta watched, stunned, as one of the kindest, brightest students Doretta knew left the room. Why was he singled out? Surely, he wasn't caught up with the anti-Fascists. And what does his being Jewish have to do with anything?

"Giordano, Doretta." She froze. "Giordano! Jewish student. Raise your hand now," professor Orani bellowed.

No one moved except to cast sideward glances to see if his target was near. Was Isabella leaning away? A chill ran through Doretta's body. She had never been singled out for anything. Slowly, timidly, she raised her trembling hand.

"You! Take your things and leave. Report to the administration office immediately."

Doretta sat, frozen. "But, professor—"

"Now, Giordano!" he barked. "You should have known that you are expelled from the university. There will no longer be Jews in public schools."

All the eyes of the full lecture hall bored into her. "Fucking Jew!" someone muttered, and another snickered. The faces of her friends reflected her own shock but not her humiliation. Not one would be brave enough to leave the lecture hall with her—who would risk the retaliation? More snickers came from the back of the room as she packed her things and rushed from the lecture hall, trying to remember to keep her head high. Then something dropped from her textbook: Sara's letter. A fellow student reached for it, but Doretta snatched it up, clutching it to her chest.

When the door closed behind her, Doretta dropped her books and grabbed her sides, still clutching Sara's letter, desperately trying to calm her stomach as she struggled to breathe. No tears! She would not give them the satisfaction, but she needed first to compose herself. Others joined her in the hall although classes were in session. No one spoke. The vacant stares and ashen faces of those who shuffled past her told her that they shared her indignity of expulsion. The words and glares of her classmates chased her down the stairs she had climbed minutes before with friends, laughing and joking about their lives as free-spirited university students. Within minutes, the life she knew had ended.

The hot air hit her as she burst through the doors onto the street. Or was it merely rage surging through her body? The pounding in her head pulsated with the rapid beating of her heart. With no tram in sight, she decided to walk home.

The thirty-minute walk gave her time to think what to do. She just wanted her mamma and prayed that her father wasn't home. Though, maybe if he saw her humiliation, he might finally wake to the sickening reality of their world.

Elena! Her stomach seized at the thought of her little sister, so happy to be back in school with her friends, now suffering the same humiliation. Summer in Cherasco had bored her. With her upcoming bat mitzvah in October, she made everyone aware that the last place she had wanted to be was in the countryside. And Michele! He had returned to school days ago, filled with promise for a military career. These new laws would dash his hopes. Never had her role as the big sister weighed upon her as it did now. How would her younger siblings and their two young cousins, who had already experienced the cruelty of anti-Semitism in Germany, cope with this? Carrying her heavy books, no longer of use to her, she ran the rest of the way, dashing through intersections. She would have to pull herself together for the children, to give them the strength they needed.

Doretta pushed open the door to their apartment building and ran past the doorman. He wore the same forced smile, more like a smirk, as when she left for school earlier that morning. Now she understood why. Was this how it was going to be? Before she reached the first-floor landing, the shrill sound of a wailing child echoed in the stairwell. Elena was already home. Doretta gasped for air and was sweating profusely, but the wails of her baby sister drove her up the remaining four flights of stairs. Through the wide-open door of the apartment and over the sound of her own heavy breathing, Doretta heard her mamma in the library, cooing to Elena, trying to calm her, but the brokenhearted child's sobs only deepened.

"*Perché*, Mamma? Perché…" was all Elena managed to say between sobs. Who knew why? How would they ever explain to the twelve-year-old why this was happening to her when they themselves had been broadsided?

From above came zia Silvana's unsteady voice, similarly trying to calm her two traumatized children who, Doretta feared, would be swept up once more into a maelstrom of hate.

Daniela's eyes met Doretta's. Neither mother nor daughter said a word. It had only been two hours since they last saw each other. Her mamma's eyes had been dry when she left, but now they were red and swollen.

Doretta joined her mamma on the divan, wrapping her arm around her, knowing that she needed comfort too. Elena buried her head in her mamma's bosom, her muffled sobs unrelenting as she clung to her. Doretta had never seen Elena cry from sadness and humiliation. Usually, she was defiant, often making Gisele cry. Doretta pushed Elena's tear-dampened hair out of her eyes and kissed her forehead. "Mi dispiace, carina. Mi dispiace."

Later, when she went upstairs, Doretta came across Friedrich, trying to console his mother, who sat on the divan in her room, her face buried in her hands. He was stroking her long, disheveled hair, normally neatly braided and pinned on her head. Gisele had stopped crying and watched them, stunned out of her own misery. Friedrich looked up at Doretta as if hoping that she would have the answer. But she was struggling to keep her own tears at bay. There was no one to console her. She ached for Luca. He would understand. He would know just what to say.

On her way to school that morning, she had fumed about her father's words and decided that she would try to find a way to leave—how dare her father threaten to lock her in her room—but not after today. She had no choice but to make peace with her father if only for her siblings' sake. Michele would return from military school soon. He was bold and daring, but Doretta knew this would devastate him. All his dreams and hopes now lay in ruins. They all needed her now, even her father, trapped as he was in his delusional world. Someone had to take control in the family. Her mamma had been so broken over the years that she already relied on Doretta for support and advice.

Barbaresco—she would go to Asili for Sara's comfort, her sage advice. The harvest, a time of camaraderie, of joy, would soon begin. No matter the turmoil in the outside world, the harvest never yielded. And Luca, she knew, would come to her in Asili. She ached for him.

Doretta went to her zia and kissed her cheek. "*Andrà tutto bene*, zia. All will be fine." Did Silvana believe that? She did not.

Silvana's eyes flashed with a fury Doretta knew was not for her. "Never! It will never be fine again, Doretta. I won't go through this again. I won't!"

She had no response for her zia, not now at least. This was familiar to her, but Doretta believed it was only the beginning of their persecution in Italy. How despicable that the first victims of these vile laws were children. Surely, the pope would call out the Fascists. But no one had stopped Hitler in his campaign for a judenrein Germany. The silence of the victors of the Great War only emboldened the two Fascist leaders. They appeared unstoppable, bent on war. How long before Mussolini would move to the next phase already underway in Germany—rounding up people into concentration camps. What then? Doretta shuddered.

Daniela entered the room, Elena trailing behind her, clinging to her mamma's hand. Elena, like Doretta, rarely retreated, but to be shamed was something beyond her comprehension. As soon as Daniela sat next to Silvana, Elena returned to her safe harbor on her mamma's lap. Gisele, to whom Elena had been a bullying older cousin since they arrived, squeezed in between the two sisters and stroked Elena's hair.

"Who needs school anyway, Elena? We'll have more time to play."

It was endearing to witness the child—already a refugee—attempt to comfort her older cousin. Friedrich stood erect, at attention, like one of his pewter soldiers. By his furrowed brow, Doretta guessed he was strategizing, thinking of a battle plan. He had one he presented to her.

"Doretta, do you think Luca can come and help me take us away from here? All of us. You too. We were a good team, Luca and me. He told me." He turned to her, mournfully adding. "I don't want to see Mamma cry."

Luca. Would Mussolini's laws defending a race he claimed existed forbid marriages between *ariani* and Jews as the Nuremberg laws had? Silvana's marriage to Fritz had become illegal even though they had married before Hitler came to power. Was her relationship with Luca doomed from the start? Was that the reason for him not reciprocating the love she professed to him?

Heavy footsteps on the stairs approached.

"What's all this?" Gabriele demanded as he walked up behind Doretta. Ignoring her, he asked, "Daniela, why is Elena home from school so early?"

It was as though the oxygen had been drawn from the room. His presence would only make matters worse.

"Did you hear me, Daniela? Answer me!" Doretta wished his clenched fists and booming voice that increased the volume of Elena's wails were meant for the Fascists. But they weren't.

Her mamma stared at him as if daring him to approach. Gone was the vacant expression Doretta had grown used to over recent years. "Papà, we have been expelled," Doretta answered softly.

"What do you mean, *expelled*?" he asked.

"As though you don't know, Gabriele." Daniela nudged Elena off her lap, strode across the room, and stood inches from her husband, her chin up. Gabriele had finally crossed the line with his wife. "See what your great Duce has done?" she shouted. "Our children have been thrown out of school. No Jews allowed. Do you still admire a man who would do this? What have *they* done to deserve this?"

"He has only done this to remove the disloyal from public life. We are immune as I told you this morning. Jews like us will not suffer under these laws."

"Like *us*? Tell me Gabriele, how do we fit into that picture?"

"By virtue of my service to the country in the Great War and my loyalty to the Party as a founding member."

Daniela clapped her hands over her ears and squeezed her eyes shut. When she opened them, she looked at her husband as if she didn't know who he was. "I will *not* stand by and let my children be swept up into this tempest, this hate that you condone."

"Daniela, you…" Gabriele sputtered, but she was on her way out the door with Elena close behind.

"Doretta! What lies have you been spreading here? I think it's time for you to go to your room."

Clutching the book in which she had placed Sara's letter, Doretta spun and faced Gabriele with the same fire in her eyes as her mamma. "My room? No, Papà. I'm nineteen years old and refuse to be treated like a child. I will not stand by silently while my siblings suffer a cruel fate you have had a hand in." Doretta started out of the room but turned and spat her words. "You are useless, Papà! *Useless.*"

As she looked down the long hall, it was as though she was peering through the wrong end of a telescope. Her room, her sanctuary, at the far end seemed further away. How different her life was now than when she walked to breakfast that morning. She passed her mamma's door—whimpering from within—and her baby sister's, muffled wailing continuing as she cried into her pillows. Doretta closed the thick wooden door to her room and leaned against it, feeling as she had when she left class, breathless and struggling not to retch. Who was that who had spoken to her father that way? Not her. But it was. The twelve sonorous gongs of the grandfather clock in the front hall announced the middle of the day. Nineteen years of life upended in four hours. She eased onto her bed and sank deep into her stacked down pillows.

She slipped Sara's letter from her book and carefully unfolded it.

I must be brief now since I am between patients, but I'll write more this weekend. I am riding today—no, Doretta, I am not pregnant…but we keep trying.

Oh, Sara, thank you for the smile.

I stopped below Villa Cristina on my way to visit the Contessa. I feel close to you in this, our favorite spot with il Re for company in the distance. I am happy beyond my wildest dreams and hope you and Luca will discover the same happiness. Well, I must go. The Contessa will be cross if I am late. Please, Doretta, come to Asili soon. I miss you and want to share my happiness.
With love, Sara.

Sara's life had changed, and joy had filled it. Doretta's, too, had changed but only because she was a Jew. She had already decided to leave for the countryside, but now she felt desperate to go, if only for a few days. She would return to face the future, to face everything. For now, alone, her tears flowed.

CHAPTER 26

Turin and Asili
September 1938

D oretta could not bring herself to go down for dinner even though she had had nothing since her meager breakfast. The family's longtime housekeeper, Ida, nervously shuttled between the kitchen and her mamma's and Silvana's rooms with trays of nothing more than chamomile tea and biscotti. The children ate their supper with Ida and her mamma's maid, Piermaria. Already Doretta had packed her small valise for her early morning departure to Asili. In the meantime, she hungered for fresh air following the afternoon alone in her room.

All seemed as it should be at six in the evening. Pedestrians were rushing home for dinner, jostling each other in the arcades along Corso Vittorio Emanuele II. She walked the short route toward her zio Eduardo's apartment near the Great Synagogue. Nothing felt normal for her. First expulsion and then the final break with her father. Mostly, she felt his loss. Although she couldn't forgive him for betraying his people, he was still her father. He used to be loving and kind, but now she no longer wanted to understand how he became the man he was. She was not even sure she still loved him. He seemed to think that his family would not be subject to expulsion because he was a *discriminato*, a Jew loyal to the Fascist Party. But Doretta had no desire to return to school, not when others had been removed.

All she wanted now was to see her beloved zio, to play duets with him, and, most of all, to hear him play for her. She would wrap herself in the music of Rachmaninoff, her favorite composer. Having fled oppression during the Russian Revolution, his feelings of loss were woven into the few pieces he wrote in his later years. Today, having gotten her first taste of the pain of oppression, the music of the great Russian master was what she most wanted to hear.

As soon as he opened the door, she stepped in and hugged Eduardo tight, breathing in the woodsy aromas of his pipe tobacco.

"Doretta…!" he said, but she wouldn't let go. "What brings you here? And so pale?"

"Oh, zio, have you not heard about the Leggi Razziali?" she asked. "We've all been expelled from school."

"Come, child, let's sit." He sank into his favorite chair, the upholstery long ago needing patching, with his radio on one side and a small table set with a bottle of Barolo and two glasses on the other.

"Zio, I'm sorry, were you expecting someone?"

He wrapped his twisted fingers around the *cavatappi* and tugged on the cork, waiving off Doretta's offer of assistance. "I'm always prepared for company, Doretta. And here you are." After he completed his familiar ritual of tasting the wine—look, sniff, swirl, sniff, taste—he poured two glasses. "Needs a little fresh air, like me. I know it's an odd choice for an apertivo, but I was about to open this special bottle of Barolo—it's from your birth year—when you arrived. I'm so pleased you're here to share it with me. No use in cellaring wines any longer."

What an odd thing for zio Eduardo, who enjoyed the luxury of aging his wines, to say.

Doretta sat in the chair across from him by which she measured her growth, remembering the joy she had the first time her feet touched the floor. Through the years, she had sat there, talking with her zio about music, life, and history. Next to Sara, he was her dearest friend.

"So, have you heard?"

"About the expulsions? The firings? I received a notice today from the university that my post as a member of the adjunct music faculty has been terminated."

Doretta flushed at her self-centeredness. She had not even thought that he might suffer the same fate as the Jewish students. "Oh, zio, I am so sorry to hear that."

"Not to worry, carissima. I was only teaching a few students and considering complete retirement. It's a good time to move to Cherasco, out of the bustle of the city. I've been alone in this apartment for over twenty years since my Golde died. I need a change. Anyway, my house sits empty most of the year. It's only used for a month in summer when your family goes to the countryside."

His eyes glistened as he studied the ruby-colored wine. "Oh my. Look at the color! Only the slightest appearance of the rust of age." He held his nose to the glass and closed his eyes before sipping. "Such elegance and finesse. Great vintage that brought us this superb wine and, of course, you." He was lost in his adulation of the wine as though it was a great work of art, which Doretta believed it was. His face shone as it always did when he savored a sumptuous bottle of Nebbiolo.

"Now, where was I? Ah, Cherasco. It will do me good to return to my boyhood home. We all deal with these things in different ways. Besides, I would be closer to the Barolo vineyards. Salute, carina." He winked and raised his glass once more. "What do you think?"

Although she had come to talk to him, to find answers, not indulge in a bottle of wine, the earthy Barolo aromas—the fine pipe tobacco zio Eduardo smoked and the lingering taste of black cherries and chocolate—relaxed her.

"It's simply beautiful. Thank you for sharing this special bottle, zio."

"What will you do now, Doretta? I hear there's a special exemption for members of the Fascist party such as your papà."

"I don't want to return. Never! How can I after all that's happened? And how can I possibly accept being treated better than other Jews are simply because of my father's blind support of Mussolini? It's just so wrong." She paused and sipped the wine once more. No longer did she want to talk about the world outside. All she needed now was music, wine, and her beloved uncle's company. "Oh but, zio Eduardo, let's not talk about all that. I want to hear you play. I want to play with you. Please."

"Oh, carina, my crippled hands do not make the beautiful music they once did. Like the edges of the wine, I am rusty with age."

"Please, zio. Please."

"A few then."

She studied him as he rose, steadying himself before he shuffled to his prized Bechstein art-case baby grand piano. How would he remove this precious instrument from the apartment? Had he given that any thought? Cherasco without music was unthinkable. The tinny console Elena banged each summer would not do for the likes of Mozart, Beethoven, and Rachmaninoff. Perhaps he would sell it and buy a new one for Cherasco, but nothing would ever compare to this work of art.

For the next hour, he sat at the piano. When he played for her Rachmaninoff's *Rhapsody on a Theme of Paganini* Doretta felt as though he transported into a lyrical world away from the ugliness she had faced that day. She joined him for one duet, but sensed him struggling. A few times, he faltered. His arthritic fingers no longer glided across the keyboard as they once had, and he sat stiffer, not moving with the emotion of the strains as he once had, but the music that filled the room and her soul was still magical.

"One more, Doretta. You choose, although I know what you will choose. I can no longer play the concerto."

"No, zio, I understand. The Greig piece. 'Notturno.' Please play it for me."

She took her favorite place beside the open lid of the piano to capture the notes as the strings freed them, feeling them flow through her body and into the room.

As the first mysterious, hesitant notes floated from the piano, Doretta closed her eyes, better to hear and allow the music to enter her soul. When she opened them, tears filled her uncle's eyes. She kissed his cheek and helped him to his feet. When had he become so frail? She had not noticed earlier the pallor in his face. Was he ill?

"Thank you, zio. I feel much better. I'm glad I came."

"The pleasure was all mine, carina. I hope you find your way. Remember, we're survivors. Come back again soon. I have an old bottle of Madama Lia's Barbaresco we can open together."

Pots and pans clanking, happy voices, and the sounds of families at dinner echoed through the stairwell as she walked from her uncle's third-floor apartment. When Doretta opened the outside door, the air that rushed in was much cooler than when she had entered nearly two hours earlier. And so was she. Little by little, with each note that rose from the piano, the heat of anger and despair had dissipated. Dearest zio Eduardo, always there to provide her with a musical tonic that chased away her troubles. As she stepped out into the night, she heard a loud noise from inside the building. Someone dropped glassware at the dinner table, no doubt. Doretta began her walk back to Corso il Re in lighter spirits.

DORETTA SLIPPED AWAY TO PORTA NUOVA BEFORE THE FAMILY ROSE. MAMMA would understand. She explained it all in the note she slipped under her door. The evening chill lingered through the night, and the first autumn fog cloaked the city. By mid-morning, she arrived in otherworldly Barbaresco on a typical September day of fine weather under vivid blue skies.

The walk to Asili from Barbaresco station in autumn, in the waning days of the growing season before contadini relieved the vines of their heavy burden, lightened Doretta's mood. There was no one season she loved more than she loved any other in the vineyards, but if forced to choose, it would be harvest. She savored the sun-drenched, verdant vines and deep purple, almost black, bunches of hanging grapes.

Giovanna spotted Doretta first. Dressed in pants and looking much like Sara, she was in the Asili vineyard with her papà, who toward the end of the growing season always carefully followed the grapes' maturation. Less than two more months of studying the clouds and praying for good weather before he and Francesco would harvest the Asili grapes. "First to burst, last to hang," the contadini always said of the Nebbiolo grape.

"Doretta!" Giovanna squealed, abandoning her work. Nico waved at Doretta and shook his head as he watched his youngest, braids flying, run through the rows of vines down the steep hill. Doretta saw Elena in the energetic girl. They were both vivacious and stubborn twelve-year-olds. But soon, their experiences would diverge. Giovanna's track was certain. She was a child of the vineyards, a member of the so-called Mediterranean Aryan race. But Elena? As a Jew, she only knew the unknown in her life now.

Giovanna hugged her and took her valise from Doretta, replacing it with her free hand. Doretta had once worried Giovanna would be jealous of her close, sisterly relationship with Sara, but true to her sweet nature, she considered it a blessing to have another big sister. In rapid-fire words, Giovanna gave her the news of Asili. "We didn't know you were coming so soon! Sara galloped off on Zeus at sunrise, but she said she'd be back for lunch. Francesco is in the vineyards...as usual. Mamma's in the house. Who knows where Maria and Letizia are? They never help. And Madama Lia will be here tomorrow. How long will you stay?" She paused.

Before she could continue, Doretta broke in. "Giovanna, slow down. Catch your breath." She noticed Luca was not among the cast of characters in Giovanna's litany. "I don't know how long, Gio. I didn't exactly let your mamma know I was coming, so I don't want to impose on her."

"Don't be silly, Doretta. You're family. Mamma will be thrilled. I'm thrilled! Sara never has time for me now that she's married. She and Francesco always go to bed immediately after dinner." Giovanna kicked at stones on the road. "And Maria and Letizia only have time for each other"—more stones went flying, propelled further this time—"and boys." They walked a little further before Giovanna asked her the obvious question she wanted to avoid. "Why aren't you in school now?"

Doretta looked away. It was a delicate subject to explain, one she had not fully comprehended yet, so best to leave that to when they were together with Sara. "I have an unexpected break, Giovanna, so of course the first thing I thought to do was come to Barbaresco to be with my dear Langhe family." It was the truth. Before Giovanna continued her litany of questions or, like her sister, read her distressed expression, Doretta spotted a tall, stocky horse with a white blaze on his face trotting toward them. The diminutive rider astride the black steed could be none other than Sara. As Zeus approached, like her baby sister, Sara squealed with joy and hopped off like a circus rider before the horse stopped. She ran to Doretta and gave her a warm, loving welcome. One month of marriage had been kind to her. Her eyes sparkled, and her face was fuller.

"Why such a hurry not to tell us you were coming, Doretta?" Sara asked, her eyes squinting as she studied Doretta. "Is everything all right?"

"It was a last-minute decision. We were given an unexpected break in classes, so as I told Giovanna, I'm here to visit my Langhe family. I thought, if your papà was already picking Barbera and Dolcetto, he might put me to work."

Sara gave Giovanna a leg-up on Zeus then linked arms with Doretta. Together, they walked up the dusty, gravel lane to the cascina, stirring Doretta's memories of long walks and sisterly talks in the summer.

As expected, Luigia was delighted Doretta had come. Like Sara, she appraised Doretta's expression. Was her anxiety that easy to read? Giovanna took her valise to Sara's old room. Now that they were married, Nico had expanded Francesco's small, simple room in the loft into a larger, homier room for the couple. The extra space was needed for the grandson he was sure would come before the couple celebrated their first anniversary. Eventually, he would convert the loft into their own small apartment as the Bosco family grew.

Francesco and Nico came in from the vineyards for lunch, as did the missing middle sisters. Francesco's face radiated joy. Doretta was glad that they had finally found happiness together.

Lunch, as always during the harvest, was short, and the men were once again off to the vineyards. Tomorrow, they would harvest the Barbera vineyards in Ronchi then wait and watch both the grapes and the sky until the Nebbiolo was ready.

Sara left with Zeus to continue her rounds through the valley, but she would be back in time for dinner and a *passeggiata* afterward. Giovanna trailed her papà and Francesco to the vineyards. With the middle sisters and their mamma busy in the house, Doretta walked through the valley and up to Tre Stelle to hers and Sara's favorite spot below Villa Cristina to take in the alpine panorama to the west. She needed time alone to think.

It had been a pleasant visit with her zio and, as always, she lost herself in his music, but it felt as though he was saying good-bye before a long trip. What did he mean, "We all have to deal with this in our own way?"

After their light supper, while Francesco tended the farm animals, the two dear friends left for a passeggiata to the village. Doretta had been edgy at table, hoping the conversation would not shift to her family. Fortunately, it had not, other than the most basic polite inquiries about her parents' wellbeing. But Sara had kept a keen eye on her from across the table as though she well knew why she was here.

As soon as they were out of earshot of the cascina, Sara asked the question Doretta knew would come.

"Doretta, in all these years, I've never known you to show up on our doorstep unannounced—not that you aren't welcome, of course. Why? Has something happened at home?"

"First tell me all about your weekend in Camogli and everything that has happened in the past month. I don't have any close friends who are married ladies. Do tell!"

Sara's face was tight and worried. "No. Later. I want you to explain why you're here. What's troubling you, cara?"

They walked in silence along the road to the village as the last rays of sun painted the mountains in an amber glow. Sara didn't push, leaving her question in the air, knowing Doretta would answer when she was ready.

"Jews. We're Jews. No longer Italians."

Sara stopped and spun toward Doretta, whose eyes were downcast, her lower lip quivering. Her voice now stern, Sara framed Doretta's face with her hands and asked for an explanation. Doretta squeezed her eyes shut, avoiding Sara's intense blue eyes that bore deeply into her. Her eyes were also blue. Her hair was chestnut. Both were defined Aryan characteristics. But she was a Jew.

"Haven't you heard?"

"Heard what?"

"The Racial Laws." She threw her hands in the air in disgust as though to sweep away the frightening reality and stood defiantly, her hands on her hips. "The Laws in Defense of the Race…the Italian race. Jews have been singled out, relegated. We're second-class citizens."

Sara grimaced. "I only saw headlines in the paper when I was at Villa Cristina the other day. You told me about the ten-point manifesto, so it caught my eye. No, Doretta. I can't see Italians standing for that. They won't let this happen."

"Don't be so sure," Doretta snapped. "When I was expelled from my class, not a single friend left with me or even looked at me. If our friends don't speak for us, who else will?"

Sara threaded her arm through Doretta's and resumed their walk toward the village, holding her closer, clasping her hand in hers.

"Zio Eduardo said there were exemptions to the expulsions because of my father's service and his party membership, but I can't go back, not after yesterday."

"If you're not going back to class, what will you do? You've had your heart set on the law. You're what they call a modern woman," Sara said, trying to keep her voice light.

"Sara…" Doretta paused, took a deep breath, and continued, her voice now plaintive. "What if these laws are only the beginning? There's talk of harsher laws to come. Some believe, though not my father, of course," she said, her voice now filled with disdain, "Mussolini will finally yield to Hitler's pressure and force us all out of Italy…or worse."

There it was. The strained relationship between father and daughter had finally ruptured. It didn't surprise Sara. Even at her wedding, she had noticed the tension between Doretta and Gabriele. Now Sara sensed that Doretta was grappling with something greater than her duty to her mamma and siblings. Clearly, there was something much bigger at stake.

"I'm glad you came. Stay here with us. There's no need to rush into anything right now, is there?"

In silence, they continued walking to the village. The sun had disappeared behind the mountains and damp autumn air swept their faces. Sara knew Francesco would look for them in the truck, but she still wanted time alone with her troubled friend. Sara had been afraid this day would come. Anything that affected Doretta and her family affected her too. They had pledged to support one another long ago.

Sara was the first to speak.

"Have you talked with Luca about this?" Sara asked softly.

"There hasn't been time! Yesterday was a blur, and this morning I left home too early to call him. Right now, I'm more concerned about my mamma and zia Silvana. And the children. Last night, zia Silvana told me she wants to leave Italy."

"That's no surprise. But where will she go? America?"

"No, Palestine. She has no one in America to help her. She's writing to Renata Goren, her old schoolmate. She helped her before, so she hopes she can help her emigrate. But, I don't know. I read that the British are limiting the number of refugees into Palestine. And, well, she has no money."

"It hasn't really come to that, has it? But I can understand how she would want to leave…for the children's sake."

"I know I'm selfish, but I don't want her to go! Mamma needs her." Doretta gripped Sara's hand. "You know—to help deal with my father."

"Madama Lia's coming tomorrow. I don't know about Luca. Please stay, Doretta, for at least a few days," Sara pleaded.

"Michele will be coming home soon from school. I should be there to protect him. He's fifteen now, and my father is hard on him. My little brother—what will he do?"

Sara shivered.

"Let's go back. You're cold."

"No. Let's walk. It's a strange feeling I get sometimes, like icy fingers dancing up my spine."

"But it's dark. We should…"

"Don't be silly. The moon's nearly full. We have plenty of light. Anyway, the only frightening thing in the dark is a mamma cinghiale. That snorting you heard a few minutes ago was a wild boar." She laughed and continued to walk, pulling Doretta along with her. "We'll walk to the piazza and wait for Francesco. He'll come…trust me."

Footsteps approached.

"*Bon-assèira*, Sara."

"Bon-assèira, *monsù* Bianco. Why the rush?" Isidoro Bianco and Sara's father had been friends since they were boys. His uncanny likeness to and similar jovial disposition of *Babbo Natale* made the major's assistant popular with the villagers.

"Just left the *municipio*." He stepped closer and squinted in the dim light. "Is that you, Doretta?"

"It's me. Who doesn't want to be in Barbaresco in September?" Doretta answered, relieved to see a familiar face.

"True. I just wish the Fascist police would stay away." He scanned the area, lowered his voice, and looked about once more. "One of them from Alba…a woman from Barbaresco, no less, showed up late today." Though he had to work with the Fascist police, their presence unnerved him as it did most in the village.

Again, Sara shivered. There could be no one else, Sara thought, but she asked anyway. "Who…?"

In nearly a whisper, he spat out her name. "Cinzia Strega. She came here to check on the village children, asking why they aren't attending Saturday youth group activities. I have more important matters to attend to, and so do their parents."

"What business is that of hers?" Sara asked.

"She claims it's her job to ensure compliance with the governmental order that all children participate in group activities. She even mentioned your sisters."

Isidoro Bianco fidgeted with his cap and continued scanning the area. Sara sensed he had said more than he should. No one was safe from prying eyes and ears. "Not to worry, Sara. No one here has time or the money for that nonsense, especially with the harvest approaching. And who can afford the uniforms?"

"Yes, I suppose you're right." Sara's voice quivered.

"It's late, Sara. Would you like me to drive you back to Asili?"

"Thank you, monsù Bianco, but I'm fine. We're fine. Francesco will come soon."

"Well, if Francesco is coming for you, I'll be on my way. My dinner is waiting. Bon-a seirà."

Sara turned to Doretta. "Let's start back. Francesco will be cross."

Lights from an approaching vehicle behind them flooded the street.

"And there he is, mio caro Francesco, my knight in shining armor."

Francesco pulled up next to them in Nico's farm truck. "Ladies, I am here to escort you back to Asili. It's much too dark for you to be out alone, although I don't know who would be foolish enough to tangle with the two of you."

Dear Francesco—certainly not the sort of man Doretta had expected Sara to marry. She could have had an easier life in the city, but even though she seemed to enjoy the luxuries Cornelia Bottero had gifted her, Sara didn't seem to need such things as Doretta did. And, this was the man she loved—as simple as that. Yet, unfathomable too.

As Francesco helped her, in the darkness ahead, Doretta spied the flash of a match struck, the glow of a cigarette. Footsteps…light. A woman? Francesco saw it, she was certain, but he said nothing. She didn't believe Sara, already seated in the small truck, saw the light. But once again, Sara shivered, slid her hand into Doretta's, and squeezed.

"Please stay in Asili, Doretta," Sara whispered.

When they arrived at Asili, Francesco bade Doretta buonanotte and slipped off to the loft.

Doretta waited a moment until the light came on in their room under the eaves.

"Sara, cara, who do you think came to see Officer Bianco?" Sara looked away, but Doretta saw her face tense. "Do you think...?"

"Yes. I believe it was her, Cinzia Strega, who kept Officer Bianco so late."

"Sara, I know how fearless you can be, but that woman...that woman is not someone to confront. She has official power. She has a weapon. Most of all, for whatever reason, she hates you."

"The reason is Francesco, Doretta," Sara said flatly.

"Jealousy?"

"Yes, I know. I nearly lost...oh, never mind."

Doretta clasped Sara's hands in hers and begged her to listen. "Promise me please, Sara, promise me you will avoid her. Don't provoke her. Will you promise?" Sara glanced away. "Sara?"

"Of course, Doretta. Of course. But if—"

"No conditions. I need you. Francesco needs you. Oh, Sara, you and I have bigger, more important battles ahead, I fear."

Sara hugged Doretta and rested her head against her. "You're right, of course, cara. Aren't you always? *Promesso...promesso.*"

SHORTLY BEFORE DAWN, THE ROOSTERS OF THE RIO SORDO VALLEY WOKE. The first loud crow that roused Doretta came from below her window. The noisy roosters were the one thing Doretta could not get used to in Asili. Another loud crow came from across the valley. The cacophony of roosters continued until the sun peeked above Monte Silva and drenched the misty vineyards with light.

She had barely slept. All had been quiet above except for Sara's giggling after two pair of boots, one heavy, one light, dropped to the floor. The bed above her creaked. Doretta covered her head with her pillow and finally drifted off to sleep. Before the roosters finished their morning symphony, heavy footsteps above signaled Francesco's departure for the vineyards.

Doretta found Sara sitting cross-legged at the table, dressed in her trousers, and sipping from a large cup. She gave a cheerful greeting and scooted over to make room for Doretta. Sara had a gift for reading expressions and a talent for hiding her own feelings. Doretta wondered what she was thinking. Luigia placed Doretta's caffelatte before her and wished them a good day as she left to tend to her animals and garden.

"Sara..." Doretta started to ask more about Cinzia Strega but stopped herself. "How did you sleep?"

"Quite well." Sara took another sip of coffee, hiding her mouth behind the cup. "And you?"

Naughty Sara. It was as though she were a child battling to keep a secret to herself. La *mia cara amica*. Doretta hoped her dear friend would still have time for her once the babies started arriving at Ca' dei Fiù. From the noises and giggles above her last night, they were trying.

"I slept fine until the roosters woke up."

"The nights are quiet here, so any sound seems loud." Again, that naughty tone in her voice.

Now, Doretta was blushing. She changed the subject, and her tone became serious. "Sara, I would like to spend the harvest in Asili. With you. And Francesco. That is if it isn't a burden on your mamma."

"Of course it isn't. Stay as long as you wish."

"I must see Luca here or in Alba. It's not only my family's situation. I'm certain the laws will impact our work with Madame Stern and Madama Lia. Surely, the Fascists will slam the door on foreign Jews. Afterward, I'll have to return to Turin, if only for a few days. Mamma will be upset, but I can't possibly stay in the apartment now. Michele will be home soon, and he'll look after her."

Sara unfolded her legs and wrapped her arms around her. "God bless you, Doretta. We thought this day might come. We'll be strong for each other. We'll—"

The crunching sound of a car speeding up the gravel lane to the cortile stopped Sara mid-sentence. Through the window, she saw Madama Lia emerge from a cloud of dust. Who was that with her?

"Doretta! Luca's here."

They dashed into the cortile, but Doretta froze when she saw Luca. His doleful expression and furrowed brow were all too familiar. Waiting for Madama Lia to join him before he greeted them, his eyes darted about, looking anywhere but at Doretta.

"Buongiorno, Sara," Madama Lia said as she kissed Sara, then Doretta, whose eyes never strayed from Luca. "Buongiorno, cara."

Luca came to Doretta and took her hands as he lingered with his light kisses on each cheek. He whispered, "Be strong, carissima."

Doretta pulled away from Luca and shook her head. "What now, Luca?" she snapped.

"Inside all," Madama Lia ordered.

An icy chill spiraled up Sara's spine, a feeling that had become all too familiar. She wrapped her arm around Doretta's waist and walked with her behind Madama Lia; Luca, head hung low, trailed them.

Madama led them to the sunroom, flooded with early morning light, her climbing roses still blooming on the terrace walls beyond the open doors. The setting was cheerful. The mood was grim.

"Doretta, sit here, next to me."

Warily, Doretta followed her directive and took her place next to Madama Lia on the divan. Sara settled next to her and took Doretta's hand. Luca remained standing until Madama Lia directed him to sit across from them.

"Doretta, cara...Luca has news from Turin to share with you."

Doretta's spine stiffened, and she squeezed Sara's hand with both of hers. "Mamma! Is Mamma all right?"

"Yes, Doretta. All is well at Corso Re Umberto." Luca's tone was calm, but grave.

"I'm confused, Luca."

He cleared his throat and continued. "It's your zio Eduardo. I'm sorry, but he's dead."

Sara gasped. Doretta cried out in disbelief. "No! This can't be. I...I don't understand. I saw him two nights ago. What...?" Doretta struggled to speak. "Luca...tell me."

Luca wrung his hands, his gaze darting back and forth between Sara and Madama Lia. Anywhere but *at* Doretta. "We aren't sure when it happened. His housekeeper found him yesterday, on the..."

"Continue, Luca. It's best from you." Madama Lia's deference to Luca surprised Sara. Was she aware that the two were more than friends?

"His doctor said it was a massive stroke. Apparently, he's been in bad health for some time but obviously hadn't said anything to your mother and zia. He was on the floor in his library, next to the piano." Luca glanced at the ceiling, and took a deep breath.

Doretta buried her face in her hands. She replayed her departure from zio Eduardo's apartment in her head. Was that the loud noise she heard from her uncle's apartment? What if she had not discounted it and run back upstairs? She might have saved him.

Luca continued with more confidence. "Eduardo had come to me late last year to make a new will. He left three envelopes I was to give to your mother, zia, and you upon his death."

He withdrew an envelope from his satchel and held it out for her, unable to take his eyes off her. Sara observed something other than compassion in his eyes—love. Doretta let go one hand from Sara's and took the envelope from Luca, his fingers brushing her hand. Sara noticed the tender gesture.

Luca sat back, waiting for Doretta to absorb the sad news. The only sound was Doretta's shallow, fitful breathing as she fought tears. Luca's eyes glistened.

Madama Lia broke the silence. She stood, and though she was small like Sara, her presence always commanded the room. "Doretta, Luca and I will drive you back to Turin now. There is much to discuss with your mother and zia."

As though sleepwalking, Doretta rose and staggered a bit. Luca rushed to her side and helped her to the Fiore cascina.

"Sara, there's much to explain that I believe you, as Doretta's closest friend, need to know. I'll be back in Asili tonight. I expect to see you after dinner. Now go help Doretta pack. We must leave straightaway."

When Sara arrived in the cortile, Doretta, standing taller, more confident in her demeanor, walked to her, only her purse in hand.

"Sara, I've left my valise in your room. I'll be back. I'll be back soon. Dear sister, I love you so." She kissed both her cheeks, touched her face, and smiled before Luca helped her into the car.

Francesco, appearing wary, approached from the barn. Together they watched the car disappear. "Giovanna came to say Madama Lia and Luca arrived. Is something wrong?"

"Zio Eduardo. Doretta's uncle. He's dead."

"Oh, carina, what…when?"

"No one really knows when, but it appears to have been sudden. A massive stroke, maybe." Sara turned to Francesco, and he wrapped his arms around her. How sad for Doretta to have lost her closest confidant other than her. Thank God, she had Francesco to help her be strong for Doretta. They would all need one another.

CHAPTER 27

Turin
November 1938

Daniela knocked again on her husband's bedroom door. It was November 22, nearly two weeks after the horrific destruction of Jewish lives and property across Germany on the night now dubbed Kristallnacht. But closer to home, it was five days since the news Gabriele Giordano had never expected—the forced sale of the bank his *trisnonno* founded nearly a century earlier and, most devastating of all, his expulsion from the Fascist Party. Nineteen years of loyal membership and service to Il Duce terminated because he was a Jew. Never had he imagined that he would be a victim of the anti-Semitic maelstrom sweeping Italy. Why, he even had Il Duce's personal assurances that he would be exempt from the crushing laws.

Within hours of receiving the news, Gabriele locked himself away, unable to face his wife and children. While he sat there alone, Daniela dealt with her own crisis: the dismissal of her Aryan domestic staff. Piermaria and their beloved cook, Bruna, both longtime employees of Giordano and Dalmasso households, would have to leave. There seemed to be no end to the string of cruel laws targeting Italian Jews. With unemployment rampant and food costs soaring—all the fault of the Jews, it was said—the new law stripped the two women of their home and livelihood. As for Ida, she refused to leave. Despite her Jewish mother's conversion to Catholicism and her own baptism that in Italy still protected her, she now claimed her Jewish heritage. She had been with the Dalmasso family since Daniela's early teens. Whatever fate awaited her mistress, Ida would accept it as well. Such was her devotion to Daniela.

"Gabriele, it's time to come out. I need cash to pay the staff, and you can't remain locked away forever." Silence. She would try again after breakfast, but should he still refuse to open the door, she would use her skeleton key. With Doretta due home from Asili after a long stay, it was time for him to end this nonsense and face the world. Doretta would help him do that.

Daniela had known this day would come. They all predicted it—even dear, departed zio Eduardo who, through the words in his letters to her and Silvana written a year earlier, had seen this coming. But, as he clung to the Fascist ideology, Gabriele failed to realize what he was really losing—his family. Now it was too late. Daniela had abandoned all hope of reconciliation in September when he failed to comprehend the seriousness of the racial laws and the pain it inflicted on their children. He had paid a dear price for his misguided loyalty to Mussolini and the Party.

When Daniela arrived for breakfast, Elena and Michele were already seated. Elena's gloomy mood weighed heavily on them all. Michele attempted to engage his little sister in conversation, but his efforts were futile. It was Bruna's last day, and she had prepared their favorite breakfast treats, not that anyone had much of an appetite, especially Elena. She had spent more time with Bruna than anyone else in the household had. Since her expulsion from school, the kitchen, where Bruna taught her to make agnolotti and tajarin, had become her classroom and the kindhearted cook her teacher.

All the children had been despondent since Silvana, Friedrich, and Gisele had left for Palestine in late October. Her sister's departure devastated Daniela, but after Renata Goren secured their passage from Genoa, it was time. Should she have gone too? Zio Eduardo had left his two nieces a substantial amount of money in Switzerland that Luca now managed. Daniela easily could have left behind this unfolding nightmare to make a new life. But how could she? Gabriele no longer deserved her loyalty, but with Doretta and Michele determined to remain in Italy now that they believed war loomed, leaving was unthinkable. Elena, though, had no say in the matter. Daniela wondered whether keeping her in Italy was a risk she should not have taken.

Eduardo's bequest offered her a compromise. She would stay in Italy, but not Turin. Soon they would leave for Cherasco. Madama Lia now owned the Dalmasso family house, and it was a refuge—for now, at least. How clever of zio Eduardo to have arranged the "sale" to her long ago. Had he not, under the Racial Laws they would have lost the house in the village their ancestors settled four centuries earlier. It was in Madama Lia's safekeeping for the

Dalmasso sisters and their children. *"Carissima Daniela,"* zio Eduardo wrote in his letter, *"after witnessing the madness in Germany, if I do not take heed of the warnings of the future and arrange what I have with Luca's assistance, I would be doing you and Silvana a great disservice. I owe that much to you, your children, and future generations of the Dalmasso family."*

"Mamma." Michele shook her arm. "Mamma!" Daniela's mind had drifted off to her happier childhood summers in Cherasco. Michele's touch and Elena's dour face across from her snapped her back to the frightening present.

"Yes, Michele."

"Is Papà coming with us to Cherasco?"

"No, Michele. At least not now. We will go and settle in. Hopefully by Christmas, by Hanukah, I mean, he will be ready to join us."

Christmas was one of Daniela's favorite seasons in Turin. Bright lights and festive atmosphere everywhere. Their Catholic friends enjoyed Hanukah parties in their home, and they delighted in the Catholic traditions. No more. Fortunately, only a few of their friends had refused her calls. Most stood by them. But no one would dine in their home or appear in public with them. Hand-delivered messages were all the communication she had with the outside world. At least in Cherasco, her children would be safe from the Blackshirt thugs. Elena refused to leave the apartment alone, but Michele often did. And he was of the age and the mentality not to dodge confrontation. She was relieved that Doretta had decided to return from Barbaresco, but she worried about her involvement in the rescue organization. Now, it was her duty to keep up the children's spirits even though her heart was heavy and she preferred the solitude of her sitting room.

"Elena, what are you doing today?" She knew the answer would be the same as it had been for two months.

"Nothing, Mamma. Nothing!" She slouched in her chair and pushed her food around her plate with her fork, her lower lip protruding. "Elena! Sit up straight and stop playing with your food." Daniela had been patient with her, but tolerating Elena's sullen behavior and perpetual frown was wearing thin. "I believe you should go with Ida to the park. You've been in the house far too long. And the weather is nice today."

Elena threw her fork down on her plate. "I'll never go outside again. Never!" Tears erupted as she dashed from the room. The sound of her stomping up the stairs and her bedroom door slamming had become part of her morning ritual.

Daniela dropped her head and rubbed her temples, trying to block out the child's behavior. Her children were the first and youngest victims of the Racial

Laws. Explaining it to them was impossible. What rational explanation was there for a country debasing a small percentage of its citizens? Despite the regime's approval of Jewish communities setting up their own schools—at their own expense—Daniela had surrendered long ago in her battle with Elena over attending school. She sought a tutor, but Aryans were forbidden to teach Jews. Finding a Jewish instructor who suited Elena's personality had thus been fruitless.

Michele squeezed Daniela's hand. "Don't worry, Mamma. I'll get her out to Caffè Platti this afternoon. Has she ever refused hot chocolate? If Doretta and Luca join us, she'll feel more secure. She adores Luca, as does Doretta." He winked at his mamma, but she stiffened.

"I didn't know Luca was coming." She picked up her fork and rearranged the food on her plate as her thoughts turned from the obstinate child to the young couple. She was fond of Luca and would be forever grateful for his brave service to the family, but she worried about his relationship with Doretta. In normal times, she would have welcomed a romance between them. What mother would not want such a wonderful man as a son-in-law? But these were not normal times. Even a close friendship was dangerous under the new law prohibiting marriages of Aryans to Jews. It was hopeless for them to fall in love.

"Gianni's driving them to the city. They'll pick up Doretta in Asili then come to Turin. Something about a meeting they have to attend." Michele did not miss the way she squeezed her eyes shut. "What is it, Mamma? Don't you like Luca?"

"Michele, of course I do! It's just, well…" She didn't want to discuss her concerns about Luca and the Racial Laws, but she knew Doretta had been educating Michele about her volunteer work with refugees. His eagerness to get involved concerned her. "I worry about the rescue work. There's talk the Fascists will disband the Commission for the Relief of Jews in Italy—"

Michele interrupted her. "I know, Mamma. I know all about COMASEBIT. Doretta told me. If they do, who will provide money to care for the Jewish refugees in Italy? Surely not the Fascists."

"What then if the rescue work becomes illegal, Michele?"

"That won't stop Luca and Doretta. And I want to—" His enthusiasm was more than Daniela could stand. Wasn't it enough Doretta was involved in an activity that soon might be illegal?

"No, Michele! I forbid it. I don't want you involved." Her voice trembled and heat coursed through her body. The daily battles with Elena exhausted her.

Michele was her only ally, and she had no strength to debate him. "Foreign Jews and those like Silvana's children who became citizens after 1918 will be forced out. Don't you believe anyone helping more Jews come into Italy will be arrested? Enough of this nonsense."

Michele folded his napkin with military precision and placed it on the table. He would say nothing more about the subject. He went to her, wrapped his arms around his mamma's stiff shoulders, and kissed her twitching cheek. "Mamma, I don't want to upset you. Let's hear what Doretta and Luca have to say." He kissed her again and brushed his hand across her gaunt face. "Now, it's time for Papà to come out. May I have the skeleton key?"

She fished out the key from the pocket of her dress, pressed it into Michele's open hand, and studied his face. Quite a man now. His face was the kind, strong one of a young man she once loved, that of his father as she remembered him from his youth.

"I'm here for you, Mamma."

After Michele departed, the table spun, and the sight of food on her plate roiled Daniela's stomach. Her family was falling apart. What else was it zio Eduardo had written?

Be strong, carina. Your brave children will be part of the fight for liberty. They are fighting for our people. You must let them go. For if they cannot fight for themselves, who will protect and defend them? The future is theirs to fight for.

How did he know what they would face? Daniela crumpled to the table and buried her face on her arm. Alone and desperate, she wept.

LUCA HAD STRUGGLED TO WAKE BEFORE DAWN THAT MORNING, BUT HIS senses stirred the moment Doretta opened the car door in Asili. All through the drive to Turin and the meeting with the rescue agency, her fragrance of roses assailed him as it always did. The meeting with Monsignor Vincenzo Barale, Cardinal Maurilio Fossati's powerful secretary, two men of the cloth dedicated to the rescue effort, was crucial. Distractions could be costly, and Madama Lia would demand a detailed report.

Doretta's two months at Asili had allowed him to see her alone often, away from Madama Lia who always had her eye on them. He suspected she didn't approve of their relationship although she had not mentioned it. "Luca, business first!" she sometimes admonished him. Business meant not only money for refugees and meetings with important rescue volunteers but also the mills. Grain prices had soared due to the Fascist government's ill-conceived attempt at making Italy self-reliant for wheat. Flour was a key staple, and keeping the government's hands off her business had become a challenge.

Doretta, too, had been a challenge. In April, the fiery law student had stunned him with warmth and passion at the doorway. Heartache consumed him that night when she dashed off, leaving him burning for more. Yes, he loved her. For weeks, thoughts of that kiss consumed him. But it had not happened again. By the time he saw her in Asili in July, he doubted that anything other than friendship was possible. Or was it? With the most recent racial proclamation, he knew it was hopeless for them. But her nearness, her touch, even holding her hand to help her from the car, tortured him. Being apart was even worse. For now, moments like this, walking arm in arm, would suffice.

"Doretta, I'm hungry. Aren't we close to Piazza *Castello*? Let's have a sweet at Caffè Cavallo Bianco. I know it's one of your favorites."

"I really should get home to Mamma. Gianni will be waiting for you there. But why don't you stay the night? She squeezed his arm and he glimpsed familiar sparkles in her eyes, like the fireflies that lit up the Langhe sky in summer. "You refused me last time."

Luca looked away, not allowing her to see his red face. To sleep under the same roof, even apart, was tempting.

"Um, thanks, Doretta, but—"

"I know, you have to be at work early in the morning. You could send Gianni back to Alba and take the early morning train."

It was all too tempting. Rather than answer, he changed the subject. "What do you think will happen if, as Monsignor Barale expects, the Fascists disband the committee? Who will care for the refugees?"

"Okay, Luca. I get it. Answer me later." She withdrew her arm and continued walking. "From what I read in the papers, which, I have to say, sickens me, Mussolini wants all foreign Jews out by March. The Fascists don't believe there will be refugees to feed."

"They'll keep coming, Doretta. The borders are porous. And no other countries will allow them. I'm amazed Frau Goren got Silvana and the children into Palestine. The British won't allow mass immigration of Jews into Palestine, particularly *German* Jews."

"And Roosevelt won't help either. The Evian Conference in July was all talk."

"I know. Thirty-two countries and no consensus. Goebbels used the conference's failure for his usual sick propaganda. *Jews for Sale. Cheap. No Buyers.* That was an actual headline in a German newspaper."

Doretta stopped dead. She gasped and staggered as though punched. Luca wrapped his arm around her waist to steady her.

"Doretta! What's wrong?" Only then did Luca see the prominent sign outside the fashionable pastry shop Caffè Cavallo Bianco: *No Jews Allowed.* So it had come to that. Italy now emulated Nazi Germany. What next? Yellow stars? "Let's go, Doretta."

But it was too late. She pulled away and rushed into the café, Luca close behind. "Doretta, no. Where are you going?"

"We'd like a table for two, please," she demanded, jutting her chin, daring the manager to refuse her. She had known him for years. The café, the oldest in Turin, had been a favorite since she was a child, and it was where Elena always asked to go when they were in the city center.

The manager glared at her. "Sorry, signorina Giordano. That, I am afraid, is not possible."

"Why not? I see tables available."

"Perhaps you might try elsewhere. No Jews allowed here."

"You mean elsewhere as in there are no anti-Semitic bastards like you running it?"

Luca had heard enough. He snatched her arm. "Come, Doretta." She jerked away. A storm raged in her eyes.

"No, Luca!" she shouted and jerked free of him. "Leave me alone."

"Signorina Giordano," the manager said, "lower your voice. You must leave, or I will call the police."

"Call them!" she shouted, her voice shaking with fury. By now, Doretta commanded the attention of everyone in the room.

"Is there a problem, here?"

Doretta froze. The menacing voice. She recognized it immediately. Baldo Volpe. She trained her eyes on the manager, avoiding the menacing man behind her. Feeling as though she would retch, she struggled to conceal her fear.

"Thank you, Officer. I was merely explaining to this woman that we have a policy not to serve Jews."

"Well then, she must leave. Now!" he barked. "Jews will soon learn their place in Italy."

Doretta seemed frozen. Luca would have to ease her out of this situation. He had seen the appalling placards plastered everywhere in Berlin and Munich, and he had witnessed men such as this viper willingly enforce them. For Doretta, this was still new, even after her expulsion from the university. She had been caught off guard. The man's nearness to Doretta, his face close to the back of her head, his nostrils flaring, unnerved Luca. He took Doretta's trembling hand, worked his fingers through hers, curled tight, and attempted to coax her away. "Come, Doretta. It's not worth it."

The man dressed in a black uniform turned to Luca and stepped closer to him, his jaw clenched, his voice menacing, but low. "Are *you* a Jew? If not, you should know fucking a Jewess is illegal now."

In a flash, Luca recoiled his arm, but Doretta blocked him and grabbed his hand. "No, Luca," she warned, grasping his other arm and pushing him away. "Not now. Not now."

Doretta didn't take her fiery eyes off of Baldo Volpe as she continued to push Luca away.

Volpe called after her. "Please review the new laws, signorina Giordano and you, too, Luca Olivero. It is my duty now to ensure you Jews comply with them until you leave Italy."

Doretta turned away from Volpe and quickened her pace.

He was shouting now, passersby gawking at them. "And tell your mother Flora Volpe no longer slaves for Jews."

By the time they reached the corner, Doretta was running. After they entered the arcade, Doretta stopped and leaned against a column to catch her breath. Luca took her in his arms and felt tremors flowing through her as she gasped for air. She buried her face against him and, like once before, her heart hammered against his chest, but out of fear, not passion.

"Doretta, you know that man. Who is he?" He held her head close, caressing her hair, trying to calm her.

"I want to go home, Luca. Take me home. *Please*, take me home."

He hailed a cab, and within minutes, they were in the Giordano apartment. Daniela gasped when Doretta, pale, her eyes glazed, and Luca entered the library.

She helped Doretta to the divan and unbuttoned her coat. "Luca, quick, a brandy for her. What's happened," her voice pleading as she put her arms around Doretta, now shivering.

"Doretta had her first encounter with a Fascist policeman. An anti-Semite. He wasn't *carabinieri*. They would never speak that way. At least, not yet."

"But I don't understand—*encounter*?"

"We finished our meeting and decided to have a merenda reale at Cavallo Bianco. Only, there is a sign now." Luca found it hard to utter the words to Daniela. "No Jews allowed."

Horror flashed across Daniela's face, and her mouth dropped open. She pulled Doretta even closer and buried her face against her daughter's. "Poverina. La mia poverina. I'm so sorry this happened."

Luca sat next to Doretta and tried to persuade her to drink the brandy. She pushed his hand away. He had poured one for himself and drained it in one gulp.

"There's more, signora Giordano. Doretta challenged the manager, and he threatened to call the police. But he didn't have to. A Fascist police officer appeared." He tried again to get her to take the glass. This time she looked at him. Her lower lip quivered, and she fought back tears. "Doretta, drink. Please." He placed the glass between her hands and wrapped his over hers. Finally, she drank. "What's more, she knew him. He called her by name."

Daniela recoiled. "She knows this man? Doretta, dimmi! *Chi*? Luca, who?"

Before she took another sip, her hands now steady, she spit out his name through her clenched teeth, though her words were barely audible. "Baldo Volpe. Flora Volpe's son."

Daniela sprang up and clapped her hands to her mouth. "No! It can't be. I knew he worked in government, but she never said what he did. Policeman?"

"He's a Fascist police officer, Mamma. I don't know which branch, but he said his job is to enforce the Leggi Razziali." Doretta put her glass down, leaned against Luca, and brushed her lips across his hand before holding it to her cheek. It was the first time she had shown affection for him in front of anyone other than Sara and Francesco. "And he knows Luca's name."

"This can't be, Doretta." Daniela threw her hands up and paced the room. "How would he know *you*, much less Luca?"

"Mamma, it's a long story. I've wanted to tell you so many times before, but I knew you would blame Flora Volpe. Lord knows what hell that woman must have endured. When I didn't see him again for years, I—"

"Years, so when was the first time you saw him?"

"When I was thirteen. Just before Sukkot. Outside the synagogue. Mamma, no one ever said such hateful words to me before and not since...until September in class, that is."

"Michele, come in. Come sit with us. Doretta and Luca have had such a fright."

"Mamma, I must talk to you. About Papà."

"Later, Michele."

"No Mamma, *now*. I tried the skeleton key earlier, and I couldn't get it into the keyhole. He's jammed something in there. Mamma! Mamma, his—"

Before Michele finished his sentence, Daniela learned what he was trying to tell her. Gabriele had taken the service revolver he carried in Caporetto from the gun case in his library.

The thud that followed a loud crack sent Doretta and Michele racing up the stairs to her father's bedroom door. Raising her hand to pound on it, Doretta leaned her head against the door instead. She knew it was too late. Too late to save him. Too late to reconcile, if a possibility for that ever existed.

Michele pushed Doretta aside and banged on the door, calling for his father, seemingly not ready to surrender to the reality that his father had taken his own life. Doretta turned away. From the top of the stairs, she saw her mother standing below, horror written on her face. Before Doretta reached her, Daniela slumped to the bottom stair and clutched the banister as she wept. Doretta froze, for the first time realizing that, despite their years-long estrangement, her mother had never stopped loving her father. Nor had she. The man who had taken his life was not her father, not her mother's mate. That man had died years before when the Fascists took his soul.

CHAPTER 28

Asili
Late August 1939

Sara suffered in the summer heat. Each evening before dinner she rested under the pergola, ensconced in her favorite chair, her swollen feet propped up. The cooling breezes that rustled the vine leaves and foretold of autumn failed to comfort her. Queasiness had plagued her these last few days. Pity her pregnancy had not begun a year earlier, on those first nights together in Liguria instead of late February when Francesco surprised her with two nights in Turin—a delayed, passionate celebration of her twentieth birthday. Already their first child would have arrived. Francesco and Nico prayed for a boy. Sara and Luigia prayed for her health and that of the baby. She had thought to try abstinence for a few months, so she could at least deliver after the harvest, but how could she? Francesco craved her body, and she his. Their passionate nights were too special for them.

How she missed Doretta. Sara had not seen her for nine months. As soon as her friend settled her mamma, siblings, and Ida in Cherasco, she had left for Switzerland. As the situation grew more desperate in Germany and Reich-occupied countries, doors to Jewish refugees slammed shut around the world, increasing the demand on their rescue funds. Madama Lia believed Doretta could help Frieda Stern more in Switzerland than in Italy. And, for now, Switzerland remained safe. The news of Doretta's encounter with Baldo Volpe in November, the same day her father took his life, had shaken Sara. Hopefully, Doretta would return before the baby arrived.

Carissima, I hope this finds you well.

The letter, dated August 15, had been opened and resealed. Doretta had sent it through Luca and without any reference to Sara's name or location. Concern for Doretta's safety and those she knew was certainly warranted.

Are you ready for the big event? I do hope to see you before then. It has been far too long. My studies fill my days.

Studies? That must be the code for her work: smuggling refugees into Switzerland.

There is much to study and I'm exhausted when I fall into bed near midnight each day. No time for anything else. The semester will end soon. Only then will I decide whether I stay on for another. I miss you terribly and want to be there for you.

Much love,
la tua cara amica per sempre.

Yes—dear friends forever.

Sara longed for more news, but she was relieved to know that Doretta was well, although probably pining for Luca. He had been a support for her and her family, Sara knew. The last time she saw her, Doretta confided in Sara that she loved him. Fate was so unkind. She prayed that the tide would turn but feared that their relationship was doomed. Sara had attended Gabriele Giordano's funeral in Turin; everyone from Asili attended. It had all happened so fast. Surprisingly, in his brief suicide note to Daniela, Gabriele had asked for Jewish rites, which meant burial the next day. Doretta had said that nowhere in his note had he asked for her mother's forgiveness. First zio Eduardo's sudden death, then, two months later, Gabriele Giordano's suicide brought Doretta and her together at funerals. The Racial Laws drove many men to take their lives, each for a different reason. Older Jewish men who had served their country courageously and, as was the case with Gabriele Giordano, placed misguided loyalty in the Fascist Party found themselves unable to face reality.

Sara admired Daniela's strength after these losses. Since her sister's departure for Palestine, Daniela had no one to turn to for support. After so many years apart during happier times, darkness had brought Silvana home to Italy. Now it had driven her far away again. Sara made it a point to visit Doretta's mamma in Cherasco at least once a month, but as the baby's arrival drew near, she limited her outings. She had not expected pregnancy to slow her down this much.

What was she going to do with her time? she wondered. Continue to collect eggs in the mornings and groom Zeus, who grew fat from lack of exercise? Tomorrow, at least, she would travel to Alba to help zia Luce. The Ferragosto holiday had left her short-staffed, and it would be the last time Sara would work again until after the baby came. Luciana had assumed suor Angelica's responsibilities after her retirement until the order's motherhouse sent a replacement. Although Sara enjoyed working with her zia, she didn't regret her choice of a simpler life in the countryside, despite its hardships. She could not imagine life elsewhere, with anyone other than Francesco.

Someone wrapped in the scent of the earth crept up behind her, nuzzled her neck, and refreshed the cool cloth draped on it. A kiss on her cheek. Dearest Francesco. He brushed away from her face a damp curl that had escaped from the pinned-up braid. From the moment she told him the news, he had doted on her. Most unusual for a Langhe contadino. One morning, after she had begun to show, with a naughty grin on his face, he teased, "How do you like my birthday present, cara?" Each day before he left for work, he kissed her swelling belly, wishing her and his child a good day. She had never seen him happier. He drew a chair close to her now and sat, caressing her chin with his calloused but gentle fingers as he dabbed her sweaty brow with another cool cloth.

"How was your day, cara? You're a bit pale, and you were restless last night." He brushed an eyelash from her face. "And your cheeks are warm and flushed." She touched his anxious face and allowed her fingers to dance across his lips until he smiled.

"Just the heat. A long day. Glad I didn't have to be in Alba today, but driving the Topolino is much hotter than riding on Zeus."

"And what a sight that would be. Old ladies' tongues would wag across Langhe from the Tanaro to the Apennines. Tiny Sara, belly like a big ball, riding that tall, plodding horse." He leaned closer, brushed his lips across her belly, and rested his cheek against her as he slipped his hand up her dress, caressing her thigh. She swatted it away.

"You just can't help yourself, can you Francesco Bosco?" She tousled his curly red hair.

"I'm impatient to hold him"—he kissed her inviting lips—"and you." She pushed him away as he only made her hotter. Nausea assailed her.

"Sara, what is it?"

"I'm fine. It's the heat. Even here in the shade. Though it's better than inside." She shifted to a more comfortable position, something increasingly difficult to find with the searing pain in her back. "Tell me about your day."

"I saw Luigi Grasso. He stopped by on that prized *baio* of his on his way from Vallegrande to the village. That bay horse...*è un po' pazzo*. Racing must have made the horse a little crazy." Francesco continued to caress Sara's belly until he felt her muscles flinch. "Oh. Was that a kick?"

It wasn't, but she let him think so. "Your brawny son has been quiet today. You've awakened him." In fact, over the last two days, the frequent kicks had stopped.

Francesco returned to his recap of the horse-loving farmer's visit. "Anyway, Luigi is rarely wrong about the weather. He said rain is coming. Hopefully not too much."

"But tell me about the grapes? When will you start the harvest?"

"Not for a few more days. They can use a bit more rain, and the cool air will be good to set—" This time there was no mistaking it. He saw her scrunched face and the way she grabbed at her belly. His voice took on a more serious tone. "Sara, time to stop working, or at least see fewer patients. Can't Cesare Costa help?"

"He's been at the hospital in Alba during the holiday. Anyway, with talk of war, we're worried he'll be conscripted. Then what will we do for a doctor in Barbaresco? Dottor Pera is far too old to see patients again, particularly with house calls."

"Really, Sara. Why Alba?"

"I promised zia Luce. Only one more day before her assistant is back from Liguria. I promise no more work after tomorrow...that is, until after baby comes." She didn't share with Francesco her other reason for going. Something was wrong. Francesco need not know; he would only worry.

"Well, I'm driving you to Alba. We'll take the Topolino. I have some errands to run before the harvest. And it's best that you don't go alone."

How she loved him. She already felt that everything would go well. "I have over two months left. Although I promise to take a break from work, I refuse to confine myself."

"It's a rare day to spend more time with you before the harvest."

Her radiant smile returned, and he responded with another kiss. This time she allowed his lips to linger on hers and hungrily returned his passion.

He inhaled her heady summertime scent that always reminded him of their first night together in Camogli. How he ached to love her through the night again. In due time.

OPEN SHUTTERS AND A GENTLE RAIN FAILED TO COOL SARA DOWN DURING the night. All through dinner, she picked at her food and finally excused herself from the table. Luigia followed her upstairs but returned shortly. "She's fine. It's hard to contend with heat at this late stage," she said. "I remember when Maria was born in late August, just when the harvest began. I was in the vineyards until the day before she came."

Francesco knew from Sara's fitfulness and the way she mumbled in her sleep that something other than the heat was bothering her. Later that night, she screamed his name and bolted upright, then fell back on her side and cuddled close, her belly against him, as though nothing had happened. Although still restless, she never woke. Worry kept Francesco awake. He stroked her hair and caressed her, watching over her until dawn broke.

She woke groggy and unsettled with no memory of her nightmare but complaining of nausea and a throbbing headache. Normally, she dashed to breakfast, but this morning she refused to eat.

"Perhaps you should stay in bed today, Sara," Francesco advised as she struggled to ready herself for the day.

She waved him away. "No, I promised zia Luce. It's my last day. I'll be fine."

Arguing with her was futile, so he did what he could to help her then waited below in the kitchen. He would ask Luigia to talk sense into her.

"Luigia, please, help me convince her to stay home today. She won't listen to me. So stubborn."

"I will try my dear boy, but I'm not hopeful. Though if she is unwell, there is no question she must stay home." The church bell in the village rang seven times. Sara had insisted they leave early, but she still hadn't appeared. Another deviation from her normal routine. She was never late for work.

"I'll see what's keeping her."

Francesco tried to open the door, but it jammed. He tried again, more forcefully, but still it moved only a few inches. Sara! He shoved with all his might and the door, blocked by Sara's body, opened. She was unconscious, lying where she had retched, her face scarlet and burning with fever to his touch.

"Luigia! Come quick!" he shouted. Fear pulsed through him. What had happened in the short time since he left her? Again, he shouted, hoping she would hear him above the din of her pots. He scooped up Sara's limp body in his arms and placed her on their bed.

Moments later Luigia rushed into the room, Giovanna close on her heels. Giovanna screamed when she saw Sara sprawled on the bed. She opened her eyes briefly, but failed to respond. Luigia pushed him aside. Francesco stood helpless, watching her undress Sara as she ordered Giovanna to fetch clean towels and cool water. Sara was shivering with chills.

"Francesco! Help me with this. We need to cool her down as quickly as possible. Did she say anything to you?"

"She tossed and turned all night. This morning she complained of a headache and said she was too queasy to eat. I found her against the door. Oh Luigia…what about the baby?"

At that moment, Sara cried out, rolled to her side and clutched her belly. "Mammaaaaaa!" She searched for Luigia's hand. "Mamma, the baby."

"Giovanna, run next door. Call the hospital. Luce must come. We can't move her. And fetch dottor Costa. We need a doctor, not only a midwife."

Francesco's heart leapt to this throat. "Oh no! Luigia, he's in Alba. Sara told me yesterday she would see him there today."

"Then we'll have to hope Gio can reach Luce, and they'll come together."

Though worried, Luigia calmed herself by arranging things for Sara and barking orders at Giovanna. She all but ignored Francesco. She thought to send him away, but there was a chance he might be useful. Sara turned her head, retched, and cried out again.

"What is it, Luigia, do you know?" Francesco asked.

"The fever. Nausea. I don't know. So many things, but…" Could it be? God, please no. She took Francesco's hands in hers and gazed into his eyes. "My dear, you must prepare yourself. Not only for the baby. But for Sara. I've seen this before. I lived it."

Francesco seemed confused but caught her tone more than her words. He dropped to his knees beside the bed. "No, God! You can't take them from me. Sara. Don't leave me."

Giovanna came shouting up the stairs. "They're coming! Zia and dottor Costa. They're coming!" Francesco cradled Sara's hands to his face. Giovanna leaned against him and wrapped her arms around as much of him as she could. For a few minutes, she stayed with him. "Hail Mary, full of grace…"

"Gio, here, take over and wipe her face. Then go for some clean linen, more towels and"—Luigia swallowed hard—"a small blanket."

266

Again, Sara shrieked. Luigia knew that soon she would give birth. She pulled Francesco away and sat next to her eldest child, writhing, clawing at her belly, calling out for Francesco who fought back tears as he watched.

"Luigia!" Francesco cried. "Blood!"

A red plume slowly bloomed under Sara.

"Francesco, out! Giovanna, take him downstairs." Their child would soon enter the world. Far too soon. Poor child. Luigia knew there was no saving it if it was even still alive. Only Sara's life mattered now.

As she sat, softly singing lullabies, choking back tears, the minutes turned to hours as Luigia cradled her pain-wracked daughter. Where were they? Dear God, please don't let the baby come before Luciana gets here. But her prayers weren't answered. Water, mixed with blood, now gushed from Sara's womb. It wouldn't be long.

She called to Giovanna. Francesco followed her back to the loft.

"Please Luigia. Don't send me away. I can't bear it."

No man should witness this, but Luigia did not have the heart or the energy to chase him away again. Sara fought to hold back her cries, but it was a losing battle.

Luigia gathered all the pillows and handed them to Francesco. "I want you to help me roll her onto her back and prop these under her shoulders. Sit here on the bed, next to her, and please, Francesco, do your best to soothe her, wipe her brow."

As she prepared to deliver her first grandchild, Luigia whispered prayers for strength. Her voice steady, she coached Sara to pant as Sara had taught her own patients to do. The baby's head crowned as more blood continued to flow. The bleeding frightened Luigia. Dear Lord, save her. Save my child. One last contraction elicited a wail that clawed at Luigia's heart. Francesco and Sara's son came into the world. He was perfectly formed, but still. Luigia choked back sobs as she met Francesco's piteous eyes. He needed no words from her.

Sara had fainted, mercifully since she would be denied the joy she had given to so many mothers as she laid their crying newborns against their breasts. Francesco cradled Sara and wept, burying his face against her while Luigia wrapped the limp body in the blanket. There had been no time to call don Emilio. Luigia held the baby close and began the *rosario*. Giovanna stood next to Francesco, tears dripping off her chin. The young discovered the cruelty of life in Langhe too early.

They heard the sound of tires on gravel.

"Mamma," Giovanna said listlessly. "They're here."

"Yes. Please go find your papà. Someone must fetch don Emilio straightaway."

Upon hearing the last request, Giovanna blanched. "Mamma! Sara won't die, will she?"

Francesco, still cradling Sara in his arms, shot Luigia a terrified look.

"No, Gio. He must come bless the baby," Luigia lied. Sara was still in grave danger.

Hurried footsteps approached. Dottor Costa and Luciana paused at the doorway with grave expressions. Luigia handed the baby to Luciana and pried Francesco away from his unconscious wife.

Luigia had never seen a man so heartbroken. Why did it have to be him? Once Francesco left, Luciana unwrapped the baby enough to show dottor Costa, who placed his fingertips to the baby's tiny neck. He shook his head then bent to examine Sara.

"She's still bleeding heavily," he said to Luigia. He took out a needle and a small vial from his medical bag. "Roll up her sleeve," he said. "This should help. Thank God I have it."

One of the reasons Cesare Costa had come to such a poverty-stricken area was the high rate of mortality during childbirth. While studying in Switzerland, he had learned about ergobasine in treating postpartum hemorrhaging, and he had used it to good effect several times in the region, though it was not easy to obtain. As he waited for the drug to take effect, which would take mere minutes, he held Sara's wrist as if to check her pulse. He gave her an encouraging squeeze. He could never have imagined that his assistant would be one of the patients he would try to save with the new drug.

In her delirium, Sara called for Francesco, called for her baby. Luigia clutched the baby tight to her breast. She remembered her own mamma holding her stillborn grandson, with a brooding Mirella looking on. They would have another child. Many more. If she lives.

The two sisters had returned for lunch from the vineyards near the cascina, where they had been helping their papà since shortly after dawn. Maria sped back into the long rows of vines to call him to the house. He came and sat with his beloved son-in-law, sharing his grief.

Letitia ran to the village and returned as a passenger in the village priest's car. He slipped into the bedroom and stood beside Sara, administering Extreme Unction to her while Luciana prayed with him.

The bleeding soon stopped. Dottor Costa had saved her life, for the moment, but she had lost a great deal of blood, and the danger of infection—or worse, sepsis—now loomed. Days would pass before they would know her fate.

The crisis that had begun shortly after daybreak continued well into the night. Once allowed back into their room, Francesco had not moved from Sara's side. The angels had taken their child to Heaven. He would fight them not to take Sara from him.

THREE DAYS PASSED WITH LUIGIA AND LUCIANA TRADING SHIFTS, WATCHING for signs of infection. Sara's low-grade fever persisted, but dottor Costa expected that. Francesco trudged behind Nico to and from the vineyards each day, working only because he had to. He spoke only when necessary and rarely ate. Nico could not console him although he tried. He knew the heartbreak all too well, and he, too, awaited Sara's fate.

On the fourth day, Madama Lia arrived in Asili. Luciana had telephoned her the first day as soon as they had felt hope that Sara might survive. Lia had recently travelled to Switzerland to visit Doretta and Madame Stern, and she ended up bringing Doretta back to Piemonte with her. And on to Asili. Luciana was overjoyed at seeing Sara's closest friend and gave them the good news: dottor Costa believed the crisis had passed. Madama Lia tilted her head back with relief. She looked at Doretta, nodded, and paused.

"Luigia, have you heard the news?" she asked.

"We haven't turned the wireless on for days. Why? What's happened?" She almost did not want to hear it. She could not bear any more bad news, not yet.

"Where is Nico? And Francesco. Please bring them in."

When the men arrived from the vineyard, Madama Lia hugged Francesco, something Luigia had never witnessed. They exchanged no words, but shared the loss together. Doretta then fell into Francesco's arms, and they both wept.

Once they were all together in the tinello, Cornelia Bottero made her announcement, feeling the weight of each word. "Hitler invaded Poland early Friday morning. Yesterday, after he refused demands to withdraw, Chamberlain announced on the wireless"—she paused, watching the faces in front of her—"that Great Britain, Australia, and New Zealand have declared war on Germany. France as well. As of September 3, the great powers of Europe are once again at war. God help us all."

CHAPTER 29

Asili
Early July 1940

Rain clouds appeared in the distance just as Sara expected given the sultry weather that day. She moved along with the passengers crowding onto the train in Alba and managed to grab a seat by the window to watch the storm unfold. It was Friday afternoon, and she was looking forward to the weekend, particularly after her visit with Cesare Costa.

The odor of passengers on the hot summer day roiled her stomach, as it often did these days. Fortunately, Francesco had not noticed. Now, during the short ride home, she had time to reflect on her day and its meaning for the future.

Infant and birth-mother mortality was high in the countryside. Had Cesare Costa not reached her in time, she and her stillborn son would now share a coffin in the Barbaresco cemetery. God had other plans for her. Otherwise, why should she, a farmer's wife, benefit from science known only to a few physicians in Italy? With Mussolini having declared war on France and Great Britain, this time allied with the devil himself, would Sara's talents as a nurse be needed at some point? Only time would tell. For now, her role was to bring new life to Asili. Cesare said the baby was due in November.

He suspected a bacterial infection—most likely salmonella—had wracked Sara's body and killed her vulnerable unborn child. He confirmed it when he cultured blood from her placenta. For months, guilt plagued her that she had infected herself accidentally by helping with the chickens. Only with her mamma and zia Luce had she shared that revelation. Francesco's mind would never be at ease over any pregnancy of hers if he knew. This time would be different. Despite the dire need for her nursing skills now that Cesare Costa would soon join the Fourth Army in France, her first duty was to her husband—to her family. She felt strong, as though she could take on anything. Francesco, however, was another matter. She hoped the news would cheer him and end the nightmares that had plagued him since her miscarriage.

At least he would not be called up. In addition to confirming her pregnancy, dottor Costa signed Francesco's medical deferral from army service—one of his last tasks before his deployment. Although he had healed far better than anyone expected, the accident had left Francesco with a slight limp that Cesare believed would prevent him from marching long distances with a heavy pack. So Sara had one less worry. She would promise Francesco that under no circumstance would she return to Alba to help with medical exams for draftees after today.

And there he stood on the platform in Barbaresco, waiting for her. Although sun, hard work, and heartbreak had aged him, Francesco was as handsome as always. But worry lines on his brow had deepened in the last year.

As she stepped from the train, steam mixed with the scent of light rain falling on the parched ground and swirled around her legs. Francesco's quizzical expression told her that he suspected something.

"What is it, Sara? You look like Gio just before she tells a secret."

"Oh, nothing. Just happy that you surprised me here. Now I don't have to walk home in the rain." She patted her satchel. "I have Cesare's certification of your deferment." Although excited to share her news, she was not about to tell him on the crowded train platform. Too many prying eyes and wagging tongues.

As they walked to the truck, Sara inhaled the earthy aromas the gentle rain released after such a long dry spell. She was anxious for time alone with him. Giving such news in a truck cab? No. Where then? After they crossed the railroad track, she knew.

"Francesco! Stop there." She pointed to the exact spot where her life had changed in November 1937. He veered left off the road as far as possible. *"Facciamo una passeggiata."*

"Walk? In this rain? Sara, no." He knew the importance of the location, but why stop here now?

"I don't care! Come." She grabbed his hand and pulled him into the high grass. He had not dared to go back there since that night. He still could not remember the details of the accident, other than waking to see Sara covered in mud, her face frantic, before he passed out again. His real memories began under blinding lights in the hospital.

"Here. Right here. I'll never forget it. On this spot, your life hung in the balance. But God wasn't ready for you. Not yet. He had other plans for us both."

Beads of rain from Francesco's saturated thick hair dripped into his eyes. Hers sparkled for the first time since before her miscarriage. She piqued his curiosity, but his patience was wearing thin. He still had work to do before sunset. "Sara—"

"Caro, your hand please." She took it, kissed the calluses and scar on his palm, and placed it firmly against her still flat belly. Dear God, please let him smile.

He whooped and swept her into his arms. "Oh, Sara! My dearest Sara." He set her down and embraced her as the rain fell harder, washing away his fear of losing her. "When?"

"He's very considerate. Not until after the harvest. Early November. And you won't have to go away to the army. What fortune your misfortune on this spot has brought us."

He winced at that. What about the others called to fight. Even Cesare Costa, who signed off on his disability, would be in harm's way, caring for wounded soldiers in France.

"What is it, Francesco? Aren't you pleased? What better news could I have for you? Cesare said that, as long as I listen to you hound me not to work, I should be fine." She did not mention his caution about the barnyard and the care she must take with her food.

Of course he was thrilled. The war, everyone knew, would not last long. France had fallen to the Germans: Great Britain would fall next, so they said. His place was here with her, with his child. This time he did not want to offend God, nor would he take this blessing for granted. A boy or a girl would please him.

"Carina, you know I am. But you know how I worry about you. So please, can we get out of this rain? It's chilly, and you're soaked." As they returned to the truck, the rain intensified, bringing much-needed nourishment to the vines. A good omen? Francesco no longer questioned God's will. Time would tell.

That night, the rain continued, giving them delicious relief from the July heat. Sara lay cocooned in Francesco's arms, bare skin against bare skin—the safest place she knew. And tonight, after their passionate lovemaking, she felt protected from the chaotic world outside Langhe. In that room, her most joyous and most tragic moments had happened. Sara prayed for joy. She prayed for Francesco and their child.

AFTER TRYING ALL WEEKEND TO REACH LUCA BY PHONE, DORETTA DECIDED to drive from Cherasco to his office in Alba. It had been weeks since she had last seen him in Turin when they met with clergy members of *DELASEM*, the new relief organization that operated openly—for how long, no one knew. Tension increased between the volunteers at each meeting. Foreign Jews who had not managed to leave Italy had gone into hiding under the protection of their neighbors or other Italians who defied the Racial Laws and risked their lives to help them.

Doretta had thought to call Madama Lia but then remembered that she was in Asili until the end of August. Although a day rarely passed that Madama did not speak with her *consigliere*, Doretta saw no need to alarm her—not yet. But she worried as each day passed that he didn't answer.

Early Monday morning, Doretta left their refuge in the hilltop city, hoping to catch Luca as he arrived at his office. The weekend of rain after the long dry spell washed thick grayish-blue mud onto the narrow road, challenging her ability to maintain control of the little Topolino as she rounded the many curves. With each mile of the drive through La Morra and the northernmost hills of Barolo, a new scenario popped into Doretta's head. By the time she drove into the Piazza Savona, panic surged through her.

She parked and then raced across the piazza, bounding up the stairs to the Olivero e Figlio law office. When she saw the door ajar, she calmed down. He was here, at work already! She pushed the door open. Papers littered the floor of the reception area along with desk drawers and upended furniture. Luca wasn't there. The rooms were eerily quiet. She switched on the light, and heard herself shout for signora Vacchetto, Luca's secretary. Oh, God. The room was nothing but chaos.

Doretta stepped over documents in Luca's office. His satchel lay on the floor, its contents scattered about. She squatted and picked up a framed photograph. The shattered glass distorted the photo of Luca as a young teen with his father. Then she spied a leather-bound journal in the dark recess under his desk. His agenda! All his meetings and calendar for the entire year. Names and addresses too!

She thumbed through the pages. Nothing scheduled for the weekend. She dashed to the office door and turned the locks then rushed back to Luca's office, locking the inner door behind her. Disoriented, she righted his chair and slid onto it. The stufa! She raced across the room and dropped to her knees. Before she strained to push the bulky firewood box aside, she checked for the barely visible white chalk mark on the floor at the edge of the box. Luca had marked it as a way to detect whether the box had been moved. It had not. Anyway, had someone found the safe, it would be open. She slid the box back into place and sat back against wall, her heart pounding. Oh, Luca. Where are you, caro? Then she heard the rattling of keys and tumbling of locks. There was no place to hide. Soft footsteps approached. Doretta nearly fainted as the doorknob rattled. More keys.

"Signorina Giordano! What are you—? What happened?" Signora Vacchetto clutched her chest and looked about the chaotic scene.

"I was going to ask you the same thing. Where's Luca?"

"My God. He…I don't know…he had some papers for me to deliver to the municipio, so I left about four on Friday. Everything was fine. He said he wasn't sure whether he would stay in town for the weekend or drive up to Val Maira."

"Ciarea…*Chi iè?*"

They both froze and locked their gazes on each other.

"Hello, who's there?" a man called again.

"*Siamo qui*, signor Rosso." Signora Vacchetto touched her heart again, and her stiffened body relaxed. "The building caretaker."

The middle-aged, squat man spoke as he shuffled across the room, making no effort to avoid stepping on the strewn documents. "Mamma mia! *Che casino*!" His bulbous, mottled red cheeks spoke of far too many hours imbibing at the card table, perhaps as recently as late into the early morning that day. "Where is dottor Olivero? Did he come back?"

"What do you mean, 'come back'?" Doretta demanded.

"Well…three men came here late on Friday. I peeked through the door when they drove up in the piazza."

Doretta's head spun as the blood drained from her head. She grabbed the corner of Luca's desk to steady herself.

"There was yelling. Then I heard signor Luca ask them what they wanted, but they said nothing to him." He shuffled into Luca's office and surveyed the room. "Two of them dragged him out and pushed him into the car. The other man stayed upstairs. I could hear them tearing up the office."

"*Them*? But you said there were only three men and two were in the car with Luca…dottor Olivero." Doretta clenched her jaw. Two days and three nights at the card table had passed. She doubted that he had more information to divulge. He would not know more about Luca.

"I think a woman, maybe a policewoman. I don't know. I heard a woman's voice upstairs."

She had had enough. Someone had kidnapped Luca, ransacked his office, and this drunkard of a caretaker did nothing? Doretta pounced with a barrage of questions.

"Why didn't you call the police? Why didn't you call signora Vacchetto? Or Madama Lia?"

The color of his scarlet cheeks deepened, and he stumbled a few steps backward, away from Doretta. "But they *were* the police, although I don't think from Alba." He looked back toward the office door and lowered his voice. "Do you think maybe the polizia politica?"

Signora Vacchetto gasped. "What would the political police want with signor Luca?"

Many things, Doretta feared. "I don't know. The local police won't be of any help now, so please clean this up and make note of anything missing. Call Madama Lia if he…or that woman…returns. And you, signor…whatever your name is, you can leave!"

Doretta grabbed Luca's journal from his desk and held it close to her heart. Over forty-eight hours had passed. If the PolPol had arrested Luca, there was no telling where they had taken him or what they might have done to him by now. She had to alert Madama Lia. It was the only thing she could think to do.

As she started her car, signora Vacchetto appeared, running across the piazza, waving an envelope in her hands.

"Signorina Giordano! I found this. On my desk."

Doretta saw the white cross of the Kingdom of Italy and an unfamiliar insignia on the envelope—as well as her typewritten name. Her breath caught as she tore it open.

My dear signorina Giordano, Well, I knew you would come looking for your Aryan lover, so I left this note for you out of courtesy. It was the least I could do.

Doretta closed her eyes and held the letter away from her. It was poison.

I warned him last year that fucking a Jew slut like you would get him in trouble. And it has. I hope it was worth it for you because that and his other offenses to the state have resulted in a long stay in a confino politico far from here. I suggest you watch your back. We are not done with you.

Unsigned. But then, no signature was needed. She could hear his odious voice as she read the typewritten words. Fighting the urge to shred it, she tossed it on the floor of the passenger side.

Signora Vacchetto gripped the car door. "What did it say?"

"Nothing…nothing useful. I'll be in touch later today."

Doretta sped off to Barbaresco. When she reached Pertinace on the other side of Altavilla, the enormity of what happened hit her. The road blurred. She stopped the car, opened the door, and dropped to her knees. Luca. Oh, dearest Luca. Doretta knew of *delations*, the anonymous method used to denounce fellow citizens, but it still made no sense. Some hid strangers at great risk to themselves, while others denounced friends and even family members. Some sent the letters directly to Mussolini or relatives of his. Now Baldo Volpe had defiled Luca's office and kidnapped him, no doubt taking him to Turin before sending him to a *confino*. In Mussolini's Italy, no proof was needed. No trial was held. The person simply disappeared. She had to find out where he had been taken. That was the first step.

When she pulled into Asili, Doretta stopped the car. She leaned her head on the steering wheel, struggling to compose herself. She had to show Madama Lia the filthy letter—she had no choice—but would Madama think that she and Luca had…

"Doretta! What a surprise to see you." Doretta startled. She had not seen Sara come from the cascina. She turned away and quickly wiped her eyes.

"Oh, Sara, you startled me."

Sara's broad smile vanished the moment she spotted Doretta's burning eyes against her pale complexion. "Cara! Dimmi! What on earth is wrong? Come on out. Let's sit."

Doretta reached for the letter, slipped it into her satchel, and followed Sara to the pergola. The cool breeze and shade helped calm her. She looked at Sara's sweet face, her eyes searching hers, and wondered what tempest she was blowing into Sara's world now.

"I don't know where to begin. Luca went missing Friday night. His office is in shambles." Sara slapped her hand over her mouth. Doretta pulled the letter from her satchel, but said before handing it to her, "Please, before you read this, remember that no one else must know its contents. No one. *Prometti*?"

She could tell when Sara reached the part that she would struggle to explain to Madama Lia. Her face reddened, and her pale, blonde eyebrows pinched. "Who—?" Doretta looked away. "*Bastardo*!"

"I have reason to believe the polizia politica have arrested Luca." She waited for Sara to absorb the news. "He's been denounced."

"What are you going to tell Madama Lia?"

"I don't know, Sara. Have you seen her today?"

"She was out riding early, but I've been inside all morning. Is there anything else you want to tell me?"

Doretta had planned to tell her about the policewoman the caretaker told them about but decided against it. She had no proof of who she was.

"But, Sara, what will I tell Madama?" Doretta looked deeply into Sara's eyes although she knew the answer.

"The truth, Doretta. The truth. And the truth is that Baldo Volpe is an evil liar. She'll understand. Now come." She threaded her fingers through Doretta's. "I'll go with you. I'll always be with you."

Their timing was perfect. As they walked from under the pergola into the bright sunshine, Madama Lia, astride her last equine acquisition from England before the war began, trotted into the cortile. When she dismounted and stood before them, dressed in riding breeches no different from those Sara wore, Doretta stifled a laugh. Despite everything that had happened that morning, it was impossible to hide her surprise at seeing Madama Lia so dressed.

"Modern times, Doretta. Modern times. Time to follow Sara's lead and ride astride. Even English ladies are riding astride to the hunt these days." She handed the reins to Matteo, her new farmhand. "What brings you to Asili today? And how is your mother?" She pulled off her riding gloves and slipped them into her jacket pocket. "What is it? Is there something you're here to tell me?"

"Madama, may we see you in the house?" Sara felt uncomfortable standing in the cortile with Matteo in earshot. Though she knew Madama thoroughly vetted new hires, one never knew these days. Any of them, for any reason, could fall victim to the same treachery they believed Luca had suffered. She had heard whispers of many denunciations, even for something as petty as romantic jealousy or family squabbles. It was the way some settled scores now.

Lia glanced at the leather-bound journal Doretta held close to her chest. "*Boh!* Let's go to the terrace, shall we? I need something cool to drink."

Seated across from the young women on the terrace, Madama Lia sat with her hands folded in her lap, her face somber while Doretta recounted what she had seen and heard at Luca's office.

"Luca said he might drive to Val Maira for the weekend, so when I didn't hear from him… What makes you think it was the polizia politica and that they arrested him?"

Doretta blushed and stared at the paper in her hands. Noise from the kitchen caught her attention. Giuseppina was preparing lunch within earshot.

"Doretta? No secrets. Especially in this house and certainly not from Gianni and Giuseppina. Now, dimmi."

"This letter was left for me on Luca's secretary's desk. A vulgar, anti-Semitic man with a vendetta against me wrote it. I've only met him twice, once when I was thirteen and again eighteen months ago in Turin"—she gripped the paper tighter—"with Luca. His mother was my mamma's dressmaker. I don't know why he hates me so."

"I see. May I read the letter?" Lia took the sheet from Doretta and stepped to the far corner of the terrace. The light breeze that blew past her carried the pleasant scents of saddle leather and horse sweat. The cheerfulness of flower boxes of cascading red geraniums and climbing roses on the wall was in stark contrast to what she read. When she finished, she folded it and gazed out in the distance before returning to her seat.

She placed the letter on the coffee table between them. "May I keep this?" Doretta squirmed, not knowing how to answer. She had no choice. She nodded. "This is very serious, Doretta. And not only because of the threat to Luca's wellbeing." Lia studied the folded letter, her forehead creased. "Are you sure the safe had not been opened?"

"I'm sure. I didn't want to open it while I was there by myself in case they came back."

"Good, but I'll have to send Gianni to remove the files when I'm certain the danger has passed. Chances are that drunken fool is an informer. You may not realize that, under the Police Agreement Act of 1936, the Italian authorities are bound to share information about German citizens suspected of crimes on Italian soil. German citizens in Italy—and even Italian citizens—involved with transferring Jewish assets out of Germany or helping them escape are subject to that law." She paused, letting the women absorb her brief education about Mussolini's reprehensible collaboration with the Nazis. Luca had smuggled false documents into Germany and aided in the escape of Silvana and her children. Was that the reason for his arrest? Might the Fascist police turn him over to the Gestapo? She shuddered.

Knots tightened in Doretta's stomach again. "Madama Lia, what's going to happen now? Do you think they would torture Luca?"

"Not OVRA, not as far as we know. But between the documents in his safe and what he knows, he could be valuable to them, particularly since Mussolini has ordered full cooperation with the authorities of the Reich." She glanced at the journal Doretta still clutched. "Doretta, what else do you have?"

"Only this. It's Luca's journal." She handed Madama Lia the incriminating book. "It was under his desk. I think he must have dropped it there and pushed it into the corner with his feet."

Lia picked the letter off the coffee table and slipped it into the journal then rose from her seat. The meeting had ended. "Leave this to me. I have powerful allies in the government. Don't look so shocked, Doretta. A woman in my position needs allies everywhere."

"Thank you, Madama." It had not been as painful as she had anticipated, but Doretta believed she had not heard the last of Madama's thoughts about her relationship with Luca.

"It's best if you return to Cherasco and stay there until I send for you. I will not call. This is a dangerous situation for you and the operation. I'll have to rethink your duties. Your language skills and writing talents could serve us well in our outreach for financial support in America." She turned to Sara. "Knowing you, cara, inactivity will be as unpleasant for your family as it will be for you." Her eyes narrowed as she tapped her finger on her lips while she considered her words. "On second thought, Doretta, when you arrive in Cherasco, pack your things and return to Asili. Michele is quite capable of looking after the family. I want you near me. Sara can help you with correspondence, and you can keep her company until the baby—" Lia froze. Had Sara told her yet?

Shocked, Doretta turned to Sara. "Are you…?"

"I am. I was so excited to see you so I could tell you, but then when you… well, I figured it could wait."

"I'm sorry, Sara, to have spoiled your surprise for Doretta."

Sara smiled, no doubt at the unusual experience of Madama Lia having had to apologize. "Please, Madama. It's quite all right."

Giuseppina, getting on in years, shuffled in to clear the tray of beverages. "Giuseppina, please show Sara and Doretta out."

With that, Luca's fate now rested squarely with Madama Lia.

CHAPTER 30

Asili
November 1940

God had smiled on Sara and Francesco. The bountiful grain and grape harvests that year and the mild autumn days made pregnancy a joy for Sara. Yet the kicking baby rarely gave Sara peace. The expectant parents had agreed that they would not refer to the baby as a son or daughter. Of course, Sara knew that Francesco pined for a son. Once, she overheard her papà say to her mamma that he worried the couple would suffer the same fate they had. Luigia had snapped at him. "Nico, how could you! Suffer? Have we suffered with our daughters? They have all been blessings. Shame on you." Sara knew her papà adored his daughters, but it was as natural for him to desire a grandson as it was for Francesco to keep praying for a son.

Despite the harvest and her healthy pregnancy, a dark cloud still hung over the Fiore farm, and over Cascina Asili, where Doretta remained as Madama Lia's guest. It had been over four months since Luca's denouncement. And there was no telling when or where Baldo Volpe might strike next. All Madama Lia had been able to discover was that he had been taken to a confino politico in Pizzoli, an impoverished village far away in the Abruzzi. Though locked away from society, at least it was not a prison. They had heard that anti-Fascists like Leone Ginzburg had been sent there too. But unlike Luca, who had never participated in overt anti-Fascist activities, those were members of the outlawed Giustizia e Libertà.

Madama Lia had returned to Alba in late August, giving Doretta the run of the cascina where she stayed in Luca's assigned room. With no one to cook for her, she dined regularly with the Fiore family.

Every other weekend, Michele drove Elena, Ida, and his mother to Barbaresco for Sunday lunch. Otherwise, they rarely left the house. Michele in particular missed Doretta's company and enjoyed their outings to Ca' dei Fiù. He spent hours walking the vineyards with Nico and Francesco, absorbing what he could about viticulture, a new passion of his. Sara suspected that it had been his father who had pushed him toward a military career. Like Doretta, Michele possessed a keen intellect, but like Francesco, the vineyards called to him.

Nico had invited the Giordanos to stay during the harvest for Michele's sake, but Daniela declined. Elena made no secret of hating village life. She referred to the medieval city of her mother's ancestors as her prison. Lush, mystical forests surrounded Cherasco, but none of it appealed to her. Her disagreeable disposition tried everyone's patience. Only a visit to Duilio Barbero for a bag of *baci di Cherasco* could appease her. Whenever she purchased a sachet of the delicious chocolate kisses, he always gave her a few pieces of other chocolate treats to taste.

At Ca' dei Fiù, however, they had harvested the crops, the wheat had been sown, and grapes had been sold for a good price—a challenge considering the unscrupulous buyers in Piazza Savona. Their own wine was fermenting, and new life would arrive soon in Asili. Despite the war raging on the other side of the Alps to the west, the Fiore and Bosco families' basket of blessings overflowed.

For Doretta, such blessings seemed in short supply. With no news of Luca, her mood was dark. Her fund-raising activities, though greatly needed, bored her. Though Sara's heart ached for her, she relished Doretta's presence in Asili during what she considered her own internal exile.

They celebrated the harvest at their pranzo domenicale. The Giordano family, including a glowering Elena, joined in the thanksgiving feast. Doretta was quiet too, keeping her sadness to herself. *L'estate di San Martino* brought them a welcome break from the autumn fog with an appearance of the sun before winter arrived. Reveling in the warmth, Doretta and Sara took a passeggiata to the village after their long lunch. They were not the only ones sauntering along *strada* Comunale, enjoying what was surely one of the last warm, sunny days before the snow flew. Sara's pace was slower than usual, and she waddled a bit, holding her stomach to feel the baby's kicks. Francesco, who rarely let Sara out of sight beyond the cortile, and Michele tagged along.

Sara loved seeing the two men together. Michele seemed lost when he first arrived. And now, he couldn't join the boys he had grown up with heading off to battle—not that he would want to given the Racial Laws and those he would be fighting for. The Racial Laws banned Jews from serving their country as their forefathers had done only twenty years earlier. But with Francesco and her papà, Michele's mood brightened.

And dear Francesco. This had been his eighth harvest in Langhe. Years in the countryside began and ended with harvests. Nothing other than the earth's bounty mattered here. But he was still Sicilian and one of military age, strong in many ways but exempt from fighting beside his fellow Italians. She knew that his gratitude for Cesare Costa's certification of his disability mixed with guilt at being home with his wife—on a farm he had always regarded as a paradise with a child soon to join them—while others his age suffered in battle.

Doretta kicked stones from her path as they walked. "I'm trapped, Sara. I'm trapped between worlds."

"What do you mean?"

"On one side is a Gentile man I love but who is forbidden to me. He rots in a confino politico. And then there are those who haunt me: Jews, suffering the worst kind of persecution. Madame Stern doesn't write that much anymore, but she did say that, since Kristallnacht, Jews are being sent to concentration camps. Many are worked to death. It's routine now!" A stone went flying further than the others. "Some are beginning to believe emigration is no longer the Nazis' method to rid Germany, the entire Reich, of Jews." Her words came faster now. "No one will have them, anyway. Something worse is happening." She paused to catch her breath. "They're going to kill all the Jews, Sara!"

Enough. Sara grabbed Doretta's wrist and pulled her over to the side of the street. "Doretta, tranquilla," Sara urged as she looked about, smiling at the black-clad crones whose nonna culture obliged them never to miss anything. "Let's walk a bit away from the village. Fewer people." She took her friend's hand and walked up to strada Ronchi, as though leading her away from her dark thoughts.

When Doretta had calmed down, Sara continued. "Tell me about feeling trapped. Explain."

They stood at the end of strada Ronchi, with the splendid vista before them and Castello di Neive across the valley. "Can't you see? Here in the country-side with so many of you looking after me, I live as though the world outside doesn't exist. This is a beautiful refuge. But this"—she waved her hand across the valley—"this is not reality. I'm powerless to help the man I love *and* the people I'm bound to through thousands of years of history." She stopped and covered her face. "I know so little about them. After Emancipation, my father's family kept very few ties with the Jewish community."

"Doretta, do you truly believe we will remain untouched in the countryside? Madama Lia said it last summer: 'Your time will come.' Don't believe for a moment she only meant me."

"But it's not *your* fight. It's not Madama Lia's fight...or Luca's." She shook her head as though trying to chase away the thought of him suffering because of her. "Anyway, look at you. You have Francesco and the baby to care for. Why would you involve yourself? And why would she, a woman who is so powerful, want to risk everything?"

Sara placed her hands on Doretta's shoulders. She studied her anguished face. *Poverina.* "*Mia cara sorella*—for yes, you're like a sister to me"—Sara brushed Doretta's flushed cheek and shook her head—"tell me how, after so many years, you think I would just be a spectator in this battle."

"You didn't answer me, Sara. It's not your fight."

Sara shook her head in frustration. "You could not be more wrong. Any human being who fails to see this as their battle may as well be on the side of the tyrants." Sara's voice grew louder. "Do you understand me now? Taking no action against these crimes is the same as helping the criminals. And don't believe for a moment it will end with the Jews if they succeed."

"Sara, I'm a Jew, but honestly I don't even know what it means to be one." For the first time, Doretta sensed a barrier separating her from Sara, who could walk freely in the world, not fearing for her life because of what she was. "Oh, my dear Sara, it's not the same. I was taught we were no different than anyone, only...only, we are. We truly are. And now that difference—our race, supposedly—is why our very existence is at risk."

"And you believe because of that—because I'm not a Jew—I can't be one with you? I know that's what you're thinking, Doretta, and you're wrong. Simply wrong."

Doretta's tight mouth finally relaxed and turned upward. "I'm sorry. I didn't mean that exactly."

Sara wrapped her arms around her. "We've been through so much together. And there's more to come, I know. But for now, let's wait and see." She stepped back and brushed Doretta's cheek again.

"But Luca—"

"I know, cara. I know. We have to trust Madama Lia and pray that she'll find a way to return him to us, to you." She leaned back and rubbed her lower back. Ever-vigilant Francesco rushed to them.

"Sara? Let's head home," he said.

"Yes, I didn't realize the time," Sara answered. "I want to say good-bye to Madama Lia and zia Luce before they return to Alba."

When they reached the cappella di San Teobaldo, Sara stopped short. She doubled over and grabbed at her belly.

Francesco grabbed her elbows. "Sara! What is it?"

When she stood, her face was already flushed. "Hurry, dearest. I knew the walk would help. It's nearly time."

He scooped her up in his arms, his long legs striding to the cascina. Doretta trotted along behind him. He felt warm wetness on his arm and nearly tripped, certain it was blood. Sara leaned up and pecked him on his cheek. "It's only nature telling you to walk a bit faster, my love."

"Luce! Luce! Where are you? It's time," he hollered when they arrived in the cortile.

The cascina door flew open, and Luciana stood there, a smile on her face. "Take her upstairs to her old room. I want her closer this time."

As Francesco raced up the stairs, Sara's arms around his neck, another contraction hit her. Francesco froze. "What is it? Are you all right? Cara, talk to me?"

When the pain had passed, she smiled at him once more, kissed her index finger, and pressed it against his tight lips. "Tranquilla, caro...papà. I've sensed it since last night and zia Luce confirmed it this morning. She believed a walk would help encourage our little one to come out."

"Dai dai, Francesco!" Luciana ordered. "You and Sara can talk later. For now, I have a baby to deliver. And this time, my boy, you'll have to get out of the way."

The room was well prepared. Clever zia Luce was rarely wrong about the timing of a birth. All day she had watched Sara like a hawk, saying nothing to Francesco, only the women of the household. Although she knew a passeggiata would ease the baby's way, she worried when they were gone for so long.

"Can't I stay, Luce? Please." For a brawny man, he whined like a little boy.

"No, Francesco. Things are different this time." She crossed herself. "Grazie a Dio. Stay close to the cascina. I'll call you as soon as your child is born."

"You're moving quickly, Sara," Luciana said.

Sara looked for Doretta, who lingered in the doorway. "Doretta, where's my mamma?"

"I sent Gio to Madama Lia's to fetch her. She had taken some soup to Giuseppina. She's under the weather today. And then she was going to find my mamma and Ida. Do you need my help, Luce?" Doretta's dark mood had evaporated.

How selfish she had been to think of herself when Sara, who had suffered greatly the first time, was about to give birth. She should have paid more heed to the warnings zia Luce whispered to her before they left for their passeggiata.

Luigia and Giovanna arrived minutes later. The joyful atmosphere in the cramped room belied Luciana's concerns about possible complications. Luciana had seen most everything in her nearly thirty years of nursing and midwifing, and she felt confident no harm would come to Sara and the baby. Before he left, Cesare Costa had given her the ergobasine, just in case.

After the initial burst of activity, Sara's labor stopped. There was no turning back. No hospital to run to. It was all up to Sara and Luciana. And God. Giovanna frequently scurried away to keep Francesco informed. After nearly two hours of nervous anticipation in the tinello, he took to pacing in the cortile. After the sun set, he went into the barn to feed and groom Zeus as a way to be near Sara. Francesco and the robust gelding had never bonded. Far too many torn shirts and bruises from Zeus's teeth kept Francesco away from him. But tonight, the horse was calm, nuzzling Francesco as he brushed him. Francesco began to understand the special bond between horse and woman. Maybe they both sensed the unseen.

Upstairs, Doretta sat next to Sara, wiping her brow with a cool rag, massaging her arms and hands, and breathing with her when the contractions resumed. Luciana knelt on the hardwood floor at the end of the bed, rosary in hand, while Luigia sat in the corner, embroidering and softly humming lullabies. The evening had turned to night, and the temperature had dropped, but the room felt stifling. Sara begged Luciana to leave the window cracked open.

Six hours had passed when they heard a soft tapping on the door. Giovanna entered with a worried look. "Sara, I've never seen Zeus so clean. Mamma, what shall I tell Francesco now? He refused to eat anything, but Papà is starving." Sara's yelp stifled their laughter. She had managed to constrain her cries of pain for Francesco's sake, but now that contractions came closer and harder, it was impossible.

"Gio," Luciana said, not taking her eyes off Sara as she waited to see the baby crown. "Tell Francesco the baby is almost here. But you must tell him— Gio, wait. You must tell him she's fine. Tell him to come into the house then come back right away."

Minutes dragged, but the birth progressed normally. Doretta and Luigia sat on the bed with Sara between them. Luigia sang the lullabies she had been humming and Doretta continued to breathe with the struggling mother.

"She's so tiny, signora Luigia. And this baby is not."

Hearing Doretta's observation, Sara, her lovely face contorted with pain, her hair dark and wet, shot a panicked look at Luciana.

"No child, you're fine. The baby's fine. You must know…"

There was no need for Luciana's warning about pain. The full-term baby now tore through her tiny body and into the world. Sara's scream subsided, and soon the raucous cry of the newborn replaced it.

Sara fell back, exhausted but elated. Luigia smothered her daughter with kisses. Doretta pressed her hands to her face and whimpered tears of relief. This was the joy she had longed for. Luciana beamed as she placed the baby at Sara's bare breast. "A girl, Sara. A healthy baby girl."

Doretta noted that Luigia's joyful expression wavered for a moment, but she understood the Langhe desire for boys.

Giovanna had dashed out the minute Luciana first held the baby girl. "Mamma, Francesco is here."

"*Aspetta*, Gio. Not yet. One moment."

A flurry of activity ensued as the three women fussed over Sara and the baby. Luciana took the sweet infant from her mamma, who reluctantly released her to be cleaned and swaddled. While Doretta tried to tame Sara's hair, Luigia quickly sponged her face, neck, and shoulders with cool water perfumed with lavender oil before helping her into the bed jacket she had knitted for her.

"Please, can I come in?" Francesco called in. The women all exchanged smiles, and Doretta giggled.

"Gio, open the door," Luciana called.

As Luigia had often noticed, Francesco was no ordinary man. When Sara told him that she had borne a daughter, he wept—not tears of dismay or anger but sheer delight, his ruddy Sicilian face alight with joy. His wife was well, and they had a healthy child. In this world, how could he not be grateful?

"Caro, you don't mind…I know you said you didn't care if—"

Before Sara finished, Francesco pressed his lips against hers then held his finger to her mouth. "Tranquilla. Tranquilla, carina. She's beautiful. Oh my, she's a little angel who looks exactly like her mamma. And her zia Gio too. Isn't she lucky?" He laughed as he drank in Sara's glowing face. "And she has blue eyes!"

"Silly, all babies have blue eyes. I did all the hard work today, now you must do something for me." She ran her fingers across his brow, trying in vain to tame his red curly locks. "What shall we name her?" Francesco flushed. Puddles of tears formed in his green eyes. "Caro! Dimmi. Why the tears?"

"Don't you remember? You said if we had a daughter, we would name her Anna after my mamma. Oh, Sara, I miss her." He buried his face against her neck and wept. She had never seen him cry for his Sicilian family.

"Of course, my love. Anna is a lovely name. And Anna she shall be."

He cradled Sara and sleeping baby Anna in his long, muscular arms. They were both precious, and the baby was tiny and delicate. Was there anything that could make him happier than this moment?

Shortly before midnight, Luigia finally called her exhausted family to the table. To her delight, and without being told, Maria and Lucrezia had laid the table, prepared plates of antipasti, and placed a pot of *brodo* on the putagè to heat. Nico blessed the food, their family and dear friend, and the new life at Asili. Anna's birth heralded a new generation on the land of his courageous ancestors.

After the excitement of Anna's arrival, the Giordano family remained in Barbaresco for the night. All but Doretta were asleep at Cascina Asili, but lights shone from Madama Lia's study. They were all so hungry and excited that no one had seen or heard a car pull into the cortile. Doretta, sitting by the window, noticed that Madama Lia was dressed as elegantly as usual. She was talking to someone. Doretta thought exhaustion had set in and her eyes were playing tricks on her—but no, it was real. Luca! He stood next to Madama Lia at the window. Twice that night, God had blessed them.

CHAPTER 31

Asili
December 1941

Cinzia Strega relished the news she carried to Asili. Did Francesco Bosco actually believe he would avoid military service? Since dottor Cesare Costa was in France, unable to support his reasons for certifying the Sicilian's disability for service, Francesco was a pigeon waiting for her to shoot. As she drove along the ridge, Asili in sight across the Rio Sordo valley, she glanced at the official conscription notice on the seat beside her. Despite his sadistic perversions, it was well worth the favors she had given the senior conscription officer to obtain a rescission of the absent doctor's medical release. For a little extra, he had allowed her to personally deliver the news. The bruises on her wrists and ankles would heal in week or so. Francesco's pain would endure. He had little time to contest the conscription. In any case, it would be of no use. She had seen to that. Baldo Volpe was right. A better opportunity, more painful than denunciation, would surely arise. And it had. Besides, his little wife was too well loved in the community to denounce him with success. Cinzia had ensnared Francesco Bosco. Escape was impossible. It was worth the wait. It was worth the roughing up.

There he stood, in the tall grass, not far past Martinenga, where he should have left this world. Well, now she gladly would see him out of *her* world. She would attend to his wife next.

"Francesco Bosco!" He raised his eyes from his work clearing a drainage ditch. Good. His expression is perfect. Stunned. Just wait. Let's see your expression once you realize you are leaving your precious wife and brat.

The day was mild for the season, but he felt as though an icy wind whipped past him. "What do you want?" He had never expected to see Cinzia Strega again. "Have you come to adjust my horse's harness once again?"

"Oh, caro Francesco…" As she strode from the car, she drew out the endearment, long and sickeningly sweet, her high heels sinking in the wet clay mud. "Now why would you say such a thing? I have no idea what you mean."

Her coquettish tone tied a knot around his stomach, still full from *colazione*. Francesco ignored her and resumed clearing weeds from the drainage. She continued toward him, a lioness stalking her prey. "Why no. I've come with news from Alba."

She made no effort to hide the nature of the paper. The Italian tricolors with the emblem of Savoia were in plain view. Her wolfish expression forced up his throat the knot in his stomach. Only to deliver bad news would Cinzia Strega take the time to drive to Asili. He tightened his grip on the handle of the hoe as he pushed evil thoughts from his mind.

"Francesco Bosco, your deferment has been rescinded. Men are needed on the Eastern Front. You're to report for duty on Thursday the seventeenth. Thursday, Francesco. Be thankful you have eight days." She held out the letter to him.

Her pointed chin and onyx eyes devoid of any kindness reminded him of the *masche* Sara's nonna Beatrice always told tales about when they visited her in Bossolaschetto. The witches, she said, roamed the forests of the Alta Langa, casting evil spells on unsuspecting peasants. But this wasn't a spell. It was his own bad judgment, an impulsive reaction to Sara spurning him. Although he had been a lonely Sicilian peasant, far from home and missing all that was familiar to him, he had known better, particularly after his brothers had fallen in with a bad lot. At least he had had the sense not to go with her to Liguria that weekend when she left him with the scar that would always remind him how close he came to disaster. A woman like her would have trapped him for sure. Only now did he realize she had indeed trapped him.

His shock, the veins of his neck throbbing, hatred in his eyes, satisfied her. Entirely within her power he was. She waved the letter that sealed his fate. "You can't refuse it, Francesco. All the details about when and where you're to report are there. If you fail to appear, you will be declared a deserter after three days. Up against the wall you would go." She raised her arm in the Roman salute then released the letter from between her thumb and index finger before sauntering to her car.

Francesco watched the paper float to the ground. Before she got back in, she added, "Sooner or later we all have to pay the price for the choices we make in life. *Buona fortuna*, mio caro Francesco."

He stood frozen, his eyes following her as she drove up the hill toward Barbaresco. Where was she going? Surely not to Asili to tell Sara. Cinzia Strega was wicked enough to inflict more pain on her. Panic surged through his body. Was she even home yet? Only from him should Sara hear this devastating news. He picked up the letter, jumped up to the driver's bench on the cartun, and smacked the dozing Romeo with the thick leather reins. Within minutes, he was back at Asili. No sign of the witch's black Topolino.

No one was about, so he spun the horse around and headed back to his work. They would all learn soon enough. Eight days. It should not have come as a surprise to him. Suspicion was high that Cinzia Strega had a hand in aiding the polizia politica who had come from Turin for Luca. If denunciations were commonplace, why had she not struck before? He would never know the answer, but having struck now, in this manner, she had likely handed him a death sentence. The question now was how to tell Sara.

He picked up his tools and returned to his work. Each blow of the hoe was a blow to Cinzia Strega's neck. Though the Eastern Front was far away and they had heard of slaughters of Italian troops, should she ever harm Sara or Anna, he would find a way home to hunt her down. He struck the ground even harder. Hate consumed him.

On a quiet afternoon on December 9, Luca picked up his satchel and donned his hat, ready to leave his office for the day. It had been eighteen months since he sat here alone on a hot Friday afternoon and Baldo Volpe violently entered his life. Adrenaline surged through his body each time he heard heavy footsteps on the stairs or a Blackshirt passed him on the street. Volpe never laid a hand on Luca, but it was clear he had power over those who would, and he was willing to use it. All to harm Doretta.

He was anxious to drive to Asili for the night to discuss the news from America with Madama Lia and Doretta. Although they mourned the many who had died at Pearl Harbor, they rejoiced at the news of America's declaration of war against Japan. Surely, in a matter of days, they would extend their war declaration to Germany and Italy. What were the president's words over the wireless that for the first time gave Luca hope? *We will gain the inevitable triumph, so help us God.* It took the actions of the faraway enemy in the Pacific, but the deployment of American troops in Europe would lead to their liberation. He prayed time had not run out.

A year had passed since he was freed from Pizzoli with no reason given for his incarceration or release, and there had been no sign of Volpe though Doretta lived in constant fear of him—not only for herself but also for those whom she loved. About town, he had seen that repulsive policewoman Cinzia Strega, but he would not give her the pleasure of thinking he was afraid of her. Luca felt sure that he was being followed, but he never carried anything incriminating on his person.

One early morning a few days after his abduction, before signora Vacchetto arrived, Gianni transferred the files from the office safe to the cellar in Madama's house in Altavilla. Although signora Vacchetto had served the Olivero family loyally for years, Madama Lia believed that there was no telling what the polizia politica might extract from her under interrogation. She knew enough already. It surprised Lia that the polizia politica had not paid her a visit. The absence of action against her led Luca to believe that Doretta—not he, not Madama—was Volpe's ultimate target.

Those months in confino in Pizzoli had hardened him. He didn't rot in a cell; in fact, he roamed the village freely and listened carefully to prisoners from Giustizia e Libertà such as Leone Ginzburg and Carlo Levi. They had been willing to risk their lives in the fight against fascism and, years ago, had become some of OVRA's most-wanted targets. Luca had placed himself at risk before but never as they had. He went into captivity as a lawyer who used his skills to help persecuted people flee tyranny. That was his only role against fascism. But now, as an anti-Fascist, he would find his place in the fight. And that place would not be simply to follow the courageous lead of Madama Lia as he had for five years. He had his own vision of how to meet the growing crisis. America's entry into the war meant the time for action had come. Soon he would make the needed sacrifice.

On his way through Martinenga, he passed by Francesco in the field. He never stopped beating the ground with his hoe, even when Luca tooted the horn. It was unusual for Francesco not to wave and flash his boyish grin. He hoped nothing was amiss between Sara and him. Doretta had told him that, once freed from the frequent need to nurse Anna, Sara returned to her punishing schedule of caring for the sick of the valley and rarely came home during the day. No doctor had come to replace Cesare Costa yet, so it all fell on her. Doretta worried about the lack of time she gave to Anna these days, but Giovanna gladly served as a nanny and doted on the child. He once over-head her say that Anna was the only child she ever needed in her life. Never would she leave Asili. Her older sisters had not yet married, but Luca knew the time approached when they would, provided there were still eligible men in their generation.

Lists of dead or missing and contradictory accounts from the Fascist-controlled press of glorious victories on the Eastern Front were all they heard. At least, Francesco remained in Asili. As for himself, Luca figured his age and time in confino politico made him ineligible to fight for now. Italy still possessed many young men for Mussolini to conscript as cannon fodder.

Doretta greeted him at Madama Lia's door. She now had her own room in Cascina Asili, far from his. At least sleeping under the same roof allowed them late nights in front of the fire, sipping brandy and grappa and trying to make sense of the tragic news that arrived at Asili on a daily basis. Five months apart had been torture, but during that time, they both came to think more rationally about their future today. Though they were careful, anyone who saw them together could tell they were in love. Time—they needed time. And peace.

"Bondì, Luca. What brings you to Asili today?" Doretta led him to the sunroom, which had a fire crackling in the hearth. "I was about to pour myself an apertivo. Join me in a glass of Arneis?"

When she handed him the glass, electricity shot through him as she brushed his fingers with hers. Although it had been years since their first kiss, her touch still felt new and exciting. He never tired of the familiar feeling. Sitting across from her, he was far enough away to avoid temptation but still within the envelope of her rosy scent.

"Salute, Luca. I'm surprised—but so very happy—to see you here mid-week. Tell me, what's going on with you in Alba?"

"Work. And more work. I wanted to see Madama…with what's happened in Pearl Harbor and all, so rather than wait for her in Alba…and, well, I didn't want to wait until the weekend to see you." Her naughty smile always warmed him, but he felt a pang of guilt knowing he also had come to tell her news that would upset her. He raised his glass once more and fought the urge to move next to her. She changed the subject.

"Have you heard anything about the Americans?"

"Only that Churchill finally got his wish. I heard only one member of Congress opposed Roosevelt's war declaration. All hemispheres are now at war.

"Where's Madama?" Luca was eager to discuss with her the surprising turn of events. What did America's involvement mean for them?

"At Villa Cristina. The Contessa's son Emanuele is a major in the Alpini. Somewhere on the French border, I think. Those are two tough women, Luca. They have a lot in common." She rose and refilled his glass, leaving a cloud of roses about his head. "She'll be home for dinner." Doretta noticed that Luca did not have his overnight bag with him. "You aren't returning to Alba tonight, are you?"

"Not if you promise to sit with me after dinner." Their eyes locked. She blushed. They had promised one another that they would not pursue a deeper relationship, but it became harder each time they were alone. He took another sip of wine. "I have clothes here. The fog's already thick in the valley." He set the glass on the low table between them and leaned closer to her. "Speaking of which, I saw Francesco working below Asili. Not a happy man. Any idea why?"

A shadow passed across Doretta's face. "Not at all. I saw him with Anna this morning. Can you believe she's walking already? He was all smiles. Maybe he's annoyed at Sara's schedule. I know he was hoping for another baby this year, but…" Best not to discuss that with Luca. Sara had confided in her that, although she enjoyed motherhood, nightmares had plagued her for months after Anna's birth. Although she had heard of illegal contraceptive devices available in Turin, Sara allowed nature to take its course, only shunning Francesco on those days she believed she might conceive. It baffled Francesco that she had not become pregnant again, but Sara was grateful she had not.

They heard a car pull up outside. "Sara's home. I'll see if she'll join us."

Within a few minutes, Doretta returned with her. Luca had not seen Sara in a few weeks, so the circles under her unusually dull eyes surprised him. But she was warm and welcoming as always.

"What brings you here, Luca?"

"Doretta asked the same. It's not so rare that I come to Asili, is it?"

She pecked his cheeks and plopped onto the divan where Doretta had been sitting. With the onset of winter, she had taken to wearing slacks again and appeared abnormally thin.

"Yes please," she replied when Doretta held up the bottle of Arneis. "It was such a long, tiring day. Many of my patients have influenza." Doretta handed her a glass of the pale yellow wine. "You still haven't answered my question. Anything in particular bring you here during the week?"

"You mean besides the obliteration of America's Pacific fleet and their entry into the war?"

"No need for sarcasm. You must admit your unannounced appearance over the years is not always the sign of good news." She flashed him a wry look and raised her glass. "Salute!"

Uncharacteristically, he avoided Sara's eyes when he raised his glass. She would sense he had indeed brought bad news for Doretta. "The war, Sara. The war. I'm alone in Alba and longed to know what my two families in Asili were thinking about it." Doretta's crossed arms and tight lips had not gone unnoticed. "That includes you, Doretta."

"Good!" Doretta winked at Luca and returned to her seat on the divan next to Sara. "I received a message from Madame Stern that the Nazis established yet another Jewish ghetto, this one near Prague." Doretta's tone turned grave, and she lowered her voice though only those within Madama Lia's circle of confidence would be in the house. "And spies have reported something about the Nazis' interest in Zyklon-B." Doretta paused. Luca saw her shudder as she whispered, "Cyanide."

"Cyanide? Madòna!" Sara exclaimed. "Are the Germans returning to chemical warfare?"

"Not exactly…" He let the answer hang in the air while he swallowed the lump in his throat. "Warfare, yes. But this time to kill Jews. I know it's hard to believe. There's also intelligence that the Nazis are converting some concentration camps and building new ones to use as"—he took a long, thoughtful sip of wine as he chose his words—"as death factories. I heard they conducted the Zyklon-B tests at a new camp in Poland in September. They named it Auschwitz."

Doretta added, "It seems that working Jews to death and starving them or shooting tens of thousands of them like they did in Odessa and near Kiev isn't efficient enough for them." Heavy silence descended upon the room. Doretta continued, her voice now wavering. "Sick, I tell you, that now they're exterminating human beings on an industrial scale!"

"Surely, the British and Americans will stop this, don't you think, Luca?"

"No, Sara, I really don't believe it's a high priority for them. If so, why didn't they do anything for the last nine years while the Germans persecuted the Jews?" The front door closed and someone's heavy steps on the staircase grew louder. Francesco entered with a wan face and haunted eyes.

"Francesco!" Never shy about showing affection for her husband, Sara jumped up and threw her arms around his waist. Francesco looked at Doretta, who squinted as though trying to read his expression. "Come, sit with us. I've missed you."

Luca could see that Doretta noticed something was wrong, but how unusual for Sara not to see it. She was giddy.

"Ciao, Luca. Ciao Doretta. No, I'm still in my work clothes." He pulled Sara's arms away and took her hand. "Please excuse us. I must speak with Sara."

A pall fell over the room.

"What is it, Francesco?" She looked bewildered.

"Come, Sara."

Doretta and Luca sat in stunned silence. Moments later, through the closed windows and shutters, they heard Sara shriek below in the cortile. Whatever news Francesco had shared was devastating.

Soon they heard Luigia's and Nico's voices and then Sara sobbing. The sun had set, and the room had grown cold. Not knowing what to do, Luca busied himself stoking the embers in the fireplace and adding wood. Only the glow of the roaring fire and a dim lamp next to Doretta lit the room. Madama Lia had entered unnoticed. The eerie glow the fire cast on her face deepened her solemn expression. Luca stood until she sat where, half an hour earlier, Sara had been beaming at Francesco. Frantic with fear, he waited for her to share the news.

"Francesco's deferment has been rescinded." She spoke as though in a trance, though her voice cracked. "He is to report for duty on Thursday, December 17."

Doretta clasped her hand over her open mouth. "But Madama," she asked, "what about his deferment?"

Madama cast an all-knowing look at Luca in the firelight. He shivered. "You mean…?"

Without another word or gesture, she rose. Luca stood, and Madama Lia left the room. Luca and Doretta exchanged meaningful looks. Neither had the strength to resist the need for comfort. After he heard Madama Lia's bedroom door upstairs close, Luca went to Doretta and held her close as she whimpered, pressing her head against his chest. It made no sense. He had never heard of such a thing. Baldo Volpe had nothing to gain from hurting Francesco. How was he even aware of Doretta's close friendship with Sara?

"That bitch! The sadistic, vengeful bitch." Doretta snarled, as though she had read his mind. "It had to be her."

Luca tightened his arms and hushed Doretta. He wanted no interruptions now. He nuzzled her until she glanced up at him and caressed his cheek. God she was gorgeous. He drowned in the blue pools of her eyes, the same eyes she once told him cursed her the day she met Baldo Volpe. The villain had stared deep into them with his own eyes, windows to a blackened soul.

He pulled her closer and covered Doretta's welcoming, full lips with his. The last time he had kissed her with such passion was that first night in the dark cortile when he had returned from Pizzoli. After months of seeing her in his dreams, her lusty nearness stirred a longing to bed her. But reason returned before they stepped off into the abyss.

The memory of thinking he would never see her again returned and stirred his desire for her once more. But not here. Not now, when Sara and Francesco's future was in tatters. He pulled away and kissed her cheek. Unable to gaze into her eyes, he pressed her head against his chest. Did she hear his heart pound as she glided her fingers across his face, through his hair? Did the wave of heat her nearness unleashed through his body flow into hers? He was content to hold her. Nothing more. For now, at least.

Doretta threaded her fingers through his and held his hand close against her chest. "Luca, why have you never spoken about Pizzoli to me? I mean, other than your life there and the anti-Fascists you met. What made you turn away from me after you came back?"

The question floored him. "Turn away from you?" He pulled his hand away.

"The reason Baldo Volpe targeted you was because of me. He wanted to hurt me through you." She sat up and scrutinized every twitch in his face to detect evasion, to see whether he would break her gaze. He did not. "Is that why you said there was no future for us when you returned?"

"Of course not! Why say such a thing? I love you, Doretta, and nothing that vermin could do would change that." Again, he kissed her but pulled away and gazed at the blue and orange flames licking the dried peach wood. "You were all I thought of."

"Then why?" She tugged his chin and drew his face back to her. "Why? I grudgingly agreed this was no time for…for romance. It was only because you'd been through too much. But doesn't today show you the peace we're fighting for may never come?" She wrapped her arms around his neck and drew close to him, once again resting her head on his chest. "Luca, caro, now, this moment in each other's arms, is all we can be sure of."

Luca ran his fingers through her thick hair, caressing her, struggling against the ache he had for her. After hearing Sara's reaction to Francesco's conscription, he had decided to delay telling Doretta about his own imminent departure. "And if I must go away again"—she stiffened, but he continued to stroke her as he broke the news he loathed to tell her—"for an important mission. In France. For Madame Stern." She melted against him.

"Is that why you came here today? When…?" For an instant, fire flashed in her eyes. "No. No, Luca. I don't want to hear any more of that. Just tell me that you love me."

His lips found hers once again. "I love you, dearest. Always and forever." And there they fell asleep in each other's arms, long after the flames in the hearth had died out.

A PALL SETTLED OVER ASILI. THE DAYS PASSED AS MINUTES. ON FRIDAY, LUCA drove to Cherasco and returned with Doretta's family. He remained in Asili until the dreaded hour of Francesco's departure. Luciana and the women of the two households did what they could for Sara and helped to care for Anna, who would turn thirteen months old on the day of her papà's departure. The couple spent little time with Anna or anyone else. The weather had turned foul, so they remained in each other's arms in their loft apartment. Nico had surprised the Boscos with their expanded lodgings after their return from a week by the sea in August. They no longer needed the extra space.

On the morning of December 17, they woke to a world shrouded by fog. Francesco had to report at Turin Porta Nuova stazione at eight o'clock that morning. With the heavy fog and the need to leave before dawn, Madama Lia wanted Gianni to drive the mournful couple and then return Sara to Asili. But Sara would not hear of it and respectfully told Madama that they wished for Luca and Doretta to go with them. Luca would drive. Francesco had asked to say his good-byes to family and friends at the farm. He wished only for Sara to walk to the train with him.

The residents of the two cascine and their friends from Cherasco stood shivering in the cortile before dawn. Francesco held his sleeping Anna in his arms and smothered her with kisses. Her eyelids fluttered and, for a moment, she gazed into her papà's wet eyes then kissed him before drifting off to sleep once more. "*Ti amo mio caro angioletto. Ti amo…*" The words choked him. He kissed her once more and handed the girl to her zia Giovanna. "Take care of her for me, Gio. Help Sara. She carries the world on her shoulders."

"Caro *fratello, assolutamente.* We'll be here when you return." Like Sara, she stood on her tiptoes to kiss his cheeks. "Come back to us soon, dear brother."

After the tearful good-byes, Francesco helped Sara into the rear seat of Luca's car and joined her, pulling her close and cocooning her with his body. He never looked back.

The long, dangerous drive along the winding roads of Langhe and Roero took twice as long as usual. The incessant fog thickened the closer they got to the Po River Valley. No one spoke, but as they entered the bomb-damaged streets of Turin, Francesco whispered endearments to Sara who, with her face buried in his chest, wept. Luca reached for Doretta's hand and threaded his fingers through hers.

The press of his hand couldn't soothe her. She swore, if the opportunity ever presented itself, she would put a bullet into that Strega woman's head, and Baldo Volpe's. What an evil duo they were. Hidden in the vineyards and using the Beretta that had been their nonno Davide's, Michele had been teaching her how to handle a weapon. Provided the gun didn't jam, she could easily take them out.

In front of Porta Nuova, cars crowded Corso Vittorio Emanuele II, a street filled with so many rich memories for Doretta and Sara. Francesco would not travel alone to his infantry-training base in Molini di Triora. And Sara would not be alone in her heartbreak as she wished the only man she had ever loved good-bye—for good, she feared.

Luca parked around the corner on via Sacchi. He and Doretta would accompany them to the track, but beyond there, only Sara would walk with him. They would wait to comfort her after he departed.

At 7:45 a.m., they arrived at the head of the track. With another hour remaining before sunrise, rushing commuters and families seeing off their sons jammed the station. Sadness permeated the air, filled with plaintive sounds of crying mothers and wives along with blaring announcements and the screeching sounds of metal-on-metal as trains pulled into the station. Strapping men who most likely had seen senseless battle themselves not long before their sons were born, stood at attention next to the women, sneaking a pass of their handkerchiefs or jacket sleeves across their eyes. Another generation of Italian sons would be sent into battle. They prayed that, unlike them, their sons would be well fed and properly clothed for winter.

Francesco scanned the crowd of young men standing in line, waiting to receive their carriage assignment. He didn't see anyone he knew. He turned to Luca, whom he had grown to love like a brother, and reached to shake his hand. Luca ignored it and hugged him tightly. He had spent little time with his own siblings since reaching adulthood. They had their own lives in Milan and Rome. The Fiore and Giordano families were his kin now, and Francesco was like a brother. "Take care, Francesco." Words to express his sorrow escaped him. Only inane thoughts came to mind. "Please write as soon as you can."

"I'm counting on you to look after my angel."

"Of course, Francesco, but as you know, she's more capable of looking after us. That is, along with Doretta." He forced a smile as he glanced into Doretta's shimmering eyes. "I'll do what I can to keep them out of mischief."

Francesco tried to smile, but then his attention returned to the throng standing in line. He had heard that many bodies were never recovered, while others were buried in makeshift graves—not in cemeteries next to their ancestors and without a priest to grant them absolution. And for what? The Nazis were the Fascists' allies, not his. People dear to him had been persecuted by those for whom he would now fight. He had come to accept his deferment as a blessing. Now he must take up arms in defense of those who cursed him and those he loved—a world gone mad.

"Caro Luca, mio caro fratello, fight hard." Though Francesco was leaving to face battle in a foreign land, he feared Luca, Doretta, and Sara would face their own battles. "God go with you." Francesco gave Luca one last brotherly hug before turning to Doretta.

"Doretta…" His voice broke. "I…"

"Hush, Francesco. I know." She kissed his wet cheeks and hugged him. "Now go."

Standing back from Sara and Francesco, Luca put his arms around Doretta, who turned and found her familiar place against him. There she hid from the world, from the sobs of women leaving the station. They would give Sara and Francesco all the privacy they could for what might be their last look at one another.

END OF PART TWO

PART THREE:

1942 – 1945

CHAPTER 32

Turin
November 18, 1942

T he first flash of white light roused Baldo Volpe from his sleep. Lightning in November? Within seconds, the walls shook as the roar of thunder rolled over the apartment, upsetting dishes from shelves. It was not thunder. Another aerial attack on Turin had begun. Flashes and thunderous explosions came one after another. Exhaustion from a long day of interrogations had sent him into a deep sleep. Why were there no sirens? Or maybe there were and he had slept through them.

Whump. Another blast. This one much closer. This was not a pinprick bombing, like those they had suffered after Mussolini declared war on France and Great Britain two years ago. Tonight was different. The bombs were different. Bigger. Bigger planes and more of them by the sounds of their droning engines.

Each morning after a bombing, Baldo passed citizens clearing rubble before going about their day. They were not about to let the cowardly British, who killed innocent women and children, demoralize them. The Volpe household was unscathed, physically at least. His mamma had less money now that all the rich Jews had fled. And her nerves were frayed. So were his, but he didn't show it.

Another blast and Baldo heard his mother cry out. He ran through the dark hallway and found her in the kitchen, illuminated by the flashes of light. She bent over shards of her nonna's china—the only possession other than her Singer sewing machine that she treasured. The only luxury her family had ever owned.

"Mamma, get dressed! We need to get to the shelter. Subito!" They hadn't taken shelter during previous attacks, and now he couldn't remember where one might be. There were so few. Another explosion. Another scream. "Quick. No time, Mamma."

"No! I won't go out into the street now." Flora's hysterics only fueled Baldo's rising panic.

"We have no choice. Get dressed!" he barked. "At least put your coat on."

The telltale whistle stopped them in their tracks. Where would it land? Seconds later, the ceiling in Baldo's room erupted in flames. Had the Allies resorted to dropping incendiary bombs?

"Run, Mamma! Now!" Baldo ran to the door of the apartment and slipped into his uniform boots, grabbing his jacket hanging on the hook. Flora darted into her bedroom and emerged clutching her secondhand, black, patent leather handbag that contained her entire life's savings.

He threw open the apartment door, and they joined others jamming the hall leading to the narrow staircase. In the dark, children were crying, and a bass voice yelled for people to get out of the way. Baldo went first, dragging his mother by her hand as he elbowed past his neighbors. Between the bomb blasts, he heard her ask to go back for her sewing machine. He jerked her forward.

"Mamma! No! The apartment's on fire." She tried to break free, but he held tighter to her hand.

As they descended, frigid air tainted with smoke and the stink of rotten eggs rushed up the stairwell now like a chimney, choking them. With only another flight of stairs to go, the building shook violently. The human stream stopped flowing. Plaster rained on them. Baldo floated in the darkened silence. Water stung his eyes as he touched the ground again. Or was it water? Had he walked off the landing to his death?

When he opened his eyes, it was daylight. Time had escaped from him. Were the flashes of light from the sun or from the bombing? The cold, hard ground chilled him. He felt sharp, searing pain in his legs. His ears were ringing, and his head hurt, deep inside. An acrid mixture from something burning filled his lungs. Where was he? Was that his apartment building? Looming above him, the walls and floors of the building seemed like pigeonholes. Heaps of rubble smoldered all around him. As his eyes focused, he saw rigid human forms, some scantily clad in nightclothes, some missing limbs, lying about him. Two young men with vacuous stares placed corpses on shutters from the blown-out building while others carted off the wounded on the improvised litters.

He struggled to sit up. Pain shot through his legs and arms, but he felt intact. His muscles slowly obeyed his commands as he felt around him in the dirt. Where was his mamma? Where was she? All he remembered was her hand locked in his. He struggled through the rubble and carnage, dashing from corpse to corpse. Some had been covered, and after pulling away their flimsy shrouds, he left them exposed. Desperation set in. He still had no idea how long he had been lying in the street. He raced to where rescuers were digging in the rubble that had been his apartment building.

"What time is it?" he shouted to a stout, bearded man as he flung pieces of concrete and plaster from the pile.

"*Mezzogiorno.*"

Noon! The first bombs fell over twelve hours ago. He dropped to his knees and struggled to help paw through the rubble. Hours seemed to pass, but they didn't get very far, and they didn't find a soul. He felt sick with terror. Without her, his world was empty. Only his mamma had loved him. He wandered away, thinking of searching the city's hospitals when the late afternoon sun reflected on a shiny object wedged in the concrete blocks. Her handbag! He fell to his belly and clawed through the rubble. Crying now, he pulled away slabs of wood and more rocks of concrete. There it was, her hand still clutching the strap of the old patent leather bag.

Someone in his squad had recently interrogated a Jew on suspicion of spying for the British. How else had they so accurately pinpointed the strategic locations of factories across town? And those leaflets the British dropped. Piemontese would not flee their city in fear. But his mamma had wanted to leave, to go her cousin's house in Salbertrand, in the mountains to the west. He forbade it. And now she was dead. He cursed the Jews, especially the Jewess who still haunted his dreams. One day he would make her pay for the sins of her people, sins he believed she committed herself.

His mamma, for all the finery she created for the Jews of Turin, never owned even one bag that looked as though it had money in it. But the one she died clutching did. He dug deeper into the rubble and grabbed the handbag before anyone noticed. Unable to hide the bulky bag under his jacket, he pried it open and ripped out the secret silk pouch she had sewn into the lining. He wondered whether he should pay the fat, hairy man to dig out her body. Not necessary. Her money was all his.

CHAPTER 33

Asili
December 1942

...quindi, mia carissima, I must close now. We arrive soon in Molini di Triora. I believe we'll be here for six weeks. Then I don't know where we'll go. I'll write every day. Promesso.

> *Ti amo per sempre,*
> *il tuo Francesco.*

Sara kissed Francesco's first letter, dated December 18, 1941, and placed it on the kitchen table next to the stack of 168 envelopes containing letters he had written since that day. He had kept his promise and had written as much as his grueling life would allow. Some letters went on for pages. Some simply reminded her of his love. Sometimes, several days' writing came in one envelope. Despite the frequent breaks of weeks between deliveries, the letters—a diary of his life in the military and declarations of love for her and Anna—had kept coming. Yet after an especially heartfelt one written on their fourth wedding anniversary, no other letters had arrived from Russia. Through his cryptic language, she surmised he was headed to some place on the Don River, nearly two thousand miles away. Had he received her letters—the photos of them with Anna taken by the sea the summer before he left?

Only one week remained until Christmas, her second without Francesco and ten years since he had walked into her life. The heavy snow rendered the narrow vineyard roads far too dangerous for car or horse, trapping her at home for the second day in a row. The blazing fire in the putagè and the aroma of simmering *bollito misto* transformed the kitchen into a homey refuge filled with sweet memories of childhood to cosset her as she read his letters a third time. No matter her schedule, she would take time each day to re-read at least one, usually many, of Francesco's precious letters. She would continue to read them until he came home.

"Mimi!" Sara still wasn't used to the name Anna had given her when she was ten months old, and baby talk came early for her. It had taken time to teach her that Giovanna was her zia and she her mamma, but one of the first words she learned was "Papà." He never tired of hearing it. When her milk dried early, Sara returned to work. Then Francesco left. She threw herself into her work, caring for the refugees who now flooded the countryside after the intensive bombings in Turin. Sometimes she stayed in Alba for days on end, helping zia Luce at the hospital. The war had arrived in Piemonte.

"Dimmi, carina."

"*Dov'è* zia Gio?"

It warmed Sara's heart that her favorite sister had assumed the role of Anna's nanny. Often, she spoke with her mamma and zia Luce about her guilt over not spending enough time with the child. She even visited don Emilio to confess her selfishness. They listened. They smiled. They reassured her that the times called for sacrifices. They needed her God-given talents elsewhere, don Emilio had said before he blessed her. Sara always returned to her work.

"I don't know where zia Gio is. Are you alone?"

"Arrivo!" Giovanna stumbled into the kitchen from a cloud of wind-driven snow, balancing a knobby pile of wood in her arms. Anna squealed and scampered to her as Giovanna struggled against the wind to kick the door closed and avoid dropping the heavy logs on the clinging two-year-old. "Anna. Cara. Wait. Let me set these down and take off my coat." She dropped the wood next to the putagè. "She was playing with Nebbia by the fire. I thought I could sneak out to fetch some more wood." Giovanna peeled off her coat. At sixteen, she was a beauty like Sara in height, eyes, and hair color, but her figure was fuller, and she was growing shapely. "Didn't you hear me go out, Sara?"

"No." Sara slipped the letters into the wooden box and snapped the lock, placing the key in her pants pocket. "I was reading."

Giovanna picked up Anna and handed her to Sara before she settled onto the bench beside her. She wished she could find a way to cheer her up—if only a little for the holidays—for Anna's sake. But Sara's sadness had deepened when she heard rumors that many soldiers marched through the deep snow in cardboard shoes. With no warm clothes to protect them from the frigid

Russian winter, many froze to death. Giovanna wrapped her arms around her sister and Anna, squeezing them both until Anna squirmed out of her embrace and scurried back to her place on Nebbia's pillow. Aside from Giovanna, the dog was the active two-year-old's most attentive and patient guardian.

"I'm sure all is well with Francesco. The weather's making a mess of mail service." She didn't believe it, nor did Sara whose eyes, now wistful and remote, had long ago lost their brightness.

"I love you, dear sister, but you never were a good liar."

At least, Sara's face softened. Giovanna spotted a few crinkles next to her eyes. Feigning shock, Giovanna clutched her heart. "Ouch! I'm not lying. Just look at the wind outside!"

A ghost of a smile crossed Sara's lips as she hugged her baby sister. Whatever would she and Anna do without her?

"Sara?" Doretta called from the front door as she stomped her feet and struggled to remove her coat and boots.

"We're here in the kitchen." She slipped the box under the table. Doretta's timing was perfect. She refused to discuss Francesco's deployment with anyone, not even Gio or Doretta. She preferred her time alone with him, through his letters.

"*Sacratu! Quanta fioca!*" Laughter erupted when Doretta, her chestnut hair and eyebrows white, entered the toasty kitchen. "I haven't seen this much snow in December for years. Look at me. And I only walked across the cortile." She kissed the sisters and sat across the table, closer to the putagè. Giovanna sprang up and grabbed a towel for her. Then she rummaged in the cupboard for a tin of chopped dried fruit and brought it over with a steaming mug of hot water. "Grazie! I need to warm my insides. That wind cut through me. I'm glad to see you didn't venture out, Sara."

"Unfortunately, I'm afraid the roads won't be passable again for days. I have so much to do at the hospital. More and more refugees. Two hospitals in Turin hit on the eighth."

Doretta's face, framed by her soaking hair, turned grim. "And an air raid shelter—if you can call them that—collapsed that night. Scores dead there. It's horrid."

"The Red Cross asked zia Luce for volunteer nurses, but it's impossible to spare anyone now. I want to help, but I just can't. And with winter arriving, influenza and that other thing the Fascists don't believe exists in Italy—hunger—will hit my Langhe patients hard."

"Have you seen the price of flour lately? Madama Lia has been diverting some to don Rossi for the poor. You know him, the priest of the *Più Società San Paolo*. It's a dangerous game they are playing with the Fascists' controls on wheat."

"It's a dangerous game the Fascists will play if they take on those two conniving soldiers of God." Again, the corners of Sara's mouth turned upward, if only a little. "I don't know how she does it, but Madama Lia is always several steps ahead of them."

"Zia!" came an insistent call from the tinello.

"Excuse me," Giovanna said. "I'm needed and I'm sure you have plenty to discuss. Ciao Doretta. *A più tardi.*"

Doretta blew on the hot fruit drink, her eyes fixed on the spiraling steam rising from the cup. "You're blessed, Sara, that Gio and Anna have bonded so well."

"I know. No different than Gio and me..." Sara's watched Giovanna carry Anna up the steep stairs. "She's a blessing." Changing the subject, she asked, "Have you heard from Luca?"

Doretta flinched. She felt guilty that Francesco, so far away, had not been heard from for months while Luca's letters arrived from France every other week.

"Yes. That's what I came to tell you. He's in a little village in the mountains north of Nice: Saint-Martin-Vésubie."

"Why in the mountains?"

"When he arrived in Nice with the money Madame Stern sent to a French Capuchin priest, Père Marie-Benoît, he was asked to stay on to help with a type of confino for Jews. Luca said there are some three thousand Jews there now."

"But isn't the Fourth Army occupying that area?"

"Yes! And that's what I came to tell you. Who do you think is also in Saint Martin?" Doretta quickly answered her own question. "Cesare Costa! He's one of the few doctors assigned to the village."

Sara brightened. At least someone they knew fared well in the army.

"Listen to this letter I just got from Luca." Doretta paused and looked at her friend. "Oh, Sara, I'm so—"

"Tranquilla, Doretta. Please read it to me. I want to hear fresh news from the war." She tapped Doretta's leg. "Read, please."

Doretta squirmed but then launched into Luca's most recent letter.

"It's surreal, Doretta. The Nazis demand the Italian army hand over the Jews for deportation. The French gendarmes are itching to carry out the arrests,

but Major-General Avarna di Gualtieri, he's representing the supreme Italian command in Vichy, is standing firm. No one is to touch a single Jew in the village. Can you believe that? An Italian general telling Oberg's thugs to keep out. I tell you, Doretta, they are like a pack of wolves, salivating, waiting for the shepherd to turn his back. Honestly, I believe Mussolini is trying to prove his army does not take orders from Germany, but who cares as long as the refugees are safe. But here we sit in the eye of the storm. The refugees live normally. Well, as normally as can be expected, but they are protected from deportation to Poland. At least for now."

"And so on. The rest is…well, just…" Doretta's face flamed. Poor Sara, so anxious for any news from Francesco and, most of all, the same words of endearment that Luca used to close the letter.

Sara shuddered. Madama Lia had shared images smuggled out of France of helpless Jews of all ages being herded into cattle cars and transported to their deaths, mostly at Auschwitz. The fear they had when Germany sealed Jews within Reich borders was now reality.

"When does Luca return?"

"No time soon, he said. For now, he's to remain there, shuttling back and forth between the village and Nice. He raves about working with the Capuchin priest. Apparently, Padre Maria Benedetto, as the Italians call him, is quite a thorn in the Vatican's side. Good for him. Follows his conscience, not orders."

"Does that remind you of a certain priest and a woman in Alba?"

"According to Luca, there are many of these clandestine partnerships. He wouldn't say exactly, of course he couldn't, but the padre and the Jewish banker who came up with the confino idea—Donati, I think that's his name—are devising some sort of major rescue plan. Luca didn't say whether he's a part of it."

They sat for a few minutes, each lost in her own thoughts about the men they loved. Doretta added more hot water to her cup and stirred the steaming fruit infusion before asking her a question to which, from all appearances, she knew the answer.

"Still no word?" Sara's pained expression answered for her. "Anna seems to be doing well."

"She is. I'm away most of the time, but…well, it's good for us both." Yes, work did help to keep desperation at bay, but it was more than that. Though Anna looked like Sara at that age, Anna reminded her of Francesco. "It's just—there are certain things about Anna that are hard for Gio to understand. Remember I told you once about my dreams where I saw things in the future?"

Sara detected Doretta's usual skeptical expression whenever she spoke of her premonitions and dreams. "I know you think it's countryside superstition, but more than once a vision in a dream became reality. Doretta…really, why don't you take me seriously?"

"I'm sorry, Sara." Doretta bit her tongue and sipped from her cup to suppress a laugh. "I do. I really do. It's a little hard to understand, but…well, why would I doubt you?'

"And it's hard for Gio to understand too. Anna is having dreams where she sees people. It's hard for her to describe it of course, but she's had some terrible nightmares. The other night, she dreamed that Francesco and…and a little boy had come to take me away." Doretta shuddered. "Of course, it had to be our stillborn baby she saw. Oh God, but this is no gift, Doretta."

Sara became quiet once more. Only the popping of wood in the putagè and the howling wind outside broke the silence. She peered into the far corner of the tinello, then, satisfied that no one was about, settled onto the bench next to Doretta. "You must promise me you'll never breathe a word of this. *Mi prometti*?"

"Of course. I promise."

"I never told Francesco why I lost the baby. Only Cesare Costa knows and, of course, Mamma and zia Luce. It was my fault." Sara choked on her words and she fought tears. "Poison. I poisoned the baby."

Sara now sobbed. An icy chill ran up Doretta's spine, but she still said nothing. *Sara? Poisoning her unborn child?*

"I was home, bored. I wanted to help. No one was around, and I knew the eggs had not been collected, so I went to the henhouse. Salmonella killed my baby, Cesare Costa said. I killed my baby…"

Doretta took hold of Sara and held her tightly against her chest, stroking her dearest friend's hair. What a burden to carry, to unnecessarily place on herself.

"Shh…Sara, don't do this. Don't blame yourself."

"I do, Doretta. Don't you see? I should have known better. My God, I'm a nurse!" She stared at Doretta, anguish contorting her sweet face. "I'm always warning my patients about that. It's all too common on farms. And it was a boy…a son for Francesco. A grandson for Papà. And now Francesco…he's gone." Her sobs resumed.

Doretta looked about, worried that Giovanna would hear Sara crying or that someone might walk in on them. She never cried. Sara comforted others and dried their tears. Doretta held her tighter, but Sara edged away.

"During my entire pregnancy with Anna, I was terrified. Then she arrived and all was good. Not until Francesco's letters stopped coming did those thoughts—thoughts about what I did—return."

Doretta held Sara's face between her hands. "Look at me, Sara. This is nonsense. You did nothing. It was an accident. It's not as though you willed this to happen like some women do to end a pregnancy."

"And it was a boy. A son. What if he never comes home, Doretta?" Sara asked, her voice now pleading. "Who will carry his name? And the farm?"

"The farm? Let's not think about that now. And Anna has his name."

"For now. But later…" Her lower lip quivered, but her tears ceased.

"Francesco will come back, Sara. He will. You must believe that."

Sara's face became hard. Her voice cold. "No! He's gone. I know it. I feel it. Anna's dreamt it. And it's time I begin to live my life without him."

"It's one thing to go about your life, Sara, but it's another to give up hope—you of all people. Francesco wouldn't want that."

Sara startled and looked about. Doretta thought it was the howling wind that caught her attention, but as she jumped from the table and ran toward the stairs, Doretta realized it was Anna, crying.

When Doretta caught up with Sara on the stairs, she heard Anna scream, "No, Papà, no! Please don't take Mimi!" They both froze. "Mimi, don't die!"

Sara turned to Doretta, her face ashen, her voice trembling. "It's that dream again. Francesco's dead…and now…" She raced past Doretta, out of the house into the snow. Francesco was dead. And he and their stillborn son had come for her.

CHAPTER 34

Turin
August 16, 1943

In Turin, a city that had already suffered twenty-eight bombing raids, Baldo Volpe's world burned. Since the bombs fell on his apartment building two and a half years earlier, he had changed lodgings three times. Now at least, summer had arrived. If forced once again to sleep outdoors or in the fields south of the city, it would be bearable. But for now, he was comfortable, safe.

After the events of July 25 when Il Duce and the glorious Fascist state fell, he had found the perfect place to lie low in the near-deserted city. There was no electricity, no water, and part of the large building had burned, but otherwise he had all the comforts of home. That it once belonged to someone who was now running for her life made it even better.

It was not only the Allies' savage bombing raids that sent him into hiding. Mussolini's precipitous arrest weeks before made Fascist leaders and police the targets of the anti-Fascists. The Bolsheviks they had worked so hard to eradicate in Turin were fearless in their power grab. For some time, there had been dangerous talk that Il Duce, now fat and fighting an ulcer, could no longer lead Italy to glorious victory. Conflicting reports about his whereabouts ranged from the island of Ponza, where he had sent many of his political enemies, to a high-altitude resort in the Abruzzi. One thing everyone agreed on was that he had vanished. The Fascist state had collapsed! Everything Baldo had ever known and defended had ended.

When the Fascist Party dissolved, cowardly members threw away their party pins and burned their cards. Paramilitary troops and OVRA officers, who had served as the guardians of the Fascist state, disbanded. Anti-Fascists attacked the OVRA headquarters at Casa Littorio, burning files, including, no doubt, some of Baldo's thick collection of documents on Doretta Giordano and her lover Luca Olivero. As far as Baldo knew, Olivero still rotted in the confino in Pizzoli, where he belonged. The release from Le Nuove prison of five hundred political prisoners, many of whom he had interrogated, struck fear in Baldo the most. He was hiding out to make sure that he wouldn't be among those taking the place of former prisoners in the fortress, having castor oil forced down their throats. The anti-Fascists were enjoying their moment as the hunters, but the worm would turn soon. When the Fascists returned to power, there would be no mercy.

He would do whatever was necessary to bring back the Fascist state. "Long live free Italy," the uncensored *il Messaggero* had proclaimed when Mussolini was arrested. What drivel. Italy had always been free! But now, because of the feeble, old Savoy king, its freedom hung in the balance. Baldo was certain Hitler would send his army south to stop the Allies who had taken Sicily. In time, Italy would fall under Reich control. That was inevitable. He had heard through sources in the paramilitary, now in hiding—just waiting for the dust to clear to re-emerge and battle for restitution of the Fascist state—that German tanks and troops were already crossing the Brenner Pass to stage an invasion. The question was when—and how far south the Germans would get.

Baldo had heard Marshal Pietro Badoglio proclaim "*la guerra continua*" in his July 25 speech announcing Mussolini's arrest. So the war would continue. But on whose side would Italy fight? Surely, the traitor Badoglio would not join with the murderous Allies to the south against Germany, already a trusted and powerful ally. Regardless, soon Italian cities and countryside would become the killing fields of two opposing powers who would fight to the death. Only one of those foes had the power to restore fascism in Italy. Only one of those foes understood the urgent need to rid the world of Jews and undesirables. If the incompetent king and his minions did not know on which side they would fight, at least Baldo Volpe knew. All that he had learned in Berlin would prove a valuable asset when the Germans finally invaded. He spoke their language, and he supported their Führer. Now all he had to do was to wait. His time would come.

Unlike the many homeless Turinese who wandered the surrounding countryside, here he sat, comfortable and safe from the anti-Fascists. How clever of him to think of it. After anti-Fascists torched Casa Littorio, where he had made his makeshift home in his office, he knew where to look for refuge, where there would be clothes and even food in the larder. He had watched this place for years, even after the Jewish occupants had fled the city. After that, the apartment remained dark.

As he lay on the luxurious bed, he recalled that day months earlier when he still had his police powers and had first entered the apartment alone. Convinced that it was indeed vacant, he showed the aged doorman the police file and photo of one of the former occupants. He demanded the key so that he might conduct a search.

Most of the valuables were gone, but some clothing and furniture remained. Even the beds had been made, with goose-down duvets and pillows, and satin sheets. Plush towels still hung on brass hooks in all four of the ostentatious bathrooms. He wasted no time looking around, and when he walked into the large bedroom overlooking the tree-lined avenue, he knew he had found what he was searching for.

From all those times he had tailed her, most of all when he stood face-to-face with her at the café, he had learned to detect her scent. Even though her family no longer owned the apartment and they were long gone, he knew this had been her inner sanctum—one he never dreamed of entering. The room oddly appeared as though she had just left and would be returning soon. He even thought he could detect her scent. Impossible. He picked up a tarnished silver frame on her small writing desk in front of the window and examined the photo of her holding the hand of a little blonde-haired girl. An expensive Mont Blanc fountain pen lay next to a box of cream-colored linen stationery with her name engraved on the envelopes and sheets of paper: Teodora Giordano. He pocketed the pen. Unusual sheepskin-lined slippers had been left under the large, opulent bed. A white satin robe hung on a hook behind the door alongside a lacy blue nightgown. It took a moment before he recognized it. Of course. Once again, he closed his eyes as he ran his fingers along the inside of the delicate lace, imagining the thin straps sliding off her shoulders. No doubt, she wore it for *him*, but no more—Baldo had seen to that. He lifted the nightgown off the hook and drew it across his face, imaging the fabric on her bare skin, stirring that now-familiar warmth over his groin as he continued to prowl around her room.

Her gown in hand, he crossed to the tall chest of drawers next to the armoire. When he slid the top drawer open, he found some of her smooth silky undergarments and handfuls of pink and red rose petals, now dried and faded but still infused with her scent. Though he knew he was alone, he scanned the room before slipping a pair of her red silk panties into his trouser pocket. The woman had no shame. He opened the mirrored door to the armoire. As he suspected, several of his mamma's dresses, some he had seen the Jewish exhibitionist wear, hung on padded satin hangers. Odd that she would leave them here when they fled Turin. In any case, where she was eventually going, she would have no use for them except as a burial shroud. The floral scent was strongest at the fronts of the dresses, several obscenely low cut. She dabbed perfume in her cleavage, no doubt—deep between her breasts. He closed his eyes and savored the image of her breasts and the fragrant cleavage between them. Oh, that feeling again that at first repulsed him but now he craved.

Her bed was still made. It didn't matter to him if his shoes soiled the starched white linen duvet cover. It was dusty anyway. He lay back on the large, soft pillows, unbuttoned his shirt, and spread the nightgown across his bare chest. The panties he pulled from his pocket were a superb addition. He hated her so, but the spell she had cast on him was impossible to break. She had power over him, but for how long?

Although he knew where to find her, time had run out on him. Soon that would change. The Nazis were experts in handling Jews, and their arrival, he believed, was imminent. Before he put a bullet in her head, as he planned to, he would ravage her as he had done in his fantasies. That, he believed, was needed to break her spell on him. It would be unlike the time in Berlin when, upon discovering he had never been with a woman, his SS buddies dragged him to a seedy whorehouse with unclean women. They said he needed an education, but instead it had been humiliating. Why put up with that when he found uncomplicated, safe pleasure elsewhere? With her under his control, there would be no repeat of Berlin. With a whore, you bought cooperation and consent; he didn't need that with Doretta. All alone, in her own bed, he then enjoyed a moment unlike anything he had imagined, taking himself to new heights of ecstasy.

Today, as he had that first day months ago and since he had taken refuge in the bombed-out apartment, he had given himself many hours of pleasure in her sanctuary. Now he was hungry. He opened one of the remaining jars of tuna he had found in the larder. No bread, but at least he had protein, water he had collected in empty bottles, and even a fine wine to drink. The cases of Barbaresco he discovered had taken the edge off the anxiety that often crept up on him during these last solitary weeks as bombs continued to rain on the city. And though she had left long ago, with the bottle of her perfume he discovered in one of the bathrooms, he refreshed her clothes and the bed with her scent. His shelter may not have been the safest, but lying on her bed with a bottle of fine red wine beside him made it feel like a posh and cozy refuge.

When he finished the tuna, he grabbed the wine bottle and retreated to her room. He slid Flora's handmade silk pouch of money, his money, off the nightstand and under his linen shirt. With the frequent nighttime air raids, he no longer slept without a shirt or wore nightclothes even though he had found a nice pair of men's silk pajamas. How fortunate to have found an armoire and several drawers filled with men's hand-tailored clothing. He had read in La Stampa that Gabriele Giordano had shot himself. What a coward. These were a Jew's clothes, but at least he had been a Fascist. In any case, Baldo had no choice. He had shed his gray police uniform as soon as OVRA had been disbanded. Soon, he was certain, he would have a new uniform and serve a more determined and expert master. All his civilian clothes, sewn by his mamma, had been lost when their apartment was destroyed. Now, he had his choice of fine, handmade shirts, sweaters, and even wool suits. Maybe he would wear her father's monogrammed shirt when he finally had Doretta in his clutches. He might pass as an aristocrat and no one would be the wiser.

Darkness would soon fall, so he lit the strange-looking candelabra with nine small candles he had found in a cupboard and placed it on the nightstand next to the wine. The room wasn't as neat as it had been that first time. Months of bombing raids and the fire that burned part of the roof had tarnished it, but the room was at the end of the apartment, far from the hole in the roof.

In the candlelight, he unfolded the letter he had received at his office days before Il Duce's arrest. It was from one of his closest friends from his days in Berlin, Gunther Schliessen, now an SS officer assigned to the Hygiene Division in Poland.

I'm hopeful soon I will be transferred out of this camp in Poland. Between the filthy Poles, revolting, lice-ridden Jews, and this damned cold, I want to go south. My superior officer tells me there is a possibility we may be transferred to Marseilles. Who knows, maybe someday we will hunt Jews together in Italy! It will be like the good old days in Berlin except this time we'll be able to…

That was all of the letter Baldo had left. Fortunately, he had stashed it in his jacket pocket the night he fled the raid at Casa Littorio, though in the ensuring chaos he lost the last page. No matter. He knew what Gunther meant. And with luck, they would be able to work together to be part of what he said Hitler called "The Final Solution."

Another sip of wine, but not too much. He had to keep his wits about him. The lingering oppressive heat of the August day made him uncomfortable fully dressed, but the gentle nighttime breeze through the open window cooled the room. It was close to midnight as he blew out each of the nine slow-burning candles, careful not to waste the wax.

FOR THE THIRD NIGHT IN A ROW, EXPLOSIONS SHOOK HIM FROM HIS DEEP sleep. Another raid. What were the Allies bombing now? There wasn't much left of Turin's industrial complex. It was only to terrorize the civilians. Had to be. And the phosphorus bombs dropped with incendiary devices did just that as they ignited fires in the shell of the city without water to extinguish blazes. He rushed to the window and peered through the shutters. In the light of the waning full moon, he spotted a formation of bombers overhead. By the sound of the engines and the size of their silhouettes, he guessed they were the large Lancaster and Halifax bombers the RAF had been flying the past year. To the left, in the direction of Crocetta, huge flames lit the sky. A bit close for comfort. He sat on the edge of the bed and pulled on his boots. Falling plaster dusted their tops like snow. He heard rumbling. Then the mirrored door of the armoire filled with dresses, stripped from its hinges, crashed to the floor. Everything went dark.

CHAPTER 35

Cherasco
August 22, 1943

Daniela had put this off long enough. She lit four matches and then blew out each one. Time was running short. She struck the fifth one, and tossed it onto the pile in the cold fireplace. The eleven colorful and even seductive silk dresses she and Doretta had worn during happier times had no place in their lives now. She took Doretta's hand and together they watched, mesmerized, as the brilliant remnants of that life of confidence and ease melted before their eyes.

In late 1938, when they fled Turin after her husband's death, they left behind most of their dresses Flora Volpe had created. To calm Elena, they fibbed and told her they would soon return. There was no need to take their entire wardrobe. Daniela tried to make herself believe the lie, and Doretta even left her room ready to receive her as though on any other day, but she knew better.

As he had done with the Dalmasso family house in Cherasco, Luca had crafted a legitimate sales transaction of their apartment on Corso Re Umberto to Cornelia Ferri Bottero of Alba. It had given them hope, but now that word had reached Cherasco that the gracious apartment building was little more than a shell in the shade of the chestnut trees, Daniela knew there was no going back. Even if the building still stood, a life again in Turin, a place where hateful signs and denials of service at their favorite haunts became commonplace, was unthinkable. Now that news of the German army marching deep into northeastern Italy had reached them, Daniela believed they would be fortunate to secure a life anywhere at all.

Though initially discounted as rumors, word that German troops entered Italy from Austria on July 26 spread like wildfire. Weeks later, when Hitler's elite First SS Panzer Division Leibstandarte crossed the Brenner Pass, panic erupted. Only the most naïve believed that Hitler would not respond forcefully to Mussolini's shocking fall from power. Never would he leave the entire Italian peninsula open for the Allies to advance northward unopposed. First, the war had come to Piemonte from the air. Daniela worried it would soon arrive in the wake of jackbooted German troops.

Although Badoglio's government had relaxed a few minor aspects of the Racial Laws, it had yet to stop the persecution of Italy's Jews. And thanks to the Fascists' Jewish census, the Nazis had a road map to ensnare Italy's tens of thousands of Jewish citizens and refugees. Daniela failed to understand how such a dysfunctional government had managed to take the meticulous census, the one thing that might lead to their imprisonment, or worse. With Fascist zealots in hiding, waiting for the Germans to arrive, Doretta and Michele knew a bloody retaliation against the anti-Fascists would come swiftly. The hunt for Jews would soon follow. They had no choice but to flee Cherasco where the Dalmasso family, silk merchants to the Royal House of Savoy, had been present for four hundred years.

Daniela, Silvana, and dear zio Eduardo had always been well respected in the village. The Dalmasso family, like so many other Jews from small villages across Piemonte, left Cherasco for Turin after emancipation in 1848. But they maintained a presence in the village where their ancestors had found peace after their expulsion from the Iberian Peninsula in 1492. Eduardo's final resting place was the Jewish cemetery not far from their house. Cherasco was home to them. The village children had been especially fond of her zio, who gathered them around his tinny piano to sing children's songs and munch on the baci di Cherasco he bought from Marco and Duilio Barbero, a rare treat during the impoverished years of fascism. After he left his touring life of concerts behind, each year during Advent, he conducted the children in a Christmas concert. Catholic, Jewish, or Protestant. He didn't care about the origin of songs nor the religion of those who sang them. Music was all that mattered to him. Sharing it with children, as he had done with Doretta, gave him great joy.

The Dalmassos' rich life in Cherasco, living harmoniously with their Catholic neighbors, had come to an end. First Turin, now Cherasco. The flames of hate lapped at the edges of all they had known. Europe itself, not Cherasco, had turned a hateful face on them. Would they return? Madama Lia said the house would always be there for them. It was theirs. For now, they thought of nothing other than outrunning the raging fire of hate that would soon spread throughout Italy.

"Doretta! Where are you?" *Now what?* At seventeen, Elena still tried her big sister's patience. Daniela knew Elena was well aware of her disintegrating world. Accepting the consequences was another matter. The difficulties of farm life combined with the responsibilities she had in caring for a small child had turned Giovanna Fiore into a reasonable and mature young woman. Surrounded by poverty, she had never known frivolity and luxury. Giovanna easily accepted sacrifices. For Elena, the cruelties and uncertainties she had known these last five years had turned her inward, thinking of almost nothing but her moods and herself. How would she rise to the occasion of not only living quietly and in relative isolation, but in life-or-death hiding? A rebellious teen's behavior could have dire consequences for them all.

"I'm in the sala, Elena." Doretta grabbed the poker and stirred the ashes. No evidence of fire remained.

"Eek, what's that awful smell? Did you burn your hair or something?"

Doretta ignored her question. "What is it, Elena? We have to leave for Asili in an hour."

"What do you think of this dress, Doretta?" Elena twirled around in the one dress Daniela knew Doretta could not part with. The mandarin orange linen dress with embroidered flowers was Doretta's summertime favorite, no doubt because Luca liked it so much on her. Though she knew Doretta fumed at seeing Elena show off in the dress, Daniela did not have the heart to tell Elena to take it off. It was the first, and now the only, dress of its kind her youngest child, now a blossoming young woman, had worn. As with Doretta, it accentuated her maturing figure. Oh but how she prayed for peace soon and that her troubled daughter might experience the joys of youth as Doretta had.

Daniela glanced at Doretta whose narrowed eyes and pursed lips signaled another argument would soon erupt between the two sisters. "It looks lovely on you, Elena," Daniela said before Doretta could respond. "Though you both could use a little weight to fill it out better," she added, hoping to remind Elena that the dress belonged to Doretta. She wondered how much of Elena's question was a search for approval or an opportunity to dig a knife in Doretta. Elena knew how much the dress she had taken—without Doretta's permission—meant to her. Never mind. If Elena was happy even for the road trip, life would be easier on them all. Anyway, Daniela knew Doretta would snatch it back at the first opportunity.

"I'm quite happy with my figure," Elena said as she smoothed the dress over her hips.

Doretta ignored her. "What is it you wanted, Elena? We have to get going."

"That's all. Thanks." With that, she strutted out of the room.

Doretta squeezed her eyes shut tight. "Mamma…"

"No, Doretta. Just ignore her. More important things to do now."

Like thieves in the night, although it was broad daylight, they would have to depart unnoticed. There was no need for subterfuge in Turin. Their longtime neighbors were sad to see them go and opposed the heinous laws that forced them to sell their property. They never even asked who had bought the apartment. It was common knowledge that such arrangements were being made. But now, unless by some miracle the Allies arrived first, the Nazis and Fascists would surely come for them in Cherasco as soon as the hunt was underway. They had to leave without creating suspicion or handing out clues. They had to disappear.

Doretta had returned to Cherasco from Asili the day after Badoglio's speech announcing the formation of the new military government. Even before news that the Germans had set foot on Italian soil reached them, Madama Lia told Doretta to prepare the family for the move to her farm in Bossolaschetto. She believed that, for the time being, they would be safe in Alta Langa. It would buy them time, so she hoped.

With the Italian Fourth Army's presence in France, and the fate of the Jews in Saint- Martin-Vésubie uncertain, Luca opted to remain there. Doretta and Michele could move the family on their own. But she needed more than Luca's help; she needed his presence. It was nearly a year since Sara last heard from Francesco, so Doretta never mentioned to her how much she longed for Luca. Sara had recently become more resolved, and the word "resistance" often crossed her lips. "I'm ready to support the resistance, though I won't fight," Sara had said to Doretta when she left for Cherasco the previous month.

For the last three Sundays, their neighbors had seen them leave Cherasco at 10:00 a.m. to drive to Asili for pranzo domenicale with the Fiore family and Madama Lia. This Sunday would be no different, at least in terms of their departure time and the lunch. After nightfall, they would continue their drive from Treiso to Benevello along the narrow winding roads through the countryside, bypassing Alba, to the forested hamlet outside the hilltop town of Bossolasco. The village was popular with city dwellers seeking relief from the August heat. Madama Lia had said never would she have imagined that her summertime haven would one day be a refuge for Jews on the run. Now she believed it would be the last place the Germans would reach and prayed the harsh winter would set in before they marched into Langhe.

"Michele, would you please bring the car around now?" Doretta went to the kitchen to help Ida with baskets of food she had prepared as their contribution to the lunch. Though they paled in comparison to the opulent meals she had created with Bruna on Corso Re Umberto, Ida had mastered the art of cooking on tight rations. She had ration cards, but what good were they when often there was nothing to buy in the markets. For years, Italy's agricultural production flowed northward to feed the German war machine while many Italians found themselves near starvation. But with the supplemental food they received from the Fiores' farm, Ida had learned to improvise. With one egg from Asili and flour from Madama Lia, she could make tajarin for a week.

Ida gave thanks for what they had. For today's lunch, she had cleaned out the icebox. They secreted tins and jars from the larder in baskets, but perishables she transformed into tasty dishes, such as brasato al Barbaresco with a scrawny piece of beef she had found on the black market, fatty *salsicce*, and *coniglio con verdure*. Luigia had generously shared a rabbit and vegetables from her garden for Ida to prepare the classic Langhe dish.

Doretta peeked into the three baskets of food. The fourth held various items they would need in Bossolaschetto. No suitcases this time. Would anyone notice the large handbags and market baskets filled with clothes they were carrying?

After Michele loaded the car parked in the narrow street, Doretta gathered them in the sala. Daniela might still be the matriarch, but Doretta had long ago become the de facto head of the family, though she shared many responsibilities with Michele. He was, after all, the man of the house.

"We're leaving now—no different than when we left last Sunday and every Sunday before." She glared at Elena, smoothing the orange dress over her curvy hips, admiring her shoes. "Elena. Are you listening?" Elena threw her snide expression at Doretta as deftly as she would a knife. It hit its mark.

Daniela looked elegant in her simple white cotton dress Luigia Fiore had made for her, in stark contrast to Elena. Doretta was proud of her mamma, a woman of substance forced to take another step down the ladder, having to make more sacrifices, having to run for their lives with her son and eldest daughter leading the way. Despite their deteriorating circumstances, Daniela's eyes sparkled once more. Her silver hair neatly braided and pinned up gave her the look of the sophisticated matriarch she was. Daniela had acquiesced, not surrendered, to her and Michele handling the family business. Oh, how she loved her mamma and wished she had lived a happier life. She and Michele would do all in their power to protect her now.

"Ida, I'm glad you've decided to come with us. You'll be safer. As we know from Silvana's experience, the Nazis don't make distinctions between converted or baptized Jews and people like us."

"Signorina Doretta, I had no decision to make." Ida kissed each of Doretta's cheeks and embraced her as she had since swaddling her minutes after her birth. "Do you believe I'd leave the only family I've ever known? You would make your papà proud." She crossed herself. "God rest his poor soul." At the mention of her father, Doretta tensed. Though fiercely protective of Daniela, Ida was a kind, forgiving woman who had prayed for the couple's reconciliation to the end. She repeatedly urged Doretta to shed the bitterness she carried. That was part of the past they were leaving behind. "Now, we must go. The food will spoil in this heat."

Hand in hand, Doretta and Daniela took one last look around the house for anything small they had missed. The courtyard burst with the bright colors of flowers in full bloom, the air sweet with the aroma of roses and lavender. Overlooked peaches still hung on zio Eduardo's lone peach tree he had adored. "Nothing wasted" was the Piemontese refrain even before rationing. Doretta plucked the unripe fruit from the tree and handed them to her mamma.

"Ida can pickle them. I'll join you in a moment, Mamma."

Daniela scanned the scene awash with color, committing to memory her ancestral home, then strode to the gate and the awaiting car. The occupants squeezed together as sardines laid in a tin. They sat with baskets piled on their laps and underfoot. It would be an uncomfortable drive to Asili, but Gianni would lighten the load and take some of their meager belongings to Alta Langa tomorrow.

As she walked to the courtyard gate, Doretta turned and ran back up the narrow wooden stairs to her bedroom. Buried under long forgotten toys in a large wooden chest, she found a small tin box containing childhood trinkets. She opened it and, without looking at it, slipped a framed, small photo into her handbag. Now she had everything she needed. She touched her hand to her heart then brushed her palm over the box as though whisking away dust—the past—then returned it to its hiding place. The photo of her with her father at her bat mitzvah would always remind her of happier times.

CHAPTER 36

Asili
September 8, 1943

"Amen." Seconds after Nico finished blessing the Fiore family's meager weeknight supper of boiled vegetables, polenta, and dry bread, Giuseppina burst through their front door, shrieking, pointing to the heavens, and then crossing herself.

"*È finita!*" She gasped and pressed her hand to her heart. "La guerra…è…è finita!"

Stunned silence. Nico glanced at the clock on the wall so he would always remember 6:40 p.m. on September 8, 1943, when he heard that the madness had ended. Giovanna rushed to Giuseppina and led her to a chair at their dining table in the kitchen. Sara poured her a glass of water then checked her pulse. Only recently had her health improved after bouts of high blood pressure that required frequent bed rest.

"I was listening…to the wireless." A sip of water. "The American general announced a surrender…unconditional, he said. Something about our soldiers resisting the German aggressor. Resisting? On our soil! Sara, what does he mean? Our boys now have to fight the Germans?" She drained the beaker and held it out to Giovanna. "Wine, please. No, I need something stronger. Grappa."

"Giuseppina, you really shouldn't—" Sara caught herself. What was the use? She nodded to Giovanna. Maybe the alcohol would settle her nerves. Sara looked at Nico. Concern etched deep furrows in his brow, and he was rubbing his neck. They knew this wasn't the end. It was merely one war ending, and a new battle beginning, against an occupier. Since Badoglio announced the new military government, they were not sure whom they were fighting, only that, as he had said, the war would continue. Allied bombings of Turin paused then resumed on August 7, but Italy was now a ship without a competent captain, adrift in the fog.

If peace with the Allies had come, then they were now at war with Germany. Shortly after Mussolini's arrest, the Nazis began to infiltrate northeastern Italy, positioning themselves for invasion. They were now the enemy and would soon march through the streets and establish their occupation. Would battles be fought in their fields and vineyards? And what of the Eighth Army in Russia? Was Francesco one of the thousands whose bodies were abandoned in the snow, never to be buried in their village graveyards? What if by some miracle he was alive, a prisoner of war? So many questions that Sara had banished from her mind now returned. If he were alive, word would have reached her by now, as it had other local families. The time had arrived to attend to the home front, to protect her family, her friends, her fellow Langhetti.

"What about Badoglio, though?" Nico demanded. "Has he spoken? What of our army?"

"Later tonight, I think. Oh, I don't know." Giuseppina gulped the grappa Giovanna had set before her and, still agitated, threw her hands in the air. "Has he given us anything but confusion?"

Sara took her pulse again—better but still high. "Where's Gianni? Are you home alone?"

"He's with Madama Lia in Altavilla. Maybe she knows more and will come to Asili tonight." She downed the remaining grappa and steadied herself on the table to rise. "So, I must get back to my cooking."

Sara pressed her hand on Giuseppina's shoulder to stop her from rising. "No. Your heart rate is still high. You need rest, not work. Stay here with us now. Gio, help Giuseppina to Papà's chair by the fire. Make her comfortable."

With no further details, was this news truly the answer to their prayers? Or was something far worse about to happen? Where were the Allies? And what of Rome? Would the Germans take Badoglio and the king prisoner? Sara and Nico followed Giuseppina, now shuffling after drinking the grappa. Supper was cold, the momentary celebratory mood past.

"The Germans."

"What of the Germans, Sara?"

"Exactly, Papà. What of the Germans? I heard from a nurse from Liguria that in early August, German troops were seen marching on foot toward Genoa."

"But the Allies are already in Sicily. Surely, they'll take Rome quickly, and Genoa. They've been bombing the port and Turin for years. There's not much left for the Germans to use against them."

"I don't know where the Allies are, Papà. Maybe they'll even drop para-troopers here tonight," Sara said, her voice now edgy. All the Germans needed was a pretext to take control. Now Eisenhower had given them one. She prayed that Badoglio had prepared his generals for the about-face. Their former enemy's commanding general had spoken, but they heard from no one in their own government. Her mind worked, knowing they had arrived at the moment that Doretta and Madama Lia had feared. "The Nazis are here, Papà. It's only a matter of days before we see them on our roads, in our villages. And I'm sure the cowardly Blackshirts will slither out of their hiding places and join them."

While Nico tuned the wireless to the *EIAR* station, still the only radio station allowed to broadcast in Italy, Anna toddled in and tugged on Sara's trousers. "*Non adesso*, cara," Sara said, and waved her away gently. Still the little girl reached for her, holding out her arms. All she wanted was love, and Sara had been away since before Anna woke that morning. Sara picked up her only child and hugged her before setting her down. Despite the child's bewildered expression, and the tears welling in her eyes, it was best for Anna if she learned to seek comfort from the many not the one. Anna ran to Giovanna and climbed onto her lap.

Less than an hour later, the entire family gathered around the wireless in the tinello to wait for Badoglio's announcement. A light rain fell, cooling the air. Tension was high.

But for Anna's soft humming as she sat on Giovanna's lap, munching a biscotto, all were silent and stone-faced. Finally, at 7:42 p.m. as the sun slipped behind Monviso, Marshal Pietro Badoglio's voice crackled through the hissing static.

"The Italian government, recognizing the impossibility of continuing the unequal struggle against an overwhelming enemy force…" Sara grew angry as Badoglio droned on. *Unequal struggle….overwhelming enemy force.* Is that what Francesco had faced in the frozen Russian Steppe against the Soviets? Had their government ever tried to find him?

"Consequently, all acts of hostility against the Anglo-American force by Italian forces must cease everywhere. But they may react to possible attacks from any other source."

That was all. Only one thing could be "any other source"—the Germans, the Nazis whom Mussolini had recklessly followed into war. Il Duce's folly had not left a single family in the area untouched. At least now, after forty-five days of uncertainty, Sara knew that soon the resistance they had been preparing for would begin. And Luca? What of him and Cesare Costa with the Fourth Army in France? Would they be taken prisoner? A tingling spread from her chest throughout her body. Please, dear God, protect them. She could not bear another loss to their tight-knit family of friends, nor could Sara bear seeing Doretta suffer as she had.

"Tomorrow I'll drive to Bossolaschetto to tell Doretta while there's still time."

"I'm sure she's aware of it, Sara. At least she will be soon. I sent Gianni up there the moment I heard General Eisenhower speak."

How long had Madama Lia been standing in the doorway? Her habit of appearing unnoticed irritated Sara. "You'll come with me in the morning," she said. "Word is the Germans are advancing toward Turin and are expected there, and in Langhe, in the next day or so. Our war has begun, Sara, and so has the hunt for our Jewish friends." The petite general turned, and without looking back, said, "No time to waste. We leave at dawn."

For four years, the distant war had plucked away the men of the village, but it was now on their doorstep. When would they gather around the wireless to hear news of peace? It was late, and the day would start early. Giovanna, twisting around her index finger a loose ringlet of the sleeping child's hair, locked eyes with her. She knew this was a watershed. Giovanna would remain in her place, but for how long, only God knew.

My beloved Francesco, even from your grave of snow, you are now the guardian angel of my dear little sister and our child. Protect them.

CHAPTER 37

Turin
September 11, 1943

Incessant sirens early in the morning woke Baldo the previous day. This morning, machine gun fire drew him out onto the street from his nest on Corso Re Umberto. With political prisoners released from Le Nuove prison roaming the streets of Turin, many with guns in hand, hunting Fascists, he worried that someone was bound to recognize him. At no time since the nighttime bombing raid that had injured him had he left the relative safety of the bomb-damaged apartment. After he woke, bleeding from a deep gash on his head, time passed in a blur. From the chilly nights and the warm sunny days, he guessed it was early September.

The noise from nearby explosions the night of his injury had muted the telltale whistling sound of the British bomb landing nearby. He had had no time to take cover. Though deep, the gash from the falling light fixture required no medical attention—not that there was any to be had in the city. The excruciating headache lessened after two days, and for some days afterward, he slept. When he looked at himself in a large shard of the shattered armoire mirror, he barely recognized the gaunt, unshaven man with unruly blonde hair that he had become. He was anxious to shed the clothes of a dead Jew and return to his familiar uniform. Although weak from lack of food, he felt rested, healed, and ready to fight if the noise outside was what he thought.

He basked in the warm sunshine as he walked up the deserted street. The sight at the corner of Corso Vittorio Emanuele II and Corso Re Umberto stopped him dead in his tracks. He hardly recognized the intersection of the two avenues. The skeleton of a tram lay in a twisted heap at the familiar spot where he used to wait for Doretta Giordano. Debris littered the arcades and the street, now lined with scorched plane trees. Turin was a war zone, with barely anyone about. Those that were wore vacuous stares, their sunken eyes wide, mouths gaping. Living ghosts, they wandered through the graveyard that once was their great city.

A line of gleaming black cars, Mercedes-Benz, he thought, with flapping red flags next to the windscreens, and motorcycles, sirens blaring, raced pass in the direction of Porta Nuova stazione. The Germans had arrived! Moments later, two large trucks sped past, following the convoy. He recognized the Italian military garb of the men, crammed like cattle on the truck bed. Where were they going?

At last, he could emerge and fight the final battle right beside them. He sprinted toward the train station to see where the occupiers were taking the soldiers. Another convoy of trucks filled with Italian soldiers sped past. This time he saw the German soldiers with machine guns at each corner of the truck beds. The terrified expressions of the passengers said it all. They were prisoners of war—on their own soil. Well, if they had refused to fight, as they must have, they were where they deserved to be.

Machine gun fire erupted! Baldo dove behind the carcass of an overturned tram seconds before smaller trucks carrying only German soldiers passed. Many of the ghostly Turinesi walking along the street crumpled to the ground. They had been shot! He raced back to his refuge. He would shave with the little water he had left, and change out of civilian clothes, particularly such rich ones as those he now wore. No longer would his uniform make him a target of retribution. He would be recognized for what he was—a proud member of OVRA. The most loyal of Il Duce's supporters, he was certain, had regained their power over the anti-Fascists and the Jews. But how? What had transpired in these last days?

An hour later, Baldo, refreshed, stood in front of Porta Nuova stazione, now swarming with German soldiers, many of whom wore the uniform of the SS. They shouted "*Raus! Raus!*" as they marched disorderly lines of scruffy Italian soldiers, their heads bent and shoulders slumped, toward the train platforms. They looked the cowards they were. Where were they being taken? Sporadic gunfire, including the *rat-a-tat-tat* of machine gun, rang out in the distance. At the last minute, as he dressed, he had decided to holster his sidearm. There would be no mistaking him for a traitorous anti-Fascist. Baldo scanned the groups of uniformed men before he chose one to approach—his age and an officer. Best of all, he wore the insignia of the SS.

"Guten Tag. Baldo Volpe. OVRA, *Mitglied, der Geheimpolizei*."

Baldo knew he was addressing a junior officer in the feared organization. Why such a menacing glare? Had he not recognized that OVRA had been the model for his country's own secret police? The sneering officer said nothing then snapped his fingers.

"I was injured in a bombing raid and then isolated, so I've been unable to obtain news. What day is this?" Strange, still no recognition or eye contact. "And can you tell me what—"

Before he could finish his question, two uniformed hulks seized Baldo. One grabbed his side arm before they dragged him off toward the station entrance. The more he struggled to free himself, the tighter their grip.

"*Halt, warten Sie mal!* Let me go! Can't you see? I am an officer. *Ich bin bei der Geheimpolizei*!" he shouted.

No response. What a nightmare! For weeks, he had hidden, preparing himself and gaining strength to serve with valor. Would they kill him as mindlessly as they did the ghosts along Vittorio Emanuele?

"Don't you understand?" His German was perfect. Surely, they did not mistake him for an enemy. He was one of them!

They arrived at an office in the station. One soldier released his vise-like grip on his upper arm; the other shoved him through the open door. He stumbled and fell to his knees; then a kick in his ribs sent him onto his back. Another, stronger one. He rolled to his side, unwittingly making himself vulnerable for the most heinous attack of all. His eyes were squeezed shut, so he didn't see it coming nor did he see who wore the boot that landed squarely in his balls. The room whirled and the voices shouting at him to stand seemed far away. He was yanked to his feet and his face crushed into the wall. Once his arms were wrenched behind his back, handcuffs were slapped on his wrists. He fought to stay alert.

"My pocket, please," he pleaded, gasping, "my papers."

The soldier who had delivered the blows to his ribs searched him and pinned him against the wall. Fear clutched Baldo's heart as tightly as the gorilla-like hand clutched his throat. The reek of tobacco and onions bursting from the soldier's mouth, inches from Baldo's face, roiled his stomach. What if his rising vomit erupted onto the thug's face or his bladder released as he felt it would after the blow to his groin? He knew rough handling from training. When hazed as a new Avanguardista, he had learned firsthand how a kick in his balls would incapacitate him. But never had fear unmanned him as it nearly had now.

"*Jetzt reicht es!*" someone barked from an inner office. When the grip on his throat relaxed, he collapsed to his knees. Unsteady and without the use of his hands, he tipped over and balanced on his aching head. "Was ist los?" the same voice, strangely familiar, barked again.

Baldo managed to turn his head slightly. Each of the two pairs of feet belonging to his assailants snapped together as a pair of jackboots, as shiny as his mamma's patent leather handbag, appeared. As hands pulled him to his feet, searing pain shot from his ribs and his groin, leaving him gasping. Though his vision was blurry, Baldo's knees wobbled at the sight before him.

"Schliessen!"

"*Lass ihn frei!*" Baldo's old friend, now dressed in a gray tunic with the insignia of an SS officer, ordered the goons to remove the handcuffs and release him. "*Folgen Sie mir,* Volpe." Gunther obviously had risen in the ranks to become a man of importance. Baldo struggled to stand, but the guard who seconds ago assaulted him, grabbed him and helped him stagger behind Gunther who, along the way, snapped orders at unseen minions to bring water and a cool cloth. The goon released him and handed his superior officer Baldo's gun before saluting and leaving them alone. Baldo collapsed into the chair before Gunther's desk.

Gunther removed the cartridges from Baldo's gun and pocketed them. "Here." He placed the weapon on the desk in front of Baldo. "You must forgive them. They're a bit edgy. Where's that warm Italian hospitality your people are so famous for?"

Though his vision was still blurry, Baldo watched in awe as Gunther Schliessen, now the strapping SS officer of an occupying force, sat at his desk and signed papers brought to him.

"Ah, *danke.* Set it here. Volpe, drink. Or do you want something stronger?" Baldo shook his head. Water in a bottle. Clean water. Something he had not had for weeks—or however long it had been since he went into hiding. The dank water he collected in empty wine bottles had twice made him violently ill. He rubbed the cool cloth over his face and neck. The luxury of running water ended after an early bombing raid. When he lifted the bottle to pour, his hand shook uncontrollably. With two hands, he was able to pour and hold the glass to his lips. Never had he felt so weak and vulnerable. He waved away Gunther's offer of a cigarette. He craved one, but the waves of bile in his stomach still assailed him, and holding one was impossible. "So Baldo, bring me up to date."

"Gunther…uh, Schliessen, you must forgive me, but first, what the Hell is going on? Communications are down in Turin, and my brother officers are isolated."

Gunther cocked his head back and snickered. "Wait, Baldo Volpe, the fierce OVRA policeman has no idea what's going on in his own city? Where have you been? In a cave?"

Blood rushed to Baldo's cheeks. His palms sweated and the pain from his injuries had not abated. The morning wasn't going as he had envisioned when the sirens woke him. "You could call it that. I'm at a loss for information. I don't even know what day it is."

Gunther snuffed out his half-smoked cigarette and leaned forward, hands clasped, his eyes boring into Baldo's. "Why it's September eleventh. With his proclamation just days ago, your incompetent leader stabbed my Führer in the back and surrendered to the Allies. But now, we, not the Allies, are your masters."

Baldo didn't know what to think. The Germans would bring order to this chaotic land and finally transform Italy into a clean, judenrein country. On the other hand, what would become of him, of his fellow officers? And where was Mussolini? Surely, Baldo's training in Berlin, proven track record of inter-rogating Jews, and now, his close relationship with an SS officer would place him in good stead with the Germans.

"Our intelligence picked up the news of the Armistice signing in Cassibile on September 3. They believe Eisenhower finally had enough of that incompetent fool and announced it the evening of the eighth. We saw it long before even Mussolini knew. Unlike the Americans, we were prepared. In early August, the First Panzer Division Leibstandarte secured the Brenner Pass. It was simply a matter of time. All too easy."

"What of the government? Are they in prison?"

Contempt coated each of Gunther's words. "Badoglio and your king… cowards…fled the capital. We are in complete control of Rome and all Italy to the north. It's only a matter of time before we push the Allies back into the sea."

Baldo's mouth dropped open. What great news, beyond anything he had imagined. "And what of Mussolini? Of his supporters? The army?"

"Slow down. Mussolini, I'm certain, will appear soon. For the time being, we're disarming your military, and sending away to Germany those who prefer to work than fight."

"And…"

"And the Jews? A high priority task, of course. For me, the highest. Dealing with them is why I'm here as an Obersturmführer in the Security Police, SiPo. In Poland, I was well trained in dealing with Jews. But of course, you know that, Baldo. Anyway, thanks to your government's Jewish census, it won't take us long to root them out and begin deportations. A Jewish census," Gunther said, chuckling. "Brilliant and, I must say, quite impressive."

What of the experienced OVRA officers? They were a small, but highly effective group overseeing a vast network of spies and informants throughout the country. With their expertise, there was no doubt the SS would partner with them.

"As in France, we're the masters, but we've found that local assistance in policing the country is great help." He leaned back and flicked his lighter. Then he paused as he contemplated the glow of the cigarette and the spiral of smoke. "I can see the question you want to ask? Am I correct?"

"You know me well, Schliessen."

"Yes, I do. And how very lucky that you found me. Saved me time, of which I have little. Following orders from the highest level in Berlin, SiPo's headquarters in Verona has demanded deportations begin immediately. So we must start…let me see, how do you call it in Italian…ah yes, *rastrellamenti*. We're to begin the roundups immediately."

Baldo had struggled not to wince at his friend's horrible pronunciation. But the SS's great efficiency did not surprise him. "I'm ready to begin, Schliessen. I've waited a long time for this."

"Excellent. Your local Fascist leaders were clever to see your potential and send you to Berlin when you were young. Didn't think you were in training for this work, hey Baldo?"

Yes, Baldo knew. He always knew he was one of them, an Aryan, more German than Italian. His mamma was from Südtirol, so his Germanic ancestry was strong. "I'm ready. Ready to work."

Gunther slapped his desk. "Great. In that case, come with me. Your first assignment. You can hone your interrogation skills."

"Who's the criminal?"

"A young, stupid anti-Fascist, a Jew no doubt, tossed a hand grenade from a window into a group of our soldiers. Of course, we caught him within minutes. Time to go hear what he knows before we—"

Baldo yelped as he struggled to stand.

"Time to toughen up, Baldo. We'll get our doctor to check you later. Now we have work to do."

As they passed the guards that had manhandled him minutes earlier, they snapped to attention and gave Gunther a crisp salute. Such great fortune that, of all the Germans soldiers swarming Turin, he had stumbled upon Gunther Schliessen. It was almost worth the beating. And Gunther would see his strength, his ability to withstand pain and continue working as he had been taught.

As they walked to the waiting staff car, Gunther broached a subject that had crossed Baldo's mind. "We'll assign you lodgings and get you some food, so after we finish with this task, get your things and report back to my office by four o'clock."

Adrenalin rushed through Baldo's body and chased away the residual pain in his balls. Not only would he work alongside the most feared, most experienced handlers of Jews, but he would be living in comfort with them. Baldo Volpe, working with the SS—he had finally realized his dream.

"We'll do great work together, Baldo. You'll be well rewarded."

CHAPTER 38

Bossolaschetto
September 24, 1943

On September 11, the Nazi First SS Panzer Division, fresh from the harsh conditions of the Eastern Front, stormed into Piemonte and unleashed a whirlwind of terror on the remaining citizens in the shell that was left of Turin. With only contempt for their former allies, now their enemies, they took as prisoners Italian soldiers who had not fled to the mountains and then turned on the civilians, leaving scores of them dead in the streets. By the late evening of that day, word of the Nazis' arrival reached the Giordano family's sanctuary in the hills of Alta Langa.

Madama Lia's cascina in the Alta Langa countryside above the Capra farm—shuttered since the death of Luigia and Luciana's mamma, Beatrice—sheltered the four Giordanos and their loyal housekeeper. Here, in a place filled with Madama Lia's carefree childhood memories, they hoped to avoid arrest and certain death. Bossolaschetto, a tiny hamlet on the edge of Bossolasco, a place of peace and serenity, was safe, at least for now.

Isolated in the ancient forests of Alta Langa, without any useful role to play in what was becoming a more organized resistance, Doretta found herself mirroring Elena's sour moods. She never had tolerated idleness. But as the head of her family, she bore the responsibility for their wellbeing. With winter coming, all she could think of was how she would keep her family safe if the Fascists led their new masters to the remote area.

In less than a month since the Armistice, *partigiani* that included many former Italian soldiers settled in Alta Langa. Doretta hoped to join one of the many brigades operating in the area, but only if she could stay near

Bossolaschetto. She had to find a role to play, even if she wasn't allowed to carry a weapon. But what if the Nazis infiltrated Alta Langa searching for the resistance fighters? Doretta stayed alert not to let their bucolic surroundings lull her into a false sense of security. The Nazis had spread quickly throughout northern Italy, and she knew their circumstances could change without warning. They had to remain vigilant.

The only country life Doretta had known was in the Rio Sordo valley. With its higher hills and denser forests, Alta Langa seemed otherworldly. Unlike Madama Lia, who spent her girlhood summers in Bossolaschetto where she learned the ways of the countryside, Doretta's short summer visits to Asili did not allow her time to learn about survival. She found more enjoyment working alongside Sara during the harvests of grain in summer and grapes in autumn. At the time, learning to grow vegetables and tend to farm animals seemed beside the point for a city girl. Now, as unregistered Jews, fugitives with no ration cards, and with food scarce, necessity became her teacher, and she learned.

Fortunately, Francesco had taught her an invaluable skill: to harness a horse to a cartun and drive it during harvests. Driving Gina, a stubborn mule, along the narrow, winding roads on the steep Alta Langa ridges, however, was more of a challenge. Unlike experienced and placid Romeo, who merely took her along for the ride, Gina had a mind of her own and was not to be trusted.

Elena shocked them when she took to milking the sheep and lone cow on the farm. Pipo Merluzzo, Madama Lia's longtime caretaker and his wife, Ornella, became her new companions. Her newfound interests blessed them all, particularly Ornella who sparked Elena's hidden passion for cooking. For the first time in his life, Michele found his baby sister's company enjoyable, so he joined Elena in farm chores. Having made certain everyone knew she hated Cherasco, Doretta feared Elena would feel the same about their remote refuge. As they moved further from Turin, deeper into the countryside, had she finally realized there was no going back? Whatever the reason, Elena's transformation made life easier for them all and lifted a burden off Doretta's shoulders. If she and Michele left to join the partisans, for the first time in her life, Elena would have to assume the responsibility for caring for her mother and Ida.

Daniela busied herself with reading many of the dusty books that Lia's father had in his library. Surprisingly, Ida had the most trouble finding her place in their new circumstances. With Ornella ruling the kitchen and Elena consumed with her cooking lessons, there was little for Ida to do other than cleaning. That is, until a fortuitous pranzo domenicale gave her a purpose and, most importantly to her, a way to contribute to the family's security and well-being.

Ida had taught them the rituals of the Catholic Mass. As far as the locals knew, they were Madama Lia's cousins, refugees from Turin, like many others who had found refuge in Bossolasco—or so they said to avoid suspicion. Informers were everywhere, and with so many strangers passing through the popular summer retreat, they would take no chances. Each Sunday, Michele drove them in the cartun to Mass at San Giovanni Battista in Bossolasco. They sat at the back of the church, following Ida's subtle cues of when to stand and kneel, hoping no one would notice that only she took communion.

Three days before the announcement of the Armistice, the family lunched at the hotel across the piazza from the church. In May, Paolina and Fabrizio Pratto, newlyweds from Milan, had opened the Hotel Paradiso. At the urging of Fabrizio's cousin, Marco Brione, the couple, experienced in hotel and restaurant work, bought the hotel from a widow whose two sons were killed in Russia in the early days of the war. Life in the countryside would challenge them, but Marco, a cultured man who worried for their safety in the city when the Fascists fell, believed they would be safer in the remote village. The timing and the location were perfect.

Not far from Liguria, holidaymakers from Genoa and Savona discovered in Bossolasco an enchanted realm where nature ruled. In summer, Mother Nature blessed them with abundant sunshine, cooled in the higher altitude. In winter, after she had given them her bounty of game, white truffles, and porcini, she unleashed her fury, leaving snowdrifts higher than most of the inhabitants. The ancient forests around the hilltop village buffered city visitors from the realities of war. The villagers need not know that the Giordanos sought protection from persecution there rather than leisurely enjoyment or charm.

The first weekend of September marked the end of a successful first summer for Fabrizio and Paolina. The petite, feisty woman had already gained notoriety for her cucina, particularly her tajarin, a rare treat in these difficult times when eggs were so precious. Soldiers billeted in the nearby barracks ignored the black market. Everyone helped each other. Paolina's trattoria became a gathering spot for visitors—many of whom remained—and villagers alike.

At least for a few hours, dining on the treats they had not enjoyed for a long time, with a cool breeze carrying the message of approaching autumn, chased away the Giordanos' concerns about the enemy beyond the forests. That day,

Ida met Paolina Pratto. The young, energetic hotelier welcomed Ida's offer of help with the hotel. Despite the nearly four-decade difference in their ages, the two women became fast friends. Most important of all, through Ida, Paolina passed along news from the outside world to the Giordanos.

Each morning after breakfast, Doretta or Michele drove Ida on the cartun the two miles to town and then fetched her in the late afternoon. Petrol was scarce, and who knew when they might need to make their escape in the aged Fiat that Madama Lia kept at the farm. Gina the mule became the family's means of local transportation. Ida brought home a few lire and bits and pieces of food from Paolina's kitchen. But, most important to her, the friendship that grew between her and other ladies of the village helped her through the transition.

It was through the Paradiso that they first learned of the details of the Nazis' arrival in Turin. A few days earlier, Ida had come home with news related by a hotel guest escaping the mayhem in Turin. He had told her of rumors spreading that there had been an orgy of blood not far away on the shores of Lago Maggiore. Doretta believed that the Fascists, in possession of the Jewish census, had abetted the massacre and helped the Nazis send a clear message that they would show no mercy—not to Jews and not to those aiding them.

And now, in Alba, Madama found herself forced to do business with the Nazis. Doretta worried about her being alone at the mill without Luca to help. The last word they received from him was shortly after the coup d'etat that toppled Mussolini. Doretta's anxiety grew with each passing day and no word of him. When news of the Armistice reached them, they worried that the Italian Fourth Army in France faced imprisonment or conscription if they failed to escape across the rugged Alpes-Maritimes in time. Would Luca suffer the same fate or worse for having aided Jews fleeing the Nazis? Waiting was all Lia and Doretta could do.

On the tenth day of the Nazi occupation, as Doretta returned from her morning round-trip to Bossolasco, Madama Lia and Gianni arrived with more supplies and news about the horrors unfolding throughout the region. Dealing with the Nazis in Alba, and their strict food controls that carried capital punishment for violations, prevented Madama Lia from making frequent visits to Bossolaschetto. Although there was no prohibition on travel throughout the countryside, Lia preferred the ruse Gianni devised. When he delivered flour to Alta Langa bakeries, he would drop her in Bossolaschetto then drive on to make deliveries. He fetched her late in the day on his return to Alba. The less anyone saw of her in Alta Langa, the better.

"Bondì, Doretta. Why the look of surprise? My trousers? This is no time for frills." Doretta sat gaping at the sight of Alba's most elegant woman dressed like a man. "These are yours. Wear them." She tossed the trousers up to Doretta. "Driving the cartun and riding a bicycle in a dress does not suit you. And there are some other provisions you'll need for winter."

Gianni had hidden the supplies for the Giordanos, much of it obtained on the black market, in sacks cleverly placed among those filled with flour.

"Still no coffee, but Gianni's now a black-market expert. He found your mother's favorite Assam tea." Gianni walked by carrying a large wooden box of clinking bottles. "Oh, and Nico Fiore sent some wine. There's a limit to the sacrifices you must endure."

"We're surprised to see you today, Madama, but what a pleasure. Will you stay for pranzo?"

"Delighted, Doretta. We will talk later. Such a pretty day and I'm in the mood for a passeggiata. Now go change into your trousers."

After lunch, they walked alone in the warmth of the afternoon, the branches of the chestnut and lime trees dappling the ground with sunlight. The late-rising autumn fog held close to the ground the forest's pungent scents of decaying leaves and prolific porcini Doretta would gather the following day. She always found it a paradox that the process of nature dying released such heady aromas. As they walked deeper into the forest, careful to avoid the favored autumn hunting grounds of local contadini, Madama Lia updated Doretta on the situation they now faced.

"The trousers suit you, Doretta." Lia noticed that Doretta seemed ill at ease in the pants. "So you've heard of the massacres on Lago Maggiore?"

"Massacres? More than one?"

"Several, from what I heard. Details are sketchy. As you can imagine, DELASEM leaders scattered, and volunteers dove underground. There are constant warnings on the radio that anyone who aids Jews in any manner will go before a firing squad."

The thought of what might happen to Madama Lia, Sara, and all who helped them sent quivers through her insides. "If Jews are in hiding, who are the couriers for the money, Madama?"

"Priests and Christian volunteers. Of course, the pope sits within the walls of the Vatican, silent for whatever reason. At least priests and nuns aiding and hiding Jews are taking his silence as approval to follow their consciences."

"Volunteers like Luca?"

"Yes. Like Luca." Her voice faded as though saying his name was painful.

Doretta wanted to ask her if there had been any word, but she knew if there had been, Madama would have told her already.

"The priests have an alibi for the large sums of money they carry. It's for the starving of their parishes. For now, nuns in convents, monks in monasteries, and simple farmers are taking in total strangers. All of them are risking their lives for these poor souls."

"What about here in Alta Langa? Do you think the Nazis will bother with the remote villages, Madama?"

"I'm afraid so. At least that's what happened in France. It's only a matter of time."

Again, Doretta held her tongue though she hungered for information about Saint-Martin-Vésubie now that word had reached them that the Fourth Army had retreated over the Alps. No one knew whether Luca and Cesare had gone with them.

"Mussolini's loyalists are now the Nazis' vicious hunting dogs. They're eager to prove their anti-Semitic credentials. So I expect them to lead the SS to the most remote villages and sanctuaries throughout Piemonte—even far up into the high mountain valleys. But we *will* resist. We must. For now, what choice do we have?"

"And the Allies?"

"They're on the mainland. No progress. We're on our own, and winter's coming."

Doretta shivered. Winter? Would winter bring the Allies' operations to a grinding halt? Any partisan initiative, even with thousands of former soldiers, was incapable of repelling the Nazis and their massive armaments for long.

"I've heard rumors in the village that partisan brigades are already forming here and in the Stura valley. Is that true, Madama?"

"True." Madama paused and seemed to look Doretta up and down. "So, Doretta. Are you ready?"

Doretta stopped, and her heart skipped a beat, but Madama resumed walking as though she had asked her something as mundane as which hat she would wear that day.

"I…I don't understand. Ready?"

"Come now, Doretta. Of course you do. You're a fighter. I've heard you say many times how much you wanted to be part of the battle for the liberation of our country, the salvation of *your* people. Well, now's the time. Like your great-grandfather, you have an opportunity to shape Italy's future. Michele thought he would never see battle. He will. That reminds me: Has he taught you to shoot yet?"

"Yes, Madama. In the vineyards at Asili, although we never actually fired the gun. Michele said I might need to use a gun in self-defense at some point although he doubts the men will allow women to fight alongside them. But if I had to..."

"Good. I think you should go hunting with Pipo. He'll teach you to shoot a rifle with real bullets. And it wouldn't hurt for you to learn how to hunt. These woods are full of partridges and pheasants. That will be great practice for you." Madama grew quiet. As the silence lengthened, Doretta squirmed. Finally, she turned to Doretta, her eyes narrow, her voice full of emotion. "We women will have to stand up and be counted, Doretta. I heard that, in Turin, thousands of women helped Italian soldiers hide from the Nazis. It's our time. I spoke with Michele last time I was here. He's anxious for action as I expected with his military training. But are *you*, Doretta, ready to fight with us?"

Who was this woman? Had the occupation unleashed something in her that Doretta had never noticed? She had always known her to be strong and confident, not afraid of anyone, but today she was defiant. Then it dawned on her. Today, dressed in trousers and boots, her graying blond hair braided and pinned up, the diminutive woman was Sara as she would be in twenty years. They were twins from a different era, different circumstances. Both women would fight, taking on boundless risks, yet neither would raise a weapon except in self-defense. One would provide funds and, she suspected, logistics. And shelter, as Doretta recognized. The other would care for the wounded. They would both follow their destinies. It was all clear to her now. Doretta would fight. She would hone her skills with a weapon. And she would gladly plant a bullet into the head of the likes of Baldo Volpe. She knew little of weapons and only recently began exploring the forests of Bossolasco. Alta Langa was so vast, so remote. But she would waste no time learning.

Her back straight and head high, her voice firm, Doretta answered the question. "Yes, Madama Lia, of course. I'm ready. But what about Sara? Will she come to Bossolaschetto?"

"Yes, Sara will come too. Soon. But never will she take a life. She will be here to save yours."

"But what of Mamma, Elena, and Ida? How can I abandon them?"

The edges of Madama Lia's mouth turned up in a wry smile. "Soon enough it will all be clear."

Lia led Doretta deeper into the forest, saying nothing further about fighting. Instead, her voice became wistful as she reminisced about her girlhood summers with Luciana Capra. She told Doretta the story of the *masca* who lived in the forest. By merely casting her evil eye on someone, Lia said, the masca would freeze their faces into tortured forms. All the villagers ran from the old crone they believed was a witch, except Luciana and her. Luciana pitied the old woman and never believed the stories told about her. The power the frail, hunchbacked woman held over others intrigued Lia.

Lia stopped and pointed up at the towering trees. "There were times it seemed God lived in the trees. We heard only the sounds of his creation. There were no cars. No planes flying overhead, no bombers. Only the wind whistling, the birds singing from their perches on the high branches, the sounds of squealing baby wild boars, of unseen animals searching for food." Lia continued walking until they reached a clearing. She plopped down and sat cross-legged. She patted the ground next to her. "Sit, Doretta." Lia raked her manicured fingers through the loose soil, scooped up some, closed her eyes, and held it to her nose, then to Doretta's. "That, cara, is God's perfume. The fragrance of the Langhe earth from which our nourishment comes."

Doretta said nothing but hung on each word from Madama, knowing the importance of this moment when Lia Ferri Bottero took off her armor, if only for a moment.

"See that chestnut tree? That's the one Luce and I climbed to find God. She said we wouldn't see Him, but we would feel His presence. I did. I truly did. From there, the view of the plains and mountains beyond confirmed that God would live in such a place. Though just thirteen at the time, I knew then God had a plan for me. For Luce."

Lia paused and grabbed a nearby twig. Doretta was surprised to see her mentor, their protector, sitting on the ground like a little girl and drawing lines in the loose soil, her eyes tracking the movement of her hand. Deep in thought, saying nothing, yet speaking volumes. "Sara knows the forests as well as any hunter." More silence. She wrapped her arm around Doretta and kissed her forehead. "And in the forests of Alta Langa, you and Sara will rise to the occasion to support the resistance." With that, she jumped to her feet, brushed off her trousers, and headed back toward the house.

The shadows had lengthened, and the air now chilled them. Pipo, a man wise to the ways of nature, warned of an early winter. Autumn, one of Doretta's favorite seasons in Asili, would be shorter than normal. Would the deep snow protect them, or would it help the Nazis set a trap? Would they, like their soldiers in Russia, perhaps even Francesco, become corpses under the snow?

As they turned into the long lane leading to the cascina, Michele, on his return trip from Bossolasco with Ida, passed them. Doretta heard the sound of car tires crunching gravel beneath. She panicked when she saw a beat-up black car with four occupants had followed Michele to the farm. The Nazis always drove either shiny black Mercedes-Benzes or armored vehicles. Madama Lia's face appeared calm, serene.

"It's fine, Doretta. Nothing to worry about."

The car stopped. Three men and a young woman emerged. Doretta didn't recognize any of them. Or did she? Skinny and dressed in rags, they wore shoes with so many holes they looked more like sandals. One of the men approached Doretta. Although a heavy beard obscured much of his face, Doretta recognized the broad smile behind the thick beard and bushy mustache of a contadino. *Luca!* She nearly fainted with joy and relief. Luca rushed to her and wrapped her in his arms.

She nuzzled him and buried her face against his chest and the rough fabric of his sackcloth jacket that might as well have been velvet. She wanted no kisses, no romance, only to find that familiar, safe place of hers again. Longing that had rendered her heart numb, vanished. Her spirit awakened. For the second time in her life, God had delivered Luca home safely.

CHAPTER 39

Bossolaschetto
September 25, 1943

After a long night of little rest and much spirited conversation with the latest arrivals at her sanctuary in Bossolaschetto, Lia and Gianni slipped away before dawn. With Jews hiding in the cellar of the mill, there was work to do in Alba. Ernst and Talia Bader, the Jewish refugees who arrived with Luca and Cesare, had also made the long, arduous trek across the Colle delle Finestre from Saint-Martin-Vésubie to Borgo San Dalmazzo in the Stura valley. The tales of their harrowing escape from the Nazis on both sides of the mountain pass captivated those who gathered before the stufa that burned all night.

In December 1942, Luca had arrived in Saint-Martin-Vésubie, a village, now a confino for Jews, forty-five miles north of Nice, deep in the Alpes-Maritimes. He threw himself into assisting Cesare, the only doctor caring for the over two thousand residents. The work gave him a sense of purpose and suppressed his painful longing for Doretta. He had left Langhe on short notice, leaving much unsaid between them. But for months, in letters he sent through Madama Lia, he had poured his heart out and told Doretta all about his life in Saint-Martin-Vésubie. After Mussolini's fall, his letters became cryptic and impersonal, no doubt for fear of censors. Rather than return to Alba that summer, Luca chose to remain in the confino. The situation grew more precarious by the day. At any moment, the Germans might swarm into the village. Cesare needed him.

"It was like Barbaresco," Cesare said. "Plenty of work, and I had a Sara to work alongside me. Her name was Marie-Claude." He paused for a moment.

"Marie-Claude LeBlanc. But she was French"—another pause—"from Maulévrier. She remained after we left on the ninth." Melancholy crept into his voice. "God only knows what will happen to those poor souls, most old and sick, who weren't able to cross with us. I'm sure Marie-Claude stayed with them as long as possible." His brows drew together, the pain inside evident on his face. He peered into the flames. "Lord knows what she witnessed."

Tell us about the crossing, Cesare," Doretta said, thinking to distract him from the loss of love. She knew how he felt now. She sighed and tightened her fingers, entwined in Luca's.

Cesare's attention returned to them. "Luca should tell that story. He's the great mountaineer from his boyhood years hiking in Val Maira."

The eyes of the room fell upon him. Sensing he was losing the battle not to wrap her in his arms, Luca eased away from Doretta and stood.

"Cesare and I started planning for an escape we knew would come as soon as we heard the news of Mussolini's arrest. We had a wireless, so we kept up with the Allies' progress in Sicily. When they didn't land in Liguria as everyone had hoped, we decided to hike up the pass to Italy any chance we had. We learned the terrain and the places for refuge along the trail to the Colle delle Finestre. We found boots, but as you can see…well, others needed them more. On the eighth, Cesare was told the Fourth Army would pull out the next morning. They were as anxious as their Jewish internees were to leave before the Germans arrived. So Cesare and I left with the other soldiers. About a thousand refugees followed us."

For over an hour, he recounted spellbinding tales of their harrowing journey and the frigid early-autumn nights at the Sanctuary of the Madonna di Colle delle Finestre where the billeted Italian soldiers gave aid and comfort to the Jewish refugees. "We remained at the sanctuary longer than we planned. There was no way Cesare would leave them." He turned to Cesare who sat on the floor, knees drawn up tight as he gazed into the fire, off in another world. "Many were dehydrated and exhausted from the climb in street shoes. Some even wore sandals."

Luca went on, telling the worst of it. They arrived in Borgo San Dalmazzo on the same day the First SS Panzer Division Leibstandarte unit massacred twenty-three civilians, including two priests not far away in Boves. The death of an SS officer in a firefight with partisans triggered the bloodshed that followed.

"That bastard commander of theirs, Obersturmbannführer Joachim Peiper, gave the order to 'teach the Italians a lesson.' We heard from French resistance fighters that the Nazis use reprisals against civilians to retaliate against the partisans. But there were no partisan brigades in Boves. *Che bastardo.*" He paused. "Mi dispiace, Madama." Even in the dim orange firelight, there was no missing Luca's expression of disgust, a fire in his eyes that Doretta had never seen in the gentle, soft-spoken man except for the altercation with Baldo Volpe years ago. She shivered at the memory."Speaking of partisans, what's the latest here?"

"Before we get to that, tell us how you reached Alta Langa, Luca. And how you came upon the Baders." Luca had already told Madama Lia the details of how the young Jewish couple joined them, but it was a story she wanted him to share. It would be a learning experience for Doretta and Michele, and perhaps Elena should she have to lead her mother to safety.

"Many of the Jews remained in the villages and hamlets—San Giacomo Entracque, the first we came to, Entracque, and Valdieri mostly—but before we heard about the massacre, Cesare and I thought to risk it on the train from Borgo San Dalmazzo to Cuneo and then figure it out from there. But when we saw Nazis everywhere in town, we raced back to Valdieri. Already the SS soldiers were combing the area for Italian soldiers and Jews." Luca stole a glimpse of Doretta. The memory of her sweet face had urged him onward during the long, painful days walking on the rocky trails and the nights shivering at the sanctuary. "That's where we met Ernst and Talia. An old farm couple had a beat-up car outside their barn. I bought it off them. And it had a full tank of petrol."

Elena, who had been silent the entire evening, yet hanging on Luca's every word, cut in, "Luca, where are they from?"

"Germany. But I'll let them tell their story. It was raining, so we went into the barn to wait for the farmer. We heard a noise and discovered them hiding behind a haystack. They had come from the sanctuary with us, so we knew they were Jews escaping the Nazis and in hiding like two hundred or so others in the village. I still can't believe what those courageous villagers, mostly farmers, did to help the refugees. And don't forget: it's a bullet, usually on the spot, if they're caught aiding Jews. Well, anyway, we figured if two of us were running from the Blackshirts and Nazis, why not four?"

"Madama Lia knew you were coming. How did you get word to her?" Elena leaned forward, a keen expression on her face.

"A local priest in Valdieri. We had to trust someone other than the farmer, although that was scary, so we went to the priest. I told him I was a DELASEM courier. That's all I needed to say. He did the rest."

Ida walked in the room, surprised to find them all still gathered around the glowing stufa. It was already four in the morning, and she had just woken to make tea for Lia and Gianni before they left for Alba. The hotel was now full of guests who had joined the others she suspected were Jews from Turin and Ferrara. Sooner or later, she worried the Nazis would show up.

And they did.

That morning as sleepy Michele drove Ida to Bossolasco in the dense fog, armored vehicles heading toward the village whizzed past them. Adrenaline shot through Michele's body. Should he continue? He had no papers on him. A man named Franco had come the previous day and asked for their identity cards. Madama Lia had told them to expect him and assured them there was nothing to fear. Ida had hers, which showed she was Aryan, but even if he did have his with him, the large "J" on it would guarantee his arrest. Since they were close to the village, he stopped. Ida climbed down.

"Godspeed, Michele," she said. And off she went, ambling along the remaining mile to the Hotel Paradiso. Michele turned the mule, but despite his prodding, he knew it would be a slow return to the cascina. What they would do now remained a mystery. Surely, Doretta had a plan. They were six Jews, including the young couple and a doctor who had deserted from the army, hiding in a home belonging to one of the most prominent women in Langhe. Their chances of survival—and Pipo's and Ornella's—were nil if discovered. "Madòna!" he called to the sky. Ida, who often called the Virgin Mother's name, had assured him she would protect them. He hoped she would listen to a terrified Jew. Didn't Ida say the Madonna was Jewish anyway?

It was already mid-morning by the time he reached the cascina. He dashed into the house, shouting to wake all who had gone to sleep at dawn. "They're here. The Nazis are here!" he cried, his voice raspy with terror. He bounded up the stairs and banged on every door. "Mamma, Doretta, they're here." No one stirred. Again, he ran through the hall, this time opening each door and shouting as he went by. This was no time for modesty.

Doretta, in her heavy cotton nightdress, bare feet on the cold wood floor, emerged first from the room she shared with Elena. "What is it, Michele?" His eyes, wild with terror, and breathlessness drove a flash of panic through Doretta. It could mean only one thing.

"They're here! They're in the village. They raced by us on the way in." He bent over, hands on his thighs, taking shallow, quick gasps before continuing.

"Four armored personnel carriers"—more gasps—"and one staff car. Those damned red flags flapping on all of them."

"Did they stop you?" Doretta asked, though she knew the answer since he was here in front of her. The thought of his arrest tore at her insides. She needed to think what to do.

"No. Ida walked the rest the way. I came as quickly as possible, but that stubborn mule... What do we do, Doretta?" Michele implored. His breathing slowed, but color had not returned to his face. In fact, everyone except Luca, Cesare, and the Baders were ashen. Think, Doretta. She needed to put to use all those hours walking the forests and planning for this eventuality. Her eyes locked on Luca's. Doretta saw he knew the drill. The threat always loomed that the Germans might sweep into Saint-Martin-Vésubie. They had to be ready to escape, day or night.

"Listen to me. Everyone. Listen. Dress immediately, make your beds, and put your things in your hiding places as quickly as possible." She looked at Luca for reassurance. "Can't leave any obvious signs we were here. And take your identity cards with you. We don't even have ours, but at least that's one less piece of evidence against Madama." Stunned silence. No one moved. "Now!" she barked. "Meet downstairs in ten minutes. We're going for a hike."

Minutes later, the group assembled in the tinello.

"Everyone's here, Doretta," Luca said. "Cesare and I checked the bedrooms. There are no signs of us."

"Good. Grazie, Luca. I've said nothing to Ornella or Pipo. Let's go."

Talia picked up wicker baskets and handed them to Elena, Doretta, and her mamma. Upon seeing Doretta's puzzled expression, she explained. "Porcini. Didn't you say the forest is teeming with them and you were going foraging today? Why return empty-handed?"

Doretta smiled and pushed Elena toward the door. "Yes! That will give us something to do. Anyway, we'll have to eat tonight." *Provided we are able to return*, she added to herself.

She led them through the cortile into heavy fog that showed no signs of lifting and down the overgrown road in the direction of the Capra farm. The fog added to the chill, but she welcomed the cover. No one had driven down the hill past Madama Lia's cascina for a long time, so there were no tracks on the road. Weeks ago, Doretta mapped a route for them to take into the dense forest down the road if they needed a quick escape. She knew of a *ciabot* in the hayfield on the other side of the forest. They would shelter in the remote, tiny shack that offered the farmers refuge from storms and storage for their tools. She had stashed blankets, tins of sardines, and even some bottles of wine. Although they couldn't stay for more than a couple of nights, the isolated location, inaccessible by road, would buy them precious time.

As the day dragged on, Doretta wondered whether she should return to scout the cascina. Though they had some bites of the sardines and sips of wine, she had brought the supplies out weeks before. Now with their latest arrivals, there was barely enough for eight people. The fog had not lifted until midday, and the sun would set in a few hours. Cold and hunger would follow. While the men remained there on the lookout, Doretta and the women foraged for porcini in the nearby forest. She could not sit still.

Foraging with Talia, Doretta drew up beside her and asked about her life on the run and in Saint-Martin-Vésubie. Their newest lodger's Italian was passable, but Doretta preferred speaking in Talia's mother tongue, French, a language she had perfected during her time with Madame Stern in the Swiss Romandie. Talia and Ernst, both from Strasbourg, met in Nice before they were sent to Saint Martin-Vésubie. They married shortly after the Allies landed in Sicily in July. Talia said they finally felt settled after years on the run, so why wait any longer.

"When we were climbing the steep path up to the pass, many people were exhausted and wanted to give up. Only hope that the Allies would be waiting for us kept us all going. And Luca."

"What do you mean, Talia?" She had yet to be alone with Luca, so he had not had the chance to tell her about his months away.

"He was always carrying someone, usually children. One time, I saw him with a small child in his arms and another clinging onto his back. Honestly, I don't know how he did it."

Caro Luca. Had Talia not told her, Doretta never would have known about the struggles he had faced helping in the escape. She had heard stories of people risking their lives for total strangers, but she knew demons lurked among the saviors. Already word had spread of bandits and informers posing as guides along the Swiss border in the Alps. Refugees paid large sums for safe passage over the mountains into Switzerland, but some of their so-called guides turned them over to the Nazis before reaching the border. The occupiers paid handsome blood money, making it a lucrative business.

"But Doretta, there's something you should know." Talia stared at her basket of mushrooms, turning them over, inspecting each one. "I'm…" Her cheeks flushed. "I'm going to…"

Doretta laughed. "A baby. New life. What's there to be shy about, Talia?"

"Well, I barely know you. You've not only taken Ernst and me in, but now I won't be able to do my share. I'll be a burden."

Doretta could not help herself. Sara had taught her long ago that emotions should be expressed. She hugged Talia and brushed away dirt from her forehead. "Don't be foolish. There's plenty for you to do to help. Anyway, new life is what will be needed when this is all over. We'll survive, Talia. I promise. And your baby...your baby will have a new world, a new homeland."

Talia crinkled her nose, but before Doretta answered the question she read in Talia's expression, Elena came running from deep in the forest. "Someone's coming!" She tripped, spilling a full basket of porcini, but sprang back to her feet and dashed toward the *ciabot*.

"No, Elena. Stop!" Doretta sprinted after her, grabbed her arm, and drew her back to the other two women. She lowered her voice and motioned for her mamma and Talia to follow her. Hopefully the men would be safe, but for them, the only possibility was to walk deeper into the forest, away from the clearing and the approaching noise.

They came upon fallen trees that offered some protection. "Elena, what did you hear? Voices?"

"No. Only noise like someone was coming. Someone with big feet."

Big feet? The forest was eerily quiet. The only sound Doretta could hear was her heart drubbing in her ears. Elena's wide-eyed expression touched her. She pulled her baby sister close and kissed her head. Parties and boys were all she should have on her mind, not this madness. Her acceptance of their challenges made life easier for Doretta and her mamma. "Don't be afraid, carina. I'm here," Doretta whispered. "I'm here." Doretta glanced at her mamma, the one Elena had always run to. Now Elena trusted only her sister and her own instincts.

Voices! A male voice grew louder. "Doretta! Where are you?" Luca! Or was it a ploy? Did someone have a gun to his head? She turned to Elena. "Listen carefully. Don't come out until I come back for you. Even if I call for you. Don't answer. Stay where you are, no matter what. Understood?" Elena nodded. Doretta knew her sister struggled to remain calm, but she would. Elena had become a fierce guardian of her loved ones. Doretta wished she had a gun. Should she make it out of the day alive, she would lose no time in asking Madama for a sidearm.

When she reached the spot where Elena had spilled the porcini, her heart stopped. The shock made her head spin. *Sara!* Sara on Zeus with Luca astride, holding the reins, and Sara behind him, perched on Zeus's haunches. Now Doretta understood what Elena had described. Zeus's footsteps would surely have been loud and heavy.

Sara slid over his rear, a mischievous grin on her face. Was this a sweet dream in the middle of a nightmare? No. Sara was here.

"Whatever are you doing here?"

"I came to visit you." She flashed Doretta an elfin grin, seen so often in happier times.

"All this way on Zeus? No, why are you here?"

"It's time, Doretta. How was I to stay in Barbaresco knowing you were all here and the countryside's crawling with Nazis and Blackshirts? Besides, it's my home too—at least, it was in summers when I was little. Mamma and zia Luce still own the Capra farm."

"But what about your work…and Anna?" Doretta glimpsed a flash of pain that ran across Sara's face when she said her daughter's name. "Surely, you don't mean you've come to stay."

"Look, Doretta, Anna is safe and loved. And she adores her zia Giovanna. Gianni will bring my things later, but I'm here for the duration even though there's word the Americans have asked that the partisan brigades stand down for the winter."

"Have they asked the Germans and Fascists to do the same?"

"I doubt anyone will stand down. But we can talk later."

"Later? Sara, the Germans arrived this morning."

"And they left. I arrived and found only Ornella in the house. She had no idea where you had gone, so I rode into town." She patted her cross-body satchel. "I have something for you from Fabrizio Pratto."

Luca dismounted and gave Sara a leg-up.

"Come, Doretta. Luca, would you give our fearless leader a leg-up?"

Doretta laughed, expelling all the tension of the day. "Wait! Mamma, Elena—I told them to wait."

"Then hurry. We'll get them."

As Doretta stood beside Zeus, her left leg bent and waiting for Luca to help her up onto the tall steed, he nuzzled her ear and kissed her cheek. She scrunched her shoulder and giggled. He spun her around and finally kissed her for the first time since their long separation. "I love you Luca," she breathed.

"My life's nothing without you." Pinned between Zeus's sweaty haunches and Luca's warm body, heat rose from Doretta's core—first fear, then passion. If this was a dream, may she never wake up.

"I love you too, carissima. You're all I've thought of. I wish we could run—"

"Um…you two. Save that for later."

In an hour, as the last rays of the sun sparkled through the trees and the fog crept up from the valley floor, they poured back into the cascina—cold, hungry, and grateful that the worst thing that happened was Elena's spilled basket of porcini. It wasn't a total loss; Elena recovered them, and Ornella showed her how to clean the pungent mushrooms and prepare *risotto con funghi*. Doretta's little sister was fast learning the art of *cucina piemontese*. In the kitchen with Ornella, it seemed Elena had made peace with the world.

Sara dumped the contents of the large envelope on the table.

Doretta picked up one of the identity cards and studied it. "I don't understand. Doretta Bottero? Daniela Bottero? And Elena and Michele too. Why 'Bottero,' Sara?"

"Well, even though your given names sound Aryan, Massimo Botti, the municipal chief, and Fabrizio decided that, as long as they were changing the identities of the Paradiso's Jewish guests, they might as well officially make you Madama Lia's relatives. See"—Sara pointed to a specific spot on the small card—"you're now Aryan. No more 'J.' Madama Lia told me you now go to Mass, so why not?"

Doretta stared in disbelief at the documents. "But, Sara, how did they know?"

"Ask Madama Lia. I don't know the details, but what's important is that you and all the other Jews in town have been aryanized. Sorry, none for Ernst, and you Talia, just yet. I suppose signor Botti will have to give you Italian citizenship before he can give you new cards."

Doretta fixed her eyes on the card. *Doretta Bottero, Aryan.* She burst out laughing. "Oh, why not, Sara? Our lives are upside down anyway, so why not new identities?" Elation flipped to panic. Doretta's stomach lurched. If the village's chief knew about them, who else in the village knew? "What about the other villagers? Don't tell me no one will denounce us and the Prattos."

"No one will betray you, or the Prattos. They're proud of their unity and self-sufficiency." Sara took Doretta's new identification card and studied it. "Certainly not like the false documents they're creating in Alba. These are official, from the municipio. I'm sure there's no Doretta Bottero on the Jewish census. You have no past—only a future." Sara pointed to the birthplace on the card. "And look, you were born in the Allied zone in Sicily. Impossible to check. Aren't they clever?" When Sara mentioned Sicily, for a moment they looked at one another. Doretta could not help but think of Francesco. She studied her dear friend who might have remained in Asili with her child and family. Instead, like Madama and Luca, she had chosen a different path. Trousers, her hair still in a singular braid—she truly resembled Madama Lia as her younger self. Both fearless women fought against the social conventions that would make them subservient to men.

They would both give anything they had to save the soul of Italy and to rid the Jewish people of the murderous Nazi scourge. Doretta was in a fight for her life. If she won, what then? Sara and Madama Lia had given her a vision of brotherhood, and she swore never to let it fade. She took Sara's small but strong hands in hers. "Cara, why are you here? You could be home. Why risk it all?"

Sara's face grew dark, her usually warm eyes empty. "For Francesco. He died fighting for a brute in a senseless war. At least here, I know why I'm fighting. I'm fighting for Anna's future." She paused, and fire now burned in her eyes. "To avenge Francesco's death. It's my destiny, Doretta."

CHAPTER 40

Langhe
December 3, 1943

"W ell, Volpe, looks like we can turn you loose." Gunther Schliessen slapped his protégé on his back. He was now an officer in the newly formed Italian SS. "With your interior minister's order, you and your brothers are now free to conduct your own rastrellamenti. Of course, roundups are more efficient if we work together."

Baldo Volpe, now a lieutenant in the Waffen SS Italienische No. 1, studied the fog-shrouded winter landscape out the window of the Nazi staff car as they crossed the Tanaro River into Alba. He had gone from Avanguardista to OVRA and now the Italian division of the feared Waffen SS. All because of the good fortune, at one of the most momentous times in history, to have been chosen as a teenager to study in Berlin. Now, thanks to Police Order No. 5 of the Italian Socialist Republic, he was free to hunt Jews with his own men. But he enjoyed the chase much more when teamed with his close friend, Gunther Schliessen.

"Tell me more about this town, Volpe."

"I don't know much about it, but my informant here tells me it's a hotbed of partisan and black market activity. She helped in the arrest of an anti-Fascist several years ago."

"Any Jews?"

"None that I know of. There used to be many Jewish families last century, but they're gone. We had them in Turin, but thankfully we're free of them now." He knew of one who had disappeared. Eventually, he would find her.

"And this woman you've set up the meeting with? Who is she?"

"A widow who inherited a great deal of money. She bought some flour mills after the war, so with that she's powerful, but she could also be dealing in the black market. I thought we should check her ledgers. I don't know much beyond what's in the dossier." Baldo opened the folder and studied the photo of Cornelia Ferri Bottero—born 1896, address Altavilla. War widow. Never remarried. Child dead at age four. "I'm sure the local police have a more detailed file on her. She's not exactly an ideal Fascist woman. I'm surprised the mills weren't confiscated. A woman owning them…" Then he noticed something he had not seen before—*Associate: Luca Olivero, Legal Counsel.* How had he overlooked the familiar name? That Jewess's lover who had spent only six months in the confino. All his hard work for nothing when he was released. No reason given. How very interesting. He would not divulge that connection to Gunther—not yet. This would be a big catch for Baldo on his own. If Olivero was suspected of anti-Fascist activity and known to be involved with a Jewish woman, perhaps this Bottero woman had some deep secrets she guarded. The hunt was on.

The cortile of the Ferri-Bottero mulino buzzed with activity when the Nazi staff car and its armored escort arrived. Idling delivery trucks spewing diesel fumes, and wagons hitched to mules and oxen lined up at a loading point, but all eyes turned on them as they emerged from the car. Had these people any idea of the power he, Lieutenant Baldo Volpe, held over them, over their employer?

The sound of creaking hinges drew their attention to a diminutive woman dressed in a heavy woolen coat over trousers, no less, emerging from behind a large carved wooden door. A cloud of the pungent aroma of caramel and molasses enveloped her.

"Heil Hitler. Obersturmführer Gunther Schliessen."

Lia had seen the Roman salute the Fascists used long before Hitler's rise to power, but to be greeted with it on her property, combined with the revolting little man's name—he might as well have landed a punch in her belly. The Nazi's piercing ice-blue eyes unnerved her. Fortunately, the large register she clutched, containing the mill's legal transactions, prevented her from returning his salute. When the officer from the Italian SS called to request a meeting to review her ledger, Lia struggled to keep panic from creeping into her voice. Normally, she dealt with the local Wehrmacht officers. What interest would either of the SS divisions have in her business? The black market, partigiani, and Jews were their interests. And they were hers as well. She would not call giving flour to the poor a black market activity, but they would.

Although Lia spoke flawless German, he was in her country now, so she replied in Italian but would have preferred Piemontese. *Don't be rude, Lia.* "*Piacere di fare la vostra conoscenza.*" Truth was, it sickened her to meet either of these two vile characters, but Lia Bottero knew how to play the game. There was a limit, however, and she would never reciprocate the salute. "*Mi chiamo,* signora Cornelia Bottero." Turning to Baldo, "*E voi?*" Part of the game was to follow the *Voi Fascista* and avoid the formal, polite pronoun, *Lei.* Ah, it pleased the Nazi lackey. He seemed vaguely familiar to her, but in his uniform, he appeared to be a perfect SS Aryan except for his dark brown, nearly black, eyes.

Parroting his Nazi handler, Baldo gave a crisp Roman salute but added "Mi chiamo Lieutenant Baldo Volpe, Waffen-SS Italia." Volpe? The officer who called her. Of course, he would be in the newly formed Italian SS. Hadn't Daniela Giordano said he had spent some years in Berlin as a teenager? He looked the same age as the Waffen-SS officer. Could they have met there? "Piacere di fare la vostra conoscenza." Nausea roiled her belly, but never did her forced smile wane.

He wrinkled his nose as though sniffing something fetid other than the sweet aroma of the wheat. It was his disapproval of her trousers, no doubt. Normally, she would greet visitors in one of her conservative wool suits, but she planned to ride later. Anyway, these times were more informal. If the pair were not so dangerous, the Fascist pig's annoyed reaction would have amused her, but this was serious—deadly serious.

"Shall we?" Lia led them into her office but hesitated before offering them a seat. For nearly a quarter of a century, many dear, respectable people had sat across from her in the two large chairs facing her mahogany desk. People who came to her for loans and advice on troubles of all kinds had sat in those same chairs that now would be defiled. Later, she would call the bishop of Alba and ask him to say a blessing over the office—over the mill.

Bile burned her throat throughout their visit. Although she did not wish to take refreshment with Nazis—like Contessa Cristina, forced to lodge German soldiers in her villa—Lia's upbringing obliged her to extend hospitality to guests, no matter how unsavory and unwelcome they might be. Besides, chamomile tea might calm her stomach.

For the next two hours, with a forced display of cordiality, Lia conducted a meeting with the two men as they combed through the ledger and toured the mill. She avoided the cellar. Although the safe with the real ledger was well hidden, she saw no need to tempt fate. Police Marshal Salvatore Libera had sounded the alarm about a roundup days ago, so they rushed the two Jews from Borgo San Dalmazzo hidden there to her cellar in Altavilla. But she knew more would arrive as the Jews from Saint-Martin-Vésubie fled into the mountains and Langhe. She struggled against her rising horror that both men were on the hunt for people she loved. But for this visit, they only showed interest in the mill's operations and her accounting for the grain that arrived and the flour that left.

As they left, a haughty red-haired woman with a bulge at her mid-section under her police uniform coat—a gun, perhaps—strutted across the cortile. This one Lia knew. She was the *Fascista* that Lia had seen with Francesco in Chiesa San Giovanni Battista in Barbaresco many years ago. Never would she forget her pointed chin, the hair of a harlot, and the contemptuous glare in her beady eyes. What was her name? Of course, Cinzia Strega, a relative of that Fascist family of card sharps in Barbaresco. The shrew who lashed out at Francesco on the train platform. The informer who led OVRA to Luca! Rage rippled through Lia, but she maintained her business-like countenance. She fought the urge to escape the evil troika but dared not move either her body or the smile that strained her facial muscles. After she greeted Lia with the Nazi salute and confirmed that she was Sergeant Cinzia Strega, she gave Lia a frosty smile. For Lia to show any sign of intimidation would be to court disaster.

As though reading her thoughts from afar, Gianni called to Lia that she was wanted on the telephone. At last, she made her escape before the vortex of bile in her stomach rose to her mouth. Luca's nemesis had been a local police informant, one who swore revenge against Francesco through Sara. She knew the entire story. And all, but for Francesco, were together in one place in Bossolaschetto. The collision of nausea and rage made Lia's head spin as she bade them farewell and hurried to close the door behind her. She would also have to warn Marshal Libera that a dangerous spy lurked in his office. Cinzia Strega might easily discover his role in helping to hide Jews in her mill and elsewhere in Alba, warning them of rastrellamenti. *What a catastrophe it would be* if the authorities discovered their clandestine rescues and siphoning of flour to don Piero Rossi of the Pious Society of Paul. The Nazis would make no distinction between the black market and the needs of the poor of Alba. They would both face deportation, or worse, all the same.

At least she knew her enemy better, now. The known was less frightening than the unknown. Before she answered the fictitious telephone call, Lia was forced to endure the Nazi salute from the three of them. All she managed was "Buona giornata" and a quick retreat.

Back at her desk, she fought the feeling that her inner sanctum had been violated. Luca was on the front line now, not in his office to advise her. She was on her own to fight the biggest battle of her life. The thought of Major von Ebnerberg, the Wehrmacht's commanding officer in Alba, flashed in her mind. Was he aware of the Turin SS's presence in Alba? Would he approve of the visit they had made to her? Since the Wehrmacht's arrival in Alba, she had reported the mill's transactions to his office. What if she found a way to ask him? Unlike Volpe and Schliessen, and despite being the enemy, he was an officer and a gentleman, a military type no different than her beloved Alessandro. Her intuition told her he did not share Hitler's racial madness although he served the Reich all the same.

But obviously, someone beyond Alba had targeted her. Why? How would she get to Bossolaschetto now? Future solo car trips were out of the question, at least for the time being. Gianni would have to hide her among the sacks of flour when he made his deliveries to Bossolasco. Easy for her to slip out unnoticed when he drove past the turn to Bossolaschetto. She buried her face in her hands. There would be no tears. No time for that. Langhe needed her.

CINZIA STREGA CLIMBED INTO THE FRONT SEAT FOR THE DRIVE TO BALDO and Gunther's next stop on their Langhe tour, Villa Cristina atop Monte Silva, the highest point in the area, the perfect spot for the Germans' rural headquarters. From the villa's observation deck, the Nazis commanded an unobstructed view of Vallegrande, the Rio Sordo valley, and the countryside for miles around in every direction. Plus, the villa had the Contessa Cristina di San Benedetto's wine cellar and the aristocratic family's farm products to enjoy. The perfect spot for officers to billet inside and for soldiers to camp on the grounds.

How Baldo detested the aristocracy. After the war, the Italian Socialist Republic, free of the parasitic monarchy, would eliminate the entire aristocratic class and seize their lands. For now, they would make use of the aristocrats like the Contessa, and their homes.

They arrived shortly before noon and joined the officers for lunch at the villa's massive carved wood table in the dining room. Pity it was foggy. Baldo was told the room's large windows looked upon splendid, expansive views. But where were the great wines and delicious food Baldo had heard of? The elderly maid served them a disgusting cabbage soup flavored only with a pork bone, and stale bread, but with much of Italy's food production being sent to Germany, this was to be expected. A sacrifice for the cause. He did enjoy the pears cooked in

Nebbiolo and the glass of Moscato d'Asti for dessert. At least something was tasty and fitting. The biggest disappointment for Baldo was that the Contessa was nowhere to be found. The housekeeper said she had left for the family's estate in Monferrato that morning. Pity. Strega had mentioned that she and the Bottero woman were old friends. He would have liked to interview the Contessa, in a style that veered—politely of course—toward interrogation. Soon.

After lunch, they climbed the stairs to the observation deck on the roof of the villa. A mere four flights up, they discovered another world. Although midday sunshine blinded him as they emerged from the dark stairway, and despite the sea of fog below, the breathtaking panoramic view of the Alps amazed Baldo. Snow-capped mountains of the Alps and Apennines in the distance ringed them.

"Quite a view. Strega, Volpe says you're from around here. Is the fog always heavy like this?"

Cinzia beamed at Gunther's attention since the Germans had barely acknowledged her. They would soon know the value of a *Langhetta Fascista*. "September through early December can be like this. No fog in summer, but the storms can be violent. Great surveillance spot, is it not?"

Gunther sneered and shot Cinzia a dismissive sideways glare before he walked away. That was the end of the conversation with her.

"Where to next, Volpe?"

"Barbaresco. Strega goes far back there. She would like to show you around." Volpe observed Cinzia's poorly disguised frown. The Germans' cool, condescending manner clearly annoyed her. He needed to keep his prized Langhe informant motivated and have the Germans accept her as a knowledgeable intelligence asset. "Strega, didn't you say the contadini around here are apolitical? Any anti-Fascists or partisans?"

Cinzia jumped at the opportunity to display her knowledge. "Monarchists, mostly, but there are some Communists among them, mostly in Barolo. The Savoy family has been tied to Langhe and Monferrato for generations. It's the partisans we have the most to worry about, maybe even Jews among them."

Now she had the SS Obersturmführer's attention.

"Jews, you say? Volpe told me there are none around here."

Baldo's cheeks burned as a flush of embarrassment crept across his face.

Cinzia lifted her pointy chin and met Volpe's glacial stare with a haughty one of her own, her expression bordering on mockery of him. "Not *from* here, but connected to the area. Turin Jews. Friends of that signora Bottero, I believe."

"Where do these friends live?"

Cinzia pointed at la Torre di Barbaresco, its top a ghostly image peeking through the ceiling of the fog. "There are two farms in a place called Asili between here and the village of Barbaresco. Look, you can almost see the tower. We'll pass it on the way to the village."

"I want to see it. Come, Volpe," Gunther ordered.

Strega's familiar behavior with Gunther began to enrage Baldo. Minutes ago, he had drawn her into the conversation to give her an opportunity to impress the German. Now, the bitch repaid the favor by embarrassing him. He would deal with her later, but for now, she had valuable information. Only one family fit her description of the Turin Jews—Giordano. And it had been months since they had disappeared from Cherasco. At least, he still had her scent. Delicious heat gushed from Baldo's groin at the thought of Doretta's connections right here under his nose.

The Turin-based convoy left the villa and drove through Tre Stelle. As they descended deep into the Rio Sordo valley, the fog grew thicker, darker. Seeing Cinzia in the front seat, relishing her role as guide along the narrow, twisting road, Baldo smoldered with resentment.

"There! Turn right there," she ordered, obviously pleased with herself. "Drive to the end of the lane."

The two vehicles pulled into the fog-shrouded cortile of the Asili compound. Baldo thought it the perfect spot to hide Jews, but they had discovered them in more remote settings, even high in the mountains. Their search techniques had been honed, making it nearly impossible to escape arrest and deportation.

No one was about.

"Two houses. Who else lives here, Strega?" Gunther asked.

She pointed to the left, slightly above the cortile. "That Bottero woman owns the yellow one up there, and over there"—she swept her hand around and muttered through clenched teeth—"the Fiores. Sara Fiore is the one I know who is close to the Jewess from Turin. I've seen her here in the village."

Baldo's heart leapt. "When!" he demanded. "When did you last see her here?" He broke out in a cold sweat. Was she here? Should he search the premises?

By her crooked smile on her pencil-thin lips, Baldo could tell Cinzia enjoyed his shock, knowing something he did not. Oh yes, he would deal with her. But first, he had to deal with the Jewess and anyone hiding her.

"Three years ago, I think. Not recently. I don't come up here so often now. Too busy in Alba."

Gunther turned to the soldiers standing beside the armored vehicle, a mixture of Blackshirts and Nazis, and barked orders. "Search the place! Both houses."

The searchers scattered. Two to each cascina and two to the barn and cantina. Baldo's two Blackshirts, Lugar P08s at the ready, disappeared into the nearby Fiore cascina. Through the open door, they heard a woman scream.

"That didn't take long. Sounds like your boys found something, Volpe." Gunther, with Cinzia and Baldo on his heels, headed inside.

A plump elderly woman stood in the cascina's tinello, her hands raised above her head, a gun at her head. A small child, sitting on pillows by the fire, wailed.

"You handle this Volpe. Your men found her." Gunther walked toward the child, who ran screaming from him to the woman who struggled to lift her into her arms. He pulled out his cigarette case, lit one, and dropped into Nico's chair by the fire. "This might take a while. Sit, old woman!"

Giuseppina, her eyes wide and face ashen, sank into the chair where she had been dozing when the gun-wielding brutes burst into the cascina.

Baldo rushed to Giuseppina, menacing her. "Who are you?" he snapped.

"I'm..." Giuseppina choked on her words. Trembling, Anna, clung to her, muffled wails rising from her face buried against Giuseppina's heaving chest.

"Well?" he barked.

"I'm the housekeeper. There." She pointed a trembling finger toward Cascina Asili. "The family is out for the day. I'm sitting with the child."

Baldo waved off the two Blackshirts. "Search the house!" He turned his attention back to Giuseppina. "Where are they?"

Giuseppina winced at the sound of the jackboots stomping overhead, doors slamming, furniture being upended. She called out from her heart to the Madonna. *Oh, Mary, Mother of Jesus, protect this child. I am old, but please protect dearest Anna.* "The women are in Alba. Signor Fiore is in the vineyards, pruning. I am...I am Madama Cornelia Bottero's housekeeper." The mere mention of Madama Lia's name helped strengthen Giuseppina's resolve. Her words came easier. "She is a very powerful woman in Alba. An acquaintance of Major Volker von Ebnerberg, the army commander of Langhe."

Baldo's and Gunther's eyes met. Baldo had not considered that Cornelia Bottero was already under the watchful eye of the Wehrmacht. There was no need to contact them before he set his appointment with the woman. The SS needed no one's permission to carry out searches for Jews and black marketers. Perhaps they had shown no courtesy to the aristocratic major, but they did not need his authority for the visit.

One of the SS soldiers called out from the entrance. "We searched the other house, the barn, the cantina, the yard. Nothing. No one is about."

"Enough of this. Where is Sara Fiore, old woman?" Cinzia had stepped out of the shadows and stood next to Baldo, interrupting his interrogation. He skewered her with his eyes. "She's lying. She knows more."

Giuseppina had not seen Sara for nearly two months. This was the first time she was questioned on her whereabouts, but she was prepared. The truth flowed from her mouth. "Signora *Bosco* is a nurse. She travels around to where she's needed."

"Isn't that her brat? What sort of mother would leave her child?" Cinzia shot Giuseppina a malevolent glare, making no attempt to mask her loathing for Sara.

Giuseppina pursed her lips. Her cheeks burned. "Signora Bosco is a dedicated nurse. She's an angel." Giuseppina wanted to stand, to stare *face-en-face* with this evil woman, but she was too weak to rise from the chair with Anna clinging onto her, the child's tight grip around her neck now painful. "This is her daughter, Anna." She spat the words, her jaw clenched. "Hers and her sainted husband, Francesco." She managed to cross herself and Anna. The woman's witch-like face darkened and a storm in her eyes raged at the mention of Francesco's name. So she knew him, did she?

The two Blackshirts returned to the tinello. Nothing had been found.

"Well, Volpe, it seems your prized informer led you to an old woman and a kid. I hope she does better next time. Let's go."

Baldo followed Schliessen out of the Fiore cascina. He stopped at the door, took one more look, turning the eyes of the hunter on everything before him. The Fiore family might lead him to Doretta Giordano. For sure, Sara Fiore could. The old woman was lying. The Jewess and the child's mother were together. That he knew. But where? The search today had been fruitless, but he would be back. And he would have Strega keep an eye on Cornelia Bottero. Somehow, they were all connected. He sensed it as if the cascina tinello were a schoolroom and all their names formed a column on the blackboard. When he found them, it would be a huge catch with many names to erase all at once. No woman was immune from a firing squad.

CHAPTER 41

Alta Langa
August 17, 1944

After she bathed, Doretta still had the stench of cow manure and urine in her hair. But with only a small amount of her beloved Fête des Roses perfume left and the danger of wearing such a strong scent on clandestine operations, she would have to endure it. And Sara, who now roomed with her since Talia and Ernst arrived, would have to endure it as well.

Cramped in the false bottom of the cattle railcar under the searing August sun, she had struggled for air during the daylong, round-trip journey to Turin from Cuneo. She had chased away thoughts of fellow Jews being packed into boxcars—as many as 150 in one car—for the final journey of their lives. The idea of their suffering clawed at her throat. Zia Silvana and her children would have faced the transports and extermination camps had Luca not rescued them from Germany years ago.

Three days earlier, among sacks of flour in Gianni's delivery truck, her journey to Turin via Cuneo had begun. She succeeded in finding her contact and then returned with a satchel filled with Cesare's and Sara's badly needed medical supplies. Hiding overnight in the cemetery in Cuneo, waiting for the cattle transport train, had been spooky, but that came with being a *staffetta*. She found the contact she knew only as Tiger waiting for her near the slaughterhouse outside Turin. The city of her birth had become a stranger to her. So many friends and relatives she had known in her childhood had vanished. But Madama Lia told her that Baldo Volpe was there, no doubt slithering around the ghost town with his Nazi comrades. Best for her not to be seen there.

Now, stinky as she was despite a long hot bath, Doretta relished her comfortable bed in the relative safety of Bossolaschetto. She pulled the sheet under her chin and rolled over, away from morning sunlight. Her body craved sleep, but her mind refused to rest. Thoughts of another winter like the last, with drifts up to fifteen feet high, chilled her. The Americans had requested that all the partisan groups stand down for the winter. Some, like the Autonomous Mauri group their men served in, obeyed. But not the Nazis and Fascists, who continued to comb the area for Jews and partisans. When the snows had melted, all hell broke loose across Langhe. The fine weather meant bloodshed as the partisans, joined by American OSS spies and escaped British POWs, took on well-armed German and Fascist battalions in Langhe. The notorious Black Brigades spread as much terror across occupied Italy as did the Nazis. Fighting in northern Italy intensified after Rome's liberation from Nazi occupation two months earlier. The enemy soared to new heights of brutality in reprisals for partisan activity. The Blackshirts worked relentlessly alongside their Nazi masters to arrest Jews. Doretta knew dangers were increasing with each mission.

But new life had come to Bossolaschetto. Talia's baby girl came on a rare occasion when Sara was home although Ernst was away fighting deep in Alta Langa. It was an easy birth, and Sara welcomed the change from tending the wounded. Bringing life into this world was bittersweet for her, Doretta thought. The rising generation would rebuild Europe when the nightmare ended, but a treacherous road lay ahead, particularly for Jews. How would the survivors return to a normal life in Christian Europe and rebuild it side by side with those who had turned a blind eye to what was done to them? Would they even want to?

Doretta heard familiar voices drifting from the forest below the cascina. Fabrizio Pratto and his Jewish "guests" often sought refuge in the nearby forest where they would await Paolina's all-clear sign—a bright red nightshirt hung on the clothesline on the valley-side terrace of the hotel. Although the Bossolasco municipal chief and mayor had aryanized the refugee Jews through their new identities, they took no chances when the Nazis arrived at Hotel Paradiso. Sometimes there was no warning, and the Jews found themselves eating in the hotel dining room with Nazis seated at nearby tables. They could hide in plain sight, but it was too risky. Fabrizio Pratto faced a similar risk as their Jewish guests did. Because of his youth, the stocky, handsome young man remained a target for forced recruitment into the murderous thug Rodolfo Graziani's Fascist paramilitary or for deportation to the labor camps in Germany or Poland. Paolina had charmed the Germans and convinced them there were no Jews or partisans in Bossolasco, but they still returned to dine on her traditional dishes—despite her alterations due to shortages—and to conduct occasional raids with Blackshirts in the area.

From the sounds of it, Hotel Paradiso had unwelcome visitors today. When Doretta finally dragged herself from her cocoon, she would take a walk to get the latest village news. For now, she would try to go back to sleep. But after only a few minutes, the sound of hooves pounding past the cascina jolted her awake. She bolted out of bed. Sara had already left.

She pulled on her trousers and boots and buttoned her blouse in a flash. Where had Sara gone? Last night, as was so often the case, Sara had slipped into bed late after tending to the wounded members of a group of *Garibaldini* partisans in San Benedetto Belbo. There were many different partisan groups in the area, and she tended to them all. Yet Sara was supposed to rest a few days before heading out again. What had happened?

Doretta raced down the stairs. No one was about. Only the click with each swing of the pendulum of Madama's ancient clock broke the silence. A note from her mamma lay on the kitchen table.

Cara, I hope you slept well. Elena, Talia, and I have gone foraging in the forest. The baby is with us. Pipo and Ornella have gone to Dogliani to barter their eggs. Baci, Mamma.

She grabbed a hunk of bread and tore into it as she sprinted in the direction of muffled voices, into the forest where the Bossolasco group usually hid. Fabrizio was not among them, and only seven of the thirty were there, all agitated and speaking rapidly over one another.

"*Aspettate! State zitti!*" She pleaded with them to quiet. "What's going on? Where is Fabrizio?"

The eldest of the group, the first to arrive from Ferrara in the autumn of 1943, spoke over the other men. "Germans and Fascists showed up at the hotel this morning during colazione," he said. "They weren't there to eat. There was no warning. Signora Paolina hid signor Fabrizio behind crates of wine in the room in the basement, you know, where that artist from Savona paints?"

Doretta needed facts, not a tour of the Paradiso. "But where is everyone else?"

"We escaped out the back door of the hotel, but the others were in the dining room. Trapped. We saw a partisan run to the communal bread oven to hide."

If the Nazis discovered the Jews, the Prattos, their guests, and…Ida, they would all be shot. It was Monday. Ida was there.

"How long ago did you leave the hotel?"

"About two hours ago. Still no sign of signora Paolina's red nightshirt sign. But we saw signora Sara."

"You did? Where?"

"Here. She came from the cascina to see us. About an hour ago. Alosio… you know, the little boy from the village the partisans call Purru? He had a message for signora Sara…news of a *rastrellamento* at a farm between Serravalle Langhe and Cissone. Blackshirts. And the Nazis. She rushed off."

Doretta's mind raced. Sara? Riding off alone to the scene of a rastrellamento, no doubt a reprisal? What if they had not left by the time she got there? And what if the soldiers that conducted the raid had also stopped in Bossolasco that morning? Cesare had moved to the hospital in Cortemilia before she left for Turin. Ernst, Luca, and Michele had gone on a mission to Liguria with others from the Autonomous brigade—railway sabotage, she feared. They had left over a week ago, and she didn't know when they would return. The women had to fend for themselves.

She dashed back to the house, grabbed her bike, and took off up the hill. Then she pulled up short. Not knowing where the raid took place—only the general direction—meant that she would have to ride along the main road. The area was crawling with Nazis and Blackshirts. Papers! She had forgotten her identification card. It was risky to have an assumed name, but to be caught without her papers would mean a trip to the barracks in Alba where further scrutiny could prove deadly. Within minutes, winded already, but her identification card in her trousers' pocket, she resumed her climb up the hill and sped off to Serravalle Langhe.

That morning, only cartun and farm trucks passed her as she struggled with the rusty old bike along the main road. When was the new bicycle Madama Lia had promised arriving? As a staffetta, a bike was her only transport to carry messages and small weapons as far afield as Cortemilia to the east and La Morra to the north. Thoughts of her early spring mission, when she pulled a small milk cart behind her to Murazzano ten miles away, helped keep her panic at bay. The false bottom of the pails had been stuffed with rounds of ammunition. That time, a German patrol stopped her on her return trip along the twisting road. They were Wehrmacht soldiers, less menacing than the Waffen-SS and Gestapo but dangerous all the same. Boys Michele's age.

Her fluttering long eyelashes, an Aryan name on her identification card, and no apparent stereotypical Jewish features, freed her from further inspection. It had shaken her, but getting past her first encounter with a German patrol and seeing how easy it was to charm them emboldened her. She had worn a sweater that day, but once summer warmth arrived, she rode with revealing tops and often in a skirt. Although her mamma didn't approve, she would use any advantage she had. She knew some slept with the enemy, but never would she go beyond flirting.

Twenty minutes later, when she arrived in the *frazione* of Manere, past the trees lining the road, she could see across the valley toward Cissone. It was a clear day with endless vistas. Smoke! Something was ablaze not far past Serravalle. At least she had some indication of where she was going. She had no idea what she would find or what she would do when she arrived, but she was certain that Sara would already be there.

Doretta pedaled through Serravalle, her strength waning from fighting the cumbersome bike and the panic that weighed her down, turned in the direction of Cissone and then coasted a short distance until something caught her eye. Ahead on the left, inside a small grove of acacia trees, she spied a riderless Zeus standing ground-tied. Sara's medical saddlebags were still attached, but she was nowhere to be seen. Doretta pulled her bike into the trees. Eyes closed, the stocky horse, his black coat now sunburned and brown, dozed, his lower lip hanging, twitching his ears as he fended off flies. Still, there was no sign of Sara. Doretta crept deeper into the brush until she came upon her, crouched near the clearing. She gasped as the horror of the conflagration below came into view. The barn and haystacks were ablaze, but the cascina was untouched. As she stepped closer, the crunch of sun-dried canes under foot alerted Sara. She sprang up, swung about, her two hands clutching a Beretta pistol aimed squarely at Doretta's chest.

"Sara! What in the name—?"

"Shh...down!" Doretta stooped and made her way next to Sara. They sat together at the edge of the grove, perched above a steep embankment that dropped to the valley floor. Nothing obstructed their view of the burning farm. "You don't believe I'm going to ride alone day and night through the countryside unarmed, do you? Neither should you." She holstered her gun and picked twigs and leaves out of Doretta's hair. "Don't think for a moment every partisan stands for good. They aren't all like our men. By the way, your brother's an excellent teacher." She gasped and grabbed Doretta's hand at the sound of a single shot of gunfire below. "They must still be shooting animals. Target practice. What are you doing here, anyway?"

"The Paradiso refugees told me that Purru had come with a message for you about a reprisal. Why didn't you wake me? This is not something either of us should do on our own."

"No time. I could only get this far without being spotted. Look, they're still there. That's the Vento family. Such kind people my nonna Beatrice knew well. Purru said it started shortly after daybreak. What time is it now?"

"I heard nine chimes of the church bells when I came through Serravalle. That wasn't long ago."

Sara handed her field glasses to Doretta, who gasped at the sight of two immobile cows on their sides and a flock of sheep looking as though their beige woolen coats had been splashed with red paint. Dead chickens littered the barnyard. "Did you see their vehicles? I see the Nazi flag. Must be SS. And I'm sure the Blackshirts are with them." Doretta handed the glasses back to Sara. She'd seen enough of many different groups vying for the most kills.

"Do you think these could be the same soldiers who leveled Belbo on the fourth? My God, but they killed many villagers."

Doretta had heard about that reprisal. She had had nightmares of the carnage she witnessed in the aftermath of others. "All because the Nazis believed a partisan lair was nearby. The villagers had nothing to do with them." That was usually the case. The occupiers used their cruelest weapon of all—civilian reprisals meant to be a warning to all—and it did not matter to them whether the villagers had indeed aided the partisans. Instead of turning them against the partisans as the occupation dragged on and reprisals continued, it strengthened civilian resistance.

"I tended to some of those people. There were children Anna's age with crazed looks in their eyes, terrified of every loud sound." At her mention of Anna's name, Sara tugged at the dried grass. "Unimaginable horror for them to witness," she said, her words barely audible, her eyes closed.

"I heard that many of the villagers scattered into the wheat fields but that not all escaped the machine gun fire."

"That's what I heard, but I don't know all the details. Apparently, there's a new brigade of Italians, Slavs, and French that's been carrying out reckless raids against the Germans." Sara froze when more gunfire echoed from the valley. "They're putting the civilian population at risk. If it was them, it wouldn't be the first reprisal they triggered…and it won't be the last."

They sat in silence for some minutes, both shocked by the scene below them.

"This twists my heart, Doretta. All I can do is sit and wait until the monsters leave. I'm powerless to help."

"Don't say that, Sara. You don't know what's happened down there. And anyway, you're the only one who can help them. But instead of going all over Alta Langa, from village to village, why not work with Cesare? You'd be safer in Cortemilia. I hear the Nazis don't raid the hospital…well, that is unless they're on the hunt for someone they believe is there."

"The hospital isn't for me. Zeus and I are happier on our own. With so many different partisan brigades in Alta Langa, some seem as ready to fight each other as they are the Nazis and Fascists. I don't want to be aligned with any of them, but of course my heart's with our own men."

Doretta had seen something of the partisan turf battles, the arguments, often violent, over which brigade would execute prisoners. Some raided farms, helping themselves to the animals and crops, while others ate in Paradiso without paying. She worried a new civil war would erupt when this one against the Fascists ended. "But you tend to them all and the civilians who are caught in the crossfire, like those poor souls down there."

Sara wrapped her arms around her knees and buried her face against them, shutting out Doretta and the sight below.

"You're already a legend here, Sara." Silence.

Not changing her posture, Sara glanced sideways at Doretta, a smile teasing the edges of her mouth. "Grazie, cara. I'm no angel. I'm only doing my job." She laid back and stared at the cloudless sky tainted with tendrils of thick black smoke rising from the barn and haystacks. An eerie stillness had settled on the farm. The cascina remained untouched although the flames from the nearby barn licked at its walls. The murderers had not left. A few armed soldiers lingered next to the vehicles. No one else was about. Had the family been taken inside the cascina for interrogation?

All Sara and Doretta could do was wait.

The *rat-a-tat-tat* of machine gun fire erupted in the valley. The cascina's roof exploded in flames. Sara sprang to her feet and sprinted to Zeus. Doretta raced after her.

"Sara! Where are you going?"

"To the farm. They need me. Someone might still be alive." She struggled to free herself, but Doretta grabbed her other arm and held tight to her thin wrists.

"Are you crazy? Stay here. You'll do no one any good." Sara jerked away.

Doretta tackled her and pinned her to the ground, doing her best to dodge Sara's flailing legs. "No! Ouch!" Sara landed her boot squarely on Doretta's shin. "Stop it! I…will…not…let you go, Sara. You'll get us both killed. I beg you."

"Let me go, I have to get closer."

"No, Sara."

A crimson flush transformed Sara's fair complexion as she struggled against Doretta. Fury flashed in her eyes. Doretta released her wrists and sat back on her heels. It was no use fighting her. But Sara didn't move. Instead, she started to cry.

"Francesco…oh my God, Francesco!" she repeated between gasps. So that was it. Their sixth anniversary, the day after the Belbo reprisal, had passed without Sara uttering a word about it. They had been apart for as long as they had been together. Had Sara been harboring hope that he was still alive?

As her ragged sobs continued, Doretta worried that someone might hear them. She sat next to Sara and pulled her into her arms, rubbed her back, and whispered to her.

"I know, cara. I know. You're so strong—we forget you may be hurting too. Cara…cara mia. Shh…"

Sara's body went limp. Only soft whimpers rose, her breathing eased. In the distance, the familiar hum of armored vehicles lumbering up the hill grew louder. Doretta panicked. They were close to the road, but still hidden within the trees and tall grass. Trees shielded Zeus from view to anyone coming up the hill. There was no time to run further into the trees. She grabbed Sara and they lay there, clutching one another. Doretta craned her neck to see the passing Nazi staff car, hateful red flags flapping, and gasped. Dressed in a gray-green Italian SS uniform and puffing on a cigarette in the rear seat of the staff car, his long, thin neck and chiseled chin were unmistakable. Baldo Volpe had arrived in Alta Langa. Minutes before, he had orchestrated a bloodbath on Langhe soil against innocent civilians. How many others had he killed?

Sara had recovered her composure. Doretta released her this time although she doubted there was anything to be done for the farm's inhabitants. Once the convoy had passed, they sprang to their feet. Sara tapped Zeus's left front leg and, as Doretta watched, he sank to the ground. Sara sprang aboard and he rose. She turned to Doretta and shrugged. "How else can I mount him out here?" And off Zeus went at a dead run with the Angel of Alta Langa on his back.

Doretta's stomach had lurched at the sight of Baldo Volpe passing so close to her. He would stop at nothing to get to her. As she stood, wondering whether she should follow Sara, don Bartolo, the parish priest in Serravalle coasted by on his bicycle. She jumped on hers and followed him.

When they arrived, they saw amidst the carnage that Sara stood clutching a hysterical child, possibly Anna's age, turning her away from the sight of her murdered family. From all appearances, she was the lone survivor. The fires had consumed all but the stone walls of the cascina and barn. Ten bodies lay in unnatural positions against the blackened wall of the farmhouse. To the far left, a woman and two teenage girls lay together. Had the mother tried to shield her daughters? An elderly couple had crumpled nearby, as though having died in each other's arms. On the other end, four small boys, the youngest not much older than the child in Sara's arms, and a man who had to be their papà, lay facing the wall. *I bastardi!* They had been shot in the back as traitors. Doretta raced from the scene to the nearby orchard and collapsed on all fours. She heaved, hoping her vomit would exorcise the evil images now burned in her mind. Blackness overtook her.

When she awoke, Sara was by her side, the sun high in the sky above, blinding her. Tender strokes of a soft cloth across her face wiped away dirt, vomit, and dried, salty tears.

"Oh God, Sara. I'm so sorry."

"About what? Being human?" She glanced at the bodies, still as they had found them. "There's nothing I can do here other than get you on your feet."

"Where's the little girl?"

"Over there. Poor child." She pointed to a woman holding her and talking with don Bartolo and others who had arrived. "She and her husband are neighbors. They were there"—she pointed to a grove of hazelnut trees only a few hundred feet down the hill from the farm—"scooping up nuts when those bastards arrived. Terrified to move, they lay on the ground." Sara rubbed her eyes and turned away from the scene. "They witnessed it all," she said, her voice unsteady, her disgust evident in her pained expression.

"Any idea why they chose this family?"

"Totally random. That's how it's done. Yesterday, the partisans—I don't know which brigade—killed a German officer between Cissone and Roddino. Ten to one—that's the rule. The child was number eleven, so I guess that's why they let her live. I wish I could say it was uncommon, but…"

They knew such brutality was not limited to Piemonte.

"I know about the ten-to-one law, Sara. Remember the Ardeatine Caves in Rome in March? Three hundred thirty innocents murdered for thirty-three

SS officers and soldiers. That was swift reprisal." Everyone knew about that massacre; the Nazis made sure of it.

"Well, I heard of another reprisal in Sant'Anna di Stazzema in Tuscany just a few days ago. I think two hundred women, children, and elderly. The numbers don't seem real."

"Enough talk, Sara. Now I'm scared. What if they return? We should go now."

"You're right. Don Bartolo will care for their souls and inform their relatives. He already said prayers over each victim."

Doretta's stomach lurched yet again, and spots from a splitting headache danced before her eyes. How would she make it home?

"Sara…" She started to tell her she'd seen Baldo Volpe but hesitated. Although she didn't want to alarm Sara, she feared Baldo was stalking her in Alta Langa. They were all at risk, so it might be best if Doretta left Bossolaschetto. Madama Lia was certain it was Baldo and an SS Nazi who terrorized Giuseppina and Anna last November on the same day they had met her at the mill. Whether he connected the Fiore family with her, she didn't know. Although Madama suspected Cinzia Strega had a hand in it, she had said nothing to Sara. If Cinzia was involved, Baldo was sure to know about Sara. Would he use her as bait to trap her?

"Let's go home, Doretta."

Doretta decided it was too important to wait. They must not be seen together. "No, Sara, I have to tell you something. Baldo Volpe is here in Alta Langa. I saw him in the staff car of the convoy." Sara stared at her as though in disbelief.

"Are you sure it was him? Why is he here and not Turin?"

"Because he knows of Luca and that I might be here with him, I suppose. If Cinzia Strega is working with him, that means he also knows about you, and…" There was no turning back. Sara deserved to know the truth. "He knows about you and your family, perhaps even Madama."

"So it was Volpe and the SS at Asili last year? Oh Doretta!"

She grabbed Sara's hands. "Listen, Sara, we have to leave. Now. If he saw us together, well, nothing would stop him from going after your family and Madama. We should leave here separately and pray he's not spying on us now."

Eyes wide, the two friends backed away from one another, each looking for her solitary way home.

CHAPTER 42

Asili
Sunday, November 5, 1944

Although born and raised in Alba, Giuseppina's heart lay in Asili where long ago she helped the newlywed Cornelia Bottero make her home in the country. In Asili, Cornelia discovered her child was on the way. Later, she retreated there when she sought solace from grief that visited her often in her youth. And now, since the Armistice, Asili was Giuseppina's home. She considered herself lucky to have left Alba long before the beginning of the partisan battles with the Fascists and Nazis for control of the city. In Asili, the twenty-three days of the partisan siege of Alba that began in October was a world away.

The visit from the SS and Blackshirts nearly a year ago had been terrifying, as she had been on her own and never would have forgiven herself if something had happened to Anna. But the young one helped her to recover and, so full of life, had drawn her back into life in Asili.

Despite her frailties, Giuseppina stayed busy, preparing the harvest feast, scant though it was compared to happier times before rationing. Today, in celebration of the harvest, she and Gianni would sit at the long, elegant table with everyone else. She had even put on her best dress and tied on a fresh, crisp apron with scalloped edges.

Anna, the reddish-blonde-haired child with eyes like fiordalisi, the purplish-blue flowers that blanketed the fields in late spring, closely resembled her mamma who in turn bore a striking resemblance in personality and looks to little Giulia Bottero. It was as though God had returned Giulia to Madama as Anna, a child sage beyond her years. Since that day the SS charged in,

Anna wanted only to be with Giovanna, to protect her, she told Lia. But it was Giuseppina she sought when her nightmares frightened her.

The most recent one disturbed Giuseppina as well. It was hard to calm the child, especially when she cried out for her mamma. Often, Anna dreamt of Nazis chasing her mother, which was no different than what Giuseppina feared for Sara. Why had she left her child, her family, and the relative safety of Asili for such a dangerous life in Alta Langa? Why follow those partisans and not the ones here in Barbaresco, if supporting the *resistenza* was her goal? Whenever she broached the subject with Madama Lia, she simply smiled and said, "Sara is Sara. She is answering a call only she has heard, and she believes her family is safer with her far away." Giuseppina would be happy to see Sara again, to see them all again, back safely in Asili. Maybe God would answer her prayers to send back another one He took too soon. Francesco belonged here with Sara and Anna.

The heavy wooden door of the cortile protested as it opened. Giuseppina did not want to live behind a locked door, so Gianni refused to oil the hinges. Better to know whenever someone entered, he claimed.

"Giuseppina…Giusi…*dove sei*?" came Anna's insistent call from the downstairs entrance.

"*Sono qui*, carina, in cucina." Sara had never liked to cook, but already at four years of age, Anna loved the feel of wet dough between her fingers, of pushing stuffing into agnolotti with her tiny fingers. And today, Anna wanted to help prepare for yet another pranzo della vendemmia. The harvest had been poor, but they had much for which to give thanks. They had lived through the first year of Nazi occupation and, if the news on Radio London was correct, they would be free of the Nazis and Fascists before the vines flowered in June.

Anna ran to Giuseppina and wrapped her small arms around as much of her ample thighs as she could. "*Bacio*, Giusi." A demand for a kiss always followed her hugs.

"Why aren't you at Mass, Anna? You're not alone, are you?"

"They went. Nonna let me come here with you. It's too cold for me to walk."

Giuseppina chuckled. When had it ever been too cold for Anna? She loved nature no matter the season. But Giuseppina was happy to have the company.

"Here, Anna. Pull your stool by me. I'll lift you."

"No!" she snapped. "Umm, scusi…no, grazie, Giusi." Giuseppina spied her flushed cheeks. "I can do it myself. Grazie." And there was Sara. Independent.

"No, dear, it will topple over. Soon you'll have to climb up yourself. You're getting so big." As she bent to lift her little helper, a dizzy spell hit her, and pain shot through her arms. She grabbed the counter and steadied herself. "Oh my, Anna, you *are* a big girl. Here, why don't I hold the stool and you show me how you can climb up. But never do that alone. Understand?"

It had been hard for Giuseppina to rise that morning, and her stomach only tolerated a small piece of bread for colazione. Well, it was no wonder, after standing hours in the kitchen the previous day. She had prepared twenty-nine harvest lunches at Asili, but this year she found the work harder. She thought to call Madama Lia's cook, Alma, from Altavilla, but she refused to admit she needed help.

At least Gianni was home for the weekend. Although two years older, he had more energy these days. He needed it to keep up with Madama Lia, who worked harder than ever but said less and less about her whereabouts. Giuseppina missed Gianni during the week when he remained in Alba to deliver flour, often to Bossolasco and Cuneo, a new task he had undertaken since the Armistice.

Well, if this is the last harvest under occupation, may it be the last harvest lunch we see no beef for a bollito misto and only two eggs to make tajarin for eleven. The month before, the partisans helped themselves to the steer Nico had bought as a calf, and eggs went missing from the henhouse most mornings. At least they left a few for the families. The various brigades fought against occupation, but many were bandits, preying on civilians and refugees. Between their thefts and the fear of reprisal for their actions against the Nazis and Fascists, farm families lived in constant fear.

"Here child, you lay out the stuffing for the agnolotti. I'll pinch." She handed Anna a pan filled with the leftovers of the week's meals from both families that she had kept in their new icebox. Nothing went to waste these days. Fortunately, from his last delivery of flour in Valle Grana, Gianni was able to bring her some Castelmagno cheese from the Martin family in Valliera, which she had not tasted in years. With the cheese and the potatoes he brought her from the mercato in Alba, *gnocchi con fonduta di Castelmagno* would be a welcome treat.

"Giusi…" Anna appeared deep in thought over something other than placing bits of food on the long, thin sheets of dough.

"What is it, child?"

"When is Papà coming home? He said soon. Do you think for *Natale*?"

Giuseppina dropped her only two eggs into a basin, where they cracked. The queasiness that had plagued her all morning intensified as she watched the red yolks spread. "What do you mean, Anna? Where did you see…?" They had learned long ago not to dismiss Anna's visions, her dreams, as merely a child's active imagination.

"Last night. He comes to me, but only when I am sleeping. He said soon he'll come home."

These questions about Francesco came more frequently. Perhaps it was because Anna was older and more aware of his absence. But Giuseppina found answering such questions difficult.

"Well, cara…" She didn't want to dash her hopes. Although they had heard nothing from Francesco for three years, and they had received no report that he was alive, neither had he been reported dead. "The war hasn't finished in Russia, carina, so it's still hard for him to write."

Anna's expression softened and her concentration shifted to the long strips of dough and the small, uneven balls of stuffing she had laid out on them. Giuseppina delighted in teaching the child the ways of the cucina piemontese.

"One day, Anna, you will make your husband and children very happy with your cooking."

"Oh no, Giusi. I won't marry. I want to be a tota like zia Luce and zia Gio. I will be a doctor." There was Sara, once more. She had married for love, but her other love—her passion and her gift from God—was the healing arts. Anna wanted to take it a step further. If any woman could, Anna would be the one.

"But Anna, look at your mamma. She is a nurse *and* a mother. You can have babies too."

"I will be too busy! Like Mimi. I don't want to leave babies alone like she does."

Giuseppina trembled and spots danced before her eyes. Now she had a throbbing headache. This was no time to get sick.

Giuseppina looked up and saw Madama Lia at the kitchen door, arms folded, a questioning expression on her face. How much had she heard? Regardless, she saved her from any further discussion with Anna about her parents.

"Anna, show me what you're making," Lia said as she kissed her cheek. "Oh, very good! I'm *very* impressed. Here, let me help you off the stool so you can wash your hands." Lia studied Giuseppina's face, the pearls of perspiration above her mouth. Her fair complexion had turned ashen these last days.

"I managed to get some scraps of meat from the Contessa's cook. It's not my usual bollito misto but tasty all the same."

"You've been working too hard on this lunch, Giuseppina. But I know it will be wonderful."

Gianni entered with an armful of wood he dropped next to the putagè. "It's beginning to snow. I thought I'd drive to the village to pick up the Fiores from Mass. Nico's in the barn. I'll be back shortly."

"Very kind of you, Gianni. I know don Emilio will scold me for missing Mass this morning. He should be here to join us for lunch shortly before noon."

Lia turned to leave then looked back at Giuseppina. Since the summer, she only saw her longtime housekeeper and companion on weekends. There had been a noticeable change in her since the previous Sunday.

"Where are your rosy cheeks these days?"

"Oh, Madama, I'm fine. It's just so hot in here with the putagè fired and those pots of boiling water."

Lia turned to Anna who stood scrutinizing the two women.

"Come, Anna. Let's let Giuseppina finish. You can help me lay the table. Wouldn't you like that?"

Anna whooped and scampered out of the kitchen to the large dining room overlooking the valley. She loved handling the heavy silver cutlery. No one other than the Contessa had such fine things.

This year, Lia was hosting the lunch. It suited her since Cascina Asili had a real dining room and a larger table with chairs, not benches as in the Fiore cascina. And today, for some reason, she wanted to use all the china, cutlery, and crystal she had inherited from her mother. Why would her mother's memory weigh so heavy on her mind these last days? Lia was all too aware of being the last of the line, the final possessor of the land and the luxuries. After the war, she would give this her attention. Cascina Asili must never fall into the hands of strangers.

"Look, Lili! Look! It's snowing!"

Lia smiled and shook her head. Only Anna called her that. It pleased her that the child had a unique name for her. She walked to the window and embraced Anna.

"Come Anna, I'll show you how to lay the table." When she opened the doors of the sideboard, Anna gasped.

"Beautiful, Lili."

Yes, it was, she had to admit. She had inherited her German great-great-grandmother's Meissen porcelain service for fourteen. What would nonna Alexandra say about the Germans today? The Baccarat crystal wine glasses had been a wedding present from her mamma. Ludovica Ferri was pragmatic. "Cornelia, if you are going to make the best wine, you must drink it from the best crystal." And, of course, there was the sterling silver cutlery from Turin's finest silversmith of the early 1800s, Carlo Balbino. It was also a wedding present handed down from her maternal bisnonna. These were dishes on which the women of her family had dined for generations. They connected her with the women she never knew but whose blood flowed through her veins and whose own strength had flowed into her. She slid the heavy silver chest from the top of the sideboard and placed it on the table. When she opened it, Anna gasped.

"Here, Sar…umm, Anna, here. I'll put everything on the table and make a sample for you. You go and do the same at each place."

"Lili, why so pretty today?"

"Why not, Anna? All these beautiful things are very special to me, but nothing is more special than the people I love, just like you."

"And Mimi?"

Clattering of metal on the floor in the kitchen startled Lia. Giuseppina was anxious today, more so than usual when preparing special meals in Asili.

"Yes, carina, your mamma. We should make every day a celebration." Being with Anna was like stepping back in time. Although Sara was never interested in such things, she was a curious child, a loving child. She missed her terribly. Though she saw her occasionally in Bossolaschetto, there was never time for merely sitting with a glass of wine and talking. Most of all, she missed their long rides together through the vineyards, fields, and forests of Barbaresco.

Never had Lia imagined that the gift of Zeus would have such a profound impact on so many lives. Nor had Lia considered how far-reaching her support of Sara's education would be. Would she have still done so had she known these nursing skills would be put to use on the resistance battlefield? Best to leave those matters to God. "Oh, Anna, I forgot the silver salt cellars. Run to the kitchen and ask Giuseppina for them, please. They're in a box in the larder."

Lia held the sterling forks in one hand and counted them. *One, two*— Anna's scream sent them crashing to the floor. She dashed to the kitchen and found Giuseppina sprawled on the floor, eyes closed, boiled potatoes scattered about her, a pot, probably the noise she heard, overturned on the floor. Anna was kneeling beside her, shaking her, pleading with her.

"Giusi, Giusi, wake up. Giusi." She turned to Lia, her eyes imploring as she continued to shake Giuseppina's arm. "Lili, don't let Giusi die."

She knelt beside Anna and took Giuseppina's wrist. Her pulse was weak, but still there.

"Anna, listen to me. Run—find your nonno—in the barn. Anna! Now." Lia sat, slid her crossed legs beneath Giuseppina, and cradled her beloved companion's head in her lap. She was powerless to help. Such an unfamiliar feeling. She bent forward and kissed Giuseppina's brow. "Giusi, cara Giusi, hang on. Don't leave me. Not now. It's too soon."

In no time, Lia heard more than one set of heavy footsteps rushing up the stairs. Gianni had returned from Barbaresco and now stood anchored at the door to kitchen. Luciana dashed past him. Anna darted in and retook her place at Giuseppina's side. Neither Lia nor Luciana sent her away. After what she had been through with Giuseppina, she deserved this moment with her.

Luciana settled beside Giuseppina and placed her fingers against her throat, moving them about, searching for a pulse. Her expression darkened.

"What happened?"

"I don't know, Luce. She looked pale to me. I was going to ask you to check her after lunch. But..."

Giuseppina stirred, her eyelids fluttered. Anna leaned across her ample chest to hug and kiss her.

"Giusi, I knew you wouldn't leave me."

Don Emilio, early as usual for lunch at Cascina Asili, rushed to Giuseppina's side.

"Suor Luciana, tell me." Luciana looked at him then bowed her head in prayer. Time was running out to administer the last sacrament. He fished out of his pocket his small stole and the purple silk-covered vessel of sacred oil he always carried with him. Luciana slipped from her neck the crucifix she always wore and handed it to don Emilio. As she watched the priest hold it to Giuseppina's lips then begin anointing her body, Lia worried the rite would take longer than the time she had left. Please, dear Lord. Not yet. Her breathing slowed. A rattle now came with each breath as the end grew near.

Once the kind priest finished, he pressed Luciana's crucifix into Giuseppina's hand and gave his place to Gianni, stunned to see his beloved wife leaving him. Giuseppina, her eyes barely open, tried to touch him, but her hand fell back. He took it, placed her palm against his wet cheek, and kissed her good-bye.

Her eyes fluttered and closed again. Lia gazed at Giuseppina, her face so peaceful. Had she passed? But then she opened them, wider than before, and glanced at Anna, the edges of her mouth twitching as she struggled to smile. "Carissima Giulia. Always such a dear child. So good…so good to see you again."

Lia shuddered. Was Giulia here among them, ready to walk with her into the afterlife? Or was it merely Giuseppina's mind slipping away? Giuseppina struggled with each breath, but managed to gaze at the tears pooling in Lia's eyes.

"Cornelia…my child. I…I love you. Always so kind to me." She struggled harder to speak. Lia prayed she would overcome this. But she knew better. "Take care of…of Anna…" She gasped for air. "Look after…her. Soon…she and Gio will need you…more than ever."

With those words, Giuseppina's chest fell and rose no more. Lia placed her fingers on Giuseppina's eyelids and closed them.

Gianni, the strong, reticent man Lia had known even longer than Giuseppina, wept like a child. She leaned to kiss his cheek then slipped a pillow Luigia had given her under Giuseppina's head. After Nico helped her to her feet, she took one more glance at Giuseppina's body, her spirit now departed, and held out her hand. "Come, Anna, come with me."

With that, Lia and Anna walked out of the kitchen, hand in hand past the rest of the stunned Fiore family.

CHAPTER 43

Asili
Monday, November 6, 1944

The sun broke over Monte Silva, revealing a snow-blanketed landscape under a blue sky tinged with shades of pink and orange. But the late autumn beauty failed to brighten the mood at Asili. News of Giuseppina's death spread over the village grapevine and through the Ferri-Bottero family businesses as far away as Nizza Monferrato. The prior day, instead of a harvest lunch, Lia had hosted a wave of visitors who arrived at Cascina Asili to pay their respects to her beloved housekeeper. Those who knew her from Bossolaschetto to Alba to Asili deeply felt the loss of her maternal and cheerful presence. Only in death had modest Giuseppina been the focus of so much attention.

With no telephone service in Bossolasco, Lia sent word to Bossolaschetto on Sunday afternoon through her mulino foreman in Alba. "Giusi has passed away. Expect a delivery in the morning," was her cryptic message. Lia knew the risk to Sara if she returned for the funeral, but she had no reason to believe that anyone suspected Sara spent her prolonged absences anywhere other than the Alba hospital. On more than one occasion when a Nazi patrol came through the hospital, Sara happened to be there picking up supplies. Her infrequent visits to Asili with Luciana on the train from Alba should quash any suspicion. No partisan sympathizer had any fear of being denounced in Barbaresco—except, of course by Cinzia Strega's family. Though she lived in Alba, her family of informers in Barbaresco served her, and she in turn served Baldo Volpe.

An afternoon of receiving mourners and saying the rosario in the evening drained Lia of emotion and strength. Not since Stefano Olivero's passing nearly ten years earlier—in another lifetime—had she felt such emptiness. Only Luciana remained and, of course, Gianni, but he was her guardian, not her confidante. He and Giuseppina had promised Alessandro to look after her until he returned, but he had not. When Giulia died, they became the only people who connected Lia to Alessandro and her parents.

Lia had drifted off during the vigil, lulled by Luciana's soft entreaties to the Virgin. She opened her eyes at a noise in the kitchen, but it was not Giuseppina. Luciana, her head bowed, her lips moving in silent prayer as she fingered her rosary wrapped around the palm of her right hand, sat beside her. And there Giuseppina lay on the table now pushed against the wall, with chairs arranged in rows for mourners to gather. In Lia's elegant dining room, the setting for so many happy occasions, they should have celebrated Giuseppina's cooking that day, not mourned her passing.

Earlier, after the sun had set, Luciana had led the mourners in the rosario as only she could do. Luciana and Lia now remained in the room and held vigil, praying for the immortal soul of her beloved companion. Lia believed that Giuseppina remained safe in God's presence. Her prayers, instead, were offered for those that Giuseppina left behind, particularly the young ones she loved.

Luigia placed a tray of hot milk and *caffè* on the small table between the two women. Minutes after Lia and Anna left the kitchen the day before, she and Luciana assumed the responsibility of caring for Giuseppina's body. With Nico's help, Gianni had laid his beloved wife on their bed she had meticulously made that morning with only thoughts of a celebratory lunch. Luciana and Luigia set out washing her body with love and tenderness, preparing her for eternal rest. It touched Lia to watch the two sisters, much like Mary and Martha, lovingly caring for Giuseppina.

Lia squeezed Luigia's hand and peered into her serene eyes as she placed the steaming *caffè* before her. "Grazie, Luigia…grazie for all your help. You and Luce." She glanced back at Giuseppina's body. "Not the least for dressing Giuseppina so elegantly. She always loved that pink suit and the blue Hermès scarf I brought from Paris the year"—a lump in her throat trapped her words—"before the war. It was one of the first they produced. Giuseppina treasured it."

The wars. The first one stole the love of her life, and now the present one had invaded her homeland. Would the spilling of blood across Europe and the sacrificing of generations of young men ever cease? And what sort of future lay ahead for Anna, for Sara, for all in harm's way? So many questions.

Luciana straightened and rubbed her back. "Bondì, Lia. Bondì, Luigia. Oh, *caffè* Grazie." She sipped from the large porcelain breakfast cup and scanned the room. "Where is Anna?"

"She fell asleep on Madama's lap, so Nico carried her home. She was still sleeping with Giovanna when I left. I was here until shortly after midnight but needed a nap. I'll make sure everything's ready for the next visitation." That was Luigia's way of dealing with grief. She cooked and cleaned. Luciana prayed.

The outpouring of love for Giuseppina was precious to Lia, but the visits exhausted her and merely delayed the reality she would have to face once she returned from the cemetery to an empty house. Gianni was shy in the presence of so many people, so she did what she could to lessen the strain on him.

Lia stretched her legs and stood, her back aching after the long night spent on the small, hard chair. She rubbed her eyes and glanced at her watch. "Oh my. It's nearly eight. Where is Gianni?"

"He left with Nico for Alba about a half an hour ago. Nico hitched Romeo to the cartun. It looks as though the snow is melting fast, but he said it was too dangerous in the truck. They were going to Alba to fetch…" Luigia glanced at Giuseppina's body and took a deep, mournful breath. "The boards for her coffin." Nico had stood by Gianni from the moment he kissed his wife good-bye. The quiet farmer's compassion touched Lia's heart deeply. "Nico told him that he should stay behind, but Gianni insisted on going. He told Nico he had a delivery to make in Bossolasco. Madama, why today…" From Lia's expression, Luigia understood he had gone to bring Sara back to Asili. What a relief it would be to have her here! If only she would remain with them and not return to Alta Langa. She missed her eldest child greatly, but she knew that Sara had to continue her work there.

"Francesco left home to fight, to give his life in Russia for a war he didn't believe in. The least I can do, Mamma, is care for the resistance fighters in Alta Langa. Fighting to liberate us, to protect my child," she had said when she told her parents of her plans.

"But why Alta Langa?" she had asked her. Her answer that her work with partisans, Jewish refugees, and victims of reprisals was a threat to those at home had puzzled Luigia. Did that have anything to do with those horrid men who had burst into the cascina a year earlier?

Lia turned to Luciana, so calm and at peace from a life of prayer but so tired too. "Luce, you should go home and rest in bed for a few hours. Please. I'm going upstairs to do the same. We have two long days ahead of us." Lia kissed the sisters' cheeks, and left the room.

Two hours later, Lia woke from a deep sleep. Gianni, despite his grief, had insisted on going about his usual morning routine at Asili, lighting the stufetta in her room and leaving a basin of fresh water for her. He had not closed the shutters left open since she rose the previous morning. Now sunlight flooded the room. Had the message gotten through to Sara? She would know soon enough. Gianni planned to drive the delivery truck to Bossolasco where Sara would meet him at the Hotel Paradiso. He would return to Asili with her hidden by sacks of flour under the canvas in the back of the truck. They had devised that plan after Doretta discovered that Baldo Volpe was lurking in Alta Langa. It was too dangerous for a flour delivery truck to be seen at the cascina in Bossolaschetto often. But how would he get there if snow still covered the roads? Gianni was clever. She would not worry.

Hours later, refreshed and dressed in the only other mourning ensemble she owned, Lia was back in the sala. Luciana, who had not gone to rest, was busy at work in the kitchen with Luigia preparing plates of food, the sight of which reminded Lia that she had not eaten since colazione the previous morning. A piece of bread and some Castelmagno cheese Giuseppina had not yet melted was all she could stomach. Only Giuseppina could coax her to eat when she was too low to manage food. Now she was gone.

She looked around the kitchen filled with familiar aromas of Giuseppina's cooking. Except it was not hers. "How is Anna?" she asked.

Luigia raised her eyes from the wooden board on which she was arranging dried meats and cheese. "She's fine. With Giovanna. I don't believe she has truly comprehended what happened, yet."

"Don't be so sure, Luigia. She understands more than you realize. Look how she insisted on staying for the entire rosario. I had a long talk with her after we left the kitchen yesterday. She's like…" Lia hesitated.

Luigia had always been so kind to her. Would she herself have been so understanding had some other woman showered Giulia with gifts and love? And unwittingly, Lia had set Sara up for the dangers she faced as a nurse in harm's way. Now they both worried, separately. Death had come to Asili, and it was making Lia see danger everywhere.

Luigia finished her sentence. "You mean she's like Sara. Oh, Madama, that is so true. Anna is such a comfort to me, to us all, while Sara is away."

The hours flew past. Mourners filed through Asili to pay their respects, but Sara had yet to arrive. Nico had returned from Alba, reporting that the roads were passable yet slow going and at times treacherous. Fortunately, the temperature had risen, and the snow had melted fast on the still-warm ground. Nico and Silvio, his farm hand, had brought the coffin into the house and placed Giuseppina into it for her last night among them.

As the shadows grew longer, there was still no sign of Gianni. Lia's facial muscles hurt after the many hours of talking. The only person she wished to speak with had not yet arrived. Anna had been absent all day, so she pulled on her heavy woolen coat and boots and walked across the cortile to the Fiore cascina. It was the first time she'd been outside since the morning before when she went to the barn to visit her horses. The cold air shocked her, but she needed it. Fog was spreading through the valley, yet Gianni had not returned. She checked on Anna, whom Giovanna said had slept most of the day, occasionally waking in tears and calling for her mamma. The adults struggled with the suddenness of Giuseppina's death. How would a child perceive it?

As Lia returned home across the slushy cortile, headlights appeared at the end of the lane. It was Gianni. When he rolled up the canvas flap covering the truck bed, Lia saw that Sara had not returned alone. Luca and Cesare slid out and helped Sara from the truck. She raced to Lia who embraced Sara as she cried.

Sara stepped back and looked about. "Where's Anna, Madama? Gianni said she was the one who discovered Giuseppina."

"She's home with Giovanna, sleeping as she has all day. Poverina Anna. So brave."

The long, sad faces of Luca and Cesare mirrored so many she had seen in the past twenty-four hours. She squeezed Luca's hand, and he kissed her cheeks. "Luca, what a surprise. Bearded again, I see. And Cesare. How thoughtful— and risky—of you both to come."

"Winter's coming and, if these early storms are any indication, it'll be harsh. This may be the last we see of everyone before the spring when the Allies should be closer." Luca turned to Cesare and slapped him on his back. "At least the good doctor might get a break if the fighting is suspended for the winter, although I believe the Allies' call for us to stand down during the winter will merely increase the raids and reprisals. What do you think, Cesare?"

"Nothing will change, Luca," Cesare said, sadness in his voice. "Nothing changed last year, so why would it now? The steady stream of casualties will continue. With the embedded Allied agents, they'll continue to fight through the winter."

Lia looked past them to Gianni who, standing alone in the middle of the cortile, appeared lost. Although he spent many days away from Giuseppina in service to Lia, he had always known that she was waiting for him. "Gianni, was it because of the detour to Cortemilia you were so late?"

Gianni slid his cap off his head and walked toward her. "Yes, Madama. I thought…" He glanced at Sara, shifting his weight and fidgeting with his cap. "I'm sorry I'm late, but—"

Sara came to his rescue. "It was my idea, Madama. I thought it safer to come through the Belbo River valley and through Benevello and Treiso instead of Alba." She touched Cesare's shoulder. "And of course, we were so close to Cortemilia that we couldn't pass through without stopping to give Cesare the sad news. The decision to come was all his. It was slow going, and we ran into a partisan roadblock just before Cravanzana."

"Well, at least it wasn't a Nazi or Fascist stop."

"Oh, but, Madama," Sara interjected, "we treat every roadblock as though it was the enemy. The Fascists have been masquerading as partisans or as Jews seeking refuge. Sadly, some partisans are just bandits who would steal the flour."

Sara pulled two envelopes from her pocket. "I almost forgot. The Giordanos sent two letters of condolence, one for you, Gianni, and here's yours, Madama."

Gianni took his envelope and held it to his heart. Lia accepted hers and slid it into her coat pocket. She shivered and rubbed her bare hands together. "It's cold. Come, we can talk inside. I want to hear all the latest from Bossolaschetto—what Doretta and Michele have been up to. Come, Gianni." She waved at him to join them. "Luigia has some food prepared for you."

"If you don't mind, Madama, I'll join later for the *vigilia*. I must see Anna first," Sara said and rushed off.

The fierce fighting had kept Sara in Alta Langa all summer. She managed a quick visit at the beginning of the harvest in September, but she had seen little of Anna since Christmas. She had planned a trip to Asili for her fourth birthday the following week, but Giuseppina's sudden passing now brought her home earlier. It would not be a festive time, but at least she was back to comfort her child.

Sara found it increasingly difficult to leave, but she knew Anna was safe. Everyone in their corner of Asili cared for Anna and showered her with love. Yet each time Sara left for Alta Langa, Anna's pleadings for her to stay clutched her heart tighter. Work helped to chase away her guilt and also thoughts of Francesco.

Christmas was little more than a month away and she hoped the fighting would ease up through the winter. Regardless, she would come home soon, for good.

Sara didn't rejoin the mourners at Cascina Asili until the following morning. Instead, she had slid into bed next to Anna and cuddled her through another fretful night. Several times, she spoke to Sara, thinking she was Giovanna, who was keeping vigil with the others. Sara cooed her back to sleep each time she woke, breathing in her sweet fragrance, wrapping wispy tendrils of her hair around her finger. In the morning, when Anna discovered Sara sleeping on her back beside her, she bounced up and straddled her.

"Mimi!" Anna squealed. "I knew you would come." She covered Sara's face with kisses. "Oh, Mimi! Ti amo, Mimi." Sara reveled in the warmth of her child against her. Anna sat up and studied Sara, her expression now serious. "You're home for good now. Yes?" It was the question she knew Anna would ask, but she had hoped not to hear it so soon.

"Let's get something to eat, Anna. I had nothing last night. You must be hungry."

Anna didn't budge. "Mimi. Please stay now. Giusi's gone. I need you." Tears overflowed the edges of Anna's eyes.

Sara pulled her against her. "I know, carina. I know. You will miss her. Now you must think of her in Heaven as your guardian angel, one who never leaves your side."

"Like you? They call you an angel."

Sara failed to stifle a soft laugh. "I'm still here on earth as you can see. I'm talking about one in Heaven where Giusi is now."

"Will you go to Heaven when you die?"

Anna's questions about such matters always rattled Sara. "I'm not worried about that right now, Anna." She forced a smile, though an unexpected foreboding snuck up on her.

"But I heard Giusi say to Gianni you might die if you didn't come home. Don't leave me, Mimi."

Sara brushed Anna's hair from her face and gazed into her eyes, a mirror of her own. "Anna, it's hard to explain, but you're such a big girl, I know you'll understand. Papà went to fight a war far away because that's where it was. But now, it's close to us."

Anna's eyes widened, alarm spreading across her face. "You mean like those bad men that came here?"

"Sì, cara. Like them. There are people like Luca and Michele fighting to make those bad people go away. And someone has to make our soldiers well again when they get hurt. That's what dottor Costa and I do." She eyed Anna's grave expression. "I'm a nurse, like zia Luce. She's in the hospital in Alba, but I have to be close to where *i nostri partigiani*—our brave soldiers—fight. I help them get better so they can go home to their little boys and girls."

"So, Mimi, you're going back?" She curled her lower lip.

There was no use delaying the answer. "Sì, carina. But soon I'll come home for good." Anna frowned as tears wet her cheeks. Sara held her close and returned the kisses Anna had given her. "Anna, I promise. A Natale. I'll come home and never leave again. Promesso." She prayed it was a promise she could keep. Francesco surely tried to keep his. And she prayed Giuseppina would safeguard Anna. And her.

CHAPTER 44

Asili
Tuesday, November 7, 1944

After an interlude of bright weather, the dense autumn fog returned on the day of Giuseppina's burial. As Lia had feared, the activity of the last few days, consoling others and grieving with them, only made the emptiness worse when she opened the door to Cascina Asili. No lyrical voice called to her from the kitchen. She heard only the squeaking hinges of the door and her tentative footsteps on the wood floor. In the kitchen, the aroma of food greeted her. It had to have been Luigia.

Against custom but for the sake of Gianni's health that, for the first time, appeared frail to her, she chose not to invite anyone over after the funeral. Instead, she opted for a quiet visit with Luciana in front of the fire at Ca' dei Fiù. After watching Sara's tearful departure and hearing Anna's wails as Giovanna took her upstairs to bed, Lia needed her lifelong friend's serene presence. It soothed her and enabled her to delay returning to the empty house.

In the sala, the divan across from the crackling fire her farmhand Matteo had laid called to her. She kicked off her shoes and sank into the deep cushions, curling her bare, tired feet underneath her. Barbaresco felt more like home than Alba did. Lia had told Gianni that Giuseppina could be buried in the Bottero family crypt in Alba, but he had graciously declined. They were both from Acqui Terme and had lived their adult lives in Alba in service to the Bottero and Ferri families, but Giuseppina claimed she was happiest in Barbaresco. "She wanted to rest for eternity here," Gianni said. It was unheard of for the reserved *Langhetti di Barbaresco* to welcome her—a city dweller and relative stranger to the village—into their hearts. Though the women of the village were always kind, outsiders—even those from neighboring villages—rarely received such an outpouring of love. But now, it was all behind her.

After the Requiem Mass, the fog descended with them into the valley below the village, shrouding the cemetery. Even la Torre di Barbaresco was in hiding. Lia had regarded the grave faces of the other mourners. Anna, fast asleep in Nico's brawny arms, rested her head on his shoulder. She recognized many of the elderly women of the village as members of Giuseppina's prayer group that often met in her sunroom. Lia had closed the mulino that day out of respect for Giuseppina. It also allowed workers to pay their respects to the woman who prepared their annual Advent supper.

At graveside, Lia's thoughts drifted from the service to those who would return to harm's way. What would the world be like when they gathered again? And would it be at another funeral? There was Luca. When she met him, she was a young widow whose only child had recently died, and he was a little boy in his father's office. How far he had come from law student to rescuer to partisan fighter. Beside him today was Cesare, who gave up an opportunity for a prestigious medical career in Turin to serve the impoverished Langhetti. Had it not been for him—his brilliance and scientific curiosity—Sara would not be with them today. She would have died in childbirth two years before Anna was born. Sara, who stood between her mother and father, had brought much joy to many, including Lia. Was it possible Francesco would return to her after the war ended? No, it had been too long. There was little hope for him. She would insist that Sara return to Asili before Christmas. Anna needed her. Lia was embarrassed to say that, now with Giuseppina gone, she also needed Sara more than ever.

One face, that of a young man who appeared to be about eighteen years old, stood out. She did not recognize him, but she had spied him lurking near Sara as she held Anna's hand and speaking with Luca outside the church as they gathered to depart for the cemetery. He had a brooding, chiseled face, and his dark eyes darted about but always landed on Sara, who appeared not to notice him. Lia scrutinized him. There was something eerily familiar about him. Don Emilio walked up then and distracted her. When she turned back, the young stranger had vanished. Minutes later, there he was again, lurking in the shadows in front of the municipio as they followed the cartun on via Torino to the cemetery. He stood, his hands buried deep in his trouser pockets and his head lowered as he kicked at a flagstone. Rather than look directly at them, he glanced sideways, his narrowed, close-set eyes fixed on Sara. Lia shuddered; spies lurked everywhere.

Didn't that Fascist woman obsessed with Francesco have family in Barbaresco? Although she hungered for quiet time with Sara, she wanted to see her and Luca safely back in Bossolaschetto and Cesare in Cortemilia inside the partisan-dominated area.

Though it was dark and he was tired, Nico insisted on driving the delivery truck first to Cortemilia then on to Bossolaschetto. Although Pipo and Ornella had come to the funeral, Sara believed it too risky to drive her and Luca home with them, particularly as darkness fell. Their presence with Jews and partisans in the cascina in Bossolaschetto created enough danger for the kindly couple. If stopped and questioned about why he was out after curfew, Nico would claim he had had a flat tire. Flour deliveries were vital. Since it would be so late when he arrived in Bossolasco, Nico planned to sleep at the Hotel Paradiso for the night. Lia would rest easy once he returned to Asili.

Now that she had time to think, Lia wondered whether that sullen young man could be a Strega. And if he were, Cinzia Strega, an informer for the SS and the Fascist security police, would soon learn whatever he knew, whatever he had heard Sara and Luca say to one another. Lia leapt up. Had she seen Sara's lips form the word "Doretta"? She had to warn her. But how? Lia sank back on the divan, unable to hold back her tears of frustration.

"EXCELLENT WORK, STREGA. EXCELLENT." BEFORE HE HUNG UP THE PHONE, Baldo Volpe commended his prized Langhe informer for discovering the whereabouts of someone he had heard referred to as the "Angel of Alta Langa." The description of this small blonde woman fit someone his partisan infiltrators had told him was often seen on a tall black horse after reprisals and partisan battles. Was she Sara Fiore, the woman Strega said was a nurse who rode a horse across the Barbaresco countryside tending to the contadini who called her *il piccolo angelo*—the little angel? She had disappeared from there in the autumn of 1943 and had been seen only occasionally since then at the Alba hospital and the village, Strega reported. She had to be the Angel of Alta Langa. And he was certain that, wherever she was, the Jewess Doretta Giordano was nearby.

Strega said her cousin had overheard the blonde woman, who had a child with her, speaking with someone that she called "Luca" about a woman named "Doretta." Of course, it had to be Luca Olivero! And the child? Was she the screaming brat he had seen at the Fiore cascina with that old woman the previous autumn? He had wanted to silence her and take the woman in for interrogation. Why had Gunther stopped him? An entire year wasted.

Baldo reached for the silver cigarette case and lighter Gunther had given him after their first successful roundup of Jews near the Swiss border. He placed one of the unfiltered cigarettes between his damp lips, flicked the lighter, and drew the soothing smoke deep into his lungs. As he exhaled, he stared at the open files marked "Luca Olivero: Political Internee" and "Doretta Giordano: Distrusted" on his desk. The files were among the few he had salvaged when the anti-Fascists ransacked the police headquarters in July 1943. He unclipped the photos from the covers of the files and placed them side by side. He could not see the blue of Doretta's eyes in the black and white photo, but he knew them well. As he had done many times before, he placed the palm of his hand on her smudged image, and, with his index finger, traced her mouth, her eyes, and her neck to the bottom of the photo above her breasts. Oh, how he enjoyed that feeling again that had not crept up on him for some time. Since those first nights of refuge—alone in her bed, among her things—he dreamt how he might love her. But of course, that was impossible. Only to break her spell over him would he defile himself. If only she wasn't a Jew. No matter how beautiful she was, he could never have her except in those final minutes of her life.

Baldo put the image of her aside but kept his palm on it as he studied Luca Olivero's photo. Like Doretta's, it was over five years old. He had lost track of him in late 1942. How much had they changed? Thanks to the Strega informant's report, he believed he was about to snag the anti-Fascist again. This time there would be no confino and no powerful rich woman to buy his release. No, Gunther would see to it that the Jewess's lover would board a transport to Auschwitz.

Baldo lifted his hand from Doretta's photo. He had taken it while she sat in a café in Turin when she was with a teenager. The dress she wore was one of his mamma's creations. Doretta Giordano, he was certain, no longer decked herself out in such fashionable clothes, hand-tailored to her voluptuous figure.

In late August 1943, he had slipped out of Turin in search of the Giordano Jews. An old document he found in their apartment—then his shelter—reminded him that her uncle had a house in Cherasco. Perhaps he would discover her there. He had no authority to arrest her then, but at least he would confirm that she was in Cherasco. The Fascists, he believed, would soon return to power. He wanted to waste no time in arresting her.

When he entered the empty Cherasco house, he smelled a faint aroma of burned meat, strongest in the sala. After searching about, there in the smoldering ashes of the sala fireplace, he had found the charred remnants of cloth he recognized as a dress he had seen on Doretta Giordano, one he remembered his mamma had sewn. It appeared as though many pieces of clothing had been burned. Had they destroyed all the dresses his mamma had so painstakingly sewn? Baldo believed he had missed them by hours. She had slipped through his fingers. But that would be the last time.

Now, he would find the nest of Jews with her and that Luca Olivero in it. They would all be deported but only after a few days as "guests" in the Albergo Nazionale. Interrogating the Jewess, with her lover observing his persuasive methods, would be a complex pleasure. He would invite Gunther to join him. But first, he needed to find the Angel of Alta Langa. That, he believed, would be easy. She would lead him to his prized catch, and that would impress Gunther.

He clipped Luca's photo back to the file cover and put it aside. It was late, and no one else was around. Tonight, he would sleep on the cot in his office and spend a little time with her. It had been too long. He unbuttoned his breast pocket and fished for her red silk panties and the vial of her perfume—the most inspired thefts of all from the ruined Giordano apartment.

"Doretta. Where are you? I know you're close to me. It's only a matter of time. It will be enjoyable, at least for me."

Many hours remained before dawn—many hours of pleasure that he had not enjoyed for some time. Soon, he was certain, he would need neither her photo nor her panties. He would have Doretta, the Jewess herself, in his clutches, and she would yield to him, like it or not. One drop of her scent on the red silk was all he needed. He kissed the photo and locked the office door before undressing.

CHAPTER 45

Bossolaschetto
Early December 1944

They lived in fear for two weeks after receiving Madama Lia's message that she might have seen a Fascist informer at Giuseppina's funeral. When she finally got word to them in a flour delivery to the Paradiso, Lia included strict instructions for everyone other than Pipo, Ornella, and Ida to remain in the cascina until further notice. Ida's sighting more than once of a young man, not a villager, nosing around Bossolasco heightened their fear. They knew that time was short before they would have to dash to a new refuge.

Shortly after sunrise on the first Sunday of Advent, Purru arrived, winded, having run through the snow from Bossolasco carrying the message from Madama Lia that they had all feared. Everyone must be prepared to depart tomorrow at dawn! Zeus, too.

Only Ida went to Mass that day. The others no longer saw a need to maintain their Catholic charade, and it was too risky for Sara and Luca lest they be spotted. They passed the day in a trance, each lost in his or her own thoughts. Although they had known the day would come when they would have to flee, the abrupt arrival of it stunned them. Each had to choose the few things they could take with them and burn or bury the rest at the vacant Capra farm down the hill. For the sake of Madama Lia, Pipo, and Ornella, they had to erase all evidence of their presence in Bossolaschetto where they had sheltered for over a year. Madama Lia's cascina had protected the Giordanos' lives. They had come to know the ways of the forest, the high, remote farm, and the Langhetti of the Alta Langa, who lived a precarious existence between the partisans and their Fascist countrymen. Now the unknown loomed, weighting their movements when they had to make haste.

No one had slept that night as each made final preparations. Sara had sensed they were not leaving together. When, shortly after midnight, Madama Lia appeared with Gianni under the cloak of the dense fog, their leader confirmed her suspicion. Lia gathered them all in the tinello, including Ornella and Pipo who had laid a roaring fire that warmed the cold, damp room. Ornella had melted the last of the chocolate Gianni had found on the black market and mixed it with hot milk. Only the flickering fire lit their troubled faces as they sipped the rare treat.

The young formed a horseshoe and sat on the floor. Sara scanned those assembled. Would this be their last time together? So much danger and uncertainty lay ahead for them. She sat across from Doretta and Luca who sat with their fingers woven together, no longer hiding their affection. Ida sat with Ornella, their expressions somber, their hands joined. As the eldest women in the house, they had grown close after Ida found her place in Paolina Pratto's kitchen.

Dressed in trousers, boots, and a pullover sweater, her blonde, increasingly gray hair swept up in a chignon, the diminutive Cornelia Bottero—their only link to the outside world—stood at the open end of their horseshoe. Sara sensed their hearts beating in unison as they awaited news of their fate.

"I know this is sudden, but ever since Giuseppina's funeral, I've been making arrangements for this moment. I received word Saturday morning from someone in the municipio in Bossolasco about a visit from an Alba policewoman the day before." Lia shot a knowing look at Sara. "She inquired whether I owned a farm in Bossolaschetto. Fortunately, he pretended he didn't know and would search the records on Monday when he had the property registry in front of him."

She paused, her eyes scanning each bewildered face before her. "It's not only dangerous for all of you, but the attention we bring to the village places everyone at Paradiso at risk. Pipo's trusted friend from the farm on the other side of the forest will help. He has an animal transport truck, so he will load Zeus and take him, Sara, Michele, Luca, and Ernst to Cortemilia. The roads are passable, for now, and he is used to smuggling weapons past checkpoints. You'll be safe. Sara will remain there. The rest of you will report to your new brigade. Cesare will have all the details for you."

"Yes, but Madama," Luca asked, annoyance obvious in his tone. "Doretta's a staffetta with our brigade. Has that changed? Where is she going?"

"I'll get to that in a moment, Luca."

She walked to Doretta, who leaned ever closer to Luca as Madama approached. "Doretta, you've proven yourself skilled at charming the guards at roadblocks, especially the Germans." Sara spied Luca grimace and shot him a look. She had overheard them arguing one summer day after Doretta had put on a revealing blouse for a staffetta mission. "Your mother and I spoke earlier. You will drive her, Elena, Talia, and the baby in my old Fiat south to Gottasecca. Here are the directions. Study them, then burn the paper. It's less than an hour from here. I don't know the farmer's name—too many intermediaries, which is good—but he and his wife have been operating a safe house for refugees since late 1943. They'll have plenty to do on the farm and they'll be safe there, I hope."

Doretta hesitated, glanced at Sara, and then took the paper from Lia's hands. A frown pulled her eyebrows closer as she studied it.

"They? But, Madama Lia—"

"Later, Doretta. I want to speak with you and Sara after we finish here."

Lia turned to Elena, whose stunned expression Sara knew came from being torn from Ornella. "Elena, your sister and Talia have trained you well. Would you agree to join Talia as a staffetta?" Elena looked first at Talia, then at Lia, and nodded. "Your cooking skills will be much needed for the fighters in your area."

Only Ida was left to hear her fate. Madama Lia took a deep breath. "Ida, you will move into the village. Ornella is making arrangements for you to stay with the nonna of a friend of hers. Your company and help are needed. There's no more room at the farm in Gottasecca. Regardless, with your identity papers and baptismal certificate, you're safe in Bossolasco." Madama Lia then added an ominous question. "Did you ever meet the boy Baldo Volpe when he delivered dresses to signora Giordano in Turin?"

Ida clutched at her heart. "Why, no. I don't think so, Madama. I met his mother, God bless her," she crossed herself. "No, I'm sure I didn't. Why?"

"Because he is the Fascist pig hunting your mistress and her children now."

Sara gasped at her words. Silence, broken only by the popping sound of burning acacia wood logs, fell upon the room.

"It will be dawn in less than five hours. There isn't much time for sleep, but I assume all preparations have been made. Hopefully the snow will hold off until you're all safely away, but we do need more snow to cover your tracks around the farm. Any questions?" The stunned silence continued. "We'll meet back here at six for colazione."

After everyone else left the room, Lia sat on the divan and motioned to Sara and Doretta to pull up chairs. Sara reached sideways and took Doretta's hand, whose tight fingers telegraphed apprehension. She had been her family's stoic leader, but now, hearing that she would be separated from her mother and siblings, Doretta, for the first time, appeared frightened. Lia instructed her that once she left Gottasecca, she was to drive northeast to Cortemilia and remain with Sara until the weather broke and she received further orders from her brigade. The brigade commander saw no reason for her to wait out the winter in cramped, cold quarters with a brigade of men. Doretta squeezed Sara's hand. At least they would be together for a while longer.

"You and Doretta will share a room in a house near the hospital. Sara, you'll be able to work in the hospital with Cesare Costa. With the Blackshirts combing the area around Mango and Calosso d'Asti for partisans, the casualties have been high. Cesare's in dire need of a good nurse. Although Zeus will be with you, you are not to return to the battlefield. Is that understood?"

Sara nodded but didn't meet Madama Lia's eyes. This was a command, not a request for a promise. If she had to, Sara would find disobeying her order easier than breaking an oath. She gave Doretta's hand an encouraging shake. Though they had to separate from the rest of the group, at least they would be close to one another when liberation finally came.

IT ALL WORKED AS MADAMA LIA HAD DIRECTED UNTIL SHE APPEARED UNAN-nounced in Cortemilia less than two weeks after their departure from Bossolaschetto. When she answered the knock on her door, Sara froze at the sight of her. Was the stress and danger of all these years finally catching up with her? She looked at Sara with such weariness, her eyes bloodshot and dull. Sara knew that only something terrible would have brought her here instead of sending a messenger.

Doretta pulled up a chair for Lia while Sara fetched hot water for a cup of chamomile tea. Only when Lia—clutching the hot drink, her hands trembling slightly—told them her awful news did they realize how close they had come to disaster.

Only a week after they departed the cascina, the SS and Fascist Blackshirts raided the farm in Bossolaschetto. When they found no trace of Jews or partisans, the Blackshirts had terrorized Pipo and Ornella, stolen what they wanted, and torched the building. Whatever farm animals they could not carry off, they shot, including Pipo's beloved cow Eloisa and his ox, Brutus.

Ornella was so traumatized that she needed hospitalization in Alba where Luciana cared for her. At least the elderly couple had not been arrested and deported. Pipo told Lia that two officers—one a Waffen-SS and one an Italian SS—had commanded the joint rastrellamento. Madama Lia felt confident that Gunther Schliessen and Baldo Volpe, who for a year had circled her like wolves, had finally struck too close to home.

Sara took Lia's cup from her trembling hands and placed it on the table beside her. When she put her arms around her and drew her close, Lia began to cry. The younger women's eyes met as Lia, for the first time, sought comfort from Sara.

CHAPTER 46

Alba
Early February 1945

As he trudged through the melting snow to the Caserma Govone, Baldo cursed the weather. For over a month, he had been stuck in Alba, waiting for a break in the storms. He also cursed Cinzia Strega and the inconvenience she had become. It had been over two months since she reported a sighting of Sara Fiore in Barbaresco. It was as if the heavy snow had buried all traces of her. Not even the heavy German army presence in Langhe, after they retook Alba from the ragtag partisans in November, helped to uncover the woman's whereabouts. She had vanished, as had his hopes of finding Doretta Giordano and Luca Olivero before spring.

When winter arrived, all military campaigns on the Italian peninsula ground nearly to a halt. Even some partisan brigades had gone deeper underground. It was a different story elsewhere in Europe despite the harsh winter conditions. Baldo had heard from both Gunther and Radio London that the Allies were pushing eastward through Belgium into Luxembourg. London even claimed that the German army was in retreat.

Gunther believed that soon they would slow the advancing enemy as they had done on the Gothic Line in Italy, and then reverse the Allies' fortunes. It was just a matter of time. But time was slipping through Baldo's fingers, as was Sara Fiore. But he would find her and discover all she knew about Doretta Giordano and the partisans associated with her. Even if he had to beat the information out of her, he would. First, he had to find her. His quest would continue. Even if the war ended soon, he believed the fighting between partisan factions would continue in Italy. He and his men had to remain ready to fight and do whatever was necessary to eliminate as many enemies as possible. And to be set to take advantage of the chaos that would follow.

From what Strega's informer reported about the funeral in Barbaresco, he had finally connected that Bottero woman with the lot of those Jewish traitors. He had sensed she was a Jew-lover when he and Gunther had visited her in autumn 1943. But try as he might, he found no pretext to bring her in for interrogation or to search the mulino. Surely, her money had bought the weak Wehrmacht officers residing in the plush accommodations of Villa Cristina. But that all changed when he discovered she had a farm in Bossolaschetto. Strega's informer followed the Ferri-Bottero mill delivery truck one day in late November. The truck stopped near the farm on the way to and from Bossolasco. All it took was a visit to the municipio in Bossolasco to confirm that she owned the farm. They had already discovered many partisan brigades hiding out in that part of Alta Langa.

The joint raid on the Bottero cascina before Christmas yielded nothing. Neither his Blackshirt team nor Gunther's mercenaries from the Eastern Front turned up anything. The old man and woman claimed that they had not seen Cornelia Bottero for months and no one else lived there. So why did his informer report seeing the Ferri-Bottero mulino truck there so often? Before they torched the building, his men combed through every nook in the cascina and barn. Nothing. Once again, Gunther denied him an interrogation he was certain would have yielded answers. All he allowed him to do was burn the cascina. His men did enjoy ransacking the house and creating the bonfire afterward. It was worth the verbal thrashing he received from the Wehrmacht major. Gunther interceded for him, and he was allowed to remain in Alba.

It had been a lonely Christmas, and he did miss Gunther's company after he returned to Turin in mid-December. The officer promised Baldo that, as soon as the weather improved, he would return to Langhe. Intelligence reported activity once again near the partisan stronghold of Cortemilia. In November, the Germans plowed under the airstrip the partisans had built, reportedly with the help of Allied spies. Gunther wanted to check out sightings of partisans near the village of Vesime, where he was certain they would try to rebuild the airstrip. That fit with Cinzia Strega's claim that they would find the nest of partisans in the area.

As much as he despised her, it was time to meet up with her again. It had been weeks since he had seen her on New Year's Eve, when she had slipped into the barracks. Her vermillion hair, her latest shade from a bottle, and matching lipstick made her look like the prostitutes he had seen in front of the Alba brothel. And the acrid perfume she wore turned his stomach. After her scorn on New Year's Eve, the only thing of his that would touch her was a bullet from his gun.

How she slipped in that night without being seen, he didn't know. Female giggles echoing through the hall earlier signaled that the guards were turning their heads the other way. He answered the tap on his door.

"We should celebrate together, don't you think?" Strega said as she strutted past him, an expensive bottle of sparkling wine and two glasses in hand. Instead of her uniform, she wore an indecently short skirt and a low-cut black blouse under her coat. He had no desire to look, but she had barely covered her large breasts. The slit in her skirt reminded him of a similar long black skirt his mamma had once made for Doretta.

"I see you're ready for bed. Good." She slipped the cork from the bottle and poured the wine. When she handed him a glass, her dark, lusty eyes begged for him. "Salute, Baldo. Here's to us! And to the success we'll soon enjoy." She swayed a bit on her stiletto shoes, wet from the deep snow. How did she walk on those things? It was obvious to Baldo that she had already been raising glasses of wine, sparkling and otherwise, that night.

"Strega, what are you doing here?" he demanded as he set the glass on the small table without drinking. "And how did you get in?"

"It's New Year's Eve. Everyone's celebrating. I didn't want you to spend it alone." She sipped the wine. "Drink up. I have some news for you."

"Just tell me and leave. Can't you see I'm ready for bed?"

"Well, so am I," she said. Before he knew it, she moved on him and dug her long nails deep into his flesh through his thin nightclothes as she cupped his buttocks in her hands.

"Hmm. I believe you might need some help. Let me." With one swift move, she pulled the belt of his robe open and reached her hand inside his pajama pants. "*Meraviglioso*! Already quite large and not even hard. I'm impressed." He was mortified—and in pain as her nails scratched his sensitive skin.

He grabbed her wrist and pushed her away, watching as she stumbled against the wall. "Go! Now!"

"But I have something of interest for you. Why not a fair exchange?"

"Exchange? For what? For doing your job?"

Her eyes flashed as anger replaced lust, the cords in her neck tightening. "Are *you* refusing *me*?" He had seen her haughty sneer before that day at the Fiore cascina when she did not know her place. "Gunther didn't."

"Put your coat on and get out. You look like a whore. And you're acting like one too. Your behavior is unbecoming of a Fascist woman."

She lunged at him, but he caught her wrist before her long, red-lacquered nails made contact with his face. She shrieked and came at him with her other hand. He pinned her arms at her side and pushed her onto the bed. Now the feeling he had grown to enjoy on his own since that horrible night at the whorehouse in Berlin emerged.

Her eyes widened and she ran her tongue slowly across her bottom lip. "Hmm...so you like it *that* way. So does Gunther."

Her mocking sneer sickened him, but the throbbing in his groin grew stronger. He would have her, even though she repulsed him. She spread her legs and pulled up her skirt revealing the uncovered apex of her thighs. The opening peeking through her black curly mound enticed him to enter. Finally, he would have an Aryan woman, to know what it was to explode inside one. It was well past time he did, and Strega was available. With dexterity, she released his fully erect member from his pajama pants and grasped it. It was only the second time a woman had touched him like that, but as he stared at her open legs, Doretta's mocking blue eyes flashed before him. He went numb as blood drained from his groin. It was like in Berlin. A cackle erupted from the slut.

"Oh, so that's why you turned me down. What would Gunther say about his big strong Italian SS officer with a useless—" Before she spit out the word, he slapped her. His fury sprang to life, stirring his groin again. She rubbed her cheek and again drew her tongue over her lower lip, now oozing blood.

He fumbled with his pants, retied his robe, and then jerked her to her feet. The echoes of her mocking, near-hysterical laughter in the stone box that was his room rang in his ears. He grabbed her coat, opened the door and tossed it onto the floor in the hall as two German soldiers walked by, snickering at him.

"Get out, you bitch!"

Again, she cackled. "Don't be ashamed, Baldo. If you would give me a chance, I could help you. I've helped lots of men with this problem."

"It's no *problem*, Strega. It's you. Now leave," he ordered, bile rising in his throat.

She extracted a handkerchief from her handbag and strutted to the mirror, watching his reflection as she dabbed at the blood and reapplied her bright red lipstick. "I see you're not interested in pleasure, at least not tonight, but I'm sure you'll be interested in the information I have on your precious Jewess?"

"Unless you know exactly where she is at this moment, I am not interested in your information or you."

She snapped her handbag closed. "Listen, Baldo—"

"It's *sir*," he snapped.

"Sir, then. I want to find that Fiore woman too, so I'll share this with you. There is no doubt they were at the Bottero cascina in Bossolaschetto. All of them. My informers in Bossolasco saw a woman who fits your precious Doretta's description with an older woman. So, as you suspected, the old man and woman were lying. I don't know exactly where they've gone, but I have someone in Cortemilia who believes your girl may be there."

He fought the urge to show interest at this intriguing development. "Come back when you have concrete information."

She strode through the open door and turned to face him. Before she spoke, he slammed the door in her face.

He was deflated—the humiliation that followed arousal. He thought to call her back, to give her what Gunther had, but he didn't trust himself not to strangle her if she mocked him again. No, he would take care of her, but not in his bed.

THE THOUGHT OF BEING FREE OF STREGA QUICKENED HIS PACE THROUGH the slush. Cortemilia—now *that* was interesting. In those final hours of 1944, Doretta Giordano's mocking blue eyes he still could not chase from his dreams had caused him great humiliation. Despite her disgusting behavior, he had wanted to dominate Strega, and she was ready. Surely, that would have broken the spell the Jewess had cast on him.

Baldo walked past the guards and across the cortile to his office. As he approached the door, he caught a whiff of a familiar, unpleasant scent. As he suspected, there was Strega, sitting on his desk, her legs crossed, that same sneer he had grown to detest plastered on her face. Without acknowledging her, he removed his wet hat and coat and sat at his desk. She was hideous—not at all like Doretta Giordano. "Where have you been?" he asked while thumbing through papers on his desk.

She slid off and stood in front of the desk. "I've been busy."

"Doing what?" He was in no mood for her games.

"Collecting information." She tossed a small notebook in front of him. "It's all there: when they were sighted, where they were sighted. We still don't know where they're hiding, but the best information of all is that Sara Fiore's father was seen two days ago in Cortemilia. He has to know."

That got his attention, but as he reached for the notebook, the phone rang. Gunther—and he sounded cheerful for a change.

"Schliessen! Moment, *bitte*." He pointed Cinzia to the door. "Leave, but come back in an hour." She snatched the notebook and marched from the room.

After his brief conversation with Gunther, he felt the exhilaration of the hunt return. He and his men would arrive from Turin the following day. They would spend a day or two in Alba, planning how best to set the trap to snare this band of partisans once and for all. After they paid the Fiore family a return visit to obtain more information and evidence of their collaboration with the partisans, they would join the Asti Fascist Blackshirts for a rastrellamento at a farm near Cortemilia suspected of being a partisan nest.

Strega's notebook provided a wealth of useful information. Tomorrow, he would extract more from Nico Fiore. Then, with the added strength of another battalion, they would put an end to the rebuilding of the partisan airstrip. Unless Strega's informants were wrong, Doretta Giordano would be among the partisans. She would not escape him.

But what to do with Strega? He had what he needed from her. Was this an opportunity to eliminate her and find a more suitable, useful informer? No way would he tolerate another woman. Although, he had to admit there was nothing like vindictiveness to motivate a woman as it had Strega. He had no idea what had sparked Strega's vendetta against Francesco Bosco and his wife, but it had been useful to him. It was to his advantage to keep her, a well-motivated informer, close to him. At least for now.

As he reached for a cigarette in his desk drawer, his hand grazed the vial of Doretta's perfume. Before his humiliation on New Year's Eve, the image of her lusty blue eyes always appeared when he smelled Doretta's fragrance. But now, the scent of roses conjured images of her mocking him, laughing at him. He loathed her and soon would break her spell over him. Such a waste of an alluring woman. And such a pity to have to kill her.

He sniffed again the rosy aroma he enjoyed when he released tension over the long snowbound weeks. Only a few precious drops remained. Where in Turin would he find more? *This was Doretta's scent*, he would say to the most posh pharmacist he found in the once-magnificent city. *Doretta is gone*, he would tell them. *But I need her perfume*. The pharmacist would understand. He closed the vial and slipped it into his trousers pocket. Tonight he would use it sparingly. He needed to reserve a few drops for Doretta to wear for him.

CHAPTER 47

Cortemilia
Early February 1945

S ara rested on the front steps outside the hospital in Cortemilia. With each deep inhale, the frosty air filled her lungs and washed away the stink of blood. After a long night in surgery with Cesare, the first morning of full sunshine in weeks lifted her spirits. All about her, yellow and white crocuses peeped through the melting snow, the first sign of spring. Red, it had seemed, had been the only color appearing on the otherwise monochromatic landscape. Blood. Blood of partisans. Blood of innocent civilians. Sara hungered for the soft colors of spring after the brutal winter. She faced the sun, closed her eyes, and let the early morning light warm her and chase away fatigue. Rumors had spread that the Allies would resume their northward march as soon as the weather improved. She could only hope.

The improved conditions might allow her papà to bring Anna for another visit. Luigia had written that it broke Anna's heart when Sara had had to leave Bossolaschetto so quickly. Then the ferocious winter weather had forced her to break her promise to her daughter. Not only had she not returned for Christmas, Cesare had asked her to remain in Cortemilia through the New Year when she had hoped to return home—for good.

On a rare break between storms in mid-January, despite Luigia's concerns about the danger, Nico and Giovanna had bundled Anna and brought her for a surprise visit. He assured her they would only stay for a few hours. How Anna had grown! Yet she seemed to leave as soon as she had arrived. Anna's pleas for her to return home and the sight of them driving away made Sara realize how painful the short visits were for Anna. Seeing her daughter and holding her after their brush with death comforted her and convinced Sara that her place now was with Anna, at home in Asili. If the optimistic news of the Allies' advance continued, in a few more weeks Sara would be able to leave for good.

Nearly two months had passed since their pre-dawn departure from Bossolaschetto in early December. Although safe for now, Sara and Doretta feared for Madama, Gianni, and Sara's family at Asili. The noose was tightening. Would the Allies arrive before it was used to strangle the life from them? Although Lia had not seen nor heard from Baldo Volpe since, they knew from reports of reprisals and other partisan battles in Alta Langa that he and Gunther Schliessen still posed a danger.

When Sara had ridden out to the partisan camp above Cortemilia to deliver the sad news of the raid in Bossolaschetto, Luca had wept. He shared Madama Lia's love for the magical place in the forested hills of Alta Langa, a place that connected him with his parents, now long gone. Was there another reason the news brought Luca to tears? Although Doretta never admitted it, nor had Sara asked directly, she suspected it was there that Luca and Doretta had first made love. Why shouldn't they? Sara believed in the sanctity of marriage, but nothing was sacred about war.

Sara stretched and walked back to her room. It was time to face what she had avoided thinking about for days. Doretta would depart in a few hours. She had been called to join the brigade near Vesime, where she was needed to assist the British officers who had arrived from Cisterna d'Asti to begin rebuilding the partisan airstrip. This would be the first time since autumn that Doretta would be working as a staffetta alongside Luca, and she was anxious to rejoin her brigade for what they believed—what they hoped—was the final battle.

The airstrip—code name: Excelsior—provided a vital link between the partisans and liberated Italy. The Germans had plowed it under in November after only a few weeks of operation. Before then, two successful flights had delivered weapons and equipment for the partisans and their Allied partners and evacuated wounded soldiers and corpses to Siena.

In early 1944, Doretta, Talia, and the men in the group joined the Second Langhe Division of the autonomous partisan formations. The men sabotaged German convoys in Liguria and Alta Langa. The women served as *staffette* carrying coded messages through checkpoints and smuggling guns and ammunition although they, too, knew how to handle a weapon. They would fight if needed. The Badogliani, the pejorative name their rival partisans in the communist Garibaldini had given them, were apolitical, which suited them all. They had seen enough of the political debacles that had set Europe ablaze. Though she remained unattached to any partisan brigade, Sara's heart rested with her dear friends.

Since fighting had resumed, the further up the peninsula the Allies advanced, the more ferociously the Nazis and Fascists fought as though caged lions. They were cornered with nothing to lose. The brutality of the reprisals intensified, many civilians of the countryside paying with their lives when the partisans sabotaged supply lines or kidnapped German and Fascist officers. Despite that, as winter drew to an end, no one believed they would still be at war when the snows fell again in November. But Sara worried that much more blood would be spilled before they seized the victory that was so near.

Sara found Doretta dressed and ready to leave. Her knapsack was on the bed, her Sten gun propped in the corner. Although Sara dreaded their separation, she knew Doretta hungered to fight alongside her brother and Luca. Soon the war would end; then, Sara prayed, Doretta and Luca could move on with their lives together.

"Sara, you should wear the Badogliani blue kerchief. Look how it matches our eyes." Doretta had left behind her life of fashion and luxury in Turin, but even though she toted a submachine gun, wore trousers and boots, and tied her long hair in a braid like Sara's, she still tried to look her best. Her unusual blue eyes, dark red hair, and generous breasts helped in her work as a staffetta carrying messages and escorting Allied special forces operatives and downed pilots through and around checkpoints. Whether friend or foe, Doretta had learned to use her looks to disarm men. Luca didn't approve, but he had to accept it.

She tied the scarf around Sara's slender neck. "Look," Doretta insisted as she pushed Sara to the mirror. "You keep it. I have another."

"I can't. I can't wear the symbol of a brigade, even though our men are with the Badogliani." Sara unbraided her hair and shook it out. "I do have to admit that blue *is* my favorite color."

"Don't argue, then. Keep it. You never know when it might come in handy." Doretta tied the other scarf around her neck and held up a small beige block as precious as gold. "You know, after the war, I'll never again throw away little slivers of soap." She dropped it into her small knapsack containing only another change of clothes and the few cosmetics she managed to squeeze into it then pulled the drawstrings shut. Though she had been tempted to bring her last vial of La Fête des Roses, to add to her sex appeal when she most needed it, she decided to leave it behind with Sara.

She plopped down on the oversized bed they had shared for the past two months in Sara's tiny room near the hospital. "You have to be careful, Sara. I've heard that, in the south, as the Allies have liberated villages, collaborators and Fascists are being shot or hanged, often both. Fascists hang captured partisans—men *and* women—from trees as a warning to civilians. And now they are the ones hanging. Sometimes partisans are mistaken as the enemy and...well, just be careful. Liberation is coming soon. God forbid anything should happen to you after all we've been through."

Sara settled on the bed next to Doretta and took her hand. To Doretta, Sara still looked every bit the little girl she met nearly twenty years earlier. For nearly eighteen months, they had said good-bye to one another each morning, knowing very well that death lurked outside. But they had survived, and on most evenings, each was able to fall asleep knowing the other was safe. That would change, starting tonight.

Doretta laughed nervously, pushed Sara's hair off her shoulders, and touched her cheek. "Why the sad face? I'm only going to the partisan camp. Not even an hour away. Even when we move to Vesime I won't be far away. And I'll be with Luca, Michele, and Ernst."

Sara remained silent, dark. "You're spooking me," Doretta said. Still nothing, but Sara's mouth twitched, a tic that Doretta knew meant she was holding something back. "Tell me."

"I had a dream, about me."

"What do you mean, Sara?" croaked Doretta, her words sticking in her throat. "Don't send me away like this. You have to tell me. I heard you cry out in your sleep two nights ago, but you didn't wake. Another dream about...?"

Sara nodded, but stared at their fingers, intertwined like their lives. "Francesco. But different. Not a sweet dream of our times together. I saw him in a blizzard. His face was obscured, but I knew it was him. He wore cardboard shoes, had no coat or hat, and his frozen beard was down to his chest." Sara's small fingers squeezed Doretta's. "I wore only that thin, silk nightgown your mamma gave me for our... But I wasn't cold. My hair blew in the wind, but it wasn't wet. I felt only joy. He opened his arms. I ran to him. And *then* I saw..." She jerked her hands from Doretta's and covered her face. "A skeleton! He's dead. I tell you, Doretta, he's dead and this was his call to me to join him."

Not since the morning they watched the massacre of an innocent family near Cissone had Doretta seen Sara so shaken. She had said many times that she knew Francesco was probably dead, but her vivid dream seemed to confirm it. Sara sensed doom.

"Sara, we're so close to the end…the end of the war. You'll know soon enough. Until then, don't lose hope. Focus on what we have to do now."

Sara reached her arms around Doretta and rested her head on her shoulder. Doretta stroked Sara's hair and held her tight.

"What will I do without you, Doretta?"

"You'll work hard, that's what. And you'll stay here at the hospital. You'll listen to Madama and leave Zeus in his stall. The angel needs to stay here with Cesare." She took Sara by her shoulders. "I need you, Sara. I can't imagine my life without you. I hate myself for not taking my mother and siblings away with zia Silvana. We could have left, and we didn't. I'm so ashamed because…I didn't want to leave Luca. I can't help but think that, had I gone, you never would have been drawn into this. You'd be home now with Anna, with your family."

"All except Francesco," Sara lamented.

Doretta looked around the tiny room, more like a prison cell than a bedroom, but at least it was clean and bright. They had spent two precious months here dreaming of the future, of happier times. "At least when we're old, we'll have stories about our adventures in the forests to tell our grandchildren. We'll make sure they know all about this time."

"Grandchildren? All the years you've spent with Luca. I know you love him. Have you never…" Even talking about Doretta's sex life brought a flush of heat to Sara's face. "I hope you plan to get working on that as soon as possible after the war…if you haven't done so already."

Now it was Doretta's turn to blush. Sexual need for Luca burned inside her. The time she spent with him in Bossolaschetto, so close, yet unavailable to one another in the close quarters they shared with so many, increased her desire for him. And he shared her longing. More than once, alone in the barn—his hands, his lips on her body giving her such great pleasure—they had come close to the point of no return. But she pushed him away. What if she was left with a child and the war continued to rage? What if something should happen to him? Soon. The war would be over soon.

"No, Sara. We haven't. But I love him more than life itself. For now, all Luca and I have on our minds is getting safely to Vesime to rebuild the airstrip.

410

Michele met with someone from the Belbo brigade yesterday who said it should be operational by the beginning of March." Church bells chimed once to mark the half-hour. "Nine-thirty. I have to go, Sara. Already late. I'm going up to the partisan camp—you know, at that farm above town—before we head to Vesime in a few days. I'll come see you soon."

"And what will you be this time? A pregnant woman delivering milk or an old hag with a sack of ammunition slung over your shoulders, balancing on a wobbly bike? Carimissa Doretta, you have become a master of disguises."

They laughed and embraced. "I love you, Doretta. What strange force drew us together?"

Doretta pulled away and giggled. "Cornelia Ferri Bottero, that's who. A tiny force of nature. Like you, Sara."

"Well, God bless her." Her voice grew serious, heavy with emotion once more. "I wish we had grown up in better times." Sara knew that, without Lia Bottero, she and Doretta would never have met except in passing in the cortile. Fascism had brought them together. The war bonded them.

"Times will be better…soon, cara, soon."

Doretta grabbed her rifle, checked the safety clip, and slung the strap over her shoulder.

Sara studied her from head to toe and handed Doretta her knapsack. "The warrior returns to battle."

Doretta knew the tears would come if she didn't escape. "I have to go, Sara. See you soon." Quick pecks on Sara's cheeks and Doretta rushed out. Sara's whimpering followed her down the hall.

CHAPTER 48

Asili
Early February 1945

Lia woke to sun beaming through the cracks in the shutters—the first time in weeks. Ever since the razing of the cascina in Bossolaschetto, through the frigid, tempestuous winter, Lia had chosen seclusion in Cascina Asili. She had lost the sense of safety she had known as a woman of means, owner of the only mulino in Alba and, most importantly, an acquaintance of Major von Ebner, commanding officer of the Wehrmacht troops in Langhe. She knew that the ferocity of the search for Jews and partisans by the Nazi Waffen and Italian SS battalions and Blackshirt brigades had only intensified over the previous months.

In the last year, at least two thousand innocent civilians—mostly women, children, and elderly men—had been massacred in reprisals throughout northern Italy. For nearly ten years, she had used her influence and wealth to help save the victims of anti-Semitism and free her beloved Piemonte from the stranglehold of the Nazis. Now she was exhausted. She had grieved for too many friends and loved ones. And for the first time, she feared for her own safety. Worst of all, she was alone. Lia was convinced that, if not for the cruel raid on Asili, Giuseppina would still be with her. It had been too much for her heart, and she never fully recovered from the terror. Yet as much as she missed her, it was Sara these days—her youth and wisdom—that she longed for.

Lia had ceased all contact with Sara and Doretta in Cortemilia. The trip she made there in December had been foolish, and selfish. The horror of knowing how close they had come to disaster had clouded her judgment. She had succumbed to fear and placed the young women, who had always turned to her for comfort and reassurance, in grave danger. She would not repeat her mistake. Sara had promised her that she would return home before spring. Nico's brief visit with Sara, too, had been dangerous, but agricultural work was still important, and his ruse of delivering wine had worked. It helped to have extra damigiane for the checkpoints—both those of the partisans and the Fascists.

A tap on her bedroom door roused her from her thoughts.

"Madama, it's eight o'clock. I have your caffè."

"Come in, Maria." Though it had taken both of the middle Fiore sisters to replace Giuseppina—and even the two working together fell short of her as a housekeeper and cook—Maria's and Letizia's presence in her house was a godsend. She never would have dared to ask, but the day after the funeral, she woke to hear Luigia and the two girls in the kitchen. They were no longer girls, of course, but young women well into their childbearing years in a time when so many young men their age were fighting or had died on the battlefields or in prison camps. Luigia feared they both would end up as spinsters, each a tota like Luciana, yet with no useful skills.

"The girls have had an easier life than most on the land," Luigia had said. "We left them in Sara's shadow too long and spoiled them." Both of the young contadini they had loved since childhood had perished in Russia. Luigia believed, and Lia agreed, that it was time they refined their rudimentary housekeeping skills to prepare them for work as maids in the city after the war. They would work and learn at least until a suitable replacement was found. Giuseppina would always be irreplaceable, in her home and in her life.

Maria popped open the legs of the breakfast tray and set it across Lia's lap. She pulled a rolled-up newspaper from her pocket and handed it Lia. "Gianni came early and brought this for you."

Lia stiffened. It was an old copy of Mussolini's defunct Fascist newspaper, *il Popolo d'Italia*, but she suspected that Gianni must have had a reason for bringing it. She unrolled it and out fell a piece of paper with a short, typewritten note on it. *Buongiorno, Madama, please come to Alba today. A new priest has arrived whom I would like you to meet.* Don Rossi's code for "more refugees have arrived" brightened her mood. She was needed in Alba. And she would go.

"Maria, please tell Gianni that I'll leave for Alba in an hour." The girl, certainly no beauty and not as mature as Sara at that age, slapped her hand over her mouth. Lia hadn't been to Alba since before Christmas. "Don't just stand there, girl, get going."

She downed the weak, tepid coffee and sprang out of bed. Sunshine and work would help her to regain her strength and confidence.

The hinges of the shutters squeaked, and a rush of cold air blew over Giovanna before Anna whooped and jumped on her bed. "Wake up, zia Gio! Look! Sunshine! It's eight o'clock and you promised."

Giovanna rolled on her back and pulled the duvet tight over her face. "Anna. Close the window. It's freezing."

Anna giggled and did as instructed. "Mi dispiace, zia Gio."

Giovanna had promised Anna that, if the roads were clear on the first sunny day, she would hitch Romeo to the cartun and drive her to Treiso if she did her chores.

"I helped nonna feed the chickens and goats this morning, so I'm ready. You promised to teach me to drive the cartun before Mimi and Papà come home after the war."

Anna rarely forgot anything, although that was not exactly the promise. Giovanna and her mamma didn't have the heart to dash Anna's hopes that both her parents would come home. Only one would return, they knew, and they would leave the explanation about Francesco's fate to her. At least her sister was safe in Cortemilia and no longer riding across the countryside, dodging the Blackshirts and the SS. At first, Giovanna missed Sara terribly, but over time, as she and Anna grew closer, the pain of her absence lessened. Giovanna considered herself blessed that she and Anna had each other as they anxiously awaited Sara's return to Asili.

"Yes, Anna, I did promise, but you know Romeo is too strong for you, and it will be some time before you can drive him yourself."

"Nonno Nico said he would build me a goat cart and make a little harness for Poco. I can drive a goat." With pursed lips and her eyes ablaze, Anna shook her finger at Giovanna. "You just wait and see, zia Gio. Not only can I drive a goat, but soon I'll ride a horse! Maybe even Zeus when Mimi comes home."

Giovanna laughed. It was hopeless to argue with her. "Yes, Anna, I suppose you can." Her hugs and tickles elicited giggles from the child. Whenever Anna unleashed her peals of laughter, someone in the family would always say that she sounded like Sara at that age. They all missed her so.

"Now go get dressed. We'll go in a few hours. It's too cold now."

By nine-thirty, Giovanna finally had to give in. She had been sitting at the table in the warm kitchen, darning socks, while her mamma kneaded dough.

They had been trying to have a quiet chat, but there was no chance that Anna would leave them alone. The sooner she left, the sooner she would be back at Asili. Zia Luce was coming in the afternoon for the weekend, and she wanted to finish her chores before her arrival.

"I'm ready, zia!"

Giovanna's heart thumped. She had seen photos of Sara at Anna's age, dressed in the same trousers and boots. Only the red streaks in Anna's blonde hair, inherited from Francesco, were her own. She wondered whether her mamma had seen in Anna what she saw.

"That's fine, Anna, but where are your coat, hat, and mittens?"

She scurried up the stairs. "Don't leave without me, zia!"

Giovanna pulled on her own coat. "No chance of that, Anna," she mumbled.

Luigia laughed. "Oh, how I see myself in you. I don't know what I would have done without your nonna Mirella to keep Sara occupied once the rest of you arrived." She placed the ball of kneaded, oiled dough into a wooden bowl and covered it with a flour-sack cloth. After wiping her white, dusty hands on her apron, she came and wrapped the woolen scarf Luciana had knitted around Giovanna's neck and pressed her face between her hands. "You, cara, are too pretty to waste away without a man to love. Is there no one who catches your fancy?"

Giovanna shook her head and tugged her braid from under her scarf. This conversation had been repeated far too many times. She would keep her heart to herself. Never would she risk the suffering Sara had endured over losing Francesco.

"I love you, Mamma. But I would never leave Asili, you, Papà, Anna, and Sara. You know very well that, when the war is over, Sara is not going to sit still." They watched as Anna bounded out of the house, shouting for Giovanna to hurry. "Someone needs to keep up with that little one of hers."

She wrapped her arms around her mother, savored the tangy aroma of yeast, then kissed her good-bye. "I love you, Mamma. *A dopo.*" As she opened the door, Anna's jabbering with Nico, drifted in. Giovanna waved and blew Luigia a kiss. "Wish me luck."

Luigia watched from the window as Nico hoisted Anna high into the air and onto the bench next to Giovanna. She tittered as Giovanna argued with Anna when she tried to snatch the reins from her. Nico needed to finish the goat cart he was making by spring or else they would have no peace. Luigia turned away from the happy scene and returned to the kitchen. She and

Luciana would begin a novena to *l'arcangelo Michele* this weekend. Divine intervention, protection from their enemies, she prayed, would bring a swift, successful end to these years of hardship and loss.

BY THE TIME THEY REACHED THE VILLAGE, GIOVANNA HAD STRUCK A COMPRO-mise with Anna. She would sit on Giovanna's lap and hold the reins with her. Fortunately, though he was a draft horse, Romeo was as docile as a lamb. His ears flicked back and forth as he listened for Giovanna's commands. She was happy that Anna had dragged her out early. It was warmer than she had expected, and she enjoyed the feeling of the sun on her face. Although snow still blanketed the vineyards, in less than two months, new life would burst from the vines. All along the ridge on strada Comunale, Anna prattled, and Giovanna listened. The child possessed boundless energy and had learned enough Italian and Piemontese to create her own language. When Sara returned and taught her English, there was no telling what linguistic gibberish would spring from her mouth.

As they reached the turn to Treiso below Monte Silva, Romeo stopped short, his ears alert to a sound inaudible to them. She pulled the slack out of the reins to keep the gentle giant from bolting. Without warning, a convoy of armored vehicles, including two trucks and a black staff car with loath-some Nazi flags, appeared from around the bend. Anna screamed and clung to Giovanna, begging her not to let them take her away.

After they had passed, Giovanna pulled Romeo to the side and comforted Anna, who had begun praying to Giuseppina to save them. Of course. Anna had been with Giuseppina when the Nazis and Blackshirts raided Asili. Not much frightened Anna except the Nazi flag and military vehicles. *Povera ragazzina.* She rocked her as she rubbed circles on her back to calm her.

"It's safe, Anna. No one will hurt you."

Anna peered out from Giovanna's embrace and scanned the area. "Are they gone, zia?"

"Yes, cara. They went away. Do you want to go home?"

"No. I want to finish our drive. Can we stop to see the Contessa?"

"Well, it's impolite to stop without an invitation, but she does have a soft spot for you. We'll see on the way back from Treiso, all right?"

"*Sì!* Anduma Romeo," she called out with a big grin. Giovanna guided Romeo to the turn then up the Monte Silva road.

Anna was unusually quiet for the next few miles, but broke her silence as they approached Treiso. "Zia Gio, I saw that man again."

"What man, Anna?" She was always going on about people she met in the village or the mercato in Alba with Luigia on Saturdays.

"That bad man. The man who yelled at Giusi."

"Where, Anna? Where did you see him? In Alba?" Giovanna tightened her grip on the reins.

"No. In that black car with the red flags."

When they had sped by, she was too preoccupied with the child and horse to see where they were headed. Had they continued straight, through Tre Stelle, or had they turned left and dropped into the valley? Were they returning to Asili?

She slapped the reins on Romeo's back, and he sprung from his lumbering walk into a brisk trot. At the first opportunity, she wheeled him around and moved him into a canter back through Tre Stelle and along the ridge above Martinenga. It was quicker through the valley, but she didn't want to risk passing them if they had stopped along the way. It was only when she neared the cappella that she heard the whirring of machine gun fire, coming from the direction of Ca' dei Fiù.

She pulled Romeo off the road and into a grove of acacia trees. Giovanna snatched Anna and dashed into the nearby cappella. Once inside, she hid behind the altar and cupped her hands over Anna's ears so she would not hear the guns. They went on firing for a long time, but it was the eerie quiet afterwards that sent tremors through her. Dear God. Please dear God. After what seemed an eternity, the machine gun fire resumed, but now it came from the valley. Gunfire from the cortile answered it. Anna struggled and screamed, but Giovanna clasped her hand over her mouth. She bent over and cocooned the child. And prayed. "Hail Mary, full of grace…"

THE MORNING HAD FLOWN BY, AND LIA'S SPIRITS ROSE TO MATCH THE SPRING-like weather. Work had always helped to chase away her sorrows. As suspected, she found new arrivals hiding in the mulino cellar. The six Croatian Jews had been moving from one refuge to another since arriving in Borgo San Dalmazzo from Saint-Martin-Vésubie nearly eighteen months earlier. Fortunately, Ernst and Talia had linked up with Cesare and Luca. But Lia knew from Alba's police marshal and clandestine rescuer, Salvatore Libera, that while hundreds of others vanished into the mountains and plains, the Nazis had arrested and deported some three hundred or so, sent to Drancy outside Paris. Their final destination? Auschwitz. It shocked Lia that, while the Allies continued bombing Piemonte and the war had swung in their favor, the Nazis resumed transporting Jews to their deaths from Cuneo in December. With the need for shelter and food still so great, she wondered why she had given in to fear and let Baldo Volpe make her a prisoner of her home in Asili. For all she knew, he was back in Turin with that Nazi companion of his.

Despite being out of the office for months, she would make a short day of it. She still had time to go riding for the first time since October. This was a good start. Soon she would begin receiving those who came seeking her advice and financial support. She wanted to help her fellow Langhetti who despaired now more than ever. Once the war ended, the need would be incalculable. She would be there for them.

Lia spied Gianni through the open door, waiting in the cortile to drive her home. She pulled on her coat and picked up the bundle of correspondence that had accumulated in her absence. Elisabetta Vacchetto, Luca's dutiful, longtime assistant who had joined her after he left for France, had sent the letters to Asili, but she returned them and asked her to tend to the correspondence. Work belonged in the outside world; it would not disturb her serenity in the countryside.

The din of idling trucks, as their drivers waited in line for their orders, drowned the screams of a woman racing across the cortile. So when Luciana, her face contorted, grabbed Lia, she dropped the bundle of letters. Luciana pulled her down with her to her knees, sobbing. "They were all shot...all...dead."

END OF PART THREE

PART FOUR:

1945–1946

CHAPTER 49

Near Cortemilia in Alta Langa
Early February 1945

Despite the grim news from Germany, Gunther said that orders from headquarters in Verona called for even more reprisals and rastrel-lamenti. Jews were still hiding in Langhe, and the SS would find them. It didn't matter that transports to Auschwitz had stopped. They would be killed on the spot. But there was one partisan Jew that Baldo intended to arrest rather than kill. Soon he would find and capture Doretta Giordano.

Baldo's men did a thorough job raiding the farm in Asili, although he regretted having left the buildings standing. At least, along with the traitorous, Jew-loving Fiore family, Baldo and his men had killed a few fighters from the partisan brigade that sprang from the vineyards as they prepared to torch the Fiore cascina and that of the Bottero woman. How unfortunate that they did not find her at home. Strega's spy confirmed that she had not left Asili since before Christmas. Next time, she would not slip through his fingers.

They had not expected the partisan gunfight, but Gunther grumbled that his men should have prepared better. What would he have done if Gunther had suffered a more serious, or even fatal, wound? The nurse at the hospital said he was lucky the bullet had only grazed him. He was still in pain, but at least he would be able to join Baldo for another mission tonight—an even bigger one.

It was a pity two German soldiers on patrol had died in a partisan ambush in the region the previous day, but at least it gave them the pretext they needed to carry out the reprisal. Although Baldo knew the family was involved in partisan activity and hiding Jews, he had no evidence to support the claim.

A pretext had been needed, and the partisans had unwittingly provided it. Any farm would do, Gunther had said, and since he believed most of the contadini had given aid and comfort to the partisans, the Fiores were as guilty as anyone they might have caught red-handed. Pity they had to shoot the girls. They were pretty. And so frightened. But the mother and father unnerved him when they faced the bullets without any sign of fear. They had prayed until the end.

Tonight's rastrellamento on the nest of partisans between Vesime and Cortemilia should put an end to his search for Doretta Giordano. His informer in Cortemilia reported seeing a woman fitting Sara Fiore's description on a black horse recently. Word was that she was a nurse at the hospital there and, as she was reported to have done near Bossolasco, rode out to tend to partisans after battles. Wherever he found Sara Fiore, he believed Doretta was not far away. They would simply set a trap for the nurse. If, as Baldo hoped, Doretta was with the partisan brigade there and he captured her, he would get rid of Sara Fiore as he had her family. He would have no more use for her. If not, he would bring her back to Turin, a more suitable place for Gunther and him to extract information. Either way, he would find Doretta Giordano *and* prevent the partisans rebuilding the airstrip. He was long overdue for a promotion. Accomplishing both on this mission would bring him everything he wanted.

They would rendezvous with the Asti Blackshirt brigade in Castino at 8:00 p.m. Although Cortemilia and the suspected partisan camp at the farm near Perletto were in Cuneo province and well within their jurisdiction, Vesime, near the location of the first airstrip the Germans destroyed in November, lay within Asti province. A turf battle with another brigade of Blackshirts would interfere with the business at hand. In any case, they would need more men. These were seasoned partisans, not the same as a defenseless family of farmers and the teenage boys in the partisan brigade that fired on them in Asili. Gunther would not tolerate surprises like the previous day. He would have preferred to wait longer—to recover and to bring in more of his men from Turin—but the intelligence they received forced them to act now.

From the backseat next to Gunther, Baldo stared at the back of Cinzia Strega's head and fingered his revolver. She sat in front of him in the passenger seat, an easy target if not for the others in the car. One bullet would shut her up. He had heard her shrill voice coming from Gunther's room in the middle of the night a few weeks ago. No telling what lies she told him. He had decided that, as long as she continued to feed him useful intelligence, he would let her be. But now that they had taken care of the Fiore family and she had tipped him off about where to find Sara Fiore, Strega's value had drained away. Soon, Gunther would have to find another whore.

"What do you think, Baldo? Will you finally make your catch tonight?" Gunther must still be hurting, but Baldo knew that nothing but death would have stopped him from leading the joint operation. Baldo shuddered at the thought of how close he came to losing his comrade—the only one he had ever met whose will to purify Europe matched his own.

Intelligence reported that the partisans they hunted—the ones he suspected Doretta Giordano followed—worked with British agents. They would capture them as well. Gunther would easily extract the invaluable information the British spies possessed. He specialized in dealing with traitors and spies. And Baldo had learned well from him. When they worked as a team, they had better success, and Baldo had to admit, he enjoyed it more.

"I don't know what you're talking about."

Strega snickered, and then coughed to hide her insubordination from Gunther.

"Sure you do."

"Bigger prizes are waiting for us like sitting ducks. She's a bonus."

"A bonus? Baldo, you've been obsessed with that Jewess since I met you. Don't tell me you're going soft on me. You have feelings for her?"

Baldo tried to hide his embarrassment, but a flush grew up his neck and over his face. Good thing the fading light hid his red face from Gunther. "No! She's a Jew bitch who needs to be stopped. That's all."

"Well, you know, these vermin are like witches. They are known to cast spells on Aryan men."

Baldo wanted nothing more than to change the subject. "I'll be happy to finish with this mission and get back to Turin. I've had enough of this place."

"I would think, as one of them, you would be glad to be fighting these bastards in your home region. Look at me. I'm a thousand miles away from Berlin. At least you speak their language!"

"I'm not one of *them*," Baldo said, staring out the window. "They're traitors, I tell you, and when we finish with the Allies, we'll finally finish with them and the Jews they've been hiding."

Gunther chuckled and squeezed Baldo's muscular thigh. Baldo moved his leg when Gunther let his hand linger a bit. He still could not believe his great fortune that their shared passion had brought them together in Berlin! And when, with a heavy heart, he bade Gunther good-bye in early 1937, Baldo never dreamed of linking up with him in Turin. Their time together in Piemonte reminded him of the old days in Berlin, except now they hunted Jews legally. And Gunther had taught him a great deal about torture. The previous March, Gunther had recommended him for a commendation for his work in Turin that contributed to the successful capture and execution of eight key partisan leaders from across northern Italy. His men had hungered for a kill, and he had not disappointed them with the rastrellamento in Asili. Pity he and Gunther had lost a few in the firefight. Tonight, he believed, would go better.

"So what's the plan? Did you speak with the commander in Asti? I don't want another surprise like yesterday. I lost two good men and"—Gunther pointed to his wounded thigh—"I don't have to tell you how close I came."

"Yes, of course I did." Baldo still smarted from Gunther's insinuations about Doretta Giordano. And in front of the others! Nothing was further from the truth. His business was to capture Jews, partisans, and anti-Fascists. She was all three. He flicked on his flashlight and held it over the map he placed across their laps. "We'll meet here near Castino." He pointed to the village north of Cortemilia, a suitable place to avoid detection. "That way, we move along here, avoiding Cortemilia, and crossing the Bormida right there before continuing to Perletto. They're here in these *rocche*. It will be easy enough to encircle them."

"Rocche?"

"Ravines. Sheer face rock cliffs. Like on the Tanaro River in Roero. The sandy walls make it easy for them to carve caves deep into the rock. The Asti brigade already conducted a rastrellamento here near Perletto. It's not far from where the airstrip was." Baldo folded the map and stashed it and the flashlight in his knapsack. "It's still muddy with snow in some places, but we can handle it."

"Damn, but these roads are winding." Gunther tapped the driver on his shoulder. "Pull over. I need to take a piss and get some fresh air. Come on, Baldo."

The sun had slid behind the mountains. They had driven deep into rugged terrain of Alta Langa, a territory the partisans increasingly controlled and knew much better than they did. Though a well-armed brigade followed some distance behind, Baldo kept his hand on his pistol, nervous in the open air. A long sigh of relief accompanied the torrent Gunther unleashed onto the muddy road.

"What is it Gunther? I'm not here to watch you take a piss."

"Tell me more about this Jewess, Baldo. I know you have her perfume. If you think I haven't smelled it in your office… It isn't Strega's. I know how she smells." He snickered and buttoned his trousers then turned toward Baldo. "I don't need a Jew lover in my brigade. So tell me, what do you plan to do when you catch her? Shoot her on site? Take her in? Fuck her?"

Bile burned along Baldo's throat. Gunther's wrathful gaze sliced through him. He had seen that look many times, but never cast on him. Gunther lit a cigarette and blew coils of smoke into Baldo's face, intensifying his urge to retch. He knew he couldn't afford to cede any ground to his friend.

"I told you. The only thing I care about is arresting her and finally extracting useful information. She's a staffetta. Those women know more about the partisan brigades than anyone. And don't forget, she's a Jew!"

"That's not what Strega said. And she said a lot. She's a good fuck, but damn she's annoying."

Baldo peered back to the car. He would deal with her later. Tonight, on such an important mission, he couldn't lose focus.

"Listen," Gunther said, "I know women can be vicious liars. So let's go kill some partisans and find this Jew you say holds so much useful information."

CHAPTER 50

Near Cortemilia in Alta Langa
Early February 1945

Darkness had settled on the sprawling base camp at the farm, situated in the forest at the top of the deep ravine. In the event of a rastrellamento, the deep ravine of the rocche offered the partisans an excellent escape route. The cascina and barn provided luxurious accommodations compared to their usual shelter in barns or out in the open. The contadino who owned it had fled with his family to Acqui Terme to avoid what he believed was certain death at the hands of vengeful Nazis and Blackshirts if they discovered the partisans there.

Reprisals came with no warning as the Nazis continued to target civilians as their favored weapon against the partisans. Yet, the partisans continued to sabotage convoys and roads and raid ammunition stores. The Nazis countered with brutal assaults on villages and farms. At least the farmer had left them well supplied with grain, polenta, and dried meats. They only worried about other partisans stealing their chickens and the scrawny cow that no longer gave milk. For now, sixteen partisans and two British agents, who would soon rebuild the airstrip nearby, made their home there.

Doretta had slept for much of the day, only waking with the bright afternoon sunshine flooding the room. She peered through the window above her bed and scanned the threshing floor where two men and a woman sat on overturned buckets, cleaning weapons; the forest was steps away from the cascina. The sunshine tempted her to take a walk, but within minutes, she fell back asleep.

Their successful sabotage mission with Major York on a fuel depot near Acqui Terme the night before had come close to disaster on their return to the base camp. They saw glimmers of light in the distance along the Bormida River road near Vesime and took cover in the forest. If it was a Blackshirt patrol, they would be forced to shoot them. They had no more use for prisoners. The Fascists had rarely honored a trade, and now their partisan prisoners never lived long enough for that. Increasingly, when outnumbered, Fascist brigades beat a cowardly retreat rather than confront the partisans. They feared only the most brutal of them operating with the Nazis, many of which still lurked in Langhe. With each radio broadcast from London, victory appeared closer at hand. As ordered, they tried as much as possible to avoid more civilian bloodshed.

Tonight Michele, Luca, and Ernst had planned on the nighttime mission with Major York and Lieutenant Martin Miller, the other British agent who had arrived recently. Miller wanted to scout the area between the former landing strip and the base camp. No one knew it better in the dark than those three young men did, especially Michele, who had become a keen tracker. Doretta had given him the nom de guerre "Scout." She would remain with the others to complete preparing weapons and equipment before their move to Vesime where they would join the other British agents from Cisterna d'Asti.

She sat up, stretched her arms, and smiled. Michele came toward her with his usual light tread.

"I brought you some polenta and tuma, Doretta."

Of course, he would always be her *little* brother, but he had outgrown her in the last six months.

"Where's the wine? Luca said a farmer brought a damigiana of Dolcetto."

"He did. Yesterday. Sorry. All gone. You work and sleep too much. And here's your Beretta. I cleaned it for you. It shouldn't jam again."

She laid the pistol aside and took the board of warm polenta and a chunk of Robiola cheese a contadino in nearby Roccaverano had given them. Though she preferred oozing gorgonzola in her polenta, she had not eaten all day and made quick work of the soft, pungent, goat's milk cheese. As the partisans strengthened their presence in the region, the contadini grew bolder and kept them well stocked. When they finished the new airstrip, flights delivering supplies and ammunition from Siena could resume. After a winter of scraping by, the partisans would be well supplied when the Allies finally arrived.

The dim lantern lit Luca's bearded face as he entered the room. Dressed for patrol, his Sten submachine gun slung over his shoulder, Luca looked every bit the handsome, rugged partisan fighter he had become. She thought him even more handsome than shaven and in his fine suits.

Michele cast a sheepish grin at Doretta, and slapped Luca on his back. "I'll leave you two alone. See you in twenty minutes, Luca?"

Luca sat next to Doretta, his eyes fixed on her as he waved off Michele. Doretta was at her most alluring when sleep still showed in her face. Her drowsy eyelids reminded him of the lusty look in her eyes before she closed them when he first kissed her. He longed for more of her, and her close proximity in the room the four of them shared caused many sleepless nights. He wanted to sleep *with* her, not near her. To feel her naked body against his in the night. To wake up with her in his arms. Soon. Alone now, he kissed her cheek, picked pieces of straw from her hair, and nuzzled her.

Doretta slid away from him. "No, Luca. You're going out on patrol in a few minutes. Be serious."

"Oh, but I am, cara. I am seriously in love with you. Each time one of us leaves the camp, it could be our last. Would you want me to die having never made love to you?"

"I don't want you to die. Period. Anyway, we could die in a rastrellamento here in our own beds." She ran her free hand across the stained mattress she had covered with fresh straw to at least block the disgusting odor of, well, she didn't want to think about what it might be. "I mean, mattresses."

"We could die in each other's arms."

She pushed him away. This *was* serious. "How long will you be gone?"

"Only a few hours. We should be back not long after midnight. We're not going far. Miller wanted us to take him to the airstrip site, but it's still too muddy. So we'll show him around the rocche."

He reached for her blue kerchief on the mattress and loosely tied it around her neck before tugging on it, drawing her closer. Finally, she yielded to his embrace, to his searching lips, his warm, roving hands that he snuck under her blouse. She enjoyed his hands on her, so gentle, so pleasing. Then footsteps approached. She pulled away and straightened her blouse. Michele called from outside.

"Luca! Anduma! Time to go. Maybe we can get some sleep tonight if we leave now."

"Arrivo, Michele," Luca snapped as he drew Doretta close to him once again. He held her face between his hands and kissed each cheek, her nose, her brow, before settling his lips onto hers. Doretta melted against him. He nuzzled her ear, her hair. "I love you, Doretta. I don't know what my life would have been like had Madama not introduced me to your family. But I do know now how it *will* be."

Doretta wondered what that life would be like. Before the Nazi occupation, she might have forgiven the Fascists. But having seen ordinary Italians denounce their fellow citizens, sending them to certain deaths, she couldn't imagine trusting them again. Going back to the way things were—that was impossible.

"I know, Luca. Now, look after yourself. And my little brother." She spread her fingers and pressed her palm against his chest. "Take my love with you and hold it close to your heart tonight, dearest. I'll be here when you return."

"Olivero!" Now Major York called for him.

He unfastened the top button of her blouse and kissed her chest, her heart. "I'll be back for more. Get some rest. A più tardi, cara." One more kiss and he disappeared into the night.

SARA DROPPED HER BAG ON THE FLOOR AND FLOPPED ONTO HER BED. HER head was spinning. From dawn to well past dusk, she had been locked away in surgery with a new doctor. On a break, she had escaped outside to soak in the bright sun for a moment, but it hadn't been enough. The cruel winter would soon end—and so, they believed and prayed, would the war. And life would begin again.

She longed to see Anna and her family, and Doretta of course. They had met briefly when she brought in a British agent who had suffered a deep cut in the arm after parachuting into the Bormida River valley. Infection, maybe the most lethal enemy given their living conditions, had already set in.

Other than that, she and Doretta had had no contact, not even messages, since she left weeks ago. Sara had ridden up to the farm a week ago, but Doretta was away. The boy wouldn't say where, but he showed her around. Poor Doretta, to have such living conditions, but they were better than most that Sara had seen.

Now she felt a familiar hollowness, as she had when Francesco's letters stopped coming. But she would have heard had anything happened to her friend. Soon, however, her papà would help fill the void. He had promised to bring Anna for a visit next time the weather broke and if it was safe. Only this time, she had decided, she would return with him. They expected the Allies soon, and other well-qualified local nurses could take her place, which was no longer in Cortemilia but with her daughter. For now, all she needed was a hot shower to wash away the stink of perforated bowels and infection.

As she stripped away her bloodstained dress, she heard someone calling her name. Tito, the orderly who assisted her in the ward, was seemingly running down the hall. But what was he doing in the women's residence? Annoyed, she pulled her dirty dress back on before answering the knock on the door.

"Tito! What's the matter? You're not supposed to be here."

"Dottor Costa…he…"

"Stop, catch your breath."

"The doctor said to tell you…there's been a rastrellamento. The partisan camp…" He paused as he again gasped for air. "At the rocche. He expects casualties…wants me to alert all the nurses."

"When? How did you find out?"

"Pepino, the old contadino. He saw a convoy of Nazi trucks. Climbing to the farm up there. Then he saw flames over the trees. Gunshots. He drove to town as fast as that old truck of his would go."

Sara gasped. Doretta. Luca. Michele. Ernst. They were all at that farm above the rocche.

Tito turned, his hurried footsteps echoing off the wooden floor as he raced down the hall to knock on other doors.

Sara leaned her head against the door frame, breathing heavily. No, she would not go back to the hospital.

AMID THE CHAOS ON THE WARD AFTER NOT ONE BUT TWO RAIDS ON PARTISAN camps that evening, it annoyed Cesare when a nurse called him to the phone. Where was Sara? All the other nurses had returned to the hospital already. He had managed only a quick bite after he closed the incision on his last surgical patient of the day. He was washing his hands at the sink when Pepino came racing through the hall. The much-loved contadino served as an early warning that patients would arrive soon. Shell shock from the Great War had left him a bit touched, but that, Cesare believed, had helped him more than once evade arrest. Everyone but the Nazis and Blackshirts knew that behind his gibberish lay a mind linked to keen senses. Much the same as a truffle hound sniffing scents buried in the dirt, Pepino heard the rumble of military vehicles long before anyone else. Cesare trusted his word about gunshots echoing in the valley earlier that night.

Now he put the receiver to his ear. Muffled words came in between gasps. It took him a moment to recognize the distraught voice of Luciana Capra. Had something happened at the Alba hospital?

"Dottor Costa..." she sobbed. "Where is Sara? I need...you need—"

"Suor Luciana, please, what is it? Is it Anna? Something wrong?"

"No," she sobbed once more. "No. Anna, praise the Madonna, is alive. Giovanna is alive. But...oh dottore." Another sob wracked her. "The rest, the rest of the family, *my* family..." She couldn't continue. A sob, then muffled voices.

"Cesare, this is Cornelia Bottero," came a firm voice. "I wanted to come to the hospital myself, but I didn't want to leave Luciana and..." She deeply inhaled. "There's been a reprisal. At Asili."

During her long pause, Cesare drew up a chair. His legs trembled as his heartbeat began hammering in his ears.

Then the emotion she had hidden from her voice overwhelmed her. The words she struggled to say in one long exhale froze the blood in his veins. "The Fiore family. All but Giovanna and Anna have been shot...dead."

Cesare couldn't think straight. He was exhausted and this seemed like another of his nightmares of maimed soldiers, of Nazis stalking the halls with pistols in hand. He knew what the enemy was capable of—beating and raping women, rounding up civilians for work camps or worse—but the cold-blooded murder of women and children...no.

"Are you still there, Cesare?"

He shook his head. No. Reality *was* the nightmare. "I'm here, Madama."

"Will you tell Sara? She needs to know this from you, not from anyone else. Maybe you can find Doretta first. She should be there."

Doretta! She was at the partisan camp Pepino said was under attack. He didn't tell Madama that Sara had not reported for work that evening. Perhaps she had gone to bathe or had fallen into a deep sleep. Let her rest while she still could. And there was no reason to worry the two grief-stricken women. But he needed more facts.

"Yes, of course. I'll tell her." He glanced at his watch. An hour had passed since he sent Tito to alert the nurses. "When...?"

"It happened yesterday, late morning. Maybe a reprisal for a shooting of two soldiers nearby the day before the rastrellamento. Giovanna and Anna had gone to Treiso." She paused, and Cesare heard another muffled sob. "Make sure Sara knows Anna and Giovanna are alive and well. Don Emilio and some of the women from the village are with them at my cascina in Asili. We're in Altavilla, but Gianni is taking Luciana there now. I'll go in the morning. Cesare, I can't talk any longer."

"I will, Madama. I will. I feel helpless—" The line went dead.

He sat, stunned, still holding the phone. How could he bring himself to rouse Sara and deliver this news?

Then Tito called from the opposite end of the hall. This night would only get worse.

"Dottor Costa. Suor Sara is not in her room. And, Zeus is gone."

CHAPTER 51

Near Cortemilia in Alta Langa
That same night— Early February 1945

Doretta slipped the darning egg out of the last sock in the pile and glanced at her watch. For six hours, she had repaired rips and tears and sewed buttons on shirts and trousers. As much as she hated sewing, as a staffetta, someone had to keep the men's clothes battle-ready and ensure that their feet stayed blister-free. She shook her hands and stretched her cramped fingers, just as she used to after hours of practicing piano or playing duets with zio Eduardo. She had had enough for the night. At least the chore had helped to occupy her mind as the night wore on.

She placed the basket of socks and her sewing kit on the floor. Luca said they would return not long after midnight, and now it was just past one o'clock. Lieutenant Miller must have gotten his way, and they went further than planned. She wished she could slip off her boots and stretch out while she waited. Someday soon, she would trade in her trousers, blouse, and boots for her silk nightgown and her goose-down duvet and pillows on a soft bed—her body curled next to Luca's.

She switched off the lantern and stood on her mattress, lifting the black-out curtain slightly to peer out the window. The orange glow of the sentry's cigarette betrayed his presence in the pitch black. At least he was awake. The day before, returning a few hours before dawn, they had stumbled upon that night's sentry snoring on the threshing floor.

Had a light flickered in the darkness? The mongrel that had followed one of the partisans home barked. The light again. Although it was well past time for the patrol to return, she knew that Major York forbade flashlights unless absolutely necessary. The dog's barking grew insistent. It yelped. The forest teemed with cinghiale and deer. The mongrel had made a habit of alerting them to the invasion of animals in the middle of the night. A single gunshot usually followed, and then they ate well the following night. Now an eerie silence settled over the camp. Doretta turned and grabbed the holstered Beretta M1934 she had kept within reach all evening. She strapped it on and she peered out again. Only darkness. The sentry had finished his cigarette.

Then something hit her forehead, and she heard the sound of glass landing on the floor. Pieces of stone around the window shot in the air. A large one hit her shoulder. She lost her balance on the soft mattress and fell, slamming her head on the hard dirt floor. The room spun as the noise continued. With her right hand, she touched the spot where the piece of stone had hit her shoulder. It came away damp, but she felt no pain. Blood poured into her eyes and ran down her cheek. The gash on her head burned and hurt worse than the wet spot on her shoulder under the tear in her shirt. When she wiped away the blood from her eye, she felt torn flesh above it. Terror—and understanding—caught up with her. They were under attack! The familiar whirring sound like a sewing machine and the unmistakable odor of nail polish remover and rust alerted all her senses. A raid had begun and she had been shot!

She heard the blood-curdling shrieks of man and beast, and the flash-bang of hand grenades near the cascina. Bursts of gunfire, followed by screams. How many of the partisans based on the farm were down? Had the raiders come upon the patrol, upon Luca? Was anyone left alive to come to her aid? Or would she have to save herself?

The machine gun fire stopped. The voices inside grew louder. The window offered the only escape, from there to the forest. She sat up and glanced at the small, square opening, the blackout curtain flapping in the light breeze, and sounds outside no longer muffled by glass. When she grabbed the curtain to pull herself up, the rod gave way and she tumbled back onto the mattress. Pain ripped through her shoulder, but she held her breath to stifle her cry. She reached up again and grabbed the windowsill. A shard of glass sliced through her right hand. She fell back once again. Her teeth cut into her lower lip as she struggled not to scream.

Slow down, she told herself—think. She slipped the blackout curtain off the broken rod, folded it thrice, and placed it across the window ledge. Battling the pain in her shoulder and hand, she tried again with all her might and pulled herself up. The window was too small to pull her legs up and then jump down. She balanced on her belly, her holstered Beretta digging into her, and tumbled headfirst out of the window. As she fell to the ground, she instinctively reached out to break her fall, widening the tear in the flesh of her palm as she hit the ground.

She froze, listening. She untied the loose knot Luca had made with her kerchief and wrapped it around her sliced palm. The voices grew louder, nearer, inside. How long before they would look outside below the window?

Doretta steadied herself against the rough stones of the cascina, but her legs failed her. The forest loomed roughly one hundred paces away. Her pursuers were near too. The skeletal underbrush this time of year would not offer much cover, but once across the clearing, she might work her way deeper into the forest now whirling before her. On her belly, with the kerchief protecting her wounded palm and her Beretta jabbing her chest, she pulled herself by her elbows across the ground still muddy from recent rains. She continued crawling, tunneling through the thick underbrush until, finally, she believed she was far enough into the forest to evade the searchers. From the shouts both inside the cascina and from the threshing floor, she knew she didn't have a moment to spare. She prayed that darkness and the woven branches entangling her would be enough to keep her out of sight.

Slowly, she rolled onto her back and held her wounded hand close to her face. The kerchief! Gone! Where had she lost it? She couldn't return for it. Her strength failed her as she felt the world slipping away. Her head pounded. She would rest a moment and her strength would return.

"Doretta." She stirred. How long had she been asleep? "Doretta." The voice whispering her name sounded like…Sara! Doretta tried to speak, but a hand clamped over her mouth. The voice, now close, whispered in her ear.

"It's me. Be quiet."

Doretta was wide-awake now. Sara's silhouette was unmistakable against the orange glow of flames that now lit the moonless night that had provided a cloak of darkness for her escape. The cascina! Sparks spiraled upward from the raging inferno into the black sky. It *was* Hell!

"Cara, you're hurt badly. Lie still. Let me check you."

"Here…think I'm shot." Doretta winced as she pointed with her injured hand to the hole in her blouse, near her shoulder.

Sara struggled against the thick brush to kneel and better examine Doretta. She too had crawled on her belly, following what she hoped was Doretta's path. Now she hoped they were deep enough into the forest not to be seen. They were trapped if discovered.

Blood oozed from a gash on Doretta's brow and a deep gash on her scalp.

Sara turned her attention to Doretta's chest and felt a small hole slightly below her collarbone under a tear in her shirt. Sara guessed that a bullet had ripped into her. Even a nick of her subclavian artery would have killed her by now. Although Doretta labored to breath, Sara heard no sounds indicating a puncture of her lung. What a relief! If they evaded capture, she had a chance. Sara reached around and ran her fingers over Doretta's back. No exit wound. The bullet most likely lodged in her scapula. It would heal once Cesare removed it. She continued to run her hands across Doretta's body, checking for other wounds. When she took her right hand, Doretta's breath caught and she convulsed in pain, yet remained silent. Thick mud had obscured the blood and the gaping wound on her palm underneath.

"Doretta, can you wiggle your fingers? I know it will hurt, but try."

A groan came from deep inside Doretta, but her fingers moved, and her face brightened. "Do you think I can still run scales?"

It was no surprise to Sara that, after the shock she had suffered, Doretta was delirious. "Sì, cara." But infection might take not only her dexterity but also her hand. Or worse. Time was short to get her to the hospital to prevent that. "I'm getting you out of here." Where had she spoken those words before? At night. In the mud. Fretting about infection as someone she loved hovered between this world and the next. She squeezed her eyes tight and when she opened them, she saw only her injured friend.

"You smell so nice, Sara."

She smiled, amazed that, with sickening odors from the fire saturating the air, Doretta still detected the scent of her own perfume on her. "Who…?" Doretta's words vanished between her short and shaky breaths, her chattering teeth. Sara peeled off her jacket and threw it over Doretta's chest. The thick wool turtleneck sweater her mamma had knitted for her would keep Sara warm.

"Doretta, listen. It's Volpe, again. Schliessen…and Strega. I saw them. So many of them."

"How did you get…?" Doretta's voice was barely audible. She closed her eyes once more.

Sara listened for approaching voices, praying Zeus remained hidden. He had never moved from a ground-tied spot, but he was known to whinny for her when she was gone too long. She had left him on the other side of the farm, well before she reached it and far away from the flames although, unlike most horses, fire didn't frighten him. Sadly, her loyal steed had grown accustomed to the odor of burning buildings, the sight of flames shooting to the sky.

Sara had had no idea where to begin her search, or whether Doretta—or their men—were even at the farm. Maybe they had left for patrol or a night-time mission. If she had not escaped from the cascina, Sara could do nothing for Doretta. But what if she lay on the ground in the open, hurt, easy prey for the vultures who now scoured the grounds for more victims?

"How did you find me?" Doretta, though weak and at times not making sense, was insistent on details. No surprise to Sara.

Thank God, she had ridden up here the previous week. Of course, she had wanted to see Doretta, but something else, an unsettling feeling, drove her to the farm. The boy they called Tiger said that Doretta was away with Luca, but he happily showed her around. Now, if she was able to save Doretta, and herself, it would be due to the knowledge she had gained that day.

She had walked deep into the forest, away from the soldiers, and around the perimeter of the farm. When the underbrush became too thick, she moved closer, darting along the edge of the forest to the corner near Doretta's room. Flames shot from the windows along with the acrid odor of burning bodies. She doubled over at the thought that the flesh she smelled burning was Doretta's. As she moved away, she spotted a kerchief, dark with blood. She snatched it up. From there, she saw a bloody trail to the forest. There might be a partisan nearby who needed help.

"Thank God you dropped your kerchief. I spotted it in the mud. And your blood on the ground. You crawled, didn't you? I followed the tracks into the forest. No, don't worry. I covered our tracks. Doretta, listen now. Was anyone else inside?"

"Don't...know."

"Where are Luca and Michele? And Ernst?"

"Away...patrol...any minute..."

Any minute was not soon enough. She had seen the orange glow of the flames as she started up the hill from Cortemilia. Surely, the patrol had seen it as well and had started back to the farm.

"They'll come around to this side eventually."

Doretta released a long, anguished groan. Her body shuddered and she passed out once again. It was impossible to move her now. Although the bleeding had stopped, her pain was increasing. Sara feared that Doretta would cry out, leading Volpe and his thugs straight to them. Where was the night patrol? Would they return in time? If so, then what? The attackers vastly outnumbered and outgunned the partisans.

The tunnel in the dried vegetation she and Doretta had followed ended there. With no possibility of moving deeper into the forest, they would have to take their chances and wait. Sara prayed Doretta's cries would not give them away. She needed morphine and Doretta's wounds needed cleaning. In her haste to run toward the backside of the farm, Sara had left behind her saddlebag. It was impossible to get back to Zeus without being seen. Although the flames that had consumed the cascina were dying down, a firestorm engulfed the barn on the far side, lighting the entire area.

Doretta still shivered. Although her breathing was labored, her open eyes searched Sara's. They had come too far to face such an ending. They could only wait. It might take a miracle to save them, but miracles did happen. Sara stretched out and held Doretta close. Whatever fate awaited them, they would face it together.

Sara was unsure of the passage of time when the sound of wheels crunching gravel roused her. The Nazi and Fascist soldiers were finally leaving. The area around the barn and cascina was dark again but for a faint orange glow still above the farm as the remaining building burned. Doretta slept, and her breathing came easier.

She waited. What if they had merely moved their vehicles and still slinked around the farm? But other than the sounds of fire consuming timber, she heard nothing. After some time, when she felt sure they had left, she crawled backwards out of the tunnel of bare vegetation. She crept toward the black shell of the cascina, and scanned the threshing floor and the open space around the forest. Not a soul was about—not the returning patrol nor the attackers. Hopefully the raiders had not seen Zeus. They were known to brutalize animals, as they did humans. She had to get to him.

As she peered around the corner of the cascina, someone grabbed her arm. Before she could pull away, sharp fingernails dug into her flesh. She tried to break free, but the woman's grip intensified. Now she had Sara by both wrists, her black eyes only inches away. Michele had taught her to raise her arms and with one swift downward thrust, free herself. She broke away from Cinzia's grip, but she wasn't fast enough to escape. Cinzia pounced and dragged her to the ground, pinning her beneath her, pressing one knee hard against her sternum. Sara struggled to breathe as Cinzia strengthened her grip on her throat and increased the pressure on her chest.

A crack rang out. Gravel shot up into her face from the spot on the ground where the warning shot landed. The claws released her throat. Sara winced and opened her eyes to see Baldo Volpe standing over her, the barrel of his semiautomatic pistol aimed squarely at her head.

"Enough, Strega. Get up. She's not going anywhere. Besides, she has important information to share with me. Behave yourself, and I'll give her to you soon."

Cinzia Strega raised her hand and whacked Sara across her face. Once she was standing, with a swift kick, she connected her boot with Sara's ribs. "That's just the beginning. You will die, you little bitch, but I'll have you begging me for a quicker end."

Volpe yanked Sara to her feet, wrenched her arm behind her back, and jammed the barrel of the pistol against her temple. Searing pain in her ribs hit her with each breath.

"See, Strega, I told you the angel was here. All we needed was patience. I'm told she never misses a bonfire. Now search her."

Strega ran her hands roughly over Sara's body, searching for a weapon. Since their arrival in Bossolaschetto, Sara had carried a pistol purely for self-defense, but in her rush that evening, had forgotten it in her room. She turned her head to avoid Strega's eyes and her glee as she handled her.

Volpe held her close against him, his forearm tight against her throat, his belt buckle jabbing into her back. "You are tiny. I could so easily break you in two. But I won't. Not yet. Now, little angel, I'm letting you go. If you try to run, you'll get a bullet in your back. Understood?"

Sara stared ahead, her mind running through all her options. If she ran, he would kill her. But at least, he wouldn't find Doretta. Surely, he knew that. Then again, he was determined, and he would continue the hunt. Cinzia would have had her pound of flesh, but he had the power and the command over the two thugs with submachine guns who stood in the distance, waiting. It was Doretta *he* wanted, not her.

He wrenched her arm higher up her back and dug the gun barrel harder against her temple. "Of course, I might shoot you now, like this. But it would be messy. So, tell me, Sara Fiore, are you going to cooperate?"

She ran her tongue along her bottom lip, tasting the blood seeping from her mouth. She nodded.

"Good. I knew you'd be reasonable."

He released her so quickly she staggered. When he aimed his gun squarely at her chest, she met his icy stare.

"Now, where is she? I know she's here. I smelled her on you."

"Who?" She relished his twisted scowl. Cinzia punched her, hard, sending her to the ground once again. Her ears rang. Another kick to her ribs made her cry out. Slowly, she staggered to her feet.

"Sara, really. As you can see, I can't always control Strega. She's waited so long to have this little meeting with you. Now, once again. Where is your friend? And don't lie. Her scent is on you."

"It's her perfume, yes." Sara winced, the pain in her side worsening with each breath. "But she gave me a bottle. I'm wearing it. Smell." She held out her wrist, but instead he pulled down the turtleneck of her heavy sweater, and leaned in to sniff her throat. He inhaled deeply—not once, but twice. Did he shudder? Sara held her breath until he stepped back. "A generous gift. But I know she's here."

"She's not. I came looking for her earlier before you arrived. I didn't plan on hanging around to welcome you."

"She's lying. Can't you see, Volpe? This isn't getting anywhere." Once again, she lunged at Sara and wrapped her fingers around her throat, digging her long nails into the flesh below her jawbone. "I've been waiting a long time for this, you little bitch. Where is the Jewess?" Her vise grip narrowed Sara's windpipe. "You *will* tell us."

"Let her go, Strega. Behave yourself if you want her when I'm finished getting what I need. She's of no use to me dead." For a split second, Volpe aimed the gun at Cinzia. Sara noticed his hand quake. "Let her go, now!"

She released Sara, who gasped, sucking in the air. Strega then turned on Volpe. "Don't tell me you're going soft on me...again. We're getting nowhere here."

Even in the dim firelight, Sara saw rage sweep across Volpe's face. The engorged veins of his neck bulged above his tight coat collar.

"Shut up, Strega!" he barked.

"Oh come now, *Baldo*, we're wasting time. Once again, you're all talk. You get all horny for the kill, but can't keep it up long enough to do it."

Sara caught his attention flickering away from her to Cinzia. Now was her chance to escape. But to where? She couldn't go in Doretta's direction, nor past the thugs to try to get to Zeus. But before she could run, Cinzia had read her mind. She grabbed her arm and slammed her pistol on Sara's head. She collapsed.

"You see, Baldo, that's how..."

Sara struggled to lift her head, but then two gunshots rang out before darkness fell completely.

CHAPTER 52

Near Cortemilia in Alta Langa
After midnight that same night – Early February 1945

Loud voices and a scream woke Doretta. She felt the cold, damp forest floor beneath her. Stiff branches scratched her face and held her down. The last she remembered, she had been in Sara's arms. Sara? She stifled a yelp as she struggled to reach for her. Her left shoulder burned.

Had Sara even been here? Or was it all a dream? The day had been so bright, but now it was close to sunset. Or was it? Loud voices nearby focused her senses. She had not dreamt that Sara had been here. Doretta had heard *her* scream and *her* voice. And the orange glow came not from the setting sun, but from the dwindling fire lit by the Nazis and their collaborators. It had all but consumed the cascina and the barn.

Doretta's body protested, but within her cocoon of tangled branches, she managed to roll to her stomach and wiggle around in the direction of the voices. She saw three silhouettes at the corner of the demolished cascina. A man and woman with a child? Were her eyes playing tricks on her? Uncertain of their distance from her, she hesitated to lift her head further. She had to get a better look. That was no child. It was Sara!

She reached under her belly and slid her pistol from the holster. Michele had cleaned it, but now it was caked with mud. She rolled on her side, and wiped the gun with her shirt. Despite the painful deep gash in her hand, she could still move her fingers. She looked up again and froze.

Although the flames had diminished, in the firelight, she could not mistake his face—Baldo Volpe with his gun trained on Sara. Just then, the woman next to him lunged at Sara and wrapped her fingers around her neck. Strega?

441

It had to be Cinzia Strega. Sara believed she worked with Volpe. And they now had Sara in their clutches. Doretta wanted to shoot her then and there, but she was in an awkward position, and with her hand burning, she didn't trust her aim. With Strega's body pressed against Sara's, Doretta had little room for error. Was it possible to get off two clean shots? She had no choice. They would either kill Sara on the spot or drag her off to an unimaginable fate.

Strega released Sara, pushed her away, and drew her weapon. Doretta steadied the pistol in her left hand and pulled the receiver back to chamber the top round of the magazine. She released the safety. Both of them had pistols in their hands, but Volpe, no doubt, had a more powerful weapon and was a better shot than Strega.

Then Strega whirled around, swung, and whacked Sara's head with her pistol. Sara dropped to the ground and lay still. Doretta aimed at the one most likely to harm Sara and squeezed the trigger. Nothing. The gun jammed! Strega stood over Sara, her gun pointed at her, only inches away. Before Doretta pulled back the receiver to eject the jammed cartridge, a shot rang out.

Doretta couldn't tell who had fired the shot. Sara lay still on the ground. Strega faced Volpe, shouting at him, her gun at her side. Doretta tried again to clear her pistol. A second shot rang out. She looked up. Now only Volpe stood. Doretta frantically struggled with the jammed pistol. Then she pushed up against the branches, trying to kneel and peer around the trees between them. A body lay still next to Sara. Had he shot them both?

Volpe bent over, picked up Strega's pistol, and placed it in his cross-body holster. Then he yanked Sara to her feet, but she collapsed again. Sara was still alive! Finally, the jammed cartridge moved and dropped out. But now it was too late. When she took her firing position once again, Volpe held Sara, one arm around her middle, her back against him, her feet not even touching the ground. With his other hand, he held his pistol against the base of her skull.

"Doretta Giordano," he shouted. "I know you're here. It would be much better for your little friend here if you gave yourself up."

Holding both Sara and his gun, it was impossible for him to use his flashlight. That didn't stop Volpe from walking in her direction and studying the ground. No doubt, Sara had made footprints in the mud earlier. Would the dwindling fire provide enough light for him to find her? With each step he took into increasing darkness and closer to her, Doretta's heart beat faster. She was trapped.

"Do you really want her to pay with her life because you're such a coward? Come out, Doretta."

Her mind raced. It was only a matter of time before he discovered her. Though she attempted to speak, the words wouldn't come out. Was she a coward? She shook uncontrollably.

"I'm losing my patience, Doretta. Come out. I just want to talk to you." He lowered Sara's feet to the ground, but still supported her. His prisoner was too weak to escape. "I'll let her go, right now." He tossed Sara to the ground as though she were a doll and walked straight in Doretta's direction.

Doretta aimed squarely at his heart and fired. And missed. Again, she fired. He screamed and grabbed his side. She knew she had hit him, but he hadn't dropped. He fired three rounds back in her direction, two that whizzed by, far over her head, and a third that she heard strike a nearby tree. Doretta aimed and pulled the trigger, but again the gun jammed. Now he knew the direction in which to search for her. But instead of advancing closer, Volpe staggered and fell to his knees. Before Doretta could fire again, he got to his feet, grabbed Sara's arm, and dragged her away, shouting expletives. She heard voices and footsteps running toward them. Did he have soldiers with him who would take up the search for her, or had she seriously wounded Volpe and they would rush him back to Alba? Or Cortemilia? All she knew for certain was they had Sara, and she was powerless to save her.

Last autumn, when hunting with Pipo, she had shot a stag, but only wounded him. It charged them then fled when she fired again. Pipo said they would have to stalk the animal until she killed it. A wounded stag, he said, was the most dangerous thing of all. Had she just sealed Sara's fate? And hers?

She heard voices from deep inside the forest. She peered into the darkness. Nothing. When she turned back, Sara and Volpe had vanished. Soon she heard the sickening sound of gravel crunching under spinning tires. Even injured, Baldo Volpe had escaped with Sara as his prisoner. She retched and then, emotionally and physically spent, collapsed.

THE SOUND OF VOICES WOKE DORETTA AGAIN. THE EYE-WATERING SMELL OF smoke was heavy in the air. The voices had come from the direction of the cascina. A familiar one called her name. She tried to answer, but her words came out as a whisper. They would not find her unless she crawled out. When she rose on all fours, her wounds screamed at her. With her left arm bent against her chest, she pulled herself out as she had entered.

"Doretta, where are you?"

Again, she tried to respond, but her raspy voice didn't carry. Finally, she reached the edge of the forest and collapsed in the mud. After some time, gentle hands rolled her on her back.

"Michele," Luca shouted. "She's here!"

She opened her eyes. Luca, kneeling beside her, cradled her in his arms.

"Cara. Mia carissima. When I saw the cascina, the barn, the bodies…" Luca's voice cracked. He choked back a sob. "I thought…Madòna…I thought you were…" He brushed away her mud-caked hair from her eye. "Doretta! What happened? You're cut badly."

"Never mind, Luca…Sara…"

"What about her?"

"Here. Now gone. Volpe." Her body shook violently. "He took her."

Luca squeezed his eyes shut at the thought of Sara in the hands of Baldo Volpe. For now, they could do nothing for her, but Doretta appeared seriously injured.

"What happened?"

"Machine guns then…voices. Fire."

He pulled his flashlight from his belt and shone it on her, discovering the small hole on her muddy, bloodstained blouse. As he had feared, the tiny hole just below her collarbone could only have been from a bullet. He took her hand, and she cried out. Luca shuddered when he saw the deep, mud-covered gash on her hand.

Michele and the others in the patrol reached them.

"Is she hurt badly, Luca?" Major York asked.

"Yes, sir. She's been shot. We've got to get her to Cortemilia," Luca said.

"From what I could see, all the vehicles have been incinerated. Even the bicycles."

"What about the radio, sir?" Lieutenant Miller asked. No Special Operatives Executive team went into the field without a radio. He slid the strap off his shoulder and placed the heavy box on the ground. "I can call London, sir."

"No, I'm afraid it will take too long for them to raise someone in Cortemilia. Can we find something not burned, and rig a stretcher? We'll have to carry her. It will take an hour on foot."

Doretta reached up and tugged on Luca's jacket. "Zeus…here. Somewhere. Call him."

"Do you have any idea where he might be?"

Whatever strength Sara had given her now ebbed. She couldn't even raise her arm. She turned her head to where she had last seen Sara. "Somewhere. There, past the clearing, in the trees."

Michele dashed off and soon they heard a loud, shrill whistle. Again, he whistled.

"He's here! I've found him. He's coming." As Michele sprinted toward the horse, he tripped and fell. "What's this? This isn't one of ours!"

Doretta closed her eyes. "Strega. Cinzia Strega," Doretta whispered. "Shot. Volpe."

Michele pulled out his flashlight. "She's been shot in the head. And there's a trail of blood leading there."

He pointed in the direction she had seen Volpe drag Sara off. So that's why he rushed away and gave up his search for her. How seriously had she wounded him?

"What do we do, Luca? What if they come back?"

"They won't. Not soon, at least. Looks like they killed everyone else. Leave her."

Michele returned running with Zeus trotting behind him. Luca unhooked the saddlebag from the back of the saddle. He dug out gauze, a bottle of alcohol, and a roll of cotton he knew Sara always had with her. She had insisted that everyone in the cascina in Bossolaschetto learn some of the basics of cleaning and bandaging wounds, and many times, he had assisted her in dire situations. He also found morphine vials in the saddlebag, but not knowing the proper dosage, he dared not administer it.

Luca set out the first aid items on the small towel he found inside the bag. Now, in the light of Ernst's flashlight, he saw the full extent of Doretta's injuries. He doused the cotton wool with alcohol and dabbed around the wounds, and poured some over the gash to flush it. She screamed for the first time that night.

"You'll be fine, cara. I'm going to take you to Cortemilia."

What if they were waiting down the hill to ambush them? He knew nothing of the raid—when, who, how many, and, of course, where they had taken Sara—but that would have to wait. Doretta appeared stable for the moment, but he knew time was not on their side. He had seen men die or lose limbs when infection invaded their bodies through seemingly minor injuries. He placed fresh cotton on her palm and bound it with gauze. Now to get her up and onto Zeus.

"Can you sit up?"

Doretta nodded. Michele and Luca got her to her feet, but they stared at one another. Zeus's back was at least five feet off the ground. Luca scanned the threshing floor that resembled a war zone, with bodies of men and beasts strewn among the debris. He spotted a low stone wall about four feet high.

"Michele, if we can lift her so she can sit on the wall, she'll be able to get her foot in the stirrup and just swing her right leg over. Doretta, do you think you can?"

She grimaced and swayed. Luca held her tighter around her waist. "I'll try…but my shoulder, I can't…"

"We'll help you. I know you're weak, but I know you can do it."

Ernst and Lieutenant Miller ran to the wall, jumped up and sat on it as Michele led Zeus over. Luca steadied her as she leaned back against the wall. He looked into glassy eyes and he realized she might faint at any moment. Ernst and Miller reached under her arms and lifted her up between them. She shrieked in pain. The horse stood stone still as Luca, between him and the wall, placed Doretta's left foot into the stirrup and helped her swing her leg over. As soon as she settled into the saddle, Michelle gave Luca a leg up. When he tightened his arms around her, he gathered the reins and held Doretta tight against him. Doretta would live through this awful night. But would Sara?

CHAPTER 53

Turin
Mid-February 1945

Sara had grown accustomed to the feel of cold steel against her head, as she had the menacing voice of the man who held the gun. Though she first knew of him as a boy over a decade ago, when he began to frequent Doretta's nightmares, she had not heard Baldo Volpe's voice until some ten nights ago.

For days after she walked through the gates of hell at Le Nuove prison, as the first rays of sun spread light over Turin, she had only seen his Nazi cohort who directed her torture. One day Volpe appeared, but he moved strangely, as though he had been injured. Then it came back to her. Though at first she thought, like all that happened that night, it was part of the nightmare she had had her last night in Cortemilia, she now knew that Baldo had been shot. Doretta had seriously wounded him.

Now, in these last several days, Sara had seen his face, his mocking eyes under his steeply arched brows capable of only one emotion: hate. And his voice had pounded her ears, as did the fists of the Nazi goons who carried out Schliessen's orders. Even in the solitude of her cell and over the constant sounds of scampering mice and anguished neighbors, she heard Volpe asking the same questions over and over again. "Where is Doretta Giordano?" "Tell me the names of Cornelia Bottero's gang." "Where is she hiding Jews?" "Who is coordinating the Allied airdrops into Alta Langa?" "Who has the codes?"

Each time either man asked for names, the same faces drifted past her. Doretta, Madama, Luca, Gianni, Pipo, Michele, Ernst, her family—their faces she saw most of all. Her tormentors stopped at nothing. Volpe had even tried to frighten her, alleging that he had arrested Madama Lia and would kill her family if Sara didn't talk. The next day, he claimed he had them all executed. Sara took comfort in knowing Baldo Volpe and the truth had never met.

Volpe's Nazi comrade repeated the lies each time she was dragged to the Albergo Nazionale for him to have his turn with her. He was more interested in Madama Lia's escape network and the location of the Jews she was hiding. Did they know for certain she hid Jews? Or was he trying to trick her into implicating Madama?

Although time was running out for them, the Nazis relentlessly pursued and punished the partisans. Suor Giuseppina had told her that the Allies had broken through the Gothic Line and had made great progress up the peninsula. The summary trial the day before resulted in a verdict that Sara believed was pre-ordained. She would pay with her life, they said, for three things—the last being the most egregious and ridiculous. Baldo Volpe accused her of grabbing Cinzia's gun and killing her. The two Blackshirt goons with him that night even testified that she, not Volpe, had fired the fatal shot. Yet she could barely stand, and Cinzia had already overpowered her twice. They condemned Sara to die at the Marinetto wall for giving aid and comfort to the enemy, hiding Jews, and committing murder.

That night, suor Giuseppina came to her with paper and a pen for Sara to write to her loved ones. She managed to slip her rosary beads and a Bible though these were forbidden to partisan prisoners awaiting execution. They would replace the comfort of Extreme Unction, also denied to prisoners. But Sara's hands trembled and the pain in her fingers, most having been stripped of their nails, prevented her from holding the pen. The nun wrote as Sara spoke.

Suor Giuseppina blessed her and whispered her assurance that God would still accept Sara into his Kingdom. Most comforting to her was that suor Giuseppina had contacted her family. They could collect her body and give her a Christian burial in Barbaresco. She knew she would join Francesco in Heaven, but she wished her mortal remains to rest next to his should his body ever be returned.

SARA STARED AT THE WALL WHERE EACH HOLE MARKED THE BEGINNING OF an onward journey for a partisan. She sensed the angels nearby. She knew as soon as they accused her of Cinzia Strega's murder that even if she divulged all she knew, she would have suffered the same fate: tied to a high-back wooden chair with a gun to her head. It seemed she was spared further torture so

Volpe could cover up his own crime. Volpe, who had proven he was beyond redemption, would continue to pursue Doretta. Sara Fiore's death would not substitute for the one he really wanted.

Cornelia Bottero had taught her to always have hope. Never give up on rescue! She had heard of such things, and now that victory loomed, the partisans were fighting with abandon. While trudging through the slush to the wall, held by only one guard, she had scanned the area for some route to escape. Once they bound her to the chair, however, she knew she had to accept her fate. Since her capture, she had prayed for the strength to hold out until the Allies arrived. She had wanted more than anything to live for Anna. But now, in these final moments, she called on Francesco just to be by her side.

Again, she heard Baldo Volpe's voice as he read out her sentence. A traitor, he called her, and as such, her life would end with a bullet in the back of her head. And he, not a firing squad would do it. His hand shook ever so slightly as the gun barrel quivered against the base of her skull. Was he hesitating?

When she heard him pull the receiver back on his pistol and the cartridge drop into the chamber, she turned to him. "I forgive you, Baldo. Take my life, but please let Doretta live in peace."

The whites of his eyes grew, and his mouth dropped open. His bewilderment was the first emotion other than hate she had seen in him. She turned back to the wall that in seconds would have one more bullet hole, and contemplated the lone dove perched atop it, the azure blue sky above. "Hail Mary, full of grace…"

CHAPTER 54

Asili
Easter Sunday – April 1, 1945

Luciana slipped out a worn envelope from her Bible. She had kept it near her since Gianni had found it in Sara's room in Cortemilia with other letters she had written to loved ones. As she had done each day since, Luciana unfolded the feather-like paper and began to read. But today was different. Lia had asked her to read it aloud to her.

Dearest zia Luce and Madama Lia, I woke from a nightmare tonight that spurred me to write this brief note to you. I write to you together because, as Doretta and I have been, you are like sisters, and together, you have given me the ability to do what I love—care for the sick and wounded. Yes, Madama, I know you paid for my schooling. How else could a simple farm girl like me have studied in Alba? Papà told me when he was here recently with Anna. Please don't be cross with him for telling me. I wanted you to know how grateful I am to you both.

Luciana stopped and smiled at Lia who stared expressionless into the distance. Had she even heard her?

And though I hope to see you soon in Asili, if what I dreamed comes true, I must ask a great favor. You both know how strong is the bond between Giovanna and my precious Anna, but please give her a place in your lives as a special child to watch over. If I don't return, Giovanna will need support, and I know you will give her much love and guidance. Please help to keep Anna's memories of Francesco alive. He loved her so.

Luciana paused and studied Sara's words written in a handwriting that appeared hurried. She had written this letter the night before her capture and the massacre at Asili. How had she sensed the dangers she faced, but not her family's?

And please, Madama, will you give Zeus a good home? He deserves it after all the miles he has carried me to care for so many. Please pray for me. My love forever, Sara.

Luciana folded the letter and returned it to her Bible. Today, Easter Sunday, a day of celebrating renewed life, Lia asked Luciana to sit with her on what Sara had called "Francesco's bench" at sunset.

Sara often said that there, above the vineyard, she had felt closest to Francesco. After his deployment to Russia, and until she left for Bossolaschetto, most dry, mild evenings, she would sit cross-legged here, rereading his letters.

As they sat in the red-orange glow of the sunset, Lia reached for Luciana's hand, but she still stared at some unknown spot in the distance, saying nothing. This was the first time the two women had been together for weeks. Since Sara's death, the lifelong friends had grown apart, each isolated in her own grief.

That morning when Luciana returned from Easter sunrise service, Lia was waiting for her. With a tortured look, she asked Luciana why this evil had visited *them*. And why had God spared Cornelia Bottero, a woman the Nazis and Fascists had kept in their crosshairs, and saved her from perishing along with the Fiores? On that day of unspeakable horror, for the first time in months, she had left Asili after receiving don Rossi's cryptic message. And why had Sara, the one dedicated to saving lives, not fighting, paid the price with her young life for giving aid to the partisans?

There was no answer Luciana could give. She struggled to cleanse the anger from her own heart, especially when she thought of her nieces. She couldn't guide Lia out of her grief. But together they might help one another to heal. Since she arrived hours after the massacre to care for Giovanna and Anna, Luciana had prayed each day for guidance, for a sign from the Holy Spirit, for healing. Before this morning, none had come.

Shortly after sunrise the morning after the massacre, after a sleepless night of tending to her traumatized nieces, Luciana stepped into the cortile to find six old women from the village on their knees, scrubbing the mingled blood of her loved ones from the cobblestones. Several men had joined them to scrub and whitewash the stone wall of the cascina before which her family had faced their executioners. No trace of the murders remained when, later that morning, Madama Lia returned from Altavilla.

When Luciana walked to Mass in Barbaresco that misty, cold morning, she believed the worst had happened to them. The next morning, Lia summoned her to Cascina Asili to tell her of Cesare Costa's message about Sara's arrest. Ten days later came the call from suor Giuseppina at Le Nuove prison that shook the foundations of Luciana's faith.

The nun who smuggled Sara's final words to her family out of the prison had contacted Lia at the number Sara had given her. She had the only telephone in Asili, and surely Sara believed that her parents should hear the news from someone who loved them. Sara faced the Martinetto wall not knowing she would soon join her parents and two of her sisters in death. Luciana thanked God for that tender mercy.

Lia had been alone when the call came. She had remained at Asili since the news of Sara's arrest, spending her days on horseback in the cold, foggy weather, retracing her rides with Sara. When Luciana looked out the window and saw Lia walking across the cortile, as though in a trance, she steeled herself for news that would shatter them. Lia spoke in a strained voice that cracked, then returned home, leaving Luciana to tell Giovanna of her sister's death. Gianni found Lia in the sala of the darkened cascina long after sunset. After telling him the tragic news, she asked Gianni to retrieve Sara's remains from Le Nuove prison the following day. Suor Giuseppina would also give him a letter from Sara to her parents to carry back to Luciana.

Long after midnight on that sleepless night, Luciana heard sawing and hammering. She wrapped herself in her sister's coat and slipped out the kitchen door. A shaft of light through the window of the barn flooded the yard. She followed the sounds and peeked through the window. Inside, Gianni was crafting Sara's coffin, stopping frequently to wipe his eyes.

This was the fifth coffin he had had to build in two weeks. Nico's childhood friend Primo Barbero had insisted on building Nico's. He had mentioned to Gianni that he felt partially responsible since his cousin, a Blackshirt from Milan, had scorned Nico at the bar the night after Sara was born. No one had ever taken his politics seriously. Until it was too late. Luciana recalled the brawny man who had lost his eldest son, deployed with Francesco in Russia, weeping like a child as he honed the wood and mumbled prayers while he worked.

The large wooden door to the cortile opened and Lia walked in with a steaming cup. She watched Gianni take it and set it on the workbench he had shared with Nico for years where they had together built Giuseppina's coffin. He stood, his head bowed, only briefly making eye contact with Madama. What Luciana observed next stunned her.

Lia held Gianni in her arms while *he* keened. In a few hours, Gianni would depart for Turin to complete the hardest task she had ever asked of him. Lia looked up, and her eyes met Luciana's. She left the window and slipped back into the cascina, knowing that she would never forget what she had witnessed.

Lia was not the only one in despair, of course, nor the only one to isolate herself. Giovanna, always so lively and the most cheerful of all the girls, had gone silent. She glowered and pulled away from Luciana's touch. She noticed how Giovanna avoided the mirrors in the house and left her hair unwashed and tangled. It was hard for everyone because of her likeness to Sara.

Despite the cold, wet weather, Giovanna insisted on riding Zeus home from the contadino who had cared for him in Cortemilia. Since then, on most days, she took to riding out shortly after daybreak and returning only at dusk. Luciana had no idea where she went, but villagers reported seeing her on the promontory below Villa Cristina at sunset, gazing at Monviso. Some days, Giovanna disappeared with Anna in the cartun for hours.

They couldn't bring themselves to tell Anna about her mother's death, but one day she said to Luciana, "Mimi is with the other angels. She's happy now." It unnerved Luciana for the child to possess a gift some might consider heresy.

As the weeks went by, Lia continued to isolate herself. All Luciana could do was pray for her. Lia attended Sara's requiem Mass and stood graveside with Luciana, Giovanna, Gianni, Pipo, Ornella, and many whom she had nursed from Barbaresco and the surrounding villages, and even as far away as Alta Langa. Although well meaning, the mourners burdened them as they struggled with their pain. Each morning, Luciana walked to the village to attend Mass. She closed each day, after the girls went to bed, in solitude, praying the rosario.

After weeks of damp, rainy March weather, today the sun overcame the clouds. Lia and Giovanna refused to attend Mass these days, even on Easter. Luciana prayed for them at Mass as she prayed for her own strength to understand God's purpose in all this. On the way home from Mass in the village, Luciana had stopped to light six votive candles in the cappella, as she did each day. When she approached the tiny chapel, a flock of swallows circled above and landed in the nearby acacia tree. Their arrival after the brutal winter reassured her. The contadini believed the birds brought good luck, something they could use. Then she spied a dove perched on the cross above the entrance. The cooing bird did not stir. In fact, it was as though it studied her as she stood before the entrance to the cappella. For a few minutes, Luciana stood, listening to the birds' soothing, sweet hum before she entered the chapel. When she emerged minutes later, the dove still perched, the gentle breeze ruffling its feathers as it watched her.

Some believed the cooing of a dove was the voice of a loved one speaking from beyond the grave. Had Sara sent a message that she was in Heaven, and peace would come soon? Luciana dropped to her knees and bowed her head in a prayer of thanks for the sign. When she glanced up, the dove had disappeared. The dark clouds that hovered over her for weeks finally lifted, and her spirit lightened.

Luciana had lost track of the time, and only traces of sunlight remained. The jagged silhouette of the mountains against the pale orange and deep purple sky faded into darkness. Lia wove her fingers through Luce's and they sat as they had done so many times before as young girls in the dense forests of Alta Langa. Lia spoke first.

"Cara, do you remember the time before the Great War when you asked me whether I thought we'd live in a time of peace? You quoted Isaiah."

"I do. And I remember sitting on the boughs of the chestnut trees, looking at the world from above, thinking how the angels must see us."

"I believed after the Great War that Europe would finally be at peace. But no. It wasn't to be." Lia struggled to hide the bitterness that had crept into her heart. It was time to cleanse herself of those emotions. She owed it to Sara. "I tried my best, Luce. I tried to put my good fortune to use to help others, but in the end…" The words caught in her throat. "All I did was place three courageous young people I so dearly love in harm's way."

She should not burden Luciana with her guilt. That she should save for confession. But she continued. "Sara would be alive." A long pause followed. "I was so selfish to draw her, Doretta, and Luca into my battle. It was as though I marched Sara to the wall myself."

Luciana released Lia's hand and turned to her. "Lia! Stop. How wrong you are. You helped Sara. You made it possible for her to heal, to relieve suffering. That's what she believed she was born to do. Her destiny."

"But I was selfish to—"

"That's not for you to say. You were an instrument of God. The lives Sara saved, the child she left behind—those are blessings from God that He worked through you. You cannot take this upon yourself. It's prideful and wrong."

Lia wrapped her arms around Luciana and rested her head on her shoulder. Too many times Luciana had reached out to her, drawn her close, and eased her tears. Why had they grown apart when they needed each other the most? "Then Luciana, it's time we *both* unburden ourselves. Did you not say despair was a sin? If so, we must put this behind us and face the challenges ahead." Lia now knew the time had come for her to return to the work that had healed her in the past.

"I don't believe I can ever put it behind me, Lia."

"No, of course not, it will always be there. But there is a way forward for us, and we must find it. We must. To live our lives, to honor our dead. This bitter grief is a danger to me—to my love of God. Do you feel in danger too, Luce?"

"I don't believe that my love of God is in danger. But if my heart does not grow lighter soon, it will break."

"My father told me a story. He had gotten to know some farmers in a remote land—a land beyond Italy. Very young children there were given animals to love, to prepare them for the love of God. A child loves an animal with abandon and sweetness, and that is the way to love God."

Luciana smiled through her tears. "Abandon and sweetness?" she asked. "Lately I have hoped my faith would just be a refuge."

"Abandon and sweetness. We could start to heal from there, couldn't we?" Lia asked Luciana who, in the gathering dark, held out her hand and nodded.

CHAPTER 55

Cortemilia
Early April 1945

I woke from a nightmare tonight with an awful feeling that something may happen to me. I know you don't believe in my premonitions, but this one was so clear. Cara, if anything should happen, please help Giovanna and my mamma care for Anna. I want so much for her to know you and, through you, the stories of our lives these last years. I have been thinking a good deal about you and Luca. You belong together and always have. He loves you, and I know you love him, so stay together always. Finally, dearest, if anything does happen to me, I want you to know I love you very much, and I am grateful for all the years of sisterhood we shared. But beware, cara, beware. I fear Baldo Volpe stalks you. The devil lives to destroy you, and you must protect yourself and those you love from him.

Much love, la tua cara amica per sempre,
Sara.

Doretta pressed the sheet of paper to her heart—the letter Sara had written the night before her arrest two months ago. She mentioned a nightmare. Why else would she have woken after midnight to write letters to her, Madama and Luciana, and Giovanna? Doretta had heard about similar letters to Francesco and Anna she had written. Gianni discovered them on top of the box with Francesco's letters to her on her nightstand when he packed Sara's belongings. Doretta had seen her writing the letters after Madama's visit to Cortemilia. It seemed natural. The war, after all, still raged, and the enemy had come so close to them in Bossolaschetto. But it puzzled Doretta that Sara had not written to her parents at that time. Madama Lia said Sara had left everything neat and orderly as though she knew she would not return to her room. Had Sara sensed the nearness of her death yet walked toward it? Doretta would heed Sara's warnings about Baldo Volpe.

She had cried all her tears, but whenever she read Sara's words, Doretta heard her voice, and her face appeared again. She was near. Tears flowed again. Yes, Sara was right. She and Luca belonged together. And Baldo Volpe still hunted her. After liberation, he would have no official power over her. Would that matter to him? His hatred toward her began long before the war, so why would its end change anything?

By the time the penicillin Major York had procured in an airdrop for Cesare worked its magic, and Doretta woke from her feverish delirium, Sara was gone. In a searing letter, Sara's zia Luciana told her of Sara's imprisonment and death, the earlier massacre of the family, and the near-miraculous survival of Giovanna and Anna, who hid behind the altar at San Teobaldo. The morphine couldn't touch her pain and heartache or help her escape the reality that each night she relived in nightmares.

Cesare had removed the bullet from her shoulder, but the painful gash across her palm had damaged tendons. The wound had healed and she could use her hand, but he said only time would tell whether she would be able to play the piano again or even do other tasks. The loss of Sara overshadowed everything. She didn't care about playing the piano or even listening to music ever again.

"Cara, I'm home!" Luca called to her.

The sun had set long ago, and Doretta had not heard him slip into the darkened room. After the rastrellamento, which had killed everyone except her and those out on patrol, he had remained in a safe house in Cortemilia near the hospital. As soon as she was out of danger from infection, Cesare moved her in with Luca. Although the Nazis and Fascists had never raided the Cortemilia hospital, Cesare feared that, if they learned of partisans recuperating there, they might sweep in and arrest them all.

Her physical wounds had healed, but Cesare and Luca worried about the profound sadness that consumed her. While the prospect of liberation charged the air and electrified the town with intense excitement, Luca still had reason to remain alert. Their enemy had proven relentless, and he worried what Volpe might do in the face of defeat.

"I received a message from your mother. It's still too dangerous for them to leave Gottasecca. She said they'll come as soon as they can. Pipo, Ornella, and Ida have been visiting her. Pipo said all's well there, although they are in despair…over you and Sara."

Doretta stretched and sat up on the divan, where she spent most days gazing out the window, and where he slept at night. In their tiny two-room apartment tucked under the eaves of a safe house, they had their own toilet and shower, a luxury they treasured. Luca referred to it as "their suite at the Ritz." Doretta slept alone, or tried to, on a narrow bed in the second room. Many a night she cried out for Sara. Luca would rush in and hold her, soothing her until sleep came again.

The owner of the house was a kindly widow who had lost her husband in the Great War and her son, her only child, in Ethiopia in 1935. In these last years, she had risked her life hiding Jewish refugees and partisans here. Many owed their lives to her. "My men died fighting meaningless wars. At least if I die, it will be for a just cause," she had told Luca when he first arrived. Luca hated having to leave Doretta alone on the days he cycled to Vesime, but the old woman checked on her and brought her chamomile tea and morsels of food that often went untouched.

Luca switched on the lamp and squeezed beside her. God, but she was lovely. Before she left the hospital, she had asked a nurse to cut her hair short. Her long hair, she claimed, accentuated the shaved spot on her head. Luca missed her flowing, dark-red tresses, but the style reminded him of the fetching short bob she had sported that day in Piazza San Carlo eight years ago—another lifetime.

Now he kissed her around the clock, as he called it. First her brow, her right cheek, her left, her nose, and then her silken lips. He still wanted her, but he was cautious. Losing Sara had devastated them all. And now, while he mourned for Sara, he also mourned for the part of Doretta that had seemed to die with her.

"Doretta, cara, it's time you stop sitting here all day. The days are warm and sunny now. Cesare said you need fresh air."

If only he would see, she was really trying to break through. It was spring after all; nature was with her, and she felt its call. Sara was with her too, encouraging her. She closed her eyes and pulled Luca close.

He felt her full lips warm against him. Her hands on his back tugged at his shirt before slipping under it. Nimble fingers danced across his back, warming his blood, before gliding to his waistline and even running across his belt. He broke away and studied her face, which was flush again with desire, beads of perspiration rising on her brow. What had changed so suddenly?

"Doretta...tell me—"

She quieted him with a warm, hungry kiss. "Hush. No words. Just love me."

He wanted to be sure, for her to be sure, but tonight her deft touch and eager kisses quickened his pulse and awakened the desire he had suppressed while she recovered.

She pressed his lips harder. "No, Luca, no words. I need..." She ran her fingers through his hair and pulled his mouth hard onto hers. Yes, Doretta's spirit was coming alive.

He scooped her up and carried her to the tiny bed they had never really shared. Though she was lusty and flirtatious, he was sure Doretta had never known a man. And she, for him, was his first and only love. Of course, as a student in Padua, he had joined his friends in the rite of passage at the local brothel. More than once he had visited a sweet, tender woman there, unlike the coarse prostitutes his friends favored. Never, though, had he applied the skills she had taught him to please a woman he loved. Once Doretta walked into his life, despite her youth, he saw no other. He knew he would wait—had been waiting—for however long it took.

She freed him from his shirt. When Luca drew back the light blanket she had clung to when he carried her from the divan, a surprise awaited him. Even in the dim light, through the sheer, pale blue cotton nightgown that covered her like gossamer, he glimpsed her full breasts and the dark triangle where her long, shapely legs met her torso. Had she planned this for today?

She usually spent the day in trousers and one of his light sweaters that always smelled of roses afterwards. Had someone brought the nightgown to her, or had she slipped out to get it when he was away? It made no difference to him. The body it covered was now his to love.

As he leaned to kiss her, she pushed him away, but held tight to his hand. She swung her legs around and perched on the edge of the bed facing him. She made fast work of unbuckling his belt and then teasingly releasing each button of his trousers from its hole. Though heat pulsed through him, he shivered. Goose bumps swept across his skin. She winced once, but her fingers never faulted. He took her right hand and kissed the healing scar on her palm, but she pulled it away and returned to his trousers. With one quick move, she rendered him naked, releasing him. She leaned forward, her lips following the fingers she brushed over him. Heat streamed from her lips through his body.

Doretta rose from the bed and reached for the hem of her gown. As she lifted the diaphanous fabric, he took it from her and finished unveiling the body he had longed to explore. She was lean and no longer as curvy as he remembered her in those form-fitting dresses in Turin, but she still possessed the body of a sensuous, desirable woman. Doretta's hands danced across his back and came to rest on his bottom, which she cupped, drawing him against her.

Once again, he gathered her in his arms and laid her on the bed. No blanket, no clothes between them—they were finally flesh to flesh, with his aching arousal pressed against her thigh. After a long kiss, she drew up her knees, signaling her need. Slowly, not wanting to hurt her shoulder, he settled against her, between her thighs, pushing her legs open with his as he lowered his weight onto her. She said nothing, but she drew in a quick, shuttering breath and bit her lip.

"Doretta...?"

She answered by pressing his buttocks, and as he pressed against the silky warmth between her legs, her mouth found his and spoke for her. His body molded against hers.

Luca's tender teacher had told him that his future wife would hurt the first time and even bleed. But there was also a way to pleasure her, and to feel when she was ready. Doretta needed no more pain. He wanted nothing but to please her. He shifted his weight and slid his hand down her silky belly to the delicate inside of her thighs. Doretta trembled when with a finger he opened her petal-soft, warm folds and slowly teased his way inside. It was as he had hoped. Her entire body relaxed, and soon he knew she was ready, but still he would wait. Now that he knew she wouldn't push him away, he felt as though they had all the time in the world.

Luca framed her face with his hands, breathing in her intoxicating scent that infused his fingers, and then smothered her cheeks, her neck, the column of her throat with kisses until his mouth settled on her generous breasts, his tongue tracing her silky skin and the quivering peaks of her chest. Her wispy sounds were full of need, and the pressure on the top of his head nudging him to her belly and beyond lit up his senses. He explored further, and as he approached her thighs, the rhythmic movement of her hips became more urgent. Her breathing came in soft pants as he nuzzled the nest of red curls and inhaled her scent once again. The fragrance of roses had always been her signature scent. What filled the air he breathed now was only for him. As he lazily explored her with his tongue, her breathing quickened, and heat rose from her body. In a flash, her body jerked, and she clenched him between her legs. With one long exhale and a sweet moan, her taut body melted. His waiting was over. He lifted himself and covered her glistening body with his. She opened her legs wide to receive him and guided him as he eased into her, fusing their bodies as one as he lost himself inside her.

LUCA WATCHED DORETTA'S BARE SILHOUETTE IN THE DIM LIGHT WHILE SHE slept. The scent of their love filled the air. She shivered. He pulled the blanket over her and kissed her cheek. Although he knew he caused her pain, Doretta assured him it was only momentary. She wanted to give him pleasure and, she added, he had pleased her as well in a way she hadn't expected for her first time. It was not mere gratification; it was euphoria beyond anything he had yet experienced. Though she had bled, she skillfully had satisfied him. How had she known? Of course. Sweet, shy Sara had tutored her in the art of loving him.

Doretta rolled toward him and stirred. The glow of a woman in love spread across her face. Her eyelids fluttered then opened, revealing her lusty blue eyes that beckoned him.

"Luca?" she said in the raspy, sleepy voice that always aroused him.

"Sì, cara." He brushed her damp, short hair from her face.

"I never thought…" She closed her eyes and inched closer. "I never thought I could feel this way, so happy, so…"

"Nor did I, cara. I love you so," he said as he drew her hips against him. The feel of her warmth against his groin stirred him. "When I came home, I never expected…well, you did surprise me."

"I need you, Luca," she said as she once again drifted off to sleep.

FOR THE FIRST TIME, LUCA'S DAY BEGAN WITH DORETTA, HER NAKED BODY against his, wrapped in his arms. Although they had slept for only a few hours, she had been peaceful, the first sleep that nightmares did not interrupt since she had moved in with him. He held her tighter, remembering the feel of her beneath him when he first lost himself in the warm, wet recesses of her body. She stirred.

Again, she opened her lusty eyes. She grinned mischievously and slid her hand down to his awakening arousal.

"Buongiorno, caro," she said as she pecked him on his lips. "What now?"

He peeked under the covers and chortled. "I think I'm ready for more now. You exhausted me, but at least I got a few hours of sleep. And so did you." He drew back the blanket and moved to lie over her, but she pressed her hand against his chest and covered herself again.

"I don't mean that." She reassured him with an open-mouthed, hungry kiss that more pleasure would come before they began their day. "Of course, again…and again…and…" She squeezed his aroused flesh and giggled.

She sighed, and a frown replaced her impish expression. "But what about us? I don't want to be your mistress."

"My mistress!" He spanked her bottom and feigned hurt. "Do you think this is all I want from you?"

"Luca, we have to be reasonable. You're Catholic. I'm Jewish. Of course, we remember when that wouldn't have mattered. But will it now…after… after all that has happened?"

Luca fell back, all desire gone, and squeezed his eyes shut. Why must she bring this up now, so early in the morning when they could be…?

"No telling what will matter now, cara. We've survived this long, but the future is anyone's guess." The specter of Silvana and her children's flight from Germany, of Doretta and her family hunted because they were Jews, flashed before his eyes. He rolled on his side and drew her close. "But whatever it may be, we'll face it together. Haven't we said that before?"

"What we said before when the world around us was on fire was one thing. But now, we have to be reasonable. I have my family to care for."

"Why should that matter? You know how I feel about your mother, your siblings. Why, Michele and I are brothers now. And Elena? She certainly isn't the moody teen she was before Bossolaschetto."

"Mamma wrote that she's like a magician, transforming whatever they could scrounge up into tasty treats for everyone to enjoy. I'm proud of her."

"Where will they go when this is over? Will she return to Turin?"

"Never, she said. Cherasco, perhaps, but never Turin. I don't know whether she'll even stay in Italy. She's mentioned leaving for Palestine to be with zia Silvana. But that's pretty much impossible. The British are only letting a few of us enter, if at all.

"Michele's a different story. He wants to travel with some of the Jewish partisans to join a group in Palestine fighting for independence. The Haganah, he called them." She paused and, with her top leg she had draped over him, drew his hips against her. The warmth from between her legs distracted him from the conversation he had known was inevitable. "Why he would want to fight again is beyond me, but all he has spoken of since we arrived in Cherasco was his dream of Eretz Israel, our homeland."

Luca's heart lurched. "Our? We? Are you thinking of leaving too?"

"Oh, Luca, I don't know. Do we have to talk about that now when we could be…?" She reached again for the evidence of his arousal, but it had vanished. She wiggled away and propped herself on her elbow. Her face was calm but not her voice. "Luca…" He turned away from her, but she took his chin and tugged him to face her. "Don't turn away from me," she ordered. "So much has happened that I still don't understand, but one thing I know…"

He squeezed his eyes shut, not wanting to see her face when she told him she was leaving for Palestine.

"Luca Olivero! Open your eyes and listen to me. Listen to me well. I love you. I want to be your wife. Whatever happens in the months, the years to come, we *will* face together." Her voice cracked.

The weight that had settled on his heart lifted.

"If you're willing to have me, Luca, then I hope you'll want to marry me, especially after…"

He expelled a deep breath and laughed, desire rising again. With one swift move, he rolled her on her back and spread her body to match his. He rested on his elbows and searched her eyes. "Oh, my dearest, you *hope* I will want to marry you? My desire to make you my wife, to be your husband who worships you, has consumed me. Yes, I want to marry you. Will you marry me?"

Silence.

"Doretta!"

She unleashed peals of girlish giggles. How nice to hear her laugh once more. He'd been worried that he would never see this side of her again after everything that had happened.

"Well, of course I will. Since we've had our wedding night, I think it would be a good idea to have the wedding! But in the meantime…"

CHAPTER 56

Barbaresco
Mid-June 1945

Doretta had chosen to walk to Barbaresco, but now on the return walk to Asili, she wished she had driven simply for the sake of her shoes. She had taken a shortcut through the valley and ruined them along the dusty trail through the vineyards. No matter—her spirits were so light, she felt as though she could almost take flight. Miraculously, the one dress her sister unwittingly had saved from her collection was Luca's favorite. The mandarin orange linen frock with cap sleeves and embroidered white flowers was perfect for such a dazzling day when she had good news for Luca. Sara would want her to shed her mourning black for the colors of the season. The summer sunshine and hillsides carpeted with flowering verdant vines helped to wash away the darkness of the war. At least for now. They all bore deep scars that Doretta believed would never heal completely. But as spring gave way to summer, despite the continued war in the Pacific and threats of civil war in Italy, their futures were taking shape.

New life had taken root in her in Cortemilia at the same time as the buds burst on the vines in Asili. In the New Year, the first without the Fascists controlling Italy since 1922, Doretta would give birth to the child of her love with Luca. They would start a family.

They had married in a small civil ceremony in Barbaresco on May 10, days after the Axis surrendered to the Allies. Their witnesses, Cesare and Giovanna, stood with her mamma, Madama Lia, Luciana Capra, Elena, little Anna, and Ida, whom Gianni had fetched from Bossolasco. The three women had taken up temporary residence at the Hotel Paradiso and would soon move into the

Capra farm with Luciana, who planned to return to the hills to host Madama Lia, Luca, and her in July. A cool summer holiday in the woods—what more could a woman with child desire?

Bossolasco had remained relatively untouched. There, in the secluded Alta Langa hilltop town, Daniela felt safest. The village had sheltered Jewish refugees since autumn 1943 with not a single villager denouncing the Pratto couple or those they sheltered. With their silence and their refusal to sell information that would have condemned everyone involved, they all helped to hide the refugees and shelter and feed the partisans, although not always voluntarily.

In each of her letters to Daniela, zia Silvana begged her sister to leave Europe and join them in Palestine. Her mother read each letter and then put it away with a thoughtful look. Doretta knew that, once she heard her joyful news, she wouldn't want to leave Piemonte. She would stay at least to meet her eldest child's first child.

They all missed Michele, who had left for Cyprus with soldiers from His Majesty's Jewish Brigade soon after demobilization. Doretta and her mother now worried that he would be drawn into another war, far away. "I won't sit by while others risk their lives to build a homeland for our people," Michele said when he broke the news of his plans. Doretta didn't try to argue with him. Michele had seen too much to sit out this struggle. She felt the same call, but Doretta could never leave Luca. And Luca, she knew, would never leave Italy.

After Piemonte was liberated on April 25, Doretta and Luca left Cortemilia for Asili, settling in with Madama Lia. Now, Luca kept mentioning her "rosy glow" and how she was "filling out." He thought it was simply her happiness with him and their marriage, which would have been illegal in Italy as little as a few months ago. A week earlier, after noticing that Doretta was turning her nose up at colazione, so unlike her, Madama Lia took her aside. "I asked Cesare Costa to see you tomorrow. He'll be here in the village."

Although a shadow often passed across her face, and Doretta could tell that she found it difficult to concentrate on the mill, Madama Lia seemed to find comfort in watching out for them and especially sharing meals and quiet evenings at home.

Doretta didn't say anything to Luca. Cesare had sent a message to her that morning and asked her to come to his office to hear the results. She worried that something was wrong, but he had simply wanted to tell her in person. When she asked when, he had even laughed sheepishly and said, "A little bit soon for a couple married just over a month ago." If all went well, she would deliver in early January, not long before what would have been Sara's twenty-seventh birthday.

With Madama Lia and Gianni gone for the day, and Luca not home from work for at least another four hours, Doretta would have the house to herself to freshen up and maybe go visit with Giovanna. Waiting to tell Luca would be torture if she didn't think of something to do. Tonight, they would dine under the pergola at Ca' dei Fiù, and Giovanna said Cesare would join them—the fourth time in a week. Lately Doretta had seen Giovanna's blue eyes brighten for the first time since the final months of the war. If they had news to share, Doretta did not want to overshadow it with her own.

Giovanna and Cesare had spent a great deal of time together since Easter. Doretta guessed that their love and admiration for Sara had brought them together. Anna was now a precocious four-and-a-half-year-old. By day, she seemed fine, but often at night, Doretta heard her screams from across the cortile. She seemed to adore Cesare. In some way, he reminded Doretta of Anna's father, but she couldn't quite put her finger on how or why. But he certainly was handsome and tall for a Langhetto, nearly as tall as Francesco was.

Had Giovanna fallen in love with Cesare? Doretta thrilled to think of it. She didn't care about the difference in their ages or that Giovanna was only nineteen. She was a beauty with a strong character and resilience. And now Doretta could only hope that life would be nothing but kind and generous to Sara's little sister. Somehow, when she thought of them together, she imagined Cesare as the helpmate. He was warm and generous, and Doretta was sure that only he would be good enough for Giovanna.

Strong-minded Giovanna intended not only to maintain Ca' dei Fiù, but Madama Lia's farm too, as her papà had. No one could have imagined that Giovanna, the youngest of four daughters, one day would have to step into her papà's shoes to save the family's generations-old farm. But a single woman, in Barbaresco, running her own farm? Doretta worried the Langhetti, even those who had known her papà, might make life difficult for Giovanna. Madama Lia, on her own in business, had wealth and position, while Giovanna was a poor farm girl. But as the wife of the beloved village doctor, no one would dare criticize her.

The shortcut joined the main road at the cappella di San Teobaldo. There had been a time when Doretta would stop with Sara at the tiny chapel filled with sweet memories. But no more. Sara was gone, and the chapel—where

Giovanna and Anna had sought refuge that tragic day—reminded her of the losses they had suffered.

Today, she stepped inside. With new life in her, Doretta needed to feel Sara's presence, to put the past behind her. How she missed Francesco and Sara and wished they were here to share in their joy. She vowed to honor Sara's wishes and tell Anna about their lives during the war. Despite the evil, they found much beauty and love that she longed to share with the next generation.

When she walked past Cascina Asili above her on the hill, she looked at the sprawling yellow building. Twenty-seven years had passed since Giulia had lived there. Soon, another child would reside in Cascina Asili. Red and yellow roses in full bloom covered the walls of the terrace. The lush grapevines woven through the pergola shaded the terrace. Tonight, they would all sit together for dinner, talking late into the night. Then she and Luca would steal away to the terrace to listen to the squealing cinghiale piglets and the hooting of the horned owl that lived in the acacia tree next to the house. They would talk about the baby and plan their future.

Luciana was due to arrive from Bossolaschetto before dinner. Gianni had driven her there a week ago to visit Daniela and to reopen the Capra farm. He left early that morning with Madama Lia to fetch her. She peeked in to Ca' dei Fiù to ask whether Giovanna needed anything for dinner tonight. No one answered her call. The house was quiet. She was busy in the vineyards, no doubt.

When Doretta entered Cascina Asili, she hurried up the stairs to the kitchen. The long walk in the hot sun had made her thirsty and, for the first time in days, she craved something sweet. She poured a glass of apple cider and grabbed a bar of torrone Luca had brought from Turin. Blades of bright sunshine flooded the sunroom at the opposite end of the hall. As she entered the room, she noticed shards of a crystal vase and roses lying in a puddle of water below an opened window. Her first thought was to clean up the mess before the water could seep into Madama Lia's shiny wooden floor.

But then she felt sudden movement, a pull of her arm, and she dropped her glass. A hand clamped over her mouth before she felt a pistol pressed hard against the base of her skull.

CHAPTER 57

Barbaresco
Later that day — mid-June 1945

"Doretta." Volpe breathed the stench of stale tobacco on her neck. "I've missed you," he said. "Why didn't you come out when I called to you in the forest? You could have saved your little friend."

Doretta's breath caught in her throat, and she nearly fainted with fear when he touched her head and combed his fingers through her hair.

"I preferred your hair longer, cara. Much more feminine."

Doretta gasped when he removed his hand from over mouth. "What... what do you want?"

"To discuss some unfinished business between us."

"I have nothing to do with you."

"Not true." He tried to caress her cheek, but she instinctively jerked her head away. He grabbed her by the hair. "I must say, you have—or had—a most comfortable bed. If only I had had your company in it."

Doretta's blood turned to ice and her skin crawled as his fingers traveled from her cheek down her throat, grazing her bare arm and settling around her waist, close to her baby. Enough! She ducked quickly and whirled around. With outstretched fingers, she stabbed at him, but he was too quick. Before her nails could make contact with his eyes, he grabbed her arm and pinned it behind her back.

"Doretta, Doretta," he scoffed. "Why must you make me hurt you?"

In the split second she had faced him, Doretta saw a man on the run. Unshaven, his hair unkempt and greasy, he had a wild, desperate look that meant that he might do anything. Through her light summer dress, she felt the coldness of the pistol against her spine.

468

"Not hospitable at all, cara." He whirled her around, slammed her against the wall, and pressed his body against her, against her baby. He brushed her cheek with his thumb. She turned her head, but he grabbed her chin and jerked her to face him. When she sensed he was about to kiss her, she brought her knee up into his groin with enough force to allow her to break free. But then she tripped and he grabbed her, pulling her down and pinning her beneath him. "You bitch," he growled, knocking her head against the floor.

It was no use. She couldn't get away, and to save her baby, she would have to seem to cooperate and buy some time.

The corners of his mouth turned up in a fiendish grin. "Are you going to behave?"

Doretta couldn't bring herself to look into his cold eyes. His weight on her was sickening, and she struggled to breathe.

He got up and jerked her to her feet. "Now, let's go. It's time."

As he pushed her up the narrow stairs, the walls closed in on her. Each board that creaked under their weight heightened her fear. The only place she could go was up to the top floor that had no escape route. If she managed to break free again, she would have nowhere to run since he blocked her from behind. When she hesitated, he thrust the gun harder against her spine.

When they reached the landing, he released his vise-like grip on her arm. She glanced through the flapping lace curtains of the open window in front of her and spotted Anna frolicking in the cortile with Fufi, the sweet mutt that had adopted Luca in their final weeks in Cortemilia. He had brought her home to Asili for Anna when he learned that Nebbia had perished with her master. Rarely did she see the dog and child apart.

Fresh terror ripped through her. Anna! Giovanna! Had Baldo Volpe come not only for her but also for the rest of the Fiore family? The Fiores would be alive if their lives had not crossed. Doretta squeezed her eyes shut to erase the image of Anna, Sara's child, now playful but soon at his mercy. She opened them again, but the image of the child was blurred. No tears! She would not give him the pleasure.

"Why...why did you do it?"

"Do what, Doretta?"

"Murder those innocents." Peals of childish laughter wafted through the partially open window. Giovanna called to Anna. If Doretta screamed, they all would die. She needed time to think of something. Where were Gianni, Madama Lia, and zia Luce? They were due back in Asili not long before dinner.

And Luca! Gianni planned to pick him up in Alba. Many hours remained for Volpe to do what he wanted and then make his escape.

"Innocent? We needed to teach the partisans a lesson. Enough of this." He pushed her away from the window. "This one right here, isn't it? I had to show myself around, but it was easy to figure out which room was yours. You're not as fashionable as you were when my mother slaved to make clothes for you and all the other Jew vermin."

Her legs faltered when she saw the neatly turned-down bed and what was laid out on it. Two hours earlier, she had smoothed the covers before leaving.

"I think it's almost as comfortable as the one you had in Turin." Her old blue nightgown and red lace panties lay spread out with a vial of Fête des Roses placed on the nightstand. He pushed her into the room and closed the door behind him.

GIOVANNA SANG AS SHE WALKED THROUGH THE CORTILE CARRYING TABLE linens for her special dinner under the pergola. With her nose buried in the bouquet of roses from her late nonna's garden, Giovanna's little helper followed. While she and Anna set the table, Giovanna heard a shutter bolt slide, but thought nothing of it. She had not seen anyone return to Asili, but she had been in the garden collecting vegetables for her dinner most of the afternoon.

And what a dinner it would be. Her life brimmed with happiness, an emotion she never thought she would feel again. Never would she forget the sound of machine gun fire on that bright late winter morning or the shock of losing Sara just weeks later. But Cesare's love would at least sustain her as she took on the tasks before her. And with the support of Cesare and Madama Lia, Giovanna believed she would succeed in preserving the legacy of Ca' dei Fiù for Anna and for her children.

In the weeks following Sara's murder, Giovanna retraced her sister's routes across the countryside astride Zeus. Sitting for hours, watching the sun sink behind il Re, she wondered about the lonely future she now faced. Anna would one day marry and leave Ca' dei Fiù, and she would be left alone, a tota with a farm and no male heir to continue the legacy of the Fiore family in Asili. As a child, long before the war set her world on fire, Giovanna had sworn not to marry. Never had she thought the burden of running the farm and producing an heir would fall to her, the youngest of four daughters. But it had. Selling the farm was out of question. She would not let her parents, or Sara, down. With all that she had learned from her papà, Sara, and Francesco, she believed herself capable of taking on the job of running Ca' dei Fiù. The problem of an heir she would leave for later.

Later came quicker than she expected when Cesare Costa began to call on her. At first, she felt uncomfortable with the older man who was once in love with her eldest sister. Had he sought her company as a substitute for Sara, a way to deal with his own grief? In no time, Giovanna discovered that he was falling in love with her, not a memory, and her own feelings for him blossomed.

After the end of the war, when Madama Lia asked her to manage her farm, she balked. How could she step into her papà's shoes at the Fiore farm *and* run Cascina Asili? Madama said she would hire more hands to work the land. Giovanna had only to oversee the day-to-day management. Besides, Madama added, Doretta would not sit still and would need to work. She had no desire to return to university in Turin, and though she knew little about farming, Doretta had a quick mind for numbers and organization. Both Madama and Luca agreed they would make a great team. But even with Doretta's help, managing Cascina Asili on its own, plus looking after Anna and the babies that would soon come to her and Cesare, would leave her no time for the most important task ahead: preserving Ca' dei Fiù. It seemed too much. But dearest zia Luce stepped in.

Luciana no longer wanted to live in Alba. Hospital work had become strenuous for her and the many memories of Sara by her side too difficult to bear. She longed for the familiarity of her sister's home in the countryside and the company of Luigia's remaining child and her granddaughter. Besides, the abundance of young former Army nurses could meet the hospital's needs. Helping Cesare a few days a week in Barbaresco, and Giovanna in Asili, would fill her days and her soul. Once Luciana made her decision, Giovanna could no longer say no to Madama Lia.

And tonight, she and Cesare would announce their engagement—no doubt making tongues wag in the village. But Sara never cared what others said, nor would she.

Carisimma Sara. How she missed her so. Although she recalled her annoyance when Anna insisted that they go for a drive that morning in early February, what would have happened if they had not? The lives of Sara and Francesco would have been in vain. But Anna lived, and through her lived Sara.

"Zia Gio, is this right?" Anna said as she placed the flowers into the vases Giovanna had set on the table earlier.

"Perfect, Anna. Help me with these napkins, and then let's go finish inside."

Giovanna returned to the hot kitchen and Anna ran out to the barn-yard to play with Fufi. The afternoon breeze blowing through the open windows and doors cooled the air. She felt closest to her mamma in the kitchen. The connection was strongest when she prepared the dishes she had taught her to make and stirred the pots in which she had cooked so many delicious meals.

As she stood washing vegetables, her mind drifted back to the shutters in Doretta and Luca's room. She was certain they had been open, as were all the others in the cascina, when she walked across the cortile to the pergola. Yet, the shutters were closed when she returned. Could that have been the sound she heard? She saw Doretta when she had left for her appointment in the village after lunch. Had she returned? If so, why would she rest with the shutters closed on such a hot day? She would finish with the vegetables and go check on her. But she sensed something was wrong.

"Anna, I'm going over to get something from Madama's kitchen. You stay here with Fufi. I'll be right back."

"Sì, zia Gio," she replied as she and the dog continued chasing the squawk-ing chickens around the barnyard.

When Giovanna was halfway across the cortile, a woman screamed and cried "No!" Doretta? Then silence.

Giovanna spun around and raced back home. Long ago, with her papà, she had learned to hunt. Since the massacre, she kept her papà's loaded hunting rifle on the high gun rack by the door. She grabbed it and started back out of the house. Anna! Giovanna froze. Should she call her inside and order her to stay put, which would terrify her, or leave her outside?

Another scream.

Her heart pounding, Giovanna pulled the front door closed and raced back across the cortile. When she reached the top of the first flight of stairs, she stopped. Eerie silence. Then she heard a noise from upstairs, heavy footsteps, and Doretta's voice again, this time pleading.

Giovanna bounded up the stairs and rushed to the closed door of Doretta and Luca's bedroom. She took a deep breath and threw it open. There on the bed was Doretta, partially clad, her hands tied to the iron bed frame above her, pinned under a man wearing nothing but a shirt. Doretta's eyes, ablaze with terror, met hers. This could be only one person—Baldo Volpe.

The man jumped up and stumbled beside the bed. Then he froze at the sight of her face. "Sara...no!"

So it was Baldo Volpe after all. Her hands had been shaking, and the rifle felt heavy, too heavy to hold up. But at the mention of her dear sister's name, Giovanna drew it level to her chest. She held her breath.

He moved to dive for his gun on the chair by the bed, but it was too late. With two bullets from her papà's hunting rifle, Sara's baby sister sent Baldo Volpe to hell.

CHAPTER 58

Asili
November 1945

"Like this, Anna. Careful, now, the shears are sharp." Pruning, the art of shedding the spent, dead canes to make way for new growth in spring, was a vineyard skill handed from father to son over generations. But Ca' dei Fiù lacked sons, and her father had died leaving Giovanna with the responsibility of teaching the next generation one of the most important tasks in the vineyard. She would teach Anna all of them over time, but it was traditional to start with this one.

Giovanna promised Anna when she turned five that she would teach her to prune. Her birthday was only a week away, so Giovanna had surrendered to her pleas. Each evening during the final weeks of the harvest, while Luciana prepared dinner, Anna had spent time kneeling on the bench of the kitchen table, snipping thin canes Giovanna had cut for her. So nimble was she that in no time Giovanna and Luciana trusted her with the shears, but only under close supervision. In a few years, Giovanna would teach her to use the coltello serramanico.

"Like this, zia?" Anna giggled and beamed as she held up the first cane she cut on her own.

"Bravissima, cara! *Il tuo primo tralcio*!" Giovanna clapped—then she winced. Yesterday, the first signs of life in her womb came with a kick that she first discounted as a muscle spasm. Cesare had chided her about spending too much time on her feet in the vineyard. But today, she felt the life within her. She placed her hand on her round belly and studied the snow-dusted mountains in the distance, the approaching clouds peeking over the summits. The scent of rain, carried on the southwesterly breeze, was in the air. Cold weather, maybe snow, would arrive by morning.

While Anna continued snipping the plant, Giovanna raised her eyes to the view from Francesco's bench. How Sara had loved it here, as did she. La Torre stood tall as guardian of the village. Majestic Monviso had sheltered partisans from the Nazis and Blackshirts. The sprawling Rio Sordo valley lay below, and Pora hill, her papà's favorite hunting grounds, seemed far off in the distance. Villa Cristina, on the crest of Monte Silva, had been returned to the noble family when the Nazis fled. Freedom had come to Barbaresco, Langhe, and Piemonte. And Italy had united once again.

But Giovanna wondered whether she would ever be free of the grief that plagued her, of Baldo Volpe's terrified eyes, especially at night. He had given her no choice, and they were all the safer for it. But having taken a life, no matter how despicable he was, haunted her. The warmth from Cesare's body next to her as he slept reassured her that she wasn't alone. Someone loved and protected her.

They had surprised many by marrying less than six months after the slaughter of her family and just six weeks after she shot Baldo Volpe to death. The courtship seemed a whirlwind even to her, looking back. But it had also seemed urgent.

The war altered their lives in so many ways, including her plans never to marry. Cesare had suffered too. They understood that, and so much more, about each other.

"*Guarda*, zia! Another one." Anna's striking resemblance to Sara, no longer a source of pain, now comforted Giovanna. She dropped the cane and patted Giovanna's belly. "You're getting fat. Like zia Doretta. Except she's *very* fat now." Anna paused then furrowed her brow as she continued to pat Giovanna's belly. "Is there *really* a baby in there?"

Giovanna laughed and tousled Anna's unruly reddish-blonde curls. "Yes, cara, there is. You'll be like a big sister to your *cugino* and zia Doretta's baby. Just like your mamma was to me." Giovanna regretted those last words. Though Anna often chatted about her mamma, it often became an interrogation. And more often than not, that led to more questions about Francesco's whereabouts. When would he return home? Now, before Anna responded, Giovanna pointed to her wicker basket on the ground. "Put your shears in there and carry the basket for me. Time to get back home. Zia Luce wants us back at noon for lunch."

Anna frowned and stuck out her tongue as though ridding her mouth of something unsavory. "Oh, but, zia Gio, I'd rather eat Zeus's hay than her tajarin."

"Anna Bosco! That's unkind." Giovanna struggled not to smile. Anna had a point. She often wondered how her mamma could have been so gifted in the kitchen, while her sister seemed to excel at burning things and ruining recipes. At least she shared Luigia's green thumb. Her prized garden had flourished under Luciana's care, keeping them well stocked with vegetables through the autumn. Now, if she could only learn to cook them. "We must be nice to her. She's trying hard. She's never had to cook for a family."

Anna crossed her arms and pouted. "But you're such a good cook, zia. Why don't *you* cook for us?"

"Why?" Giovanna laughed. So many questions from this one. Sara had once said that Anna reminded her of Giovanna, questioning everything from her first words. Anna stared, waiting for an answer. How sad that it was nearly a year since she had last seen her mamma. "Because I don't have time. There's too much work around the farm. Besides, it would hurt zia Luce's feelings. You don't want to do that, do you, Anna?"

"No, but—"

"Zia Luce's here to help care for you and the babies that are coming soon. I can't do it on my own, even with zia Doretta's help."

"I can help with babies." Anna puffed out her chest. "You watch and see!"

"Yes, I know, cara. You'll be a big help. But zia Luce also needs us the same as we need her."

Anna's faced softened. She uncrossed her arms. "She does?"

"Yes. When families hurt, they comfort one another." She waited while Anna, her reddish eyebrows knitted tight together, processed her words.

"Then I'll *try* to like her food, but it won't be easy. Won't *you* make something special?" That wheedling tone—it had to go. They all had to watch themselves not to spoil Anna.

"I'm cooking your birthday lunch next Sunday. It won't only be pranzo domenicale, but a celebration for you!"

Anna jumped and hooted. "Is papà coming for my birthday?"

Anna must have had another dream about Francesco. Instead of fading into the past, he seemed more present in her dreams than ever. "He said he's coming home," she sometimes said. Nearly seven months had passed since the war ended in Europe, and yet there was still no sign of Francesco. Luca had inquired, but the army had no answer, no classification for him. Luca did learn that the Soviets had not released many prisoners of war from the far eastern provinces until after the Japanese surrendered in August.

They had no way of knowing whether Francesco had suffered that fate. But as the weeks turned into months, any glimmers of hope that he had survived the brutal prisoner-of-war camps had faded.

She took Anna's hand. "Sit here, Anna."

They sank to the ground between the rows of skeletal vines. It was time for another talk about her parents. "Now, Anna, remember when we visited your mamma's grave on All Saints' Day?" Anna nodded. "You remember what I told you about Heaven?"

"But Papà's not in the *cimitero*. You told me that's where we went while waiting to go up to Heaven"—her spine stiffened, and she declared—"so he can't possibly be dead."

To Anna, it made perfect sense, but Giovanna believed more with each passing day that Francesco's mortal remains lay somewhere on the Russian steppes, never to be identified, never to rest next to Sara and their stillborn son in Barbaresco.

"Well, Anna, there's always hope, but you're a big girl and can understand your papà may be going to Heaven from a place faraway, not from our cimitero here in Barbaresco." The intensity in Anna's eyes, mirrors of Sara's, unnerved Giovanna. *Enough.* "Lunch! I'm hungry. And I don't care who's cooking. Anduma, Anna."

Anna sprang to her feet and grabbed the basket. As Giovanna watched her scamper up the hill, a wave of sadness washed over her. She had to admit that she, too, had held out hope, especially after Sara was taken from them. And he was the only brother she had ever known.

Before Giovanna got to her feet, Anna, without the basket and with her little arms flailing, ran screaming back to her. Anna wrapped her arms around Giovanna's waist and buried her face against her. She pointed toward the cortile and wailed. "A man! A man! On a horse! Oh, zia Gio, save me!"

This was what happened whenever a stranger appeared in the cortile. Lately a few had come by seeking work, and it always upset Anna. Giovanna picked up the girl and started walking home. When she reached the bench above the vineyard, the man who had frightened Anna came into view. Her knees buckled, and she nearly dropped her load. This man was no stranger.

Giovanna struggled to steady herself while Anna clung to her, keeping her off balance. Oh, Sara. Cara sorella, do you see? She dropped to the bench, cradled Anna's face in her hands, and kissed away her tears.

"Hush, carina." Giovanna struggled to control the excitement rushing through her, the quiver in her voice. "He's a friend. I promise. Run along and go help zia Luce. Don't be frightened. Tell zia Luce I'm coming soon."

Leery, Anna walked slowly up the hill, glancing back at Giovanna. When she got close to the house, she sprinted around the side to the kitchen door.

"Zia *Luuuuce…*" Anna hollered. Luciana would come out soon.

Giovanna refocused her attention on the tall man, his red beard, and long hair, clothes in tatters. He had dismounted and stood next to the emaciated white horse as if afraid to come closer.

"Francesco!" she screamed as she rushed to him.

Wrapped in his arms, her arms around his bony body, she did not care about the stink of the road or his filthy clothes. Francesco was home. Finally, a miracle in Asili. When she heard the squeak of the front door's hinges, Luciana appeared, with the frightened child peering from behind, clutching her long skirt. Anna let go of Luciana and slowly started toward Giovanna.

"No, Anna! Wait." Luciana grabbed her arm and drew her back toward the house. The two stood at the door, wariness on both their faces.

"Oh, Sara, carissima." Francesco pulled Giovanna closer and drew her face to him as he bent to kiss her, but Giovanna pulled away.

"Sara?" she scoffed. She had had enough of people mistaking her for or comparing her to Sara. "Francesco, it's me," she said, clearly annoyed. "Your little sister Giovanna. Don't you recognize me?" Francesco had left home when Sara was close to Giovanna's age, but in the moment he had seen her, he did not find it strange that Sara had not aged.

"Gio? Little Giovanna? Let me see you, carina. How you've grown. I'm sorry." He embraced her again and laughed heartily at his error. She could not share the mirth in his reaction. Again, she stepped back. "Where's Sara?" he asked as he looked about the cortile. "Out on Zeus?"

Giovanna said nothing. It had fallen to her to break the news to him. She looked over at Luciana, still standing at the cascina door. "Francesco…tie the horse."

Alarm flashed through his eyes. At that moment, Gianni, who had been standing at the garage door, watching the stranger with Giovanna, approached.

He studied the stranger's face, and took the reins. "Welcome home, Francesco," he said, then turned and led the horse to the barn.

"Come with me." She took Francesco's hand and led him to the bench they named for him. "Sit."

The howl of an anguished man brought Luciana running. When she saw Giovanna holding him—Francesco, she now knew—in her arms, she turned and walked slowly back to the cascina. She shut her eyes and, when she opened them, Anna stood at the door.

"Zia Luce, is that Papà?"

Luciana closed her eyes again and prayed. Dear Lord, please make me worthy.

CHAPTER 59

Asili
New Year's Day 1946

L ia sat by the fireplace that Gianni had just laid with old Moscato root-
stock. How brilliantly it burned. She felt warm in the woolen shawl
Luigia Fiore had knitted for her only two Christmases ago. At dawn,
she woke, thinking of many things but mostly of her neighbors and especially
of Sara. What an honor it had been to be a part of their lives.

It would be a lonelier pranzo di *Capodanno* this year, but at least they had
Francesco with them again. Ornella who, with Pipo, moved to Asili before
Christmas, had prepared what she considered a light meal of five dishes. This
year, *cotechino e lenticchie* held more importance than ever. The sausage and
lentils would bring them good luck in 1946. Although they still had no beef
to make a *sugo*, Ornella's tajarin—nearly as tasty as Giuseppina's—would taste
delicious all the same under sage and Pipo's fresh butter.

Francesco had already brought bottles of Barbaresco from his first and last
vintages with Nico and placed them on the long dining room table. That was
his tribute to the Fiore family. She hoped it would bring him some comfort.
He was trying. He thought of others. This gave her hope on the first day of
a new year.

Soon, everyone would gather in the cortile. She barely had enough time to
finish reading Frieda Stern's latest letter. No matter the cold, they would walk
to Barbaresco for Mass and a visit to the cimitero afterward.

*I have so missed you, cherie, and look forward to our time in Crans-sur-
Sierre. Don't you recall how magical the winter is there? We could use some*

480

magic. It seems like yesterday we spent our winter school breaks at my parents' Villa Petit Paradis on Plans Mayens. Remember how we laughed at those etiquette lectures? All we ever wanted was to be plainspoken.

You will be pleased to know the United Nations has made great strides with the orphanage in the American Sector in Germany. They converted the Kloster in Markt Indersdorf. Oh, Lia, you must visit the orphanage with me in spring. These orphans who witnessed such savagery are now well cared for, but the resettlement work is daunting. No one wants Jewish child refugees. So sad, cherie.

I wonder whether you've heard any news from our dear friends in Palestine. Silvana and Daniela have repaid me tenfold by their tireless work helping with resettlement, as little as is allowed these days. They are busy working with Renata Goren, who got there first, you may recall. I hear Ida, Elena, and Talia go periodically to one of the kibbutzim, I forgot the name, to teach the children how to cook. But you have probably heard that from Doretta.

Speaking of whom, how is she? I know how she misses Sara, but the baby will be a great comfort to her. To all of you. You must be so delighted that you will soon have a baby under your roof.

Yes, soon. Lia had spied Doretta singing and folding baby clothes in the nursery Luca and Gianni had set up for her. Her belly was a thing to behold and very low. She was showing all the signs that soon she would deliver.

I hear Daniela plans to return for a long visit once the baby is born. Do you think Daniela will ever be able to convince Doretta and Luca to emigrate? She said she will never live in Italy again, but I do believe, once she holds her grandchild, her heart will say otherwise.

Oh, Frieda dearest, we have much to discuss in Crans-sur-Sierre later this month, Lia thought. She cringed at the thought of Luca, Doretta, and the baby leaving Asili.

…So cherie, I must close. I miss you terribly, dearest Lia, and count the days until we meet in Valais next month.

My love always,
Frieda.

Lia watched the orange and blue flames dancing in the fireplace. Yes, children had a way of showing what really mattered in life. She was tempted by Frieda's continuing work in Germany and with children. Sometimes Lia felt that she had given her all, but behind her grief, she felt the same old energy. She wondered how she would participate in a venture she did not direct. She would discuss that with Frieda in Switzerland. Soon. "La mej," as her father used to call her, was not quite ready to retire.

Lia thought she heard footsteps and looked behind her. No one. The sun was just beginning to rise. Although she always found refuge in her sala, this was where Doretta had come face-to-face with her would-be murderer. Young Giovanna had saved her and her unborn child in an upstairs bedroom that probably no one would ever enter again. Lia shuddered to think what that must have been like for them. They still suffered from the shock, she knew, but they were strong women whose babies would soon help them to heal.

They had received their share of miracles that year too. Luciana believed divine intervention had saved Doretta and delivered Francesco from the horrors of the Soviet prison camp near Michurinsk. Few Italian prisoners of war had survived German or Soviet labor camps. That Francesco should arrive on a white horse, a week before Anna's fifth birthday, unnerved Luciana. But she no longer questioned God's plan.

"Madama," Luca called from across the room, snapping her back to the present. "It's time. Cesare is driving Doretta, but I'll walk."

"Oh, Luca. You scared me. How's she feeling today?"

"She had a restless night. Cesare believes she's starting labor, but she said no."

Lia rose from the divan and stood with her hands on her hips. "Well then. Should she even go? It's freezing and damp outside." Lia, stop it, she told herself. Luca and Cesare would care for her.

"I told her she should rest." Luca's frustration with his wife showed in his voice. "But Doretta won't be swayed."

"At least she isn't walking to the village. It's good of Cesare to drive her."

"That was no easy task, convincing her. Stubborn…"

"Are you talking about me again?" Doretta toddled down the stairs, pecked Luca on his cheek, and greeted Lia with two kisses on both cheeks. "Buongiorno, Madama. Buon Capodanno."

Though heavily pregnant, Doretta seemed full of energy and looked splendid. She had ignored all the country customs of confinement and drab clothing. Lia was certain that glamour would always color her personality as it did her clothes.

"Buon Capodanno, Doretta. I heard you had a restless night, but you look lovely. Radiant."

"Grazie, Madama. Do you like my dress? I know it's extravagant for a maternity frock, but I'm certain I'll need it again." She winked at Luca and handed him her coat.

The unspoken language of love flushed Lia's cheeks. Yes, more babies will come. And soon.

"Why yes. The lace collar is lovely on you."

"I found it in Turin on my last trip in September and was saving it for this occasion. And what about this mantilla? Luce gave it to me for Christmas." She wrinkled her nose as she studied the fine black lace. "I think it's a hint that the baby should be baptized."

Luca chuckled and gave a helpless shrug.

"What are you laughing at?" she asked.

Lia had some thoughts about that. But only if asked would she venture to give any opinion.

"And the locket. The silver is so lovely pinned against the black." She remembered giving it to Doretta for Hanukah in 1933, so many lifetimes ago. "Is that a new scent you're wearing, Doretta?"

"Madama! You noticed."

"It suits you."

"Thank you. It's Acqua di Parma. Citrusy and soft." She held her wrist to her nose and closed her eyes as she inhaled deeply. "The baby will like it. Luca brought it from Rome on his last trip." She frowned at Luca who stood holding her coat open, waiting for her. "Luca, you look as though you've never seen me dressed up."

"Let's just say it's been some time, cara. You look lovely...not that you don't always," he quickly added. He helped her into her coat. Forgetting himself in Madama's presence, he nuzzled Doretta's ear when he pulled her tresses from under the coat collar. "Now, why won't you let me drive you to the cimitero? And why Mass?"

Doretta gave her husband a playful slap. "Oh stop it, Luca. We've already been through that. I'm going to be there for Sara, and her family. Cesare's driving me to the village."

As if on cue, Cesare called to her from the entrance.

"And I want to walk with everyone from the church to the cimitero." She held up her hand before Luca spoke. "I'm ready." Once bundled, she slid the strap of her handbag onto her forearm, pulled on her gloves, and wrapped a wool scarf over her head and around her throat. Then she was down the stairs and out to the cortile, leaving Luca's protestations hanging in the air.

Luca shook his head and rolled his eyes. "*Che donna*!"

"Luca, mio caro, the ways of women…oh, never mind." She grinned and threaded her arm through his. "Come, let's join her."

Everyone huddled together, bundled against the elements. Gianni tried to persuade Madama to ride in the car, but she would have none of it. The wind was up, but the mood was warm, almost festive.

"Gianni, park the car close to the church so we can get the berries and greens out afterward," Lia directed. "Anduma!" She waved her gloved hand, and they set off for the village.

Lia and Luciana linked arms and walked together, their heads close. Giovanna and Luca walked behind them with Francesco and Anna trailing. Well along in her pregnancy, Giovanna had not slowed down. All through the damp, cold December weather, she worked alongside Francesco, pruning vines and tending to the alchemy of wine making in the cellar. "Nonna and mamma always worked until they had their babies. So will I," she always answered when Cesare pleaded with her not to work so hard.

As they turned onto via Rabaja at the cappella, Lia leaned closer to her friend. "Luce, about Francesco—has he said anything to you?"

"Not much. All he said was that in autumn of forty-two, he was taken prisoner. Many of his comrades died on the way to the camp. That's all he could bring himself to say."

"To think after that, what he came home to…"

"I think of it often. He's still a bit lost."

"Give it time. He's only been home for what, six or so weeks?"

"And Anna keeps him busy." A brief, soft laugh broke from Luciana. "Nonstop talking about her mother and dragging him on long walks in the vineyards. They even went out in the cartun so she could show him the skills Gio taught her."

"She no longer wants a goat cart. She wants to learn to ride, Francesco told me."

"Well, she's old enough, but not on Zeus. Perhaps old Romeo. The old boy can't go much faster than a plodding walk."

"No, I was thinking of a pony. I could—"

"Lia…" A grin appeared on Luciana's otherwise placid face. "Surely, you're not thinking of another nurse flying through the countryside on horseback."

Oh, what Lia would not give to send Sara's child to boarding school in Switzerland. Freida Stern could watch over her. Francesco could never afford to educate her, nor would he think of sending her away from Asili. Lia saw that she would have to step back, to help only if asked or if she could see a way that wouldn't amount to meddling, much less put others in danger.

"Nothing like that, Luce. I promise. Only, I still have Sara's saddle, and Gianni could adjust the stirrups to fit her. It would help Francesco to have the little one occupied in the mornings. Horses help everything, don't they?"

"They seem to."

"And what of Giovanna and Francesco? I haven't seen them together much. Only when they are working, and there doesn't appear to be much conversation between them."

Luciana shrugged. "Hard to say. But her likeness to Sara must make it difficult, and not only for him. And now Giovanna's happily married and carrying a child."

Lia glanced at the procession behind them. Francesco, leaning over to listen to Anna, lagged, keeping some distance from Giovanna. Whom did he see when he looked at her face?

"By the way, Lia," Luciana said, "he had a letter from his cousin Renzo Bosco the other day." She drew closer to Lia and lowered her voice. "It seems he has been *very* successful in New Orleans. I believe it's the cousin who was pushing Francesco to go with him to America before he came to Langhe."

"Oh yes. Sara mentioned that he was still pestering Francesco to leave Italy after they were married."

"Leave Italy? For America? Sara never would have. But we forget, Lia, though we may see him as a Langhetto, he will always be Sicilian."

"How recent was the letter?"

"July, I think. It was waiting for him. According to Francesco, Renzo had returned home from deployment in Europe shortly before he wrote it. But that was all he said."

Lia shuddered. The thought of Francesco leaving and possibly taking Anna with him made her clutch Luciana's arm, squeezing it through the woolen sleeve. Francesco needed more time to adjust to life without prison guards, to life without Sara, and to the vineyards without Nico. Surely, Francesco would never feel at home in that hot, teeming American city. Francesco belonged on the land—on *terre di Langa*. And he always would.

"Luciana…" The words caught in her throat. Luciana gave her a look to say, *I know*, and slipped her hand into Lia's. They walked on in silence.

Don Emilio's sermon, a message of God's love and promise for eternal salvation for the coming year, inspired Lia—a perfect prelude to their walk to the cimitero to pay respects to their loved ones. Out of the corner of her eye, Lia noticed Doretta wince twice during the service, but she still insisted on making the fifteen-minute walk despite the cold. Luca walked with his arm around her, while Cesare and Gianni followed in their cars.

The bitter wind picked up as they entered the cemetery. There were the five graves that shouldn't be there. Her beloved Giuseppina rested not far away. Lia pulled out her handkerchief and then looked for Anna, the sweet child whose mother now rested with her ancestors. She had her head down but held tight to her papà's hand. Poor child. As Lia watched, Anna also reached for Giovanna's hand and pulled her near. Giovanna leaned down and kissed her cheek.

Around the headstones of the Fiores and Giuseppina, they distributed the branches of holly berries Gianni had handed them at the church. Then they gathered at Sara's grave. Luciana would lead them in prayer. Lia recited her own silent prayer of thanksgiving. They had suffered great losses, as had many of their neighbors and so many others, but they had come through together. Lia thanked God for each person around her.

Lia, standing behind Doretta at the foot of Sara's grave, saw her grab Cesare's arm. "It's time," she whispered. Cesare glanced at the puddle at Doretta's feet. It was, indeed, time.

Doretta threw a smile back at Lia. "Perfect it would happen here," she said. "Sara's laughing now, I'm sure. She would have told me to walk and walk, as I did with her that day. And I've done it. Now I can have my baby." Cesare dashed to the car with Luca shepherding Doretta. The others rushed to Cascina Asili to await the birth. Lia and Luciana looked for Francesco, but he lingered by Sara's grave. Anna still held his hand but bent to pull an object from beneath the holly branches.

"Look Papà. An angel." She handed the tiny wooden statue to Francesco. His expression, at first solemn, brightened as he studied the hand-carved figurine. "Why would someone leave a wooden angel here? And look, an envelope."

Francesco squatted next to her. Lia and Luciana held hands and stood back from them, trying not to eavesdrop. He opened the envelope and removed a single sheet of paper.

"Read it, please, Papà."

With undying gratitude to the angel of Alta Langa who saved my life in the forests near Bossolasco. Gino.

"Who's Gino?"

"I don't know, Anna. Probably a partisan. You know Mimi saved many, many people in her life, especially during the war. Don Emilio said lots of people come to her grave to pray and thank her."

"Is Mimi the angel?"

Francesco nodded, pulled out his kerchief, and wiped his eyes.

"People all over Langhe called her 'the angel of Alta Langa.'"

Anna scrunched her nose and pressed her finger against her lip, her tiny face contorted in deep thought. "*Why…?*" Francesco was fast learning that Sara's inquisitive nature ran strong in their daughter. The questions never stopped.

"You know what a guardian angel is?"

"Sì, Papà. Zia Luce said it's an angel always there to save you."

"That's right. And that's what Mimi was—a guardian angel, but here on earth. Now she's *our* guardian angel until we see her again…in Heaven."

"Papà?"

"Sì, carina?"

"Will you teach me to ride so I can save people like Mimi did? And zia Luce can teach me to be a nurse."

"We'll see, carina. But I thought you wanted to be a doctor like Cesare."

"Yes, Papà. I'd like that."

Francesco gazed at the sky, at la Torre—the landmark that led him to Barbaresco, to Sara—and shook his head. A shy grin creased his leathery face. He wrapped his arms around his daughter and lifted her from the cold Langhe earth where Sara slept.

Pipo and Ornella had already returned to Asili. Luciana left this arrival to Cesare. Doretta's delivery no doubt had electrified the atmosphere in Lia's cascina.

"Gianni," Lia said. "Luciana needs to return straight away, but drop me off at the cappella."

Before Lia climbed into the rear seat with Luciana, Anna darted in front of her.

"Ca ma scüsa, Lili. I want to sit between you and zia Luce."

That was a first. Her eyes met Francesco's. They both knew this likely meant that Anna no longer feared for him. She had always spread her affection, and she took what they gave her as her due. So this was a comforting sign, particularly today.

When Lia got out at the cappella, Anna's chatty voice still rang in her ears. Already, she spoke both Piemontese and Italian, and Lia had heard Luca teaching her a few words in English. Lia felt sure that, like her mother, Anna Bosco, would never meet a stranger.

Although anxious to return to Asili, Lia wanted some time alone. She had not visited Giulia's and Alessandro's graves in Alba for some time. A prayer for them in the cappella would have to do today.

Alone in the tiny chapel, reminiscing about those whose lives had touched hers, Lia lost track of the time. As she walked along the lane, Lia looked across the snow-covered vineyards that carpeted the slopes of the Rio Sordo valley. Under all that snow, life was resting, getting ready. The vines would come alive in spring, as they did each year whether there was war or peace. Already the village buzzed with talk of new vineyards and new plantings—the coming years would be important ones for their noble grapes and their humble village.

"Lili!" Anna shouted to her from the cortile. *Lili.* Maybe it was time for the children to have a less-imposing name for her. Perhaps even the adults. Lili would do fine. Now, Anna's excitement told her all she needed to know. Doretta was not one to hesitate or tarry when she had a task to accomplish. Anna raced to meet Lia halfway along the lane.

"Lili! It's a girl! Sara! Like Mimi. Her name is Sara." Anna stopped and scrunched her face as she studied Lia's face. "Why are you crying? Aren't you happy?"

"Sì, carina. *Molto felice.* People cry when they're happy too."

Small fingers searched for hers. Hand-in-hand, they walked on. Lia indulged in thoughts of what the future might hold for this Sara while Anna was already planning her own.

"Lili? Will you teach me to ride?"

Lia swooped the child into her arms.

"Ti amo, Anna. Ti amo."

THE END

GLOSSARY

A dopo. *Italian.* See you later.

A più tardi. *Italian.* See you later.

acqua borica *Italian.* boric acid water

agnolotti (del plin) *Italian/Piemontese.* little ravioli, usually stuffed w/meat, vegetables, cheese (plin: pleated or pinched)

agrodolce *Italian.* sweet-and-sour

Al vostro servizio. *Italian.* At your service.

Allora *Italian.* So then…

Alzati! Adesso! *Italian.* Stand up! Now! (imperative)

Am fa piasi' cunosla. *Piemontese.* I'm pleased to make your acquaintance.

amica/o *Italian.* friend (feminine/masculine)

amore a prima vista *Italian.* love at first sight

Anch'io. *Italian.* Me too.

Anch'io ti amo. *Italian.* I love you too. [also written **t'amo**]

Andiamo a tavola. *Italian.* Let's go eat. (Let's go to the table)

Andrà tutto bene. *Italian.* All will be well.

Anduma! *Piemontese.* Let's go! [*Italian:* **Andiamo!**]

angelo *Italian.* angel

angioletto *Italian.* little angel

antipasto/i *Italian.* food/s served before the first course

aperitivo *Italian.* beverage (usually alcoholic) drunk before evening meal to stimulate **appetite; aperitif**

ariano/i/a/e *Italian.* Aryan (male / male plural / female / female plural)

Arrivo! *Italian.* (I am) Coming! (imperative)

Arvëdsi *Piemontese.* Goodbye [*Italian:* **Arrivederci**]

Ascolta! *Italian.* Listen! (imperative)

Aspetta! *Italian.* Wait! (imperative)

Aspettate! State zitti! *Italian.* Wait! Be quiet! (imperative to more than one person)

assolutamente *Italian.* absolutely

Auf Wiedersehen. *German.* Goodbye.

Auguri! *Italian.* Congratulations!

B

Babbo Natale *Italian.* Father Christmas; Santa Claus

baccalà *Italian.* cod (usually dried and salted for easy keeping)

baci *Italian.* kisses [singular: **bacio**]

baci di dama *Italian.* Lady's kisses; two buttery hazelnut cookies sandwiched together with gianduja (sweet hazelnut chocolate paste)

baci di Cherasco *Italian.* kisses of Cherasco; crispy, irregularly-shaped dark chocolate and hazelnut sweets that are a Langhe tradition.

bacialè *Italian/Piemontese.* matchmaker

baio *Piemontese.* bay horse

bambinaia *Italian.* nursemaid; nanny

basta *Italian.* (that's) enough [imperative: **Basta!**]

Basta così! *Italian.* That's enough! (be quiet!)

Bastardi! *Italian.* Bastards!

bastardo *Italian.* bastard

ben arrivati *Italian.* welcome (plural)

benvenuto/a/i *Italian.* welcome (masculine/feminine/plural)

biova *Piemontese.* type of soft bread

birocc *Piemontese.* type of two-wheeled cart

biscotto/i *Italian.* cookie/s

bisnonna *Italian.* great-grandmother

bisnonno *Italian.* great-grandfather

bitte *German.* please

Bitteschön *German.* You are welcome.

bogia nen *Piemontese.* people who are not adventurous and prefer to stay in their comfort zone

boh *Piemontese.* great utility word meaning "I don't know" or "I'm not sure."

bollito misto *Italian.* a slow-cooked mixture of poached meats and vegetables served primarily in winter

bon-a seirà *Piemontese.* have a good evening [*Italian*: **buona serata**]

bon-assèira *Piemontese.* good evening [*Italian*: **buonasera**]

bondì *Piemontese.* ciao; hello

Bondì, monsù, an dua ca alè la cassin-a dei fiù? *Piemontese.* Hello, signore. Where is the Cascina dei Fuì?

bosco *Italian.* woods

botte/i *Italian.* large wood barrels generally 10–300 hectoliters, usually made of Slavonian oak

bottero *Piemontese.* wine barrel maker; cooper [*Italian*: **il bottaio**]

brasato al Barbaresco *Italian.* beef braised in Barbaresco (or **Barolo** or **Nebbiolo**)

bricco *Italian/Piemontese.* top of a hill

brindisi *Italian.* a toast

brodo *Italian.* broth

Buon Natale *Italian.* Merry Christmas

buona fortuna *Italian.* good luck

buona giornata *Italian.* have a good day

buona serata *Italian.* have a good evening

buonanotte *Italian.* good night

buonasera *Italian.* good evening

buongiorno *Italian.* good morning

C

ca' *Piemontese.* farmhouse [*Italian*: **cascina**]

Ca' dei Fiù *Piemontese.* farmhouse of the flower [**Ca'**: farmhouse; **Fiù**: flower]; pronounced "cah-day-few"

Ca ma scüsa *Piemontese.* Excuse me.

caffè *Italian.* coffee; coffee shop

caffelatte *Italian.* coffee with hot milk

cane *Italian.* dog [**bravo cane**: good dog]

cantina *Italian.* winery; wine cellar [plural: **cantine**]

Capodanno *Italian.* New Year's

cappella *Italian.* chapel

capra *Italian.* goat

carabinieri *Italian.* Italian national police

carissima *Italian.* dearest (feminine)

caro/a *Italian.* dear (masculine/feminine)

carina *Italian.* term of endearment; darling (feminine)

cartun *Piemontese.* type of wagon (four-wheeled)

casalinga *Italian.* housewife

cascina/e *Italian.* farmhouse/s

Casellario Politico Centrale *Italian.* Central Political Records archive

castello/i *Italian.* castle/s

cavatappi *Italian.* corkscrew

Che casino! *Italian.* What a mess!

Che donna! *Italian.* What a woman!

Che nebbia! *Italian.* What fog!

chi *Italian.* who

Chi iè? *Piemontese.* Who's there?

chiesa *Italian.* church

chinino *Italian.* quinine water

ciabot *Piemontese.* little buildings in the vineyards used to store tools and give shelter from sudden summer storms to workers

ciarea *Piemontese.* ciao; hello

cimitero *Italian.* cemetery

cinghiale *Italian.* wild boar

cognata *Italian.* sister-in-law

colazione *Italian.* breakfast

colpo di fulmine *Italian.* struck by lightning (love at first sight)

coltello serramanico *Italian.* a special curved, wooden-hand knife used to harvest grape bunches

confino politico *Italian.* internal exile (usually in a godforsaken village or island, not prison)

coniglio con verdure *Italian.* rabbit with vegetables

coniglio *Italian.* rabbit

consigliere *Italian.* adviser

contadino/i *Italian.* (peasant) farmer/s

cortile *Italian.* courtyard

cotechino e lenticchie *Italian.* slow-cooked pork sausage with lentils (traditional New Year's Day lunch dish)

cucina *Italian.* kitchen; cuisine [as in **cucina piemontese**: piemontese cuisine]

cugina/e *Italian.* cousin/s (feminine)

cugino/i *Italian.* cousin/s (masculine)

cugnà *Italian/Piemontese.* marmalade of figs, pears, grape must, hazelnuts eaten w/cheese

D

Dai *Italian.* Come on! (different uses but usually expression of impatience)

damigiana/e (di vino) *Italian.* bulbous, narrow-necked, 3- to 10-gallon bottle/s; "demijohn" in English

danke *German.* thank you

DELASEM *Acronym.* Delegation for the Assistance of Jewish Immigrants

delation *English.* denouncement

Dell'acqua (minerale) per favore. *Italian.* Some (mineral) water, please.

digestivo/i *Italian.* digestive/s (after-dinner drink to aid in digestion)

dimmi *Italian.* (you) tell me

discriminato/i *Italian.* outcast/s; marginalized

dolce *Italian.* dessert; sweet

Dona eis réquiem *Latin* Grant them eternal rest. (blessing at end of Catholic funeral)

donna di Langa *Italian.* a woman of Langhe

dopo *Italian.* later [**a dopo**: see you later]

dottor *Italian.* title for medical doctors and lawyers

dottore *Italian.* doctor

Dov'è... *Italian.* Where is...

Dove sei? *Italian.* Where are you?

E

è finita *Italian.* it's over [**la guerra è finita**: the war is over]

È un po' pazzo. *Italian.* He is a little crazy.

Ego conjúngo vos in matrimónium. *Latin.* I now pronounce you husband and wife.

EIAR *Acronym.* Ente Italiano per le Audizioni Radiofoniche; only broadcast radio station allowed by the Fascist government.

en caul birth *English.* rare birth with amniotic sac still attached to baby's head; veiled birth

Entlassen! *German*

Entschuldigung. *German.* Excuse me.

F

Facciamo una passeggiata. *Italian.* Let's take a walk.

fasces *Italian.* bundle of rods with a projecting axe blade; symbol of Italian Fascist party

ferragosto *Italian.* August festival on the 15th

festa di maggio *Italian.* May festival

festa *Italian.* feast; festival

fiordaliso/i *Italian.* cornflower/s

fiore/i *Italian.* flower/s

fiù *Piemontese.* flower; pronounced "few"

493

Folgen Sie mir. *German.* Follow me.

forno a legna *Italian.* wood-fired oven

fratello/i *Italian.* brother/s

frazione *Italian.* hamlet

G

Gasthof *German.* inn

gianduiotto *Italian.* long, triangular-shaped, hazelnut chocolate; traditional confection in Turin

gianduja *Italian.* sweet hazelnut chocolate paste [*Piemontese:* **giandoja**]

Giustizia e Libertà *Italian.* Justice and Freedom (anti-Fascist group based in Turin)

gnocchi con fonduta di Castelmagno *Italian.* gnocchi with melted Castelmagno cheese

Grazie a Dio! *Italian.* Thank God!

Grazie *Italian.* thank you

grazie mille per tutto *Italian.* thank you very much for everything

grissino/i *Italian.* typical breadstick/s in Piemonte [*Piemontese:* **ghersin**]

Guarda! *Italian.* (you) Look!

guten Tag *German.* hello; good day

H

Halt, warten Sie mal. *German.* Stop, wait a minute.

I

i nostri partigiani *Italian.* our partisans

Ich bin bei der Geheimpolizei. *German.* I am (with the) secret police.

Ich bin hier für... *German.* I am here for...

Ich heiße.../Mein Name ist... *German.* My name is...

Ich liebe dich für immer. *German.* I love you forever.

il piccolo angelo *Italian.* the little angel

il problema della razza nell'Italia Fascista *Italian.* the problem of race in Fascist Italy

il Re di pietra *Italian.* the Stone King [**il re**: the king]

il tuo primo tralcio *Italian.* your first branch (vine)

In nómine Patris, et Fílii, X et Spíritus Sancti. *Latin* In the name of the Father, and of the Son, and of the Holy Spirit.

insalata piemontese *Italian.* a mixture of tuna, tomatoes, and parboiled garden vegetables

Italianità *Italian.* the Italian spirit, character, or essence; term favored by Mussolini

J

Ja *German.* yes

Jetzt reicht es *German.* That's enough.

judenfrei *German.* free of Jews (initial stated goal of Nazis and Mussolini to rid Germany and Italy of Jews)

judenrein *German.* cleaned of Jews (of Jewish blood) - the goal of the Wannsee Conference and "The Final Solution of the Jewish Question" to exterminate Jews by systematic murder

K

Keine Worte. *German.* No words. (hush)

L

l'arcangelo Michele *Italian.* the archangel Michael

l'estate di San Martino *Italian.* The summer of St. Martin (Indian Summer)

la guerra continua *Italian.* the war continues

la mej *Piemontese.* the best (term of endearment)

landò *Piemontese.* a type of carriage

Langhetto/a *Piemontese.* Man/woman from Langhe [plural: **Langhetti/e**]

Langhetti di Barbaresco *Piemontese.* Men (or men & women together) from Barbaresco

Lass ihn frei! *German.* Set him free!

Le Leggi Razziali *Italian.* The Racial Laws of 1938 (Laws in Defense of Race)

letto matrimoniale *Italian.* queen bed

lire *Italian.* Italian currency pre-Euro (singular: **lira**)

lo spirito *Italian.* mixture of 90% alcohol and boric water

località *Italian.* locality (hamlet)

M

Madòna *Piemontese.* the Madonna (Virgin Mary)

marito *Italian.* husband

masca *Piemontese.* witch [plural: **masche**]

masche *Piemontese.* witches

Massaie Rurali *Italian.* largest fascist women's group consisting of rural women (peasants)

meine liebes Schatzli *German.* my dear darling

meraviglioso *Italian.* marvelous

mercato *Italian.* market

merluzzo alla salsa verde *Italian.* salted cod with green sauce

mersi *Piemontese.* thank you [*French:* **merci**]

metodo classico *Italian.* champagne method of producing sparkling wine where a natural second fermentation take place in the bottle

mezzadri *Italian.* sharecroppers

mezzogiorno *Italian.* midday

mi chiamo… *Italian.* my name is…

mi dispiace *Italian.* I am sorry.

Mi prometti? *Italian.* Do you promise me?

mi scusi *Italian.* Excuse me.

mia cara amica *Italian.* my dear friend (feminine)

mia cara sorella *Italian.* my dear sister

mia povera sorella *Italian.* my poor sister

minestre da bate el gran *Piemontese.* literally, "soup from the beating of the grain;" soup made when the grain harvest was threshed, separating the grain from the shaft.

mio caro *Italian.* my dear (masculine)

Mischling/e *German.* person/s of mixed race (e.g., Aryan with Jewish); Nazi pejorative meaning "mongrel."

Mitglied der Geheimpolizei *German.* member of secret police

molo/i *Italian.* pier/s

molto felice *Italian.* very happy

Molto gentile da parte tua. *Italian.* (It is) very kind of you

monsù *Piemontese.* signore

mulino *Italian.* mill (e.g., flour mill)

municipio *Italian.* city hall

N

Na do madh'in'zot. *Arbëreshë.* If God wills.

Natale *Italian.* Christmas

nocciole tostate *Italian.* toasted hazelnuts

non adesso *Italian.* not now

Non è possibile. *Italian.* It's not possible.

nonna *Italian.* grandmother

nonno *Italian.* grandfather

O

OVRA *Acronym.* Opera Vigilanza Repressione Antifascismo; Mussolini's secret police

P

panettone *Italian.* a sweet bread originating in Milan served during the Christmas holiday season

partigiano/a *Italian.* partisan male/female [**partigiani/e**: partisan/s]

Pässe bitte *German.* Passports, please.

passeggiata/e *Italian.* stroll/s [**passeggiare**: to stroll]

pazzo/a *Italian.* a crazy man or woman

pelle d'oca *Italian.* goose bumps

Perché *Italian.* Why?

Perdona la mia gelosia. *Italian.* Forgive me for my jealousy (for being jealous).

Perdonami amore mio. *Italian.* Forgive me, my love.

pesche della vigna *Italian.* peaches from the vineyard

piacere *Italian.* to please

Piacere di fare la voi conoscenza. *Italian.* Pleased to make your acquaintance. (Pleased to meet you.)

Piasì *Piemontese.* Pleased to meet you, …

piccola vedova *Italian.* little widow

piovra *Italian.* octopus

polizia/e *Italian.* police

polpettone di tonno cotto *Italian.* tuna loaf

povera ragazzina *Italian.* poor little girl

povero/a *Italian.* poor

pranzo della vendemmia *Italian.* harvest (celebration) lunch

pranzo di nozze *Italian.* wedding lunch

pranzo domenicale *Italian.* Sunday lunch

pranzo *Italian.* lunch

primavera *Italian.* spring

professore *Italian.* professor [title: **professor**]

promesso *Italian.* I promised (note: past tense is used in daily language for present tense of "I promise")

prometti *Italian.* you promise

putagè *Piemontese.* wood-fired cooking stove that doubles as a source of heat

Q

quindi *Italian.* therefore; so

R

rastrellamento/i *Italian.* raid/s; search and round-up (literally "rake")

Raus! *German.* Out!

Razzismo Italiano *Italian.* Italian racism (cornerstone of Fascist racial ideology)

Rebecchine di Gerusalemme *Italian.* polenta and anchovy fritters

Resistenza *Italian.* Resistance

Risorgimento *Italian.* 19th century political movement; Italian unification

risotto alle lumache *Italian.* snail risotto

risotto con funghi *Italian.* risotto with mushrooms (e.g., porcini)

rocche *Italian.* fortress-like cliffs; deep chasms due to geological erosion

rosario *Italian.* rosary

S

Sacratu! Quanta fioca! *Piemontese.* My God! What snow!

salsiccia *Italian.* salsiccia [plural: **salsicce**]

salumi *Italian.* Cured meat products primarily made from pork, but also beef; charcuterie

Salute! *Italian.* Cheers! (literally: to your health)

scelti *Italian.* chosen one (Avanguardia honor)

Schatzli *German.* sweetheart; dear

Scusami *Italian.* Excuse me.

secondo *Italian.* second (masculine); main course [plural: **secondi**] [*English*: **entrée**]

Setesse! *Piemontese.* (you) sit!

Siamo qui. *Italian.* We are here.

Siediti, Generale…per favore. *Italian.* (You) Sit down, General…please.

Sono arrivata. *Italian.* I have arrived.

Sono qui. *Italian.* I am here.

Sono tornati. *Italian.* They have returned.

sorella *Italian.* sister

sorellina *Italian.* little sister

Sporca ebrea! *Italian.* Dirty (female) Jew!

staffetta/e *Italian.* courier/s; specifically, women couriers in the Resistance (literally: "relay race")

stalliere *Italian.* groom

stazione *Italian.* railway station

strada *Italian.* street

strega *Italian.* witch

stronza arrogante *Italian.* arrogant bitch

stufa *Italian.* wood-fired stove (also used for heating) [also, **putagè**]

stufetta *Italian.* heater

subito *Italian.* immediately; at once

sugo *Italian.* sauce

suocera *Italian.* mother-in-law

suocero *Italian.* father-in-law

suor *Italian.* sister (as in nun or nurse)

T

taboret *Piemontese.* a term of endearment for a small woman

tajarin *Piemontese.* Piemontese traditional egg-rich, golden pasta (thin ribbons)

Tante *German.* aunt

tanto/i *Italian.* much; a lot

tartufo bianco *Italian.* white truffle

terre di Langa *Italian.* land of the Langhe

Ti amo. *Italian.* I love you.

Ti ho sempre amato, ti amerò per l'eternità! *Italian.* I always loved you, I will love you forever!

tinello *Italian.* a place for the family to gather in a cascina

tisane *English.* infusion of herbs, fruits, roots, bark, spices, or flowers steep in hot water

torre *Italian.* tower (Barbaresco tower is referred to as **la Torre di Barbaresco**.)

torta di nocciole *Italian.* hazelnut torte

tota *Piemontese.* unmarried woman (spinster)

tranquilla *Italian.* Be calm (quiet).

trisnonna *Italian.* great-great-grandmother

trisnonno *Italian.* great-great-grandfather

Troppo mal di cuore. *Italian.* Too much heartache.

tu *Italian.* you (singular, informal)

tua cara amica per sempre *Italian.* your dear friend forever

tuma *Piemontese.* type of soft or semi-cheese (literally: "made by the farmer himself") [*Italian:* **toma**]

tutti a tavola *Italian.* everyone to the table to eat

tutti *Italian.* everyone

tutto *Italian.* everything

U

Ura ed disne! *Piemontese.* Dinner! (time to have dinner)

V

vaccaro *Italian.* cow herder

Vai! *Italian.* Go!

vedova *Italian.* widow

Ven si! *Piemontese.* Come here!

vendemmia *Italian.* harvest; vintage

Vielen Dank. *German.* Thank you very much.

Vieni qui! *Italian.* Come here!

vigilia *Italian.* vigil; wake

vitello *Italian.* veal

vitello tonnato *Italian.* thin slices of rare poached veal w/a tuna sauce

voi *Italian.* you (plural)

Volo. *Latin.* I want (marriage vow response meaning I do/will)

volpe *Italian.* fox

W

Was ist los? *German.* What's going on?

Z

zia *Italian.* aunt

zio *Italian.* uncle

LATIN MARRIAGE VOWS

N. vis accípere N. hic praeséntem in tuam legítimam uxórem (marítum) juxta ritum sanctae matris Ecclésiae

[Name], do you take [Name] here present, for your lawful wife (husband) according to the rite of our holy mother, the Church?

Ego conjúngo vos in matrimónium. In nómine Patris, et Fílii, X et Spíritus Sancti. Amen.

By the authority of the Church I ratify and bless the bond of marriage you have contracted. In the name of the Father, and of the Son, + and of the Holy Spirit.

AFTERWORD

Thank you for journeying with me through Piemonte during its darkest days where—despite the horror—love and charity endured. I hope my characters—good and evil—touched you deeply.

Although Italy's Fascist-era and wartime history bears a dark stain that has yet to be fully expunged, when liberation came to Italy in April 1945, eight out of every ten Italian Jews survived. No country other than Denmark and Bulgaria saved as many of its Jewish citizens. The number of Italian clergy, government and military officers, soldiers, and ordinary Italian citizens who risked their lives to help Jews during the Nazi occupation far outnumbered those who aided the Nazis in their brutal hunt for and deportation of Jews after September 8, 1943. High in the mountain valleys of western Piemonte, simple farmers who had never met a Jew hid refugees at great risk to themselves and their villages. Although Mussolini's motives for keeping the door open to Jews fleeing the spread of Nazi terror throughout Europe were to obtain the foreign currency they brought, not out of Christian charity, the fascist country was the last in Europe to allow Jewish refugees in, saving countless lives before the sanctuary closed to them after the Racial Laws began in September 1938.

As I grew up the fourth child of parents who were born in New Orleans, Louisiana, in 1920 and 1921, both world wars loomed large in my childhood. My nonno Joe Manale fought in France during the Great War. My daddy joined the Navy in 1944 after working for Andrew Higgins in New Orleans building landing craft used on the beaches of Normandy and PT boats for the South Pacific where Daddy later served. As far as I knew, only Germany and Japan were America's enemies, and only Germany was to blame for the Holocaust. My mom's Sicilian family with roots in Contessa Entellina had no kind words for Mussolini and told only stories of America's role in liberating

501

Sicily. Although I learned early in my life about the Holocaust, neither my parents nor anyone in my Sicilian family ever mentioned the Holocaust in Italy. Did they even know the extent of the horrors Jewish Italians and refugees suffered during the Nazi occupation of central and northern Italy? They are all gone now, so I cannot ask them; but I suspect, in the absence of high-profile prosecutions in Italy such as the Nuremberg trials, the truth was slow to surface.

I came by most of my stories that inspired *Angel of Alta Langa* in a highly unusual way. Over two decades, they were told to me by Piemontese wine family members who witnessed the horrors for themselves and those who learned of the tragedies and triumphs from their parents and grandparents. Rarely were these stories discussed outside the family, but as time marched on, I got a sense that members of Piemonte's greatest generation wanted to share what they had experienced before it was too late. It was truly a priceless experience to learn the stories from those who lived it.

My Piemonte odyssey began in the cold, rainy, early days of November 1999 when I made my first trip to Langhe with my momma and my schnauzer, Otis, alongside for the adventure. Little did I know that this marked the beginning of a career change from law to writing that would take over ten years to materialize. It was also the first milestone in my journey to write *Labor of Love: Wine Family Women of Piemonte and Angel of Alta Langa*.

In 2003, Giovanna Rizzolio drew back the curtain for me when, in her kitchen at Cascina delle Rose in Tre Stelle, a frazione of Barbaresco, she told stories of her nonna Beatrice Rizzolio, and Carlo and Maria Ravera during the Nazi occupation and their amazing feats of selfless bravery. All three were honored in the Garden of the Righteous among the Nations at Yad Vashem in Jerusalem. As is written in Ecclesiastes 3:1, there is a time for everything. Though I wanted to learn more and do what had not been done—record these precious stories before they were lost—it was not the right time in my life. But eventually, that changed. Released at Ca' del Baio in Treiso (Barbaresco) on June 2, 2016, *Labor of Love* was my first project in a race against time to learn and share all that I could from those who had borne witness to the Fascist era and Nazi occupation.

Through *Labor of Love*, I shared the timeless relevance of stories of struggle and triumph, but I recognized life never stands still. People would die. Children would be born. Generations would end, and new generations would begin, but I knew that, as long as the stories continued to be told, traditions would not die, and the lessons of the past would not be forgotten. And I pray they will not be repeated.

The warm reception *Labor of Love* received from the families and readers across the world overwhelmed me. But I felt my job was unfinished. Within the hours upon hours of interviews, reams of notes, and stacks of books that laid the foundation for *Labor of Love* were the seeds for a novel I believed could reach beyond the wine and tourism world to people who possessed a passion for history and great stories of courage in the face of evil. It took a pandemic and my seclusion at home in the Rockies—far from my beloved Piemonte—and the support of my husband, Dani, and my editor, Elatia Harris, to coax the novel out of me. *Angel of Alta Langa* is my pandemic silver lining.

Although fictional, my *Angel* draws upon stories of actual people and the events they experienced between 1918 and 1946. My characters are inspired to varying degrees by people I know, read about, or chronicled in *Labor of Love*, and who are long gone, but they are all products of my imagination. A few minor but important characters were real people. In addition to honoring the wishes of their families, choosing fantasy names enabled me to be more creative when I integrated them into the world of my fictional characters.

Madama Lia, Sara, Francesco, Giovanna, and Baldo were cornerstone characters. Everyone else was built around them. Doretta, I must confess, was not initially part of the plot outline, but as I began to write, she appeared suddenly to play a crucial role in Sara's life. I cannot imagine what I would have done without her. I've learned not to question the muses when they speak to me. Although the other characters (except the evil trio of Baldo, Gunther, and Cinza) in varying degrees carry the DNA of people I know, Doretta was a woman unto her own. I love her dearly.

A word about Francesco's red hair: yes, there are Sicilians with blonde and red hair and blue eyes—thanks, no doubt, to the Norman influence centuries ago. My grandfather Joe Manale had red, curly hair and green eyes. Giulio Inglese of Abbazia Santa Maria del Bosco in Contessa Entellina is quite tall and his wife, Anna Salerno, is petite. Since I imbued Sara with much of Anna's personality, stature, and looks, it felt natural to give Sara a tall, handsome husband like Anna's.

Although Fabrizio and Tina Pratto are fictional characters, they are based on Rina and Demetrio Veglio who, in my opinion, have not received the attention they so richly deserve for their courage in hiding Jews in plain sight in their Hotel Bellavista in Bossolasco during the Nazi occupation. They have been recognized by the Jewish community of Turin, but there is no mention of them in Yad Vashem, which puzzles me. The entire village of Bossolasco deserves a place with the "Righteous among the Nations." All the villagers of Bossolasco stood alongside the Veglios in protecting the lives of those who sought refuge from the Nazis in their bucolic, hilltop village in Alta Langa. Had someone denounced the Veglios and the town officials, the Nazis most likely would have massacred the villagers and burned Bossolasco to the ground. But no one denounced them—a miracle of humanity since a handsome bounty was paid to those who exposed Jews in hiding and those who helped them. When, in 2013, I first learned of these saviors—these angels—I set my sights on learning more about them and perhaps one day writing their story or, as I have done here, incorporating it into a novel.

A quick word about nonna Mirella. She is an amalgam of the grandmothers of her era who saw the absence of sons in a family as a curse. But, like many of the grandmothers of modern times whose sons and daughters have given them only granddaughters, Mirella came to appreciate the value and strength of Sara. Although Piemontese mothers still wish for grandsons, today's wine family women of Piemonte stand shoulder to shoulder with their fathers, brothers, and husbands, doing their part to make Piemonte wines some of the most sought after in the world and to preserve the legacy of their ancestors who farmed the land.

People often ask me from where in my imagination Zeus emerged. There are skeptics who think a nurse on horseback who cares for contadini is a bit fantastical. Actually, there was real-life, present-day inspiration for Sara and Zeus. His name is Roberto Anfosso. In May 2014, kismet directed my path across the good doctor's in Piazza Vittorio Veneto in Castiglione Falletto, just next to the Vietti winery gate. I had just dined with Maurizio Rosso, and as we crossed the piazza, we spotted a tall man whom Maurizio appeared to know astride a black horse. Little did I know that when Maurizio introduced me to dottor Anfosso, Zeus was born.

Fortunately, in my sixty-four years, I have never met anyone close to Baldo or Schliessen's vile character or someone who spouted such anti-Semitic views in my presence. Unfortunately, we have much proof they do exist. Creating them and placing words in their mouths that I would never speak much less think proved to be the most challenging part of writing *Angel of Alta Langa*. I spent many hours in prayer, meditation, and consultation with my Israeli-American husband over the portrayal of Baldo. Should I forego the words he would have spoken? The first time I wrote Baldo's dialogue found in chapter seven, it sickened me. How could I continue, I asked myself over and over? In the end, Dani and my developmental editor, Elatia Harris, supported me in my belief that it would be unrealistic not to have written the evil trio as the real-life villains they truly were.

One of the first decisions I had to make was whether to create fantasy place names. I quickly abandoned that idea. I set out to write a novel set in Langhe, specifically Barbaresco and Bossolasco, and that I would do. As I mention in my Ringraziamenti, Asili was chosen as the main setting of *Angel of Alta Langa* because of my close friendship with the Grasso family of Ca' del Baio in Treiso and my desire to pay homage to Giulio Grasso's mother, Fiorina Cortese, who was born and raised in Asili. The frazione of the village of Barbaresco and its tiny cappella di San Teobaldo have always enchanted me. The view, the vineyard, and my sense of the people who once lived there combine to make it the perfect setting for the farms of the Fiore family and Madama Lia. One note: I did take literary license and grow Nebbiolo in Asili a few decades earlier than the vines actually were planted. There were vineyards all around the slopes of the Rio Sordo valley, but the area next to the two cascine were covered with fruit orchards before the war. Ronchi and Martinenga, however, were thriving vineyards at that time.

The inspiration for Madama Frieda's villa in Camogli is the Hotel Cenobio dei Dogi. It sits along the shore at the eastern edge of the tiny fishing village exactly as I described it, but the villa was not a hotel until 1956. In 1985, I first visited this magical village, staying in a terrace room just like the one I described that the honeymooners occupied. We've been back several times since, and it remains a wonderful getaway.

The first massacres the Nazis conducted on Italian soil occurred in Piemonte on the shores of Lago Maggiore in the north, and in Boves to the south near Cuneo shortly after the announcement of the Italian Armistice on September 8, 1943. The first victims were Jews, easily discovered with the assistance of the Fascists and their meticulous Jewish census. The Boves massacre was a reprisal conducted by the infamous, bloodthirsty Waffen-SS officer Joachim Peiper, also responsible for the Malmedy massacre during the Battle of the Bulge. Other reprisals occurred in Langhe throughout the occupation.

Did a bloody reprisal occur in Barbaresco? No, but one was narrowly averted in August 1944 thanks to the intercession of the bishop of Alba. The fascist il II Cacciatori degli Appennini brigade under the command of

Colonel Aurelio Languasco conducted a rastrellamento in Barbaresco on August 5, 1944. They took thirty villagers hostage, threatening to execute them and burn the village and countryside if the three Germans and five Fascist soldiers the partisans kidnapped from the Barbaresco train station were not released. If not for the quick thinking of the bishop who sprang into action, searched for the partisans and their prisoners, and convinced the partisans to release them, Barbaresco's name would be among the long list of villages that suffered massacres at the hands of the Nazis and Fascists between autumn 1943 and liberation on April 25, 1945.

Research during the pandemic, as I've mentioned elsewhere, was daunting but not impossible. Thanks to the internet, Amazon, and online used-book stores, I managed to add to my already large cache of research material on Piemonte and Italian history. The list of books and scholarly articles that I used as reference material is too long to include in this book, but I have provided a list of some of the books I found particularly helpful—ones I thought readers would seek to expand their knowledge of this era.

My hope for *Angel of Alta Langa* is that it will find readers across a broad spectrum with an interest in stories about strong characters who lived through one of the darkest periods in modern history. I drew most of my characters' DNA from people I know in Piemonte and Sicily. Today, with concerns over the erosion of freedoms and sometimes fevered scapegoating of groups of differing skin color, religion, or even political opinions, it would serve us well to pay attention to their cautionary voices calling to us from the past through the characters of *Angel of Alta Langa*.

RECOMMENDED READING

A listing of all my reference material that formed the foundation of *Angel of Alta Langa* would be quite long and include not only books but also scholarly journal articles, blogs, and websites such as The United States Holocaust Museum, Yad Vashem, and The Jewish Virtual Library. The list below contains a selection of valuable reference books I recommend to readers seeking more information on the history of Italy, particularly Piemonte, from the beginning of the Fascist era through the end of World War II.

Banfield, Edward C. *The Moral Basis of a Backward Society*. New York: The Free Press, 1958.

Basani, Giorgio. *Il giardino dei Finzi-Contini*. Turin: Giulio Einaudi Editore, 1962. Translated by William Weaver as *The Garden of the Finzi-Continis* (New York: Harcourt Inc., 1977).

Caracciolo, Nicola. *Gli ebrei e l'Italia durante la guerra, 1940-45*. Rome: Bonacci Editore S.R.L., 1986. Translated by Florette Rechnitz Koffler and Richard Koffler as *Uncertain Refuge*. (Champaign, IL: University of Illinois Press, 1995).

De Felice, Renzo. 1961-1993. *Storia degli ebrea italiani sotto il fascismo*. Turin: Giulio Einaudi Editore, 1951-1993. Translated by Robert L. Miller as *The Jews in Fascist Italy: A History*. (New York, NY: Enigma Books, 2001).

Dusio, Andrea. *Rina and Demetrio's Century: Passion, Hard Work and Success of the Renowned Couple, Owners of the Albergo Restaurant Bellavista in Bossolasco and Their Famous Langa Cuisine*. Translated by Christopher Winner. Rome: Banda Larga, 2010.

Dutto, Alessandro. *Storie Piemontesi*. Boves, Italy: Arabafenice, 2014.

Fenoglio, Beppe. *I ventire giorni della città Alba*. Turin: Giulio Einaudi Editore, 1952. Translated by John Shepley as *The Twenty-Three Days of the City of Alba*. (South Royalton, VT: Steerforth Press, 2002).

Fenoglio, Beppe. *Il partigiano Johnny*. Published in English as *Johnny the Partisan*.

Fenoglio, Beppe. *La Malora*. Turin: Giulio Einaudi Editore, 1954. Translated by John Shepley as *The Ruin*. (Marlboro Press, 1992).

Fenoglio, Beppe. *Una Questione Privata*. Turin: Giulio Einaudi Editore, 1963. Translated by Howard Curtis as *A Private Affair*. (London: Modern Voices, 2006).

Fox, Elaine Saphier, ed. *Out of Chaos: Hidden Children Remember the Holocaust*. Evanston, IL: Northwestern University Press, 2013.

Hoffman, Suzanne. *Labor of Love: Wine Family Women of Piemonte*. Colorado: Under Discovered Publishing, 2016.

Holland, James. *Italy's Sorrow: A Year of War, 1944-1945*. New York: St. Martin's Press, 2008.

Levi, Primo. *Si questo è un uomo*. Turin: De Silva, 1947. Translated by Stuart Wolf as *If This Is a Man*, (Orion Press, 1959).

Mo, Tiziana. *Le parole della memoria*. Turin: Omega Edizione, 2005. Translated into Italian from Piemontese by Corrado Quadro.

Moorehead, Caroline. *A House in the Mountains: The Women Who Liberated Italy from Fascism*. New York, New York: Harper Perennial, 2020.

Pavese, Cesare. 1950. *La luna e I falò*. Turin: Giulio Einaudi Editore. Translated by R. W. Flint as *The Moon and the Bonfires*. New York: New York Review of Books, 2002).

Petrini, Carlo, ed. *Atlante delle vigne di Langa*. Bra, Italy: Slow Food Editore, 2000, 2008.

Revelli, Nuto. *La strada del davai*. Turin: Giulio Einaudi Editore, 1966 and 2004. Translated by John Penuel as *Mussolini's Death March: Eyewitness Accounts of Italian Soldiers on the Eastern Front*. (Lawrence, KS: University Press of Kansas, 2013).

Revelli, Nuto. *L'anello forte: La Donna: Storie di vita contadini*. Turin: Giulio Einaudi Editore, 2007.

Rosso, Maurizio and Chris Meier. *The Mystique of Barolo.* Turin: Omega Edizione, 2002.

Roth, Chaya H. *The Fate of Holocaust Memories: Transmission and Family Dialogues.* New York: Palgrave MacMillian, 2008.

Sarfatti, Michele. *Ebrei nell'Italia fascita.* 2006. Translated by John and Anne C. Tedeschi as *The Jews of Mussolini's Italy: From Equality to Persecution.* (Madison, WI: Wisconsin University Press.)

Slaughter, Jane. *Women and the Italian Resistance: 1943-1945.* Denver, CO: Arden Press, 1997.

Stille, Alexander. *Benevolence and Betrayal: Five Italian Jewish Families under Fascism.* New York: Picador, 1991.

Zargani, Aldo. *Per violino solo.* Società editrice il Mulino, 1995. Translated by Marina Harss and published as *For Solo Violin: A Jewish Childhood in Fascist Italy* (Paul Dry Books, Philadelphia, PA, 2002).

Zimmerman, Joshua D., ed. *Jews in Italy under Fascist and Nazi Rule.* Cambridge, United Kingdom: Cambridge University Press, 2005.

RINGRAZIAMENTI (ACKNOWLEDGEMENTS)

Writing my debut novel seemed like a great idea at first. I had the plot, the assistance of a great editing team and, of course, more time than I ever imagined to research and write, thanks to a once-in-a-lifetime—hopefully—pandemic. What I didn't consider was how daunting the research would be with libraries and museums shuttered, the interlibrary loan system shut down, and my inability to travel to Piemonte and Sicily. Fortunately, I had something the pandemic could not deprive me of: over two decades of living in Switzerland, twenty-one years of experience in Piemonte, and many willing wine family members to help me mine the information I needed for this book. In cyberspace, I was able to purchase books I needed, access resources, and connect with people on the ground that I otherwise would have been interviewing over a glass of wine in Barbaresco, Alba, Turin, Bossolasco, and Contessa Entellina. Thanks to those who were my eyes and ears across Italy and America I succeeded in compiling the needed, often elusive, information about the period between 1918 and 1946 in northern Italy, Sicily, and Germany. I added all what I gleaned from the long-distance research to my large cache of hundreds of hours of interviews and research for my first book, *Labor of Love: Wine Family Women of Piemonte*, helping me bring the characters and the world of *Angel of Alta Langa* alive.

I want to thank those people near and far who generously gave me their time and their patience to field my nonstop questions. It's a long list, so I'll start from the beginning that *was* the beginning—the wine families of Piemonte.

I am eternally grateful to them all for the role they played in helping the *Angel of Alta Langa* fly. Thanks go to all the families in Langhe, Roero, Monferrato, and Alto Piemonte who over the years have welcomed me into their homes and so graciously shared with me the history of their families and their patrimony. I owe a debt of gratitude to them for their generosity of time, food, wine, and warmth they have showered on me since that cold November in 1999 when I first set food on Langhe soil.

The two people I have known the longest in Piemonte are the patriarch of the noted wine-producing di Grésy family, Alberto di Grésy, and his cellar master, Jeffrey Chilcott. Alberto gave life to many characters by recounting stories of life in Barbaresco during the first half of the twentieth century told to him in his youth. Jeffrey, who quietly celebrated thirty years in Piemonte in 2020, speaks fluent Piemontese, a rarity among the youth of Piemonte, much less a foreigner. Jeffrey shared his knowledge gleaned working alongside *contadini* in the vineyards of Martinenga. Both Alberto and Jeffrey are our longtime friends, responsible for opening up Piemonte to me and making the stories of the past and dreams for the future come alive.

I owe the inclusion of traditions, many of the experiences of the Fiore family and their neighbors, and the building blocks of my characters' DNA to many friends and acquaintances from Langhe, Monferrato, and Roero. Sadly, many of those Langhetti born in the 1920s who shared stories with me for *Labor of Love: Wine Family Women of Piemonte* are no longer with us.

In 2003, Giovanna Rizzolio of Cascina delle Rose in Barbaresco first told me the stories of her nonna Beatrice Rizzolio who passed away in 1995. Without that enlightenment, I doubt my writing career ever would have begun. It shocked me to discover that no one had recorded the stories about the courage and defiance of Beatrice, who hid Jews under the noses of the occupying Nazis, and many of the *donne di Langhe* who were her friends and cohorts. Failure to share the stories meant they were in danger of dying out as so many have. Through her feisty granddaughter, Beatrice, who was declared Righteous among the Nations by the State of Israel in 1975, inspired me to write *Labor of Love*. The fruit of that vine is *Angel of Alta Langa*. Though they lived quite different lives, Beatrice inspired the character Cornelia Ferri Bottero.

The Grasso sisters of Ca' del Baio—Paola, Valentina, and Federica—along with their mamma Luciana and zia Natalia, helped with information about Langhe traditions and *cucina piemontese*. They added to the stories their late, beloved nonno Ernesto told them, which they shared with me, and those their nonna Fiorina once told me about the hard life in Asili between the two world wars. Nonna Fiorina was born and raised in Asili, and today her family still owns the yellow cascina at the end of the lane. Although it wasn't until the 1950s that vines were broadly planted there, I chose Asili as the setting for Cascina Asili and Ca' dei Fiù to honor nonna Fiorina's memory and pay homage to the Barbaresco wine her family produces from the Asili vineyard today. The sisters' great-great-grandfather (*trisnonno*) Giuseppe "Pinin" Grasso inspired the character Aldo Fiore, the great-grandfather (*bisnonno*) of Nico Fiore. Nico's gentle, kind manner, his dedication to the terroir, and most of all, his abiding love for his daughters are those qualities I found in Giulio Grasso, the patriarch of Ca' del Baio. Giulio and Luciana have no sons, but Pinin Grasso's legacy is already secure with Paola, Valentina, and Federica. Paola's husband, Carlo Deltetto, graciously answered my rapid-fire questions, even in the middle of the *vendemmia* in 2020 and in the aftermath of the tragic hailstorm of July 2021. The spirit of the generation of Langhetti about whom I wrote—their ancestors—is alive and well in these young people. I am grateful to them for the inspiration and support they gave me as I struggled through the many months of isolation while I wrote *Angel*.

The Albino Rocca sisters—Daniela, Monica, and Paola—helped me in many ways, particularly acting as conduits of information from don Paolo Doglio of the parish of San Giovanni Battista in Barbaresco, providing excerpts from books unavailable to me and organizing a Zoom interview with their cousin Giancarlo, who related stories from his father, Alfonso Rocca. I will forever be in Daniela's and Monica's debt for timely responding to my plethora of emails and texts and for providing me with invaluable insight and research material.

Thanks also go to Giancarlo Montaldo, former mayor of Barbaresco and former president of the Enoteca Regionale del Barbaresco. Giancarlo's fountain of knowledge about the history of the Langhe never runs dry, and he has always been generous with sharing that knowledge. The details of the story of the rastrellamento in Barbaresco in August 1944, first told to me by the late Albino Rocca, would have remained a mystery to me without the help of Giancarlo and Monica Rocca. I am truly grateful to Giancarlo for his support of my work on both *Labor of Love* and *Angel of Alta Langa*.

Aldo Vacca, president of Produttori del Barbaresco, provided me with information about the Barbaresco in the early twentieth century and connected me again with his uncle Adriano Vacca of Cantina del Pino, one of the last of the villagers who lived in pre-war Barbaresco and who bore witness to the cruelty of the Fascist Blackshirts and their Nazi overlords. Through Adriano's daughter-in-law, Franca, Adriano added to the hours I spent with him and his late son Renato in March 2012. Much of what came to be Ca' dei Fiù came from the pages of my journal from that interview. I will never be able to eat a peach again without thinking of Renato and how he introduced me to the delights of *pesche della vigna* (peaches of the vineyard).

Alberto Bianco, surveyor and former mayor of Barbaresco, brought the village of the twenties and thirties to life in my mind with vintage postcards he scanned and emailed to me. He provided old maps of Barbaresco, helped me with proper street names of the times, and filled in gaps regarding the partisans in Barbaresco during the Nazi occupation.

Ornella Correggia of Matteo Correggia winery in Roero, shared captivating stories of her childhood in Bossolasco, particularly about the *masche* and how the locals used everything nature had to offer, even the twigs and leaves on the ground in the forests nearby. Ornella introduced me to Bossolasco in March 2013 over lunch in her tasting room. When I first visited the hilltop village in Alta Langa in May 2014, red and yellow climbing roses covered the walls of buildings that line via Umberto I. I fell in love at first sight.

In 2013, I first learned from Ornella that Jews took refuge in Bossolasco during the Nazi occupation. But it was Giuseppe "Beppe" Veglio who, in November 2017, shared with me details of the courageous exploits of his parents, Demetrio and Caterina (Madama Rina) Veglio—proprietors of Hotel Bellavista in the center of Bossolasco—the village officials, and the villagers themselves during the Nazi occupation. Despite the bounty the Nazis offered, not a soul renounced the Jews or those hiding them in Bossolasco. In 2010, Beppe published *Il Secolo di Rina e Demetrio* (The Century of Rina and Demetrio) as told to Andrea Dusio in honor of his parents who inspired the characters Paolina and Fabrizio Pratto, and their Hotel Paradiso. Nowhere other than in Beppe's homage to his parents have I found details of the true stories of Jews hiding in plain sight in Bossolasco from late autumn 1943 until liberation in April 1945. I'm deeply grateful to Piemonte Pioneer Amy Marcelle Bellotti for introducing me to Beppe. The treasure trove of information I learned from him laid the foundation of *Angel of Alta Langa*.

Barbaresco producer, Claudia Cigliuti helped fill in gaps in my knowledge about partisan activity on Bricco di Neive that I had learned from her parents, Dina and Renato, and her zio Giuseppe Cigliuti, when I wrote *Labor of Love*. The perilous nighttime journey of Claudia's nonno Leone Cigliuti under the noses of the Blackshirts and Nazi occupiers to take a severely wounded partisan—nom de guerre "Stambecco"—to the hospital in Cortemilia helped me set the scene for the penultimate, crucial chapters.

Lucrezia Scarsi and her father-in-law, Marco Monchiero, of Monchiero-Carbone in Canale, added to information Marco shared with me for *Labor of Love* about his nonna Clotilde "Tilde" Raimondo who also contributed to Madama Lia's DNA. Like Madama, Tilde's father nicknamed her *la mej*. Like Madama, Tilde was a visionary, a determined woman with her own mind at a time when such things were not acceptable.

Maurizio Rosso—historian, author, and owner of Cantina Gigi Rosso—helped me with historical accuracy and once again gave moral support as he had with *Labor of Love*. Maurizio's dear companion, Maria Grazia Promio, whose late father Mario was from Bossolaschetto, planted the flora of the forests of Alta Langa in my mind.

Chiara Boschis of E. Pira e Figli in Barolo and Marina Marcarino of Punset in Neive are two dynamic wine family women and role models for many young wine producers—women and men—following in their footsteps. The two *donne di Langhe* provided cultural color, helping to enrich my characters and their lives. I am blessed to count these women as friends. They continue to inspire me with their hard work and dedication to the land and the rich Langhe heritage they have inherited. They are worthy stewards of the Langhe terroir and the agricultural legacy of their ancestors.

I owe a debt of gratitude to my dear friend Isella Zanutto, sommelier and former director of hospitality at Marchesi Alfieri in San Martino Alfieri where I first crossed paths with her. She provided invaluable assistance to ensure equine, cultural, historical, and linguistic accuracy. Isella also read the early drafts of chapters, catching glitches and adding to the cultural flavor of the book.

My photographer from *Labor of Love*, Pierangelo Vacchetto, who is a prolific author of books about Langhe—particularly Barolo—and Alta Langa, once again stepped up to help me with research, particularly with regard to San Lazzaro hospital in Alba, Barbaresco history, and stories of the partisans.

Arbëresh was the language of my maternal great-grandparents who immigrated to New Orleans in the late 1800s. Anna Fucarino of Contessa Entellina helped educate me about the Greek Byzantine church and the Arbëreshë words and phrases I included in Chapter Five. Anna made it possible for me to give a taste of this language she tirelessly campaigns to preserve. Lilliana Barbetta, and her lively husband, Paolo—also from Contessa Entellina—helped with Arbëresh and the culture of their village, including what Francesco's mamma might have served at his wedding had he married there. When in doubt, Lilliana went to papas Nicolas, pastor of SS Annunziata e San Nicolò church in Contessa for assistance. Giulio Inglese of Abbazia Santa Maria del Bosco explained how the animals were cared for on his family's farm. I'm grateful to Giulio and his family for allowing me to use the Inglese family name and their home in the forest above Contessa Entellina. Giulio's wife, Anna Salerno, was my inspiration for Sara. Although Sara's DNA also consists of elements of noted Barolo wine producers Silvia Altare's and Chiara Boschis's personalities, it was Anna I visualized throughout my writing. I owe a great deal to all of these Sicilians who, with Antonino Montalbano of Vivere Slow, and all the tenacious residents of Contessa Entellina, continue to inspire me with their dedication to preserving the village and their culture by promoting wine and nature tourism in their region.

For Luca Olivero's journey from Turin to Munich by air, I turned to aviation reinsurance attorney, Philip Chrystal, my former colleague at Swiss Reinsurance in Zürich. Philip is an avid collector of all things having to do with commercial aviation from the dawn of the industry, so he was able to plot Luca's route. He not only provided me with the flight times and routing based on an actual Ala Littoria timetable from that era, but Philip also guided me on the specifications of the type of aircraft the airline used on that route.

My dear, long-time friend, Lucia Hofbauer and her stalwart Scottish companion, Martin Miller, helped to bring alive Lucia's birthplace, Rosenheim in Bavaria, where I created Lorelei Volker's home. Without them, Luca's journey from the town, over the border, and into Austria never would have been possible. Lucia also checked the accuracy of my use of the German language.

Father Patrick Riviere, a young Catholic priest from my hometown of Thibodaux, Louisiana, and Francesca Vaira of Barolo, helped greatly with Latin and Italian funeral and marriage rites.

Cherasco resident and licensed tour guide Sara Matteodo, with the assistance of history professor Bruno Taricco who, according to Sara knows every stone in Cherasco, helped me draw an accurate picture of this beautiful hilltop village. Cherasco, like Bossolasco, captivated me from the moment I reached the top of the hill in 2004.

Rabbi Barbara Aiello, an expert on Italian Jewish genealogy, provided me with a list of Jewish surnames in Piemonte from which Dani chose the name of the Giordano family of Turin.

Attorney Marco Calabrese in Rome assisted me with inheritance issues that impacted Madama Lia's complicated situation and guided me to other useful resources along the way.

Prolific novelist, childhood friend, and fellow child of the Louisiana bayou country, Jack Caldwell, helped me safely cross many of the minefields I encountered as I wrote my debut novel. I'm grateful to him for his generosity in sharing with me his wealth of knowledge and experience.

I never could have kept up the pace—and my faith—without my dedicated team of beta readers on both sides of the Atlantic who read the first drafts of each chapter as they emerged. By waiting impatiently for additional chapters, my first draft readers—Claudia Kiely, Alisha Quinn Bosco, Shelby Key, Shawn Marie Fleishon, Jane Block, and Isella Zanutto—were the best cheerleaders a writer could have. Their candid critiques and support motivated me throughout the long hours at the computer.

I owe a debt of gratitude to my team of medical advisors: beloved Barolo wine producer and former pharmacist Giacomo Oddero and his physician-daughter Mariavittoria Boffa, registered nurse and fellow Louisianan Leslie Culicchia, and my dear friend Dr. Howard Fleishon MD. They helped me choreograph injuries and calamities that I inflicted on my characters and told me how to treat their wounds and ailments. Dott. Boffa's daughter, Isabella, served as translator, helping me learn from her mother and grandfather about the pharmacological agents used in pre-war Langhe and about the medical services available—or not—in Alba during that time. I'm grateful to Dr. Fleishon for his patience and generosity as he fielded my macabre emails queries regarding causation and treatment of fatal and life-threatening wounds.

No book project of this magnitude would be possible without the help of a stellar editing and design team, which I was blessed to have. This is my second collaboration with Elatia Harris, my first writing a novel. Elatia gave me the courage to begin and was by my side in cyberspace from when Sara was a mere idea floating in my head, and I know she will always be there to support me as an editor, mentor, and dear friend. With her help, I got past the numerous speedbumps and seemingly insurmountable obstacles, which included a few crises of confidence. Day and night—and often in the wee hours of the morning—Elatia was there to guide me. She calls herself the godmother of the Angel. And that she is.

Elatia connected me with my copyeditor, Olette Trouve. I discovered quickly that copyediting a fictional work is far more painful than a nonfiction book. Therefore, I owe a large debt of gratitude to Olette for patiently staying the course with me and lending her expertise to refine my *Angel*.

This was my first collaboration with cover and interior book designer, Ellen Pickels. Ellen is not only a talented designer, but she is also a gifted editor and proofreader. Her nickname, "the Grammar Queen," is well earned, but to me, she will always be the Grammar Empress. Ellen excelled in patience and skill in proofreading a manuscript of this length and complexity, particularly the glossary.

Also urging me to begin my *Angel* odyssey was my sister-in-law, Ilana Ben Shachar and her husband Aaron. In his late seventies, Aaron, a retired, highly successful attorney in Tel Aviv, penned his first novel, giving me the courage to do the same.

Throughout the book, I employed many words and phrases in Italian, Piemontese, Arbëresh, German, and Latin to give readers a sense of these languages my characters would have spoken. It was a daunting task to weave three languages and a dialect into dialogue and prose. Fortunately, in addition to those mentioned above, I had the help and support of Anna Olivero, Adult Language School Director at the Italian Cultural Center of Minneapolis and Asti native who spent her childhood climbing the craggy rocks of Monviso with her brother, Mario. Until the very end, Anna coached me with my Italian and meticulously combed through the manuscript and glossary, making corrections as needed for Italian words and phrases to insure I had the correct daily usage.

Although Zeus was a product of my imagination, I had many photos of Hanoverian horses to help bring him alive in my mind. But it was artist Clare O'Neill's work in beeswax and fire, "Wild Abandon," that I most turned to when I wrote about Zeus. Although not the same breed, Clare's image was most like Zeus in manner. That's why Clare's *Wild Abandon* graces the back cover. I'm grateful to her for her talent and her generosity in allowing me to share Zeus's inspiration.

Jane Block and her daughter Katie came to my rescue when time and logistics challenged me in finding a cover image for Sara. Although everyone will have their own image of Sara, as I do as well, Jane's photograph of Katie alongside the Stone King, Monviso, gave my cover the feel I sought.

The *Angel of Alta Langa* never would have come alive without the undying support of Dani, my best friend and husband, who believed in me even when I did not. On our long hikes throughout the lockdown, Dani patiently listened as I rattled off ideas about the plot and the characters, often changing my mind midsentence, then offered his incisive input. As my most loyal reader and toughest critic, he gave me invaluable feedback on the drafts and the final manuscript. I am forever grateful to my partner of thirty-six years for sacrificing my presence and the many evenings the muses kept me from preparing dinner for him.

As with everything in life I attempt, I give thanks to my late parents, Gloria and Bob LeBlanc, and honor their memory. My daddy gave me my dogged work ethic and my momma gave me my Sicilian genes. Without my momma, I never would have known that Contessa Entellina, a village now so much a part of my life, existed. As momma would say, "I am truly blessed."

Finally, I want to give thanks and honor those Piemontese who lived under Fascist tyranny and Nazi occupation and risked their lives for strangers. Many saviors perished, as did innocent victims of Nazi reprisals. In the words of Beatrice Rizzolio when asked why she did not travel to Rome to be recognized as a Holocaust savoir in 1975, "I didn't do it for an award. I did it because it was the right thing to do." May we never forget those who refused to be silent witnesses to the horror of the Holocaust. May we never forget the evil that plunged the world into war and holocaust—and the good that overcame it.